PRAISE FOR *ALL THIS I WILL GIVE TO YOU*

Winner of the Planeta Prize 2016

"*Twin Peaks* in Galicia."

—*La Razón* (Spain)

"An extremely tight and sagacious investigative work. There is not a single fact or turn in the novel that should not be there or that is missing from the novel."

—*La Vanguardia* (Spain)

"The author has outdone herself. This is a story of elongated narrative, a palpable smoothness in the way she writes, in the clarity of her ideas on the paper. She moves at light speed. You can easily see her mind working as an experienced chess player: while she develops one plot point, she is already thinking about the next one."

—*El Correo Gallego* (Spain)

PRAISE FOR DOLORES REDONDO

"The queen of the literary thriller."
—Carlos Ruiz Zafón, author of *The Shadow of the Wind*, *The Angel's Game*, *The Prisoner of Heaven*, and *The Labyrinth of Spirits*

PRAISE FOR THE AUTHOR'S BAZTAN TRILOGY

Nominated for the International Dagger Award

"Utterly compelling."

—*Publishing Perspectives*

"Eerily atmospheric."

—*Sunday Times* (UK)

ALL THIS

I WILL

GIVE TO

YOU

ALSO BY DOLORES REDONDO

ALL THIS
I WILL
GIVE TO
YOU

DOLORES REDONDO

Translated by Michael Meigs

Text copyright © 2016 by Dolores Redondo Meira and Editorial Planeta, S. A.
By Agreement with Pontas Literary & Film Agency
Translation copyright © 2018 by Michael Meigs
All rights reserved.

Previously published as *Todo esto te daré* by Planeta in Spain in 2016. Published in agreement with and Pontas Literary & Film Agency. Translated from Spanish by Michael Meigs. First published in English by AmazonCrossing in 2018.

Published by AmazonCrossing, Seattle

www.apub.com

Amazon, the Amazon logo, and AmazonCrossing are trademarks of Amazon.com, Inc., or its affiliates.

ISBN-13: 9781503902541 (hardcover)
ISBN-10: 1503902544 (hardcover)
ISBN-13: 9781503901230 (paperback)
ISBN-10: 1503901238 (paperback)

Cover design by David Drummond

Printed in the United States of America

First edition

This novel was awarded the Planeta Prize for 2016 by a jury composed of Alberto Blecua, Fernando Delgado, Juan Eslava Galán, Pere Gimferrer, Carmen Posadas, Rosa Regàs, and Emili Rosales.

For Eduardo, forever.
To my father, a Gallego in every sense of the word;
to my mother, and to their love despite the disapproval
of their families:
it made me even prouder of them, and it was proof that love
conquers all.

A LIFE PRESERVER

The knock at the door was loud and peremptory. Eight decisive blows, one after another, warning that someone expected to be admitted immediately. The sort of insistence you'd never hear from an invited guest, a worker, or a delivery driver. He would remember it later with the bleak reflection, *typical behavior of police demanding to be let in.*

He stared for a couple of seconds at the cursor blinking at the end of the last sentence. This had been a good morning for work, the best of the last three weeks. Though he hated to admit it to himself, he especially enjoyed writing when he was alone at home with nothing else to do, free of the usual interruptions, so he could go with the flow. That's what happened when he got to this point in a novel. He was expecting to finish *The Sun of Tebas* in a couple of weeks. Maybe earlier if all went well. And until then the story would take over and obsess him every minute of the day. He'd have no time for anything else. Each of his novels had brought him to this intense pitch and this sensation, at once intimate and destructive. He loved it and feared it. He knew it made him hard to live with.

He glanced toward the hall that led to the apartment's front door. The blinking cursor seemed about to burst with the pressure of all the words still behind it. In the moment of deceptive stillness he began to hope the untimely visitor had given up. But no; he sensed the silent presence out there of the intruder's demanding energy. Determined to finish one more sentence, he put his fingers to the keyboard. The insistent pounding resumed and echoed in the narrow hallway. He tried to ignore it but had to give up.

Irritated less by the interruption than by the arrogant insistence, he got up and muttered a curse at the guard at the front gate. He'd told the man more than once to make sure he wasn't interrupted at work. He angrily yanked the door open.

A man and a woman in police uniforms took a step back when he glared out at them.

"Good morning," the male officer said, glancing at a little card barely visible in his big hand. "Is this the residence of Álvaro Muñiz de Dávila?"

"It is," answered Manuel, surprise overcoming his exasperation.

"Are you a family member?"

"I'm his husband."

The policeman glanced at his companion. Manuel saw his expression, but by this point his natural paranoia had already kicked in. He didn't care whether they were surprised.

"Has something happened?"

"I'm Corporal Castro, and this is Sergeant Acosta. May we come in? It would be better if we spoke inside."

This was a scenario familiar to any writer: Two uniformed police officers wanted to come inside for a private talk. They must have bad news.

Manuel stepped aside. In the cramped hallway the two troopers looked immense in their green uniforms and military boots. Their soles squeaked against the varnish of the dark parquet floor like those of drunken sailors balancing on the deck of a tiny boat. He led them to the living room where he'd been working. He started to escort them to the sitting area but stopped so suddenly they almost bumped into him. He stubbornly repeated himself. "Has something happened?"

It was no longer a question. Between the front door and the living room the inquiry had vanished and now it was almost a prayer, an echo of the voice in his mind pleading, *Please, no; please, no; please, no.* He prayed, even though he knew all pleading was useless. Prayer hadn't stopped cancer from devouring his sister in nine short months. Feverish and exhausted, she'd still been determined to buck him up, console him, and take care of him; she'd joked even as death became visible in her face as she lay back against a pillow, as if already in her coffin. "Looks like I'll take just about as long to leave the world as I did to get here." In the humiliation of his weakness he kept praying to some inept superior power as he trudged like a humble servant to the doctor's cramped, overheated office to be informed his sister wouldn't survive the night.

He'd known prayer was useless, but he'd made one last desperate attempt. He'd folded his hands in mute supplication even as he heard those words, that sentence, the final judgment from which there would be no last-minute reprieve.

The corporal stood surveying the magnificent collection of books filling shelves that completely occupied two walls. He took a look at the desk and then his eyes turned to Manuel again. He gestured toward the sofa. "Maybe you should sit down."

"I don't want to sit. Go ahead and tell me." He realized he sounded curt, so to take the edge off his comment he added, "Please."

The policeman hesitated, clearly ill at ease. He looked off somewhere beyond Manuel's shoulder and bit his upper lip. "It's about . . . your . . ."

"It's about your husband," the woman intervened, taking charge. She didn't look at her colleague but couldn't have missed his ill-concealed relief. "Unfortunately we have bad news. We're sorry to have to inform you that señor Álvaro Muñiz de Dávila was in a serious traffic accident this morning. He was already deceased by the time the ambulance got there. I'm very sorry, señor."

The sergeant's face was a perfect oval. She'd combed her hair to frame that shape and had gathered it into a bun at her neck. A few wisps had begun to work free. He'd heard her perfectly clearly: Álvaro was dead. But for a few moments he was surprised to find himself intrigued by the serene beauty of this woman. The impression was so strong that he almost mentioned it. She was extremely beautiful but apparently not conscious of that fact. Her sympathetic attitude and the astonishing symmetry of her features made her even more gorgeous. Later he would recall that impression and marvel at the trick his brain had played in an effort to preserve his sanity. He would remember time stopping as he took refuge in the exquisite lines of that feminine face, a drowning man flailing after a life preserver, even though he didn't know it then. That eternity lasted only one precious instant and didn't block the avalanche of questions already surging into his mind. But he said only one word. "Álvaro?"

The sergeant took him by the arm—later it would occur to him that she must have used the same practiced maneuver to detain suspects—and escorted him unresisting to the sofa. She gave him a gentle push on the shoulder, and when he was seated she settled beside him.

"The accident happened in the early morning. The car ran off the highway, it appears, along a stretch of straight road with good visibility. There doesn't seem to have been another vehicle involved. According to our Monforte colleagues, he may have fallen asleep at the wheel."

He listened with careful attention, trying to grasp and retain the details, trying to ignore the chorus shouting louder and louder in his mind: *Álvaro is dead, Álvaro is dead, Álvaro is dead!*

The woman's beautiful face no longer overrode the catastrophe. From the corner of his eye he saw the corporal absorbed in examining the various objects on his desk. A glass with coffee dregs still holding the little spoon, the invitation to a prestigious literary award ceremony he'd used as a coaster, the cell phone he'd used to talk to Álvaro just hours before, and that blinking cursor awaiting the completion of the last line of prose he'd written as he, poor idiot, had told himself things were going so well. But that was no longer important. Nothing mattered if Álvaro was dead. It had to be true because that sergeant had told him so, and the Greek chorus in his head kept chanting it in deafening crescendo. That's when he grasped the sergeant as if grabbing a life preserver.

"Did you say Monforte? But he's in—"

"Monforte, in Lugo province. They called us from there, although in fact the accident occurred in a small town in the Chantada area."

"It's not Álvaro."

His emphatic reply drew the attention of the corporal, who forgot the things on the desk and turned a disconcerted face toward him. "What?"

"It can't be Álvaro. My husband went to Barcelona yesterday afternoon to see a client. He's in marketing and public relations. He's been working for weeks on a project for a Cataluña hotel group. They set up several promotional events, and this morning he had a presentation to make. So he couldn't possibly have been in Lugo. There must be some mistake. I spoke to him last night, and the only reason we didn't talk this morning was, as I said, his meeting was very early and I don't get up early, but I'll call him right now."

He brushed past the corporal on his way to the desk, ignoring the officers' exchange of knowing looks. He fumbled through the mess on the desktop. The spoon rattled against the glass; the rim was indelibly stained with coffee. He located the cell phone, tapped a couple of keys, and listened, his eyes fixed on the sergeant. She watched him with a pained expression.

Manuel stayed on the line until it stopped ringing. "He must be in his meeting," he explained. "That's why he didn't pick up."

The sergeant rose. "Your name is Manuel. That's right, isn't it?"

He nodded as if accepting a formal accusation.

"Manuel, come here. Have a seat next to me, please."

He went back to the sofa, the phone in his hands, and did as he was told.

"Manuel, I'm married too." She looked down briefly at the muted gleam of his wedding ring. "And I know from experience, especially because of my profession, that we're never entirely sure what our partners are doing. It's something a person has to learn to accept. There's no use being tormented by uncertainty. Surely your husband must have had a reason for not telling you. We're certain it's him. No one answered because our colleagues in Monforte have his phone in custody. They've had your husband's body transported to the medical examiner's office at Lugo Hospital. And we have positive identification by a relative. There is no doubt whatsoever. We're talking about Álvaro Muñiz de Dávila, age forty-four."

He'd kept shaking his head as Sergeant Acosta spoke, attributing her incorrect assumptions about Álvaro to the tarnished brilliance of his wedding ring that afforded her the opportunity to pontificate about marriage. He'd spoken to Álvaro just a few hours ago. Álvaro was in Barcelona, not in Lugo. Why in hell would Álvaro be six hundred miles away, all the way across the country, in Lugo? Manuel knew his husband, he knew where Álvaro was, and there was no way Álvaro was on some damned road in Lugo. He hated pronouncements about couples, he hated absolutes more than anything, and he was starting to hate this smart-ass little sergeant.

"Álvaro doesn't have any family," he countered.

"Manuel . . ."

"Okay, I suppose he comes from a family just like everybody else, but he hasn't been in contact with them for a long time. Nothing at all, zero. It's been like that forever, since long before Álvaro and I met. He's been completely independent since he was very young. You're all mistaken."

She was patient with him. "Manuel, your name and phone number are on the *Aa* speed dial on your husband's phone."

"*Aa* speed dial?" he repeated in confusion.

He remembered now. They'd set it up years ago. *Aa* was the key combination the public safety authorities had invented. It linked to the name and number of the person to be informed in case of an accident. He checked the contact list of his own phone and there it was: *Aa* linked to Álvaro. He stood there for a time examining carefully each of the letters of that name. His vision blurred with the weight of his unshed tears. He flailed about, seeking some other life preserver.

"But no one called me . . . They'd have had to phone me, wouldn't they?"

The corporal seemed almost pleased at the opportunity to explain. "They used to do it like that, until a couple of years ago. They telephoned the indicated person, and if there wasn't anyone specified they called the number marked 'home' or 'parents' and informed them. But it was very traumatic for the recipients. More than once those calls provoked heart attacks, accidents, or . . . unintended consequences. We're trying to do it better. Now the standard procedure requires a positive ID; you notify the post closest to the residence of the deceased, and we always come as a pair. One is always an experienced officer, as in this case, and we deliver the information personally or escort the individual to identify the body."

So this whole parade of *Sit down and keep calm* wasn't real. It was standard operating procedure for the delivery of the worst possible news. The officers were merely following a protocol. His protests were pointless, because there'd never been any possibility of appeal.

For a few moments they sat motionless and silent as statues. At last the corporal gestured to the sergeant, who said, "Maybe you'd like to call some relative or friend to go with you."

Manuel looked at her, confused by the suggestion. The idea seemed as foreign as if she were speaking underwater or from another dimension.

"What do I do now?" he asked.

"As I told you, the body is at the medical examiner's office at Lugo Hospital. There they can tell you what steps to take, and they'll release the body for burial."

Pretending an assurance he was far from feeling, he got up and went to the door, obliging the officers to follow him. He promised to telephone his sister as soon as they left. He knew he had to look like he was in control of himself if he wanted to get rid of them. He shook their hands and withstood the sharp glances that weren't quite in keeping with their affable farewells. He thanked them again and shut the door.

He leaned his face against the warm wood, certain that they were listening on the other side. From this angle he noticed something he'd never particularly paid attention to before: the narrow hall opened to the living room in just the way a long-stemmed flower reached for the light. This was the home he'd shared with Álvaro for the past fifteen years; seen from this neglected vantage point it seemed immense. The light that flooded through the window threw the outlines of the furniture into sharp relief and spread a liquid brilliance that made it seem to dissolve into the walls and ceiling. That was the precise moment when the beloved familiar space ceased to be his home and turned into an ocean of frozen sun, an infernal arctic night that made him feel like an orphan again, as he had that other far-off night in the hospital.

He'd told them he was going to call his sister. He smiled bitterly at that. If only he could. Vertigo rose through his chest like a hot, unwanted animal squirming in his lap, and his eyes filled with tears at the knowledge that the only people he wanted to telephone were both dead.

He suppressed the urge to weep, went back to the living room, took the same seat as before, and picked up his phone. The screen lit up and offered the option of telephoning Álvaro. He stared at it briefly, let out a long breath, and looked for another number in the contact list.

Mei's sweet feminine voice answered his call. Mei Liu had been Álvaro's secretary for more than ten years. "Oh, hello, Manuel, how are you? How's your latest novel going? I'm biting my nails, I'm so impatient. Álvaro told me it's going to be incredible—"

"Mei"—he interrupted her chatter—"where is Álvaro?"

There was a sudden brief silence on the other end of the line. Manuel knew she was about to lie to him. He even had one of those flashes of clairvoyance that reveal the stage machinery that moves the world. The mechanism that mercifully remains hidden from us for most of our lives.

"Álvaro? Why . . . he's in Barcelona."

"Don't lie to me, Mei!"

The renewed silence on the other end of the line was proof to him she felt caught and was racking her brains for something to put him off.

"I'm not lying, Manuel. Why would I lie to you?" Her voice had risen, and she sounded close to tears. Excuses, questions, any possible evasion to avoid answering directly. "He's . . . he's in Barcelona, in the meeting with the board of directors of that hotel chain in Cataluña."

Manuel clenched the phone so tightly that his knuckles turned white. He closed his eyes and with a great effort resisted the desire to fling it away, destroy it, smash it into a thousand pieces to silence the lies coming through the line. He tried to control himself when he spoke again, to resist the urge to shout.

"Two police officers just left here. They told me Álvaro couldn't be in Barcelona because he got killed last night in a traffic accident, and now he's in the morgue in Lugo. So you can goddamn well tell me, because there's no way you don't know. *Where is Álvaro?*" He drew out every syllable in a long, low hiss in an effort to contain his anger.

The woman's voice broke and turned into a wail so shrill that he could hardly understand her. "I'm sorry, Manuel, so sorry!"

He broke the connection. Mei could have been his third possible life preserver, but she'd failed him.

THE ARCTIC SUN

The waiting room smelled of despair. Two rows of plastic chairs faced one another and left hardly enough room to pass. Respiration and fetid body odors floated in a cloud of stinking vapor that blurred the grieving faces of those waiting. Disconcerted, he went back out into the hallway. The security guard at the counter there kept an eye on him. Manuel nodded to indicate he intended to stay in the hall. He'd dismissed the idea of making his way to the last available seat. That would have meant negotiating the knees and feet of people waiting and muttering a long string of apologies to those skeletal presences. He chose to remain standing to avoid all those eyes. He also chose to lean against the wall close enough to the door to make sure of a reasonable volume of fresh air, even though he had to put up with the stern vigilance of the guard.

Lugo had received him with sullen skies the color of chalky water, as if the town were an extension of this miserable room. The clouded weather and temperature in the mid-60s were a brutal change from Madrid's blinding sun and muggy skies. This early September weather seemed almost artificial, a literary trope orchestrated to create an atmosphere of oppression and despair.

Lugo had no airport. He'd thought about flying to Santiago de Compostela, the closest one, and renting a car there, but with the nameless dread lurking inside him he felt incapable of waiting two hours for the flight. That dread would have exploded in the cramped cabin of an airplane.

The hardest thing had been to open the clothes closet, push aside their suits, and locate the little suitcase. He'd filled it hastily with the absolute necessities, or at least that's what he'd thought. Later he found that in his hurry he'd grabbed four useless garments and forgotten almost everything he really needed. He thought back to the fugue state of his last few minutes at home. The quick check for flights from Madrid, the hastily packed suitcase, and the deliberate refusal to look at the photo of the two of them that stood on the chest of drawers. He hadn't examined it then but couldn't get the image out of his head now. A mutual friend had taken it during a fishing trip last summer. Manuel was looking distractedly out over the silver surface of the sea, and Álvaro, younger, slim, his olive skin gleaming in the sun, watched him and smiled his typical smile, so subtle and so discreet. Álvaro had gotten it framed, and Manuel had taken endless pleasure from it. That photo showed Manuel at his most typical—distracted, as if he'd just missed a moment of great meaning he'd never be able to recover. The instant captured by the camera had confirmed his suspicion he'd never been entirely present in his own life. Today that image amounted almost to an indictment.

The vigil at the morgue, a never-ending immobility, imposed a sudden halt. He'd rushed to travel, deluded by the confused thought that one minute more or less might change the fact that Álvaro was dead. He'd gone through the house like a sleepwalker, stopping to survey each room and confirm the presence of things that had belonged to Álvaro and in some way embodied him: his photography books, his sketchbooks on the table, and the old sweater hanging on a chairback, the one he wore at home and had refused to throw away even though it was faded and frayed at the cuffs. He studied each item, almost surprised they still existed now that Álvaro was gone. As if somehow with his disappearance they'd have ceased to exist and vanished into thin air. He glanced quickly over his own desktop and without thinking gathered up his wallet, cell phone, and phone charger. Perhaps most surprising was his present certainty that he hadn't saved *The Sun of Tebas* or the morning's work he'd thought had gone so well. Then came the ominous task of entering the name of that dreadful city into his car's navigation system. He drove nearly three hundred miles in silence in less than four and a half hours, interrupted only by persistent calls from Mei that he didn't answer. He couldn't recall whether he'd turned off all the lights at home.

The sound of a man weeping made him acutely uncomfortable. The man's face was buried in the neck of a woman who had to be his wife. He was whispering unintelligible words. Manuel saw the woman's tired expression as she rubbed the back of the man's head. He saw the expressions of others in the room who were pressing their lips together, breathing deeply and gulping for air, like children trying to endure pain.

He hadn't wept. He didn't know if that was normal or not. There was one instant just after the sergeant and corporal left that he'd almost surrendered to tears, when before his frightened eyes the contours of his home blurred and began to dissolve. But weeping required warmth, or at least some sort of arousal; the arctic chill that had invaded his house had frozen much of his heart.

Two men in elegantly tailored suits stood at the counter. One was a few steps to the side as the other muttered in a voice so low the security guard had to lean over to hear him. The guard nodded and without hiding his interest in the visitors pointed toward the waiting room.

The one who'd consulted the guard exchanged a couple of words with his companion. Both came toward the room.

"Manuel Ortigosa?"

The man's polished elocution and the expensive suit caught the attention of everyone in the waiting room. These men were too well dressed to be physicians or policemen. Manuel nodded.

The one who'd addressed him held out his hand. "I'm Eugenio Doval. Allow me to introduce señor Adolfo Griñán."

The other shook his hand as well. "Could we have a word?"

The introductions only confirmed his suspicion they weren't physicians. Manuel motioned toward the waiting room and the other people there, offering to accompany the strangers inside.

Ignoring the frankly curious expressions of those within, Griñán looked up through the room's turbid haze to the ill-defined yellow stain across much of the ceiling. "Dear God, no! Not here. We greatly regret we didn't get here earlier and you've been obliged to endure this ordeal alone—is there anyone with you?" he asked, though his initial survey of this mourning company had apparently answered that question for him.

Manuel shook his head.

Griñán looked back up at the stain on the ceiling. "Let's go outside."

"But they told me to wait here."

Doval sought to reassure him. "Never mind about that. We won't go far, and perhaps we can inform you of certain aspects of the situation that you need to know."

The prospect of answers overcame his reluctance. He followed them out of the room, sensing the bleary gazes of the room's company on his back. They were probably asking one another who the hell those two men were. As if in tacit agreement, the three of them walked in silence past the vigilant guard at the counter, went down the hall, and turned a corner into a space the hospital had furnished with vending machines.

Doval gestured toward those large colorful devices. "Would you like something to drink?"

Manuel declined the offer and turned uneasily to look back toward the waiting room.

The one named Griñán stepped up to him. "I'm a bonded administrator and property manager. I oversaw your husband's business undertakings, and I'm also the executor of his will." He gave Manuel a look as grave as if he'd just listed the military decorations he'd earned.

Manuel didn't know what to make of this. He took some time to study the man's calm, impenetrable expression. Manuel turned to Doval in hopes of an explanation or perhaps expecting to detect a glint of amusement that would confirm they were putting him on.

"I know that all this is a shock for you," Griñán acknowledged. "As the contracted manager of don Álvaro's estate, I'm aware of the circumstances of your relationship."

That put Manuel on his guard. "What are you trying to say?"

The administrator wasn't offended by Manuel's reaction. "I know you'd been married for years and you'd lived together for a long time before that. What I want to make clear to you is that I'm quite aware that much of what I'm about to explain is going to be completely new."

Manuel sighed and crossed his arms across his chest in a defensive posture. He was fed up with all this. He'd used up his last reserve of self-mastery in the conversation with Mei, but he'd consider a truce with anyone capable of shedding at least a little light on the reason his husband was now lying dead on a slab in the morgue in this godforsaken place. He glanced again at the counter and the security guard watching them, then looked back at the two men.

"Can you tell me what Álvaro was doing here? What he was doing on that road so early in the morning? Can you tell me that?"

Griñán glanced at Doval, who stepped forward with a somber expression. "The reason Álvaro was here is that he was born here and his family home is here. I don't know where he was going when the accident occurred, but as the police must surely have told you, it appears that no other vehicle was involved, and everything seems to indicate he might have fallen asleep at the wheel. It's a pity; he was forty-four years old with his whole life ahead of him. He was a charming young man, and I thought the world of him."

Manuel had a vague memory of seeing Álvaro's national identity card and the mention of his place of birth. A place to which he had no ties at all. Manuel couldn't remember his ever mentioning it. But why would he? When they first met, Álvaro had been categorical about it—his family refused to accept his life-style and sexual orientation. Like so many others, he'd broken every tie to his past when he moved to Madrid to live his own life.

"But he was supposed to be in Barcelona. So what was he doing here? As far as I knew he hadn't been in contact with his family for years."

"As far as you knew," Griñán murmured.

"What does that mean?" Manuel snapped, offended.

"Look, Manuel—may I call you Manuel? I always advise my clients to be candid and aboveboard, especially with their spouses. After all, their spouses share their lives, and spouses are those most affected by bereavement. Álvaro's case was no exception. I'm not the person to judge the reasons or guess the motivations that drove him to act as he did. I'm simply the messenger, and I accept the fact that what I'm going to say isn't going to win me any points with you. But this is my duty. I made a promise to Álvaro, and I will carry it out in every detail." After a dramatic pause he continued. "Álvaro Muñiz de Dávila had been the Marquis of Santo Tomé for the past three years, since the death of his father, the previous marquis. This title is one of the oldest in Galicia. His family's estate is only a few miles from the site of the accident, and although I wasn't aware he was here, I can vouch to you that he visited regularly and was conscientious in attending to his obligations."

Manuel found each successive statement in this account more absurd than the last. He failed to suppress a sneer. "You're putting me on!"

"I assure you every word I've said is true, and I stand ready to provide proof and documentation to corroborate any part of it."

Manuel looked back and forth between Griñán and the security guard down the hall. He felt extremely jittery. "So you're telling me my husband was an aristocrat—what was it you said, a marquis? With an estate and land holdings, and a family I've never heard of?" His tone became brutally sarcastic. "All that's left now is for you to say he had a wife and children."

The man raised his hands in protest. "No, for the love of God! As I told you, Álvaro inherited his father's title upon the patriarch's death three years ago. That's when I first met him, when he took over the affairs of the family. You must understand that a title of nobility is encumbered with heavy obligations, and Álvaro did his duty."

Manuel was frowning. He realized as much when he pressed his icy fingers to his brow in an effort to mitigate the headache that had begun to throb behind his eyes. Now it was creeping across his skull like a white-hot lava flow.

"The police told me a relative identified the body."

"That's right, his brother Santiago, the middle brother. Álvaro was the eldest. Francisco, the youngest, died not long after their father. He fell into a deep depression and evidently had problems with drugs: an overdose. Misfortune has dogged the family in recent years. The mother is still alive, but she's in delicate health."

Manuel's headache was getting worse.

"This is unbelievable," he muttered aloud to himself. "How could he have hidden all this for so long?"

Doval and Griñán exchanged dismayed glances. Griñán was the one to reply. "I can't help you there; I don't know why Álvaro decided on this course of action. But he left very clear instructions about what was to be done in case he died, as now unfortunately he has."

"What does that mean? Are you saying Álvaro thought he was going to die? Tell me straight out, please. Remember what I'm dealing with here. I've only now learned that my husband, who just died, had a family I knew nothing about. I don't understand a word of this."

Griñán seemed to share his pain. "I know that, Manuel. It must be a terrible blow for you. I'm referring only to the fact there's a will with his last wishes, as is appropriate for someone in his position; it's drawn up as a precaution. We prepared a first version when he accepted the title and all it implied. It's been modified several times since then to take into account arrangements made for the interests of the estate. Álvaro left specific instructions for what was to be done after his death. Of course we will arrange a reading of the will at the appropriate time, but he left instructions that within twenty-four hours of his death a letter concerning his last wishes was to be read, a measure that, if I may say so, will greatly assist the beneficiaries and relatives, since this preliminary declaration will advise them of arrangements before the will is probated. The codicil to that document stipulates that the terms of the will are to be made public before ninety days have passed."

Manuel stared at the floor, his expression a mixture of dismay and frustration.

"We've taken the liberty of reserving a room for you at a hotel in town. I imagine you've not yet had time to make arrangements. I've summoned all the family members to my office tomorrow morning for the reading of the document. We'll send a car to pick you up at the hotel. The funeral and burial will be the day after tomorrow in the family plot on the As Grileiras estate."

Manuel's head was about to explode.

"What do you mean—a funeral? Who decided that? Nobody consulted me. I ought to have something to say about it, shouldn't I?" His voice had risen, and he didn't care whether the security guard could hear it.

"This is the family tradition—" Doval began to explain.

"I don't give a goddamn for their traditions. Who do they think they are? I'm his husband!"

"Señor Ortigosa—" Griñán interrupted him. "Manuel—" he said in a conciliatory tone. "This is one of his instructions. Álvaro wanted to be buried in the family cemetery."

The swinging doors that had been closed behind Griñán and his assistant were suddenly flung open. The men turned to look. Two police officers appeared. This time both were men, one hardly out of his teens, the other well into his fifties. The young man was very slim; the older could have been a caricature of the stereotypical backwoods cop. He was scarcely five feet tall, probably a holdover from the days when the height standards hadn't been rigorously enforced. Manuel thought incongruously that the prominent potbelly stuffed into the perfectly ironed uniform would be a distinct disadvantage to someone presenting himself today for the challenging entrance exam for the Úbeda Police Academy. To make things worse, the man's mustache was mostly gray, matching his temples and the sideburns so meticulously shaped, probably with a straight razor, by a barber who obviously hadn't updated his tonsorial techniques in an extremely long time.

"Police Lieutenant Nogueira." The officer looked scornfully at the expensively tailored suits of Doval and Griñán. "Relatives of Álvaro Muñiz de Dávila?" It sounded more like a declaration than a question.

"We are his legal representatives," Griñán stated, extending a hand that the officer ignored. "Manuel Ortigosa," he said, gesturing with the same hand, "is his husband."

The officer made no effort to conceal his surprise. He jabbed a thumb over his shoulder. "The husband of . . . ?" He looked at the young trooper, who was diligently pretending to be searching his notebook for a blank page. Nogueira was clearly disgusted to see the younger man offering him no support. This did nothing to alter his own attitude. "As if I didn't have enough to deal with already," he said under his breath.

Manuel gave him a defiant look. "You have a problem with it?"

The officer didn't reply but looked again to the young trooper for support. This time the younger man just shrugged, apparently not understanding why this should be an issue.

"Take it easy," the lieutenant snapped. "The only one around here with problems is the guy on the slab in the morgue."

The attorneys responded with disgusted looks. Manuel's gaze burned into the policeman.

"I have to ask you some questions."

Manuel waited to hear them.

"When was the last time you saw him?"

"The day before yesterday in the late afternoon when he left on a trip. We live in Madrid."

"In Madrid," the lieutenant repeated, looking over to make sure the young trooper was taking notes. "When was the last contact you had with him?"

"Last night at about one. He phoned me, and we talked for ten or fifteen minutes."

"Last night. Did he tell you where he was or where he was going?"

Manuel took his time before answering. "No. I didn't even know he was here. He was supposed to be in Barcelona for a meeting with a client. He is . . . was in public relations, and he'd developed a campaign for a hotel chain, and—"

"With a client."

The man's tiresome tic of repeating some of his words came across as arrogant and downright insulting, although Manuel knew his own reaction was less because of the man's arrogant tone than because the policeman was forcing him to confirm in so many words that he'd been lied to.

"What did you discuss? Do you remember what he said?"

"Nothing in particular. He told me he was very tired and was looking forward to getting back home."

"Did he sound particularly tense, irritated, angry?"

"No, just tired."

"Did he say he'd had an argument with someone?"

"No."

"Your . . . husband, did he have any enemies? Anybody have it in for him?"

Manuel turned in dismay to the attorneys before he replied. "No. I don't know. Not that I know of." He felt fatigue overpowering him. "What's the point of all these questions?"

"Not that he knows of," parroted the lieutenant.

"You're not going to tell me anything? Why are you asking about enemies? Perhaps you think that . . . ?"

"Is there anyone who can confirm you were in Madrid last night at one in the morning?"

"I already told you I lived with Álvaro and I understood he was in Barcelona. We lived by ourselves, and I didn't go out yesterday, I wasn't with anyone, so no, I can't prove I was in Madrid, but your colleagues can tell you I was there this morning when they came to deliver the news, but—what's this all about?"

"Nowadays we can determine the exact location of a telephone when it connects with another, to within a couple hundred feet. Did you know that?"

"That's all very good to hear, but I don't see what you're driving at. Can you tell me what's going on? Your colleagues told me that Álvaro fell asleep at the wheel, he ran off a straight stretch of road, and no other vehicles were involved." He was starting to sound desperate. The refusal of this man to answer him with anything but more questions was driving him crazy.

"How do you make a living?"

"I'm a writer," he said dully.

The officer tilted his head to one side and smiled slightly. "A lovely hobby. And how do you make a living?"

"I just told you. I'm a writer," he insisted, losing his patience. This guy was an idiot.

"Writer," he repeated. "What color is your car, señor?"

"It's a blue BMW. Are you implying there's something suspicious about the death of my husband?"

The officer waited to answer until the youngster had finished writing the latest note.

"When there's a traffic fatality, the judge authorizes holding the body in the same locality, and there's no autopsy unless there's sufficient reason to suspect foul play. The rear part of the car of your . . . husband," he said with a sigh, "has a recent minor dent with signs of paint from a second vehicle, and—"

The doors swung open behind him, and another uniformed officer interrupted.

"What do you think you're doing, Nogueira?"

The others stiffened to attention.

"Captain, Manuel Ortigosa is a relative of the deceased and has just arrived from Madrid. I was taking his statement."

The new arrival stepped past the others and gave Manuel a firm handshake. "Señor Ortigosa, I'm the chief of police. I'm sorry for your loss and any annoyance Lieutenant Nogueira may have caused you in his eagerness." He accompanied the apology with a swift look of reproach. "As our colleagues informed you, there is no doubt whatsoever the death of your husband was an accident. No other vehicle was involved."

Though the broad-shouldered figure of the senior officer partly blocked his view, Manuel did see a grimace of annoyance behind Nogueira's mustache.

"But the lieutenant just said they wouldn't have brought him here if there hadn't been something suspicious about it, like the rear of the car."

"The lieutenant leaped to conclusions. Wrong conclusions." This time the captain didn't deign even to look at his subordinate. "He was brought here out of deference to his position and to the family, who are very well known and respected throughout the region."

"Are they going to do an autopsy?"

"That won't be necessary."

"May I see him?" Manuel entreated the officer.

"Of course," the police officer replied. "I will escort you."

Placing a hand on his shoulder and giving him a slight push, the captain guided him, passing through the group of the four men and going through the swinging doors.

The hotel room was white. Half a dozen pillows were artfully arranged upon the bed. All the lights in the room—track lights, overheads, and accent lights—were illuminated, casting such dazzling brilliance on the bed that they created a sensation bordering on unreality. It was a painful extension of the arctic sunlight that had taken possession of their home that morning and had stayed with him, virtually blinding him on the three-hundred-mile drive to Lugo. The overcast sky here had provided his eyes some relief, alleviating somewhat the impression so typical of a migraine of viewing the world through a hundred-faceted prism, where every image was blurred and distorted.

He turned off almost all the lights, took off his shoes, inspected the meager supplies in the minibar, and called room service to ask for a bottle of whiskey. He was well aware of the employee's disdain when he turned down the offer of something to eat to accompany the bottle. Nor did he fail to note the expression of the uniformed waiter who delivered it and looked over his shoulder to check the condition of the room. The man had the expert eye of someone who recognizes a guest who's going to be a problem.

The administrator had insisted on accompanying him from the hospital to the hotel. During the drive Griñán tried without success to fill in all the blanks. Words washed over Manuel but merely confirmed the existence of gaps, of quantities of information he needed to know and Álvaro hadn't told him. Griñán dogged Manuel's steps as far as the reception desk where Doval, who'd already set everything up, was waiting. They accompanied him to the elevator doors. Griñán suddenly seemed to realize Manuel must be exhausted and yearning for solitude. He and Doval excused themselves.

Now, alone in his room, Manuel served himself a double shot of the amber liquid and shuffled his way to the bed. He didn't bother to pull back the covers. He heaped the pillows against the headboard, leaned back on them, and downed the contents of the glass in two swallows like medicine. He got up, went back to the desk, and poured another drink. He started to return to the bed but had a better idea: he took the bottle back with him. He closed his eyes and cursed. Even with his eyes shut he kept seeing that midnight sun, its dazzling image burned into his retinas, as brilliant and formless as some repugnant ectoplasm.

He hesitated, faced with the choice between the need to think and the desire to obliterate all thought. He opted for the latter. He filled the glass and drained it so quickly that his stomach heaved. He almost threw up. He closed his eyes and found to his relief that the overwhelming solar brilliance was starting to fade. But in compensation the echo of all the conversations of that day returned to play out in his mind, blending with memories of things that had actually happened. Other images offered themselves, and dozens of tiny trifling details he'd overlooked or perhaps hadn't actually overlooked at all now began to make sense. The fact that three years had gone by since Álvaro's father had died, with the death of Álvaro's younger brother shortly afterward . . .

There was that September three years ago when Manuel had become convinced he'd lost Álvaro forever. He could recall every minute and every detail: the change in Álvaro's face that betrayed the unacknowledged fact that some weight as heavy as the world had fallen upon him; his disconcerting composure when he announced he had to go away for a few days; and his reticence as he calmly folded garments and placed them in his suitcase.

"Where are you going?"

The silence that met each question, the grieving expression, and the faraway look of someone who was no longer the man with whom he was sharing his life. Pleas had done no good. Demands and threats were useless. Álvaro was already on his way out when he turned to say, "Manuel, I've never asked for anything, but now I need you to trust me. Will you?"

Manuel had nodded, knowing he was too quick to give in, aware his answer wasn't an unqualified yes and it wasn't completely sincere. But what choice did he have? The man he loved was leaving, slipping through his fingers like sand. He felt no certainty in that moment other than that Álvaro was determined to go. Since he was going to leave in any case, agreeing to a pact was the only hope of binding him, the only chance that the linked obligations of freedom and mutual trust would hold them together.

Álvaro left home with a small suitcase, leaving Manuel plunged in a violent tempest of emotions, plagued above all by the fear Álvaro would never return. Then came the unhealthy brooding. He wondered what he might have done recently; searched for the tense instant in which the equilibrium had been disturbed; felt the weight of the eight years of difference in their ages; blamed his exaggerated attachment to books and a secluded life that perhaps were just too much for someone younger, better-looking, more . . . and he cursed the feckless-ness that had kept him from realizing that his world was crumbling. Álvaro was gone for five days with only the occasional hurried nighttime telephone call, his vague explanations relying on the pledge of trust he'd forced out of Manuel at the last moment.

Uncertainty gave way to frustration and pain. They alternated relentlessly and dragged him into that state of emotional vulnerability he'd thought he'd never have to endure again after his sister died. On the fourth night he lin-gered, inconsolable, by the phone, unable to step away, conquered by despera-tion, reduced to the point at which you give up and bare your throat to the executioner.

He clearly heard the pleading in his voice after he answered the phone. "You said just a couple of days . . . now it's been four."

Álvaro sighed. "Something has happened, something I wasn't expecting, and things have gotten more complicated."

He summoned his courage and asked in a whisper, "Álvaro, are you coming back? Tell me the truth."

"Of course I am."

"Are you sure?"

On the other end of the line Álvaro took a deep breath and let it out in a long, slow exhalation, a sound of infinite fatigue. Or perhaps of irritation? Annoyance at being forced to confront and resolve something bothersome and inappropriate?

"I'll be back, because that's where I belong and it's what I want. I love you, Manuel, and I want to be with you. I want to go home more than anything in the world, and what's going on right now has nothing to do with us."

There was such desperation in his voice that Manuel believed him.

THE DROUGHT

Álvaro came back one morning in mid-September, but for weeks it was as if he hadn't really returned at all. It was like jet lag, as if his essence had been left in some remote place and only the empty shell of a soul without breath or pulse had come back home. Even so, Manuel embraced the body that was his homeland, kissed those sealed lips, closed his eyes, and silently expressed his gratitude.

No explanations or excuses. Not a single word was spoken of what had gone on during those five days. The first night, while they lay in close embrace, Álvaro said, "Thanks for trusting me." Those words barred any possibility of an explanation for why he'd subjected Manuel to that hell. Manuel accepted it the way living flesh accepts a caress. He was so grateful and relieved; to his shame he embraced that humiliation and felt the euphoria of a condemned man who's just been pardoned. Remaining silent, he again gave thanks for the miracle that had calmed his terrible distress and the stomach cramps he'd suffered for days on end. Over the following weeks, that torment manifested itself as nausea every time the two were apart, a pathetic reminder with a horrible weight of panic. It lingered for months, and Manuel was unable to write a word during all that time.

Frequently he would regard Álvaro in silence as they watched a film or when his husband was sleeping. He was looking for some trace of betrayal. A relationship with another human being leaves upon the skin an indelible mark that's subtle but impossible to erase. Jealousy is primeval; writers have poured out rivers of ink describing it and the blindness of those afflicted. He devoted stolen moments to the search for some sign he knew would destroy his heart.

There were a few. Álvaro was unhappy, deeply sad and unable to hide it. He began coming home earlier, and on a couple of occasions he delegated to Mei the job of presenting projects when they involved firms outside Madrid. He turned down Manuel's suggestions of going out for a film or dinner with the excuse he was too tired. And Manuel accepted the excuses, because Álvaro really did seem tired, beaten down almost, as if he were carrying a great weight on his shoulders or dealing with some terrible guilt.

The telephone calls began. Manuel had always picked up the phone without a thought, with the exception of mealtimes, intervals they'd always designated as private time. Álvaro began leaving the room to answer the phone. This offense was offset somewhat by his obvious displeasure at receiving the calls, but the demon of doubt continued to torture Manuel. Sheer panic prevented him from sleeping on those nights.

In those bygone times Manuel had become paranoid and watched for the least sign that would unequivocally confirm infidelity. Obsessed, he analyzed Álvaro's every expression and gesture whenever they were together. Álvaro's emotional attachment had neither lessened nor increased; any such change Manuel would have found suspicious. Sometimes remorse is accompanied by an effort to compensate, so as to make amends for shame. Nothing of the kind occurred. On the few occasions that Álvaro took trips, he never spent more than a single night away. Except for those times Manuel insisted that he take two nights, urging, "There's no need for you to knock yourself out by driving such a distance. Stay another night and come back in the morning."

And when Álvaro was away, Manuel subjected himself to lengthy, exhausting walks that sometimes lasted all day. He intended them to overcome his desire to run after Álvaro, to tail him and turn up unexpectedly in the distant city where his husband was staying. They helped reduce the desperation of his welcoming hug upon Álvaro's return, for sometimes Manuel was so driven by anxiety that his embrace of welcome was almost physically painful. To a casual observer everything would have appeared to be in its place, for their lives went on just as always. Álvaro tried to smile, but when he managed to do so, his smile was faint and melancholy and weighted with a tenderness that encouraged Manuel to believe Álvaro would stay, that behind that expression Manuel was finally seeing the man he loved. The mere thought would be enough to sustain Manuel for days.

Only one sign, a single new clue, mystified Manuel. Frequently after a return, Manuel would catch Álvaro observing him, almost certainly aware he was reading without taking in a word or sitting at his desk pretending to write. Álvaro would look at him and smile confidently with that smile of a clever little boy. When asked about it, Álvaro would shake his head with a shy refusal to answer and then would embrace Manuel as fiercely as a shipwrecked sailor clinging to a floating timber. That ardent hug left no space between them, blocked any gap through which doubt might slip, and caused Manuel's heart to skip a beat. Manuel wanted to take that sudden fervent embrace as assurance and relief, but he didn't dare see it that way.

Emerging from pain requires determination. Calls from his editor had become more frequent, and his excuses of alleged pains, colds, and medical tests were no longer working. His conscience wouldn't let him exaggerate them, so he couldn't keep it up. The novel then in draft, to become a grand success in just a few months, would be his best yet. Reading had been his refuge throughout his life, from the time his sister and he had been orphaned as small children and continuing through the years they'd lived with an elderly aunt. When his sister reached the age of adulthood, she took charge and moved them into their parents' house that had stood empty all those years. Reading was the fortress from which he could defend himself as he struggled in a losing campaign to control the exultant instincts of his sexuality. Reading was a defense, a shield his timidity could use to arm itself, a guide to seeking relationships.

But writing was infinitely more than that. Writing was an interior palace with secret sites, gorgeous places, a complex of unlimited spaces. He explored them, laughing, running barefoot, and stopping to touch the beautiful treasures stored there.

He finished his academic studies summa cum laude and was invited to lecture on Spanish history at a prestigious university in Madrid. Not once in all those years of preparation or in his brief teaching career did he feel the need to write. In order to write he would have had to embrace the immensity of grief.

There's a type of open grief that's public, one of tears and mourning; and there's another, immense and silent, that is a million times more powerful. He was certain he'd experienced such open grief: his rejection of the injustice of losing his parents, all the miserable cold of childhood loneliness, the grim public mourning that marked him and his sister as bereaved and damaged, and all the fears that arose in his spirit and made him weep night after night in panic as he clung to his sister and made her promise she'd never abandon him, made her pledge that this suffering was the price they were paying to become invulnerable.

He knew that somehow they'd both embraced that belief. And their lives validated it as they grew up. Nothing bad could happen anymore, and they were blessed with bold happiness. Sometimes he imagined that time as the odyssey of the last remaining soldier, the heroic valor of being the last survivor. Somehow he'd managed to convince himself that the death of their parents had filled their quota of catastrophe, and somewhere there was a book that recorded the accumulated disasters and hurts until they reached a level that couldn't be exceeded. But he'd been mistaken. When they were both adults, destiny struck him at his only vulnerable point.

One of those last afternoons in the hospital she told him, "You have to forgive me for failing you. I always thought you were my weakest point, and the only hurt that could destroy me would have to come from you. But now it turns out that I'm the one who's failing you."

"Don't say that!" he pleaded through his tears.

His sister's voice was inaudible under Manuel's sobs. She waited patiently for him to calm down and then motioned to him to come closer, closer, until her chapped lips brushed his cheek. "That's why when I'm gone you must forget me. Try not to think of me or torture yourself with memories, because when I close my eyes I always see you again as a six-year-old weeping and impossible to console, broken and quivering with fear. I'm afraid that when I leave you alone you'll start crying again like that. You wouldn't let me sleep then; now you won't let me rest." He tried to pull away, not wanting to hear what he knew was coming. But it was too late. Her long, slim fingers wouldn't let him go. "Promise me, Manuel, promise you won't suffer. You won't let me become your greatest weakness. Don't ever let anyone be that to you."

He made that pledge to his sister like a crusader vowing to do battle. And when she closed her eyes, his grief was immense and silent.

❧

He'd been asked dozens of times why he wrote, and he had a couple of good answers, more or less sincere, that he trotted out. The satisfaction of communicating, the need to put oneself into the lives of others. But they weren't the truth. He wrote to maintain his vows under that truce, the armistice imposed as he made his way back to the palace, the only redoubt immense grief could not conquer, and the place where he wasn't breaking his promise. There was no single moment of decision. It wasn't something he'd thought out, and it wasn't the culmination of a desire he'd always cherished. He'd never dreamed of becoming a writer. One day he sat down with a blank sheet of paper and started filling it with words. They welled up like the water from a mysterious spring and eventually became a series of books. He couldn't name or locate the elusive source, for it changed constantly in his imagination. Sometimes it resembled the turbulent surface of the North Sea, other times it was like the Marianas Trench, and sometimes it appeared as an elegantly civilized Moorish fountain in some sun-drenched patio in Andalusia. All he knew was that the sea or trench or fountain originated somewhere in his mind. That's where he'd discovered the palace. He could enter it whenever he wished, and that storehouse of happiness and perfection inspired him and took him away, providing the perhaps inexhaustible, sparkling source of new expression.

When the sales of his first novel reached numbers that made it impossible not to continue, he asked for two years' leave from the university. Though no one said so, the assumption was that Manuel would eventually ask for an extension. The administration and faculty organized a party to mark his departure. They quickly forgot the annoyances that the articles and photos in the Sunday papers and cultural reviews had created for the entire university by profiling the young academic whose first novel was at the top of the bestseller list. With touching concern for his future, they came up in groups or individually to wish him luck and to warn him solemnly of the dire consequences of failure and the pitiless cruelty of a publishing world they'd never experienced or even tried to. For they were denizens of the ivory tower, that safe and welcoming place where they'd all greet him with open arms whenever he returned. Because they were sure he'd eventually be coming back after his little fling with literature's great prostitute, the popular novel.

One must make a conscious decision to feel pain. He knew that he'd been lying to himself, claiming he couldn't write, saying he was suffering too much to achieve the necessary state of grace. Nothing could be more wrong, because the truth was exactly the opposite. The palace was the site of ritual expiation, the healing place where wounds were cured. Three years ago in his uncertainty over Álvaro he'd obstinately refused to go back there. Because of that masoch-istic stubbornness he'd wasted away like an angel sleeping outside the shelter of paradise. His soul was dirty and disheveled; his clothes were in tatters, and his body was crosshatched with bloody wounds. He would try to stanch the blood flow one moment, but in the next he would whip himself anew, inflicting just as many bloody cuts to exorcise his pain.

Months had gone by with no sign of the threat that only Manuel had believed to exist. Life had continued. Moments of gloom were diluted in the tranquil routine of daily life, and Álvaro was able to smile again. The mysterious telephone calls to Álvaro had ended. Whatever had happened and whatever had been threatening to destroy his world, the shadow had lifted. He was sure of it.

His editor was pressing him, insisting he commit to a delivery date for his next novel, even if only an approximate one, any response at all. With Álvaro still at his side, he went back to the palace and resumed his writing.

FENG SHUI

He'd read in a book about feng shui that it's a serious error to place a mirror in such a way that it reflects the image of a person who's resting or sleeping. Evidently, the interior decorator for this hotel had been completely ignorant of that principle. Manuel's face was clearly reflected despite the dim lighting. He found no relief from stiffness. Neither the nest of pillows nor the whiskey he'd drunk had loosened his limbs. In the mirror his body looked cramped and tense. That pale face and the way his two hands clutched the almost empty glass to his chest made him resemble a corpse arranged for viewing. In his mind he saw Álvaro on that morgue slab.

As soon as he'd seen the body he was certain it wasn't Álvaro. The feeling was so strong that he even started to turn to say so to the police chief, who'd remained a discreet two steps behind him. The morgue technician, intimidated by the presence of such authority, had turned back the sheet covering the body, tucked it neatly across the chest, and retreated to his place.

Álvaro's face had a waxy sheen and—was it a trick of the light?—a slightly yellow tinge, like a mask of the man he had been. Manuel had stood there, absorbed, aware of the presence of the police officer behind him but not knowing what to do. He wanted to ask if he was permitted to touch his husband's body, but he knew he'd never be able to find the words. He'd never again kiss that face now transformed into a crude copy of the man he'd loved, the man now beginning to fade away before his eyes. Even so he forced himself to keep looking, conscious that his brain was refusing to recognize Álvaro in a stubborn effort to deny his death. Something was wrong with his perceptions. He couldn't comprehend what was right in front of him, but the crudest details stood out with extraordinary clarity. The hair, for example: It was a bit long, wet and combed back. Why was his hair wet? The curly lashes splashed with drops of water and stuck together by that moisture. The bloodless lips, slightly open. A little cut above the left eyebrow, defined by clean edges that were too dark. And nothing more. He was tormented by the monstrously perverse anomaly that held him there unmoved like a disinterested observer, but he became aware of a growing pressure in his chest that made it more and more difficult to breathe.

He wanted to weep. He knew that somewhere inside him the barriers that held back lamentation were cracking and that at any moment the stout walls erected against all that anguish would give way. But he couldn't weep. He despaired at that knowledge; it was like trying to breathe without lungs, gulping vast quantities of oxygen that went nowhere. He wanted to shatter into pieces. He wanted to die. But there he stood, immobile as a statue and incapable of locating within himself the key to open the chamber where his pain was locked away.

Then he noticed Álvaro's hand, visible at the edge of the sheet. He studied the long dark strong fingers. The hands of the dead do not change. They lie there full of their caresses, half-open and inert, as if in sleep. Manuel took that hand in his and felt the chill that had wicked up from the slab, up through the hands and fingertips to leave them icy. But it was Álvaro's hand. A focus of their love. He felt the smooth outer surface, so different from the surprisingly rough palms. "You must be the only marketing man in the world with the hands of a lumberjack," he used to tease Álvaro. And as he lifted that hand toward his lips, he felt the walls that restrained his grief yield violently in so many pieces that he'd never be able to put them back together. The rush of his desolation, like a tsunami of mud and rock, swept everything before it, ravaging the narrow confines of his soul. He touched his lips to the icy skin but then noted a band of lighter skin where Álvaro had worn his wedding ring for so many years.

He turned to the technician. "The wedding ring?"

"Excuse me, sir?" The technician stepped forward as if to hear better.

"He was wearing a wedding ring."

"No, sir. I inventory everything during registration. He wasn't wearing any personal item except a watch. It's with his belongings. Do you want to see them?"

Manuel carefully put down Álvaro's hand and covered it with the sheet so he wouldn't have to look at it. "No."

He moved past the two men and left the room.

A HOSTAGE TO FATE

Manuel was thirty-seven years old and had published six novels when he first met Álvaro. He was promoting *The Man Who Refused* each of the last three weekends of the Madrid Bookfair, which ran from the end of May to the middle of June. He was autographing copies.

He paid no attention to Álvaro the first time he saw him. He autographed the novel on a Saturday morning, and during the afternoon session he gave a routine smile when Álvaro came to the head of the line. He opened the book to the page where he usually placed his signature. "But look—I've already signed it!"

The young man smiled but said nothing. Manuel took a closer look. The fellow looked to be in his late twenties. Chestnut hair that was long enough to hang like a curtain to either side of large eyes that shone like those of a mischievous boy. The little smile was polite, the expression was contained. Manuel autographed the book again and extended his hand for a handshake. The other's tanned hand was firm. Manuel was captivated by the murmured *Thank you* mouthed by those moist lips rather than spoken, the words lost in the cacophony of the PA system and the chatter of other readers waiting impatiently in line. When the same visitor returned Sunday morning, Manuel looked at him in surprise but didn't say anything; but when the young man turned up again in the afternoon to place the novel in front of him, Manuel began to suspect something. This must be some kind of joke, a hidden camera trick to make fun of him. He autographed the book with a serious expression and held it out, studying the man's face for some sign of deceit.

Mornings and afternoons he was assigned to sessions at the stands of different bookstores, and Álvaro turned up at each of them with his book under his arm. Manuel's reaction progressed from his initial surprise to suspicion to curiosity to amusement. The game kept him in suspense, making him look forward to the man's return and wonder if he'd ever see him again. During the long intervening week Manuel occasionally found himself wondering at that fan's insistent enthusiasm, but by the following Saturday he'd forgotten about it.

Then he found the man in front of him yet again. He was bewildered. "Why?" he managed to ask as he accepted the book held out to him.

"Because I want you to autograph it for me," the young man answered patiently.

"But I've already signed it for you," Manuel replied in confusion. "This is the fifth time."

Álvaro leaned over so the others behind him in line wouldn't be able to hear. Manuel felt the young man's lips brush against his hair. "I'm back!" he said. "So you'll have to sign it for me one more time."

Manuel pulled back, disturbed, and peered at his face, trying to remember whether they might have met somewhere else.

"You?" he asked, disconcerted as he looked down and read the dedication. "Álvaro?"

Álvaro nodded with a smile and left with the latest autograph, evidently content.

Manuel was no monk. He'd sworn he'd never let anyone become important enough to make him fear loss, but that was no obstacle to getting laid. He'd had acquaintances who were one-timers, men who never stayed over and would never think of moving in.

The following day he scribbled his telephone number after his autograph.

He waited all week for a call that never came. Meanwhile he imagined all sorts of possibilities: perhaps the young man had felt somehow offended; maybe he never bothered to examine the dedicatory notes written each time; perhaps it was just a game and the boy shut the book and paid no further attention to it.

Manuel couldn't get the man out of his mind as he anxiously waited for Saturday to arrive. The session began at noon and was scheduled to last until two. Readers came one after another. He wrote notes and signed them, posed for photos he'd never see, and he waited.

In the closing minutes he looked up and spotted Álvaro. His heart almost skipped a beat. Manuel had trouble concealing his agitation when Álvaro reached the front of the line. He'd decided to say something, maybe invite him for coffee or a beer after the signing, right there in one of the crowded bars of the overheated enclosure of the fair. But when Álvaro stood in front of him, he had trouble maintaining his calm, and so Manuel just looked at him instead of saying anything. Álvaro wore a white shirt and had rolled the sleeves halfway up his forearms, further accentuating his tan and his muscles. Manuel took the book from him and sluggishly turned it to the usual page to inscribe it again. He caught sight of his note with the telephone number and saw Álvaro's decisive, confident handwriting for the first time with the reply: *Not yet.*

Without caring if anyone overheard him, he looked up into Álvaro's eyes and asked in anguish, "When?"

Álvaro stood there meeting his gaze and said nothing. Feeling defeated, Manuel looked down, scrawled a signature, and held out the book. He was disappointed and a bit annoyed.

He liked games as much as anyone. The exquisite tension of anticipating seduction heightened pain and pleasure and imposed a self-discipline almost Confucian in nature. He found it extraordinarily alluring. But Álvaro's attitude confused him. Nothing the man did suggested a willingness to go further. Each morning and each afternoon he limited himself to standing in line, waiting patiently like any other reader to get up to the author with no other goal than to get an autograph.

Manuel decided not to play anymore. For the rest of the weekend he limited himself to executing his signature on a different page each time and handing back the book with the same pleasant smile as at first, the same smile he offered every reader, and he refused to allow himself to be trapped into doing more. By the end of the Sunday sessions, he'd decided that the young man was a harmless stalker, either an ardent fan or a collector of autographs.

The last weekend was in the middle of June. The central avenue of Retiro Park was practically coming apart beneath the constant flow of visitors. He gave autographs all Saturday morning and afternoon, and Álvaro didn't appear. At the end of the Sunday-morning session, he was convinced Álvaro wouldn't be back, a prospect that created a curious emptiness in the pit of his stomach. The publisher had arranged for a farewell luncheon in a nearby restaurant, but Manuel scarcely touched his plate as he tried to follow the conversations, most of which were writers' anecdotes about other autograph sessions. The press relations agent came up to him as the meal ended.

"Manuel, you're looking under the weather. Has this all been too much for you? You've been signing every single weekend." She took out a thick sheaf of paper and consulted it. "It's your turn to sign at the Lee Bookstore booth. If you're not feeling well, I'll make excuses for you. They're lovely people, and they'll understand. It's your last session and only the real latecomers will be there."

He went. The metal stands were stifling in the heat of that June afternoon. The proprietors left the back doors open in unfulfilled hopes of creating a cooling draft. But the high temperature didn't appear to affect the visitors. Like some great multimembered living thing they slithered their way past the stands, carrying with them their noise and the radiant heat of their bodies. At eight o'clock the place was jammed to the bursting point; by nine they were almost all gone. The crowds were quickly replaced by squads of workers taking apart the concession stands and carrying away dispensing machines in the open backs of freight trucks and pickups. This time the booksellers hadn't lowered the metal shutters on their booths, and they'd stacked up dozens of cardboard boxes into which they were busy collecting everything that had constituted a branch of the store throughout the duration of the fair.

He lingered and took farewell of his hosts, feeling satisfied at the outcome of the fair. It had broken all sales records for the third consecutive year. Then finally he had no excuse to stay. He walked away from the stands and looked for the nearest bench so he could sit to observe the central aisle and the activity of those taking the stands apart.

Álvaro sat down beside him.

"I was afraid I wouldn't get here in time," he said and excused himself with a smile. "I'm lucky to find you still here."

Manuel's heart suddenly pounded so hard that he felt his pulse throbbing in his throat. He wasn't sure if he could even speak. "I'm waiting for my press agent," he lied.

Álvaro tilted his head to one side and met his eye. "Manuel, your press agent left a while ago. I saw her going out as I was coming in. She went out into the park with a group of authors."

Manuel nodded slowly and smiled. "That's right."

"And the real reason is . . . ?" His eyes still had all the sparkle of the youngster he'd been not too many years before. Manuel would recognize that same audacity and confidence many years later when he at last saw a photo of Álvaro as a boy.

"To tell you the truth, I wanted to see you again," Manuel admitted.

"Will you sign this for me?" he said, holding out the book again.

Manuel looked back with a smile. *Here we go again. What was the point of all this?* he asked himself once again.

"You'll have to keep on signing it until you write another one this good."

IMPASSE

The administrator's offices occupied a whole floor of an imposing building in the center of town. As Griñán had promised, a driver with a limousine picked him up at the hotel and drove him the short distance to the executor's place of business. Doval escorted him to a small room adjoining a larger conference room and insisted on providing him with a coffee he sipped reluctantly and a tray of pastries he wasn't going to touch. The very thought of food made him feel ill, even though the last decent meal he'd had was breakfast at home the day before, before the corporal and the handsome woman sergeant turned up to deliver the worst imaginable news.

He rose and grunted, but his head was all right. An old woman who'd taught him to drink whiskey had given him good advice: "Whiskey is the perfect tipple for a writer. It lets you think when you're drunk and doesn't leave a hangover. So the next day you can go back to writing."

He stepped up to the glass door between the two rooms, attracted by the rattle of chairs against the floor and the obvious unease of Griñán, who was overseeing the setup of the room. The administrator's worried look wasn't at all in keeping with his earlier affability. It was as if he'd ordered the staff to set up a display of coffins instead of chairs. Griñán caught sight of him through the glass door, smiled, waved, and came toward him.

"Señor Ortigosa, you look like hell."

Manuel couldn't help smiling at the candid evaluation of a reality of which he was all too aware. "Call me Manuel, please," he replied.

Griñán smiled. "Excuse my frankness. All my fault; I should have foreseen you'd have trouble sleeping, given the situation. Completely to be expected. My wife, who's a physician, gave me this for you." He held out a tiny metal pillbox. "She made me promise that I'd ask you if your blood pressure is normal and whether you've had any heart problems."

Manuel shook his head, checked the pillbox, and noted that Dr. Griñán's precautions went well beyond perfunctory inquiries about his circulatory system. The little box contained only two pills.

"Take them just before bedtime, and you'll sleep like a baby." Griñán closed the door to the adjacent office. "You'll wait here. I think that'll be best. Doval will seat the immediate family. With the blinds down they won't be able to see anything in here. After they're all seated, I'll escort you to your place, and we'll begin. That way you won't be in the room as they're arriving. I think that will make this easier for everyone."

He turned on a little desk lamp and gave Manuel a worried glance as he lowered the blinds. Griñán sat down next to him. "There's one thing you should know," he said in a concerned tone. "They, too, have been shocked by all this, just as you have. And for them perhaps it was worse, not so much because you were in a relationship with Álvaro—that they could have taken for granted—as for the revelation that you and he were married."

"I understand."

Griñán shook his head. "The noble line of the Marquis of Santo Tomé is one of the country's most ancient noble families and beyond all doubt the most important of Galicia. They regard their name as sacred. The old marquis, Álvaro's father, was extremely strict, and he considered the preservation of family honor more important than anything else. Absolutely anything," he repeated with emphasis. "Álvaro's homosexuality was unacceptable to him, and he was aware that the title would revert to his eldest son. Through his long wasting illness, he continued to insist we not inform Álvaro until after his death. Perhaps that will give you an idea of how vindictive the gentleman was."

"If he despised Álvaro so much, why didn't he disinherit him and pass the title to one of his other sons? For example, the one who inherits it now?"

"Disinheriting the eldest son would have caused a scandal. He found that unthinkable, and in my view he was right. Oh, well, you'll get to know them soon enough." Griñán got up and turned off the desk lamp. "Let's go." He moved to the glass-paneled door. "What I'm trying to convey is that they're cut from very different cloth."

"Are you warning me they'll be hostile?"

"Hostile? No. They'll be frigid. They don't mix with others; it's like oil and water. You shouldn't take it amiss. It's nothing personal." He peered through the blinds. "Álvaro entrusted me with his affairs from the day he came into the title and the estate. My office provides legal and management advice as well as a certified accountant who makes sure the books are balanced and all the numbers, taxes, and donations are properly recorded. Álvaro's father had attended to that with the help of an attorney who was an old friend of the family." He shook his head. "The attorney ran all the businesses. Back then they occasionally came to consult me about the manor house and the agricultural holdings. More than once I had to deal with affairs more domestic in nature, and still today every time I run into them I have the impression that in their eyes I'm nothing but a servant. A sort of lackey. You'll see what I mean." He shrugged. "That's their attitude toward everyone outside the family."

"Was Álvaro like that as well?"

Griñán looked back at him from the door. "Of course not. No, Álvaro was a businessman. A very wealthy man in his own right. He had his two feet planted firmly on the ground, and he was brimming with ideas about how to run the place." For a moment he appeared lost in thought. "I'm afraid that on more than one occasion his ingenuity surpassed my understanding. He always wound up surprising me with the outcomes. Over the past three years the Muñiz de Dávila account has become the most important of all those we manage." He gave Manuel a confident smile. "And I hope it will continue to be so." He looked out at the adjoining room, stood, and motioned sharply for Manuel to accompany him.

Manuel gave a puff of annoyance and went to join the group.

A number of people were taking seats in the adjoining room. An elderly woman, frail and dressed in black, probably in her seventies, was escorted by a man who was obviously Álvaro's brother. The gentleman was shorter and stockier and his features were less delicate, but he had the same chestnut hair and green eyes as Álvaro. His right hand was in a cast.

"The old woman is the mother, and as you've probably guessed, the man is Álvaro's brother, the new marquis. The woman with him is his wife, Catarina; she comes from a noble family that's fallen on hard times. They've barely managed to hold on to the family mansion. But theirs is also a name of renown. It's not surprising that the dowager marquess adores her."

A little boy perhaps three years old came running into the room chased by a young woman who was extremely thin but very good-looking. The boy zigzagged through the chairs and wrapped himself around the legs of Álvaro's brother. The man lifted him high in the air and provoked shrieks of laughter from the child. The elderly lady glared at the young woman, who responded with a shrug and a cheerful smile.

"The girl is Elisa. She was engaged to Fran, the youngest son. She was a model or a beauty queen, something to do with fashion in any case, and the boy is little Samuel, Fran's son and the only offspring of the family, at least for the moment." He gestured toward Catarina, who was delightedly contemplating the child and her husband, who without paying attention to the old lady's indignation was tickling the youngster. Little Samuel shrieked and twisted about in the man's arms. "Although they hadn't yet married, because of the child, Elisa has been living with them at the manor since Fran's death."

"Do they know I'm here today?"

"Considering the circumstances, I was obliged to inform them of your existence, just as it's my duty to explain things to you. So they know about you, but they don't know why."

"And tell me: Why am I here today?" Manuel didn't bother to hide his curiosity.

"You'll find out almost immediately," Griñán replied. He looked out at the room where Doval had already taken a seat to one side of the table facing the rows of chairs. He opened the door. "We're all here. Shall we go in?"

Manuel took the seat in the back of the room that Griñán had reserved for him. It gave him the advantage of seeing everyone there without feeling exposed. He was grateful for Griñán's precaution, even though it wasn't enough to suppress the nausea knotted in his stomach or the clammy feeling of his palms. He wiped them on his trouser legs in an unsuccessful effort to dry them and asked himself again what the hell he was doing there. How would these people react when he had to look them in the face?

The executor, Griñán, strode through the rows of chairs without a word. Clearly conscious of the ceremonial nature of the occasion, he stood behind the table. "First of all, both señor Doval and I wish to express our deepest sympathy to you for the terrible loss you have just sustained." He paused and carefully seated himself as Doval opened an imposing leather portfolio, extracted a large envelope, and handed it to him. "As you are aware, I was charged with administering the affairs of don Álvaro Muñiz de Dávila, Marquis of Santo Tomé, and I am the executor of his will." He took a sheaf of documents from the envelope. "I have invited you here for the reading of the last wishes of don Álvaro Muñiz de Dávila before seeing to the execution of the instructions of his will. As I previously informed you, this will take some time, given the complexity and the number of holdings that constitute his estate. The document I am about to read is not his legal will, strictly speaking, but it does provide important information. Allow me to add that it faithfully reflects the provisions of the will. It was the desire of the honorable marquis that this be read immediately in the event of his death. Which has come to pass." He put on spectacles that had been positioned on the table and looked about to see if there was any objection. When he saw none, he continued. "Before I proceed with the reading, I am obliged to outline for you certain relevant circumstances I believe unknown to you. You are not unaware of the state of the family finances following the death of the previous marquis. A series of unfortunate business decisions and investments had left your fortune severely reduced, and a number of unpaid mortgage obligations and other overdue debts were about to result in foreclosures of all of the real estate, including the manor of As Grileiras, the Arousa summer house, and the vineyards and winery in Ribeira Sacra."

The old lady cleared her throat, obviously annoyed. "I don't think it's necessary to go into details. We all know the situation my husband left us in." Her voice was sharp. She directed an angry look at the child. Bored and seated on a chair too tall for him, he was kicking his feet.

Griñán nodded, looking at her over his reading glasses. "Very well. Over the past three years don Álvaro undertook a heroic effort and put his personal fortune at risk, against my advice, I have to acknowledge, in order to forestall the catastrophe that was about to befall you. He bought up all the loans, renegotiated the mortgages, paid them off, and brought all of the various business affairs under professional management. As of today the estate is free of debt. Don Álvaro has been providing family members with monthly allowances, and he has instructed that these are to continue. And there is an endowment to finance the education of your little Samuel." He paused. "I take the time to explain these matters so that it is clear that don Álvaro purchased, settled, and paid all family debts with his own funds."

Both the matriarch and the new marquis nodded in acknowledgment.

"And that as a result, all of the real estate holdings became his personal property."

The mother and son exchanged a glance. There was an uneasy stir in the room.

"What does that mean?" the son asked.

"It means that all of the land and buildings to which banks and creditors had held title became the personal property of your brother."

"All right. And so?"

"I was of the opinion that you would need to keep that fact in mind as I read the present document. It is very brief, with an attachment listing the allowances and other specific bequests. I will read those to you. The principal document states, *I name as my only heir and the heir of all my assets my beloved husband Manuel Ortigosa.*" He paused. "That is the entire text."

For a couple of seconds time seemed to have stopped. The silence was absolute. Then Griñán raised the scroll of papers held in his hand like a baton and gestured toward where Manuel was seated.

Everyone turned to look at him. The child started applauding.

The old woman stood up, went to the little boy, and slapped him. "Teach this child manners, or he'll wind up like his father!" she hissed at the young woman.

The dowager marquess left the room without another word. The boy's pursed lips opened in a wail, and the embarrassed young woman quickly gathered him into her arms. The new marquis got up, took the child from her, hugged him, and kissed the flaming red spot on his cheek.

"I'm very sorry," he said, without addressing anyone in particular. "You must excuse my mother. She is in delicate health."

He left carrying the little boy, who was still in tears. His pale wife followed him. The young woman was the only one who turned for a moment to say goodbye before leaving the room, leaving Manuel with the feeling that something extraordinary and beyond his comprehension had just taken place before his eyes.

Griñán removed his spectacles and looked at him, letting out his breath in a low whistle.

"*That's* why I'm here," Manuel said, suddenly enlightened.

Griñán nodded. "As I told you, they don't mix. Don't be alarmed by their reaction; one could hardly expect otherwise. As I explained, all this was as much a surprise for them as for you, since Álvaro hid much of his life from them. Perhaps the news about their money was something of a shock. But that's the extent of it." Griñán tilted his head to one side, reflecting. "Perhaps the only one disturbed by the fact they won't have their own fortune is the dowager marquess, even though she's lived that way half her life thanks to the 'abilities' of her husband." He grimaced. "The others won't trouble you. They've never been a problem. Álvaro was quick to size them up: as long as their allowances are big enough to live in the style to which they're accustomed, they'll be content. Knowing that, Álvaro provided for annual increases that will keep them more than satisfied. Of course, he also provided for the operating costs of the manor of As Grileiras and the Arousa summer house."

He got up and handed the documents to the patiently waiting Doval, who slipped them into the portfolio. Griñán came around the table, negotiated his way through the chairs, repositioned one, and seated himself next to Manuel.

"I saw earlier they had no idea Álvaro was married. Once they come to terms with that fact, however, they'll see it was logical for him to will his fortune to you, especially considering that he used his own money to put affairs in order. He paid off family debts from the fortune he earned with his brilliant successes in marketing and public relations. Anyone with any brains at all will see it's entirely logical that the fortune Álvaro made as a married man should go to his spouse."

He shook his head. "Logic is one thing, however, quite apart from the immense resentment they must feel upon finding that they now depend financially upon someone from outside the family, and I mean 'outside' as they conceive of it. But they'll get used to it. They already adapted when the father willed the businesses and holdings to Álvaro even though they'd assumed he would be disinherited." He pursed his lips. "Maybe Santiago will feel a bit disappointed at inheriting a title without a fortune, but I guarantee you he'll pose no problems. He's never had the least interest in business. That's why I always said that the old marquis never considered willing the holdings to him."

"They seemed to be very wealthy," Manuel said tentatively.

"Well, now *you're* the wealthy one," the executor reminded him.

"I mean, after all, not all noble families are rich. Where did the family fortune come from? What were the father's business interests?"

"As I said, this is one of the most important noble families of Galicia. Its history goes back hundreds of years, and from the very first it was very closely allied with the Church. They're owners of vast land holdings, and they own an extensive and important art collection."

"Like most of Spain's noble families," Manuel commented. "Always reluctant to part with their works of art. And ownership of an enormous amount of land between Lugo and Ourense probably means more expenditures than income. Unless it's properly administered."

Griñán appeared impressed. "I forgot that you were a historian. Indeed, many noble families have wound up in financial difficulty for those very reasons, but Álvaro's father was very fortunate in business dealings as a young man. He was granted concessions, agricultural land, commissions. Unfortunately he was less successful in preserving his wealth than he was in acquiring it."

Manuel was intrigued. That kind of talk could be risky for a man in Griñán's position. The implications were obvious. "In other words, business dealings during the decades of the forties, fifties, and sixties. During the Franco era." Griñán nodded almost imperceptibly, so Manuel went on. "Nobles who maintained their allegiance to the royal family in exile didn't do as well back then."

"The marquis managed to accumulate a considerable fortune, but times change. The usual unfortunate story: extravagant spending, bad business deals, gambling. There were rumors he maintained at least a couple of mistresses in grand style. He may not have had such a good eye for investments in his later years, but he was no fool. He always found a way to maintain his family in the comfortable circumstances they were used to. But then the upper classes always do, don't they?"

Manuel remembered the family's reaction in the meeting room. "Santiago might have been offended."

The administrator waved his hand in a sign of dismissal. "The old marquis knew his middle son had no head for business. People tell stories about terrible public humiliations the old man subjected him to. It's true the old marquis found Álvaro's inclinations unacceptable, but he knew his eldest would be capable of taking care of the family. He also knew Álvaro had more talent in his little finger than all the rest of them combined." He smiled. "One doesn't cancel the other, but as I said, the man was obsessed by the duty of preserving the honor of the family name, which in the last analysis means maintaining the family lifestyle. He was ready to do anything for that, including willing it all to Álvaro." Griñán nodded thoughtfully. "The old fox knew what he was doing. In three years Álvaro not only cleaned up the estate's finances but also turned around disastrous operations in agriculture and wine production. He made them extremely profitable."

"What I don't understand is how he managed those businesses from Madrid," Manuel said almost to himself. He shook his head in amazement.

"By telephone, most of the time. Álvaro knew exactly what changes had to be made. My office provided him a team for legal counsel, administration, and management through the network of firms that regularly work with us, a team of real professionals. We all knew what had to be done, and whenever some key decision or binding commitment had to be made, I was the one to consult him via his private number. Not even the general manager had it. I served as the channel of communication."

"And the family?" Manuel asked, indicating the seats they'd occupied.

"I alone was involved," replied Griñán. "Álvaro made his desires clear on that point from the very first."

A shadow passed over the kindly face of the executor. Manuel was about to ask about it, but Griñán got to his feet. "Well, that's enough for today. The driver will take you back to the hotel." Manuel declined the offer of a ride. He wanted instead to walk through streets overhung by that odd sky of rain clouds, so he could think about what Griñán had said.

"Very well," the executor said. "Take the pills and get some sleep. You need it. I'll come by tomorrow to pick you up and escort you to the funeral. We'll have time to talk after that. But believe me when I say that it's a relief to the whole clan not to have to take charge of the businesses. Not a single person you've seen today has lent a hand or shown the least interest in them. Family members don't work; they've never worked, unless you count raising gardenias, hunting, or horse riding as work."

Manuel left the management offices expecting gentle breezes outside, but instead the odd, cool September weather of Galicia gave him a rude shock. Instead of providing the mild reassurance he needed in order to think, it made him feel tired and hungry. His eyes burned from the brilliance reflected from the clouds. He felt like an orphan, a traveler from afar, alien to a city that refused to accept him. He hurried to seek refuge from the light, the voices, and the cacophony of the Greek chorus in his head.

He took the two pills Griñán had given him and consumed half a bottle of mineral water. As he shed his clothing he looked down from his hotel room window at the facades of the buildings along the street. The cruel, inescapable light of the gray noonday sky overwhelmed their colors and decors. He closed the curtains and went to bed. He slept almost immediately.

He dreamed of a six-year-old boy who couldn't stop crying. The child's weeping awoke him, and in the darkness it took him a few moments to remember where he was. He slept again. The sky was completely dark when he again became aware of his surroundings. He rang room service and ordered a huge quantity of food. He devoured it while watching the evening news on television. After the meal he went back to bed and fell asleep again. He next opened his eyes at 5:00 a.m., just in time to see Clint Eastwood on the screen pointing a finger at him and pretending it was a pistol. The effect was just as threatening as if it were a real gun.

He felt clearheaded. For the first time since the beautiful sergeant in Madrid arrived with the bad news, he had overcome the sluggish confusion that had surrounded him as he trudged onward like a soul in purgatory. He settled into a curious serenity, relieved at last of the noisy mad-ghost voices that had hounded him since the sergeant told him of Álvaro's death. He recognized that serenity as his natural habitat. His lucid mind and unassuming thoughts were always distracted by noise and disorder. He sighed, realizing he was alone in the silence of the night. Completely alone. He looked around.

"What are you doing here?" he whispered to himself.

There was no answer. Eastwood gave him a steely glance with an unmistakable message: *Get out of here. This is no time to look for trouble.*

"I will," he said aloud to the television screen.

It took only forty minutes to shower, shave, and pack his few belongings. He settled before the television and waited patiently until seven o'clock. Then he picked up his phone. He'd kept it turned off since the day before, but now he was going to call Griñán. The phone listed forty-three missed calls, all of them from Mei. It began to vibrate as he looked down at it. He thought of not answering, but he knew Mei wouldn't give up. He accepted the call, lifted the phone to his ear, and said nothing, too tired to deal with it.

She sobbed before she spoke. "Manuel, I'm so sorry. You have no idea how much this hurts. These have been the worst days of my life. I loved him, Manuel, you know that."

He shut his eyes and just listened. He said nothing.

"I know you have every reason to be angry with me, but you should understand I was just doing what he told me. He said it was for your own good."

"For my own good?" he exploded. "Lying to me for my own good? What kind of people are you? What kind of people would claim something like that is good for me?"

Mei's distress on the other end became twice as loud. "I'm sorry, I'm so sorry! If only I could do something . . ."

Mei's abject apology just made him that much angrier. He rose in fury, unable to contain himself. "Go ahead and be sorry. The two of you fucked up my life, the one I have now and everything I had before. Now I know. Everything I thought I could depend on was just one lie after another, and I was the only one being kept in the dark. I hope you enjoyed yourselves!"

"It wasn't like that!" Mei shrieked, still racked with tears. "It's not like that at all! Álvaro loved you and so do I, and you know we'd never do anything to hurt you. Álvaro told me that's how things had to be, because he wanted to keep you safe."

"Safe? Safe from what, Mei? What kind of crap story are you trying to put over on me now?" he shouted. He remembered where he was and desperately rubbed his face. He lowered his voice. He told her almost in a whisper, "I met the family. They're not monsters, Mei; they don't have two heads, and they don't eat children. What I found here is a group of people as surprised and frightened as I am by what happened. The only person safe in this whole mess was Álvaro. Safe from explaining, safe from the life with me he was ashamed of, safe to live his double life as a Spanish grandee!"

"A grandee?" Mei responded. "What on earth are you talking about?" The surprise in her voice sounded real.

"I'm astonished you didn't know. Álvaro's family are aristocrats. He was a marquis."

"I don't know what you're assuming, but the truth is that I knew hardly anything. Three years ago he told me his father had died and he had to take charge of the family businesses. From then on he ran them from this office. He said his family members were horrible, and he had no contact with them except for the businesses. He warned me they were very destructive, and he wanted to protect you from them, so you were never to know anything about them. I was supposed to avoid mentioning anything about them in front of you."

"And that seemed normal to you?"

"Manuel, what was I supposed to do? He made me promise. And it didn't seem so strange to me. Lots of gay men are estranged from their families. You know that."

Manuel couldn't find the words to respond.

"Manuel, I'm coming, I have my tickets and I take the train today at noon—"

"No."

"Manuel, I want to be with you, I don't want you to have to face this alone."

His refusal was obdurate. "No."

"Manuel!" She again burst into sobs. "If you don't want me there, at least let me tell some of your friends . . ."

He sagged into the armchair, exhausted. The air escaped from his lungs in a long miserable sigh. "And what are you going to tell them, Mei? Since I still have no idea what I'm doing here or what happened? What was Álvaro doing so far from home? I just want it all to be over so I can go home."

She dissolved in tears on the other end of the line. Dazed with fatigue, he listened to her and felt an entirely justified envy of her ability to weep. His anguish seized his voice so fiercely his throat seemed to be tearing apart. He vomited all his anxiety in a rush of bile and resentment. "I'm fifty-two years old, Mei. I promised myself this would never happen again. I never thought Álvaro would be the one to make me feel this way. This is more than I can handle. I've been here for two days, his funeral is in two hours, and I'm still not able to weep. You know why? Because I don't understand a thing, because none of it makes sense. This is insane; it's a goddamn tasteless practical joke."

"Stop fighting it, Manuel," she urged him in a low voice. "Crying will do you good."

"He wasn't wearing his wedding ring, Mei. The man who died here wasn't my husband anymore. I can't weep for him."

~❦~

Griñán, the executor, answered his call immediately.

"I have to talk to you. I've made a decision."

"I'll be there in half an hour. At the hotel café."

When he shut the door to the room behind him, he was carrying his packed suitcase. He had no intention of returning.

Griñán was punctual. He ordered a coffee. As he seated himself he noticed the suitcase. "You're leaving?"

"Right after the funeral."

Griñán looked him over as if to judge his resolve, and Manuel asked, "Correct me if I'm wrong: You're now my legal representative, aren't you?"

"Unless you decide to entrust your affairs to another professional."

Manuel shook his head. "I want you to inform Álvaro's family that I'm not accepting the bequest. They don't have to worry, because I don't want anything. I don't want to hear another word about any of this. Do everything necessary, so I can complete the formalities as soon as possible, and send any paperwork to my home. I'm sure you have the address."

Griñán smiled.

"What's so funny?"

"I was just thinking how well Álvaro knew you. I can inform the family if you wish, but your husband included an instruction that you're not to be permitted to renounce his bequest until three months after his death or—which is the same thing—until his will is probated."

Manuel glared at him for a moment, but then his tension ebbed away. It wasn't Griñán's fault, after all; Álvaro was to blame.

"This is unbelievable," he said wearily. "All right then, tell the family, and you can send me the documents in December."

"As you wish," was the response. "That way you'll have time to think it over."

He'd been determined to keep his cool with Griñán, but this was just too much. He lost it. "There's nothing to think about. Álvaro hid his identity from me. He concealed his life. Now I discover I've spent almost fifteen years with a man

I didn't know, who has a family I didn't know existed, and I find myself heir to a fortune that doesn't belong to me and I don't want. I've made my decision, and I'm not going to change my mind."

The executor looked down, his face studiously neutral as he sipped his coffee. Manuel looked around and saw the few other customers doing their best to pretend they hadn't heard. He'd been berating Griñán at the top of his voice.

⁂

In his BMW he tailed Griñán's Audi for forty minutes on the highway and another fifteen through a settled area. The forecast of rain had resolved itself into a sky of billowing clouds that offered sufficient cover to filter the sunlight and impose a palette of muted colors. The town wasn't large. The countryside and landscape were a series of rural clusters along the road with barns along their outskirts, flanking the highway or the train tracks. After they'd turned off the main road there were fewer barns, and the perspective opened to vast fields of emerald green enclosed by walls of ancient stone and fences so picturesque they'd have been the delight of any photographer. Manuel was surprised by the beauty of the small cultivated groves of trees, their leaves shaded between green and silver. He guessed they were eucalyptus. The gorse bushes, nearly black and dotted with distinctive yellow flowers, contrasted with the pink heather along the road. Griñán turned right onto a wide, graded gravel road that led toward a forest. A hundred yards farther he stopped the car outside an immense iron gate that stood wide open. Manuel parked behind the Audi, got out, and approached the administrator. Griñán stood waiting at the entrance, his face lit with almost childish enthusiasm.

"We could have driven in together," he explained as they walked through the gate, "but I didn't want you to miss your impression when you saw it for the first time."

Flanked by hundred-year-old trees, the unpaved drive was covered with pine needles. Here and there open pine cones clung to thin branches overhead like wooden roses. The ground sloped gradually upward toward an open area with a carefully manicured lawn and a one-story stone structure where rounded arches in a facade enclosed two magnificent wooden doors.

Manuel looked at Griñán, who was expectantly awaiting his reaction.

"It's very beautiful," he had to admit.

The executor smiled in satisfaction. "It is, but this is merely one of the outbuildings. The stables are down there." He stopped and pointed to the right. "The house is there. Señor Ortigosa, that is As Grileiras manor, the house where your husband was born and the residence of every Marquis of Santo Tomé since the seventeenth century."

The rectangular building was triple the size of the first one. Its small windows were deeply inset in walls of light-brown stone. It was situated at the crest of a gentle hill that dominated the grounds and contrasted with the deep vale extending behind it. The flat plain before the manor was planted with a thick little grove of ancient olive trees that blocked the view at ground level but would not, he was sure, obstruct the panorama visible from the upper floor. A line of wrought iron lamps and stone planters full of flowers was situated in front of the structure, much in the style of the Vatican, and they were surrounded by a hedge of shiny leaves and white flowers so fragrant he could smell their aroma even at this distance.

"Those are gardenias. As Grileiras has the most extensive collection of these flowers in Europe, perhaps unmatched anywhere in the world. Catarina, Santiago's wife, is an expert; since the day of their wedding she's taken care of their cultivation and has even won prizes in the most prestigious competitions. Next to the pond there's a magnificent greenhouse where she has succeeded in cultivating some really interesting hybrids. We can visit it afterward if you wish."

Manuel walked to the exterior hedge to admire the waxy cream-colored flowers and glossy leaves. He picked a flower and ran a fingernail along the hard stem. Cupping it in his hand, he inhaled a perfume so thick it almost dripped through his fingers. Griñán's explanations, that parade of offspring and in-laws, the family devoted to class distinctions he'd never encountered—this constellation seemed absurd and hostile, and the shame and humiliation of the encounter almost drove him away. Not even his need for answers would be enough to motivate him to stay in this place one minute beyond the required time. Concealing that reaction in deference to the friendly executor, he asked, "What does *As Grileiras* mean? It sounds like something to do with crickets."

"It does, doesn't it? But that's entirely misleading." Griñán smiled. "*As Grileiras* in Gallego, also known as *herbameira*, are magic herbs with marvelous healing powers, just short of miraculous. According to the legends, they grow along the banks of ponds, lakes, and fountains. The expression comes from the word *grilo* or *grelo* referring to the first little shoots of the plants."

Manuel took in the fragrance of the flower, slipped it into the pocket of his double-breasted jacket, and trailed after Griñán.

"The cemetery is about two hundred yards from here, next to the estate's church."

"They have both a cemetery and a church?"

"Actually it's something between a small church and a large chapel. A few years ago lightning struck the steeple of the village church, and the family allowed people to use this sanctuary for some months while the other was being restored. The parish priest was delighted. He held daily masses in addition to the usual Sunday service, and I believe that many more people came for the mass here. For the pleasure of being admitted to the marquis's manor grounds, you know. People here follow such things very closely."

"What things?"

"Well, the holy mass is a class-conscious ceremony, after all, so the humbler the congregation, the better. The Marquises of Santo Tomé have owned these lands for centuries. Half the families of the region have worked for them at one time or another, and there still exists a feudal notion of protection granted by the lord of the manor. When you or your ancestors have worked for him, that's considered to confer a portion of his honor and distinction on you and yours."

"A distinction for the ignorant."

"Well, don't be so sure," Griñán disagreed. "The majority of today's Spanish aristocrats are extraordinarily discreet, except for the handful who appear in the tabloids. The rest live private lives. However, in certain circles of society it's still considered a boon to be able to flaunt one's friendship with nobility. An aristocrat's recommendation or sponsorship for a business deal or a diplomatic appointment remains an advantage very few are willing to forgo."

Many villages had churches smaller than this one. The avenue bordered by century-old olive trees ended at the perfectly circular open space of the church and cemetery. The church entrance was directly in front of them, but the building also had a side entrance flanked by two narrow stained glass windows and reached by three awkwardly steep steps.

A stiff breeze scarcely screened by the ancient trees had blown pine needles across the access path. The wind blew insistently across the bare esplanade that stretched around three sides of the church. The space behind was dedicated to the cemetery. Simple stone crosses stood in the well-kept grassy plot. Manuel's quick count added up to about twenty of them. There was nothing else other than an ominous mound of earth alongside a recently dug grave. There was no fence to enclose the cemetery. After all, what for? Everything here belonged to the family.

So this was where Álvaro had wanted to be buried. Manuel didn't blame him— what alternative could he as Álvaro's bereaved husband have offered? Maybe a service at the funeral home by the M-30 highway and a small plot in Madrid's huge, crowded Almudena Cemetery. He couldn't recall ever having discussed the subject. Despite the undeniable beauty of the surroundings and the tidy simplicity of the weathered gravestones, there was a desolation about the place. But wasn't that true of any cemetery? Confronted by stark reality, he was forced to admit his preconceptions: for some reason he'd been expecting an elaborately ugly family crypt.

"They're very devoted Catholics, like most of the aristocracy. And like the rest of their ilk, they make provisions for a simplicity and austerity beyond this life in stark contrast to their preferences in this one." Griñán accompanied him to the church entrance. A crowd of probably more than a hundred people was gathered outside.

He saw people whispering discreetly to one another, pulling their dark jackets tight against the wind gusting across the open space before the church. Many turned to look at Manuel and his escort, but no one approached them. Doval, the executor's diligent assistant, had been sheltering from the morning chill in the lee of the wall, and he came out to greet them. Manuel noticed for the first time that both men were dressed in impeccably tailored black suits. His own double-breasted blue jacket and rumpled shirt made him feel out of place, and he became aware that the crowd was studying him with a morbid curiosity. Disapproving looks condemned his informal dress. The touch of Griñán's respectful hand on his shoulder comforted him and guided him to the entrance to escape the inquisitive inspection of the locals.

"There aren't many people here. Of course, it's quite early," the assistant sought to explain.

"You said there aren't many?" replied Manuel, careful not to look back but aware of a growing murmur. The crowd seemed to have doubled in the short time they'd been there.

"The family desired a simple private service," Griñán declared. "Since his death was unexpected. In other circumstances . . ."

Manuel gave him a miserable look. The administrator turned away his gaze, tactfully declining to go into more elaborate explanations. Doval came to his assistance.

"We can go inside. The family is about to arrive." He immediately realized his error and did his best to correct it. "I do beg your pardon. I meant to say the *rest* of the family."

The church was packed. He'd already been impressed by the number attending when he thought those outside were the only ones there; once inside, he realized that they'd been outside only because the church was already full. He looked down, overcome and disoriented, grateful as a lost child for Griñán's firm hand guiding him along the center aisle toward the altar. They passed someone weeping in deep distress. Looking for the source of those sobs, he was astounded to see a group of women in deep mourning wailing and clasping one another. Their lamentations were reflected and amplified by the vaulted ceiling. He stared at them, thunderstruck. Of all the things he'd imagined for this day, he'd never expected to see people dissolved in tears over Álvaro's death. What were all these people doing here? Who were they? He found it incredible that funerals like this could still take place. On the rare occasions he'd attended funerals, those present were family members and no more than a couple of dozen friends and acquaintances of the departed. Most often the simple service was held at a funeral home before cremation. With no more ceremony than that.

What was all this? He silently cursed that region's hidebound traditions, the unlettered rural preference for funerals at the manor, the servile respect Griñán seemed to appreciate but Manuel found embarrassing. But at the same time, he realized that the presence of all those gathered here to share his grief made him feel less isolated, rejected, and offended.

From their first days together Álvaro and he had been that sort of mutually self-sustaining couple who didn't engage in much socializing. The lengthy periods of reclusion required for his writing and his preference to stay home after his promotional tours had led them in recent years to reduce their circle of acquaintances. There had never been very many. They had a few friends, of course, but he'd turned down Mei's idea of announcing Álvaro's death to them. He'd found ridiculous the prospect of anyone coming and seeing him in the humiliation he so desperately wanted to escape; even worse was the thought of explaining to friends a situation he himself found impossible to understand. He advanced and found the pews packed with many men, eyes watery, clutching ironed handkerchiefs. Pained looks from sad eyes as bleary as those of old dogs were directed at the dark, brilliant coffin.

Struck by the sight of it, he abandoned the executor's comforting touch and approached the casket, grateful that it was closed. Hypnotized by the brilliance of the polished wood and by the rise and fall of sounds of female lamentation, he reached out and brushed his fingers across its surface just as a murmur interrupted the eerie wailing and quiet sobbing. A whisper rippled through the church like a spreading plague. The family made its entrance.

He looked around and saw that only the first two rows were unoccupied. He took a seat on the right. The murmur suddenly died away. He turned to look and saw that the matriarch leaning on her son's arm had halted. Dressed in full formal mourning, she was whispering something to Griñán, who quickly came to Manuel and leaned over to relay the message of sharp reproof. "You can't sit here; it's reserved for the family."

Rising in confusion, Manuel took two steps toward the aisle, about to bolt. He stopped short. His initial feeling of stupidity gave way to indignation.

"I *am* part of the family. If they don't mix with others, that's their choice. The man in that coffin is my husband, and unless I'm mistaken, as of now this pew belongs to me. It's my property. Tell them they can choose to sit here or elsewhere in the church. I'm not moving."

Griñán turned pale. Manuel sat down again in the same place, so furious he had to clench his hands together to hide their shaking. He heard whispers in the hushed silence that had installed itself among those attending and then the sound of steps resuming their course. To the first pew on the left.

He didn't look at them once during the ceremony.

It lasted almost two hours. The funeral mass, a service for a single departed person, was officiated by a priest about forty years old who seemed to know the family well. Manuel assumed from the priest's apparently real chagrin that he'd actually known Álvaro. The officiant was assisted by an unusually large number of other priests. Manuel counted nine of them, all elderly and remote. In curious ritual fashion they hovered at a respectful distance in a semicircle behind the altar, assisting the younger priest.

Manuel remained seated throughout, indifferent to the priest's promptings, drained by the effects of his rage and the disorienting emotional intensity of those behind him. He heard moaning. Rise, sit down, up again, sit down . . . He looked up for a moment and found that the women lined up in the aisle for their turns at communion were peering at him. He withdrew into his shell, looking down, fighting to contain his increasing distress, and resisting the urgent desire simply to get up and leave.

Once the service was over, a pallbearer team of men with calloused hands and ironed handkerchiefs lifted the coffin and carried it to the cemetery. Manuel was grateful to find the breeze had moderated in the course of the morning. The sun had found its way out between the low clouds massed above.

"I've already informed the marquis of your decision," Griñán whispered as they exited the church.

Manuel limited himself to a nod, wondering when Griñán could have done so. It must have been in the course of the funeral ceremony. After all, as Griñán had told him, the Muñiz de Dávila account was one of the most important of those he managed. Mindful of that, the executor had probably been quick to put himself forward in the expectation of continuing the arrangement with the new owners.

Manuel hung back and let the others go ahead. They gathered in a circle around the grave. He watched them from the edge of the cemetery, unwilling to come any closer. The energy expended in the dispute over the church pew had left him drained and unwilling to chance another confrontation.

In contrast to the never-ending funeral service the burial went quickly. The prayer for the dead, that was all. Because of the massed crowd, he didn't witness the lowering of the coffin. The crowd began to disperse. The priests dutifully greeted the family and then walked toward the side entrance to the church, certainly to disrobe in the sacristy.

He felt a small hand slip into his. He looked down and discovered the family's little boy. Manuel leaned down to speak to him, and the tiny one threw his arms around his neck and kissed his cheek. The child ran off toward his mother, who was waiting at a distance, and turned to smile before they took the path back toward the manor house.

"Señor Ortigosa."

He turned to find that Santiago, the new marquis, was standing before him.

Some distance behind the marquis, Griñán gave Manuel an encouraging gesture as he walked away in the company of the women.

"I am Santiago Muñiz de Dávila. Álvaro was my brother," he said and held out a right hand partly covered by a cast.

Taken aback by this, Manuel just looked at him.

"Don't worry, it's not serious. Just an accident while riding. A broken finger and a few scratches."

Manuel cautiously took the man's hand, feeling the rigid shape of plaster under the binding.

"Señor Griñán informed me of your decision, and the least I can do is to offer you my thanks and those of my family. I want to apologize if we've seemed cold or impolite. We've been overcome"—he looked toward the grave—"by the events of the past few days."

"There's no need to apologize. I know how you feel."

Manuel said nothing more. The brother took leave with a slight nod and hurried to catch up with his wife, who was assisting the matriarch. The wife gave way, allowing him to replace her at his mother's side.

The young priest crossed the cemetery toward him. Only the burial team remained, the foreman and a group of workmen smoking as they huddled together against the side of the church.

"I'd like to speak with you for a moment." The priest paused. "Álvaro and I have been friends since childhood. We went to school together. But just now I have to take these things off," he said, indicating the voluminous liturgical vestments. "If you'll wait, I'll be back in just a minute."

"I don't know," Manuel replied evasively, looking toward the way out of the church clearing. "I'm actually in a bit of a hurry."

"It'll take just a minute, I promise," the priest replied, breaking into a run toward the side entrance of the church.

Manuel glanced at the workmen smoking and chatting cheerfully, but he saw that the foreman, the only one not wearing overalls, was staring at him. Manuel had the odd feeling that the man was about to leave the group to come tell him something. But after a moment Manuel simply acknowledged the man with a nod and walked toward the open grave. He wandered past the crosses and read the inscriptions as he went.

Apparently Griñán was right about the posthumous austerity of the nobility. The graves were marked only with the names and the dates of birth and death. No mention of titles or distinctions. Some were from the 1700s, and the only aspect that differentiated those from the more recent ones was the color of the stone used for the crosses.

Next to the open grave stood colorful flower arrangements that would be placed over it. They bore ribbons that proclaimed the names of the sponsors, clues to how much they'd cost. The arrangements were piled high, a perfumed funeral pyre. Without thinking, he reached into his coat pocket and extracted the waxy gardenia he'd picked on the way there. Its strong perfume diffused into the air and dominated all the rest. Manuel stepped close enough to see the coffin, now partly obscured by the handfuls of dark earth the family had tossed upon it during the prayer for the dead. There were no flowers in the grave, as might have been expected, suggesting that Griñán's comment about austerity was accurate. After all, the brilliance of these expensive floral tributes was being reserved for display during the burial, when everyone could see them.

He looked again at the now dull surface of the coffin with its crucifix and image of a wasted, dying Christ. He raised the flower to his lips, took in the aroma, lightly kissed it, and held his hand out over the grave. He closed his eyes as he searched within himself for the fiercely defended chamber where his pain was confined. He couldn't locate it. He sensed a presence behind him. He closed his hand around the flower as if to shield it.

He turned toward the priest, who stood waiting a few steps behind him. In street clothes the man looked even younger, although he was still wearing his clerical collar.

"If you need more time . . ."

"No," he responded, walking toward the man as he returned the gardenia to his jacket pocket. "I've finished here."

The priest's eyebrows rose in surprise at his curt tone. Manuel saw that and forestalled any possibility of the expression of compassion likely to follow. "As I mentioned, I don't have very much time," he said in a rush. Suddenly the melancholy of the cemetery was unbearable. He wanted to flee.

"Where's your car?"

"Parked by the gate."

"Then I'll walk with you. I'm leaving as well. I have to get back to my parish."

"Oh, I thought that . . ." Manuel waved toward the church.

"No, I'm here today as a guest, because I'm a friend of the family. The local parish priest is one of those who assisted with the mass. This church really isn't a part of any parish. It's for private use and is open to the public only on special occasions."

"Ah. When I saw so many priests, I assumed . . ."

"Yes, I suppose it was a bit of a shock for someone not used to it, but it's a tradition of the region."

"Folklore," Manuel muttered contemptuously under his breath.

He wasn't sure the priest had heard him until he noticed the distinctly cooler tone of the man's reply. "It's their way of honoring the dead."

Manuel said nothing. He pressed his lips together and looked impatiently toward the path that led out of this place.

They started walking.

"My name is Lucas," the priest said in a newly amicable tone as he held out his hand. "As I mentioned, I went to parochial school at the seminary with Álvaro. With all the brothers, actually. It's just that the others were younger, and I had less in common with them."

Manuel shook the man's hand briefly but didn't stop walking. "Seminary?" he asked, surprised.

"That's right," the priest replied with a smile. "But don't get any funny ideas. In those days all the wealthy boys of the area studied at the seminary. It was the best school around; and besides, since the marquis's family have always been patrons of the center, it was only logical that their kids should study there. It had nothing to do with a calling to the priesthood."

"It looks like it did, at least in your case."

Lucas laughed heartily. "But I'm the exception. I was the only one in my class who wound up going into the Church."

"You're wealthy also?"

More amusement. "Another exception. I had one of the scholarships endowed by his honor the marquis for the deserving poor."

Manuel found it difficult to imagine Álvaro at a seminary. From time to time his husband had told stories about his time at university, at a Madrid boarding school, or in high school, but he'd never mentioned his primary school. The thought of a childhood in that rustic setting seemed paradoxical in comparison with what Manuel had assumed. He heard the gravel crunch beneath their feet as they walked. Lengthy pauses and silences between them didn't bother him at all; they calmed him. With the wind blocked by the trees, he felt the noonday sun beginning to warm his back. It intensified the aroma of gardenias exuded by the hedges around the manor.

"Manuel—can we be less formal with one another? I'm forty-four, the same age as Álvaro."

Manuel didn't reply. He made a vague gesture that didn't settle the question. He knew from experience that such a proposal was not infrequently a preliminary to greater intrusion.

"How are you feeling? How are you?" The priest addressed him with familiarity.

The questions caught him by surprise, not so much for their content as for the fact that this was the first person who'd wanted to know. Not even gentle Mei with her load of guilt and regret had asked him that. And though he'd vented his pain and confusion to her as if spitting into her face, the truth was that he hadn't stopped to ask himself that question.

How was he?

He didn't know. He had an idea of how he'd expected to be: crushed, knocked down, and sunk deep. But instead he was apathetic and profoundly disappointed, somewhat offended by everything he'd had to endure. That was all.

"Fine."

"Very well. But we both know that can't be true."

"In fact it is. All I feel is unhappiness and disappointment at everything that's happened. I just want to get out of here, get my own life back, and forget all this."

"Indifference," commented the priest. "Sometimes that's one of the stages of grief that death brings. It comes immediately following denial and before negotiation."

Manuel was going to contest that, but he remembered himself opposing every statement from Sergeant Acosta as she delivered the news of Álvaro's death, his refusal to accept that news, searching for a life preserver or some way out, rejecting the notion with tortured reasoning.

"It seems you're an expert in such matters," he commented disdainfully.

"I am. I deal with death and bereavement every day, as well as other illnesses of the soul. That's my profession. But it's not just that; I was Álvaro's friend." He paused to look for any reaction from Manuel. "Probably one of the very few people who stayed in contact with him over the years and knew the realities of his everyday life."

"Then you knew more than I did," Manuel whispered. He was suddenly upset.

The priest stopped walking and looked at him with a grave expression. "Don't be so hard when you judge him; if Álvaro concealed his family matters from you, it wasn't because he was ashamed of you. It was because he was ashamed of them."

"You're the second person to say something like that to me, but I don't know what that means. I've seen them, and they don't seem so terrible."

The priest smiled but held up a hand. "Álvaro was not in contact with anyone from the manor after he went to the boarding school in Madrid, just out of his childhood. Every time he returned, his family's rejection became more intense, until finally he didn't come back anymore. His father died without agreeing to see him, although despite that Álvaro inherited the title and its obligations. He came back, took charge of the family holdings, established allowances for family members, and disappeared again. I believe that other than his executor, I was the only one who knew how to find him." He began to walk along the path again. "I know he was happy with his life. He was happy at your side."

"And how can you be so sure?" Manuel attacked him. "Were you his confessor?"

Lucas closed his eyes for a moment and took a sharp breath, almost as if he'd just received a blow in the chest.

"Something like that, but not in a formal sense." He took a moment and regained his calm. "We talked about you a lot. About everything."

Now it was Manuel's turn to stop walking. He responded with a wicked smile and explored that unwelcome topic. "Let's see . . . why are you telling me all this? What do you want? Maybe you don't see how absurd it is for a priest to try to comfort me for the fact that my husband was hiding his life from me? How do you expect me to feel when I hear he trusted you more than he did me?

The only thing that's obvious to me is that I didn't know the man I shared my life with. He was deceiving me the whole time."

"I know how you feel."

"You don't know a goddamn thing!"

"Maybe I don't and maybe I do. What I do know is that right now you're rejecting everything I say, but I also know that a few days from now things will be different. Come see me when that happens," he said. He held out a card with the address of a church in Pontevedra. "You knew the real Álvaro." A broad gesture indicated everything in the majestic avenue dominated by the entrance gate. "All the rest was just show."

Manuel crumpled the card in his fist and nearly threw it on the ground. But almost without thinking he slipped it into the pocket that held the fragrant flower. That was the only thing he intended to carry away from that place. In secret.

They passed through the gate and went out to the road in silence.

A man was leaning on the trunk of Manuel's car. At the sight of them he straightened up, took a couple of steps in their direction, and then stopped.

There was something familiar about him. Not until they were almost face-to-face did Manuel place him. This was the police lieutenant who'd grilled him at the hospital until the captain intervened. Manuel didn't recall his name, but he did remember the man's obvious dislike. And the beer belly the uniform had certainly concealed better than his current attire: pleated pants worn very low and a thin V-neck sweater that revealed the buttons of his shirt like a row of rivets affixed to his hide.

Over the years Manuel had developed a sixth sense for bullies and louts, and he was sure this guy was going to cause him nothing but trouble. Even so, he was almost more surprised by the reaction of the priest.

"What's he doing here?" Father Lucas whispered.

"Manuel Ortigosa?" the man challenged him, although it was obvious he knew the answer. "I'm Police Lieutenant Nogueira." He flashed a badge and pocketed it again. "We met yesterday at the hospital."

Manuel was wary. "I remember."

"Are you going somewhere?" the man said with a gesture toward the suitcase visible in the backseat.

"I'm going home."

The officer shook his head, evidently troubled by the answer.

"I need to speak with you," he said, as if he were trying to convince himself of that fact.

"Speak," Manuel replied with no sign of concern.

The officer gave the priest a baleful look. "In private," he added.

It appeared that the man's dislikes were wide ranging. Either that or the two knew one another too well already.

The priest refused to be intimidated. He ignored the unfriendly attitude of the other man and addressed Manuel. "If you'd like for me to stay . . ."

"That won't be necessary, thanks."

It was obvious the priest was reluctant to leave. The officer looked like a shady character. But faced with the choice, Manuel opted for the one with a uniform.

Even so the priest lingered. He shook hands again in farewell without a glance toward the officer. He spoke as he got into the little gray SUV parked behind them. "Come see me."

Manuel watched him drive off and then turned to the officer.

"Not here," the man said. "There's a bar in the village just before you get onto the main road. With parking in front. Follow me."

INERTIA

In contrast to the cool weather outside, the strong noonday sun had turned the car interior into an oven. Manuel parked in a dirt lot next to the officer's old BMW and half a dozen dusty station wagons. He got out, tossed his jacket onto the seat, and locked the car. He headed for the bar entrance, but the lieutenant stopped him.

"This will do," he said, standing on a terrace with plastic chairs and worn umbrellas. "Wait here."

He returned almost immediately with two black coffees and dishes filled with something that looked like meat stew. He lit a cigarette before he initiated the conversation. Obviously that was why he'd chosen the terrace.

The officer stirred two spoonfuls of sugar into his coffee. "You're on your way out of town?"

"The funeral and burial are over. There's nothing to keep me here," Manuel replied, his voice indifferent.

"You're not planning to stay with the family for a few days?"

"They're not my family. They're my *husband's* family." This time the officer seemed unmoved by his insistence. "I didn't know them before . . . before this."

"Yes, that's what you said at the hospital," the man replied pensively. "Did you get a call from headquarters?"

"Yes, this morning. They said everything was ready. I could come collect his things, and they'd mail me a copy of the police report in case I needed it for the insurance."

"Sons of bitches!" the lieutenant snarled and jabbed his cigarette toward Manuel. "They did it all right, they did it again! What balls they've got!"

"Did it again? What?"

The officer countered his question with another. "What did you think of your in-laws?"

Manuel was reluctant to commit himself. "I didn't have time to form an opinion," he lied. In fact he did have an impression of them, but he certainly wasn't about to share it with this fellow. "We exchanged a couple of words, that's all."

"Uh-huh. No surprises there."

"Would you like to tell me what this is all about?"

Nogueira took a long, noisy drag on his cigarette and consumed the tobacco all the way to the filter. He tossed it under the table and ground it underfoot, even though there was an ashtray on the table. He gave Manuel an angry look. He pulled over one of the plates of stew and speared a piece of meat.

"About? It's about the fact that Álvaro Muñiz de Dávila didn't have an accident, or at least it wasn't just an accident." He put the piece of meat into his mouth. Manuel sat there amazed and alarmed while the man finished chewing. "His car went off a straight stretch of road, and it's true there was no indication he'd tried to brake. And no sign any other driver was involved. But as I was about to tell you in the morgue before my commanding officer butted in, we noticed the vehicle had a broken taillight and traces of white paint."

"I asked the captain about that when he called this morning. He thinks it could have come from a bump in a parking lot, entirely unrelated. He said it could have happened several days earlier."

"Right, he would say that." The man devoured another piece of meat. "And how did he explain the laceration señor Muñiz de Dávila had in his side?"

"Laceration?"

"An injury. A stab wound that left only a small puncture mark. He could have gotten to his car without any problem and tried to escape his attacker, but the wound was fatal. The internal bleeding weakened him. Maybe it killed him before the car ran off the road. Assuming no other vehicle ran into him from behind."

"The captain didn't mention a stab wound."

"Certainly not. Spanish aristocrats don't get stabbed to death. That's for drug addicts and prostitutes. But the fact is that the body of Álvaro Muñiz de Dávila had a puncture wound in the lower right abdomen. The medical examiner spotted it during her preliminary check of the deceased. She's a friend of mine; if I ask her to, she'll tell you. She's as disgusted as I am by this sort of thing."

"This sort of thing? But what are you trying to tell me? The injury wasn't from the accident? Was he attacked?"

The man looked around carefully before replying, even though they were alone on the terrace. "There is at least one very suspicious aspect to his death."

"And why are you telling me? Why did they say his death was an accident? And why aren't they investigating?"

"That's what I'm trying to tell you. There is a series of extremely suspicious events connected with this death, and they aren't being investigated. And it's not the first time either. The name of the great Muñiz de Dávila family has to be kept pristine and above suspicion at any price, even when it's smeared with their own shit. That's the ancient and shameful tradition."

Manuel weighed the man's words and tried to understand. "You're telling me . . ."

"What I'm telling you is that there've been social divisions since the world began. There are the miserable masses who work themselves to death to get to a crappy retirement not worth having, and then there are the others—the land-owners, princes who've lived off our sweat for generations and do whatever they damn well please. And never face any consequences."

"But Álvaro didn't even live here. He wasn't—"

"He was one of them." The lieutenant cut him off. "You already said you didn't even know his family existed. One thing I do know: according to what little I've been able to gather, Álvaro was living a double life. I don't know what he was mixed up in, but in more ways than one he was absolutely not what he seemed to be."

Manuel sat in silence, watching the man across the table and trying to assimilate this. He did his best to make sense of the tale but felt no indignation. The man was expressing exactly what Manuel had concluded earlier in the day. Past forebodings of betrayal had become reality, shaking him so profoundly that he was determined to follow Clint Eastwood's advice—*Get out of here. This is no time to look for trouble.* Álvaro had lied to him and led him by the nose. There were lies everywhere in this huge steaming pile of shit, and yes, he was the imbecile who'd swallowed everything, hook, line, and sinker. Acknowledging he'd been a fool was the hardest thing of all. But now that he'd accepted it, what more could be expected of him?

"And now what happens?" he asked listlessly.

The man stared at him and threw his hands up in disbelief. "What's the matter with you? Weren't you listening to me?"

"I heard every word."

The man sputtered in impatience. "I'll tell you what's going to happen: nothing! They'll close the case. In fact they already have. Álvaro Muñiz de Dávila officially died in a traffic accident, and that's that."

"But you don't agree with that conclusion, so you'll keep investigating . . ."

The officer lit another cigarette and took more of those noisy sucking drags. He pushed away the cup with dregs of coffee, as if it contained an idea he found offensive. "Yesterday was my last day. I'm retired. I have a month of vacation, and then I report to the inactive reserve."

Manuel nodded, understanding now why the man hadn't come to him in uniform. He was officially no longer a police officer, even though when he'd approached Manuel by the parked cars, he'd identified himself by his rank and flashed his badge. Which raised a different question: Why was he here? He'd already made perfectly clear how much Álvaro's family disgusted him, and he made no secret of his homophobia, so what was he after? Manuel straightened up and pushed his chair back to indicate that the conversation was over.

"Lieutenant Nogueira," he said, cautiously granting the man his former rank, "I've heard you out, and I thank you for your concern. But if the case is closed as you admit, and you're the only one who disagrees with the official version, why are you telling me? If you couldn't convince them, what could I possibly do?"

"A lot. You're a member of the family."

"That's not true," Manuel replied bitterly. "I'm not part of his family now, and it seems I never was."

"But you are, with full legal rights," Nogueira countered vehemently. "With your help we could get something done about an investigation that has been dropped."

"You just told me that you're no longer on active duty."

Nogueira's expression darkened for a moment, just long enough to suggest he could become very aggressive if pressed. But he mastered his emotions. What he said next must have cost him a great deal. "You were his . . . his husband. You could even demand an autopsy."

Manuel looked at him in surprise and rejected that before he said a word. "No, no, no, you don't understand. I've just buried that man, and he shared my life almost as long as I can remember. That's probably nothing to you, but I also had to bury with him all that our life together represented. It's immaterial to me now. I don't care what he was mixed up in or who was with him in his last moments. None of it matters. I just want to leave this place, go home, and forget it all." He got up. "Thank you for your trouble, but I just don't have the energy for this." He held out his hand, but the man made no move to take it. Manuel looked him straight in the eye, shrugged, and turned to go to the parking lot.

"Álvaro was murdered," Nogueira called out behind him.

Manuel stopped but he didn't turn.

"It wasn't an accident. He was murdered." A moment of silence. "And if you do nothing, the murderer goes free. Can you live with that?"

Manuel's shoulders sagged. For a moment his feelings and desires seemed to count for nothing; he was trapped by circumstances; and a terrifying, inexplicable power was smashing reality into his face. Sheer inertia had sent him hurtling toward the real world, and now some mindless force was compelling him along a random path chosen by an indifferent universe. Everything in these surroundings was hostile; he should be following Eastwood's advice and avoiding trouble. But whatever his desires, here was this hateful nobody loading onto his back the weight of the worst possible crime. He felt the shock of this new bombshell buffet him, shake him through and through, and nearly flatten him to the ground. Perhaps it took a minute for him to go back; perhaps it took only a few seconds. He retraced his steps and sank again into the same chair.

If Nogueira was pleased to see him return, he showed no sign of it. He continued smoking slowly, inhaling deeply.

"What do you want to do?" Manuel asked.

Nogueira threw down the cigarette and leaned forward, placing both elbows on the table. A small black notebook appeared in his hands. He opened it to a page covered with bold handwriting.

"The first thing we do is go talk to the medical examiner to show you that what I've been telling you is accurate. After that the objective is to reconstruct everything Álvaro did over the past two days: where he was, with whom, who he saw, and, if possible, what he did here on his previous visits. His routine here, where he went. I'll guide you, but you'll have to do almost all of it by yourself. Nobody will suspect you. You're entitled to the information, and it's perfectly normal for a family member to ask about the circumstances of the death of a loved one. If anyone objects, well, that gives us something to work on. But first and foremost I have to warn you it's possible you might not like what you turn up. Murder investigations have a way of stirring up a lot of muck that otherwise would stay hidden."

Manuel nodded unhappily. "I expect as much."

"And one other thing. Whatever does turn up might not be in your favor. I have a hunch, and I'm rarely mistaken, that Muñiz de Dávila was up to his neck in shit. But if anyone finds out I'm pushing you to take an interest, I can get into serious trouble. I've spent too many years in uniform earning that pension. It's important to keep this totally confidential between the two of us. And the examiner. I trust her completely, so I'll know that any leak came from you. If that happens, I'll find you, haul you off behind the mountain, and shoot you dead. Got that?"

"I understand," Manuel replied. He didn't doubt the man for a second.

Nogueira checked his watch. "The medical examiner is a real pro with lots of experience. Her shift ended at three o'clock, so she's probably home now. She'll be expecting us."

"What made both of you so sure I'd agree?"

Nogueira dismissed the question with a shrug. "I'd have found it strange if you hadn't. And suspicious as well." He gave Manuel a side glance. "Leave your car here, we'll use mine. They rent rooms here; it's both a bar and an inn, so you can stay here for now. I'll need information about the bank accounts and a report of the most recent movements of your . . . family member. And whether he had debts. His father, the old marquis, got mixed up with loan sharks and their associates. Those people seem to have been out of the picture for a couple of years, but you never know. Anyhow, it'll be interesting to see who inherits, although I assume it's too early to know yet. Maybe that administrator who was with you the other day can tell you something if you play your cards right. After all, you were Álvaro's . . . family member. You need to go to the hospital and the police headquarters as soon as possible to recover his personal property. Ophelia has to examine his clothing again. And we'll check his cell phone—make sure it's included with his effects. It wouldn't be a bad idea for you to ask the victim's telephone company for a list of his calls. Just pretend to be him and go back as far as possible. If they make difficulties, you can threaten not to pay the latest bill."

Manuel stopped him. "That won't be necessary. I have internet access to all our bills. I can review the times and details of all the calls."

Nogueira looked at him appreciatively. Suddenly Manuel found the retired officer's goodwill more offensive than his skepticism or derision. Manuel's face flushed with shame, and he looked away. He'd almost said they never kept any secrets from one another.

I'm an imbecile.

Nogueira continued his list. "Bills, personal schedule, calls, belongings. And ask for the return of his car. It'll be in the storage yard, and I'd like to take a look at it." He tucked away his notebook, leaned back, and lit another cigarette. "I guess that'll do for a start."

Manuel leaned forward in deliberate imitation of Nogueira, planting his elbows on the table where the lieutenant's had been. "Two things. First, I'm the heir to all the worldly goods of Álvaro Muñiz de Dávila. The executor gave us a preview of the will yesterday. The businesses have been turned around, and in fact they're in excellent shape now. This morning I instructed the executor and communicated to the family my decision to renounce the inheritance as soon as the will is probated three months from now."

Nogueira's eyebrows went up in astonishment. Manuel had a hunch the man wasn't often that surprised.

"Interesting. That sets you up as the principal suspect and at the same time clears you of any motivation. At least as far as the assets are concerned." He smiled slightly, as if at some private joke.

Manuel's face was stony. "And second, Álvaro was not my cousin or my brother-in-law. He was my husband. If that word offends you so much that you can't pronounce it, refer to him as Álvaro. But don't let me hear you call him 'your family member.' And especially not 'the victim.'"

Nogueira threw away his cigarette butt. He got to his feet. "Can do." He looked with regret at the other bowl of stew sitting untouched on the table but went to the car anyway.

Nogueira's BMW was old and the exterior was shabby. Telltale white spots on the roof showed that humidity had taken its toll. But the interior was spotless. The mats appeared to have been newly vacuumed, and the leather dashboard had been polished recently. An air freshener hung from an air-conditioning vent. Lieutenant Nogueira was clearly one of the rare smokers who don't indulge inside the car. He drove and said nothing. Manuel would have preferred some music to cut the heavy silence that only served to amplify the sounds of their breathing and emphasize the paradox of finding themselves together. But he wasn't going to ask for it.

The main road wound through curves and changes of grade. Nogueira drove at exactly the speed limit. When he turned off the main road, he slowed down significantly and took the opportunity to extract a cigarette from his packet. He held it unlit between his lips for several miles until at last they pulled up before a house enclosed by a fence. Four dogs ran up barking. They were different in size and appearance, but all were wary of the new arrivals. Nogueira got out, lit the cigarette, put a hand through the gate, and unlatched it. He walked toward the house, shooing away the dogs now trying to welcome him. When they caught sight of Manuel they forgot about Nogueira.

A woman in her midfifties came around the side of the house. She was slim and stern looking. A cloth hairband held her midlength hair away from her face. She scolded the dogs halfheartedly and welcomed Nogueira with a kiss on either cheek. She ushered the lieutenant inside, held out a strong plain hand, and gave Manuel a smile. He liked her immediately.

"I'm Ophelia," she said. Only her first name. Nothing about her position, profession, or family name.

She'd been expecting them, just as Nogueira had predicted. Cooking aromas from the kitchen made it clear she'd been preparing a meal, but she'd set the table with a white cloth, three coffee cups, an ample selection of pastries, and a bottle of muscatel. She filled three small glasses.

"I'm glad that you decided to hear me out. We weren't sure how you'd react."

Manuel just nodded. "I never dreamed I'd have to hear such a thing. You can imagine how I feel. It's just too . . . too . . ."

"We understand." She took a sip of coffee. "I assume that Lieutenant Nogueira explained to you the serious consequences we'll face if anyone finds out that we revealed confidential information about an investigation. Or a non-investigation. Or whatever the hell you want to call it."

"You have my word," Manuel assured her. "No one will hear it from me." He remembered Nogueira's threat. The officer cleared his throat and gave Manuel another warning look.

"I was on overnight duty at the hospital last Saturday and Sunday. At 1:45 a.m. the traffic police notified me of an accident. We went to the scene in an ambulance but it was too late. We brought him to the hospital." She sighed and then continued. "What I'm about to tell you may be very painful. If it's too much for you at any point, just tell me to stop."

Manuel looked at her and nodded slowly.

"The car ran off the road. There was no curve and no skid marks or signs of braking, either on the pavement or in the field. The vehicle ran about one hundred and fifty feet through the open countryside and came to stop against a boundary wall. Your husband was dead. There was a cut on his brow, probably caused when his head hit the steering wheel as the car collided with the wall. The position of the vehicle, the minimal damage from the collision with the wall, and the fact that the airbags didn't inflate led us to conclude he was unconscious when the car left the pavement and it was no longer under power. I was struck by the fact that the cut above his eyebrow had hardly bled at all, since such facial cuts usually produce a copious flow of blood. I noticed the ashen color of his skin, looked for other injuries, and noted that the lower abdomen seemed swollen. That's often an indication of internal hemorrhaging. No other obvious injuries, but when we put him on the stretcher, I found a tear in his shirt. It turned out to correspond to the opening of a wound less than an inch wide and probably more than six inches deep. In my judgment, that type of injury was incompatible with the conditions of the accident. I found nothing in the vehicle that might have caused it. No postmortem examination is done when the cause of death of a traffic accident victim is evident; I issue a death certificate and that's it. I asked them to bring your husband's body to the forensic medical examiner's office because I suspected he might have died before his car ran off the road, not afterward. As soon as we identified him as a Muñiz de Dávila, I knew the news would spread like wildfire. We transferred the body from the emergency room to my work space. I was preparing to do the autopsy when I received instructions to cancel it. The identity of the deceased took priority over procedure. I was told the death was an accident, and I was not to distress the family by performing an autopsy. I objected, of course, but they told me that the 'request' came from on high and no appeal was possible."

Manuel couldn't believe it. "They told you to stop the autopsy?"

The medical examiner's mouth twisted in a bitter smile. "They're a bit more discreet than that. They strongly suggested that I spare the family's feelings."

"Against your professional judgment," Nogueira added.

"Correct."

"Where did the recommendation come from?" Manuel asked. "Perhaps from the family?"

"I doubt it," Nogueira interjected. "But there would have been no need. I already tried to explain to you. The Muñiz de Dávila family has been a power here for centuries, since the days of feudal lords, I guess. Later they ruled as landowners in a region where living conditions haven't exactly been easy for any except them. Try to understand, there's a sort of absurd reverence for what they are and what they represent. For centuries those families' abuses, scandals, excesses, and even minor crimes have been overlooked. They can count on indulgence and don't have to ask for it. It's just one of their many privileges, granted without their having to be inconvenienced by the need to ask for special treatment."

Manuel exhaled in one long slow breath, intertwined his fingers, and tried to take that information onboard. "Doctor, do you believe that Álvaro was murdered?"

"I'm certain of it. That type of wound isn't self-inflicted. He was stabbed with a long narrow blade, something like a stiletto or an ice pick. He got to his car but bled rapidly. The hemorrhaging was internal, so no blood was visible except from the cut on his brow. He passed out, and that's why he ran off the road. I don't know where he was going. Perhaps he was aware of the seriousness of his injury and he was looking for help; the regional hospital is another thirty miles away along the same road. Or perhaps he was trying to escape his attacker. We have no way of determining where the attack took place or how long he'd been on the road by the time he lost consciousness."

Manuel hid his face in his hands. A fever suddenly flared through him and plunged him back into his malaise. He pressed his chilly hands to his eyes in search of momentary relief. He remained in that posture until he felt the physician's small strong hand on his knee. He dropped his hands to look at her. Her gaze was steady and sympathetic. "Was he in much pain? I mean . . . a wound that deep seems . . . horrible. How was he able to drive after that?"

"It would have caused no more than a momentary pang, an instant of intense pain that went away almost immediately. This type of injury, although almost always fatal, usually isn't particularly painful. Quite often the injured party isn't aware of its seriousness until internal bleeding causes him to lapse into weakness and apathy. By then it's too late. Blunt force traumas of this type don't bleed outward the way cuts do; the body's natural posture tends to compress the incision, and the external lesion isn't much larger than a bad insect bite. The initial pain ceases when the shaft is pulled out, leaving only minor discomfort. These types of wounds have been extensively documented. It's a type of injury common in prisons. Some prisoners fashion weapons from everyday objects, simply by filing and sharpening them into something like an ice pick. If there's a fight, someone might get such a stab wound and not realize the seriousness of the injury; hours later he will collapse in his cell and die. All too often such wounds escape detection. But Lieutenant Nogueira came to the same conclusion and initiated a homicide investigation. He was told, however, to drop it. When we heard about you, we thought perhaps you'd want to know the truth."

"And you believe they 'recommended' forgoing an autopsy essentially as an attempt to block the investigation of a murder?"

The physician's expression was one of disdain. She said nothing for a moment. "To tell the truth, I don't think so. It's more likely that we're all some-how victims of a prevailing attitude of abject submission to authority. It's more deeply rooted in our society and customs than we'd like to admit, an uncured contagion that suggests some things will never change. Mayors' sons never receive traffic tickets, do they? I suppose it was like the widespread custom of ignoring the excesses of politicians and high-class celebrities. Someone realized who the man was and took the initiative to stifle suspicions of anything that might besmirch the family's good name."

Manuel was astonished. "Even though it might mean letting a murder go unsolved?"

"If it had been obvious, they wouldn't have dared. But as I said, I had to look hard to detect signs of violence. Álvaro was wearing a black shirt, so the cut in the fabric was virtually invisible. There were no signs of external bleeding or obvious injury. The slight swelling of the abdomen that led me to suspect internal bleeding would have escaped a layperson. There were no signs of struggle or self-defense, and he'd run off an open stretch of road. Of course, Lieutenant Nogueira noted something was amiss, but to a less experienced person this would have been an open-and-shut case. A driver falls asleep at the wheel and there's a faint smell of alcohol, so it's reasonable to suppose he might have had too much to drink. That's exactly the sort of scandal people here are more than willing to cover up for families like your husband's. I hadn't even begun the autopsy when I heard there was an official version being put around. And I can tell you, few things are harder to stop than an 'official version' once it's gotten started."

"Just one more thing," Manuel said. "Why are you two doing this? I know that it's the right thing to do and all that, but even so you yourself admit you might get into a lot of trouble."

She didn't hesitate. "I know it may sound like a cliché if I say my job makes it my duty, but that's the truth of it. Every time I have a victim before me on the autopsy table, I fully assume my professional responsibilities. If I don't fulfill those obligations, nobody else will."

The doctor was right, and her motivation was entirely credible. Manuel nodded and caught Nogueira's look of disapproval. The man clicked his tongue in displeasure. But what was the policeman's own motivation if he didn't feel a sense of obligation to the victim, a sense of duty? Manuel had no idea, but the man's motive had to be a powerful one. After all, the lieutenant was doing his best to stifle his contempt for the upper classes, his homophobia, and his rebellious tendency to question the established order. Manuel hoped the police officer's motives weren't both covert and malicious.

"Anything else?"

She nodded. "Professional responsibility, added to the fact I don't like anyone interfering in my work or subverting my authority. The decision whether an autopsy is required is a matter of routine legal procedure, but once the body is on my table, I'm in charge. I don't like it when someone interferes with my business and tells me what to do." She glanced at Nogueira. This time he approved.

Ophelia served another round of coffee. They drank in silence. The main business had been dealt with, and the gathering drifted into that inevitable feeling of uneasiness that arises when strangers are brought together by chance or fate. Manuel rose and shook the doctor's hand and thanked her again for her willingness to help. On the way to Nogueira's car he saw that the dogs were sprawled on the porch, drowsy in the afternoon sun, apparently having lost interest in Ophelia's visitors. At the front door Nogueira took leave of Ophelia with a quick kiss on the lips and a light pat on the rump. She smiled and closed the door. Manuel wondered if the easy affection between the two might also have influenced the doctor's decision. He assumed it had, at least in part. What was still unclear to him was the lieutenant's motivation. He still had the feeling the man was up to no good.

THE SECRET GARDEN

Manuel woke very early. The television was still on. After two frustrated attempts the night before, he'd given in to the obvious: he wasn't able to sleep in the foreign silence of the inn, because it echoed with the mix of inconclusive conversations he'd sat through. And he kept hearing in the distance the insistent weeping of a six-year-old boy. He'd turned the television volume down low and left it on as background noise, a bridge and an escape to the everyday, available if anguish overwhelmed his dreams. Over the preceding hours the dead weight of Eastwood's advice had been replaced by a sort of spiritual mission, a justification for staying.

He'd eventually collapsed into five hours of dreamless sleep that brought rest, relief, and nothing to remember. He showered, shaved, and took out his last clean shirt, just as wrinkled and unpresentable as the one he'd worn the day before. It looked passable after he covered it with his double-breasted jacket. He took a last look at the list he'd drawn up before going to bed, then folded it together with the copy of Álvaro's phone bill the hotel manager had printed out for him. When he put them in his pocket he encountered the gardenia, now soft and limp. He put the fading flower on the coffee table. He was ready for the meeting he'd set up with Griñán by phone the night before. At the last moment, just as he was about to leave, he came back and shut the flower in a drawer.

Griñán's Audi was parked at the entrance to As Grileiras. Manuel started to pull in behind it, but the administrator reached out and waved him on into the drive. The two vehicles stopped next to the hedge that enclosed the manor house.

The man got out and hurried to open Manuel's door, a satisfied smile sketched upon his face. He'd made no comment the previous evening when

Manuel said he'd decided to stay a few more days and visit As Grileiras. When they agreed on a time to meet, Manuel could almost see a smile spread across the face of the man on the other end of the line. Manuel hated being predictable, but even more he hated seeming so. Nevertheless, he decided not to contest Griñán's probable interpretation of his motives, since it provided cover for doing what had to be done. He intended to finish this business once and for all, as quickly as possible.

"So you decided to stay?" Griñán didn't hide his satisfaction that Manuel seemed attracted by the property.

"I think perhaps that's saying too much, but the truth is I'm curious. I'd like to see the place where Álvaro grew up."

Griñán stood there staring at him. Manuel strode away along the path to escape his scrutiny.

"That's all?"

"And perhaps to take the opportunity to learn a little more about his family."

"Oh, unfortunately I expect that that'll be more difficult," the administrator apologized. "Santiago and Catarina left on a trip this morning, and the dowager marquess has been secluded since the funeral."

In Manuel's mind arose the memory of the matriarch leaving the cemetery, ignoring the arm her daughter-in-law offered, erect of posture as if she didn't need support, walking toward the manor without looking at the younger woman. His disbelief must have been visible in his face, for Griñán was quick to explain. "I telephoned to announce you yesterday after you informed me of your intention to visit. I hope you don't mind. I did so with the intention of avoiding unexpected encounters that might have been distressing to both parties. His excellency the marquis asked me to convey his regards. He requests you excuse him, because today's engagement was made some time ago."

So good old Griñán with his friendly winks and flattery had already chosen his loyalties. He'd lost no time finding an opportunity to be useful to his new master, who in the passage of just a few hours had become *his excellency the marquis* instead of *Santiago*, and very conveniently happened not to be at home today. And the worst of it was that Manuel hadn't asked to call on the family; he'd only expressed his desire to see As Grileiras. So here they were.

The drive ran past the caretaker's lodge into an open area and curved into a horseshoe shape where a stone entryway invited them to approach the horse stalls of the main stables. Two men were inspecting the rear hooves of an impressively handsome horse.

"That's the veterinarian," Griñán explained. "The last horse Santiago bought has been nothing but trouble since the day it arrived."

"An unfortunate purchase?"

Griñán grimaced and tilted his head to one side to signal something between agreement and uncertainty, but he didn't elaborate. "The man with him is Damián, the caretaker, who's a jack-of-all-trades: stableboy, gardener, minor repairs, and maintenance. He locks the manor gates at night and opens them in the morning so the nonresident staff can get in. This is where he and his wife, Herminia, live. She's the cook and housekeeper. She was nanny to all three children when they were small, and she still manages the household."

"How many people work on the estate?"

"Well, that depends on the season. The caretaker family lives in their lodge. Estela, the dowager marquess's nurse, lives here; although you saw the old lady at her best yesterday, she suffers from terrible arthritis that sometimes leaves her prostrate for weeks. The nurse is sturdy enough to carry her when necessary. Her room is adjacent to the dowager marquess's quarters, for obvious reasons." He began counting on his fingers. "And then there's Sarita, who comes every day to help Herminia with the housework; Vicente, who assists Catarina with her gardenias; and Alfredo, who's a combination steward and farm manager. You'll have seen him yesterday at the cemetery, overseeing the burial. He's mostly in charge of hiring temporary labor for plowing and farmwork, gardening, pruning, and whatnot." He frowned as he searched his memory. "There's a man who comes from time to time to take care of the orchards, and a dairyman too. On a normal day there might be eight or ten people attending to different things. They harvest chestnuts, potatoes, apples, and olives." Griñán shrugged. "These estates were designed long ago to be completely autonomous. As you've seen, this one has its own church and cemetery, like a little independent village. As Grileiras has its own wells, arable lands, and cows, hogs, and sheep in a rustic barn about a mile away. There's also a mill on a waterway and an olive press."

Manuel noticed that the two men outside the stables had stood up and stopped chatting in response to their arrival.

Griñán introduced him by name but didn't explain the reason for his visit.

The veterinarian gave him a firm handshake. Damián's grip was gentler and more tentative; he took off his English-style cap and wadded it between his fingers, which were as thin and dry as vines. As they walked away Manuel felt the man's watery gaze still fixed on his back.

"They don't seem very surprised to see you here," Manuel commented.

"We have a bookkeeper in our office who follows the details of the estate and its daily operations. My responsibilities as administrator don't bring me around as often, but I like to drop by from time to time. I find the place enchanting."

They walked in silence. The gravel crunched underfoot as they took the path through the trees to the church. When they came to the circular clearing Griñán stopped, hesitated, and waved toward the direction of the cemetery.

"Perhaps you'd care to . . . ?"

"No," Manuel answered, studiously not looking in that direction.

The path around the right side of the church was narrow and sloped downward, so Griñán was forced to lag behind Manuel. The older man grumbled about his inappropriate footwear. Manuel took the opportunity to move ahead—not far, just a couple of yards to distance himself from the executor for the first time since they'd arrived. He'd had the impression of being under constant surveillance, like a prisoner in transport or a visitor who wasn't entirely trustworthy. Behind him he heard the man call out in a voice agitated by the effort of trying to keep up.

"As Grileiras wasn't always called by that name. In the seventeenth century it was known as the Santa Clara estate, and it's recorded as having been the property of a wealthy abbot, a family ancestor favored by the king. He willed it to his only nephew, the Marquis of Santo Tomé, who had a winter residence constructed on the estate and called it As Grileiras. That must have made the abbot turn over in his grave. As I mentioned, the name of the estate is drawn from the folklore of the region."

When he crested a slope Manuel was delighted to find a long stretch of perfectly-laid-out chrysanthemum beds and beyond them the agreeable disarray of an English garden. His steps slowed involuntarily as he listened to the murmur of the breeze through the tops of the towering eucalyptus trees on the far side. The terrain then sloped downward through a densely wooded area. A shady path brought him to a small clearing with a still green pond. The roots of several weary ancient trees had given way, leaving the trunks inclined here and there over the banks of the pond. He stood for a moment, moved by the beauty of the place, and then looked around for the administrator. "This place is . . . incredible!"

Clearly winded from trying to catch up, Griñán looked down in dismay at a lichen-covered stone bench but at last lowered himself onto it. "An Atlantic garden in the English style. At least a dozen landscapers throughout history contributed, each one in his time, to achieve its beauty." He fanned himself ineffectually. "And to think that my wife is worried about her heart. She'd do better to worry about mine."

Manuel didn't look back at him. Engrossed by the calm power of the garden, he looked all around. He was fascinated. How was it possible that such a place should exist as part of someone's home? How could this wonder be someone's private garden? He was surprised to find himself thinking Álvaro had been lucky to spend his childhood here. His imagined recollection of his husband's childhood brought to mind an unwanted recollection of his own.

The silent house of the elderly maternal aunt who took them in after their parents died in a traffic accident. The foibles of an old woman who could scarcely stand the sight of them. The smell of boiled greens that over the years had permeated the walls and couldn't be scrubbed away. Whispered conversations on the upstairs balcony, the only place he and his sister could talk, and Madrid's summer sunsets, little more than a glint of dying red light fading across the house fronts opposite. They'd found them beautiful.

A century-old ficus had place of privilege at the near edge of the pond. Its two-toned leaves shone, forming a strange cascade, and its veined living roots gave it majesty and sweep, as if it were ruled by its own desires and not by any passersby who had the liberty to walk away.

Attracted by the grandeur of that tree, Manuel stepped forward and touched the trunk, its bark as fine and warm as a living animal. He turned again toward Griñán but didn't see him. He smiled for the first time in days. He looked down the path and made out the shape of an ancient water mill. He set off in that direction, resisting with difficulty the impulse to break into a run. He descended a stair guarded by two sandstone lions that the ravages of time had rendered as smooth and round as shapes drawn by a small child, and he went around the building of ancient tile, attracted by the splash of water over a mill wheel. Ferns grew along steps that presented a succession of communicating pools of greenery, each thicker and denser than the previous one. Every turn in the road opened up new paths that beckoned him into their labyrinth with the alluring promise of undiscovered niches, fountains, and views.

Manuel smiled, enraptured, admiring at every step the studied carelessness of the garden, the serenity of its beautiful chaos, the sylvan taming of that leafy glade. He imagined a happy childhood in this place. And suddenly the twists and turns weren't merely the experience of this present moment; they belonged to him.

He passed his hand through the stream of water a stone angel was pouring from an amphora. Within the music of falling water he heard his sister's laughter as she splashed him with icy drops as brilliant as pearls from a broken necklace. He envisioned the games, races, shouts, hiding places, and ambushes possible in this landscape. He followed the path, looking around at every turn, convinced that if he'd arrived just an instant earlier, he'd have seen his sister slipping away through the ferns stifling giggles, her bangs plastered to her perspiring brow. He closed his eyes, trying to preserve that vision and trying to impress upon his memory the sound of her laughter, for he heard it as clearly as if she were standing at his side. His face was wreathed in smiles as he went forward, welcoming the memories and the promise of youthful joy floating in the magic of that place. If only he could have had that imagined childhood. That yearning desire was not oppressive. It held no bitterness or rancor but was, instead, melancholy, a nostalgia for something that had never been and now never could be. But it was so lovely . . .

He found his wandering had taken him back to the lily pond. Sitting to wait for Griñán to catch up, Manuel realized this was the first time since his sister's death the thought of her hadn't caused him pain. Now at last he saw a childhood that was happy, although entirely fictitious; this was what it must mean to believe, to have faith. He hoped with all his heart that there was a heaven for her, for the two of them. It would be this garden, a paradise where someday they'd be united to frolic without care in a lush and welcoming Eden.

Manuel heard Griñán on the path before he saw him.

The administrator arrived all out of breath. He'd taken off his jacket and was carrying it carefully folded across one arm. "Are you all right? I thought you'd gotten lost."

"I needed to be alone. But I'm feeling fine." As he said it he realized it was true.

Griñán made an understanding gesture and murmured something.

Manuel made way on the bench for the administrator. In a moment of benevolent patience, he gave the man some time to catch his breath before he got up again.

"Toward the left," the executor pointed, determined to prevent Manuel from wandering off again. "That's the way to the greenhouse."

Dozens of sturdy little trees of all different sizes were planted around the structure. Dangling from branches or tacked to trunks were cards indicating each sapling's species, age, and variety. Some were budding or flowering, a display ranging from thick dark buds and little green acorn-like shapes to the perfection of pale-petaled gardenias wide open and ready to fall. Because the gardens showed such a marked English influence, he'd expected a greenhouse constructed of wood with oval arches, perhaps in the shape of a pentagon. But this structure partly sunk into the hillside had been constructed of gray Galician stone with typical striations, glittering lines against a dark background. The windows were set in white wooden frames, and the roof was of double-paned glass. The inside wasn't visible, for the panes seemed to have been splashed with mud and dirt up to the height of a man's head.

"The old marquis had it constructed for Catarina as a wedding present when she and Santiago came to live at the manor. He'd heard her say that she missed the greenhouse of her parents' estate, so he arranged for this one. It's more modern and ten times larger. It has watering pipes suspended from the ceiling, forced-air heating, and a full stereo system. That was the old man's way—everything on a grand scale."

Manuel didn't respond. He wasn't impressed by extravagance. Wealthy people in positions of power were often given to waste and excess; he was repelled by such attitudes. Even so, he had to admit to himself that the gardens testified to a love of beauty. The conscious shaping and training of this environment was evidence of extraordinary patience. The closely monitored anarchy that allowed these glades to flourish, carefully untamed, hinted at the spirit of the men who'd commissioned it.

Griñán pushed the door open. It wasn't locked. A little bell tinkled above their heads, and from inside they heard music playing from a high-quality system. "I expect Vicente is at work."

Along with the music a heavy sweet aroma arose to meet them, so intense it was dizzying, the concentrated scent of hundreds of flowers forced to bloom by the artificial warmth of the interior space. Five long worktables stretched away from the entrance and were loaded with hundreds of pots. There were many different species; he recognized some although he couldn't recall their names. But above all there were gardenias—in all possible stages of growth, from tiny sprigs with burlap-wrapped stems to bushes as tall as those in the gardens outside.

A fairly tall young man walked up the center aisle carrying what looked like a bag of potting soil. When he saw them he put it down, took off his gloves, and gave them each a strong handshake. "Hello! I suppose you're looking for Catarina. I regret she's not here today. If I can help you with anything . . ."

"We're just taking a stroll to show Manuel the estate."

Vicente gave a little start but quickly concealed his surprise. "Have you seen the lily pond? It's a magic place."

"So is the entire garden," Manuel said.

"Yes," the man responded vaguely, his gaze lost in the depths of the greenhouse. "It's too bad Catarina isn't here. I'm sure she'd have been very pleased to show you around. We've achieved remarkable advances in hybridization over the last two years." He motioned them to follow as he walked back into the interior. "Catarina has an extraordinary gift, especially with the gardenias. She never had any formal training or education in the science of it, but she has a rare talent for knowing exactly what the plant needs at any given time. Over the last year she's been recognized by leading publications as a master propagator. *Life Gardens*, the professional journal, called her the world's best producer of gardenias." He showed them a bush less than two feet tall with flowers as large as outstretched hands. "We've gotten impressive results. Not only in size and longevity of the bloom but also in the scent. Two perfume manufacturers in Paris are negotiating to use our flowers for their creations."

Manuel listened with feigned interest, but he was struck more by the man's expression and gestures, the way his body language changed when he mentioned Catarina. Trailing behind, Manuel noted that the gardener's walk had changed: the awkward gait typical of a tall man had shortened, and he seemed to glide between the worktables. The man reached out to touch the hard, brilliant leaves of the plants; when he spoke of Catarina's talent, he'd virtually caressed the gardenias. Manuel watched him wipe a white spot of powdered lime from one leaf, gently rubbing his thumb against it. The man's voice was full of admiration.

Manuel wasn't moved by gardeners' fascination with the craft of cultivation or disease-resistant hybrids, but he had to admit that the surreal, strong masculine beauty of those strange flowers was riveting. They seemed to call out to be touched. Those muted, pale petals evoked the fragility of human existence.

He remembered the waxy touch of the flower he'd been about to drop onto Álvaro's coffin and had instead carried around in his pocket all day. There was something addictive in the warm texture of the milky surface of a gardenia petal. It invited a caress the way that contact with human skin made one aware of its evanescent vulnerability. Without thinking, he lifted both hands to touch the open petals of the bloom he stood before. His fingers felt their yielding surface. He leaned over, almost bowing formally, and took in the scent. Like some magic spell, it transported him to that moment after Álvaro's funeral when he'd held the first such flower in an instant of graveside farewell, looking down at the coffin in which his own heart was being buried. The vision faded. He opened his eyes and found the greenhouse had become a blur of vague shapes. As if impelled by irresistible centrifugal force, he staggered back two steps and collapsed. He didn't lose consciousness. He perceived the shapes of two men hurrying to him, and he felt a cold hand pressed to his brow. He blinked.

"It's the heat and humidity," Vicente said. "You're not the first one to react that way. There's a difference of at least twenty degrees Fahrenheit with the outside. The humidity makes it a bit difficult to breathe if you have high blood pressure, and then there's the perfume of the flowers."

Exhausted and embarrassed, Manuel let them help him up from the sandy floor. He brushed off his already mistreated clothes. He knew he must look deplorably rumpled and unkempt.

"What have you had to eat today?" Griñán asked sternly.

"A coffee."

"A coffee," the administrator repeated, shaking his head as if lamenting the inadequacy of that response. "Let's go to the kitchen and get Herminia to give you something." He held Manuel's arm in a firm grip and steered him to the exit.

The manor house facade was structured around two symmetrical arches. One was the principal entrance; he assumed that the other must once have been the opening that granted carriages access to an interior court, for it had been bricked up. Next to it a fat black cat lurked around a Dutch-style door with an open upper section. The smells of cooking that wafted through it persuaded him that maybe Griñán was right in urging him to have something to eat.

Two women, one old and the other young, were busy at the ovens of a modern kitchen. Somewhat paradoxically the central feature was a wood-burning stove.

"Good morning," Griñán called through the doorway. The women turned with expectant looks. "Herminia, look and see if you have something to feed this man of ours. He's feeling faint."

The woman came to the door, drying her hands on her apron. She opened the lower section and stood there smiling as she looked Manuel over. He remembered her from the funeral, for she'd been wailing with the group of women. After a moment she leaned forward, took his hand, and drew him into the warm room, ignoring the administrator. Looking back and forth from Manuel to her young assistant, she brought him to the kitchen's great wooden table.

"Oh, my dear, you have no idea how much I've been thinking about you recently! And all you've been going through. Sarita, clear the table and bring Manuel a glass of wine. And you, dear, sit here and give me your jacket." She took it and hung it on the back of the chair. "Just let Herminia take care of you. Sarita, cut him a slice of the big pie."

Overwhelmed by this rush of affection, he let the women take over. Looking over his shoulder, he saw Griñán grin and heard him say, "Herminia, I'm going to get jealous, with all this attention for Manuel and none for me."

"Don't you pay any mind to him." She deliberately ignored Griñán. "He's as shameless a flatterer as that fat cat over there. And just like the cat, if I don't pay attention, he's in the kitchen eating everything he can get hold of. Sarita, fetch a bit of pie for señor Griñán as well."

Sarita put a pie as big as a tray on the table and set to cutting pieces under Herminia's vigilant gaze.

"Bigger than those, woman!" the cook cried. She took the knife and cut the pie herself, depositing slabs on sturdy white earthenware plates and placing them before the men.

Manuel had a taste. A bed of onions lay under tender fragrant pieces of meat, and the cornbread crust gave it a distinctive aroma and consistency. Clearly one was meant to eat it with one's hands.

"You like it then? Eat. Have some more!" The woman put another thick piece on his plate. She turned to Griñán, lowered her voice, and changed her tone. "Sarita has a message for you. Sarita, what do you have to say to señor Griñán?"

"The lady dowager wants to see you," the girl said timidly. "She said to tell you as soon as you arrived."

The executor straightened up in his seat and took a last regretful glance at the steaming hot yellow crust with its onion-and-meat filling.

"Duty before pleasure," he said as he got up. "Save it for me, Herminia. Don't let the cat get it." He left through a door that opened onto an interior stairway.

Little Samuel came running in, closely followed by his mother. He wrapped himself around Herminia's legs.

"Well, who's this?" the cook exclaimed. "Look, if it's not the king of the castle!" She tried to lift the boy.

But the child was suddenly struck shy when he noticed Manuel. He ran to hide behind Elisa, who smiled with evident maternal pride.

"Mama!" the child whined.

"What's the matter?" she teased him. "Don't you know who this is?"

"Uh-huh . . . it's Uncle Manuel," the boy said.

"Aren't you going to say hello?" she prompted him.

The boy smiled. "Hello, Uncle."

"Hello, Samuel," replied Manuel. He was overcome by the boy's gentle innocence and the weight of that single word.

The boy took off toward the door.

"He's full of beans today. We'll see if we can wear him down a little," Elisa called in farewell as she rushed after him.

Herminia looked after them and then turned to Manuel. "Elisa's a good girl and a fine mother. She was Fran's fiancée—Fran, Álvaro's little brother. She was pregnant when he died."

Manuel remembered what he'd heard from Griñán: death by overdose.

"He didn't live to see his son," Herminia went on. "Elisa's been with us since then, and as for Samuel, let me tell you—" She smiled. "You've seen already. He's a little ray of sunshine. He's brought a bit of joy to this house." Sadness crept into her expression. "And heaven knows we need it."

Sarita, standing behind her, sighed as well and placed a hand on Herminia's shoulder. The cook quickly covered it with hers and tilted her head to express gratitude and affection.

Griñán looked very concerned when he returned. He didn't touch the pie and took only a quick sip of wine. He made a show of checking his cell phone. "Look at this! I'm sorry, Manuel, something unexpected has come up at the office. I have to go back to Lugo."

The false note in his voice was so obvious that neither of the women would look at him. They busied themselves with the first thing that came to hand to dissociate themselves from his little charade.

"I have things to do as well," Manuel lied. "It's quite all right."

Manuel rose and collected his jacket. Herminia gave him a big hug before he even started to say goodbye. He was obliged to lean over and hold on to her until at last, uneasy with her excessive display of affection and afraid she'd never let go, he pretended to hug her back.

"Come back and see us," she whispered in his ear.

He donned his jacket and caught up with the administrator, who was waiting for him outside.

"Uncle!" He heard behind him the little boy's shrill voice.

Manuel turned and saw Samuel come running in that clumsy manner of small children, looking every moment as if he were about to fall flat on his face. Those cheeks flushed with the morning chill and the arms held out in insistent appeal brought a smile to his face as he reached down to receive the boy. He lifted the child high, deeply moved by the boy's enthusiastic attention. Against his chest the boy's body was as solid and uncontrollable as a huge fish, the little arms wrapped around Manuel's neck like strong sprouting vines. The boy kissed his cheek with a smack that left the moist cold trace of his lips. Manuel held on to him, overwhelmed and not at all sure what to do as he waited for Elisa to catch up with them.

"I thought I could keep up!" she excused herself cheerfully as she tried to catch her breath. The youngster reached out, jumped down, and hurled himself toward her; she opened her arms and received him. "Come back to see us. We'd both love that."

He nodded and then joined the administrator, who accompanied him in silence back to where they'd parked. When Manuel reached the car he turned to look back and saw the mother and son looking after them. Before he got into the car he waved, and they waved back.

THE LABORS OF THE HERO

The police weren't surprised to see him. As soon as he mentioned Álvaro Muñiz de Dávila, an officer escorted him to the captain's office. He hid his surprise at the sight of a copy of one of his novels on the desk. The captain expressed his condolences once more, brought out a cardboard box, opened it, and read out the inventory of the contents. "A wallet, eighty euros in cash, two sets of keys, identity documents, two cell phones, and a bag with the clothes, belt, and shoes removed at the hospital after his"—he cleared his throat—"his admission."

"Two cell phones?"

"That's not correct?"

"I suppose so," he admitted in tacit acknowledgment of Nogueira's cynical views. Why not? Two sets of keys, two phones, two lives. Why should he be surprised?

"I'm sorry, we haven't located the wedding ring."

Manuel nodded without knowing what to say. He stood up. "I'll also need the keys to the car."

"Of course. And please sign this receipt. It's part of the routine when we transfer possession." The captain clicked a ballpoint pen and held it out.

Manuel scrawled his signature. The captain held out the keys but then took them back at the last moment. "Señor Ortigosa, would you autograph this for my wife?" He gestured at the book, with an uncertainty quite unlike the confidence he'd manifested up to that point.

Manuel looked at the dust jacket. He and Álvaro had chosen it from two designs proposed by the publisher. Back in the days when every cover design and every translation into another language were miracles to be celebrated with champagne toasts.

The captain fell all over himself with apologies and jolted Manuel out of those memories. "I know this is hardly the best time to ask and maybe . . . if you'd rather not . . . I shouldn't have asked."

"Of course," Manuel said, pocketing the keys and picking up the book. "What's your wife's name?"

⁊⋇⟇

He put the cardboard box into the trunk of his BMW. He would deliver it to Nogueira that night so the medical examiner could check the clothing. He put the two cell phones into his jacket pocket. He went out to the parking area to look for Álvaro's car. It was in the very back between two patrol cars, and from a distance it showed no sign of any accident. He didn't intend to drive it away, since to do that he'd have to leave his own car behind. He hadn't foreseen that complication. He went up to the vehicle and shaded his eyes to look inside. The interior looked clean and orderly except for a few dark spots on the seat and the steering wheel. He pressed the remote and unlocked the car.

And Álvaro was there. Manuel sensed his presence as if they were standing shoulder to shoulder—the scent of his skin, the imprint of his life, his very essence. And it was as physical and real as if his ghost were about to appear or had just vanished.

Manuel reeled back in astonishment, his head spinning from the distinctive scent. His heart raced, his eyes filled with tears, and his knees buckled. He backed away, holding on to the adjacent patrol car and sliding in retreat along its entire length. He gasped in fright at the impact of the presence linked to the odor trapped in the cramped interior, as if a crystal bottle of strong perfume had suddenly exploded. He shut his eyes, trying to retain every atom of aroma, as it rapidly faded and lost itself in the vulgar smells of the rest of the world, robbing him of the miracle of Álvaro's instantaneous presence.

Devastated, he shook his head and mentally cursed the torment that had played such a trick on him. In a final attempt to hold on to his husband, Manuel lunged forward and shut the car door, denying himself that aroma in a final attempt to keep the little that remained from vanishing forever. He sank down, shattered by Álvaro's absence, his eyes filled with tears of rage. He became aware of a young patrolman watching him, hesitant, concerned and yet afraid to approach.

"Are you all right, sir?" the officer asked with careful formality.

Manuel looked at him and almost broke into laughter. Here was that famous writer on the ground with his back against a police cruiser, weeping desperate tears, and the kid was asking if he was all right.

Yes, I fucking well am.

He groped in his pockets for a handkerchief he knew wasn't there and encountered the ominous shape of the second cell phone from the undisclosed life. The touch of it was enough to exorcise Álvaro and replace him with the memory of a stranger he'd once thought he knew. That humiliating realization cut short his blubbering with the power of a magic spell. He looked back at the car door, clicked the remote to lock it, and pushed himself to his feet. He brushed off the dirt. "Yes. Don't worry, I'm fine. I just got a little dizzy."

The young man didn't say anything. He pressed his lips together and nodded.

Manuel sat motionless behind the wheel of his own car, too exhausted to drive and too confused to make any decisions. In his hand he held the latest model of an iPhone he'd never seen before. He inspected it anxiously. It was as sleek and black as some repulsive beetle guarding a secret that humanity couldn't live without. He turned it on and the display warned that the battery was almost dead. He plugged it into his car's phone charger and used his own cell phone to call Mei.

"Manuel?"

"Mei, Álvaro had a business phone, different from his personal one."

Mei didn't reply immediately, and that provoked him. "For the love of God, Mei, I'm not asking for confirmation. I have it here. Álvaro's dead. There's no reason to cover up for him."

"I'm sorry, Manuel, that's not what I was thinking. It's just that I can't get used to the idea . . . Yes, he had a second cell phone."

"I assume it was billed to the office, since I knew nothing about it."

"Yes, the statements came here. The firm paid."

"All right, I need the itemized statements for this phone."

"If you have the phone, you can use the app and see them yourself. But if you want me to send them, I can do that. Give me your address."

"I'm staying at an inn. I'll text it to you as soon as I hang up. I'll need his appointment book with his meetings and travel."

"Those are on his calendar in the iPhone. But I'll send you a hard copy."

He switched on Álvaro's business phone and swiped through the icons until he located the calendar. It displayed a jumble of notes, color-coded deadlines, assignments, and meetings. The confusing mess of notes and dates provided no hints or obvious clues.

"I need your help, Mei. How can I find one particular piece of information in all of this?"

"Well, that depends. What are you looking for?"

"The trips to Galicia. His administrator said he came here regularly. They have to be in his calendar."

"Every two months," she answered, clearly expecting an angry reaction.

He liked Mei and knew she liked him. And she'd adored Álvaro. Now that his initial anger and astonishment had subsided, he realized that in her place he also would have done anything Álvaro asked. He was sure she was struggling, but he was still too resentful to admit he might eventually forgive her. He kept his voice neutral. "I don't see anything in his calendar about that."

"They're listed as meetings with *The Hero's Works*."

The Hero's Works was one of the agency's principal clients. Manuel couldn't remember exactly what they did. He had the vague idea it was something to do with chemistry, but the name was so bizarre that it had stuck in his memory. Álvaro's calendar confirmed that for the last few years, meetings with *The Hero's Works* had been blocked out for two or three days every other month.

"So he took advantage of those meetings to travel?"

"Manuel, *The Hero's Works* was Álvaro's. Its principal activity was processing, marketing, and exporting wine."

"In other words . . . ?"

"He owned it."

Manuel's face burned with humiliation. The tears he had wanted to shed boiled away and disappeared.

※

92

The shower stall was so narrow he could hardly move. The thick plastic shower curtain with the pattern of squares was marked by a streak of mold along the bottom like a soiled hem. Manuel overcame his disgust long enough to wet it and push it against the wall, determined to counter its intrusive inertia and make it stick there to keep it away from his body. A powerful jet of water erupted from the showerhead and obliged him to contort himself to get completely wet. The stream was so forceful it battered his head, but he opened the tap all the way, shut his eyes, and let the hot water wash over his exhausted limbs. It hammered his shoulder like an invisible fist, a sensation that felt oddly comforting. His shoulders, hands, and legs throbbed painfully, and a constant burning sensation lurked behind his eyes and in his lower back.

He felt himself getting sick, and he knew only sheer rage kept him going. He felt it boiling slowly inside, distilling itself into bitterness as if through a fragile glass retort that reduced it to drops of pure poison destined to become the only food for his soul.

Rage was necessary. He needed it to keep him from fleeing, to resist the impulse to get in the car and just leave behind him this place and its lies, all the pain, and the idiotic pact he'd made with the deactivated officer who despised him and everything he represented.

The rest of the room was adequate enough. The towels and sheets were clean; the furnishings were spartan and old-fashioned; the wooden floorboards creaked in some places. One of the walls featured a door with a dead bolt that clearly led to the room next door and hinted of a justification for the cramped single iron-framed bed he found hateful. The overly soft mattress was so thin the boards of the bed frame beneath were visible in its contours. It was entirely too reminiscent of his childhood bed in his old aunt's house, a place of sleeplessness and despair.

Just now it was covered by plastic bags of purchases he'd made before visiting police headquarters. Two double-breasted jackets; three pairs of pants; half a dozen each of shirts, socks, and underwear. He chose what to wear today and stowed the rest in the closet. He left on the nightstand the book he'd purchased at the shopping center. Normally he was a firm supporter of independent bookshops, but today he didn't want to take a chance on being recognized by a clerk—he was in no mood to make small talk. He'd opted for the friendly smile of a teenager more likely to recognize someone from *Dancing with the Stars*.

Disappointed with the selection and feeling too distracted for a novel or an essay, he'd gone through the shelves. In a fit of annoyance, he chose a book he was surprised to find there. He'd already read it, but as often happened when he was deep in his writing phase, it seemed a good idea to revisit something familiar. It was a special edition of works by Edgar Allan Poe that included *The Tell-Tale Heart*, *The Black Cat*, and *The Raven*.

He'd bought something else as well. He'd placed it mechanically on the dark surface of the desk, the most logical place. He'd avoided looking at it as he arranged the garments and decided what to wear.

Two packets of paper and a package of ballpoint pens. That was the title he'd given one of his earliest articles, the only time he'd ever written about the process of literary creation.

Shortly after the publication of his first novel, as sales were approaching half a million copies, editors of a famous literary magazine persuaded him to describe his process, to evoke the laboratory of his alchemy and reveal his magic. *Two packets of paper and a package of ballpoint pens*—that's how he'd summed up everything a writer needed in order to create a novel. He'd said it because he believed it, because he'd lived it. He knew that writing is driven by human necessity and erupts from the poverty of the soul, from an interior hunger and cold that can be tempered by writing, if only for a time. The criticism from his literary colleagues had been brutal. Who was this new arrival to offer them advice, this wannabe, this performing monkey with a typewriter? Wasn't the very number of copies sold the irrefutable proof he was nothing but a producer of run-of-the-mill popular trash?

Many books and interviews later he'd perfected his technique with interviewers. He received them in a room with walls covered with bookshelves, a plate-glass table, light slanting through a transom window, white orchids, and silence. He wrapped his calling in a halo of revolting artificiality and extolled the worst of vices as aids to creativity: alcohol and drugs, violence, and dabbling in various abhorrent behaviors.

The truth was that he believed in the exultation of loneliness, inspiration born of misfortune, the pride of the scorned, and motivation encouraged by the sneers of others. All were powerful motivators and fonts of creativity. He also believed they were effective only if concealed. Those subterranean rivers of cool water or burning lava swept away everything within the writer. Revealing them would be as obscene to him as claiming that a well-lit office, a computer, or a PhD in literary criticism were sufficient in themselves to make anyone a writer.

He had to acknowledge that he'd always occupied the best room of their home and had been pampered like a sultan. He had a beautiful desk, excellent light, and orchids most of the time. And Álvaro's silent presence, reading while Manuel worked at his desk, had been his reassurance, the symbol of ideal perfection and happiness that sometimes distracted him and robbed him of inspiration when he looked up and took in their surroundings. But he also knew as well that those things were superficial.

As he lost himself in the blank whiteness of the writing paper, he wondered when he'd stopped paying attention. When had he forgotten that writing was engendered by pure misery, pain beyond words, and secrets dying inside? The essence of the magic of creation was suggesting them without ever revealing them, never allowing the nakedness of the soul to become a pornography of emotions.

He went to the desk in his unadorned room, feeling the warmth from the shower rapidly dissipating. The towel about him was becoming cool to the touch. He reached out and ran his fingertips across the silky surface of the wrapping of the packages of writing paper. Two packets of paper and a package of ballpoint pens, no more.

He sighed and retreated.

He wiped the steamed-up bathroom mirror with a towel and stood before it as he buttoned his shirt. It was almost time. He put on one of the new jackets and lowered the volume of the television. He'd left it on; that was a new habit. Before going to the door he picked up his soiled double-breasted jacket to remove his wallet and the cell phones.

He found something else in the pocket. He recognized it as soon as he touched it, but he had to examine it in order to make sure. The flower was a bit worse for wear from being in his pocket, but even so it was still smooth, firm, and redolent with its elegant masculine aroma. A gardenia.

He held the flower for a few moments, glanced at the jacket and then back at the gardenia, and wondered how the bloom had gotten there. Puzzled, he opened the drawer and confirmed that it still contained the flower he'd deposited there that very morning, bedraggled but unmistakable. He put the two gardenias side by side on the dull surface of the nightstand and studied them.

He decided at last that something must have happened when he fainted in the greenhouse. He'd been admiring the gardenias and perhaps, when he fell, a flower had been . . . but then that seemed absurd. The flowers in the greenhouse had been twice as big as these . . . and yet . . .

It had been a strange day of experiences just as bizarre as those of the previous one. Everything in recent days had been so unreal that it was difficult to reconstruct sequences from the chaos that had overtaken his life. Perhaps he'd simply picked the flower and stuck it in a pocket without realizing what he was doing.

A sudden knock at the door gave him a start. He opened it expecting to see the innkeeper's wife who'd dropped by from time to time, perhaps concerned he might be lonely. She'd offered to fix him something to eat, had delivered fresh towels, or had let him know the soccer match was starting on television, even though he'd told her he wasn't much of a fan.

Mei Liu, her face marked by fatigue and almost unrecognizable, stood outside his room. Her expression was half apology and half apprehension.

"Mei—why are you here?"

His question was one of resignation instead of reproach; his tone was surprised but gentle. He opened his arms and took her in. She burst into tears. As he held her he felt his anger ebb away completely. It would surely come back redoubled in the course of the day, but the warmth of her body comforted him unexpectedly and provided something he hadn't been aware he was missing. It made him aware that since the moment of Álvaro's farewell and departure, he hadn't really embraced anyone. Except little Samuel.

It took him quite a while to calm Mei. The tissues he provided one after another contained her tears at last. She took her first look at his room. It must have seemed stark and unhappy to her, for she asked in a sad, choked voice, "But why are you staying here, Manuel?"

"I'm here because I have to be here. But how about you? Why are you here?"

Mei freed herself from his arms and went to the window. She dropped her purse and took off her thin coat. She looked outside and then back around the room. Manuel saw her focus on the blank sheets of paper stacked on the old desk. She looked at them in silence for a few moments, almost as if she were drawing from them the words she was about to say.

"I know you told me not to come, and I tried to respect your wishes, but . . . Manuel, I don't ask for forgiveness, but I want you to understand. As soon as he had to take over his family's affairs, Álvaro asked me to keep them entirely separate. The fact is, from the moment he described his approach, it never occurred to me it might hurt you like this. I'd never have been a part of it. It seemed to me he was being forced to deal with something purely commercial, and he just didn't want to discuss it."

"All right, Mei, I suppose you're right. I guess that perhaps someday I might understand. It wasn't your fault. But you already told me all this on the phone. Why did you come?"

She nodded and even gave him a woeful little smile of acknowledgment. "Because I have something to tell you, something I remembered when you called to ask about Álvaro's other telephone."

That caught Manuel's attention.

"He kept that iPhone on the desk. It didn't ring very often, and he picked it up when it did. Once or twice I answered it. Each time I did, I found myself speaking to the same man, someone with a strong Gallego accent who spoke perfect Castilian Spanish. He was very educated and polite; you can always tell that much from someone's voice. It was señor Griñán. You must have met him."

Manuel nodded at the description of the administrator.

"Last Friday Álvaro and I were in his office. He'd gotten a call from Griñán that morning. I know that's who called because I heard Álvaro greet him. But in the afternoon he got another call. The person on the other end of the line was shouting so loud I heard him across the room. I couldn't understand what he was saying, but he was obviously very angry. Álvaro sent me out of the room, but you know his office and mine are separated only by a glass partition. He listened for a while, said a few words, and then ended the call. He was worried when he came out; I knew him well enough to see that. He muttered an excuse about going out for a coffee or something and left the office.

"Then the phone rang again. I want you to understand he'd authorized me to take those calls. I promise you they were usually just routine messages like 'Tell Álvaro to call me,' or 'Tell Álvaro I mailed him the documents for the firm,' and I would just answer, 'Yes, I'll tell him,' or 'He's in a meeting right now.' I just mean that even though Álvaro generally picked up, there was nothing out of the ordinary about this." Visibly nervous, Mei bit her lower lip. "So when it rang, I wasn't exactly sure what to do. The number displayed on the screen was really strange, only three or four digits. But anyhow, the administrator's office has lots of extensions and sometimes he'd use one that didn't display caller ID. So I picked up.

"It's been years since I heard it, but I immediately recognized the sound of coins being accepted by a pay phone. It wasn't Griñán on the other end. It was a different man. He sounded really agitated and didn't give me a chance to say anything. As soon as the call was connected he said, 'You can't ignore him, you hear me? He has proof. He knows you killed him and he'll tell the world if you don't do something.'"

Mei said nothing more. Her body sagged like that of a marionette when its strings are cut. She had to grab the windowsill to stay on her feet, as if what she'd just said had emptied her completely.

Manuel was astonished. "'He knows you killed him'? Are you sure?"

Mei nodded and closed her eyes for a moment. When they opened again her face was submerged in grief. "I didn't say anything. I just disconnected. The phone started ringing again right away. I guess the man on the pay phone thought the call had been dropped. I didn't answer. I went out for a coffee as an excuse to get out of there. When I got back Álvaro had already returned. There were no more calls, but later I saw him talking on that same phone. When he finished, he came out and told me he had to move up the meeting with *The Hero's Works* and was getting on the road right away. He was 'officially' spending the weekend in Barcelona at the Cataluña hotel group's convention."

Manuel stood there in silence, at a loss for words. He had the pressing sensation of having stepped through a mirror into some disconcerting parallel world where logic no longer prevailed. *He knows you killed him.* But who knew? Killed? Killed whom?

He put his icy hands to his brow and felt it burning again with the interior fever that had been devouring him. Mei was looking down, but his gesture hadn't escaped her. He disappointed her the way he'd disappointed everyone who'd expected him to collapse in pain. He knew; and he saw it again in her surprise at his next question. "Mei, did you know that Álvaro had that much money?"

She stared at him, plainly stunned.

Manuel realized he needed to clarify. "I'm referring to . . . well, I know that the firm had signed important deals with sports clubs, pharmaceutical manufacturers, and . . . well, like that contract with Chevrolet and the other automobile firm, the one from Japan. What was it again? Takensi?"

"Takeshi."

"Right, that's the one. But his executor told me Álvaro was very wealthy and said it was his own money."

Mei shrugged. "Yes, I guess you could say he was very rich."

"Well, I knew things were going well for us, but I never imagined . . ."

"After all, Manuel, you were busy with other things. Your travels, your books."

With other things. Was there a reproach hidden in Mei's response? How could he have lived in such ignorance? With his back turned to everything? So all those who knew him must have interpreted his ignorance of the circumstances of his own life as due to a fundamental flaw in his character? Were his travels and books excuses enough to have remained oblivious of all that?

He tried to entertain those questions, but his mind was mired in a sort of defensive torpor that inhibited him from accepting the tale of excess and violence Mei had just told.

"Manuel, I really should leave now."

He looked up and saw she had put on her coat and was looking for something in her purse. She held out a medium-sized personal agenda with a black cover. He looked it over quickly and left it on the coffee table, so he wouldn't have to see Álvaro's handwriting.

"I already went through it," she said, jutting her chin toward the agenda. "It's the same as the one on the cell phone. But you don't have to take my word for it. You can check it yourself."

There was no resentment in her voice. Her humble acceptance of guilt both broke his heart and irritated him beyond words. She kept her eyes fastened on the purse she was helplessly turning over in her hands, now without a purpose. When she noticed him watching, she slowly turned toward the window, stopping a tear with a fingertip almost as if she wanted to push it back beneath her eyelid. Manuel realized that he didn't even know where she was staying or how she'd gotten to Galicia.

"What hotel are you staying in?"

"I'm not staying. I'm going back to Madrid."

Manuel checked the time on his cell phone.

"But it's late. Even if you leave right now, you won't get there until two in the morning."

"After we talked I felt really terrible. I thought about calling you back to tell you all this, but I realized I needed to come tell you in person, because you loved Álvaro. And I love you, Manuel. I can't stand the idea that you think I betrayed you."

He returned her gaze, profoundly moved, but he remained seated on the edge of the bed, watching her rummaging in her purse again as a pretext to stay. He told himself to get up and embrace her again, but he didn't do so. He wasn't yet entirely ready to forgive her. "I didn't say you betrayed me. And I'm grateful you came all this way to tell me this."

Reluctantly accepting the evidence that if she were ever to receive absolution from Manuel it wouldn't happen today, Mei slowly secured the clasp of her bag and placed the strap over her shoulder. "Then I'll be on my way."

Manuel felt her pain. "Why don't you stay tonight? You can take your time on the drive back tomorrow."

"I didn't tell anyone I was coming, not even my husband. It was . . . an impulse. As soon as I put down the phone, I knew I had to come see you."

Mei went toward the door. Only then did Manuel get up to follow her. He caught her as she put her hand to the doorknob.

"Mei, right now I'm in no shape to think clearly. But don't think I'm not grateful. We're sure to talk again, maybe a little later, but right now . . . I can't."

She went up on tiptoes and he leaned over to kiss her. He gave her a brief farewell hug and closed the door after she'd gone.

THE SUN OF TEBAS

Álvaro was reading on the sofa, barefoot, with his trouser legs rolled up. He was a speedy reader. He'd started early that morning, and by noon nearly half the pages of the four-hundred-page manuscript of the novel were stacked beside him.

Manuel was in the kitchen. Álvaro usually took care of their meals, but they switched duties on the days when he served as Manuel's reader. Today Manuel's duty was to make sure everything around his husband was in perfect order, so Álvaro's reading wasn't interrupted.

Manuel went back to the living room. For a few minutes he pretended to be consulting a weighty book on Italian cuisine. In fact he was watching Álvaro from the corner of his eye, monitoring his husband's facial expressions and the intense focus with which he devoured page after page. Manuel was hoping for a hint of the emotions Álvaro was experiencing.

"You're distracting me," Álvaro muttered. He didn't look up from the typed pages.

Taking that as an invitation rather than a rejection, Manuel put down the heavy volume that he'd been using as a pretext and went to Álvaro. He perched on the armrest of the big chair.

"Tell me how it's going."

Álvaro declined to be lured. "I will. But you have to let me read it to the end."

"You already know the end hasn't been written. I'll finish it after you've read everything here, just like always."

"You know perfectly well what I mean. I'm not going to say anything until I've read every single page. So clear out and let me read."

Manuel was preparing gnocchi, principally because the recipe was tedious and complicated. Peeling and dicing the potatoes, boiling them, putting them through the food mill, preparing the dough, the strips of meat, the small molded balls of dough, the sauce. The recipe was simple, but the steps were complicated enough to keep him busy for hours. Even so, he eventually ran out of things to do. He stepped onto the terrace to look for cats on the rooftops of Madrid, sorted his sweaters, glanced without interest through the newspapers, even started an abortive attempt to read one of the many books in the pile he'd postponed reading until he finished his novel. Meanwhile he kept taking furtive looks into the living room where Álvaro sat reading.

Manuel loved seeing him like that. Shirtless and relaxed while the sunlight of that long day shifted its way across his back, endowing his short mane of chestnut-brown hair with a luster and illuminating the calm concentration in his face. Álvaro turned page after page, placing each one face down at his side in a stack that by now was taller than the one yet to be read. The last of the August daylight was fading away when he put the final page on the stack.

Manuel placed a bottle and two wineglasses on the table. He carefully filled them and handed one to Álvaro. "And so . . . ?"

Álvaro stretched out his right hand and placed it over the pages he'd just read. "It's very good, Manuel."

"Really?"

"Your readers will love it."

Manuel put down his glass and leaned forward. "And you? Did you love it?"

"It's very good."

"That's not what I asked. Did *you* love it?"

Manuel caught Álvaro's gesture of pushing away the finished pages, similar to that of a croupier at a roulette table. Álvaro leaned forward to meet his gaze. "If you're asking if it's like *The Man Who Refused*, then no, it's not that good."

"You just said it was good."

"Yes, and that your readers will love it."

"But why don't you?"

"Manuel, you write very well. You're a pro, but this isn't . . . it isn't sincere. It's not of the same quality as *The Man Who Refused*."

Manuel rose, turned his back to his husband, and walked to the center of the room. "I've told you a thousand times I can't write another novel like *The Man Who Refused*."

"You can't—or you don't want to?"

Manuel came back to the sofa and turned to face him. "I wrote *The Man Who Refused* because I had to. It was necessary, a price I had to pay. I had to drink the bitterness of that pain and those memories before I could tell the story: my childhood, how we were orphaned, living with that old aunt who detested us, and how we thought nothing bad could ever happen to us again because we'd already survived the worst. Until my sister died."

"It's your best novel, but you've refused to be interviewed about it."

"I was reliving my life, Álvaro, my own life. An incredible amount of grief went into writing about that. I don't want to write about it. I don't want to ever go through that again." He rose and took a few steps away.

Álvaro followed him. "It's not a matter of living through it again, Manuel. You're safe now. I'm with you, and you're not six years old anymore. *The Sun of Tebas* is a good novel, and your readers will love it, but it's insincere. If you don't want to hear my opinion, you shouldn't have asked for it."

"Of course I want your opinion. I write for you. But I want you to understand me too. I believe in literature that reflects reality, but I refuse to make a spectacle of private pain."

"And that's your mistake. It's not a matter of drawing attention to yourself. No one but you needs to understand your sources. But when you write from the heart, every reader perceives it. Even if subliminally. Why do you think *The Man Who Refused* is still considered your best novel?"

Manuel dropped onto the sofa and put his face in his hands. His fingers slipped up into his hair. "I don't know," he said at last.

Álvaro settled close beside him. "Yes, you do know, Manuel. Sure, somewhere inside you there's still a six-year-old who wakes up in tears. I know that child misses his parents and the sister who's no longer there to console him. I know how reality pains you, and I know that's probably what makes you a magnificent writer: your ability to shelter in that endless palace of your imagination and bring back one story after another. But there's a man who confronted that pain, a man who consoled that boy, a magnificent, sincere man who buried his parents and his sister and did it with a novel. I fell in love with that man. You can't tell me to stop admiring that strength. That would mean giving up the best thing that ever happened to me."

Manuel looked at him, obstinately opposed. "Don't you realize I've spent my whole life trying to flee from that life, trying to forget it all? I'm successful. I have thousands of readers, money, this home—enough for the rest of my life. And you admitted my fans will love *The Sun of Tebas*. It's exactly what they want. Why must I suffer to write when I can choose to be happy instead?"

"Because it's the truth."

That was too much. Manuel got up again. "I'm not looking for truth, Álvaro. I had more truth than I could stomach when I was a boy and all my life before I met you. I want what we have now." He collected the bulky pile of typewritten pages and pressed them to his chest. "This is the truth I want. It's all the truth I can bear."

Álvaro remained very quiet for several seconds, gazing at him. He closed his eyes and sighed. He got up and came to Manuel. "Forgive me. You're right." He took the manuscript from Manuel's hands and embraced him.

"Forgive me, Álvaro, but it's just that you don't know what it was like to endure a childhood like mine."

"No," his husband whispered. "No, I don't know what that was like."

THE NET

A couple of dozen locals crowded the inn's lively bar. He made out the figure of Lieutenant Nogueira in the press of bodies. The man was chewing a piece of fried bacon held in several paper napkins that gleamed translucent with streaks of grease. He downed the last bite and helped it along with a swig of beer. He took two or three more napkins from the dispenser and meticulously wiped his lips and mustache.

"Best if we talk outside," he said by way of greeting.

Manuel nodded. He saw Nogueira signal the waiter for drinks, indicating that they'd be on the patio.

The retired officer lit a cigarette as soon as they stepped outside. He drew in a deep drag with the satisfaction of a tobacco addict. He gestured toward a table in the dark corner farthest from the entrance.

"How did it go at As Grileiras?"

"Not very well. Griñán warned the family of our visit the night before, so the mother was too infirm to receive visitors, and Santiago and Catarina were away on a trip. The only one of them I got to see was Elisa, Fran's wife. Just for a moment, because she was running after the child. We said hello but that was about it."

Nogueira clicked his tongue in annoyance. "That Griñán! I took a dislike to him as soon I saw him at the hospital."

"I don't know. I think he's just doing his job." Manuel was defending the executor, even though to his mind the man had been entirely too quick to ingratiate himself with the new marquis.

Not that anyone could blame him. Manuel had to admit that the man's obsequious attitude toward him as presumptive heir had changed entirely too quickly to seem sincere. Manuel was annoyed to find he'd been naïve. His first impression of Griñán had been positive. The man's admiration and respect for Álvaro had seemed genuine, and Manuel wasn't yet ready to believe the man's attitude was motivated solely by the desire to maintain a juicy account. But no way was he about to get into all that with Nogueira.

"He gave me a short tour of the estate. That garden is incredible."

"Yes," the officer agreed. "It's really precious."

Manuel was astonished. The expression *really precious* wasn't one he'd expect to hear from Nogueira.

Nogueira's face hardened when he became conscious of Manuel's surprised look. He took his time finishing his cigarette. "But don't confuse an escorted tour with real collaboration. First he warns the family; then he runs you around the garden to distract you."

"Well, I did meet some of the people who work on the estate. The caretaker and the veterinarian; Catarina's assistant at the greenhouse with the gardenias; Herminia, the watchdog who keeps an eye on everything in the house; and Sarita, who does the housework with her."

"Were you able to talk with them?"

"With Herminia for a while, just a few minutes. She was very affectionate," he commented, remembering that overenthusiastic embrace. "The rest of the time Griñán was right on my heels," Manuel admitted. "Despite all his efforts to keep me mostly out of sight, I believe the old dowager was quite sharp with him. She had him summoned to her 'lodgings,' and when he came back he was in a rush. He invented an obviously false pretext and insisted we leave. It was obvious even to Herminia."

Nogueira shook his head.

"I went to the police headquarters," Manuel went on. "I have a box in my car with his clothing and personal effects."

"That's good. I'll take them to Ophelia."

"The car's still there. I'd have had to leave my own in order to drive it away. I'll take a taxi there tomorrow."

"I should have thought of that," the officer said, annoyed with himself. "Give me the keys, and I'll ask a police friend of mine to bring it here and leave the keys at the bar. I'll take it from there."

Manuel looked away for a moment, inhaled deliberately, and slowly let the air out before answering. He was finding it difficult to admit he'd been deceived. "They gave me two cell phones. I recognized one but didn't know the other one existed. It seems to be the one he used for his business here." He took the iPhone from his pocket and placed it on the table, unable to suppress the vision of Mei answering that strange call. "His setup here is a network of private companies running all of the real estate, the ranches, the dairy, and the agricultural operations. Nothing to scoff at." Manuel pushed the phone across the table to Nogueira. "His personal calendar shows all his visits here. They were noted as meetings with *The Hero's Works.*"

Nogueira took the phone but observed Manuel closely as he continued filling in the lieutenant.

"*The Hero's Works* is the enterprise that manages all the rest, as well as two wineries and a company that exports Galician wine. Phone usage was billed to his office, so I never had a clue. And that," he added with a bitter smile while pointing at the iPhone, "is how I found out about all those meetings with *The Hero's Works*. Álvaro's secretary recorded them on his business calendar, along with meetings with other clients. Every other month, like clockwork, Álvaro left for a couple of days to meet a VIP client who happened to be himself. Every other month for the last three years."

The arrival of the waiter with the drinks plunged him into a dark silence that echoed with Mei's words: *He knows you killed him.* He sipped his beer and ignored the inevitable plate of snacks that materialized with every order in that place.

He wondered whether he should tell the officer what Mei had said. He was undecided. He knew it was significant, but on the other hand he realized that in the lieutenant's eyes the reported fragment of conversation would be enough to condemn a Muñiz de Dávila once and for all. He looked up to see Nogueira peering at the iPhone calendar, repeatedly swiping a finger across the screen. The officer looked up, rose, and moved his chair next to Manuel's.

"Look here." He pointed to the screen. "Just like you said: he had regular meetings with *The Hero's Works*, two days every other month except each September. In September the calendar is blocked out up to five days, see? Always around the same time of month. The most recent meeting was scheduled for the second and third of July. But none after that until the end of September."

"Griñán told me about the schedule for meetings. He also said Álvaro didn't ask him to attend, so he didn't have any of the particulars."

Nogueira sighed. He put down the cell phone, finished off his little plate of snacks in two bites, and had another swallow of beer. He eyed the other saucer. "You're not going to eat yours?"

Manuel shook his head and watched the lieutenant gulp down a concoction that looked like macaroni with meat and tomatoes. Only after finishing it, lighting another cigarette, and taking another deep drag did the man seem satisfied.

"Did you get a list of the calls for this phone?" he asked.

Manuel took the cell phone, turned it on, and examined the icons. "No need. The phone has an app that lists all calls made and received, even if they're deleted from the main listings."

The history showed a fair number of calls had been made with this cell phone, but there were few incoming calls: three from a four-digit number, most likely the odd number Mei had mentioned, and two others from a different number without caller ID. All on the day Álvaro had left for Galicia.

Manuel lifted his eyes from the screen. "What do you think?"

"The four-digit number's a pay phone," Nogueira said, confirming Mei's hunch. "We might be able to identify it, but that wouldn't be much help. We'll try anyway. Maybe its location will give us a clue. The other's from a landline, and it's from this area code."

Nogueira had taken out his notebook and scribbled down the numbers. He took out his own phone and punched the digits. He lifted it to his ear and then passed it to Manuel quickly enough to convey the end of the recorded message: ". . . the administrative offices are open from eight in the morning to four in the afternoon. If you wish to make an appointment, please leave your number after the beep, and we will return your call."

Manuel held out the phone as the familiar beep sounded. Nogueira ended the call.

"Administrative offices of Adolfo Griñán. Don't you think it's a very interesting coincidence that his administrator happened to call and he decided to travel that same day? And according to his own declaration," Nogueira continued,

"Griñán was the only one who could reach Álvaro on this number. Álvaro was there because Griñán called him. Maybe Griñán was the one using the pay phone."

Manuel thought about that. Mei was sure the caller wasn't Griñán. And then, those words: *He knows you killed him.* Sharing that confidence with Nogueira would amount to an accusation that would tarnish Álvaro without opening up any other options.

No, not yet.

"All right then, tomorrow, first thing, without calling ahead," Nogueira ordered him sternly, "I want you to go to those offices, interrupt whatever our friend the administrator is up to, and demand an explanation. Don't give him time to think up an excuse. Just tell him you know Álvaro was here because Griñán called him, and see what he comes up with. I said already I didn't care for him one bit."

Manuel agreed with a pensive nod. This wasn't a triumphant discovery, as Nogueira seemed to think, but at least it was grounds for a bluff.

"And go back to As Grileiras. What assholes! You have every right to; after all, you're the legal owner. Surely without that clown Griñán hanging over you, someone will be willing to open up."

Manuel gave Nogueira Álvaro's car keys, the two cell phones, and the rest of the personal items, and watched the man leave. He thought of Griñán and the man's eager servility. He also told himself he wouldn't mind going back to As Grileiras.

⁂

The office receptionist smiled to welcome him. He returned the courtesy and walked down the hall to Griñán's office. He nodded left and right, greeting those in the office, both secretaries and the senior staff. It seemed they'd all heard the rumor that he was a famous writer, given their eagerness to see him. His unexpected appearance elicited those shy smiles and admiring looks he'd seen so often.

Doval intercepted him at the door to the office with a smile. "Señor Griñán didn't tell me you were coming this morning," he said.

"That's because he doesn't know I'm here."

Doval was momentarily perplexed but quickly recovered. "Oh, then please be so kind as to have a seat here in the waiting room. I'll tell him you're here."

"No, I don't think I'll be so kind today. It seems my kindness is all used up." He pushed past the secretary and put a hand on the doorknob.

"But you can't just—" Doval protested behind him and put a hand on his shoulder.

Manuel went rigid, let go of the knob, and slowly turned around. "Keep your hands off me." There was a threat in his voice.

Doval pulled his hand back as if he'd received an electric shock.

The door suddenly opened, and he found himself face to face with the executor, who failed to conceal his consternation.

"Señor Ortigosa! I wasn't expecting you. What can I do for you?"

"For starters, you can begin by not lying to me anymore," Manuel replied with a hard look.

Griñán's usually affable expression vanished. He looked at his assistant posted close behind Manuel's back and said, "Doval, I'll take care of this. I'd forgotten I had something I needed to discuss with señor Ortigosa. Bring us coffee."

He stepped aside so Manuel could enter and closed the door behind them.

"I wasn't lying to you," Griñán affirmed with great seriousness. He took care to make sure the door was properly shut.

"Álvaro came to Galicia because you called him," Manuel snapped, without allowing the man time to reach the shelter of his desk.

Griñán looked down in silence. When he spoke again his voice held a deep regret that seemed sincere. "I'll be sorry for that for the rest of my life. But I didn't lie. I didn't know he was here. Not until they told me."

"Why did you call him?" Manuel's tone was unremitting harsh.

Griñán dragged himself to his desk chair and with a gesture invited Manuel to have a seat. "There was a financial matter to discuss. Santiago needed a rather large sum of money, he came here to ask me for it, and I passed the request along to Álvaro. In my role as administrator I have a discretionary fund of up to ten thousand euros per month for ranch and farm operations. It's from a contingency reserve. But the amount requested was much greater than that."

"How much did he want?"

Griñán reflected. "Three hundred thousand euros."

"Did he tell you why?"

A shake of the head. "He didn't want to tell me, but he certainly was in a hurry. Whatever the reason, it was very important to him. I telephoned to inform Álvaro. That's all. I didn't lie to you. I didn't learn that Álvaro had come here until Santiago telephoned me about his death."

On his way out Manuel encountered Doval carrying coffees on a silver tray. He turned back toward the administrator. "Griñán, don't call As Grileiras this time. Remember, I'm still the owner."

ARTISTS

The turbid light from the overcast sky of recent days was gone. Sunlight slanted across the sky. The silver-blue shapes of new eucalyptus and the greens and blacks of the furze bushes stood out sharply as Manuel drove past. So did the ancient lichen-covered stone walls, leaning wooden fences, and houses—the latter seen less and less frequently as he left the city behind. Everything glowed with an unfamiliar rarefied patina. Manuel leaned forward and peered up at the sky. The blue clouds looked like paint strokes extended until the paint ran out, leaving long random streaks of white. *There must be a strong wind up there.* At ground level not a leaf was stirring, but the air was heavy and humid. It would rain soon.

He parked in the same place they'd left their cars the day before. His BMW could be seen from the manor, but he didn't care. As Nogueira had admonished him, this was no courtesy visit. He had questions and he wanted answers.

A red Nissan drove toward him from the outbuildings, scattering gravel as it neared the entrance. The driver's face seemed familiar, perhaps from the funeral. The vehicle coasted almost to a stop as it came abreast of him. The driver made no effort to hide his look of surprise. Manuel fully expected him to stop and say something, but instead the Nissan accelerated and left the estate.

Manuel closed the car door and lingered for a few moments, attracted by the flowers. Their brilliant white made the gleaming green hedge seem almost black in contrast. He recalled the two gardenias he'd returned to the desk drawer before leaving the inn the previous night. The pallid smoothness of those petals was strangely attractive. He raised a hand to run a finger across the extravagant bloom of the flower just as Herminia appeared in the kitchen doorway and waved to invite him in. She must have heard his car.

The fat black cat sat motionless on sentry duty before the kitchen entrance. Manuel grinned as he saw Herminia trying to run it off.

"Get out of here, you rascal!" she called out and stamped her foot.

The animal glided away only a couple of feet before settling again. It pretended not to notice them and licked its tail to demonstrate its indifference.

"Come in, *fillo*, come in and let me get a look at you," she exclaimed as she pulled him into the kitchen. "I'm worried sick about you. All I can think of is how you must be feeling. Sit down and have something to eat." She placed a huge round loaf of Galician bread before him, cut a dark fragrant slice, and added some cheese and chorizo sausage.

Manuel smiled. "I'm really not hungry; I had breakfast at the inn."

"You want something warm instead? I can cook up a couple of eggs in no time at all."

"No, honestly, I'm not hungry."

She gave him a pitying look. "Of course. How could you have an appetite after all you've been through?" She sighed. "Maybe a coffee? Surely you'll accept a cup of coffee."

"That's fine," he agreed, for he expected that otherwise Herminia would keep pushing food at him. "I'll have some coffee. But first I'd like to discuss something with Santiago."

"They're not back yet. They telephoned this morning to say they're returning this evening."

Manuel nodded thoughtfully.

"There is one person who's always here, though," the cook volunteered. "The Raven."

He looked blankly at her.

"The Raven," the woman repeated and jabbed a finger at the ceiling. "The old lady up there keeping an eye on everything."

Manuel nodded to show he understood. Into his mind came the sinister warning from Poe's poem in the collection he'd happened across the day before: *Nevermore.* He obediently took a place at the table. The cook laid out breakfast pastries on a platter tidily covered with a cloth napkin.

"Elisa and the child are here," Herminia said in a much warmer tone. "They'll be over at the cemetery. Elisa spends almost all her time there."

She laid out the coffee service and poured two cups from a pot that apparently was always kept hot on the wood-burning stove. She settled beside him and gave him an affectionate look.

"Ay, *neno*! You're unhappy, no matter what you say. You think I don't know you; I can see that, but I knew my Álvaro and so I know you. The person who chose my darling was bound to have a huge heart."

"Did he ever mention me?"

"He didn't have to. I knew there was someone, of course; I could tell it from his smile, and it was obvious in his eyes. I raised this family's children. I've seen them born and grow up and become men, and I've loved them more than anything on earth. My baby's heart held no secrets from me."

"It did from me," Manuel said, almost to himself.

She extended her hand and covered his. Hers was dry and warm. "You mustn't be so hard on him. It's not my place to say so, because I've loved them all, and each was a good man in his own way; but Álvaro was always my favorite. Even when he was a little fellow he had more energy and courage than the others. Everyone knew. And that character of his was always bringing him into conflict with his father."

"Griñán told me. Unfortunately some parents just won't accept their children the way they are."

"Griñán said they didn't get along because of whom Álvaro liked, whom he loved?"

"Yes," Manuel replied hesitantly. "Or at least that's what he implied."

The cook got up, opened a cabinet, took out her bag, rummaged in it, and took a photo from her wallet. She placed it before him on the table. It was old but well preserved. The corners were curved by the contour of the wallet where it must have been tucked away for many years. It was a picture of three boys. One was looking at the camera. The other boys were looking at him.

"The tallest is Álvaro. The others are his brother Santiago and his friend Lucas, who's now a priest. These two are about ten years old and Santiago is eight."

Manuel tentatively touched the photo with one finger. This was the first image of Álvaro's childhood he'd ever seen.

Manuel had told his husband more than once, *You must have been an amazingly handsome little boy.* The reply was always, *Just ordinary.*

But the boy with huge eyes and sun-bleached curly chestnut hair Manuel saw in this photograph was anything but just ordinary. He was smiling happily at the photographer and had a comradely arm flung around Lucas's shoulder. Santiago, half hidden behind his brother, hung from Álvaro's left arm as if trying to attract his attention.

"My husband, Damián, took this picture right here in front of the oven with the camera I gave him as a birthday present. This photo is nothing particularly special, but I've always thought it was the best picture of my boys."

The charisma of the boy in the center looking back at the photographer was obvious. Lucas was smiling with the happy adoration of a youngster ready to follow his friend to the ends of the earth. The smallest boy was scowling. There was something excessively jealous in the way he hung on his brother's arm. He looked afraid the photo would make Álvaro forget him.

Herminia was moved by Manuel's unfeigned reaction. "I doubt it really had anything to do with his relationships," she continued. "I won't claim that wasn't a point of contention, but maybe if Álvaro had been the sort to accept parental counsel and advice, things might have turned out differently. The conflicts with Álvaro were nothing new. They started when he was very small. You should have seen him. He wasn't much more than knee-high, but he was always defying his father, talking back, disagreeing, and glaring at him. Álvaro's attitude infuriated the marquis. I don't think the old man ever had a lick of affection for anyone. He hated Álvaro but he admired the boy at the same time." She paused and gave Manuel a somber look. "Maybe I'm not making myself clear. The old marquis was the sort of man who valued courage more than anything. Even if it was the courage of an adversary."

"I do understand what you're saying. But I just don't understand how character differences could justify exiling a child from his family."

"It was a good deal more than that. Álvaro's father was used to dominating others, and in this family everyone danced to his tune. Except Álvaro, and that's something the marquis couldn't stand. I remember one time, when Álvaro must have been eight or nine. Santiago, two years younger, was a very shy but impulsive child. One day he took a lighter from his father's office and had the brilliant idea of setting fire to a pile of hay in the stables. He stamped it out, but not carefully enough; after he left, it flared up again. Luckily one of the stableboys saw him doing something back there and was smart enough to check what the boy might have been up to, so they put it out quickly.

"When their father heard about it he went out looking for Santiago with a belt in his hand. Santiago was terrified and hid somewhere. Álvaro walked up to his father and said he was the one who'd done it. I'll never forget the look on his father's face. It was as if suddenly the incident itself wasn't important anymore; he focused only on his oldest son and what the boy had told him.

"The marquis became very stern. 'You know what I think? I believe you're lying. I think you want to deceive me, and I'm not going to let you make a fool of me.' His father made him stand there before the front door of the manor, all day long. Didn't let him sit or eat or go to the toilet. In midmorning the rain started, but even then he wouldn't let the child back inside. He came out every two hours holding his black umbrella overhead and asked, 'Who was it?' and got the answer, 'I did it, father.'"

As he listened, Manuel had no trouble visualizing the boy Álvaro had been, the child with the light-colored hair and proud look who'd defied his father and stood firm.

"I don't remember exactly when this was, but it was winter. It was cold outside. By five thirty night began to fall and a terrible storm broke. There was thunder and wind and so much lightning that by six the electricity went off and didn't come back until the next day. Santiago was so scared at dinnertime that he went to his father in tears and confessed. The marquis didn't even look at him; he turned his back and sent the child to his room. Everyone went to bed but the marquis and me. He didn't say a word to me, either, but not for anything in the world was I going to go off and leave the child there alone. At one o'clock in the morning the marquis came down here to the kitchen. That was unheard of. Neither of the parents ever came in here. To this very day the lady dowager won't set foot in the kitchen.

"The marquis was carrying a candle, and that flickering candlelight made him look even more ferocious. He stood in the kitchen door and said, 'That child has more balls than all the men I know, put together.' I could hear pride and admiration in his voice. He told me to wait until he'd gone to bed, and then I could bring the youngster inside.

"I got a glimpse of that same expression sometimes as the years passed. He hated Álvaro, but there was something in the boy's defiance the old man appreciated. But don't you ever mistake it for affection. He didn't love either of his older boys. He outright despised Álvaro, and he systematically humiliated Santiago from the very first, even though the poor dear followed him around like a little puppy, ready to lick his feet if it would elicit the least little bit of affection. And in return the child got nothing but contempt. Never in my life did I ever see him look at Santiago with the respect he had for Álvaro."

Manuel was intrigued by the demanding attitude of the little boy in the photo. "How did Álvaro and Santiago get along?"

"Very well. Excellently, in fact; they loved one another immensely. Santiago was younger, of course." She nodded at the photo. "And he was shorter and a bit chubby. Whenever the other kids teased him, Álvaro inevitably defended him. Álvaro took care of his brother, took him by the hand as soon as Santiago learned to walk, and you might even say Álvaro never let go. Santiago adored him, worshipped the ground he walked upon, thought everything Álvaro did was wonderful. Santiago has always been the most sensitive and sentimental of the three. He nearly fell apart when his brother Fran died. But I've never seen him as devastated as the night we lost Álvaro. He was almost out of his mind. I was afraid he was going to do something crazy."

Manuel recalled the couple of glimpses he'd had of Santiago over the past two days. "I don't know; they seem very different."

"And that they were, but they were allied, even if it was in a strange way. For Álvaro it was a sort of duty, a feeling he was responsible for his brother. Álvaro had lots of friends outside the estate, but Santiago wasn't sociable at all. If it hadn't been for Álvaro, the poor child would have spent his entire childhood alone."

"Did they spend a lot of time with their youngest brother?"

"Álvaro was eleven and Santiago nine when little Fran was born. Álvaro got along well with him, though obviously they didn't spend much time together. The family sent Álvaro off to boarding school in Madrid not long after Fran's birth, and from then on he came home only during his vacations. The first chance they had to really become acquainted was when their father died, but Fran outlived the old man by only two days. My poor little tyke! You see, Fran was the only one the marquis cared for, if you can call it that, and their father made the terrible mistake of spoiling him rotten. Gave him everything." Her face showed deep pain. "But I do have to admit we all treated the child that way.

Perhaps because of the age difference between him and his brothers, he became everyone's darling, the plaything of the family. He was a lovely one, always laughing, singing, and dancing; he had a sweet and cheerful character. I can still see it now, how he would come in here, hug me, and kiss me. He'd untie my apron and ask for money. And I'd give it to him." She nodded, almost rocking, grieving and accepting her portion of the blame.

Manuel was surprised. "In other words, they brought him up wrong."

"Well, yes, I suppose; I gave him money whenever he asked. So did his brother, and so did all the others. And you can be assured there was never any shortage of funds around here. Fran got his driver's license as soon as he was old enough and a fine automobile when he turned eighteen and became an adult. They had no problem affording travel, riding lessons, fencing, polo, hunting, whatever the boys wanted. Their father kept them well supplied with cash, because the sons of a marquis couldn't go around without their spending money. But Fran . . ." Her face twisted in terrible pain as she shook her head once more. "Fran never had enough, and we all turned a blind eye until it was too late. One day I went to clean his bathroom and found the door locked. Nobody answered. Finally my husband and one of the other employees broke the door down and there we found him, lying on the floor with a syringe dangling from his arm. Alive, thank God! He was a drug addict. Both of them were, Fran and his girlfriend, Elisa."

"Nobody suspected? They hadn't noticed?"

"Haven't you ever heard of those so blind they would not see? Fran put up a good front. All of them suspected something, or at least it had occurred to them. That's when it became obvious the boy was going downhill. The marquis located a very good, very expensive clinic in Portugal, and Fran agreed to go, but only if Elisa went too. They were gone for almost a year and came back only on special occasions like Christmas and the marquis's birthday. Not for long; they had to go right back to their program at the clinic. And not even then did his father's attitude change. Fran was always the apple of his eye. His mother could hardly stand the boy; she refused to look at him. She made no secret of her opinion that anyone with Fran's failings was lower than dirt. But with his father it was different. That wicked man seemed to realize for the first time that his son was especially vulnerable. Which he was, in my opinion. Some people can overcome any difficulty, and Álvaro was one of them; but others, like Fran, are too easily overwhelmed in this life."

"And Fran died during one of the visits home?" Manuel prompted her.

"The old man realized his health was failing fast, so he had Fran called home. It was cancer. He'd been ill for several years, but the doctors had kept him in reasonably good shape. He lived a fairly decent life, until the monster within finally woke up. The sickness spread to all his organs and laid him so low the end was in sight. For about two months he suffered like a dog. Toward the end he was given heavy doses of morphine. Fran came back home to be with him and stayed at his side for days on end, even though the old man had no desire to see anyone. And Fran took it like a man; he hardly slept at all. He held his father's hand, wiped the man's drool, spoke to him. The two of them were inseparable until the night his father died."

The cook broke off, lost in her memories and shaking her head, as if trying to expunge those unpleasant visions. "I've never seen anyone cry like that. He stood there clutching his father's hand until at last the old marquis slipped away. Fran started weeping in a way that broke my heart. All of us went into the room—the rest of the family, the doctor, the priest, the undertaker. We found ourselves in tears as well, but I tell you that the only tears shed in that room for the father were Fran's. He wept like a child, sitting rigid and exposed. Tears ran down his cheeks, but he seemed not to be aware of them, like a lost little boy. We should have realized that's exactly what he was, a child who'd gotten lost in the dark and was scared half to death. And then there was his mother's face when she came into the room and saw him crying like that. I'll never forget her expression of deep, black contempt. There was nary a trace of pity or consideration in that old woman. She looked away in disgust and left the room. The day after the funeral they found him dead of that overdose. Lying across his father's grave."

Herminia stopped and moaned. Manuel waited patiently for her to resume her story. She'd closed her eyes and was squeezing them tight, fighting back her tears. But without success. They trickled from beneath her lids and streamed down her face.

The woman sat wordless and unmoving. Finally she sighed and covered her face with her hands. "I'm sorry," she managed to say in a broken voice.

Deeply moved and pained by her doleful story, Manuel wavered indecisively between the impulse to take her in his arms and the feeling he was intruding in a stranger's grief. Torn, he placed a hand on her arm and pressed gently in a sign of support. She felt his touch and covered his hand with hers, slowly regaining her composure.

"Forgive me." She wiped her tears away. "First Fran, now Álvaro . . ." She reached for the photograph that lay on the table.

· "There's no reason to apologize, Herminia." Manuel pushed the photo across the table toward her.

She gazed at him with great affection. "Poor fellow, I should be consoling you. You can keep it, *fillo*," she said as she pressed his hand.

He flinched. He didn't want her pity. "No, Herminia, it's yours. You've kept it all these years."

She insisted. "I want you to have it."

A feeling of great depression descended upon him as he stared into the eyes of the boy in the photo. The child's pure gaze pierced him from that great distance and faraway time, a dagger of knowledge painfully striking home. He hid his reluctance and accepted the photo, but to avoid further exposure to its force, he slipped it into the inside pocket of his jacket. Keenly aware of Herminia's gaze, he tried to redirect the conversation. "And Elisa?"

"The child saved Elisa. She was already pregnant, in her first trimester, but that was enough to sustain her. She kept herself clean, and she's completely recovered. She's a marvelous girl, and as for the child—what can I tell you of a boy I love like my own grandchild? He's wonderfully bright. Only three years old and he can read already. Elisa taught him. Sometimes he says things that make him sound like a little grown-up. Of course, he's with adults all day long here on the estate."

Manuel reacted with a grimace of disapproval that just seemed to encourage Herminia all the more. "I don't say that's necessarily a bad thing. This is a fine place to educate a child. But he hasn't gone to kindergarten, and Elisa won't hear of him leaving the estate. I suspect she's never even taken him to a playground. Children need to be with other children if they're not to turn out strange."

Manuel gave her a surprised look, but she didn't meet his gaze.

"But she's always in the cemetery, you said."

"Every day, morning and evening. In summer she stays until sunset. She plays with the child on the lawn in front of the church. But it gives one a strange feeling to see her, always alone, playing with her toddler son in the graveyard."

"How does the family treat her?"

They heard Sarita come in and both turned around. The girl held an armful of rags and cleaning products. Herminia's voice assumed a different tone. "Sarita, please go up and clean the windows in don Santiago's study."

"You said to clean the refrigerator," the young woman countered.

"You can do that later."

"But if I don't, I'll never get done today!"

"Then you'll just have to do it tomorrow," Herminia said tartly. "Go do the study now."

The girl went to the back stairway door, opened it, and passed through, and then leaned back against the door to push it shut.

Herminia remained silent for a couple of moments, her eyes fixed on the door. "She's a good girl, but she hasn't been here long enough. Just like Griñán. By the way, neither Sarita nor I were fooled by the excuse he made up to get you to leave."

"We were speaking about Elisa," he reminded her.

"Yes. The family treats her well, very well, in fact, and of course it's because of the child. Santiago and Catarina love him. They haven't had children yet, so they're just crazy about Samuel, who's an angel. You've seen him. Sweet, always smiling, always happy. Álvaro adored him and would spend hours talking with him. It was so cute to see Samuel explaining things to his uncle with all the seriousness of a grown-up."

"And?" He pointed to the ceiling and lowered his voice. "I saw her in Griñán's conference room, and she didn't seem too kind either to Elisa or to the child."

"The Raven?" She shook her head. "She's not kind to anyone except maybe to Santiago's wife, Catarina, whom she adores. But the child is Fran's son and her grandchild. He has Muñiz de Dávila blood, no matter how much she may curse that connection and do her best not to like him. He's a Muñiz de Dávila. For the moment he's the only heir because Santiago has no children. For all of them, including her, that overrides any other consideration."

❧

He followed the path through the trees. Under the increasingly leaden sky, the occasional rays that had found their way through the treetops had become rarer and rarer. The shafts of sunlight that had colored the ground the previous day had yielded to dull gray reflections from the sky above. The leafy tunnel was dark but offered no promise of light at the end of it; though this long-enclosed space protected him from the stiff breeze, the rapidly falling temperature gave him goose bumps. *Rain is coming soon*, he thought. And he contemplated the deep sadness they assumed he was suffering. Griñán and Herminia, in any case. He also had expected to feel such grief.

He was sad, certainly, but not the way he'd expected. If the thought of losing Álvaro had occurred to him a month before, he'd have been sure he wouldn't be able to survive or bear the pain. Memory of previous losses would have convinced him of that. He remembered how, after his parents' sudden death, his sister had slipped into his bed every night to embrace him. He had been unable to stop crying at the never-ending grief of loss, the savagely cruel prospect of living as a pair of unloved orphans. For all the years after cancer carried off his sister, he'd thought he'd never love again. And then Álvaro had arrived.

His refusal to mourn Álvaro as the days passed was his refusal to accept that he'd been betrayed. It was also because he didn't understand what had happened, who had murdered Álvaro or why, or even what was happening now. And suppressing that grief had undeniably given him the dispassionate perspective from which to observe all this. That comforting detachment had been broken today when an old photo transported him unexpectedly back in time and space. He'd been struck by the impact of those eyes he knew so well, the assured and certain gaze brimming with the self-confidence he'd loved from the first but had been trying to forget. That courageous look, the look of a hero.

He put his hand to his pocket to make sure that haunting photograph was still there. Its slightly bent edges set themselves into the soft lining of his jacket. And into his heart.

He heard them before they came into view. Samuel's pealing laughter at play was unmistakable as he threw a ball again and again against the church door. Elisa stood before him pretending to tend the goal, and the ball repeatedly bounced past her to the child's chortling delight. He celebrated each goal by flapping his arms and running in circles.

The boy saw Manuel and came running. Instead of leaping into his arms as he'd done the day before, Samuel grabbed his hand and pulled him across the lawn. "Goalie! Goalie! You be the goalie!" His mother stood before the church door, smiling. "Mama, no more goals! Uncle, you be the goalie now."

An amused Elisa shrugged and pretended she was giving up in defeat. She picked up her jacket from the front step and yielded her place to the newcomer.

Manuel took off his jacket and placed it by the door. "You're in for it now, kid. I'm an unbeatable goalie!"

The boy rushed out to the middle of the clearing with the ball under his arm.

They played for a quarter of an hour. The boy yelled his head off every time Manuel stopped the ball and celebrated even more gleefully each goal he was allowed to score. Elisa looked on, smiling and encouraging her son, until Samuel began to slow down. By fortunate coincidence, just then four kittens, only a few weeks old, appeared on the trail and diverted Samuel's attention. Manuel left the boy playing with the kittens and went to Elisa.

"I'm lucky you turned up," Elisa said. "I was tired already, and the poor little fellow gets fed up playing only with me all the time."

"Don't mention it. It was a pleasure." He turned to watch the boy and grinned when he saw that all four kittens were black.

"How are you doing?" Elisa asked him and sounded as if she really wanted to know. She wasn't just greeting him or being polite.

"Fine."

She tilted her head slightly to one side. He knew what that meant: disbelief. The gaze of someone who's searching for a sign you're lying. She looked back toward the graveyard and stepped off in that direction. He followed.

"Everyone claims you'll get over it. They say things will get better over time. But it's not true."

He didn't reply because in fact that was exactly what he was hoping: to put everything behind him and clear up the circumstances of Álvaro's death, so reverence, order, tranquility, and oblivion could reign. He knew Elisa wasn't talking about him; she was speaking of her own grief.

"I'm sorry," he said with a vague gesture toward the cemetery. "Griñán told me what happened, and today Herminia described the circumstances."

"Then you don't know the truth," she said sharply. Her voice was milder when she spoke a moment later. "Herminia's not a bad soul. I know she really loved Fran; but neither she nor Griñán knows what happened. No one does. They think so, but nobody knew Fran as well as I did. His father spoiled him and sheltered him from everything his whole life long. Everyone in this family saw him as a little boy. That's how they treated him and how they expected him to behave. I'm the only one who saw Fran as the man he really was. And it wasn't suicide." She looked directly into his eyes as if challenging him to disagree.

"Herminia said she'd never seen anyone in such deep despair."

Elisa sighed. "And she's right. It frightened me after a while to see him like that. He did nothing but weep. Said nothing and refused to eat. It was all we could do to convince him to accept a little broth, but he was adamant. He sat up all night with his father's body, accompanied the coffin to the church, and he and his brothers were the pallbearers who carried it to the grave. After they lowered the coffin into the grave, he stopped crying. He refused to say a word after that. He wanted to be alone. He pushed us all away and sat there on the soft earth by the grave, where he stayed all day. He refused to listen to reason. He just stared as they filled in the grave and then wouldn't leave. Finally, when night fell, Álvaro convinced him to come inside the church. That night before going to bed I went to see him and brought him something to eat. He was calm; he was coming to terms with his loss. He told me not to worry, everything would be all right. His father's death had made him understand many things. He asked me to wait for him at the manor; he needed a little more time, because he was there with Lucas. He said he needed to talk to Lucas first, and then he'd come to bed."

"Lucas, the priest?"

"Yes, the one who officiated at Álvaro's funeral. He's been a friend of the family since they were small children. Fran and the whole family are devout Catholics. For me it's not so easy to explain why I'm not a believer, but religion was important to Fran. It helped him enormously in his drug-treatment program; and for me, obviously, anything that helped him or made him stronger was a good thing. Though when your partner prefers to speak to a priest instead of to you, that's hard to accept." Manuel nodded in agreement. Those were his feelings exactly.

"Lucas told me the same thing he told the police," she continued. "He heard Fran's confession, and then they talked for an hour. When he left, Fran was entirely calm. There was nothing to suggest that he was contemplating suicide. I never saw him alive again. When I woke up the next morning and realized he wasn't there, I came back here. And I found him." She turned away to hide her tears.

Manuel lingered behind to give her some breathing space. He went to look for Samuel. The boy was still amusing himself with the kittens. After a while she returned and stood at his side. She was calm once more, but her eyes were still wet.

"Elisa, do you have friends or family? Anyone outside this place?"

She left Samuel with the kittens and began to stroll. Their steps turned toward the cemetery. "You want to know why I don't just leave. Why stay here? My mother spends practically the whole year in Benidorm with her sisters. We don't get along very well, and after my father died she moved to the coast. We call one another at Christmas and on birthdays. She thinks my life must be fabulous. That's what she tells everyone." Elisa gave a rueful little laugh. "I have a brother who's a decent man. He's married and has two girls, but, well, I lived a fairly wild life for a while, and we haven't spoken for years. I don't have anyone else. Our friends from those days are all dead, or they might as well be. There's nothing for me out there. And besides, Samuel's family is here."

Manuel remembered Herminia's comment about a child growing up surrounded only by adults. "Samuel could visit the family if you lived somewhere else."

"Sure. But it's not just that. I can't leave." She ran her hand along the edge of the cross where Fran's name was engraved. "Not yet. Not until I'm sure."

"Sure of what? What do you think happened?"

"I don't know," she said in a tired whisper.

"Herminia told me the doctor certified it as death by overdose."

"I don't care what the doctor said. I knew him, Manuel, I knew him better than anyone else in the world. He wouldn't have sent me off alone and pregnant to wait for him in our bed if he was planning not to come back."

Manuel stopped short, realizing that they were before Álvaro's grave. The flowers from the funeral drooped in the cellophane wrappers. Only the chrysanthemums showed any vigor.

He'd felt the same way. He'd thought he knew a man better than anyone else in the world.

He turned his back to avoid the name chiseled into the stone cross.

Sarita, the housemaid, appeared on the path. She stopped to greet the boy and exchange a few words, then came down the walk to the cemetery.

"What is it, Sarita?"

"Elisa, the lady marquess told me to bring the boy to her. She wants to see him."

"All right." The young mother lifted her eyes and gazed at the distant windows of the imposing manor.

A figure wrapped in black stood barely visible on the second-floor terrace. Manuel heard Herminia again: *The old lady up there keeping an eye on everything.*

Samuel toddled off holding Sarita's hand without saying goodbye. Manuel watched them disappear into the distance, feeling a bit pained but surprised at the same time to find himself affected by the boy's departure. He saw Elisa's slight smile as she observed him.

"He's very special, isn't he?" she said.

He agreed. "Why's he named Samuel?"

"I suppose you're really asking why he doesn't have his father's first name."

Manuel gave her a questioning look.

"Around here you don't name a child for someone who's died. It's not an honor; it's a curse." She spoke with great seriousness, though she smiled as if to counter the bluntness of her declaration. "Well, every name belonged to someone else, sometime. There's always someone who had the same name and is gone now." A shadow passed over her face. "But Fran died a violent death, too young and certainly before his time. Many people around here believe the superstition that if you give a child the name of someone who died violently, that dead person's ghost will carry him off."

Manuel's jaw dropped in astonishment. The fact that she was not a practicing Catholic was apparently no buffer against local tradition. He was so struck by her words that he found none with which to reply; and by the time he'd composed himself it was too late. Elisa was on her way along the shaded path through the trees to catch up with her son.

"Elisa!" he called.

She looked back and did her best to give him a smile of farewell. She wasn't too convincing.

He stood there alone in the cemetery, feeling the wind that had buffeted the high clouds earlier now manifesting itself, ruffling his hair and stripping petals from the withered flowers to reveal the straw framework that clever hands had covered with asparagus leaves and wire twists to anchor the flowers. Hundreds of tiny red petals blew across the graveyard, where they appeared for all the world like shocking splotches of blood. The sight of the wire used to fasten the decapitated flowers was a sudden reminder. His recent experiences seemed to have given him a hard-won vantage point from which to detect the world's deceptions: the wires, the ropes sustaining the scenery, the hanging counterweights, the dusty glow of the footlights, the shared illusions we want to believe.

"Everything is false," he muttered, looking up. "It's all lies."

He picked up his jacket from the church step just as the rain began. He was about to hurry to the sheltered path, but beneath the beating of the rain he heard a sound of great pain, a hoarse, visceral groan, and the unmistakable sound of a man weeping. He realized that the church door he'd thought was locked was slightly ajar. The scent of candles and wood wafted forth as at the funeral service, mixed now with impassioned sounds of lamentation, as pain and profound grief gave in to despair. Manuel raised one hand to the gleaming varnished surface of the door. The stark metal handle was shaped like the point of a spear thrust through the door from the inside, sharp as the pain of the man within.

Manuel held himself back. A variant of Herminia's words answered the question of who was lamenting inside: *The man who was always weeping.* The man with the hard eyes, the mournful, tender heart that had adored his brother as only a younger child can adore another. The only person of adult age entitled to the honor of the key to that sacred space: Santiago. So he was here on the estate after all. Herminia had lied to him or hadn't known of his return.

Manuel pushed the door tentatively and it silently opened an inch or two more. Three dozen candles burned furiously on a stand to the right of the altar and threw a light that made identification easy. Santiago knelt on a prayer stool, his face buried in his hands as he wept, a garment of some sort pressed to his face to stifle his sobs. Manuel felt a mixture of shame and aching pain for the man. He was so struck by the sight of such raw pain that for the first time he was thankful he himself hadn't been able to weep. At least he'd endured his bereavement and hadn't allowed it to overwhelm him like this.

He ran through the pounding rain toward his car.

⤜✲⤝

The rain and the sudden drop in temperature seemed to have kept away the bar's usual clientele. Few were here tonight. Granted, the hour was later than yesterday. Lieutenant Nogueira had insisted on meeting after eleven. Manuel was indifferent to the choice of hour. After returning from As Grileiras, he'd lunched on the inn's soup and beef filet and then slept all afternoon, plunged into torpor by the dim light of the long rainy day. Daylight was dying away when he awoke. He shut his eyes and tried to hold for an instant longer to the dream image of his sister lying beside him in close embrace. It was no use; she was gone. He looked through the window at stones darkened by water and soaked trees patiently withstanding the lashing rain. It all looked as sad and static as those bleak Sundays of his childhood in his aunt's apartment.

Manuel opened the window and took a deep breath of humid air laden with smells of loam and rock. The prevailing deep silence made those scents seem even more pungent. He again told himself this was perfect weather for writing, and he even looked around for his materials.

The brilliant white sheets of writing paper gleamed on the somber desktop, still untouched in their transparent cellophane wrappers. He was jolted by the sudden realization that his reluctance to put pen to paper was ridiculous. His refusal was part of a strange masochistic pleasure in suffering that only prolonged this torture of his soul. He was that foolish angel sleeping in the open and refusing from sheer pride to return to paradise. He went back to bed and huddled under the covers, leaving the window open. He reached out with one hand to pick up the collection of Poe's macabre writings. He was killing time until his meeting with Nogueira.

⤜✲⤝

The retired policeman sat there with a beer and a plate with what looked like the remains of a bar snack. Manuel ordered a draft beer and almost sent back the slice of omelette the waiter delivered with it. "You want it?"

128

Nogueira nodded and didn't bother to thank him. "You should take it while you can, man. Free food's a blessing."

Maybe not. Manuel glanced at the potbelly that bulged against the man's thin sweater. *And that's about all you've got on your mind.*

"You remember what I told you the first day?"

"Your promise to haul me off behind the mountain and shoot me? How could I forget that?"

Nogueira stopped the fork halfway to his mouth. He was not amused. "A real comedian today, aren't you? Keep that in mind. I was dead serious. We've got a lot to lose in this case."

"I know that."

"And don't forget it. Today we're going to pay a visit to a lady friend of mine who has something to tell you."

"Ophelia?"

A sour grin gleamed behind Nogueira's big mustache. "No, not that kind of friend. I'm warning you—you're probably not going to like what you hear."

Manuel nodded. "Got it."

The policeman paid the bill, exited the bar, and paused in the shelter of the awning at the entrance. He lit a cigarette and smoked with evident pleasure. "We located the phone booth, the one with the strange number used to call Álvaro. Not that it's of much use. It's in Lugo; there's no telling whether the caller is from that area or was just covering his tracks."

Manuel nodded again but made no comment.

"What did the administrator tell you?"

"He admitted he telephoned Álvaro. But he claims he didn't know Álvaro was in town until Santiago called to tell him about the accident. He said Santiago had been urgently requesting a large amount of money, more than the firm was authorized to pay out."

"How much?"

"Three hundred thousand euros."

"Wow!" Nogueira liked that. "That stinks to high heaven! Did he say what he needed it for?"

"No, he refused. But he told Griñán he needed it right away."

"And when he couldn't lay hands on it, he must have said he couldn't wait another week for his brother's scheduled visit," Nogueira concluded. "What did Santiago say?"

"He wasn't back," Manuel lied. "He returns tonight." The writer didn't share the scene of Santiago in the church covering his face to stifle his howling desperation.

"Are you sure Griñán didn't warn him?"

He recalled the administrator's contrite expression at the conclusion of their conversation. "He didn't. And he won't."

"Good," the officer snorted. "So we've made a little progress at least. There's only one thing that doesn't add up. Why didn't Santiago just phone Álvaro?"

"He didn't have the number. The only way the family could contact Álvaro was through Griñán."

Nogueira seemed inclined to dispute that, but he dropped the matter. "We'll take my car." He snuffed out the cigarette in a container of sand by the entrance and strode out into the rain toward his parked vehicle.

A STRANGE WORLD

The quiet swish of wipers at low speed was the only sound that disturbed the silence.

Manuel waited until they were well on the highway. "I managed to spend some time with Herminia and Elisa. They both told me about Fran, the youngest brother."

Nogueira's nod indicated he was listening.

"Herminia's story was more or less like what Griñán said. Fran was devastated by his father's death, and he killed himself by overdosing on heroin." He paused to choose his words. "But Elisa is certain it wasn't suicide. She said Fran was clean, done with drugs. He reassured her, told her everything would be all right. Of course, someone thinking about suicide might say that too."

Nogueira didn't comment. He clicked his right turn signal, drove into an open lot, and stopped the car. Through the rain-soaked windshield the blinking neon lights of a bar were visible. There were few cars in the lot.

"That's exactly the kind of crap I mentioned the other day." His voice was testy.

Manuel waited in silence.

"I told you already. This wasn't the first time they papered over something the Muñiz de Dávila family might have found painful. I was in charge of the team that responded to the call from As Grileiras before dawn. We found the young addict dead across his father's grave. The syringe was still in his arm. The family and employees gave us the same story. The father died and they'd buried him the day before. Fran was terribly stressed, they said, and after the burial he said he wanted to be alone. Everything we got from the relatives suggested he was depressed. After a year in rehab with his fiancée, he'd come back for the old man's final days. Everybody claimed father and son were very close, and they all assumed that instead of dealing with it, the boy took the worst possible way out. Only the fiancée found it hard to believe. She told me the same thing she said to you. I wasn't too surprised. Suicide is always hard on those left behind. But when we removed the body I concluded she was right."

Manuel looked at him in astonishment.

"Yeah, there was a syringe in his arm, but the boy'd been struck hard on the head. The toes of his shoes were scuffed and scratched, as if he'd been dragged. We initiated a routine investigation but got called off. The bosses 'suggested' it would be a shame to cause additional suffering, considering it was obvious how the youngster died. The lab tests did in fact confirm an overdose killed him. Inside the church we found the kit used to prepare the fix, so it was officially decreed that he'd collapsed there but then managed to stagger out to the cemetery. They concluded that on his way through the graves in the dark, he must have stumbled and hit his head. A good hard blow, one that left him dazed but not unconscious. He dragged himself as far as his father's grave, passed out, and succumbed."

Manuel shrugged. "And what doesn't fit about that story?"

"What I find strange . . ." The officer heaved a huge sigh. "What I find strange is the scuff marks on the shoe tips. Suppose he did smash his face against a gravestone; maybe he could have crawled to where we found him. But his trouser legs were clean. Wet, yes. After all, it rained that night. But they weren't soiled. If someone drags himself across the ground or goes on all fours through the wet grass in that cemetery, his trousers aren't going to be clean. How come the only marks were on his shoes? The blow to his forehead was produced by a round, blunt object that crushed the bone without breaking the skin. An oval object, smooth and even. It didn't break the skin. I checked all the crosses and gravestones in the cemetery, one by one, and nothing out there corresponded to that kind of injury."

Manuel listened closely. His estimate of this strange man was rising steadily.

"And there's the issue of the key. Get this: the family tradition is for male heirs to receive a key to the church the day they're born. It's a silver key, cruciform, set with precious stones, a symbol of their long and faithful support of the

Church. I hear the family has produced generations of prominent churchmen. The original owner of the estate was a famous abbot from around here.

"When they found the boy that morning, the church was locked. I thought that was strange too. Given his supposed physical state, how did the door get locked? We didn't find the key on the body. We searched every inch of the path from the church door to the site where the body was found. We even searched the whole lawn with a metal detector. It wasn't anywhere."

"Someone locked the church and took the key," Manuel said.

"His brothers didn't need his key; each of them had his own, engraved with his initials. They showed them to us right away, no problem."

"And there were only three keys."

"Four. The old marquis was buried with his, another of their crappy traditions. I suppose Catarina's kid will get one once he's born, but at that time there were only the three brothers. We talked to Fran's friend the priest, supposedly the last person to see him alive. He told us he heard Fran's confession and afterward they had a bit of a chat. He declined to describe the conversation under the pretext of the sanctity of confession, but he did say that Fran didn't act like someone thinking about killing himself. And the upshot of it all is that officially the youngster died of an overdose because he was distraught at his father's death. Which once again demonstrates the deference the Muñiz de Dávilas get whenever there's even a hint of scandal. Those in charge accepted the version offered to them."

"But why? What reason could someone have for moving Fran's dead body? Were they trying to hide the way he died? So they could pretend he wasn't a drug addict?"

Nogueira wasn't having it. "No, that's absurd. Everyone in the whole region knew Fran was hooked. And believe me, for a lot of us it somehow made the family seem more human."

Manuel didn't understand.

"Listen, in the 1980s and '90s thousands of young folks in Galicia got into drugs. The drug dealers owned the place. Damn few families didn't have a son or daughter mixed up in it, or even several. It was tragic, and it's not over yet. We were stumbling over dead young junkies all the time. It was an epidemic; that shit was everywhere. A rich kid, good-looking the way Fran was, was a gold mine for some dealer. The fact that one of the marquis's boys got into drugs generated a lot of sympathy. People could tell themselves money can't save you from calamity; see there, the rich are just as vulnerable. Like there's some divine justice that affects everybody the same way."

That much Manuel could understand. "And then?"

"No matter how much they were paying for the clinic and rehab, it's obvious the kid was up to his neck in that shit. Life beat him down, and he had a relapse. But I think his girl's right; he wasn't trying to kill himself. He was just trying to dull the pain. He hadn't shot up for a while, so he misjudged the dose. He probably died inside the church. Injected himself and passed out. The curved sides of the kneelers in the pews correspond pretty closely to the shape of the injury to the head. And then, who knows, maybe some family member cleaned up the mess. Though come to think of it, whoever it was didn't even have to get his hands dirty. It could have been an employee, maybe the caretaker, some trusted soul. Somebody finds the body and sees what has to be done."

"But why? For what reason?"

Nogueira's long-contained rage finally burst through. "I already told you! This goddamn family doesn't have junkies or whoremongers or rapists; but if they do, they make sure everything looks as pretty as possible. What's really deplorable is that they don't even have to ask. It's been that way for centuries, and it's not about to change. They're the Muñiz de Dávilas; you owe them that respect; you have to spare them pain, embarrassment, and shame. And don't even mention the sacrilege of finding their junkie son dead of an overdose in the middle of the church. Such things don't happen. But a son destroyed by grief, dead on the grave of his father, that's a fine romantic tale, so that's how it goes. They have this weird talent; they step out squeaky clean from shit that would swallow up any of the rest of us."

Manuel looked off into the unseen distance through a windshield blurred by heavy rain. He told himself he'd stumbled into a different world. A strange unknown world. A world where behavior, response, and relationships were judged by different standards. Here he was, an outsider surrounded by chaos and unable to react. It was a nightmare. He knew that his unexpected numbness gave him the impartiality to ponder and analyze everything Nogueira was saying. He was an unwilling participant in the developing chaos, but his cold indifference allowed him to watch from afar without going mad, without allowing himself to be swept away by destructive passion. He blessed that sense of detachment.

"Is that what happened with Álvaro?"

The officer didn't have to stop to think twice. "Yes, it was partly that, the way we said. But this time there's a difference. Their deference to family sensibilities is covering up something more serious than a suicide disguised as an accident. This time it's murder."

Manuel started to say something, but Nogueira cut him off. "Let's go." He pointed toward the neon lights blinking above the bar entrance. "This is the place."

The pink and blue neon lights across the front of the building had been barely visible through the steamed-up car windows, but up close they flashed and dazzled. Manuel turned to Nogueira with a questioning look.

"Right," the man answered. "It's a pickup joint, a real dive. I suppose you've never been in one, at least not one this low class."

Stationed at the door was a tall nameless guy with greasy hair and skin as white as an albino. His cowboy boots and blue polka-dot shirt wouldn't have looked out of place at Nashville's Grand Ole Opry. He gave them a sloppily casual two-fingered salute. His smile bared teeth that gleamed eerily white in the blue neon light. He towered over them.

The place was intended to look elegant, but it smelled of mold, cheap air freshener, and even cheaper perfume. Despite the low light inside, Manuel saw that the paint was peeling along the baseboards. The warmth inside did nothing to counter the moisture glistening on the walls. The humidity was invisible but almost tangible, an intensification of the oppressive feeling that had enveloped Manuel since he arrived in Galicia.

A dozen men sprawled in armchairs of imitation leather. They were variously involved with about the same number of scantily clad women. Another two men at the bar were buying drinks for girls who'd sidled up to whisper in their ears. Nogueira was pleased to find an open corner at the bar. He took a seat and motioned to Manuel to do the same. He openly surveyed the clients.

A bartender in his fifties attended to them promptly. "Good evening, Lieutenant. What'll it be?"

"A gin and tonic." He jerked a thumb at Manuel. "And—?"

"A beer."

"A beer!" said Nogueira scornfully. "Have a drink, man!"

"A beer will do," said Manuel to the bartender, who nodded and got busy with the drinks.

"And, Carlos, tell Nieves we're here."

The man gestured toward upstairs. "She's busy, but she won't be long."

Soon afterward a woman came down a set of stairs from some obscure locale above. Manuel caught the envious looks of some of the girls and the sudden tension that made them straighten up.

It was hard to guess Nieves's age; she could have been anywhere in her thirties or forties. Her blonde hair was cut so it fell straight across her shoulders. She was short and not particularly shapely. Her relatively wide-set eyes might have been blue, but of a shade that the dim bar lighting made look almost black. The hard set of her mouth suggested the merciless determination needed to run a place like this. Nogueira greeted her with a kiss on either cheek, and Manuel shook her hand.

Nogueira was quick to pay when she asked the bartender for a drink. She sipped it.

The policeman was in a hurry. "So tell him what you told me yesterday."

Her expression was provocative. "All of it?"

He did his best to hide the smile that flickered beneath his mustache. "You know what I mean."

The woman feigned innocence as she made eyes at them across the rim of her glass. "As you like. But remember I'm sharing this as a special favor to the lieutenant." With great dignity she declared, "If there's one thing I insist on in this house, it's discretion."

Nogueira nodded, still impatient.

"Lots of VIPs here, you know?" she confided, instantly undercutting her previous assurance. "Top brass from the military, board members of big corporations, mayors . . ."

Nogueira's exasperation was becoming more evident, but he tried sweet talk. "Come on, darling little Nieves." He broke into Gallego. *"Que non temos toda a noite."*

She pouted. "I know we haven't got all night. Listen, señor, yesterday I reminded the lieutenant that don Santiago is a well-respected regular client. He visits us at least every other week, sometimes more often. Sometimes his brother comes with him."

Nogueira held up his cell phone with a photo of Álvaro. "When was the last time?"

"His brother? It's been a while. Months. But don Santiago was here maybe two weeks ago." She tapped the screen image with one bright-colored artificial nail. "Yes, that guy. I don't know his name, but he's the one. The good-looking guy."

Manuel stared at the photo in disbelief. "Are you sure?"

"Not a doubt in the world. He liked to take 'Baby' upstairs. She isn't a baby, really," the woman added quickly. "She's nineteen, but we call her Baby, because she's the youngest by a long shot. And hardly developed at all." She waved toward a girl who was giving a client a languid lap dance. "She's busy right now."

Baby did look young. A long sweep of brunette hair covered her shoulders, and her dark-skinned legs were thin. An unsuspected strength became evident from her rippling muscles as she teased the john. Manuel leaned over and caught a glimpse of delicate feminine features. He found he was attracted despite himself by her sensuous dance moves and the suggestive fluttering of her hands.

Nieves's voice seemed to come from far away. "Don Santiago usually goes with Mili, but he doesn't mind an occasional switch. Mili's not here tonight. Her mother's dying. For the second time this year," she added with malice. "If she croaks, Mili'll be back in a couple of days; and if it's another false alarm, she'll be back tomorrow. 'Cause I already warned her it's about time for her mama to make her mind up once and for all whether she's going to kick the bucket."

"All right," Nogueira replied. "At least we can talk to the other one."

"You'll have to wait your turn. Right now she's busy. Looks like it might take a while."

Baby couldn't have heard the brothel owner's comment, but she rose and enticed her client to the back stairs. She looked back toward Manuel, and for a fleeting moment their eyes met. She ascended the shadowed stairs, unaware of the abyss her dark glance had torn in his heart. His eyes followed her until she melted into the shadows. He woke from his trance and turned to Nogueira. "Let's go."

"Be patient, man, it won't take long. Never mind what little Nieves says. Around here 'a while' is never more than half an hour."

The owner gave him a wry little smile and sauntered out to benches where men were lounging. She paused, turned, and eyed Nogueira. Nothing was said. She gave him a little nod of invitation. The policeman responded immediately. "Won't be long," he muttered. He tossed a fifty-euro bill on the bar to feed the tab and gestured to the barkeep to keep the newcomer supplied.

Disconcerted and feeling completely out of place, Manuel accepted the glass of draft beer the bartender delivered with great ceremony. He'd have preferred to drink straight from a bottle. Unwilling to meet the bartender's eyes, he took a swallow. With an ominous hiss on his palate, the bubbly liquid blended with the unpleasant tang of air freshener from a vaporizer above the bar. He stared at the foam rapidly subsiding on the amber surface of the beer. He left his glass on the polished wooden surface of the counter and went outside.

The rain had settled into a regular rhythm likely to continue all night. He cursed his lack of foresight in not driving his own car. He looked bleakly at Nogueira's old BMW. Lit by the hectic neon lights, the vehicle looked like a reject from a carnival ride. The opaque windshield was a sign the interior was still warm. The temperature had fallen. The almost tangible presence of humidity enveloped him like a clammy shroud, even in the shelter of the awning. He went out into the rain and walked to the edge of the road. The road was hung in both directions with uncertain mists that obscured the hot brilliant neon. He was only a few yards from the club, but the mist had already covered up its gaudy beckoning call. The lot was almost deserted, but traffic was heavy. Cars sped past with little heed for the beating rain. He sensed a malevolence in their unceasing flow, as if every few seconds a new driver were deliberately trying to blind him by projecting those shafts of dazzling brilliance against the curtain of rain.

It would be foolish to walk along the highway. He went back into the parking lot, acutely aware of the absurdity of the situation. He didn't want to be there, but there was no escape. He looked around. About ten cars stood in the lot, and there was no departing driver he could ask for a ride out of there. The cowboy had gotten up from the plastic-covered barstool by the door and was peering at him. Manuel gave up and went back to the entrance, wishing for the first time in his life that he was a smoker. At least that would have given him an excuse to hang around outside. He pretended to search his pockets. "Thought I'd lost my phone."

The man went back to his stool with a dismissive gesture that showed he accepted that explanation for the odd behavior. Manuel completed his little pantomime by taking out his phone. The pale flower that came out of his pocket at the same time fell to the mud like a dead butterfly. Manuel squatted, astonished, and reached for the flower. He completely forgot the cowboy and his own awkward little pantomime. Even in the glare of neon the gardenia proclaimed the perfection of beauty, despite a smear of mud across one petal. Gently he wiped it clean with one finger and marveled at the firm delicacy of the flower. He raised it to his face, closed his eyes, and inhaled its heavy sweet scent.

The roadhouse door opened and released a blast of music, heat, and rank odor from the interior. The client who came out for a smoke got into a lively conversation with the cowboy bouncer. Manuel jabbed at his phone pretending to write a text, withdrew along the covered porch, and turned the corner of the building. He found a covered niche and took shelter there for a while. He gazed blindly at the unreal world of the parking lot and the neon reflections in its puddles. He held his phone up and kept the screen lit to maintain the fiction. He had no desire to attract the cowboy's attention. He kept his other hand in the interior pocket of his jacket and slowly stroked the smooth surface of the soft petals. Their aroma would linger on his skin for many hours.

Nogueira burst from the entrance and took out a cigarette. The cowboy quickly gave him a light. The policeman looked around until he found Manuel. "What the fuck are you doing there? I thought you'd left!"

Manuel didn't reply. He put his phone back in his pocket and walked past the bouncer and out into the rain on his way to the car.

Nogueira stood watching for a moment, then muttered a curse as he tossed his newly lit cigarette into a puddle. He unlocked the car and they got in, but Nogueira didn't start the engine. He fumed silently and then smashed a fist against the steering wheel. "I warned you. I told you it could happen. All kinds of dirty business could come to light, I said. I warned you." His repetitions sounded like an effort to divest himself of blame.

"You did warn me."

Nogueira exhaled a great gust of air. "I talked with the girl. She said—"

"I don't want to know."

The retired cop looked at him in frustration.

"I appreciate what you're doing, and yes, you warned me, but I don't want to know. Because I already do, don't I? You can spare me the details."

Nogueira started the car. "Whatever. All I'll say is that she confirmed it."

"That's just great."

Nogueira shook his head. He pulled away from the bar but then braked to a halt, as if he'd suddenly remembered something. He pushed himself up against the seat belt and twisted enough to get a hand into his pants pocket. He took out a gold ring and slipped it back on his finger. The neon sign of the brothel reflected off the matte finish of his wedding ring.

Neither said a word during the drive back. Nogueira had already given him guidance about what to do the next day, and Manuel was too disheartened for conversation. His thoughts flitted between the opposing poles of the gardenia in his pocket and the funereal gleam of Nogueira's wedding ring. He couldn't imagine that a man like this could have someone waiting for him anywhere. Manuel found something profoundly perverted in the man's act of returning to his finger the wedding ring he'd taken off to visit the roadhouse. He thought back and couldn't remember if the policeman had worn that ring when they'd visited Ophelia. He'd certainly taken an affectionate farewell of her. Manuel wondered if Álvaro had practiced the same deception; that might explain why the ring was missing. Maybe that was the custom here among men who frequented prostitutes.

Nogueira must have read his mind. The man glanced at his ring at least twice. He rubbed it with his thumb as if suddenly noticing it and feeling an insistent itch.

Manuel looked down at the wedding ring on his own hand. Why hadn't he taken it off? A sudden heavy sigh broke from him under the weight of shame and hopelessness.

At the inn his only words were "Good night."

Nogueira courteously wished him the same.

For the first time.

❧

The energy-saving bulbs of the small lamp fixtures came on with a dim glow that would grow stronger and brighter as the minutes passed. He stood in the open doorway to his room. The single bed, narrow as that of a monk, revived memories of the sleepless nights of his childhood. He went to the desk, pulled out the uncomfortable desk chair, and seated himself.

He opened a packet of paper and sniffed it without taking out any of the sheets, following the little ritual that had become his custom prior to starting a novel. He caught the subtle whiff of bleached paper, that indecisive perfume that achieved its full bloom only when blended with the distinctive aroma of ink. As if conjured by that odor, the memory of clutching four hundred sheets of his printed work rushed back. *The Sun of Tebas*, the novel he'd almost finished when they told him of Álvaro's death, lay three hundred miles away, untouched since then. A couple of short chapters remained to be written, maybe as few as twenty-five pages. His readers would adore it. It was good, but not as good as all that. *I can't write another novel like* The Man Who Refused, *he'd told Álvaro. This is all the truth that I want and can bear.*

He took out a fistful of blank sheets and placed them before him on the desk. He pushed the rest to one side. He took one of the ballpoint pens from the package and wrote the title across the top of the first page.

OF EVERYTHING HE REFUSED

The knock at the door was loud and insistent. Eight decisive blows, one after another, warning that someone expected to be admitted immediately. The sort of insistence you'd never hear from an invited guest, a worker, or a delivery driver. He would remember it later with the bleak reflection, typical behavior of police demanding to be let in.

He stared for a couple of seconds at the cursor blinking at the end of the last sentence. That had been a good morning for work, the best of the last three weeks. Though he hated to admit it to himself, he especially enjoyed writing when he was alone at home with nothing else to do, free of the usual interruptions, so he could go with the flow. That's what happened when he got to this point in a novel. He was expecting to finish The Sun of Tebas *in a couple of weeks. Maybe earlier if all went well. And until then the story would take over and obsess him every minute of the day. He'd have no time for anything else. Each of his novels had brought him to this intense pitch and this sensation, at once intimate and destructive. He loved it and feared it. He knew it made him hard to live with.*

He glanced toward the hall that led to the apartment's front door. The blinking cursor seemed about to burst with the pressure of all the words still behind it. In the moment of deceptive stillness he began to hope the untimely visitor had given up. But no; he sensed the silent presence out there of the intruder's demanding energy.

SMOKE

Nogueira smoked and looked out at the dark night. He wore only an undershirt and briefs. The streetlights along the road to his house were so distant from one another that their wide orange pools of light were isolated and independent. They never overlapped. He'd left a single lamp on in the child's bedroom, a small one that cast only a faint pink light. He assumed that anyone looking from outside would see his shadow, an enormous silhouette, looming behind him on the wall. He held the cigarette across the windowsill, and each time he wanted a puff he leaned out to keep the smoke outside. She detested smoke. And he hated having to smoke his last cigarette of the day this way, for often this was the moment of reflection and insight when pieces of the puzzle fell into place. Lately it'd become an excuse for not thinking of other things. The light outside was too dim to reflect off his wedding ring, but that gold band burned his finger like a white-hot brand. How can something in plain sight become invisible, only to materialize once more when someone notices it? Something gradually worn away to invisibility manifests itself because the glance of a stranger revives its essence. He inspected the ring on his finger and shook his head. He knew he couldn't escape that insistent question. It wouldn't let him sleep tonight.

He took a last long drag. He pulled at the cigarette so hard the heat seared his lungs, and then blew the smoke out sharply, sending it swirling as far from the house as he could. He stubbed it out against the exterior wall and put the butt into a plastic bag that was already half full. He closed the bag, folded it, and deposited it on the windowsill, leaving the window open a while longer to make sure the stink of tobacco wouldn't be detected. He looked back toward the interior and grimaced at the smile of Minnie Mouse watching him from the bedspread. One by one he removed the stuffed animals from their pile on the pillow, opened the covers, and slipped into bed. He turned off the little pink-shaded Disney princess lamp.

BREAKING THROUGH
THE SURFACE

Manuel opened his eyes to an entirely dark room. He realized he must have turned off the television sometime during the night. In his sleep he'd heard the boy crying, and she'd come to console him again. He left the bed and groped his way to the window, visible only because of the crack of light between the window sash and the outside shutter. He opened it, pushed back the shutter, and looked out.

The rain must have stopped hours earlier. There were some puddles, but the ground appeared to be mostly dry. Long shadows showed that the sun had only recently risen. He searched the bedsheets for the TV remote but couldn't find it. He went around the bed and opened the desk drawer. He took out his watch but didn't touch the withered gardenias that seemed to beckon to him. He shut the drawer quickly but couldn't escape the heavy floral scent. The perfume mixed with a musty odor like that of a sacristy chest, a blend of mothballs and ancient wood. The mix of smells evoked the confident gaze of the boy in the photo. Now, surrounded by dry petals, that print seemed more than ever the photo of a dead man.

He looked into the mirror. His face was ashen, the aftermath of the insomnia that had kept him writing until dawn. He looked over his shoulder at the closely scribbled pages that covered the desktop. Others had slid to the floor, so that an avalanche of paper now presented a snowy track across the room to the bed. He gazed stupidly at them for a couple of moments. When he turned back to the mirror his eyes were as clouded as the early-morning sky of Galicia, masked by a film of pallid sadness. He rubbed a hand across his face in an effort to shake off his fatigue. He raked his fingers through his short dark hair and noticed there was much more gray at his temples than just a few days before. His cheeks were dark with what was now a salt-and-pepper morning shadow. His lips were as bright and red as those of a sad clown. When he tried to smile, no more than a mild tremor crossed the mask his face had become, as rigid as if a drunken dentist had injected him with too much novocaine or his face were paralyzed with Botox.

"You can't keep this up," he told the man in the mirror.

He pushed the flowers aside. In the back of the drawer he located the card the priest had given him at the gate of the estate. He took the photo and slipped it into the inside pocket of his jacket, feeling the bent corners catch the pocket's satin lining and cling to it like a living creature.

He went down the hall and followed a trail of bedsheets deposited before open doors until he found the innkeeper's wife. She was humming a little tune as she cleaned guest rooms. Her almost childish treble was such a contrast with her bulk that it brought a grin to his face.

Manuel leaned through the doorway and held out the card. "Can you give me directions to this address?"

Dutifully she studied it. When she looked up, he saw her curiosity had been piqued. "That's where they exorcise the *meigallo*. Did you know that?"

He was confused. "The what?"

"*O meigallo*: demons, the evil eye, the company of the devil."

Manuel blinked in wide-eyed surprise. He looked again to see if the woman was teasing him. She wasn't.

"Explain that to me, if you'd be so kind."

"Of course I'll explain," she said in a kindly voice. She dropped what she was doing and came out to him in the hall with the card still in her hand. She pointed to it. "This has been a holy site of pilgrimage almost since time began. No other place in Galicia is more sacred. That's where people go to have *o meigallo* or *demo* cast out."

He leaned to peer into her face to see if she was sincere. He found it hard to believe such superstition could exist in this day and age.

She gave him a stern look in return. "See here, I'm telling you God's honest truth."

Manuel accepted that but didn't know what to say.

"God is real, but so is the devil. Evil hearts summon him or he comes on his own, creeping into our lives and making us miserable."

Manuel reached out for the card, intending to take it back. He'd had enough of this superstitious talk. But she held it tight and didn't let go. She backed away with a stern expression. "You can't fool me," she scolded him. "You're one of those nonbelievers, aren't you? Then let me tell you a story."

Manuel glanced up the hall, ready to walk away from her and her story. But the innkeeper's wife had been friendly and helpful to him since the day he arrived. And after all, he was a writer; writers should never refuse a story. He shrugged.

"I have nephews in A Coruña. Well, only one nephew, actually; he's a math teacher and his wife's a wonderful young woman, a social worker. They've been married for almost eight years, and they have a little girl who's five now. Anyway, after she turned four about a year ago, the child started having nightmares. She'd wake up screaming in terror about people in her room, bad people, horrible people who shook her awake and frightened her. Her parents dismissed it at first. They thought those nightmares came from something that happened in kindergarten, maybe some child was bullying her. That kind of thing happens, you know. But the nightmares continued. The child screamed and the parents rushed to her room and tried to wake her up. But even with her eyes open the poor baby kept shouting there were people in the room. She pointed behind her parents but they saw nothing. The terror reflected in her little face seized them as well.

"The pediatrician said those were nighttime terrors, very vivid nightmares some children have. They imagine things even when their eyes are open. He gave them plenty of the usual advice: keep her away from stress, avoid active games before bedtime, no heavy meals late in the day. He even recommended warm baths and massages. But the nightmares continued. Nothing changed. They were desperate, so they consulted other doctors. Finally someone referred them to a psychiatrist who specialized in treating children. After examining the girl, the doctor told them she was perfectly healthy, and told them sometimes children with a lot of imagination convince themselves they see things. It wasn't a bad diagnosis, but it wasn't enough for the parents, so the psychiatrist prescribed a sleeping pill. A very mild one, he said, but it was a drug, after all. For a child.

147

"You can imagine their concern. They came back home devastated, and they told my sister, who happened to be there visiting a very dear friend. The friend offered some advice. 'Look, why don't you take her to the shrine?'

"They told her, 'Oh, we don't believe in hocus-pocus. We couldn't possibly take our daughter to an exorcist.'"

"What did she reply?"

"'I'm sure you never imagined you'd take your four-year-old to a psychiatrist and drug her either. Go ahead and give it a try, people. You're Catholics, the child was baptized, and you were married in a church. And after all, it wouldn't hurt any of you to attend mass once in a while.'

"They took a while to decide. I think they'd already started giving her the pills, but those weren't working. They were desperate. So they went to the shrine, and it happened to be a festival day. After mass the father took the child to the priest and told him of their problem.

"He gave them good advice. 'They're about to take the Virgin from her altar and parade her around the church for the festival. Hold the little one by the hand, run under the platform carrying the figure of the Virgin, and come out on the other side.'"

"That's it?" Manuel asked.

"That's it. They stood outside in the crowd and saw more than one person doing exactly what the priest had described. People ducked under the processional platform with the statue of the Virgin and crossed to the other side. It seemed like a harmless game, so the father took her hand as the procession approached. The child screamed and threw a tantrum, struggling and shrieking, 'No, no, no!' The parents crouched by her, totally aghast, not knowing what to do, completely confused and horrified by the child's suffering. The priest ran to them, grabbed the screaming little child, took her in his arms, and crossed beneath the platform.

"You can explain it any way you like, but when they came out on the other side, the child wasn't screaming anymore. She was as sweet and calm as could be. She didn't remember a whit of what had been afflicting her."

Manuel took a deep breath.

"What can I say?" The woman sighed. She handed the card back to him. "I don't know if my nephew and his wife are better Catholics now, but the girl's nightmares are gone. Every time there's a festival they take her back to cross under the Virgin's platform."

❧

He drove almost thirty miles along the main road, passing through a small town and several extended villages. The story he'd just heard at the inn played in an endless loop in his head. A couple of times he passed signs pointing out places of touristic interest or architectural distinction. He turned onto a secondary road and drove for miles through the unmarked countryside. He was sure he was hopelessly lost, but the GPS insisted he go on. He didn't mind; the beauty of that morning in the countryside intensified his feeling of successful escape.

Half a dozen humble cottages surrounded the church and its annexes. He drove around the exterior of the grounds and a deserted parking lot of impressive size, then took the drive to the main entrance. He parked in the shade of a rank of plane trees that hadn't yet shed their broad green leaves. He got out and surveyed the double set of stairs that led up to the sanctuary.

A noise distracted him. He turned and on the other side of the street running along the far side of the parking lot he saw a pair of elderly men open an aluminum door to enter a structure identified as a bar only by a faded tinplate ad for Schweppes that would have fetched a good price at an antique store. They hadn't noticed him. Before taking the stairs he went to the dusty trunk of a plane tree and pulled off a chunk of bark. He knew the irregularly shaped yellow wound would again look like the rest of the trunk in just a few days. His sister had loved doing that. They would wander through the parks of Madrid taking turns stripping plane trees of their scaly coverings. Sometimes they found one almost intact, its bark so cracked and buckled that it looked as if the tree were struggling to push its way out through that covering. They took real pleasure in breaking off the scaly pieces; the challenge was to see which of them could pull off the largest one that stayed in one piece. He smiled. Then he smiled again, ruefully this time, aware that in these days of uncertainty revisiting painful memories he'd suppressed so long had become one way of assuaging his pain.

He turned the jagged chunk of bark over in his hands as he climbed the stairs to the shrine. He didn't try the door of the main entrance, for he assumed it would be locked. He walked around the building instead. Thousands of signs of the cross had been scratched into its walls, from the ground up to as far as a man could reach.

A woman with very short hair came out of the side entrance, pulling her wool jacket around her in a gesture so exaggerated it verged on the manic. She stopped, stared at him, and declared, "The church is open, but you have to use this entrance. If you want to buy candles or liturgical items, I'll have them out in just a moment." She pointed to a stone structure with a sign: SOUVENIRS OF THE VIRGIN.

"No," Manuel declined, perhaps a bit too brusquely. "In fact I came to see Lucas, but I don't know if this is a good time. Maybe I should have telephoned ahead."

She looked disappointed and then mystified, but then suddenly grasped his meaning. "Oh! You're here to see Father Lucas; of course he's here. Go in and call him. He's busy in the sacristy." Forgetting about him, she yanked out of the pocket of her shapeless jacket a ring with more than twenty keys and headed toward the rough-hewn door of the souvenir shop.

The midmorning sun that had warmed the outside poured into the church nave from high windows. Shafts of light cut through the dusty air of an interior so dim he had to stop for a moment for his eyes to adjust to the gloom.

A number of people, almost all women, stood or knelt at the front pews. Though they resembled one another, the distances between them showed that each was here alone. He walked toward the front, keeping to one side of the pews so he wouldn't have to cross in front of the altar or get too close to the worshippers.

The side chapels featured colorful primitive images, and on some he saw bizarre anachronistic votive offerings of images of parts of the human body. There were heads, legs, arms, even yellow wax figures of infants or adults. They made his skin crawl. Vending machines offered imitation votive candles as sadly diminished replacements for the massive tapers that surely would have burned in here in olden times. The slot required a fifty-cent piece. He dropped one in for the pleasure of seeing the little plastic candle light up beneath the cover of transparent polymer, for all the world like a meter keeping track of prayers to the saints. He went up the side aisle toward the sacristy, passing the praying faithful and hearing their quietly muttered supplications. He looked to see whom they were addressing and saw upon the altar the effigy of a surprisingly young and happy Virgin with a year-old child in her arms. Both were smiling, and the colors of her gown and adornment were those of joy and celebration. He stood trying to reconcile that surprising sight with the picture on the church website of a suffering Virgin crushed by the weight of responsibility and plunged in inconsolable grief. He'd expected that alternative view because the site was so ancient and the traditions of this region so foreign to him.

When he entered the sacristy he saw a woman who could easily have been the sister of the one he'd spoken to. She sat at a little table arranging stacks of folded papers, no doubt the order of service for Sunday mass.

He interrupted her work. "Hello. I'm looking for Father Lucas."

A chair scraped in the adjoining room, and the priest stepped out. He smiled at the sight of Manuel and came forward with his hand extended. "Manuel! I'm so pleased that you decided to come visit."

Manuel shook his hand firmly but said nothing.

The woman behind the little table had the strict look of an old-fashioned schoolteacher. Her prim air was further accentuated by the calculating way she surveyed him with a mixture of reproof and misgiving. She scratched her head in an almost cartoonish effort to jog her memory and kept her eyes fixed on him.

"Won't you come in?" Lucas asked as he gestured toward the room from which he'd come. Seeing Manuel hesitate, he offered an alternative. "Or perhaps you'd prefer a stroll and a tour of all this? The weather is gorgeous after the downpour last night."

Still silent, Manuel turned and crossed the nave toward the exit. The priest bowed for a moment in the direction of the altar and crossed himself. He made his way around a group of the faithful and caught up with Manuel.

The sun did indeed seem more brilliant and the air more inviting when they stepped out of the church. Manuel took a deep breath of the morning air. In tacit accord they began to walk along the exterior wall.

"Manuel, what a joy this is! In truth, I was hoping you'd come, though I wasn't entirely certain I'd see you again. I thought perhaps you'd left. How are you doing?"

His reply was entirely too quick. "I'm fine."

The priest pressed his lips together and tilted his head. Manuel was familiar with that response by now. It was one he'd seen each time he answered that question. Manuel waited, refusing to initiate the conversation. He knew that Lucas wouldn't give up. No one ever had. He'd seen after the funeral that as a priest, Lucas felt even more justified than others in pushing against his reserve.

Lucas looked up at the bell tower. "What do you think of the shrine?"

Manuel smiled, but he wasn't going to be won over by that gambit. "It's impressive enough when seen from a distance," he conceded.

"And close up?"

"I don't know." He reflected, cautious. "It gives me a feeling that's a bit . . . don't get me wrong, it's . . . intimate, but somehow disquieting. Like an old hospital, a mental asylum, or a geriatric ward."

Lucas seemed to ponder that. "I know what you mean, and I agree. For centuries this place has been a refuge from human misery. It wasn't built to hail God's glory but rather to call for victory over sin."

"Sin," Manuel murmured with a touch of mockery. "Is it true they do exorcisms here?"

The priest halted, which obliged Manuel to do the same. "Folks come here seeking all sorts of solace for what ails them," he said sharply. "But that's hardly what you're looking for, is it?"

Manuel regretted his impertinence. He let out a long breath of air and wondered why he felt the urge to attack this man and his beliefs. Elisa's unhappy comment came to mind. *It's hard to accept when your partner prefers to speak to a priest instead of to you.* Yes, perhaps that had something to do with it. Lucas wasn't to blame.

He resumed his pacing; the priest, still offended, didn't follow him immediately. Manuel tried to put his thoughts in order before speaking, but he hadn't come with any plans or expectations. He noticed the piece of bark still in his hand, an unexpected talisman, and he held it tightly. He absentmindedly picked at its surface with a fingernail, shredding edges that yielded with faint cracking sounds. He didn't need to hear them, for those quiet yielding protests were recorded in his memory. He hadn't thought of them for years, but to his surprise that sound was still fresh and familiar.

The priest joined him and broke the silence. "Listen, Manuel, I was Álvaro's friend. His death is a great loss to me. I'll mourn him the rest of my life. I know how you feel, and I'm glad you've decided to visit, that you're still here. But, if you're going to stay, stop acting like a haughty intellectual and show some respect. Many people here loved Álvaro. The fact you didn't know of their existence in no way invalidates their feelings. I wasn't going to mention it because I didn't think you'd appreciate it, but Herminia saw to it there were nine priests at the altar for the funeral. The family told me of his death and I informed the parish priest; the lady dowager said they'd pay for a simple ceremony. Herminia paid honoraria for the other priests from her own pocket. An average of fifty euros per officiant, in honor of a man she loved like a son. She made sure he got a proper mass, so the family wouldn't bury him in silence and shame. She was the one who announced it. She attended to Álvaro's reputation in a land where even the humblest funeral mass is conducted by at least five priests. Any fewer is an insult to the memory of the deceased."

Manuel was astonished.

"Yes, Manuel, that rude tradition, that folklore you sneer at, is an expression of respect. It's pure love. In the same way the workers at the winery paid for a novena of masses here at the shrine. In all sincerity, I can't imagine any greater act of love for the dead than caring for their welfare beyond the grave. I believe you're a good man. You're wounded and in pain, but that gives you no right to mock. So tell me, Manuel, why are you here?"

Manuel sighed, pressed his lips together, and acknowledged the stinging rebuke. *Entirely deserved*, he thought.

"I'm here because of Elisa."

"Elisa?" the priest murmured, surprised but cautiously receptive.

Manuel didn't want to explain the real reasons behind his decision to stay in Galicia, but he didn't want to lie either. He was ashamed of his presumption and wished with all his heart he could share his thoughts, but it was still too early to address the question directly.

"I went back to the cemetery in As Grileiras yesterday." It was only half a lie. "And I met her there. She's obsessed by the idea that her fiancé didn't commit suicide."

Lucas kept walking in silence, looking down, apparently not surprised in the least.

Manuel was fishing for information and decided to let out a bit more line. Since Lucas seemed willing to discuss the strange circumstances of Fran's death, he might also be ready to talk about Álvaro. The priest had said he was the only person from Álvaro's past who'd had more than simple business dealings with him.

"Do you remember the policeman who was waiting for me after the funeral? The truth is, he also hinted there was something not quite right about Fran's death."

The priest looked him directly in the eye.

Aware that he was being inspected to judge how much he knew and how much he was hiding, Manuel twitched the line again. "He said he questioned you, but you didn't tell him anything."

"It was privileged information, from—"

"Of course. Under seal of confession, he said. And he also told me you didn't believe Fran was the type to kill himself."

"That's still what I think."

"If you think there's something suspicious about his death, since Fran is gone and Elisa's in pain, why not tell her the truth?"

"Sometimes it's better to say nothing than to mislead with only part of the truth."

Manuel's anger awoke. His self-control was being tested to the very limit. "Then tell me something, priest—do you intend to mislead me too? Or will you tell me the truth? I don't want to waste my time. I'm pretty fed up with everyone feeding lies to me—Álvaro, his secretary, Herminia . . . and besides," he said, turning slightly to look out at the valley below, "you're right, it's a glorious day. I could think of a million better things to do instead of standing here listening to tall tales."

Lucas's expression was stern, almost fierce. He surveyed Manuel for five or six seconds and then began to walk once more.

Manuel realized he'd raised his voice. He was furious with himself. He emptied his lungs in a great gust of air, and in two vigorous strides he caught up with the priest. The man was saying something but in so low a voice Manuel had to lean close to catch the words.

"I cannot tell you what he told me under seal of confession," Lucas said firmly. "But I will tell you what I saw, what I felt, and what I concluded."

Manuel didn't reply. He knew it would be useless to say anything. A comment from him might even induce Lucas to change his mind and retreat into stubborn silence.

"I officiated at the old marquis's funeral mass in the church on the estate. That ceremony was also deeply affecting, but in a different way. Álvaro was down front, very serious, already aware of the weight of the responsibilities that had been left to him. Santiago was in mourning but not in the same way. He was frustrated and angry, as if by dying his father had bitterly disappointed him. I've seen that reaction before; often the children assume their parents will always be with them, and their different reactions can be astonishingly unpredictable. Often, it's anger. And then came Fran . . . Santiago needed his father, but Fran worshipped the man. His grief was indescribable.

"It was obvious they were all worried about Fran, maybe because in a way they knew in their hearts his grief was more real than anyone's. After the funeral Fran didn't want to go back to the manor; he stayed by his father's grave all alone. Álvaro walked me to the church door and said he was very worried about Fran. I reassured him. I knew this was normal; it was pain that he had to face and endure. It's the price we pay for loving." He gave Manuel a sideways glance. "I urged Álvaro to call me if I could help his brother, but only if Fran agreed to see me. Often someone in pain adamantly rejects any offer of help out of fear that comes from some mawkish sentimentality or hidden judgment. You of all people know exactly what I'm talking about. Fran phoned me late that night, after ten, and asked me to come see him. It must have been past eleven when I got there. The church door wasn't entirely shut. I pushed it open and found him sitting in the front pew with an untouched sandwich and a Coca-Cola at his side. The only light was from the candles for his father's funeral. He asked me to hear his confession, and he made a good one; that of a grown man, not of a spoiled child. He was aware of the pain he'd caused and repented his sins with a firm intention of reform. I gave him absolution and communion. Afterward we returned to the pew, he smiled, and he ate the sandwich. 'I was famished,' he told me." Lucas searched Manuel's face. "You understand the significance of that? He'd been fasting in preparation for confession and communion. He hadn't gone to confession in years, but he knew how it should be done. A man who's that observant of the rules would never have committed suicide. I know it's difficult to explain that to an agnostic or to a police officer, but believe me, it's true. Never would he have taken his own life."

Manuel weighed all this as they resumed their walk. He hadn't failed to notice that Lucas had called him an agnostic.

Ahead of them at the side entrance to the sanctuary, two women were waiting, the same two he'd assumed were nuns. It was obvious the women had been anticipating their return. Their nervous smiles, bright eyes, and the restless nudges they exchanged betrayed an almost childish excitement.

Lucas appeared momentarily alarmed by this, but he quickly perceived what they were on about. He whispered an apology to Manuel.

The woman who'd been at the sacristy table was the first to speak. "You're Manuel Ortigosa, aren't you?"

Manuel smiled and confirmed it. After all these years he still felt flattered and grateful to be recognized in public. Perhaps it was absurd of him, but he couldn't help it.

"When you came in I thought, 'That man seems familiar to me somehow,' but I couldn't put my finger on it. Then I heard Father Lucas call you Manuel. Well, I went running out to tell my cousin." The other woman smiled in embarrassment and wrung her hands. "She discovered your novels and made us all read them, everyone in the catechism group, the rural women's association, all our female cousins . . ."

Manuel held out a hand. They rushed giggling and vying with one another to take it. The one who'd remained silent was holding back tears. He hugged her, genuinely moved by this sudden outburst of adoration.

She burst into tears. "You must think I'm a silly goose," she said between sobs and hiccups.

"Not at all, my dear. You move me deeply. Thanks ever so much for reading my books and recommending them."

The woman wailed even louder in the arms of her chatty cousin.

"It's too bad we didn't know you were coming. We'd have brought all your books to autograph, but maybe you'll be coming back?"

"I don't know," Manuel answered evasively, looking into the distance.

Lucas rescued him. "That's enough now. You two stop bothering the man, you're confusing him. Manuel isn't here to sign autographs." He took Manuel's arm and sought to guide him past the women.

Manuel's protest of "It's no bother at all" provoked more smiles of delight from his adoring fans.

"At least maybe we could take a picture?" blurted the tongue-tied one.

Ignoring Lucas's exaggerated expression of annoyance, Manuel stepped between them, accepted her cell phone, and took a selfie with them. He had to handle the phone because they were too flustered to manipulate it.

He said goodbye and walked away, leaving them wreathed in smiles, standing there and holding one another by the arm as the men departed. Manuel and Lucas walked until they were out of earshot.

Manuel was the first to speak. "I've thought about it, and I think you're right that Nogueira didn't fully consider Fran's behavior that night, including the fact of his confession. He might even be assuming Fran was clearing his slate before taking his own life. It's known that some individuals intending suicide put their affairs in order before taking the last step."

"But not out of concern for others. Those who kill themselves lack the empathy to put up with life and with other people. A good deal of what was troubling Fran had to do with the family, and he felt deeply responsible for them. Whatever was on his mind, he wasn't ignoring a problem; he was trying to solve it. It's a sad truth that I've known individuals who decided to end their lives, but never, not one single time, did I see that attitude. And I chatted with him for a full hour after his confession." He paused to recall the conversation. "Mostly about his father, his brothers, and his childhood. All his happy memories. We even had a good time laughing at some of his mischief. He said that when his father died, he realized how important it is to have someone close to you. He realized the instant his father's hand slipped from his that he was nobody's son anymore. He was alone. And at the same moment he saw Elisa sitting at his side, he saw that bulge in her belly where their baby was growing. He said he knew then that his role had changed. From then on he was the father. It was his responsibility to take his child's hand.

"He'd finished the sandwich when I left, and I saw the expression of a man beginning a new life. Not of someone about to end it all."

"Then how do you explain what happened?"

"Certainly not as suicide."

"An accident perhaps?" Manuel recalled Nogueira's theory. "Maybe he was looking for relief, something to take the edge off, and he got his dose wrong."

"You weren't there, Manuel. I was and I saw him. He wished me good night and said he was going to stay a little while longer to put out the candles and lock up."

"You're suggesting that someone . . . ?"

"I have no basis for such an allegation," the priest replied gravely. "But under seal of confession he told me certain things that may have put him at risk."

"You're referring to whatever was worrying him about his family?"

The priest nodded.

"Did he provide details?"

"No. Just that the person or persons involved might have been there and he knew about it."

"Person or persons," Manuel repeated impatiently. "Who?"

"I wouldn't tell you even if I knew!" responded the priest in an offended tone. "Let me remind you I'm strictly forbidden to reveal secrets learned during a confession. But the truth is that he didn't say."

"But you said he confessed!"

"The sacrament of confession is completely different from a police interrogation. The individual is invited to relieve his conscience, and that's no easy matter. Sometimes a full confession requires several sessions. Fran hadn't taken communion for years, and I wasn't about to pressure him, especially when I saw a lost sheep returning to the fold. I assumed there would be plenty of time for him to work through his concerns and quiet his conscience." Lucas paused. "In any case, and this is just my impression, I felt he was still letting things come to a head. He said he was afraid something terrible might happen. He wasn't entirely sure of his suspicions. That may be why he was measuring his words."

"And after that? You said good night and left him there alone?"

"Well . . ." The priest seemed to be wrestling with something.

"No?"

Lucas hesitated a long time as if trying to decide whether to put it into words. Manuel was expecting a tremendous revelation.

"I took the unlighted path through the trees. I used my phone as a flashlight. I thought I heard a sound, so I looked back. I saw the figure of someone going into the church."

"Who was it?"

"I don't know. I was probably two hundred yards away in almost total darkness. The only light inside the church came from candles. The door opened, and I got only a glimpse of someone going in. Then the door swung shut."

"You know who it was," Manuel said.

"I'm not sure. That's why I chose not to mention it."

"Who was it?" Manuel insisted, determined to have an answer. "Tell me!"

"I thought it might have been Álvaro."

Manuel stopped short.

"That wouldn't have been strange," the priest quickly added. "I already told you that on the morning of their father's funeral Álvaro told me how worried he was about his brother. I remembered that when I heard Fran had died. The more I thought about it, the less certain I became, and finally I wasn't prepared to declare I'd seen Álvaro."

"And?"

"So I asked him."

"You asked Álvaro?"

"I did. He said it couldn't possibly have been him, because he'd been nowhere near the church that night. So I decided I must have been wrong. I don't know who it was. Someone I confused with Álvaro, that's all."

"He told you he hadn't gone to the church, and you believed him."

"Álvaro never lied."

"You'll forgive me, Lucas, but from my current perspective that sounds like a bad joke."

Lucas pretended not to have heard. "I told him Fran was worried about something having to do with the family. In other circumstances I wouldn't have said even that much, but Fran had just died, and . . . well, Álvaro needed to know. He'd become the head of the family. He listened carefully, and his reaction suggested to me that he knew what Fran had been talking about."

Manuel stepped in front of the priest and stopped, determined not to allow him to evade his responsibility. "Let's recap. Fran tells you he's worried something very serious might be going on, and then he turns up dead. You tell Álvaro as much, and now he's dead too."

Lucas scowled. The very idea was deeply repugnant to him. "The deaths weren't related. That night was three years ago, and Álvaro died in an accident."

Manuel knew that trusting someone always means taking a leap of faith. It's like throwing oneself off a precipice. He could rely only on pure instinct, the quality that had brought the human race through ages when a wrong choice meant death. He felt himself reduced to the primitive hunter who persists within us all. The last five days had utterly destroyed the world he'd thought solid and lasting, leaving him at the mercy of a numbing inertia. And there was nothing he could do about it.

Manuel shut his eyes and released a steady stream of air that curiously resembled a prayer of appeal. "Maybe not."

"But . . ."

"It's what keeps me here, it's why I can't leave. There are certain things that suggest Álvaro's death wasn't an accident."

Lucas's expression was sympathetic. "Manuel, I know that sometimes it's difficult to accept."

"Goddamn it, listen to me! I'm not talking about some fantasy of mine; there's a policeman who finds it suspicious. Otherwise I'd have gotten the hell out of here long ago."

Lucas spoke to him slowly and patiently, as if addressing a child. "I accompanied Santiago to the hospital. I was there with him when they confirmed that Álvaro was dead. The police said it was an accident. His car ran off the road, a straight stretch, with no other vehicles around. It was an accident, Manuel."

"Sure, Fran's death was accidental, too, even though he'd been knocked on the head and his shoes were scuffed because he'd been dragged. The church door was locked, and no key was found. Even though the boy couldn't hold himself up. I have the distinct impression that for this family there's always been a deep dark gap between the official version and the truth. Don't you think so?"

Lucas's face lost all its color. "I didn't know that." He took a deep breath and released it in a rush. "What do they think happened to Álvaro?"

Manuel felt a strong desire to tell him everything, including the fact that "they" were limited to the medical examiner taken off the case, a retired policeman, and himself. He wanted to lay out every last detail and share all his torments. But he'd formally pledged to Nogueira and Ophelia he would keep them out of it. Trust has to go both ways, and he'd get little or nothing from Lucas unless he gave him something in exchange. But it was still too early to open up completely.

"I don't know. That's what I'm trying to find out. I don't even know if I can trust you, or if I'm making a huge mistake by telling you."

The photo of the boy with the calm gaze clamored suddenly from his jacket pocket as if it had come alive. He clasped his hand to his chest as if he'd just been struck by a terrible physical pain.

Lucas met his gaze. His eyes were steady. "You can trust me."

Manuel studied his face and thought about it. "I already have. That's the honest truth. But sometimes confessions take time and several sessions. Isn't that what you said?"

"I'll help you with whatever you need. Don't shut me out."

Manuel nodded. "I have to think about it. Right now I'm really confused. I could get into big trouble if anyone hears that I told you this much."

"What are you mixed up in, Manuel?"

"What was *Álvaro* mixed up in? That's the question to ask!"

"I can assure you it was nothing evil."

"Assure me? You think you can assure me?" His voice rose. "And how do you think you can assure me? Maybe you knew everything about him? Did you know he wasn't wearing his wedding ring when he died? Did you know he used to go out whoring with his brother?" His mind was echoing Mei's account of the words someone had said from a pay phone, under the impression he was speaking to Álvaro. *He knows you killed him.*

Lucas closed his eyes. His response and emotion were evident. He covered his face with his hands.

Manuel stayed on the attack. "That's right, Lucas, your married, gay buddy hung out with whores. He even had a favorite hooker. What do you think of that? Still want to stand up for him? You want to look me in the face and tell me he never lied?" He was shouting now. Tears of indignation erupted from his eyes and he trembled in fury.

Manuel turned his back on the priest and took a couple of angry steps. He didn't want to let the man see him cry.

Lucas dropped his hands and opened his eyes. He was devastated. "I didn't know," he whispered.

"Doesn't matter," Manuel responded bitterly. "If you had, you wouldn't have told me. Right?"

"Manuel," Lucas said in a conciliatory tone, coming up behind him, "what I do know is that the Álvaro I knew was an honorable man. Perhaps he had a reason for taking whatever measures he did."

Manuel stubbornly rejected that objection, his eyes fixed on a blurry vision of the distant valley.

"I know you don't want to hear it, but I understand what you're going through. Numb indifference and false calm, depression, insomnia or constant sluggishness, and sometimes anger or rage—those are normal feelings." He placed a hand on Manuel's shoulder.

Manuel shrugged it off in a fury and turned to face him. "Don't you go breaking my balls with your cheap psychology. I don't need some exorcist priest with a degree in theology to tell me it's perfectly normal for me to be angry. Of course I'm angry. I'm so damn angry that I'm surprised I don't just explode. But more than that I'm frustrated and disgusted by all the lies. How am I not going to be in a rage when at every step of the way I get new evidence that the man I thought I knew was a complete stranger to me? A fabulously successful businessman from a family of aristocrats, Catholics devoted to the church and the whorehouse! How can I help being furious when every day I wake up with the feeling I'll have to face another stinking pile of his shit?" He spewed out indignation. "With the added provocation that since he's not here to explain, I'm the one who has to bear the weight of his fucking shame. And to top it off, he has the gall to will it all to me like a grand lottery prize or compensation for the insult. 'Here you go, you're heir to all my fucking crap.'"

His bitter, resentful harangue surged forth from his innermost being like boiling bile vomited up from his deepest gut. He'd lost control. His mind fought with itself in the knowledge he'd been blinded by black wrath. He'd never felt such searing emotion; it overwhelmed him and yet strengthened him at the same time. He subsided into silence, shaking, his jaw rigid and clenched to the point of pain.

He'd lost it. He needed to get away. No hope remained. "Do you really want to help me, priest?"

"In whatever way you wish," Lucas replied with a mildness in total contrast to Manuel's anger.

"No more lies. Not even by omission." Manuel walked away.

"I give you my word," Lucas said behind him.

Manuel left the grounds of the shrine without looking back. He felt Lucas's eyes on him until he turned the corner of the wall at the front stairs. He forced himself to slow his pace as he descended toward the shade under the thick crowns of the plane trees. *You can't go on like this*, his inner voice told him all the while. The serene authority of those towering trees calmed his spirit. He plunged again into the unending shade of the trees like a wounded animal seeking refuge.

Trying to regain his calm, he took a deep breath of the air that was rapidly shedding the invisible humidity of the preceding day's rain. It smelled now of hay and wood. He knew his inner voice was right; he was destroying himself with every step. He felt the ache in every muscle of his body, the physical toll taken by his outburst, and the mental damage inflicted by these struggles. Mei, Nogueira, Lucas . . .

Exhausted, he looked around in search of help. The faded tinplate advertisement with rusted edges visible across the street beyond the parking lot presented itself, both tempting and incongruous. Surrendering to his fatigue, he allowed its quaint appeal to influence him. He turned his steps in that direction, hoping for the respite he so desperately needed.

There were two men behind the bar. The older one was cutting bread and cheese on a board while carrying on a lively conversation in Gallego dialect with the locals Manuel had seen entering earlier. Two other men had joined them. All were drinking wine in bright white porcelain cups. The bar ran the entire width of the narrow, cramped room. A table and three chairs stood on either side of the door in a public space that measured not much more than ten feet by twenty feet. A small handwritten card tacked to the only other door identified it as the access to a toilet. Behind the bar a door stood open to a kitchen in the house behind. A woman of the same advanced age as the bartender was busy there. The domain over which she reigned featured a massive wooden table and delicate old-fashioned curtains partially drawn across the kitchen window. No bottles were on display behind the bar. A set of shelves more fit for a garage held white cups and pitchers. The walls of the bar were decorated only with small family photos in unmatched frames, a lugubrious funeral home calendar, and a chalkboard proclaiming *Soup Today*. The aroma from the kitchen confirmed that promise. The contrast between the spick-and-span kitchen and the casual, half-finished installations of the bar showed that husband and wife had staked out their respective territories.

He jutted his chin toward the cups of wine the men were drinking. "Okay to have some wine?"

The young man filled a cup, and the older man laid slabs of cheese and a thick slice of bread on a plate. He slid it down the bar without a word. Manuel sipped the wine and tasted the cheese—very creamy but with a surprisingly intense and long-lasting flavor. He finished off the snack, realized he was still hungry, and asked for more wine.

The men carried on an animated conversation and laughed from time to time. When he listened closely he could make out some of the talk in Gallego, but he quickly lost interest. From where he stood watching the lady of the house tending to the kitchen—he assumed the older man leaning on the bar receiving his friends like a godfather was her husband—Manuel began to feel he'd slipped into the house of folks who were treating him with just the right amount of indifference to put him at ease. The tempest battering the shores of his soul gradually subsided, and his self-awareness reasserted itself.

He inspected his hands for evidence of the tension that had tormented him. There was none. He noticed, however, that the nails of his thumb and index finger were stained a brownish-yellow color from his nervous picking at the chunk of plane tree bark, scraping off small crescent-shaped pieces. Childhood memory reminded him it was useless to try to scrub those stains away, for they'd linger under his nails for days as tenaciously as walnut stains.

"Could I have some soup?" he asked.

The younger man motioned him to one of the tables. He gave Manuel a pitcher of wine, half a round loaf of fragrant brown bread, and two cloth napkins, one as a placemat and the other for his lap.

Manuel sat with his back to the door with a good view of the television, where a program from Galicia's regional broadcasting service was playing with the sound muted. A bowl was placed before him almost immediately. He wouldn't have dared to try to lift it with both hands. The young man warned him it was very hot.

The strong, salty aroma of the brew enveloped him. He tried a spoonful and then eagerly slurped the steaming liquid. Each spoonful comforted him with the deep flavor of greens and the strong taste of lard. The soup had the powerful consistency of a dish meant to strengthen body and soul, a welcome relief for travelers, and a source of warmth on winter nights. After finishing half of it he set down the spoon, picked up the bowl with both hands, and drank directly from it. He swallowed repeatedly and felt the fiery drafts of cauterizing brew descend to his stomach. His field of vision narrowed to the inside of the bowl, and his sensations were reduced to the most elemental. With the soup, he ate heavy dark bread so flavorful that he seemed to be tasting real bread for the first time in his life. Instead of dessert he had another piece of cheese and a pot-brewed coffee in a glass the lady of the house brought to him from the kitchen. She had to go outside and walk around the house to deliver it.

He paid a ridiculously small amount for that feast. He thanked the family sincerely when he said goodbye. He felt restored, as if he'd gone for a time to that ideal home portrayed in Christmas ads, the place of comfort we all yearn for. He stepped outside, returned to the towering plane trees, and pulled off another section of bark. He ceremoniously placed it on the dashboard of his vehicle where he could keep it in his sight.

Now he knew he'd be returning to As Grileiras.

CAFÉ

He drove up the driveway and parked next to the gardenia hedge. Two other vehicles were there, the veterinarian's black all-wheel-drive SUV and a white pickup drawn up to the garden entrance with its tailgate lowered.

Santiago was walking toward the stables. He wore a tight-fitting blue long-sleeved shirt and trousers tucked into riding boots.

The newest marquis stopped in midstride and stared at him. Santiago's expression clearly indicated he was offended and saw Manuel as an intruder. His disapproving stare of reproach and physical posture were those of an archangel defending the gates of paradise.

Manuel refused to be intimidated. He took his time removing his jacket and laying it carefully on the backseat. He locked his car and strode confidently toward the new marquis.

Despite his defiant posture Santiago was the first to speak, an indication he was unnerved by Manuel's unannounced visit. "I didn't know you were still in the area. I thought you'd left after the funeral."

Manuel smiled. "I'd intended to, but I needed to clear up a couple of things."

"Oh." A shadow of uncertainty showed in Santiago's face.

Manuel very nearly asked the marquis to share his thoughts. "I thought you might help."

Perhaps the suggestion Manuel was still planning to leave encouraged Santiago. He was positive but far from effusive. "Of course, if I can."

"You certainly can," Manuel said firmly. "Álvaro was here because of you."

Santiago looked away for the first time, for just a moment, but when he met Manuel's eyes again he was composed. His eyes glinted with steely dislike.

"I have no idea what you're referring to." He shifted as if to resume his walk toward the stables.

"I hear you asked the administrator for three hundred thousand euros. That's a huge sum. He telephoned Álvaro. Whatever was going on was serious enough for him to drop everything and come here."

Santiago looked away again and pressed his lips together in a childish pout. He obviously wasn't used to having to account for his actions and looked as though he found this particularly annoying. Manuel had had his share of confrontations with surly students in his years as a university lecturer, and he knew how to handle such recalcitrance. He took pleasure in insisting. "Look at me!"

Santiago did so. His eyes burned with anger at this humiliation.

"Álvaro came but he didn't give you a cent. I want to know what you wanted it for."

Santiago's pout narrowed to a sneer; he sniffed loudly and squinted in scorn. "That's none of your—" He bit his lower lip.

"Surprise, surprise. Yes, in fact, it is my business." Manuel kept his tone even.

Santiago exhaled. "Very well." He blurted out his reply as if trying to spit out the explanation and end this disagreeable conversation as quickly as possible. "It was for a horse. Last year Álvaro agreed to add to the stables. As an investment. The administrator knew about it, and in the course of a few months we added a number of horses. A few days ago I had the opportunity to make a good deal on a racehorse, but the decision had to be made quickly. I asked my brother for the money, but because of a recent unfortunate business deal he didn't trust my judgment. He didn't approve the deal. That's all."

"And he came all the way out here to tell you he wasn't going to authorize the funds?"

"I don't know what made Álvaro tick. You think I could tell you? You certainly know he had lots of business dealings. He never told me when he was going to pop up or disappear." Santiago's expression relaxed into the wicked ghost of a smile. "And apparently he didn't tell you either."

Manuel looked at Santiago with renewed interest, intrigued to find that this guy seemed to have guts after all. He wondered how long the man's courage would last. He ignored Santiago's gibe and challenged him instead. *"And am I my brother's keeper?"*

Santiago jerked up his chin. In alarm or indignation? Was he surprised or intimidated when Manuel quoted Cain on the death of Abel?

Yelps and laughter from little Samuel distracted them. Catarina appeared with the boy in her arms. At her side, Elisa and Vicente were carrying armloads of flowers to the pickup. The boy shouted anew in his shrill voice, "Uncle! Uncle!"

The group turned to look at Manuel and Santiago. Catarina came to the edge of the drive, the boy struggling in her arms. As soon as she put him down, the little fellow galloped toward the two men. When Samuel was a couple of yards away, Santiago opened his arms and leaned down to receive him, but the boy eluded the marquis and wrapped himself around Manuel's legs instead. Manuel looked down in consternation, moved and yet disturbed by the embarrassing situation the boy in all his innocence had provoked.

Santiago straightened up. He rubbed the boy's neck but got no reaction; he turned without a word and headed back to the manor. He paused briefly when he got to his wife, leaned over as they stood shoulder to shoulder, and muttered a few words. Catarina looked down and trailed after him without speaking. Manuel didn't hear their exchange, but perhaps Vicente and Elisa had. Manuel saw them exchange a glance. Elisa quickly busied herself with the flowers, but Vicente went to the pickup and slammed the tailgate shut so hard that he startled the women. Everyone turned to look at him, Santiago included.

Manuel lifted the boy, hugged him, and chatted, all the while keenly aware of the tense situation. The marquis went quickly out of sight, but the others were strung out in a long line, with Catarina halfway between him and the duo of Elisa and Vicente. A seemingly interminable pause probably lasted only a couple of seconds before Catarina hesitantly approached him. As she came forward Manuel saw her pretending to arrange her hair while wiping away tears with her forearm. Her eyes were still glistening when she got to him.

"Hello," she said, and held out a small, firm hand with close-trimmed nails and scratched green nail polish. She was short but not heavy; her frame was muscular. Her tan was evidence of long hours of outdoor work. "I'm Catarina. We saw one another for a moment at Griñán's office, but it wasn't a day for . . ."

"Very pleased to meet you," he said, shifting the boy to the other arm so he could awkwardly shake her hand.

"I'm sorry I wasn't there the other day when you visited the greenhouse. Oh, and I hope you're feeling better. Vicente told me you got dizzy."

He smiled and made a dismissive gesture. "I have no idea why."

She smiled back and seemed relieved to speak of something other than what had just occurred. "It's not unusual, what with the heat, the humidity, and the heavy perfume. The atmosphere in the greenhouse can be just too much."

"You have gorgeous flowers," Manuel said and gestured toward the pickup. "Do you sell them?"

"Yes," she responded with pride. "Most of them go to perfume manufacturers and other cultivators, but sometimes we do flower arrangements for special occasions. We're taking these to my parents' estate. There's a wedding there this weekend, and I enjoy doing the flowers." She paused and a shadow passed over her face. She looked back at the big house and bowed her head in apology. "Santiago doesn't like to see me working."

Manuel nodded at that incongruous remark as if he understood or accepted it. The pickup's engine started and put an end to the conversation.

"We have to go." She held her arms out for the boy. Samuel flung himself fearlessly into her embrace. "I hope you'll come back to visit. I'm always at the greenhouse in the morning."

"Perhaps I will."

Manuel stood relaxed where he was, watching as they got into the vehicle and left. Elisa and the boy waved as the pickup passed him. His eyes followed them as they drove out of the estate and silence settled over the premises.

The sun was high and a mild breeze rustled the trees. Birds were quiet, stunned by the unexpected heat of that September afternoon. He took out his cell phone and called Griñán.

A drowsy voice responded. Manuel checked his watch and found it was four in the afternoon. He'd probably interrupted the man's siesta. *So what?* "I just spoke to Santiago. He doesn't deny asking for the money and tells me it was for a horse. Claims you were aware of it, all part of Álvaro's plan to improve the stock at the stable."

"All right . . . give me just a moment." That confirmed it—the man had been sleeping when the phone rang. "That's right . . . over the past year they bought several horses with that idea in mind, including an English nag that was a disaster. Santiago made that decision and spent close to three hundred thousand." Griñán paused. "They haven't bought any others since." He seemed to search his memory. "They did discuss buying a breeding mare two or three months ago. Horses aren't my responsibility, but purchase prices are. I can tell you right now that given the expenses and what the other horses cost, a breeding mare wouldn't have cost three hundred thousand euros." He cleared his throat. "And besides, if the money was for the purchase of a horse, don Santiago would have told me so. As he did before."

Manuel said nothing for several seconds while he turned the administrator's doubts over in his mind.

"Manuel, I hope you were discreet enough not to tell him you got the information from me."

"Believe me, Griñán, right now that should be the least of your worries." He ended the call.

He shaded his eyes and squinted toward the upper floor of the manor house. He thought he saw a dark figure by a window. The tall dark figure didn't move. It stood motionless as a statue, not making itself obvious but not hiding its presence either.

She's always up there, keeping an eye on everything.

Noise from the stalls attracted his attention, and Manuel remembered that Santiago had been headed in that direction when he'd caught sight of Manuel. Santiago had changed his mind about riding after that. Manuel bowed toward the distant window with mock formality, reoriented himself, and walked to the stables.

The veterinarian, a man probably less than forty years of age, was the same one who'd greeted Manuel on his previous visit. The vet was guiding a handsome horse into a stall. Manuel waited until he'd latched the gate and then approached him.

The vet appeared pleased to see him. "Oh, yes, I saw you the other day. You must be . . ."

"The new owner," Manuel replied assertively. He couldn't take half measures when he was looking to enlist the man's cooperation. And after all, he did own everything here.

The man took a deep breath, pulled off a suede glove and held out his hand, clearly revising his assumptions. "Oh! It's just that . . . I thought, well . . . It's a pleasure to make your acquaintance."

"I have some questions about the horses, and perhaps you can help me."

The man smiled again. "Of course! That's one area where I certainly do have some expertise."

"How many horses do we have here?"

"Twelve, for the moment. Most of them are Spanish horses. Fine animals." He waved toward the row of stalls. "There's also an Arabian mare and *Slender*, an English racehorse. That's the one I was attending to the other day when you came by with señor Griñán."

Manuel kept it casual. "I heard there was some problem."

The vet puffed in exasperation. "*Some problem* is an understatement. *Slender's* back legs have a congenital defect. It wouldn't be so serious in any other type of horse, but he's a racehorse. The pain makes him unfit for racing."

"How long ago did they buy the horse?"

"Just over a year ago."

"You said it's a congenital defect—in other words, the horse was born with it. Why didn't they return it or at least ask for their money back? Surely that's a valid reason for canceling the sale."

The vet had nodded as Manuel spoke. He turned toward the inside. "Come with me." He took Manuel on a tour of the stables, stopping to show him each animal. A gold-colored plaque with the name was attached to the gate of each stall. "This building houses some fine specimens: *Noir*, for example, is a robust Arabian mare, spirited and with a noble character. *Swift*, *Orwell*, and *Carrol* are Spanish horses they purchased last year, and I assisted Santiago with each purchase. They're well-tempered specimens, obedient and excellent in shows."

They came to a closed stall. The veterinarian pulled back the bolt and opened the upper section of the door. The horse inside shied away and then quieted, standing sideways, watching them distrustfully with a dark eye. It was significantly larger than the others they'd visited.

"Don Santiago bought *Slender* last summer while I was on vacation. He didn't tell me how much the horse cost, but I'm sure it was far more than the animal was worth, at least as a racehorse. We registered him in two races but had to withdraw. Don Álvaro got very annoyed and told us not to buy any others unless I vetted them first. Don Santiago doesn't want to admit he made a mistake, so he keeps me examining the horse, trying different anti-inflammatory treatments, massages, even ice packs, as if the defect were an injury that could be cured. *Slender*'s a good horse; maybe a bit high strung, but that's typical of such animals. He tolerates a jockey, but he's a disaster as a racehorse. A precious but expensive disaster."

The vet shut the stall door and they went back to the stable entrance.

"I understand there was some talk of buying a mare."

"Yes, that's right. I proposed buying a Spanish mare. I put don Santiago in contact with a breeder I know, and we were close to closing the deal. But the mare is pregnant now, and we won't be able to carry out the transaction until after she's foaled. We might buy both the mare and her colt. We'll have to see."

"How much was the breeder asking for the mare?"

"Well, there's always a difference between the asking price and the deal that's struck, but I think we could get her for maybe forty thousand euros. The colt is another matter. The price for the package could go up if the colt looks good, or it could go down; the negotiation will have to take into account the fact that it'll be months before the mare will be available."

"Did Santiago recently mention the opportunity of buying another race-horse? A week ago, more or less?"

The vet seemed surprised. "Another racehorse? No, and I doubt he'll want to, considering what happened with *Slender*. Why do you ask?"

"Santiago told me that a few days ago he was offered a top-of-the-line horse, but the deal had to be concluded quickly."

"That may be, but I doubt it. Or at least, no one mentioned it to me. No, I don't believe don Santiago has gone alone to see a horse. Especially not if the deal had to be concluded quickly. He knew perfectly well there wasn't a chance in the world don Álvaro would agree unless I'd already certified the animal." He pondered for a moment. "Maybe if the seller was in such a rush, another buyer snapped it up before he could call me in."

A lateral corridor intersected with the main walkway, and Manuel stopped when he heard barking coming from one side.

"Those are the hunting dogs. They get excited when they hear unfamiliar voices. Would you like to see them?"

Manuel strolled past the kennels where dogs were leaping against the bars, yelping and whining. He put a hand out for them to sniff. Manuel and the vet reached the end of the passageway and the last enclosure, where a small mongrel peered out at them from the depths of its hay-strewn cage. The mutt was a pitiful sight. It trembled visibly, shaking with fear.

"And this little fellow is Café. The poor mutt pretty much stands out among the rest of the pack."

"Café?"

"Álvaro brought him here a year ago. Said he found the little fellow along the highway. The dog was lucky, because he wouldn't have lasted long at the animal shelter."

The veterinarian opened the cage. "Come on, Café! Don't be shy, little guy."

Very slowly and with much nervous licking of lips, the little animal crept up to them.

"I suspect someone beat him a lot, judging from his behavior. Álvaro was the only one who'd gained his confidence."

Manuel held his hand out and kept it still. The tiny creature sidled closer and finally placed his head beneath Manuel's palm. "What's wrong with his back legs?"

The vet shrugged. "Lots. Malnutrition for one; he's been stunted since birth, although he's doing better now. I'd say he's two years old, maybe three, and was probably a mess well before he got here. He's much better now; you should have seen him when Álvaro brought him in."

The animal lifted his head, and those dark watery eyes regarded and evaluated him. Manuel saw why Álvaro had brought the creature home. Maybe there was hope yet. "You little miracle," he whispered.

"Sorry, what did you say?" The man had gone back almost to the far end of the passage. Perhaps he was impatient to leave.

Manuel made no move to quit the place. "Just one more question . . . did you see Álvaro the day he died?"

The man nodded. "About noon, as I was leaving."

"Did you happen to discuss anything? Maybe the horses or Santiago?"

"No, he just asked me about Café."

Manuel nodded without looking up from the dog. "Thanks very much. I'm sorry to have detained you."

"It's been a pleasure. My phone number's on the board at the entrance. Don't hesitate to call. About anything at all." The vet started toward the main passage but paused. "Just one thing. Please make sure Café's pen is very firmly latched. Don Santiago was very annoyed the one time he saw the dog running loose."

Silence settled over the stables. Nothing was to be heard other than the weary sounds of a late summer afternoon, the snuffling breath of the horses, and the creaks and pops as their muscular bodies stirred.

"Café," Manuel murmured. The dog's tail wagged cautiously, as if reluctant to become too excited. "You don't know it, but you're a total surprise." He kept his voice low for his first conversation with a canine. "Want to take a walk?"

Manuel walked toward the exit, looking back each step of the way to be sure the little animal was following. As he stood at the stable trying to decide which way to go, a red Nissan SUV turned into the main driveway, the same vehicle that had passed him the previous afternoon. Again today the man behind the wheel seemed startled to see him. The Nissan slowed, passed him, and then pulled over.

Manuel waited expectantly, checking behind to make sure the dog was still there. The man got out and walked up to Manuel with his hand held out.

"Don Manuel, maybe you don't remember me, but we saw one another at the funeral. I'm Daniel Mosquera, the manager of the winery, and I've been looking for a chance to say hello. Yesterday I thought I saw you . . . and, well . . ." The man finally let go of his hand. "I was surprised, that's all, because don Santiago said you were leaving. And the sight of you yesterday . . . well, what can I say? It was a surprise!"

He took Manuel's hand again and shook it vigorously, grasping Manuel's forearm with his other hand.

Manuel was taken aback by the wine expert's enthusiasm. The man spoke again. "I'm really happy you're still in these parts," he said in farewell. He took a couple of steps toward his car and then looked back. "Excuse my asking, but do you plan to stay?"

Manuel appreciated frank talk. "For the time being." He smiled.

The winery manager wrinkled his brow, obviously trying to decide something. He shook his head as if dismissing a thought but immediately changed his mind. "Are you doing anything right now?"

"Nothing at all." Manuel smiled again.

"Then come with me. Oh, wait . . . what's your shoe size?" Once he had that information, the manager disappeared into the stables and came back with a pair of rubber boots and a bulky gray jacket equipped with a fur hood that would have suited an Eskimo. Manuel picked up the little dog and settled into the passenger seat.

Daniel drove several miles in the direction of Lalín, talking all the way. He turned off onto a road that rapidly became all twists and turns. The vehicle tilted alarmingly through the curves and turned so sharply that it left tracks visible in the steep sides of hills that fell away below them to the Miño River.

Looking down, Manuel could see hundreds of terraces trimmed with rough Galician stone that looked like a profusion of grayish steps up the steep hillsides. Grapevines grew on trellises that occupied the narrow flat space between one step and another. Handbuilt stone walls were visible as far as one could see. Eventually the vehicle descended to the riverbank and shuddered forward along a narrow road apparently hewn with great effort from the steep wall of the mountain. The SUV stopped in the private parking space of a house with its own pier. When they got out, Café immediately pattered ahead of them onto the floating jetty to which a motorboat was moored.

They boarded the boat and Daniel piloted the vessel downriver. Café stared forward undaunted from the prow, like a diminutive live figurehead.

"But where are we going?" asked Manuel. He waved toward the steep hillside. "I thought you said we were going to visit the vineyard."

"And that's where we're headed," Daniel responded, clearly amused.

"By boat?"

"Of course! This is the Ribeira Sacra, Manuel, the one that gives the name to the region's wines. Taking a boat along the river is the only way to get to many of the plantings along its steep banks."

"There's no other way?"

"You can reach our winery and warehouse by road." He pointed toward tracks so narrow they looked hardly wide enough to accommodate a single vehicle. "But some vineyards are accessible only via the river. Others are so steep that in harvest season the workers have to be lowered to them on ropes."

The wine expert smiled. "You won't believe it, but when I first came here I hated the place. I'd been working at a huge winery in the center of Spain, nothing like any of this." The memory of his own naïveté seemed to amuse him. "The old marquis hadn't been much interested in wine production, but three years ago Álvaro established the outlines of a colossal project that's become a model for many in the industry."

"Álvaro hired you?"

Daniel nodded, busy at the helm. "He had zero experience in the world of wine, but he was blessed with a natural genius for understanding this region, its needs, and its special qualities. From the very start he proclaimed it in the name of our winery, the brand name he chose to evoke his concept of heroic viticulture." He glanced at Manuel, seeking a complicity his guest couldn't offer.

Manuel avoided the implied question. "I'm sorry, Daniel, but I have no idea what you're talking about."

"Álvaro had a different idea. He wanted to pay homage to strength and dedication by recognizing the work of those heroic early vintners. Álvaro registered the trademark *Heroica* for our winery and all our products to honor countless generations of small producers."

Café abandoned the lookout's position and came back to them.

"Yes, Café," the enologist said, "we're almost there." He slowed the engine and allowed the boat to approach the bank under its own momentum. He shut it off and moored to a thick post on the shore. Water beat like tumultuous applause between the terrace wall and the side of the boat. A soft breeze rustled the leaves, the mooring cable creaked rhythmically against the post with each wave, and birds warbled.

Manuel pulled on the thick socks and rubber boots Daniel handed him. The terraced steps that rose above them looked like the jagged teeth of a broken zipper. Many of the terraces looked too narrow to accommodate a human foot.

The winery manager heaved himself across the lowest stone wall and held out a hand. Manuel picked up the dog, grabbed Daniel's hand, and scaled the wall, not without some difficulty.

The enologist turned to the slope. "Climb slowly, one foot at a time. If you sense yourself starting to lose your balance, just lean forward. It's impossible to fall."

Café was quickly ahead of them. Manuel discovered that the challenge was the unpredictable placement of the hewn blocks of stone bordering the terraces and the lunatic succession of different elevations that played tricks on his vision.

He advanced in fits and starts. The phone in his pocket began ringing, a sound completely alien to this setting. When it stopped, he heard Café barking above him to celebrate a successful climb.

He joined Daniel on a terrace more than three feet wide and turned to look down at the river. From this height the surging green energy of the trellised vines resembled the waves of an emerald ocean, their movement intensified by the breeze. Way down on the dark deep waters of the river, their boat bobbed and pulled at the mooring line.

They heard the hum of an engine and voices from below. A strange vessel emerged from the river canyon, carrying three girls who couldn't have been much out of their teens. They were laughing as they bailed water from the vessel with plastic pails. Their absurd vessel looked like a wooden fish crate.

"That boat is typical of the region. It has no keel," Daniel explained. "It's used to transport the grape harvest by river. The thing could flood completely, but it's as unsinkable as a pontoon jetty."

Mostly to reassure Manuel, he cupped his hands about his mouth to make a megaphone. "Hey, girls! Everything okay down there?"

They turned, looked up, and laughed even more merrily. "Everything under control!" one called, and assured him in Gallego that they'd be fine. They kept bailing.

The two men watched in silence as the young trio disappeared in the distance and took their cheerful noise with them.

Manuel's cell phone rang again, and this time he took it out in time to see that the call was from Nogueira.

"You can answer it if you like," Daniel said.

"Never mind. It's not important."

And it wasn't. He didn't want to listen to Nogueira in this place. Not here with girlish laughter still floating on the breeze, and where a dog that now belonged to him was celebrating their conquest of the slope. Manuel's recuperation from the extreme emotions of the previous day had entailed a confession, a bowl of soup, an abused dog, sailing a river, and scaling a steep canyon wall. He wasn't going to let anyone, not even Nogueira, spoil it now.

The cellar master had been leaning over from time to time to try the consistency of the grapes hidden under the leaves. He rolled a grape between his thumb and forefinger. "We start harvesting this weekend. I'd like it if you could come along, and I'm sure the others would appreciate it as well."

Manuel accepted a grape from the enologist. It was firm and fragrant, with a fresh green aroma that belied the warmth he felt as he held it in his palm. "The others?"

"The rest of the winery employees."

"Sure," Manuel responded without stopping to think. "Yes, I'll be glad to participate." Then he suddenly had misgivings. "Though I don't know if I'll be of any help. I've never been to a grape harvest."

Daniel was grinning openly. "You'll help, believe me. You'll be of great help to us."

They used the same technique to descend the mountainside. It was easier than Manuel had expected when he looked down. The sun still warmed the slopes, but the river was in shadow by the time they reached the boat. As soon as they set off upstream he felt chilled.

"Here's your explorer's jacket." Daniel had already put on one like it. "The days are still warm, but from late August on, the temperature drops quickly."

Manuel slipped on the jacket and zipped it up all the way. When he thrust his hands into the pockets, his jaw dropped in surprise. He didn't have to look to recognize the firmness of the petals or the creamy smoothness perched on the hard woody stalk. Daniel was piloting the craft, apparently unaware of his consternation. Manuel was quiet for the rest of the trip, studying the silent waters. He made an unsuccessful effort to see the place as sinister, but he simply became more profoundly aware of its beauty.

On the drive back from the jetty, Manuel looked at the enologist. He had no reason to distrust Daniel. They'd become acquainted only this afternoon. What could have motivated the cellar master to stuff gardenias into the pockets of the jacket he'd brought for Manuel?

Daniel let him off next to his BMW and set a time to pick him up the next morning. "Keep the boots and jacket. You'll need them tomorrow."

"But aren't they for here?" Manuel pointed toward the stables.

Daniel's expression was pained. "No. Those are Álvaro's. He always took them when he went out to the countryside." Something seemed to occur to him. "And by the way, he didn't find the dog along the highway."

"Excuse me?"

"Café . . . That's the official version. But actually Álvaro saw that little dog every time he drove to the winery. The poor thing was always tied up outside a shack by the road. No water or food. Belonged to a despicable old fellow who lived alone. One afternoon on our way back to the estate, Álvaro stopped and walked into the yard. I saw him yelling at the old geezer, then he took out his wallet and gave the man some money. I have no idea how much. Álvaro came back to the fence, untied the dog, and had to carry him to the car. I was sure the animal wouldn't survive the night. And yet," he added, turning to Manuel, "there the little fellow is."

Café sat turned away on the path, head lowered, watching them sidelong.

"Thanks for telling me," Manuel murmured.

Daniel lifted a hand in farewell and disappeared into the darkness.

Manuel stood there in the dark for a time, letting his eyes become accustomed to the low orange light cast by the lamps around the manor, far too dim to light the drive. As he took out his phone to use his flashlight app, he noticed he'd missed a total of five calls from Nogueira. He felt a malicious satisfaction at not responding.

He walked a few steps toward the stables and then realized Café wasn't following. He turned and used the flashlight to locate the dog squatting beside the car. He hunched down and held out his hand. The little animal nuzzled his palm. Manuel sighed, stood up, and opened the car door.

Café jumped up and almost made it inside. The scrabbling pooch wound up hanging from the passenger seat. Manuel gave him a little boost and watched him curl up there.

He looked one last time at the manor before he started the engine. On the second-floor terrace he saw the profile of a dark figure that remained motionless as he rolled out onto the drive on his way to the highway.

He drove through the night regretting his decision every minute of the way and asking himself what on earth he was going to do with this dog.

◈

Back at the inn he gratefully accepted the blanket, a pitcher of water, and a beefsteak the innkeeper's wife had saved for him, along with some scraps for the dog. Those looked almost as appetizing as his own meal. After dinner he laid out the blanket for Café, put the television on at reduced volume, and telephoned Nogueira.

"Goddamn! I've been trying to get hold of you all afternoon. Where are you hiding?"

Manuel pressed his lips together in spite and shook his head in annoyance. "I've been busy."

"Busy," the officer echoed with that tic that he found so annoying. "Were you at As Grileiras?"

"Yes, but before that I went to see Lucas. Father Lucas. I had lots of questions for him after you and I spoke yesterday."

"I knew it!" exclaimed a jubilant Nogueira. "And thanks for the initiative. I don't know what he told you, but your priest telephoned me after your visit. He gave me a detailed account of the night Fran died. What they discussed and what he thought about it. Not a word, of course, about what Fran said in his confession."

Suddenly alarmed, Manuel quickly said, "I didn't give him your name." He wondered if the priest had mentioned seeing someone go into the church and his guess that it was Álvaro.

"Never mind. It's not much more than what we knew already, but I have to admit that he's reinforced my doubts about a suicide. But it doesn't disprove the theory of a simple accident. Father Lucas is almost certain Fran wouldn't have been so stupid as to get mixed up with drugs again, not with all the pressure he was under. But one thing is sure: he's convinced Fran didn't kill himself, and I'm inclined to credit his theory, at least for now. All the more so, considering that someone else went into the church after the priest left."

Manuel held his breath as he waited for Nogueira's next sentence, all the while reproaching himself for caring what it might be. What did it matter to him if suspicion fell on Álvaro? Hadn't he been the first one to think that? Could he face the possibility that Álvaro might have been implicated in Fran's death? He resisted the thought, but after all, didn't he have every reason to draw that conclusion? Álvaro had hidden him away like some shameful secret. How important had it been to his husband to keep up appearances? Did Álvaro feel as strongly as his father had about keeping the family's reputation untarnished?

You know he didn't, his conscience admonished him.

And he heard again Elisa's declaration about Fran: *I knew him better than anyone else in the world.*

Hush! he ordered his conscience.

"Lucas said he wasn't close enough to see who it was," Nogueira continued. "But it still changes things. That person had to be the last one who saw Fran alive. But no one mentioned it when the boy turned up dead the next day." He sighed. "Oh, well—what did you get from As Grileiras?"

Manuel breathed normally again, feeling both relieved and guilty. "Santiago wasn't at all pleased to see me there. Even less so when I asked him about the money. He started to say I had no right to demand explanations."

"Ha!" exclaimed Nogueira with great satisfaction.

Manuel could hear the smile in the man's voice. That amused him; the policeman was pleased to hear of the humiliation of a Muñiz de Dávila. Manuel didn't disagree, and wondered why he felt the same way.

"Finally he admitted he'd asked for the money. Santiago says—and Griñán confirms—that over the last year they've been acquiring horses to build up the stables. He claims there was a sudden opportunity to buy a horse, and that's why he needed the cash."

"Three hundred thousand euros for a horse?"

"An English racehorse. A year ago Santiago bought another that cost them almost as much."

"Fuck!"

"But that deal was a fiasco, because the horse has a congenital defect and it'll never be able to race. For some reason he had no recourse, so the investment went right down the toilet. After that Álvaro refused to let his brother buy any horse unless it was first certified in writing by an expert. The vet and Griñán both told me so, so his story about Álvaro coming to look into the possible purchase of a horse is completely unbelievable. They both say Santiago knew Álvaro wouldn't agree. Without a certification from the vet he wouldn't even have considered it."

"So little brother was telling a lie."

"Well, he's not that reckless. He covered himself, since he admitted Álvaro would have refused him the money for that reason."

"But he already knew there'd be no money without the vet's approval. His brother wouldn't even bother to consider it. So why even ask? What sense would it make for Álvaro to come all this way just to confirm that?"

"That's what I was thinking," Manuel said.

"Anything else?"

"Let's see . . . there's the fact that Santiago doesn't like to see his wife working."

"He doesn't like it? Don't screw with me, the woman cultivates flowers! If she had to wipe dirty butts in a hospital the way my wife does . . ."

That was the first time Nogueira had breathed a word about anything to do with his family. Manuel made a mental note and suppressed a desire to challenge the man. *Yeah, it bothers you that your wife wipes butts in a hospital, but you go off to the whores. And you take off your wedding ring to try to hide your sin.* "And Catarina's assistant doesn't like the way her husband treats her. This morning the couple played out a nasty little scene. The guy could hardly contain himself."

"You think they're getting it on?"

He sighed at the man's simplistic view of the world. "I have no idea. The man obviously admires her, but I doubt it's like that." He remembered Vicente's anguished tone as he spoke of her at the greenhouse. "Nogueira, I was going to say that maybe today's not—"

"Right, that's exactly why I was trying to contact you. We can't get together today."

Manuel felt a childish disappointment. He'd so wanted to cancel on the man that he'd mentally rehearsed his refusal to play sidekick. He'd expected to rouse the lieutenant's ire.

"You remember I said I'd get someone to bring us Álvaro's car from the depot? Ophelia and I looked it over, and now we're going through the calls on his phone."

"I thought we'd already gotten everything from the call history."

For a moment Nogueira said nothing. When he did speak it was with the reluctant tone of someone giving out confidential information. "Listen. Almost everyone has a cell phone, but almost nobody understands what the thing really does. Álvaro's phone is the latest generation. Like the others, it records the numbers called, incoming calls, and duration of connections. It also has an app that records its exact location for each connection. In addition, and this is more complicated, we're trying to identify the owners of the numbers he called and those who called him."

"Would that help?"

"We're just getting started. But we've finished with the car and that's why I really needed to speak to you."

Manuel waited for it.

"Ophelia says she remembers that when she examined the body at the accident site that night, the car had a GPS navigator. We haven't located it."

"Right—Álvaro had a portable GPS. He'd had it for years. He could have ordered an onboard system when we bought the car, but he preferred the old one. He said it had all his usual routes recorded and it was a hundred percent reliable."

"Do tell." The policeman clicked his tongue in displeasure. "I don't know if you're aware of it, but all onboard GPS systems these days come already loaded with a full set of maps and addresses; if they're deleted or if you do a factory reset, the older routes can be recovered from memory."

"So what?"

"Sometimes individuals who don't want to be tracked for some reason prefer a portable GPS they can remove or destroy without having to pull it out of the dashboard."

"There's another possibility."

This time it was Nogueira's turn to wait for it.

"Maybe someone stole it. A traffic accident where a lone driver dies, a portable GPS no one's paying attention to and nobody would ever miss . . ."

Nogueira's voice was sharp. "I don't know what you're trying to imply, but cops are called in to deal with thousands of accidents in this country every year, and we in the police make sure that every one of us is above reproach. We put our lives on the line to help others, and all too often we're the losers. I personally guarantee the absolute integrity of every police officer in the region. The *Guardia Civil* doesn't shelter thieves."

"I'm only saying what might have happened."

"Not possible. But what certainly *may be* possible is that it might have been stored in another box that they forgot to give you. Go and ask for it. We need to know where he was and where he was headed when he died. The GPS may have that information."

"I'll phone tomorrow."

"I'll pick you up late tomorrow night, around midnight. The hooker we have to interview is on the job tomorrow evening."

Manuel wanted to protest. He'd sworn to himself the previous night he wouldn't go back there for anything in the world, but today he knew he couldn't avoid it. He had to. Not really to prove Nogueira wrong, but because the man's dedication to the truth was greater than his. Despite their differences. Over the course of the day, his insistence that the priest had to tell him everything had become a hope that Lucas hadn't shared everything with Nogueira. That thought and his guilt over withholding information made him feel he had to follow Nogueira's game plan.

He said goodbye and ended the call.

He needed to escape this reality, and he found a way. He put pen to paper for an uninterrupted four hours. The dog sat motionless at his feet. Manuel occasionally looked down and thought that perhaps it hadn't been such a bad idea after all to yield to the impulse to bring the creature back with him.

❧

OF EVERYTHING HE REFUSED

His shoulders sagged. For a moment it seemed his feelings and desires counted for nothing; he was trapped by circumstances; a terrifying, inexplicable power was smashing reality into his face. Sheer inertia had sent him hurtling toward the real world, and now some mindless force was impelling him in a random direction chosen by an indifferent universe.

❧

It was almost 2:00 a.m. when he gave in to the dog's continual yawns, stopped writing, put on his heavy jacket again, and took Café outside to do his business. Back in the room he carefully removed the contents from the jacket pockets and put them into the desk drawer. He stood and regarded the gardenias as if the simple act of examining them might unravel the secret of their unexpected appearance. He closed the drawer very slowly, his eyes on the flowers until the drawer clicked shut. He suddenly remembered the photo he'd been carrying all day and fished in his pocket for it. The bent corners again snagged the satin lining of the jacket. The young man's confident gaze hypnotized him. He spent several minutes contemplating it, studying the boys' expressions, their body language, the frank camaraderie of the older boys that shut Santiago out, the younger one's possessive clutch, and the protagonist—that young man who had the clean, spirited, proud look of a prince in a fairy tale.

He opened the drawer to deposit the photo, but at the sight of those flowers he decided to stow it in his jacket pocket instead. He turned out the lights and went to bed, leaving the television on but with the sound off. He wondered briefly if the flickering images would bother the dog and then felt stupid for posing the question to himself. Café nestled watchful on the blanket, head down between his little legs. Manuel's heart went out to the dog, much to his own surprise. He was sorry for Café but wasn't so sure he liked this newfound pet. The dog's watchful liquid gaze made him uneasy. He wasn't used to owning an animal, and he was sure this animal knew it.

This was an unexpected first for him. Many children had pets, but the circumstances of his own childhood hadn't permitted that. And later he'd never felt the urge to take on the responsibility for a dumb animal that he saw others willingly assume. He guessed he liked animals, but in more or less the same way he liked violins, for example, or Botero's sculptures. He had no particular interest in acquiring them. He glanced at the lit television screen and decided to leave it on.

As soon as he closed his eyes he felt something spring onto the mattress. He sat bolt upright and looked at Café. The animal stood on the foot of the bed. Man and dog remained there unmoving, studying one another, posing the question and waiting for the answer.

"Well, I had to pay extra to keep you here, so I guess you're entitled to a bed."

The dog curled up at his feet. Manuel lay back with a smile. A minute later he took the remote and clicked off the television.

That was the first night since his arrival in Galicia that he didn't dream of the young boy in tears.

ABOUT A MAN'S WORK

Heroica was constructed as a long tumble down a steep slope. A visitor arriving from the highway would see it was very well tended, but the first impression was of a little residential folly dreamed up by an ambitious architect, a place that might be the perfect winter hideaway for a reclusive writer. It was, in fact, an industrial operation.

A team of twenty men or more was waiting on the steps and along a narrow gallery. They turned when they heard Daniel arriving with Manuel.

"Bos días," Daniel greeted them in Gallego dialect as he got out of the car.

"Today don Manuel will be accompanying us to the vineyards," the cellar master told the assembly. The men responded with nods and gestures of welcome. Manuel returned the courtesy.

"Let's get going while I give Manuel a tour of the operation here," the enologist announced briskly. "Then he and I'll go down with a group to the *muras* of the *ribeira* so the boss can see how we work."

After passing through vast rooms with tanks and enigmatic equipment, they climbed to a wide exterior balcony overlooking the gorge. The view from there gave one the sensation of hanging in the void. Manuel saw the workmen descending the steep slope in the tentative rays of a morning sun.

In a corner of the balcony stood a display of bottles and labels. Manuel picked up a bottle with a stark white background interrupted only by the proud sweep of silver letters in Álvaro's distinctive handwriting proclaiming *Heroica*.

They left the winery and went toward the river, passing the first terraces. Daniel greeted by name each of the half-dozen workmen. He ushered Manuel to a terrace where no one was yet at work and demonstrated how the grapes were harvested. "I'm sure you'll enjoy the work. It's the most primitive and yet the most human task; especially when you think that humans were gatherers before they were planters, fruit eaters before they were meat eaters."

Manuel accepted the proffered small sickle and made a couple of awkward attempts.

Daniel had no complaints. "Don't worry. It takes practice to judge exactly how firmly you have to grasp the bunch without crushing the fruit, but other than that you don't look at all like a first-time harvester."

Manuel worked in silence at a distance from the others, concentrating on the task. The scent of the grapes became more intense as they warmed in the morning sun. He was aware of the ripe aroma of old vines, earth and granite, and fragrant herbs that grew along the edges of the terraces. The morning hours slipped away in silence.

"Hey, señor marquis!"

Manuel turned in surprise and looked uphill toward a terrace where a rural workman was holding up a wineskin. The man waved the leather pouch. "Want some wine?"

Manuel smiled and accepted. He stepped to the edge of the terrace and reached up for the wineskin. "I'm not a marquis." He grinned as he took it in hand.

The man shrugged as if in disbelief.

The wine had a strong bouquet, probably accentuated by the flavors accumulated over time in the leather wineskin. Cool and fragrant, it left an almost perfect acid tang in his mouth.

At lunchtime the workers shared fragrant chunks of brown bread and rough-cut pieces of cheese.

While they were eating, Manuel saw one of those curious floating contraptions go by on the river. Daniel gave him a wink and turned to one of the oldest workers.

"Abu, yesterday we were up on the Godello *muras* and saw your daughters in one of their floating crates. They were bailing like mad, and Manuel thought they were going to sink." He was greatly amused.

Manuel looked up in surprise.

"Eso no hunde, home!" Abu exclaimed. The old fellow turned to share the joke with the others. He reiterated, "That thing won't sink, man! If the folks on the *Titanic*'d had one of them things, they'd still be afloat out there!"

The men laughed.

Manuel smiled. "So those were your daughters?"

"They were and they still are," Abu replied with the assertive scornful tone Manuel was beginning to recognize as typical of the region. "And for sure they'll be coming back soon enough. They're harvesting our plot."

"So you have your own grapes as well?"

"Everybody around here has grapes in Ribeira Sacra, even if just on a tiny little scrap of land. The work's harder than it looks. My family's grapes are nothing like *Heroica* grapes. It's just a *pedaciño pequeno,* a tiny bit of land, on a really steep slope. But it's enough for my daughters to support themselves. At least they won't have to leave the way others have."

As the day wore on, the heat of the burning sun high overhead was reflected by the river in dazzling optical illusions. They kept filling the crates and toting them to the edges of the terraces. After that they formed a human chain to pass the crates down to the stone wall at water's edge to be stacked on the strange floating container boat.

At about five in the afternoon the enologist called an end to the day's work. The men began to climb the slope, reinvigorated by the prospect of a hearty meal.

Manuel picked up Café and began climbing behind Abu. Though at least twenty years older than Manuel, the fellow scrambled deftly up the incline. Once at the crest, Manuel put the dog down and leaned over to catch his breath.

"You're doing a fine job," Abu told him, and then followed Café toward the picnic area.

The boisterous gathering of thirty people at the big table was a celebration. Baked potatoes and green salad awaited them on the table, quickly supplemented by trays loaded with meat the warehouse team had grilled over fires fed with roots from their own grapevines. Wine was poured freely into glasses that clinked in toasts to the new harvest.

They ate without ceremony or much talk. There was no dessert; instead fragrant pot-boiled coffee was brought to the table.

Some of the men got up to stretch their legs. A foreman glanced at Daniel, received an encouraging nod, and spoke to Manuel. "Look here, señor marquis . . ."

Manuel raised a hand. "Manuel. Please."

"Okay, then, don Manuel." This was plainly costing him some effort. "I know Daniel gave you a tour, and señor Griñán has lots of information." The fellow chose his words with great care. "I think you've had a bit of a look at the way we work, and how important every single plant is, every square inch of earth."

Manuel nodded gravely and heard the man settle into his exposition.

"Well, right now the winery is working flat out, but things aren't the same in winter. Recently we've been studying the possibilities of purchasing the vineyard next door. Along with the vines there's a house with more than two acres of land that's never been planted."

The man picked up a wine cork from the table and began fidgeting with it as if he were facing invisible barriers. He was getting to the hard part.

"Don Álvaro told us he'd decided to buy it, but then he had his accident, and the owner says she knows nothing about it. So maybe he didn't have the time to give instructions to Griñán, and . . . well . . . the thing is, it would mean more work for us building the terraces, and the plantings would give all of us work for the whole winter. We could renovate the house, too, and, well . . . we were wondering if you plan to proceed with the project . . . or not."

The man fell silent and seemed to be holding his breath.

Everyone was watching the new owner.

Manuel picked up his coffee to buy himself some time. It was already cold, but he took a sip anyway. "Well," he said, "I wasn't aware of any of this. I'm afraid Griñán didn't mention it . . ."

"But do you think it could be done?" asked someone in the crowd.

Manuel felt cornered. The eyes, gestures, and expectant physical posture of these men were begging for reassurance he couldn't provide.

The foreman spoke up. "The owner said another producer might be interested. We can't let him get the jump on us, at least not here along our stretch of the river."

Daniel joined in. "I accompanied Álvaro for the discussions. Everything indicated that the deal was about to be struck. I'm sure of it."

"I don't know when I'll be able to speak with Griñán." Manuel knew his reply was evasive.

But the men reacted as if he'd given them the answer they were hoping for. The foreman took his hand, looked him straight in the eye, and thanked him. The workers rose to leave but each of them stepped forward to shake his hand.

Daniel held him back for a moment as the others departed. "You know, I remember that while the two of us were talking with the owner, Álvaro was fidgeting with his cell phone as if he were expecting a call. And his phone did ring when we were on our way out afterward. He stepped away, so I didn't hear much."

"What time was that?"

"Our appointment with the woman was for four and didn't last long, maybe twenty minutes." He shrugged. "Look, I know it probably doesn't mean anything, but I did overhear Álvaro say, 'Don't you try to threaten me.'"

THE MARQUIS

The men went to their cars, and Manuel was grateful for Daniel's offer of a ride home. In the Nissan it was all Manuel could do to hide his pain until they'd gotten past the last of the workers and clear of the winery grounds. After that he grimaced. "Good God, my whole body aches!"

Daniel chuckled and leaned over to open the glove compartment. "There's ibuprofen in there and a bottle of water in the door."

Manuel wasn't about to complain. He popped a tablet out of the blister pack and washed it down.

"Take two. You can have the rest. You'll need them tomorrow morning. *El Abu*'s right. The work's harder than it looks."

"It looks plenty hard already." Manuel was in a mood. "Tell me, Daniel. Do you refer to me as 'the marquis'?"

"No need to be offended." He smiled. "It's a compliment. The men around here have worked for the marquis's family for centuries, and unlike folks like you, they've never seen it as serfdom. They consider it part of a social contract. The old marquis, Álvaro's father, wasn't at all interested in wine production, and he didn't take it seriously even when the official denomination was established in 1996. He kept the winery running because everybody else did. The business wasn't very profitable, but it didn't cost much—the wages of a few day workers, that was all. The estate always has plenty of those. Álvaro took over and everything changed. How can I explain it? Two thousand years of tradition; the folks here have kept at it out of pure pride and their love of the land. Suddenly someone arrives and he appreciates what you're doing and the nobility of it, recognizes who you are, and endorses all of that. And not just that. He fixes it so you can earn a living doing what you love. That makes him very important to you."

Manuel listened but said nothing.

"Yesterday during our tour you said you didn't know if you were going to be of much help. I said you would be. And indeed you were. Your presence here today was very important to these men. When Álvaro died, our world almost collapsed. We knew that the new marquis, just like his father, doesn't give a damn about our wine. He'll keep the operation going, of course; the aristocratic class finds it cool and chic to own vineyards. It's a mark of distinction for a family to have its own wine. But that's not what we're talking about. Álvaro raised the profile of this winery, made it not only visible but prominent, and he came to the vineyards just as you did today. That gives those men a promise of continuity, a belief in the future for the project Álvaro initiated. It gives them hope for their own lives and aspirations."

Manuel listened carefully and pondered Daniel's words but still said nothing. He inspected his own hands. They were chafed, sunburned, and itchy, sensations that on the whole weren't entirely disagreeable. He sympathized with the enologist's view. Indeed, harvesting grapes did have that odd mixture of the primitive and the civilized that brings a man to peace with himself. More important to him was the fact that laboring in the vineyards that day had offered him subtle reassurance of possible reconciliation with the Álvaro he'd thought he knew. Café had offered a first glimpse; discovering the nature and extent of *Heroica* provided another. The quiet pride in the winery operations, the hard challenges of tending the earth, the name of the wine, the label with its confident, passionate sweep of the letters; all those, taken together, spoke to him of Álvaro, the man he admired, and reminded him of everything that had set Álvaro apart, ennobled him, and won Manuel's heart.

But right now Manuel was in no position to offer these men hope. One long day in the sunshine along the riverbank couldn't compensate for the fact that he was an outsider. His own proper place was very far away.

"I'm afraid my presence here may have misled you all . . ." He sighed. "I'm not going to go into details, but this is all new to me. A week ago I had no idea this world existed. I don't know when, but sooner or later I'll have to go back to my own home and life."

As he said that, he remembered the strange light invading his living room and breaking his fragile hold on reality, their empty bedroom, the photo of the two of them on the dresser, Álvaro's clothes in the closet like garments discarded before an execution, and the blinking cursor waiting, perhaps forever, for him to finish the sentence . . . And he realized he didn't want to go back. Or live in that place anymore. He had no home. He shook his head at those thoughts.

His movement must have looked like a repudiation of the cellar master's comments. Daniel didn't say another word for the rest of the trip.

※

Manuel helped Café up onto the bed and stretched out beside him. The next thing he heard was a strident hectoring noise that shook him from the profound sleep that had overcome him as soon as his head touched the pillow.

The golden late afternoon light that had illuminated the exterior upon his arrival was gone, and the only source of light was a streetlight near the window. He fumbled about the bedside table, trying to find his cell phone and stop its alarm. He punched the phone, but the ringing continued, unabated. At last he finally realized that an old-fashioned telephone on the battered desk was ringing. This was the first time he'd noticed it. He staggered to the phone, confused and disoriented and wondering what time it was, what day this was. He lifted the receiver and put it to his ear.

"Señor Ortigosa, you have a visitor waiting for you in the bar."

He hung up and switched on the desk lamp. He was amazed to see it was past midnight. He splashed his face with water that smelled of drainpipes. He was sluggish and out of sorts, as if after a sleep of twenty hours or twenty minutes he'd awakened on some different planet with a denser, heavier atmosphere. The only clear sensations were the aches of his suffering muscles. Slowly he returned to this painful existence; his legs burned and his back muscles were on fire. He ignored the cracked and clouded drinking glass above the bathroom sink, cupped his hands for water, and washed down another two ibuprofen tablets.

Café stood alert next to the door. Manuel looked down at the dog, doubtful for a few moments, but he recognized the creature's stance as very like the haughty, patronizing attitude of the Muñiz de Dávila family.

"Why not?" he said. He switched off the light.

❧

He suspected that Nogueira had polished off a couple of plates of the inn's greasy bar snacks while waiting for him. Through the window he saw the man smoking with his characteristic concentration, dragging deep to extract some vital but unavailing essence.

"Jesus, you look like hell! What have you been doing?" That was all the greeting the officer gave him.

"Harvesting grapes along the Ribeira Sacra."

The man said nothing, but his lips twitched behind that big mustache, and he nodded slowly with a surprised expression. Was he in fact impressed?

Nogueira tossed his cigarette butt into the sand-filled receptacle. "Let's go." He walked toward the almost empty parking lot.

"Aren't you going to tell me where the calls came from?"

"Later will be better," Nogueira said, dismissing his request. "Let's get going. The girl will be busy later tonight, and getting to her'll be complicated." He saw the dog trailing after them. "What the hell is that?"

"'That' is my dog," Manuel replied with studied indifference. "The name is Café, and he's with me."

"Definitely not in *my* car."

Manuel stopped and looked him up and down. "I was planning to take mine so you could stay afterward. If you want."

He saw Nogueira put the hand with the wedding ring behind his back. "I already told you we'd discuss the phone calls afterward."

"Okay." Manuel clicked the remote to unlock the car, swung the rear door open, and lifted Café into the backseat.

Nogueira hesitated for a moment, surveying the parking lot.

"And please drive. As a favor to me. I can hardly lift a finger." Manuel felt the leaden weight of his legs.

That seemed to pacify Nogueira, who walked decisively around the car to the driver's side and got in. "Key?"

"There is no key. It starts automatically." Manuel showed him the button, pushed it, and the engine came to life.

Nogueira watched without comment as the side mirrors swung out. The BMW's electronic systems registered the reduced light, turned on the headlights, and adjusted them. The policeman said nothing, but Manuel saw he was enjoying this. The loving care with which the lieutenant treated his own car showed why he was as pleased as punch to be riding in the latest model. Nogueira peered into the rearview mirror. "Where'd you get that thing?" he asked, plainly referring to Café.

Manuel smiled, looking forward to astonishing Nogueira. "From As Grileiras. This was Álvaro's dog. Apparently he picked it up as a stray." He offered the simple version. Though the notion of a rescue was more heroic, he assumed Nogueira would sneer at such charity.

Nogueira raised an eyebrow, baffled, and peered again into the rearview mirror even though the dog was invisible in the gathering darkness. "A dog like that at As Grileiras?"

"For the last year, more or less. He found the dog in a terrible shape along the road to the winery, took it to the estate, and had the vet take care of it. Santiago can't stand the sight of it."

"Well, for once I have to agree with the fancy-pants marquis. That's the ugliest fucking little dog in the whole damn world."

"Nogueira!"

The lieutenant looked at him with a candid grin that made him look twenty years younger. "Oh, give me a break, writer man. You gotta admit the dog is butt ugly."

Manuel turned to look. Café was perched stiffly on the backseat as if participating in the conversation. His rough fur bristled with static electricity. One ear hung limp, and a fang jutted up from his crooked jaw. Manuel exchanged glances with Nogueira and grinned, conceding the point.

❧

The jammed parking lot at the roadhouse was lit by the hectic pink and blue neon of the bar sign. They drove in and had to park at the far end. Nogueira turned off the engine. His hands ran down along the steering wheel in a gesture that was practically a caress. "Wonderful vehicle, señor. It must have cost you a fortune."

"I sold a lot of books last year." Manuel smiled but anticipated a sarcastic reply. He didn't get one.

"You have every reason to be pleased." Nogueira ran his fingertips along the dashboard.

Spurred by the officer's good mood, Manuel decided to chance it. "Nogueira, I don't know if this makes sense to you, but the thought of Álvaro in that place is really painful to me."

"Want to wait here?"

"If you don't mind."

Nogueira made no comment. He opened the door, got out, and walked to the entrance. From the car Manuel saw Nogueira's fake leather jacket change colors with the neon as he crossed the parking lot.

Manuel helped Café to the front seat and looked for music on the radio. He settled down to wait, remembering all too well Daniel's friendly warning that he'd ache all over the next day.

A sharp rap on the window startled him. Out in the electric blur of the neon he saw a face he recognized as that of the prostitute they'd called Baby. He started to get out, but she blocked the door and signaled to him to lower the window.

"Hey!" Her hoarse voice disappointed him; perhaps she had a touch of laryngitis.

He didn't know what she wanted.

She hunched down by the car to peer in and spoke before he could find anything to say. "You know who I am?"

"Yes."

"I got something to tell you, and I can't do it inside there."

He saw she was wearing only a thin satin robe over her underwear.

"Get into the car. You'll freeze out there."

"No, if you open the door, the Mammoth over there," she said, jabbing a thumb toward the albino cowboy on guard at the door, "is going to notice the light. He'll come snooping. Anyhow, this is against the rules. The boss doesn't want us out in the parking lot. No freelancing allowed."

Manuel nodded to indicate he understood. He used the moment to get a close look at her. She really was beautiful: those big saucy eyes studying him to evaluate his age, his clothing, his importance; that full mouth, looking so innocent, with pink lips like those of a child, no lipstick required. Her soft dark mane of hair, natural in color, cascaded down either side of her face. Its perfect oval reminded him with startling clarity of the beautiful sergeant who'd forced her way into his home to deliver news of catastrophe. Perhaps that was a sign, he thought, a signal to warn him that news from someone this beautiful would be equally disastrous. If so, it would be reason enough to hate such beauty.

He made no effort to hide his distrust. "What do you want?"

"We never did it!" she blurted.

"What?" He was confused.

"Your boyfriend and I never did nothing."

Manuel's mouth worked but nothing came out.

"Double negative," the girl said, grinning at a joke that for the moment only she was capable of understanding. "Well, yeah, sure we did something. We talked. What I mean is, we never fucked."

Manuel still found nothing to say.

"The brother's different, he's a regular. Comes by a lot, and your boyfriend came with him."

"He was my husband," Manuel managed to say in a choked voice.

She kept talking; he was sure she hadn't heard him. "The first time don Santiago was really drunk and really insisted he pick one of the girls. He chose me, but when we got to the room he said he'd come upstairs to avoid explaining something to his brother. Said he was faithful to his love and we weren't gonna do nothing. Don Santiago already gave me the money, but your guy paid me some more and made me promise not to tell. Hey, I don't care, you know? And I wouldn't have minded with him anyhow, he was really good-looking. But when I saw you the other night I realized it wasn't just on principle." She smiled with a little tilt of the head. "He visited a couple more times, maybe three, max, and it was always like that. We went upstairs, talked a while, he paid me extra, and that was it. The other night I saw you and Nogueira, and today the boss told Mili and me you wanted to ask about his visits. I can't admit it in front of the boss. She says we always have to provide the goods, 'cause there's some of 'em who ask for their money back afterwards. That wasn't the deal. But she'd give me hell if she knew I got paid double, so . . ."

She reached up with a slim hand and grabbed the car door to steady herself. Her artificial nails were jet black.

"Why are you telling me this?"

She gave him a beautifully bewitching smile, surprisingly melancholy for a girl of her tender age. "There's not many decent johns around here, and your guy was one. You deserve to know."

Manuel nodded gratefully.

"I gotta go back. They're probably already asking where I am. I don't smoke, so I don't have that excuse." She opened her eyes wide in consternation. "I don't take drugs or any of that stuff either. I try to live a healthy life . . . and save my pay . . ." She stood there fixing him with her gaze but saying nothing more.

"Oh!" His aching muscles protested as he twisted in his seat to fish his wallet out from the back pocket of his jeans.

He took out fifty euros, thought about it, then added another fifty. She nipped them through the window with the deft assurance of a Las Vegas croupier.

"All the best, buddy," she said. "That's a good-looking dog you got!" She crouched, made her way along the parked cars, and disappeared from sight.

Manuel raised the window and looked at the mutt. "Hear that, Café? For a hundred euros anybody can be good-looking!"

The dog's tail wagged, but as usual the pooch wouldn't look directly at him. It was the same attitude Manuel had, pretending that none of this was of any importance.

The pain of unknowing cripples you.

That agony had pierced him like an incessant drill ever since the beautiful sergeant informed him of Álvaro's death. The evidence of betrayal and a scarcely hidden derision in the voices of Nogueira and Santiago had poured salt on his wounds. Acid shame had burned its way through his guts in a cruel, unrelenting advance of unbearable humiliation that annihilated his very essence. He'd been determined to ignore it, to flee from this corrosive situation, and to walk away with his head held high. He'd shouted in his defense that all of this was foreign to him; it had nothing to do with his life. Manuel, so offended by Álvaro's deliberate deceptions, had also demanded others not reveal the truth. He also had lied.

He'd invented those pretexts to persuade himself he could flee from untruths, but what he was really trying to escape was reality. He'd refused to accept the warning signs that the inexorable corrosive process was consuming his guts and would eventually overwhelm him. And later he'd set himself this impossible investigation as a refuge from which to continue the struggle. He'd embraced the fiction that some supernatural force was driving him, that some irresistible inertia was impelling him to take on this task.

By fooling himself he'd committed the greatest sin one can commit against oneself. He'd violated moral principles instilled in childhood, ideals of honor and dignity he'd held sacrosanct. He'd lied to the only being in this world entitled to know the truth: himself.

Uncertainty is caustic.

Like an idiot he'd thought he could live with the weight of the unresolved dilemma. He'd assumed it wouldn't affect him. He'd thought he could get on with his life uncrippled by despair and unhurt by the fear of not having been loved. And suddenly a beaten dog, a steep slope of vineyard, and a baby-faced prostitute had offered antidotes for his affliction, had become the balm to counteract the pain. He was still faced with the specter of the unknown Álvaro: the man who bought Café from a tormentor before the brutal old man could beat it to death or starve it, the man who worked the vineyard side by side with his rural employees, the man who paid the prostitute so he wouldn't have to go to bed with her. Those Álvaros were as alien to him as the Marquis of Santo Tomé, the man with a second cell phone and no wedding ring. A vast number of questions called for answers, and perhaps now, for the first time, he wanted those explanations. Manuel had the impression that Café, the vineyards along the river, and the prostitute were discordant notes, exhibits for the defense that described another reality, one he hadn't wanted to contemplate, blinded as he was by the shame and humiliation of betrayal. He had just begun to acknowledge that reality with the admission the girl hadn't even heard: *He was my husband.*

He reached out to Café and held his hand still until the dog sidled close enough for him to brush his fingertips over its coat. He caressed the dog and saw the distrust gradually subside. The animal responded to Manuel's affection and closed those funny little eyes for the first time.

"If only I could," he whispered. Café opened his eyes. "Close my eyes, I mean, Café. If only I could shut my eyes."

He saw Nogueira coming across the lot and checked his watch: not more than twenty minutes had passed. Hardly time enough for a drink. Manuel had returned the dog to the backseat by the time the policeman opened the door and admitted the night chill along with the sickly sweet stink of the roadhouse.

"Okay, that's taken care of. I talked with the girl." He settled himself into the driver's seat, gripped the wheel as if about to depart, but didn't turn on the engine. His wedding ring remained plainly in sight on his finger. "She confirms what our little Nieves told us yesterday. Santiago visits a couple of times a month and usually takes her upstairs. What I found particularly interesting is what she told me about the man's routine. It's a bit out of the ordinary."

Manuel's eyebrows rose. "So there's a standard operating procedure?"

"It's like this," Nogueira explained patiently. "A guy comes here with one thing in mind. That's obvious, but most of them enjoy the routine of coming in, taking a seat at the bar, ordering something, checking out the girls and offering one a drink, imitating the usual pickup routine. Except that here you know you can pick up any of them you want."

"A hundred euros makes anyone good-looking," Manuel commented, with a backward look at Café.

"Doesn't have to cost nearly that much. The thing is, Santiago goes about it in exactly the reverse order. He gets here, he grabs her by the arm, they go upstairs; it's only afterward he treats himself to a quiet drink."

"So he's in a hurry when he gets here."

"Right. Which makes me think that maybe he's trying to beat the clock."

"You think he takes a little blue pill to make sure he can perform?"

"The girl says that he even phones in advance to make sure she'll be available. But I think that if it was just a matter of the little blue pill, the guy would be more at ease."

Manuel's expression betrayed his puzzlement.

"Viagra kicks in after thirty minutes to an hour and lasts between three and six hours. That doesn't mean the guy is going to have a hard-on for six hours, but when sexually stimulated he'll have no problem getting it up."

"You sound like an expert."

Nogueira shrugged and jutted out his chin. "So what are you insinuating? You think I need that shit? I don't. My equipment's in great shape."

"I didn't say that," Manuel replied in his defense, although with a mocking little half smile like that he'd seen earlier on the officer's face. "I recognize the fact that you know a lot about the subject."

"What the hell! I know a lot about a lot of things, but that's because I do my work. I read, I study, I'm an investigator. You got that?"

Manuel nodded but the smile remained on his face. "Loud and clear, good buddy."

"What I'm saying is that it's strange our little marquis is always in such a hurry. And by the way, the girl says he wasn't able to finish up a couple of times. That really pissed him off. He blamed her, and she says it got pretty brutal."

Manuel recalled what he'd seen in Santiago's face during their heated discussion: the cruel rictus of the mouth, the eyes narrowed in contempt, the angry stride, and the way he'd stopped for an instant by his wife to say something that reduced her to tears.

"Did he hit her?"

"She's not saying that. He's a good client, and she doesn't want to risk losing him. But he can get really shitty sometimes, and that's exactly what suggests to me he's not taking the love pill."

Manuel nodded. Nogueira continued with his theory. "Maybe he's ashamed of going to the doctor about his problem. That would mean undergoing tests to confirm your heart is up to it, that the problem isn't physical—something, say, like a blockage in his . . . well, you know. And checking to see that the guy's not allergic, either to the medication or its principal ingredient. More than one pill popper has given himself a heart attack or started to see the world in a blue haze. But lots of times men reluctant to confess their problems to a doctor turn to a stimulant. Cocaine, for example. No heart-to-heart with your physician required for that. The result is immediate, but the effects aren't consistent, and the duration is shorter, especially for a habitual user."

"Did you ask the girl?"

"Of course, but I knew what she was going to say. Our little Nieves has taught them their lessons well. Never in a million years would they admit anyone was taking drugs in there. They know they're talking with a cop, and for them, no matter how friendly we act, a dog is still a dog. And then I wasn't able to locate the other girl. She must be busy."

"She was here with me."

Nogueira's expression showed his surprise.

"She suddenly popped up next to the car and made me promise not to tell her boss. So I hope you'll be just as discreet. Otherwise she'll be in big trouble."

"Sure. Don't ever think I'm so close to little Nieves that I'd burn a source." He was clearly offended.

"I'm not thinking anything. I'm just telling you."

Nogueira nodded.

"She says Álvaro went upstairs with her when Santiago absolutely insisted on it. A couple of times. But all they did was talk. Álvaro paid her double not to say anything. But that doesn't mean her boss knew."

Nogueira nodded slowly, his hands tight on the wheel. He said nothing.

Manuel gave him a suspicious look. "You don't look too surprised. Funny, I'd swear that just a couple of days ago you were trying to make me think Álvaro was a regular with the prostitutes."

Nogueira started the engine, pulled out, and left the neon lights behind. The dim light of the car interior illuminated his face enough for Manuel to make out the closed expression behind the lieutenant's mustache. The policeman drove for a while in silence, apparently concentrating on the unlit road and on avoiding the blinding headlights of the cars coming the other way.

Manuel wasn't worried. He was starting to get used to Nogueira's repressed hostility and the signs that the man held information close until he found it opportune to fire it like a spread of close-counted torpedoes directed at a target's waterline. And besides, even though he was keeping something back, he drove with the delight of a child with a brand-new toy. Manuel noticed that they'd gone past the turnoff to the inn, and he assumed that the man was prolonging the drive for the sheer pleasure of it. He was surprised when a few miles farther along, the lieutenant pulled up before a bar busy with a Saturday-night crowd of locals and suggested they have a drink.

The average age inside was over forty. There were many couples, although there were also groups of single women. The size and the elegance of the glasses, as well as the music, reminded him strongly of the 1980s, and the volume was kept low enough to permit conversations. Manuel estimated that they were about a dozen miles north of As Grileiras in a recognizably heterosexual setting, far enough from the estate to minimize the risk that someone might see them as something other than a couple of middle-aged men sharing a drink in a bar any Saturday night.

Manuel noticed a secluded area in the back that would probably be good for conversation, but he wasn't surprised when Nogueira opted for the uncomfortable metal barstools and ordered a couple of gin and tonics. The waitress dropped bright-colored berries into them. Manuel could hardly keep from laughing at the sight of Nogueira pulling out the cocktail straws and planting both elbows as he hunched over the bar, for all the world the picture of an old-fashioned gigolo.

"West End Girls" by the Pet Shop Boys came on the sound system. Manuel took a swallow of his drink. It was bitter and slightly perfumed. *Good Lord, this is like summer camp.* "Are you going to tell me why we're here?"

Nogueira turned with an innocent expression. "You got anything better to do? It's Saturday night, we're having a drink and a conversation like . . ."

"Like a couple of friends?"

Nogueira's face tightened. Then he sighed and seemed somewhat distressed. "I already told you we have to talk about the phone calls."

"Go ahead and talk." Manuel didn't drop his slightly condescending tone of infinite patience.

Nogueira settled on the uncomfortable barstool looking straight ahead. He partly covered his face with one hand in an attempt to hide the fact they were discussing something sensitive. He spoke in a low voice. "I already said that the most interesting thing was to establish not only who called him and who he talked to, but also the origin of the calls."

Manuel took another swallow of his gin and tonic. This time it didn't taste so bad.

"First of all I have to say that since I'm not on active duty anymore, and because the case is closed, my resources are limited. But we've identified quite a few numbers, and we're working on the rest. He got calls from Griñán and Santiago; and he made calls to the seminary where they studied, which the family still supports, to the Ribeira Sacra winery, to Griñán, to Santiago. And . . . to a known drug dealer."

"A drug dealer?"

"Right. A pusher, really; you can hardly call him a dealer. He dabbles in it just enough to pay his bills, and he's been known to the police for a long time."

"Why would Álvaro phone a dealer?"

"Well, you can answer that question better than I can."

Manuel stiffened. "Álvaro didn't take drugs."

"Are you sure?"

"Absolutely."

"Not everyone who takes drugs looks like a down-and-out junkie. There're lots of different types of drugs. He could be using something, and you wouldn't notice it until it got to a critical level."

"No," Manuel said decisively. "That's impossible."

"Maybe . . ."

"I tell you, absolutely not!" he answered, raising his voice.

The officer looked back, manifesting the calm that he'd shown earlier, and gestured to urge him to take it easy and lower his voice.

"Sorry," Manuel apologized. "But there's nothing to discuss. He didn't take drugs."

"Okay, right." Nogueira accepted his testimony. "There might be other links . . . When Fran died, the same guy turned up in connection with the aborted investigation. We knew he'd supplied Fran in the past, but because they slammed the case shut so fast, we never got to interrogate him."

"And what reason could Álvaro have had for having any contact at all with him? Especially since his brother died three years ago?"

"As I said, there are other possibilities." Nogueira picked up his glass, took a hefty swallow, contemplated it, and then took another. "Toñino deals in smuggled goods, mostly to earn a living, but he's known to be a male prostitute."

And there it came, the torpedo fired at the waterline. Now he understood why Nogueira hadn't challenged the report that Álvaro hadn't gone to bed with Baby. He'd tucked that explosive bit of information away in his inventory of humiliation so he could fire it for the greatest effect.

Manuel left his drink on the bar and walked away through the crowd. Nogueira caught up with him by the car. "Where are you going? We haven't finished our talk."

"It's finished for me," he said abruptly, heading for the driver's door and making it clear that he wasn't going to allow Nogueira to drive.

When the lieutenant was buckled into the passenger seat, Manuel started the car and drove out onto the highway.

Nogueira didn't shout, but he did raise his voice. "I told you that if we started nosing around in the past of the Muñiz de Dávilas, lots of shit might come to light."

In the rearview mirror Manuel saw Café curled up and quivering.

"I accepted that. What I don't understand is the reason for this insane delight of yours. You can hardly hide your pleasure."

"Insane?" Nogueira replied, indignant. "Listen! I've been as diplomatic as I know how to be. I brought you all this way and gave you a drink to deliver the news as gently as I could."

"You, diplomatic?" Manuel said bitterly. "That's a laugh!"

"Maybe you'd have liked it better if I told you in the roadhouse parking lot why your husband didn't fuck the girl?"

"It would have seemed less like gloating than bringing me all the way out here to flaunt your two possibilities: either he was a drug addict or he went off with that . . . Don't fuck with me! You're enjoying this."

⁕

Nogueira remained silent and didn't say another word until Manuel pulled up to the policeman's old BMW in the now unlit parking lot of the inn. When he did speak it was with the same icy calm as in their first encounters. "You should go back to As Grileiras. Talk to Herminia. She's a gold mine of information, more than she knows. And it'd be terrific if you could take a look at Álvaro's room in the manor house. See what you can turn up: documents, drugs, receipts, restaurant bills, anything that can give us a clue about what he did, with who, and why."

The officer got out. Before closing the door he leaned back in. "You're right about some things. Maybe I do take an insane pleasure in the disgrace of those sons of bitches. But you don't know everything. Just remember that. Maybe I'm not your friend—but I'm the closest thing to a friend you've got around here." He closed the door, got into his car, and drove off.

Manuel leaned over the steering wheel in the darkness, feeling ridiculous. Like those times when you know you're wrong and yet still persist, your face burning in shame and your heart pumping with adrenaline. For the second time that night he said the words that had once been his pride, then his grief, forever true, and now again his disgrace: "He was my husband."

He looked out at the night with blind eyes, taking in the panorama of interior desolation. He realized at last that the place where he'd been hiding no longer offered any shelter. He'd single-handedly destroyed the redoubt where he'd taken refuge. He was the one who'd rejected the false consolation he'd imagined just hours before, when he'd sworn never to lie anymore. Yet he'd fled from the raw truth like a teenager refusing to see the flaws of his beloved. Is truth true for us only when it shows us what we were expecting to see? When revelation provides relief from the inimical advance of unknowing? And therefore, instead of being balm to our wounds, isn't the unvarnished truth all the more devastating?

Like a patient Job not expecting an answer to a rhetorical question, he'd asked himself again and again in recent days who Álvaro was. Tonight he'd received the answer as well as the implied punishment: *He was my husband.*

Tears burned his eyes. For the first time he let them flow, silent and so unceasing that they bathed his face, drenched his goatee, and dripped to the floor mat. Always before he'd repressed those tears and proudly refrained from weeping, but now his resources were exhausted.

He felt the gentle nudge of the dog's nose against his arm. The creature had moved closer, and tiny rear legs scrabbled against his thigh. It pushed into the hollow of his folded arms and finally reached a place that until now had been invaded only by his despair. The dog fully entered the domain of his embrace. Helplessly he held Café tight, feeling the little dog's heartbeat as he wept into the mutt's rough fur. He had the impression that the bent edges of the old photo in his jacket were sinking like claws into his chest.

THE RAVEN

He woke suddenly, as if a cable holding him fastened to an anchor in the depths had given way. He rose like Lazarus to a room bathed in melancholy light from the window he'd forgotten to shutter the night before. The funereal white cast of the light was oppressive.

Manuel leaned back against the pillows, his shoulders aching with the miserable morning chill, and his nerves afflicted by an anguish known only by those who wake at dawn. His despairing look at the old iron radiator was rewarded with a hollow clanking as the heat came on. He had no idea what day it was and didn't really care. He'd felt that same numb indifference every morning since his arrival. Café sprawled asleep at his side, apparently unaffected by the dawn chill that had slunk into his room like an unwelcome guest. The warmth of that little body was perceptible through the thin bedspread and lumpy wool blanket.

Headache and backache. He reached out, located the ibuprofen tablets on the bedside table, and choked two down without water, grateful to feel the pain of the effort. His hands were still cramped from the labor of the previous day, and each move brought sharp new pains in his leaden legs and stiff lower back. Physical suffering distracted him from the deeper pain he sensed drifting upward from the obscurity where it had been anchored. Unbound and unattached, that anguish rose like the ghost of a ship sunk long ago. Within his chest a heavy weight occupied the space where heart and lungs had been. Pain's monstrous bulk, saturated with secrets of the abyss, pressed against his ribs and obstructed his breathing. He saw now there was nothing he could do. He had opened Pandora's box, and its contents had dispersed the hope briefly encouraged by Café's rheumy eyes, the vineyard workers' trust in him, and the assurances of a prostitute. Hoping beyond hope, he'd imagined that in some remoteness not yet perceived, there might exist an explanation, a justification, a great grand heroic rationale that would explain and excuse the deception practiced on him, that would reveal to him everything had served some greater good.

He leaned forward to pet the dog and perceived the first faint emanation of warmth from the ancient radiator. The chill in the room had raised goose bumps on his naked shoulders. He picked up the phone and a moment later heard Daniel's cheerful voice on the other end of the line.

"Good morning, Manuel! Ready to labor in the vineyards another day? Or are you planning to spend today in bed like some of the first-time harvesters?"

"I'm calling to let you know that I can't participate today. Something's come up I have to deal with, and there's no way around it. I can't come."

He heard the disappointment in Daniel's faraway voice. "This afternoon the local producers will be delivering everything they harvested during the weekend. It'd be a shame to miss out on the experience."

The weight of the man's disappointment induced him to make a half promise he might not be able to keep. "I'll see if I can come by in late afternoon . . . but I'm not sure I'll be able to make it."

Daniel didn't reply, perhaps because he heard in Manuel's voice that something of significance was afoot. Manuel's somber tone was enough to convince him it was something sufficiently weighty that it couldn't be denied.

The noxious vapors that had roiled the upper atmosphere had by now descended and left their volatile moisture everywhere. The world seemed depopulated. During the drive, only a couple of other cars loomed up going the other way. He squinted in search of sunlight in that swirling sky. It broke through infrequently with a sharpness as painful as if composed of showers of ground glass. The sun did little to drive away the cold. That chill would linger until mild midday warmth lifted the mists for good.

He parked by the gardenia hedge, just as before. After a couple of unsuccessful attempts to coax the dog out, he left Café in the BMW. He took a moment to admire the waxy gleaming shapes of the gardenias. A film of morning dew had resolved itself into large trembling drops, like tears that seemed to float across the petals without touching them. The luxuriant late-afternoon perfume of the flowers was not yet evident, for the air was heavy with scents of wood and composted earth beneath the dense shrubbery. Manuel leaned over, trying to recapture the sweet aroma of the flowers, and he found himself slipping his hand into the now empty pocket of his jacket.

Someone slammed shut the tailgate of a pickup. He looked across the hedge and saw the vehicle parked by the garden entrance. He remembered that on his previous visit he'd glimpsed a logo on the pickup's door, an image of a basket overflowing with flowers. The vehicle was white. He went toward it and saw Catarina lifting a burlap bag, apparently heavy, from the back of the pickup. She swung it over one shoulder and entered the garden.

Rounding the vehicle, Manuel noticed that a front quarter panel had been recently replaced. The color of the paint and the pristine new turn signal were distinctly different from the faded white and scratched surfaces elsewhere. He took the path to the greenhouse and found a bag, probably the same one Catarina had been carrying, propping open the greenhouse door. He called out, even though he knew he couldn't be heard over the music playing inside. Even with the door open, the intensity of the gardenia perfume was still overwhelming and provoked confused impressions that ranged from memories of the flowers shut away in the desk drawer to the almost drugged sensations of acceleration and overarousal he'd felt when he'd visited the greenhouse the first time. He went down an aisle between the tables in search of Catarina. He was sure she was still there. There was only one way to go directly through to the outside garden. There was a pause in the music, and he heard a woman's raised voice.

Vicente and Catarina stood arguing in the next aisle. It was clear she was the one in charge; his replies were inaudible, subdued, and emotional.

"It would grieve me a great deal to have to make such a drastic decision. I appreciate your talent, and I'm delighted to work with you. I see you as a consummate professional, and it would be a great loss if I had to do without you."

Manuel couldn't make out Vicente's response, but Catarina's reply was firm. "I understand your feelings, and I'm flattered, but I need to be very clear. What you want is never going to happen. I'm Santiago's wife, and he's the man I'm going to share my life with. I don't believe I've ever encouraged you in the least. Maybe I wasn't sufficiently clear because I didn't want to hurt your feelings. But I'm telling you now."

"He doesn't deserve you." The gardener's hoarse voice was choked with emotion.

"I love my husband, with all his faults. Not for a second have I ever thought of leaving him."

"I can't believe it, Catarina." He sounded ready to break into sobs.

"Well, there are no two ways about it. Either you give up any such hopes, or we'll have to stop working together." She turned and strode in Manuel's direction.

Manuel swiftly backed away several steps. He pivoted as if he'd just arrived and called out anew, "Is anyone here?"

Catarina stepped out of the side aisle with a smile. From her sunny expression no one could have guessed that just a few seconds earlier, she'd been arguing with Vicente. "Manuel! I'm pleased you accepted my invitation."

He offered her his hand. "I saw the open door."

"Right. I went to the barn to get some mulch. We needed some, and everything is closed today." She walked to the doorway and picked up the bag she'd used to keep the door open.

"Would you like some help? That looks heavy."

She turned and smiled in amusement. "This one? It weighs nothing at all. Why is it that men are always trying to keep us women from exerting ourselves? I'm stronger than I look." She hefted the bag onto a pile of similar ones.

Manuel saw that Vicente had taken refuge in the glassed-in room at the back. He stood with his back turned to them, pretending to work. Ignoring her assistant, Catarina took Manuel's arm and gave him a tour of the greenhouse, plant by plant, smiling like a schoolgirl. Manuel paid close attention, surprised to find her so sympathetic. He responded with droll comments and even laughed once or twice. Catarina definitely wasn't cut from the same rigid, formal, and pretentious cloth as the others at As Grileiras. Yet he could see why the Raven adored her: she had a sort of innate noble grace that was the picture of distinguished sophistication. Her elegant white blouse had touches of garden soil on it; her marine-blue trousers were simply tailored but looked very expensive. Behind a curtain of undulating, dark medium-length hair, a pair of diamond studs sparkling in her ears matched the huge and undeniably genuine diamond of her wedding ring. Her open smile, radiant eyes, and candor proclaimed her a woman entirely sure of herself.

"You did a fine job of hiding it, Manuel," she said with a smile, "but I believe you overheard us."

Manuel looked at her and nodded. This Catarina was a woman very much to his liking.

She shrugged. "Well, since you heard everything, I don't need to explain. These things happen."

⁂

He discovered that the corpulent black cat had chosen to post its vigil upon the top step before the kitchen door. Because that spot was protected by a little overhang, it had escaped the morning dew. Today Manuel accepted Herminia's embrace and the exuberant enthusiasm that had seemed excessive to him a couple of days before. He smiled in appreciation but gently declined her offers of food, coffee, and sweets. After taking time to respond to her fulsome welcome, he said, "Herminia, I have a favor to ask." His solemn tone stressed the importance of the request.

She put down the cloth she'd used to dry her hands. "Of course, *fillo*, anything at all."

"I'd like to see Álvaro's room."

His request took her breath away. She stood paralyzed for a couple of seconds. She went back to the stove and lowered the heat beneath a bubbling pot of stew. She patted the pockets of her apron, found her keys, and went to the door to the rest of the manor. "Come with me."

Opposite the kitchen door rose a monumental wooden staircase he'd assumed was the principal access to the second floor. Herminia walked past those stairs and went through a second door into a large square entry hall that led to a vast open two-story covered court. The entry was dominated by two facing archways that encompassed, respectively, the massive wooden front door and the access to a majestic white-stone staircase. The pale, chalky gleam of the staircase contrasted with the stone terrazzo of the entry floor and the mahogany wall paneling. Two lesser stairways halfway up the main stairs led to either side. The sweep of the main stairs crested at a hanging gallery that ran around the upper story of the main room. Doors off the gallery led to the various upstairs rooms.

He followed Herminia up the stairs, looking down over the balustrade at the sparsely furnished great room with walls hung with tapestries and a profusion of paintings. He was impressed to see how light falling from deep windows set in the stone of the upper floor sculpted pathways through the air, casting sharply defined shafts of sunlight that warmed the stone tiles of the entrance. The dark wood banister seemed both delicate and massive, reminding him of Renaissance courtyards. He speculated that this area might have served as a carriage court in an earlier age. Herminia took him into a wide side hallway lined with heavy doors. All were shut, plunging the passage through this wing of the house into sudden darkness. She didn't sort through her key ring, so he assumed she'd had the appropriate key in hand since they left the kitchen. She inserted it gently into the lock of the first door, which opened with an almost inaudible click. Herminia entered the darkness with the confident step of someone who knew every inch of the house. Manuel supposed that after so many years of service, she could walk through the manor blindfolded, taking care of her tasks with never a false step. Disoriented by the pervasive darkness, he waited in the doorway, not daring to enter.

He heard the sound of a window swinging open. Herminia pushed back the shutters and the room presented itself. He was impressed. He hadn't been sure what to expect, but it certainly wasn't the room he saw before him. Wood so dark it was almost black glistened in the doorframe, the flooring, and the window casements. Austere furniture of the same material, certainly antiques, stood out against the monastic white of undecorated walls. The space breathed of centuries of history and magnificent conservation of its high-quality furnishings. Even so, they differed little in their essence from those of his grim little room at the inn.

The single bed looked almost too narrow for a grown man, though the carved wooden headboard and side rails gave it the appearance of a bit more volume. The thick, white down comforter did little to offset the bed's stark appearance. A dressing table featured a large mirror in a frame presumably of pure silver, and a heavy dark wardrobe matched the bed. The bedside tables held matching lamps: scantily clad nymphs sculpted in bronze lifted their arms high to hold up shades of Venetian glass. A crucifix hung at the head of the bed. Displayed on the opposite wall were an incongruous flat-screen television and the door of a heavy wall safe they hadn't bothered to hide behind a painting.

He couldn't help feeling both mystified and relieved. The bedroom had the clinical anonymity of a hotel room awaiting a new guest. The space was clean and aired, with a neutrality any guest could make his own. Not a single personal object was to be seen. Nor was there anything to suggest who the previous occupant might have been.

He looked around for anything that might confirm Álvaro's presence. He found nothing. It occurred to him that perhaps in the days since the accident, someone might have collected his things. Herminia stood silent behind him. He asked her.

"It's all just the way he left it. Nothing's been touched." She murmured something about needing to tend to the kitchen and left, closing the door behind her.

Manuel went to the window and took in the view across an ancient seedbed and the garden sheds behind the manor. The tops of the trees in the wide hollow behind the house descended and spread out like a magic garden.

One by one he opened the drawers of the dressing table, only to find them all empty. In the immense closet the few shirts Álvaro had brought hung perfectly ironed on heavy hangers next to two jackets he'd left behind. They hung abandoned within the closet. Their movement in response to the opening of the door created a disturbing impression. He wanted to touch them, to feel the soft fabric, to let his fingertips search for the elusive presence of their owner. He stood regarding them for a couple of seconds, and then he firmly closed the doors to break the spell. He was struck by the thought that everything Álvaro owned should have disappeared with him.

Perhaps that thought was really a wish. Life would be much easier if our dead didn't leave their belongings behind like so many empty nautilus shells. If every trace of their existence were erased along with them, their names could be forgotten and consigned to oblivion, like those of the pharaohs of ancient Egypt.

The adjacent compartment held two pairs of shoes and an overnight bag matching the one Manuel had filled hastily with whatever useless garments came to hand. He leaned over and confirmed his suspicion—it was empty. Inside one of the night tables, he found the book Álvaro had been reading, and he recalled seeing his husband toss it into the suitcase. The other night table held a handful of receipts for frugal purchases. Manuel recognized the logo of a gasoline company. He didn't stop to go through them; that he could do later.

In the adjoining bathroom he found Álvaro's toiletries bag in a drawer stocked with towels and wrapped bars of hand soap. The single toothbrush left in a water glass was the only sign anyone had regularly used this bathroom.

He took a look at the safe. It was an electronic model with a plain front and a four-digit keypad. Locked. He didn't bother to try to guess the code.

He sat on the bed and unhappily surveyed the room. It would have surprised him less to have found himself in a teenager's bedroom, frozen in time, where faded posters and forgotten toys were souvenirs of the rapid transition to puberty. This space contained not a single trace of Álvaro. A profiler would have been at a loss, for these objects offered no hint of the occupant's character. Man and dwelling place had remained strangers to one another. Upon consideration, he couldn't help feeling relieved at this evidence that Álvaro's transit through here had been so evanescent it hadn't left a trace. Manuel had searched his memory a thousand times or more trying to recall Álvaro's gestures and expressions, and he was certain now he'd never seen anything related to As Grileiras. It was somehow satisfying that Álvaro hadn't left an imprint upon this place. This was not his bedroom. This wasn't his house.

Manuel gathered the cash receipts and credit card slips and stuffed them into his jacket pocket. He checked the overnight bag and, after a moment of hesitation, he opened the wardrobe and searched the two jackets hanging next to the shirts. In one he found another couple of cash receipts, and in the other there was a gardenia that had withered and yellowed but still retained its familiar perfume. The dry flower's decadent dead beauty reminded him of a butterfly—the typically firm petals had become so limp they were almost transparent in his hand. The specter of that dead butterfly sent a chill up his spine; it was as if something wet, clammy, and disgusting had landed on him. In a superstitious reaction, he pushed the flower corpse into a pocket and unthinkingly rubbed his hand on the fabric to wipe away any trace of death.

He started for the door but changed his mind at the last moment. He went to the safe, and following a hunch he punched in the date of their wedding. One, two, two, five: December 25, Christmas Day. The safe gave a distinct beep as it popped open. A little light went on inside. Imprisoned in a small frame leaning against the back of the space was the photo of the two of them, a copy of the one on the dressing table in their room, the photo he hadn't had the heart to contemplate when summoned here. Álvaro's wedding ring sat on a copy of *The*

Man Who Refused. Manuel recognized the bright-colored dust jacket devised by his publisher and the worn edges of the same copy he'd autographed for Álvaro fifteen years before. Beneath it were some papers.

"*The Man Who Refused*," he muttered, and a little smile crept across his face. "*The Man Who Refused*." The presence of this novel in this place at this moment was as deeply meaningful to him as the careful safeguarding of the wedding ring.

The wall safe was at chest level, so he didn't need to lean over to make out the first letters of his own name engraved within the ring along with the date Álvaro had chosen as the code for this hiding place. Manuel reached out and put his finger through it. The metal was warm, as if only a few seconds had passed since its owner took it off.

Shouting echoed in the corridor. He took the ring, left the book, and closed the safe. The door clicked shut with a quiet beep of acknowledgment. He opened the bedroom door and suddenly came face-to-face with a furious Santiago, who was about to seize the door handle. A woebegone Herminia was visible over the man's shoulder, watching from the landing.

Santiago stepped up to him. His face was deeply flushed with a red that extended like some virulent infection all the way back to his ears and neck. He'd been shouting outside as he approached, but he choked with rage as he addressed Manuel.

"What are you doing here? Who gave you permission? You can't come in here as if you . . ."

Manuel expected a punch. Any other man in such a fury would have struck him, but Manuel saw that the blaze in Santiago's face was merely frustration, an infantile temper tantrum in response to an impossible situation. Manuel noticed that the door at the end of the hall had opened and a motionless black silhouette was watching.

He tried a conciliatory approach. "I just wanted to visit Álvaro's room."

"You have no right!" Santiago shrieked in a voice higher and even more congested than before.

"Yes, I do. Álvaro was my husband."

That very word jolted Santiago. Then frustration in his face was replaced by an arrogant, cruel sneer that Manuel had seen before. It lasted only a moment but betrayed a hatred and contempt for homosexuality. He was too much a coward to put those feelings into words. His features twisted in a childish pout.

"You said you were going to leave, but now you're back again. Showing your disrespect and sticking your nose into everything like a common thief. What did you take from there?"

Manuel opened his hand to reveal the gold ring, and without thinking slipped it onto his ring finger to accompany his own ring. Santiago brushed rudely past him to inspect the bedroom.

Manuel put up with the affront but didn't budge. He looked at Herminia. She responded with a silent apology and rolled her eyes in the expression one uses when a child is crying with fatigue or a friend has had too much to drink.

Santiago must have found the room as barren as Manuel had, for he came out immediately. "What were you doing in here?" he shouted. "What were you looking for? Herminia! Why did you let him in?"

She remained calm. "Who am I to stand in his way?"

Frustrated again, Santiago confronted him. "You can't be here. You can't just turn up anytime at all, you can't!"

Manuel kept his gaze level. "I can. And I'll come here as many times as necessary until I get some straight answers."

Santiago's face turned an even deeper red, but then his expression suddenly changed from that of an impending apoplectic fit to one of indifference. He looked as if he'd suddenly lost all interest. Or perhaps the opposite: he looked as if he'd just found the solution to his problems. "I'm calling the police."

Manuel's grin at that preposterous declaration stopped Santiago cold. Halfway to the staircase the young marquis hesitated, apparently surprised to see his threat hadn't had the intended effect.

"Oh really? And what are you going to tell them? To come take away the owner?" The mocking smile that accompanied his question was a crushing blow to the man's self-regard.

Santiago walked back to Manuel, ready to burst into tears. "So that's how it is then? I should have guessed from the first that a down-and-outer wouldn't give up something he doesn't deserve." He almost spat the words: *"It's because of the money!"*

The door at the end of the hall swung entirely open, and now the light from inside the room illuminated the profile of a tall slim figure.

"That will do, Santiago! Stop behaving like an idiot." The voice was polite and firm and brooked no discussion.

"Mother!" Santiago protested with the voice of a helpless child.

"Señor Ortigosa," the female voice from the depths of the hall addressed him. "I would like to speak with you. Would you be so kind?"

All trace of anger had disappeared from Santiago's face. Even so he tried again. "Mother . . ." It was obvious from his plaintive tone he wasn't expecting a reply.

Manuel hadn't felt threatened by Santiago even at the height of the marquis's fury, but he had an idea the man could turn violent if humiliated. Manuel nodded an acceptance of the invitation but didn't take his eyes off the young marquis. He waited two long seconds until at last the man turned and went to the stairway. At the last moment Santiago slammed his fist into the wall. The cast on his hand cracked and released a shower of plaster dust.

The figure at the end of the hall was gone but had left the door open as an invitation to enter. Standing in isolation on the landing, Herminia gave him an unhappy look, shook her head like a long-suffering governess, and followed Santiago down the stairs.

Manuel calculated that the dowager's suite must occupy the entire upper floor of the west wing. A row of tall windows overlooked the front lawn, and others faced the cemetery. The gauzy lace curtains permitted one to see everything outside. A huge fireplace of rough Galician stone dominated the interior wall. The roaring fire was boxed in by blackened stone slabs. The room's baseboards and molding were of the same dark wood as elsewhere in the manor, visible only around the doors and windows, in those few places along the wall not covered by Persian carpets in tones of red and gold, and in the imposing crossbeams that held up the ceiling. The room connected to a glassed-in terrace. Before the doors to the closed-off terrace was the tall thin figure of the woman, initially only a dark profile but with features more defined as he approached her.

She wore black trousers and a thick high-necked sweater snug about her body. She looked delicate, as if feeling chilled or suffering from a cold, but that was only a misleading impression conveyed by her clothing. She appeared to be comfortable despite the extreme warmth of the room. Her hair was in a tight bun, and her only jewelry consisted of heavy gray pearl earrings.

She made no move to shake his hand but spoke in a firm, courteous voice. "I am Cecilia de Muñiz de Dávila, Marquess of Santo Tomé. I believe we haven't yet been properly introduced."

"I'm Manuel Ortigosa, your son's widower," he replied in the same formal tone.

She stood looking at him. A slightly peevish smile appeared as she gestured toward the sofa before the fireplace and took an armchair. "Do excuse Santiago," she said after she'd settled herself. "He's quite temperamental and has been so since his childhood. Whenever vexed, he would fling his toys and break them, and then he'd weep for hours. But don't be taken in. My son has no guts. He's a fraud from head to toe."

Manuel couldn't hide his surprise.

"Yes, señor Ortigosa, it is a disgrace to me. All my children have been disappointments." She glanced behind her. "I hope you will join me for tea."

Manuel turned and saw a woman step forward. He hadn't noticed her earlier. She wore an old-fashioned nurse's uniform of sturdy white cotton with long sleeves. Bulky stockings of the same color covered her legs, and a starched cap was perched upon a short dull hairdo lacquered in place like a helmet. The aroma of spray perfume hovering about her brought to his mind the unpleasant sickly-sweet odor of his elderly aunt.

The employee laid out the tea service on the table before them, poured tea for each of them, herself included, and placed cups before them. She took a seat across from the dowager and said nothing.

"Do you have children, señor Ortigosa?"

He shook his head.

"No, of course, I suppose not. Then allow me say that you're more fortunate than I." She took a small sip of tea. "Despite all that the popular press has to say on the subject, most of the time children are a disappointment. Few people would ever admit it, of course, I suppose because they consider their children's failures to be their own. Such is not my case. I do not blame myself in the least for their failings. Believe me when I say that all their shortcomings come from their father. My husband was perfectly incompetent in almost everything: finances, the children's education . . ." She turned toward the nurse. "How could I blame myself for unacceptable behavior such as that we just witnessed?"

The nurse nodded gravely.

"Even so, I ask you to forgive him. He's never had a sense of proportion; he's a moron. The poor fool had convinced himself that now with his brother dead, perhaps he would be given the management of our affairs; a responsibility for which, allow me to say, he is totally unfit. We are fortunate that his brother was more apt."

"You mean to say you approve of Álvaro's decision?"

"I mean to say that although my husband was riddled with shortcomings, one virtue did stand out: that of knowing to whom to entrust his affairs. I suppose that is an innate virtue of the ancient nobility, a quality acquired over the course of centuries. Otherwise how could one explain the continuation of such great houses when we've been forced to confide even the simplest matters to third parties? If it hadn't been for their unerring instincts for delegation, the Spanish aristocracy would have died out long ago. My husband made Álvaro his heir, which was the proper choice. I must therefore assume that the same inherited capacity was behind Álvaro's decision to put you in the seat of command."

Manuel considered her declaration. Was that what had happened? Perhaps a candidate's outstanding qualifications could indeed outweigh any other considerations, even when the individual was as despised as Álvaro had been. "I understand that the relations between Álvaro and his father were not exactly the best."

"Not exactly the best," the marquess chuckled maliciously and looked at the nurse. "Señor Ortigosa, tell me, what is the opinion of your own parents concerning your . . . what is the expression? . . . your tendency? I expect that you're not going to tell me they're among those unhappy souls who pretend to accept your aberration."

Manuel very carefully placed his cup and saucer back on the table, sat back on the sofa, and met her gaze with calm assurance. "I'm sure that they would have referred to it as 'homosexuality,' which is the correct term, but they did not have the opportunity. My parents died in an accident when I was very small."

That did not faze her. "The more fortunate for them. Believe me, I envy them, and why not? Álvaro's relationship with his father was not exactly a good one, and the fault was not that of my husband. Álvaro was a constant headache from the day he was born, and one could say that he took a malevolent delight in opposing us in everything. The upshot was that I had two sons who were gutless and one who made up for both of them but took the wrong path."

Manuel shook his head slowly as he heard her.

"Go ahead and say it," she challenged and provoked him. "Say what you're thinking."

"I think you're a perverted, unnatural monster."

The marquess chortled as if she'd heard a good joke. She gave the nurse a look of disbelief. "Did you hear that? *He* called *me* unnatural! Me!"

The nurse smiled scornfully, as if she'd heard something completely absurd.

"A deviant, a coward, and a mental midget so spoiled by his father he never grew up." Her tone had changed; her voice was bitter. "Those are my sons. God didn't grant me a daughter, and that's the cross I've had to bear. Three incompetents unable even to give me a proper heir."

"Samuel," murmured Manuel almost under his breath, knowing she was referring to the child.

"Correct." She leaned toward the nurse as if explaining. "Little bastard Samuel. You know what they say, señor Ortigosa: the children of my daughters are certainly mine, but the children of my daughters-in-law are not necessarily so."

Manuel was astonished and disgusted by such crudeness. "You are despicable!"

"Well, I suppose it depends upon your point of view," the dowager marquess answered with a faint smile. "Those are exactly my feelings concerning you."

"And Catarina?"

"Catarina's a girl from a good family who have suffered financial reverses. But we're none of us immune to such things, are we?" She gestured indifferently toward herself. "Even so, she's an aristocrat with a good upbringing and more heart than many men. She knows her place in this house better than anyone. I have no idea what she could possibly have seen in my son."

"And you will consider Catarina's child to be your proper grandchild?"

Her face screwed up in a grimace of extreme disgust. She flung her cup and saucer on the table. They clattered but didn't break. "Catarina's worth far more than my son. She's the only person in this house, other than myself, who knows her proper place. Would that she'd been my daughter; I wouldn't hesitate for a second to trade all three of them for her."

Manuel's head moved from side to side as he disagreed, unable to comprehend this vileness.

"You see me as a monster, señor Ortigosa? You think I'm cruel? Then consider this: if my husband appointed Álvaro to run the affairs of our estate, it wasn't out of a benevolent heart but because the marquis smelled in him the cruelty and strength required to preserve his legacy, our family line, and everything it represents. *At any cost.* And I assure you," she said, sitting erect and holding her head as if wearing a crown, "Álvaro didn't disappoint. He achieved all we expected of him and more. So if you see me as a soulless monster, know that your beloved Álvaro far exceeded me. He didn't disappoint. His father knew he wouldn't, because he'd proved himself capable of it before. He would not flinch from doing whatever was required, no matter what. He proved that long ago." She took her time and looked him up and down. "No matter how abhorrent I find it, I must accept that if Álvaro judged you should become the heir of everything, he had his reasons. I shall accept his decision, and so shall we all. Take no heed of Santiago; today's incident was merely the tantrum of a spoiled child. He will get over it, and he will understand that this is the best solution for us all."

The unpredictable behavior of this elderly woman, this veering from extreme contempt to flattery, seemed to him both ill and unhinged. This was like trying to converse with a lunatic. She was placid and conciliatory once again, and she spoke without smiling. But her tone was vibrant, with the steely determination and inbred tradition of a bloodline that dated back many generations.

"You'll be faced with no confrontations or legal quibbles from our side, so you will be free to spend your time picking grapes and playing at making wine if that's what amuses you," she commented, revealing she was aware of his visits to the vineyards and the winery.

For a moment Manuel wondered if Daniel had been her source, but then he remembered climbing into the cellar master's vehicle in the afternoon and catching sight of her black-robed figure watching like Poe's raven from the perch of her particular bust of Pallas.

"Enjoy the inheritance, manage the businesses and assets, and apply yourself to assuring this elderly dowager financial security to the end of her life," she added with a smile, as if she found that prospect particularly amusing. Her gums were bright red, as if they'd been bleeding. Manuel was surprised to find himself contemplating the ferociousness they symbolized. The marquess made a dramatic pause; the smile vanished utterly and her mouth set in a short straight line. "But if you think by doing so you will become a member of this family, let me warn you that you are mistaken. You are alien to this place, and nothing in all the property deeds in the world will change that. This will never be your home, nor will my family be yours. Now get out of my house and never come back."

The two women got to their feet and went to the doorway closest to the fireplace. The nurse opened it and stepped aside to leave it free for her mistress. The dowager turned and glanced back as if surprised to find him still there.

"You're dismissed," she said. "I'm sure you can find your way out." She entered her bedroom, followed by her assistant, who gave him a last disparaging glance before shutting the door behind them.

He sat there for a while longer before the fire and the tea setting. Anyone who happened to look in might have thought a cordial conversation had taken place. He felt drained, as if that brooding old raven, that species of vampire, had put her thin lips to his neck, drunk his blood, and sucked his life away. Each demeaning word and each mocking expression emitted by that malevolent many-headed hydra had been intended less to hurt him than to amuse her. She'd played him for a fool. He quivered with indignation. He circled the sofa, his shoes sinking into the thick carpet, and he had the sensation that someone was watching him. He left that lair swearing *Nevermore*.

He closed the door behind him and walked toward the light that fell in broad luminous shafts across the stairs. He saw that the door to Álvaro's room stood slightly ajar. He pushed it open and entered, went to the night table and picked up the book. He quickly punched the code into the safe's keypad, opened it, and collected everything inside, including *The Man Who Refused*. He pulled the back off the little frame, removed the photo, and without a backward glance slipped it and the documents into the book. He remembered the ring. He lifted his hand and saw it secure next to his own, the two gleaming together like a single band. He fled.

Overwhelmed by these trials, he dropped into a chair by the housekeeper's wood-burning stove. "Herminia, I'd be grateful for a cup of coffee. The marquess's tea was more than I could take. She probably brews it with hemlock."

The housekeeper stood before him deeply distressed. "And now you've met the Raven. I can't tell you how sorry I am. Santiago was in the stables. He saw you go into the kitchen, and he came to question me. I couldn't lie to him."

"Of course not, Herminia, don't give it another thought. Santiago is a lunatic, and I wasn't too surprised."

"That's what I wanted to talk to you about." She put a chair before him and sat down. "You know, I cared for those children from the day they were born. I loved them more than their own mother did. I know Santiago has a good heart."

Manuel started to object but she interrupted him. "Very impulsive, I admit, and that's due to his lack of character. When he was small he was Álvaro's little lapdog, and he spent all his teenage years trying to win his father's affection. My poor little tyke has always been a nobody in this house. Álvaro was the one with character; Fran was the charmer; and Santiago, poor thing, was the weepy little fatso his father couldn't stand. And the old man made no secret of it. Can you imagine growing up like that? And even so I swear he loved his brothers more than anything else in the world."

"That's no longer relevant, Herminia."

"Listen to me!" she insisted. "When Fran died, Santiago went to bed for three days, moaning and weeping and blubbering constantly. I thought he was going to wreck his health. And then last week! When they told us about Álvaro and his accident, he rushed to the hospital; and when he came back home after the horrible experience of identifying his brother's body, he came to me. Not to his mother but to me, Manuel, because he knew I'd share his feelings. He stood right there in the kitchen door, looking at me without a word. 'What happened?' I asked him, 'What's happened to my boy?' He broke down and started slamming his fist against the wall, out of his head with grief, shouting that his brother was dead. Santiago didn't fall off a horse, Manuel. He smashed his hand battering that wall. He broke several fingers. So don't you go telling me what I already know. No one knows him as well as I do. He hasn't gotten over it. He thinks I don't know, but since Álvaro died, every afternoon he's hidden himself away in the church and cried his heart out."

Crushed by grief? Or by guilt?

As if she'd heard his thoughts Herminia added, "I think he feels partly to blame, because they had an argument the day of the accident."

Manuel gave her a questioning look.

"It was nothing," she said. "A silly quarrel. Santiago was here in the kitchen having a coffee. Álvaro came in and said to him, 'Who do you think you're fooling with those candelabras?' Santiago didn't say anything, but his face got red as a beet. Álvaro stalked off toward his car. And Santiago went upstairs, slamming the door behind him. I don't know anything about art. It's all a mystery to me. The new ones look just as good as the others, but maybe they're not. Like I said, I'm no expert, but Santiago went to a lot of effort to replace them. He's the kind of person who needs approval, and he was offended when his brother refused to give it. But of course that's one of those things that later, when something so terrible happens, loses importance and sounds trivial. But knowing him the way I do, I'm sure he's torturing himself because they weren't on good terms when his brother died."

Manuel turned and studied the wall by the entrance. He detected spots of lighter color where Herminia must have scrubbed off the bloodstains.

"Where is he now?"

"Damián drove him to the hospital so they could repair his cast. He's always flying off the handle like that. He's been that way ever since he was a baby."

"And what's up with Catarina? He doesn't seem to treat her very well. And she told me he doesn't like the fact she works."

"You need to understand, some things are different for them; they're not like us. These days it might seem strange to most of us, but for them it's shameful to have to work. Catarina's family is one of the oldest and most distinguished in the country, but for various reasons things haven't gone too well for them in recent years, and they've had to find other ways to support themselves. They sold a lot of their land, and not much is left except the grounds around the manor. A couple of years ago her family converted the manor house into an event hall for weddings, conventions, and that sort of thing. With a restaurant. Santiago finds such changes unbecoming. Catarina doesn't seem to have any problem with it, but you just have to understand that Santiago considers it demeaning. The way folks like us would feel if we were reduced to begging."

"There's no comparison, Herminia. There's a huge difference between converting a manor house into a banquet hall and having to beg for your supper and shelter."

"For you and for me, yes, but they see it as degrading. Santiago has refused to set foot on the property since they opened it to the public. In any case, that's not the only reason Santiago's concerned about Catarina working; he wants to protect her."

She lowered her voice in response to Manuel's look of surprise. "She has problems, women's matters, you know." She studied the kitchen table, unwilling to meet his gaze. "They'd been trying for quite a while, and at the end of last year she got pregnant, but she had a miscarriage soon afterward. You can still see it affected her. I was with her that day. She was right here when she suddenly felt a sharp pain and started bleeding. In the hospital they treated her and had to scrape it out. She seems to have recovered. She asked me not to discuss it, but all you have to do is see the way she looks at Samuel to know how much she wants her own child." She sighed. "But Santiago—well, I told you already what he's like. It affected him deeply, and ever since he's been trying his best to persuade Catarina to stop working. The doctor told them there's no reason to be concerned, a first pregnancy miscarries sometimes, and they're not likely to have a problem next time, but Santiago is obsessed with her treatment and her health. He's always in a fret, as if it was his fault. That's how he is. He blows everything out of proportion."

Manuel nodded. "And Vicente?"

Herminia pretended not to capture the nuance. "He helps Catarina."

"I think you understand me. The other day when Santiago scolded her, Vicente looked as if it were all he could do to keep from saying something. As if Catarina were particularly special to him."

Herminia just looked at him.

"Do you think there's something between those two?"

"She has no feelings for Vicente, but maybe he thinks differently. I've seen how he looks at her. He's a young man, she's a beautiful woman, they're together all day long working with the flowers in the greenhouse, and no one else is around. But she's devoted to Santiago to the point of self-sacrifice. She's always taken care of him like that. When Fran died, she was the one who coaxed Santiago back from his depression. She spoon-fed him for weeks, almost dragged him physically out to the garden. They'd sit together by the pond for hours, her talking while he just listened with his head hanging. And now it's happening again. Sometimes I hear Santiago weeping, and she's always there consoling him, calming him. The girl has infinite patience. You've seen it, how sometimes Santiago has his whims. It doesn't surprise me that Vicente might feel inclined to try to protect her. And maybe he has even stronger feelings." But then she dismissed the notion. "But unless he's a pure fool, he should have learned his lesson by now."

"Why, Herminia? What happened?"

She met his question with a shrug. "So maybe you are onto something."

He waited for an explanation and at last the woman exhaled a puff of annoyance. "Look here, *fillo*, I've been a servant in this house since before I got married. I brought up the boys, I cooked for them, nursed them when they were sick—dedicated my whole life to the estate. But I've never for a minute made the mistake of thinking that I was one of them or supposing that I was a part of all this. We are employees, they pay us well; but no matter how many hugs and pats you may see, no matter how many secrets we know or how many messes we clean up, we'll never be anything but servants. Anyone who forgets his place around here gets a swift reminder."

Manuel couldn't help taking that personally. Herminia was asserting the same doctrine as the dowager but from another angle. The presumed superiority of an aristocratic class deeply offended Nogueira, but everyone else accepted it. Manuel was only now beginning to understand the depth and extent of it. "Herminia, are you trying to warn me?"

She looked at him with an expression of alarm. "No, I'm not talking about you, *fillo*, or Álvaro either. He was like us. I'm referring to Vicente."

"Vicente?"

She clicked her tongue in annoyance. Manuel couldn't tell if she was bothered by having to discuss the situation or annoyed that she didn't have all the information. "Look, I don't know what actually might have happened, but they fired him last December."

"They fired Vicente?"

"Just before Christmas, from one day to the next, without any discussion or explanation. It was very sudden; they just said Vicente wasn't working here anymore. You can imagine the effect on the rest of us here on the estate. Not that it was the first time they'd fired someone, but it's not usually done like that. Some of the people in the village have been coming to do seasonal work on the estate for twenty-five years. The custom is always to hire the same ones, and some families have priority."

Manuel recalled Griñán's comment that employment on the estate was seen by many as a mark of special privilege.

"I remember a couple of times. They fired a stableboy and a woodcutter, one for mistreating the horses and the other for theft. It was just the same, harsh and immediate. With one difference: Vicente was given his job back two months later."

"What explanation did they give?"

"The same as when he was fired—none at all. All I know is that Catarina hired him again, and I suppose he was grateful to her. But believe me, if anyone in this house knows her place, it's Catarina."

Manuel's jaw dropped. He'd heard the same comment about Catarina just minutes before but from a completely different source. The Raven. He himself had perceived Catarina's grace and charisma.

Herminia got up and served coffee. Manuel took a long, slow swallow. His mind filled with thoughts of Catarina, the way Santiago had made her cry, and the heavy, dizzying perfume of those hundreds of flowers.

"I found withered gardenias in the pockets of Álvaro's jackets."

She smiled sadly. "A habit he had ever since he was little. I always had to check his pockets before I washed his clothes. I was always finding flowers there."

"Who knew he had that habit?"

"Who knew?" Herminia shrugged. "Well, Sarita and I, since we do the laundry. Anybody in the house might have seen him tuck a flower into a pocket. Why do you ask?"

"No reason at all." He avoided her question. "Herminia, another thing—that room, Álvaro's bedroom. Was that where he'd always stayed when he was at the manor house?"

She interrupted her bustling about the kitchen and came back to him. "No, of course not. It's just a guest room. It was kept locked when he wasn't here. When Álvaro was a boy his room was off the gallery next to his brothers' rooms. His father sent him off to boarding school in Madrid, and the old man ordered the staff to clear the room and store all his things in the cellar."

Manuel imagined what a great affront that must have been, the unspoken message Álvaro would have received when he was little more than a child, and the warning it must have sent to the rest of the family.

"As if he'd died or were never coming back," he said aloud.

"I do believe that in a way from that day on, Álvaro was dead to his father. The few times Álvaro came back to the estate, he always stayed in the guest room."

"But why, Herminia? How old was he? Twelve? What happened that day?"

Herminia looked down for a moment. "I don't know. 'From that day on' is just an expression. There was no particular day. I've never understood it, but perhaps now that you've met the Raven, you may have a clue or two of the old man's character."

Manuel nodded, still inwardly shuddering at that old woman's mean-minded attitude. "Herminia, I'm sorry I caused a problem, and I hope you won't get into trouble because you admitted me. But if you do, let me know; I won't let them make you take the blame."

She smiled. "I already know why Álvaro chose you."

Manuel didn't understand.

"When the old marquis died and Álvaro took charge of the estate, he gave me and my husband the caretaker's lodge for as long as we live. And a very generous allowance that will be enough to allow us, if we choose, to retire anytime we want. Nobody's going to kick me out. Álvaro already made sure of that."

He allowed Herminia to hug and kiss him, then readjusted his clothing and brushed a couple of imaginary spots from his jacket. What moved him even more were the words she whispered in his ear: "Please watch out for yourself."

He went toward the door but paused to look more closely at the pale spots on the wall where Santiago had broken his hand. "About that one thing you told me concerning the night Fran died: you said you were sure he'd taken up his drug habit again. What made you think so? You have access to the whole house. Maybe you saw something?"

"I didn't find syringes or needles or the sorts of things he used at his worst, if that's what you're asking. But I knew that nothing good was going on, because I saw his supplier. I saw that man the night Fran died, but he'd already been sniffing around the estate for days. I told the police. I was sure it was him. I know him well, he's a boy from Os Martiños. I've always respected the family, they're good people, but, well, you know . . . When the demon of drugs gets into a house, nothing can be done."

"Where was he?"

"Elisa took a snack out to Fran, but I wasn't about to go to bed and just leave my boy there. When I finished here, I went to my cottage to get a coat and go see him. That's when I looked out a window toward the stables, and I saw that rascal slinking along the back road. He was trying to stay hidden behind the hedges, and he took the road that leads directly to the church. You can imagine what I thought."

"Did you go all the way to the church?"

"I intended to, but then I saw Elisa come out of the manor and head that way."

"Elisa? Are you sure it was Elisa?"

"This old lady's eyes are perfect, thank you. I saw her by the light from the house lamps when she came out. Then she used a flashlight to find her way, so I had a perfect view of her."

"So you decided not to go there."

"My dear, if a young lady goes looking for her fiancé, an old lady has no business getting between them. I stayed home and watched television with my husband."

"Did you see her come back?"

"In fact, I did. The truth is that I kept an eye out, and I saw her come back not too much later. I suppose Fran didn't want to come back with her."

"Do you think she saw the drug dealer?"

"I doubt it. I always worried about Fran, but when they came back from that clinic, Elisa was cured and pregnant, and she took her health and her future with Fran very seriously. She'd never have left him alone with that lowlife, for she'd have known very well what the man was up to."

Manuel weighed her declaration and was about to step out. "Herminia, did you see Álvaro that night?"

"Of course. I saw him at dinner before he went to bed. Why do you ask?"

"Never mind. No reason." He turned back to the door. "No reason at all."

He stepped out into the morning, where although the mists on the estate grounds were beginning to dissipate, the light was murky and the temperature hadn't yet begun to rise. He walked toward his car, regretting that he'd left Álvaro's jacket at the inn. Café wagged his tail anxiously, leaped out of the vehicle as soon as Manuel opened the door, and scampered down the road. Manuel looked after the dog and saw Elisa and the boy appear. The Raven had called him *the little bastard*, and that epithet echoed in Manuel's mind as he stood in the middle of the road and saw the boy's excitement at the sight of the animal. The dog was equally enthused, bounding in delight but not willing to let the child get close enough to pet him.

Manuel looked toward the upper windows of the west wing and felt a dark satisfaction when he saw the gloomy figure posted in her glassed-in terrace. *On the bust of Pallas.* Manuel went forward, scooped the giggling boy up in his arms, and raised him high in the air. He hugged the child, perfectly aware the dowager was watching and would see him taking the boy's side. In that moment he became aware of a deep and genuine affection for the child.

When he looked up again, the Raven was nowhere to be seen.

Elisa seemed delighted to see him. She took his arm and they strolled. She waited until Samuel had run well ahead of them in pursuit of Café. Then she said, "Thank you, Manuel."

That surprised him.

"Lucas visited me yesterday and told me some of the things Fran said that night. Things I knew and was always sure of, but that I really needed to hear."

Manuel could only nod.

"He said you made him realize he should tell me. I think you know how much that means to me. All the pain and suffering these years have brought, the doubts; because though I was convinced, I won't deny that there were moments I gave in to those doubts. Thank you, Manuel."

"Elisa . . . that night?"

"Yes?"

"You didn't mention that you went back to the church later."

"I suppose Herminia told you she saw me leave the house. I saw her at the window of her cottage. The reason I didn't mention it is that I didn't enter the church. Just as I got to the churchyard Santiago was coming out. He told me Fran was fine, but he was praying and didn't want to be disturbed."

Manuel halted, and she was forced to do the same. She looked at him.

"But did you even see Fran?"

"I saw him closing the church door after Santiago."

"Did you tell this to the police?" he asked, even though he already knew the answer.

"Really, I don't remember if I did; anyhow it wasn't important. I wasn't allowed to enter the church, and I've always felt guilty about accepting that. I shouldn't have paid any attention to Santiago. I should have been at Fran's side." The self-accusation in her voice told him this wasn't the first time she'd thought this.

He offered her his arm again, and they resumed their walk. "Did you see Álvaro that night?"

"Álvaro? No."

"Or anyone else?"

This time she was the one to halt. "What's this all about, Manuel? What are you aiming at with these questions?"

He couldn't hide the truth. Not from her.

"In the days before Fran died, a drug dealer from around here was seen snooping around the estate. That night Herminia saw him walking in the direction of the church."

"But that can't be," she said, confused. "You heard what Lucas said. Fran didn't commit suicide. He wanted to live; he wanted to share his life with me and his son."

"But one thing doesn't disprove the other," he replied, recalling what Herminia had said. "Perhaps he wasn't yet completely over his drug habit, the way you were."

"Oh, no, Manuel, you're wrong. You're mistaken!" She dropped his arm and went ahead of him to the boy.

She took Samuel's hand and set out toward the manor without saying good-bye. When they reached the entrance, Samuel turned and gave him a little salute.

Manuel opened the car door, carefully helped Café inside, and placed the book he'd recovered from the safe on the driver's seat. Feeling watched, he looked up and again saw the dark profile of the Raven upon her watch. He took out his cell phone and called the number he'd added to his contact list that same morning.

"It's Manuel," he said when Lucas answered the call.

"Good morning, Manuel."

"Hi," he said, his eyes never quitting the figure in black watching him from the glassed-in terrace. "I'm at As Grileiras, and I just talked to Elisa. She thanked me for encouraging you to tell her what happened."

"I did exactly what I promised you: no more lies. Not even by omission."

"That's the other reason I called. Nogueira said the two of you had a discussion, and from what he said, it seems to me you didn't mention your doubts about the identity of the person you saw that night."

"I already told you, Manuel, it could have been anyone."

"But you thought it was Álvaro. Often when our mind tells us something, it's because somehow we've gathered enough information to reach that conclusion."

"What are you insinuating, Manuel? We already talked about this. I thought we saw it the same way."

"Lucas, I think we should talk." The suggestion seemed absurd, since after all they were talking at that moment, but Lucas understood what he meant.

"What are you doing this afternoon?"

"I promised the cellar master that I'd drop by the winery."

"Terrific. We can see one another there," he said. "But right now I have to excuse myself."

"What's the rush?" Manuel asked plaintively. He'd gladly have prolonged the conversation.

The priest took a moment to respond.

It came like a bolt from the blue and suddenly Manuel understood. That's why Catarina's workshop had been closed and there was so little traffic on the way to the estate.

The only thing that remained to be explained was how he could have forgotten what day of the week it was. That very morning he'd lamented the fact that the days were slipping past, sterile and undifferentiated.

"It's Sunday, and almost time for the noon mass. I'm officiating."

Manuel was grateful that Lucas ended the call without mentioning what was haunting them both: a full week had passed since Álvaro's death.

PLASTIC

Nogueira parked in front of his house. The warm lights of the ground-floor windows should have made him feel welcome, but he didn't go in right away. He sat behind the wheel unhappily contemplating his front door. He'd been retired for less than a week, and he was already finding his new status unbearable. Fifty-eight years old, and for the last two years his wife had been nagging him to stop work; after all, given his years of service, the regulations made him eligible to put in his papers, and retirement would give him more time with their daughters. Maybe his relationship with the younger one would turn out better than that with her sister. He'd known it was a bad idea, but he signed the papers anyway. He owed it to Laura, considering the way things were.

He opened his pocket notebook and scanned what he'd written, asking himself all the time what would become of him at the end of all this. He tried to put it out of his mind. When he put away the notebook, he looked down at his wedding ring. Noting its dull gleam, he used his thumb to rotate it, maybe to see if there was a brighter section. He looked toward the front door and sighed. He dutifully got out of the car and walked to the house.

The warm aroma of lemon pound cake greeted him when he opened the door. Muted television babble came from their small living room.

"I'm home!" He didn't expect a reply, and he didn't get one. He hung up his jacket and went to the kitchen. Two hours of driving around aimlessly had left him hungry.

The kitchen was spotless, as always. Not a crumb, not a single unwashed plate, no dirty spoons, not even a plate of leftovers in the refrigerator. He looked into the oven, just in case. It was still hot and fragrant, but there wasn't a trace of that cake. He raised the slide of the breadbox and found a small round loaf of the salt-free bread he hated. It looked so artificial and bleached, as if they'd radiated it to death. The contents of the fridge were equally bleak: an Arzúa cheese, chorizo sausage from Lalín, a piece of cured Galician pork, some ham, a piece of hard red morcón sausage. You'd think the bitch bought it with him specifically in mind.

There was a container of something that vaguely resembled beef stew and another with the ham-and-cheese balls in cream sauce that he liked so much. He'd become an expert in identifying mystery food obscured by the wrapping. His wife packaged the food she prepared in yards and yards of plastic, enveloping it like a patient spider. He was absolutely certain she was making sure he wouldn't be able to get it open. At times he'd hung around the kitchen watching her cook exquisite dishes and stow them away. She didn't mind that, but as soon as he laid a finger on one of her little bundles, she knew it. The way a spider senses something quivering at the far extreme of its web.

To test that theory he reached out and picked up the container in which his wife had so perfectly preserved the cheese dish. He didn't even get it out of the fridge before a voice called out sharply from the living room over the sound of the television. "No snacking! The greens for your dinner are almost ready. If you can't wait, then eat an apple!"

He shook his head, again both alarmed and impressed by her almost extrasensory perception. He shut the refrigerator and stared unhappily at a basket of apples as red and brilliant as those in a fairy tale. He stepped toward the living room and whispered to himself the next thing his wife would say.

"Or you could have some herbal tea." He heard the satisfaction she took in that suggestion.

He looked into their little living room. The armchairs sat before the television. His wife, seated in the farthest one, greeted him with a nod. His daughters were side by side on the big sofa. The smaller one stood on the sofa cushion and stretched to give him a kiss, but she eluded his attempt to hug her. The older one glanced up and acknowledged him with a little flip of her hand. The second armchair, his own rightful place, was occupied by the scrawny, gangling teenage boy Nogueira had despised ever since they'd first met, his older daughter's unavoidable boyfriend. The boy didn't even say hello. Nogueira tolerated that lack of respect, even preferred it. Empty cups stood on the coffee table along with more than half the cake he'd smelled as soon as he entered the house. He adored that cake, even though for six years he hadn't been allowed to have any. Nobody made it as well as his wife did.

The youngsters were watching some insipid Hollywood TV series, and his wife was reading in the warm glow of the standing lamp. She held the book half open, and he recognized the face in the photo on the dust jacket.

He pointed at it. "Manuel Ortigosa."

His wife's look of surprise gave him an immediate feeling of importance.

"I know him." He saw her interest, so he doubled his bet. "He's a friend of mine. I'm giving him a hand with something."

"Xulia!" His wife turned to their older daughter. "Scoot over and give your father room to sit down."

Pleased by that concession, Nogueira did as she'd directed.

Intrigued, she gave him an inquisitive look. "I had no idea you knew Manuel Ortigosa."

"Manuel? Sure, woman, we're good friends."

"And, Xulia," his wife said, again addressing their older daughter, "go to the kitchen and fetch a plate and a fork for your father. Maybe he'd like a little piece of cake."

SKELETONS

The farewells and the revving engines of the winery crew's pickups faded into the distance. Through the window Manuel saw the enologist in lively conversation with a couple of the last to leave. The conversation was inaudible, but the satisfied expressions on both sides showed him the transactions had gone well.

The entrance to the winery and the parking area next door had been crowded with vehicles when he'd arrived that afternoon. The narrow road offered hardly enough maneuvering room for the station wagons and tractors towing small trailers painted in gaudy colors. He left his car at the top of the drive and walked the rest of the way. Cultivators engaged in lively talk stood between the vehicles and bright-colored trailers piled high with grapes. He saw curiosity in growers' eyes as he passed them. They were also checking out the fruits of their competitors' harvests. Grapes glistened like jewels in the brilliant early-afternoon sun.

Daniel was stationed by the loading docks, where the sliding doors had been pulled all the way open. He watched laborers hoisting cartons of grapes onto the industrial scale and warehousemen carrying them to storage after the weighing. He looked up, caught sight of Manuel, smiled, and beckoned energetically. Daniel greeted him heartily. "Hey, Manuel! You're just in time; we're only getting started with the processing. Come over here, and I'll explain how it works."

Manuel watched the growers setting up tightly packed towers of crates, five layers high. Daniel recorded the weights in a receipt book along with the grower's name, and after the weighing he tore out the carbon copy and gave it to the owner. The process was repeated until the grower's entire harvest had been weighed. Then day workers carried the crates inside and dumped the grapes out on a steel table. Four men were stationed there, their sleeves rolled up to their elbows. Lucas was one of them. They were picking out leaves, twigs, dirt clods, and stones that had wound up mixed in with the harvested grapes. The official enologist from the Institute of Denomination of Origin monitored the table and cataloged the grapes. The grower stood next to him. Manuel observed the process at first, but soon he felt the need to participate, attracted by the busy flow, the constant rhythm of the work, and the laughter of men celebrating a fine crop. As they handled the dark grapes covered with must, the quality of the harvest was evident to everyone.

He rolled up his sleeves and went to the table. Daniel, who'd stayed by the scale and kept an eye on him, gestured to a worker to give him a work coat. After the employee secured it about him, he looked like a surgeon ready for the operating room. He found the work intense. All afternoon he participated as the grapes were dumped into the press. It rapidly crushed them. Sweet juices rich with sun and fortified by the mists gushed along channels to the chilled tanks waiting below.

The sun had already set by the time the last load was processed. He'd happily identified with the jubilation over the excellent harvest and felt a warm, contented glow. He waved to Lucas. The priest still had his sleeves rolled up and was helping a warehouseman transfer to storage the pomace of emptied grape skins they'd accumulated; it would be used for brandy or shredded for fertilizer. The two of them exited the pressing room, stepped into the warehouse, and encountered cool darkness in the adjoining space. They were drawn as if by a magnet toward the balcony overlooking the slope. The last rays of the September sunset threw the topography into sharp relief. The vista from that vantage point still displayed summer's exuberant growth, but it seemed to Manuel there was a hint the warm days were waning.

They heard the murmur of voices next door, laughter, and hissing sounds as men hosed out the tanks with scalding water. The workers there were shrouded in steam that stirred the aromatic must of the grapes and sent it swirling up in a white perfumed cloud that hovered just below the ceiling.

Manuel smiled undeterred in the darkness as he groped along the wall to locate the light switches, hearing the scrabble of Café's little claws against the stone floor. He was starting to regain his taste for life, and it was largely due to this place. He'd arrived wounded and dispirited, oppressed by the stark emptiness of Álvaro's room, pained by Elisa's anger and cold departure. He'd been wounded by her rejection, which had brought to mind the Raven's admonition: *This will never be your house, nor will my family ever be yours.*

That pronouncement had the weight of a life sentence. He'd realized his ache wasn't because of Elisa's reaction but rather because of the vacancy that the touch of Samuel's little hands had revealed. Manuel had been charmed by the boy's shrill voice shouting in enthusiasm, the row of his perfect little teeth exposed in that wide smile, the laughter that bubbled up from deep inside, and the thin arms that wrapped like sturdy vines around his neck in a powerful embrace.

And he'd been wounded deeply by the old woman's spite. He reminded himself that she'd intended each word charged with deliberate venom to cause the maximum possible damage. None of it was spontaneous. She must have planned and rehearsed the encounter for days. Her pronouncements had had the calculated rhythm of something rehearsed, a dogmatic declaration carefully prepared. The way the sinister nurse followed the hag's nonsense and approved like a dutiful disciple was evidence that each and every word came from the black space where her heart should have been. He remembered the studied cruelty and a malevolence that must have been carefully, slowly, and lovingly distilled. The performance had been awaiting the moment she could lure him in as an unsuspecting spectator to a scene only he hadn't seen before.

He knew that by brooding on her talk he was granting her the victory, something he needed to avoid at any price. Her poison was designed to be drunk in just that way, in little sips that amounted eventually to a lethal dose. Like a busy bee at a fatal flower, he couldn't resist the hidden malevolence.

He knew why. Even while he'd listened to her, he'd perceived in all that nastiness and hate the poison dart of her rancor, the capsule of mortal toxin and indisputable truth. She knew that candor is the sharpest dagger. She was no fool, and her rant, no matter whether excessive or subtle, whatever its effect in the telling, had been calculated to guarantee her own financial well-being.

She knew that hate alone was far less devastating than coarse candor. His brief encounter with her perverse sincerity had left him mangled and bleeding. He'd come away injected with an unwelcome entity as real as a virus and more terrifying than demonic possession: the unvarnished truth.

Manuel poured two glasses of wine, offered one to the priest, and gestured toward the deck chairs on the terrace. Lucas accepted the glass with a smile. They sat there for a while in silence, content to take in the quickly darkening profile of the hillside. The shadows lengthened and absorbed the remaining light as the two of them drank their wine.

Lucas eventually broke the silence. "You know, since Álvaro took charge of the winery, each year I've spent at least one day at the harvest. And we always ended it like this, sharing a bottle of wine right here."

Manuel looked around them as if, somewhere in the folds of time, he might detect the insubstantial image Lucas was describing. "Why?"

"What do you mean, 'Why?'" asked Lucas, disconcerted.

"Why would a priest participate in the grape harvest?"

Lucas smiled a bit as he pondered the question. "Well, I suppose I could quote Saint Teresa de Jesus. She told us God is present among the cooking pots, so surely God must be present in the vineyards as well." He paused and mused. "I can find God anywhere; but when I come here, when I work shoulder to shoulder with the men, I'm just one more laborer. I believe that physical labor confers a dignity fundamental to all human beings, a nobility that's diluted by dull daily routine. I regain that nobility when I come here."

They sat silent again for a time. Manuel refilled their glasses. He felt it as well: *Heroica* gathered in a single word, the acts, virtues, and processes so often ignored in daily life. They converged in this place like sharply drawn lines. They endowed it with a sense of the holy, making it a place where weakness, fear, and the abject ruin of the outside world were alleviated and washed away. A place where one could be robed in the fresh tunic of a hero.

He watched Lucas smile peacefully and lose himself in the undulating horizon. Manuel almost regretted having to interrupt that tranquility.

"I already told you on the phone, but I want to thank you again for speaking with Elisa. And with Nogueira."

Lucas dismissed the remark as if it were of no importance.

"I didn't know you two were acquainted. You and Nogueira." Manuel stopped to put his thoughts in order. "Well, I saw you recognize one another after Álvaro's funeral. But I didn't know you were acquainted well enough to have his phone number."

"Well, 'acquainted' would be an overstatement," the priest replied. "I remembered him from when Fran died. He was one of the first to get there that morning when we found Fran dead. First there was an ambulance, then the police turned up right away, and I came to give Fran extreme unction. I didn't have a very favorable impression of the policeman. He wasn't overtly hostile, but he was fairly cold and abrupt. I don't know why, but I had the impression of an enormous dislike behind his otherwise professional attitude."

"I know exactly what you mean." Manuel remembered the policeman's mocking sneer.

"After we ran into him at the entrance to As Grileiras, I went home and looked for his number. I knew I had it somewhere. He'd given me his card after he interviewed me, in case I remembered anything else."

"And you kept it for three years?"

Lucas said nothing.

"Did you ever think about calling him?"

Lucas shook his head but not very convincingly.

Manuel's expression became very serious. "That's why I wanted to talk to you." He paused. "I know what I said the other day at the sanctuary, but I'm starting to have some doubts."

An echo in his mind: *He knows you killed him.*

"Doubts? Why? I thought we both concluded it couldn't have been Álvaro. But even if it had been, what difference would that make? It wouldn't be strange for him to go check up on his brother. And one thing we both agree on: Álvaro couldn't have been implicated in any way in what happened to Fran, or, if Nogueira's analysis is correct, the moving of the body." Lucas fell silent and watched Manuel stare at the floor. "Or could he?"

Manuel drained his glass with a long swallow. "I'm not so sure."

He knows you killed him. Manuel clenched his jaws and tried to resist the implications.

Lucas looked concerned. "You're not so sure, but about what? You can't tell me you've changed your mind from one day to the next and now have doubts, unless you explain. I thought we made a pact to hide nothing from one another."

Manuel exhaled slowly, fixing his eyes on a horizon that by now was nearly invisible, reduced to a profile against the night sky's barely visible blue glow. He turned to the priest.

"You remember what I said about Álvaro going to the roadhouse with his brother?"

Lucas nodded unhappily.

"I talked with the prostitute. She said they let everyone think that they'd had sex, but that was just to satisfy Santiago. I believe it, because the man's so judgmental when it comes to homosexuality, a pure homophobe. Every time I say 'my husband' he almost has a stroke."

"Well," Lucas said cautiously, "perhaps that was a relief for you."

"It didn't last. A few hours later I discovered from his phone records that he'd been in contact with a local hustler."

Lucas didn't hide his disgust.

"You know what a hustler is, right? A male prostitute."

"Of course I know. The fact I'm a priest doesn't mean I'm ignorant of the world. But I find that even more out of character for Álvaro."

"Lucas, I think you're still idealizing him the way you did when you were in school together. But Álvaro lived on his own in Madrid for many years, and when we met he told me that for a while he'd been, as he said, 'out cruising a lot,' with all that implies. After we became close, that was a thing of the past. He told me everything about those days and said he wouldn't try to hook up ever again. I believed him for a very good reason—he didn't need to do that anymore."

"And what's changed now to make you think otherwise?"

"What's changed? You might as well ask me what *hasn't* changed, Lucas. I have the feeling I don't know who Álvaro was. It's like I'm discussing a stranger."

"I think that's where you're wrong. I stayed in contact with him throughout all those years, and I don't believe he changed at all. He was the same valiant, righteous young man I first met. Nothing of what you're saying makes sense to me."

Manuel didn't respond. He felt frustrated, isolated, and misunderstood. He filled their glasses again. "In any case, I think you should tell Nogueira what you saw that night. Or what you thought you saw."

"I understood that you were of the opinion it'd have a negative impact on the investigation. That as soon as he heard it, he'd stop looking for any other solution."

"Yes, I remember what I said, but now I know there were other people in the church and the surroundings that night." He counted them on his fingers. "Herminia was about to go there, but she stopped when she saw Elisa go out for a second time. Elisa saw Fran and Santiago taking leave of one another at the church door just as she got there. Fran went back inside, and Santiago said her fiancé was fine and asked her to go back to the manor because Fran was praying and didn't want to be disturbed. And from her window Herminia saw the dealer I mentioned before, who just happened to have been Fran's supplier when Fran was addicted."

"Shit!"

Manuel glanced at him, surprised by that language, and smiled faintly. "Nobody claims to have seen Álvaro; I specifically asked them. Of course I still haven't had the opportunity to find out from Santiago if he saw anyone other than Fran and Elisa, and I doubt I'll get the chance. Even if I do, I doubt he'll cooperate. He wasn't at all pleased to see me back at As Grileiras this morning."

"What happened?"

"I went upstairs to Álvaro's room to collect some papers." He found his thumb rubbing the twin wedding rings on his left hand. "Santiago went wild when he caught me there."

"Did he hit you?"

That question surprised Manuel. "It's odd you should ask. No, he ranted and raved for a while in pure frustration; then he exploded and slammed his hand into the wall. I was almost sorry for him. They told me that's how he usually responds when someone opposes him." He remembered the spots that had been bleached out of the kitchen wall.

Lucas leaned forward to emphasize the seriousness of what he was about to say. "Manuel, you must be careful. I think it'd be better if you stayed on the sidelines and left the investigating to Nogueira. After all, that's his job."

"The authorities officially closed the case. As a traffic accident. And Nogueira has just retired. He stepped down two days after Álvaro died."

"So? I can understand your concern; given the circumstances, it's normal for you to want to know more. But what's Nogueira's interest in this?"

Manuel shrugged. "I really don't know. I've never known anyone like him. To tell the truth, I don't much like him. He's disgusting sometimes." He smiled. "And I'm sure you feel the same way. But anyway, I think he's one of those men with an odd sense of honor, someone who refuses to leave a job unfinished. That's why you should talk to him and tell him what you saw. No matter how much I rack my brains, I can't find any justification for assuming Álvaro was implicated."

Lucas shook his head, put off by the suggestion.

"Anyway, Santiago isn't the most hostile opponent I've run up against. Despite what you may think."

Lucas studied him again, attentive.

"The marquess invited me to tea in her suite. I could take ten showers and scrub myself raw, but I wouldn't be able to wash away the slime and venom she spewed all over me. I've heard of parents who hate their children, but I've never met one before."

"She's always been a difficult woman."

"Difficult? It's beyond disgusting to have to listen to her. Every word drips with malice and contempt. She makes no secret of her feelings. I don't think she disliked Álvaro any more than the others; she seems to have despised her three sons equally. But she led me to understand that because of his unbending character, Álvaro gave them the most headaches." He snorted in anger. "That's saying a lot, considering that another son was a drug addict. Even so, I can't imagine any justification for banishing a boy of that age from home, separating him from his family and acting as if he were dead." He glared at Lucas. "Did you know that after they sent him to boarding school in Madrid, they took his room apart and stored his things? Álvaro didn't come back often, but when he did, he had to sleep in a guest room. As if he were a total stranger with no right to be there." Manuel shook his head at that unbelievable treatment. "You were classmates. Do you think it was because his sexual inclination was starting to manifest itself?"

"At twelve Álvaro wasn't stereotypically effeminate or delicate or even particularly sensitive; if that's what you mean, I'd have to say no. Just the opposite, in fact. He was slim and wiry, not particularly muscular. I remember he always had skinned knees. He didn't particularly go looking for trouble, but he wasn't afraid of it either. The few times I saw him get into a fight with another boy, it was always to defend his brother Santiago."

"Herminia told me that Santiago didn't have many friends when he was little."

"Mostly because he was a loudmouthed little troublemaker. He usually got away with it because Álvaro was there to intervene. I remember none of our crowd could stand Santiago. He was a pest, always hanging around us. Typical, I suppose, of little brothers. He seemed fascinated by everything Álvaro did. I remember that more than once during breaks or after school, we'd do everything we could to distract him and get rid of him. I guess we weren't terribly kind, but we were all just children. You know how it is. But there's no doubt about it—Santiago was a pain."

"His mother made no secret of her feelings. She said that two of her sons were born without character, but Álvaro had enough for all of them put together. Though she claimed that he was perverted."

Lucas emphatically rejected that, pressing his lips together and shaking his head. "I know what the marquess meant to say. Álvaro was forever disobeying and defying his parents. Especially when it came to his friends, all of them kids from the village, from poor families. We were always roaming around the estate, going up the hill to explore or swimming in the river. From today's perspective that might not seem so serious, but for Álvaro's father the dictates of social class were that certain lines could never be crossed. He took as a deliberate affront the fact that his son stubbornly insisted on associating with unacceptable companions. Between the ages of eight and twelve, Álvaro was always being punished, but that didn't deter him. He'd escape through the estate gardens and walk cross-country to the old abandoned barn where we used to meet him. His father was always threatening to send him to boarding school, and finally he did exactly that." Lucas shrugged. "On the other hand, it wasn't uncommon for unruly sons of well-off families to be exiled to expensive boarding schools where they associated with other troublemakers of their own social class. He came back during vacation breaks the first year, but after that maybe only at Christmas. He never stayed longer than two or three days. They sent him back to Madrid."

"They left him in Madrid over summer vacation?"

"He went to camps and summer programs, but he never came home. Once he was legally an adult, he didn't set foot on the estate again until his father died. At least that was the official version."

Manuel put his wineglass down on the little table between the deck chairs. He leaned forward for an explanation.

"No doubt you were told that Álvaro's sexual orientation was a surprise to them, and so was the fact that he was married to you."

"Yes."

"Well, it wasn't that much of a secret. Álvaro didn't come home, but his father still covered his expenses, financed his education, and provided the funds to set him up in his professional career. After that Álvaro was completely independent. I don't believe the old man's actions were inspired by generosity or fatherly concern; I think he simply would have found it a blot on the family escutcheon for the son of a Spanish aristocrat to wind up working as a supermarket clerk. Or, worse, for such a thing to become generally known. I'm sure that the old marquis found it less distasteful to support the lifestyle of his black-sheep son than to have the boy mix with the common people." Lucas grimaced. "The two of them scarcely said a word to one another the few times that Álvaro came back. Communications were broken off entirely after that. But his father was always fully informed about Álvaro's life in Madrid." He studied his glass. "The old marquis was one of those men who keeps a close eye on everyone, friends and enemies alike, certainly those who pleased him but especially anyone who caused him trouble. And Álvaro was a problem." He finished off his wine. "I said Álvaro had no contact with his family until the old marquis died, but that's not entirely true. Álvaro did come back one time. His father summoned him for a discussion ten years ago."

Manuel straightened up in his seat. He took a deep breath and looked out into the blackness below the horizon and the clear September sky now sprinkled with sparkling stars, a promise the next day would be sunny.

Ten years. He would never forget that time. They'd already lived together for years, but after the passage of the 2005 law on marriage equality, they set the date and got married on Christmas of the following year. This coming December would mark their tenth anniversary.

"Tell me about it."

Lucas nodded, pained by the weight of words he knew to be hurtful even before they were articulated. He owed this to Manuel, for he'd sworn there would be no more lies.

"The old man offered him a deal. He more or less told his son, though certainly not in so many words, that he was aware of Álvaro's 'condition' and the life he was living in Madrid, because for all those years a detective agency had been providing him full reports. He said he'd given Álvaro the freedom to live as he pleased all that time. He even hinted that he knew of your existence. None of it really mattered to him. 'Every person has his own vices; I know it well because I have my own: gambling, betting, women . . . A man has to get it out of his system.' Álvaro couldn't believe his ears. 'I'm very ill. Cancer's not going to kill me right away, but it'll get me eventually, and when that happens, someone in this family's going to have to take the reins and see to the estate and the businesses. Your brothers are good for nothing, and if I will it to your mother, she'll just give it all to the Church.' He said he knew they hadn't gotten along since Álvaro was a child, but he'd always admired Álvaro's courage. Though he was certain that the marquess would never accept anything concerning his 'failing' and he himself found it difficult to understand, he could put up with the fact his son had weaknesses just as he himself did. At that point in the conversation Álvaro was beginning to think that perhaps, just perhaps, after all, his father, a man of the older generation educated in a different tradition, was admitting—insofar as such a man was capable of acknowledging such a thing—that he might be wrong.

"'You must come back home, Álvaro. I will put you in charge of all the family affairs, and I will execute a living will with you as the heir to everything except the title, which you'll receive after I die, and I'll do all of this immediately. Soon I'll no longer be able to tend to our affairs, and I want to take advantage of the time remaining, knowing that everything has been secured and you'll take care of our interests when I'm no longer here. You're the only one qualified and able to do so, and I know you'll safeguard the family honor, come what may. Come back home, marry a young woman of good family, and keep up appearances. Marriages of convenience are a long-standing tradition of the nobility. My marriage to your mother, arranged by my parents and hers, is the best example of the fact that such a pledge can be very convenient for both parties. You'll be free to go off for flings in Madrid to help you blow off steam.'" Lucas paused. He studied Manuel's eyes, conscious of the impact his revelation was having and hoping to see some sign of acceptance of it.

"Manuel, I said you were misjudging Álvaro, that he was ashamed of them, not of you. Álvaro had been expecting a reconciliation, and his father's first words had seemed to promise a change of heart. He was crushed by the man's hateful attitude and adamant rejection. Álvaro stood up, looked his father in the eye, and answered, *All this I will give you if you fall down and worship me.*"

"The offer that the devil made to Jesus when he laid the world at his feet," Manuel murmured.

Lucas nodded emphatically. His pride in his friend had been evident in the way he'd unconsciously straightened up to imitate Álvaro's defiant attitude. "His father didn't answer. He looked away, shaking his head in total disgust. And of course you know what happened then. Álvaro went back to Madrid and married you. For years he had no contact with his family, convinced that his refusal and disobedience meant he'd broken with them forever. He was astounded when after his father's death, Griñán called to say he'd inherited everything."

"And at last Álvaro accepted," murmured Manuel, sickened by the thought.

"I don't think he had any choice. What his father said about his brothers was true. Even as Álvaro was trying to decide what to do, Fran's sudden death complicated things horribly. Truly, Manuel, I don't think he had any other option; but he did choose, and his choice was exactly the opposite of what his father wanted. He returned to live his true life in Madrid with you, leaving his hidden second life here."

"But why, Lucas? You're telling me all this as if he were a hero: his father's rejection, his decision to live his own life and choose me over all that his father was offering. But why prolong it? Why keep hiding me from the eyes of his family if his father was dead? To spare the feelings of his mother and his brother? For God's sake! This is the twenty-first century. Do you think it'd have been more traumatic for them to meet me three years ago than to face me now, in these circumstances?"

Lucas was upset. He'd obviously have given anything to be able to give a satisfactory answer to that question.

Manuel sighed in resignation. The alcohol had gone to his head, and the wine had dulled his emotions sufficiently for him to take a logical approach to a story that in other circumstances would have angered him and clouded his judgment. "His mother told me their father chose Álvaro as his heir because of Álvaro's innate propensity for cruelty and the marquis's conviction he'd do anything necessary, anything at all, for the sake of the family. And she said something else: Álvaro had shown himself willing to defend his family's sake before, on more than one occasion. You just said his father found him capable of doing anything to protect the family interests. Why were they so sure, Lucas? His mother told me her husband hadn't made a mistake about him. What does that mean? What was this propensity for cruelty on Álvaro's part that prompted his father, despite Álvaro's disobedience, to make him the head of the family?"

Lucas stubbornly shook his head. "Pay no attention to her, Manuel. It's meaningless. She said it only to hurt you."

Manuel had no doubt of that, but he was also sure the Raven was telling the truth.

Daniel materialized behind them in the darkness. "We've finished for today. The warehouse team is locking up, and we'll be back early tomorrow." He noticed the empty bottles on the table and added, "I can leave you a key if you're staying awhile longer. But I think it would be a good idea for me to give you both a ride home."

Manuel got laboriously to his feet, staggered slightly, and gave them all a slightly foolish grin. "You know, that would probably—would probably be a good idea."

THE AESTHETIC OF
THE UGLY

Manuel became aware of the piercing brilliance of the morning light before opening his eyes. He was annoyed with himself for again having failed to close the wooden shutters the night before. He looked out upon a sullen gray dawn that belied the initial impression of luminosity. He heard the rattle of rain against the window. A timid sun peered between passing clouds with a momentary beam that shifted like a searchlight to illuminate here a tree or there a building, like a scene in experimental theater.

He couldn't summon the energy to check the time. It looked early, the start of yet another day. It occurred to him that time had changed for him, and he was on a calendar of blank pages, all of them the same. The early confusion and lack of control of the first few days had been replaced by an immobile calm that reestablished balance by accepting whatever came and assuming that nothing mattered. Álvaro's death had removed anything that might have differentiated one day from the next. Acceptance gave him peace. It meant acknowledging absence and embracing the void. Dwelling in that merciful nothingness kept his soul from being torn to bits.

Café's quiet snuffling and the rattle of rain against the windowpane assured that tranquility. Manuel heard the steady breathing of the little body pressed against his thigh. He pushed himself up a bit and was surprised to find that the shutters hadn't been the only thing he'd neglected the night before. The bed was rumpled and wrinkled but the bedspread was still in place. He hadn't crawled under the covers or even gotten out of his clothes.

He reached down to pet the dog. "Thanks for bringing me home, Café."

The dog's eyes opened for that evasive little glower. The little creature yawned.

"It must have been you. I don't remember a thing."

Café's only answer was to leap off the bed, go to the door of the room, and sit there in perky expectation of a walk. The cell phone on the night table vibrated and beat a hollow tattoo on the thin wood of the tabletop. Manuel picked it up.

Nogueira's voice was impatient. "I'm almost to your hotel. Get ready. We've got work to do."

Manuel held the cell phone up close enough to make out the time. Nine o'clock in the morning. Baffled, he looked first at the dog waiting patiently before the door and then back at the phone.

"I don't recall setting a time."

"We didn't. Something's turned up."

He studied his reflection in the mirror. He needed a shower and clean clothes. And a shave. "Listen, Nogueira, it's going to take me a while. Ask the innkeeper to fix some eggs with chorizo. They're from his own hens. And you can put it on my tab."

"Fine, but don't dawdle."

Before the lieutenant rang off, Manuel looked over at Café waiting stolidly by the door. "Nogueira, the dog needs to go outside. Get out of your car and prop open the door to the bar so he can get outside. Hurry. He knows the way."

He smiled as he clicked the button to cut off the lieutenant's protests and let the dog out.

⊱✦⊰

Nogueira was seated next to the picture window sipping coffee. A madeleine sat next to his cup. An empty plate gleaming with grease showed he'd had breakfast as suggested. Manuel declined the offer of food and gulped down a cup of coffee. They got up, and he grinned when he saw Nogueira scoop up the untouched pastry the innkeeper had served with his coffee. He looked skyward and took his time, letting the lieutenant have his inevitable cigarette. He admired the calm, gentle rhythm of the persistent rain the Galicians call the *orballo* and remembered the starry sky of the previous evening that had seemed to promise no precipitation today.

"Let's take my car," Nogueira said.

Manuel gave the lieutenant a sidelong glance much like Café's usual expression. He remembered vowing not to go with Nogueira again unless he had an avenue of escape. But his car wasn't at the inn. After the two bottles of wine he and Lucas had shared the previous evening, Daniel had driven them back with the promise a couple of his employees would get their cars back to them.

"And what about Café?"

"I put down a blanket," the officer said without looking at him, clearly aware of Manuel's surprise.

Manuel helped the dog settle in his place, got into the car, and said nothing until they were well out on the main road. "Are you going to tell me where we're going this early in the morning? I thought the roadhouses were closed at this hour."

Nogueira gave him a baleful glance, and for a moment Manuel thought the man was thinking about making him get out of the car and walk back in the rain. But Nogueira's reply was entirely calm. "We're going to call on Antonio Vidal, aka 'Toñino.' The hustler who Álvaro telephoned."

Manuel pushed himself up in his seat and started to say something, but the policeman forestalled him. "I called a contact at headquarters this morning to make sure of the address. He told me a family member reported Toñino missing a few days ago. We're going to check it out."

Manuel mulled that over in silence, vexed at being pushed step by step through this investigation of Álvaro's movements. An inner voice admonished him not to go there, to avoid this because any discovery would be hurtful. He turned a deaf ear. He pretended he didn't care and glanced at the lieutenant. Nogueira turned off the main road and seemed lost in his own thoughts. Manuel saw his pushback had had positive effects: the blanket so the dog could accompany them in his car, the way Nogueira had stifled his protestations when obliged to wait. Given the policeman's general attitude, those might be interpreted as apologies or at least the equivalent of a truce. If Nogueira could control himself, then Manuel was determined to do the same.

The Os Martiños neighborhood spread across a hillside where the paved road quickly ran out and became a track of poured concrete for a mile or so. The rough surface made the car jolt and vibrate. Then the track became a dirt road from which gravel driveways led to single-story houses. Some of the inhabitants had done their best to dignify their dwellings with geraniums in plastic pots and pathways of loose tile leading up to their doors. Tiles had sunk unevenly into the muddy ground. Most of the houses had that disorderly, unplanned appearance he'd begun to suspect was typical of Galicia. It was worse here than elsewhere. Unfinished construction and piles of building materials by the gates gave the structures an air of dour pretension made that much worse by the rain that rendered the drenched houses as perfect depictions of misery.

"Galician *feísmo*," Nogueira commented.

"What?" replied Manuel, jolted out of his reverie.

"*Feísmo*. The aesthetic of the ugly, they call it. This fucking tradition we have of leaving everything half-finished. Comes from the custom of parceling bits of land out to all the offspring so they can build their own houses. They throw up some walls and a roof and eventually get the place habitable; they marry, and they keep adding to it bit by bit. No plans and usually without permits or qualified labor. Construction is ruled by the necessities of the moment, not by any notion of harmony or beauty. That's the aesthetic of the ugly. *Feísmo*."

Manuel looked out at brick walls with rough smears of mortar along the joints, windows mounted in the facades, many still chocked in place. Abandoned heaps of cement, sand, or rubble stood by the entrances of many of the houses.

"But, *feísmo*?"

"You can't tell me it's not ugly as a pig's butt."

"Okay," Manuel said. "That kind of construction suggests a weak economy. Maybe."

"Weak, my ass!" Nogueira exclaimed. "Drive through here any day, and you'll find cars costing fifty thousand euros parked in front of these houses. It has nothing to do with a poor economy. It's a culture of 'What the hell, that's good enough' and 'That'll do.' A lot of the time it's the next generation that winds up finishing the house."

Nogueira checked the address in his little leather-bound notebook and stopped before a small cinder-block house on a square lot. A television antenna jutted up from the roof like a flagpole planted on a mausoleum. A white balustrade separated the entrance to the house from the door of a garage that looked as if it hadn't been opened in years. The area around the house was laid with a scattering of tiles that extended perhaps six feet into the yard. Concrete-block planters on either side of the door held spindly trees. A wide dark oil stain discolored the tiles. The place looked deserted, but they saw the face of an old woman watching them from the window of the house next door. She made no effort to hide her curiosity.

"Let me do the talking," Nogueira warned him before they got out. "You say nothing, and they'll assume we're on official business. We won't do anything to make them think otherwise. And leave the dog in the car." He checked the floor behind them. "He'd make them suspicious."

Café gave him one of those glowering sideways looks.

They hurried across the yard in the rain. Nogueira ignored the doorbell and instead hammered on the painted wooden door. The quick series of demanding knocks brought back to Manuel the memory of the knocking on his own door that had started everything.

A woman of about seventy opened the door. She wore a wool housecoat and an apron. Her eyes were cloudy with cataracts. The right one looked as red and rheumy as that of some great fish.

"Good morning!" Nogueira greeted her in the official voice he'd used during all his years as a policeman. She muttered something in reply but he kept talking. "Did you report Antonio Vidal as missing?"

The woman raised both hands to her mouth as if trying to stifle her question. "Did something happen? Did you find my Toñino?"

"No, señora, not yet. May we come in?"

Her reaction showed she assumed they were from the police. She opened the door wide and stepped aside. "Please do."

The house had a single main room. The woman had furnished it as a dining room too elaborate for such a place. It was dominated by a large oval dining table with eight chairs. A polished dark sideboard held a full set of fine porcelain dishes that had probably never been used, a vase with artificial roses, and a small wooden shrine with the figure of a saint. It was one of those passed from one family to another; according to the local tradition, parishioners take turns hosting and venerating such displays in their homes. A small oil lamp flickered before the shrine. A row of medicines stood at one end of the sideboard.

She pulled a pair of chairs out from the table. "Please have a seat."

Nogueira remained standing. Manuel stepped away to examine the lamp set on a block of cork and a bowl where the fragment of a playing card was floating on a layer of golden oil over clouded water.

"I thought you weren't going to do anything, because he's had problems with drugs. Nobody cares what happens to him nowadays." She looked toward Manuel.

"Was it you who contacted the authorities?" Nogueira asked.

"Yes, I'm his aunt. Toñino's lived with me for the last twelve years. Just the two of us. His father died, and the mother, well, she ran off a long time ago, and we never heard from her after that. The doctors said my brother died from a heart attack, but I think he really died of a broken heart. "The woman shrugged. "She was a bad one."

"Your name is Rosa, isn't it?" Nogueira asked, cutting short the recital of family history the woman clearly was willing to continue.

"Rosa María Vidal Cunqueiro, seventy-four years of age this coming May," she recited. She pulled a handkerchief from her apron pocket and put it to her right eye. A glob of thick sticky fluid oozed from her cloudy eye like an enormous tear.

Manuel couldn't stand to look at it.

"Very well, Rosa María. You signed a statement a week ago Monday, declaring your nephew missing. Is that correct?"

Manuel looked over at Nogueira. In addressing the woman he'd adopted a different tone, one Manuel hadn't heard before. His voice was vibrant, patient, and caring, as if he were speaking to a small girl.

"That's right," the woman said gravely.

"And how long has Antonio been missing from your home?"

"It's been, it had been, since Friday night when he went out. But I don't make a fuss, you know, because he's young, and he always goes out on the weekends. He always lets me know when he's not going to be back at night, so I won't worry. Sometimes he stays over with a friend, but he always telephones, even if it's late at night. But I began to worry when he didn't come back on Saturday."

Manuel started at that. He released a long low whistle of pain as he turned to look out a window set excessively low in the wall. It offered the desolate prospect of the rain-soaked front yard. A writer knows how to add things up, and the coincidence of the boy's disappearance with Álvaro's visit upset him.

The policeman noticed his reaction but concentrated on the old woman. "And you haven't heard from your nephew since?"

"No, señor. I've already phoned all the friends I know and all their families." She pointed toward the old-fashioned wall phone. Someone had used surgical tape to post next to it a list of phone numbers written in huge digits.

Nogueira pretended to remember something. "What's the name of that friend of your nephew? The one he's always with?"

"You mean Ricardo. I called him right away, and he didn't know anything."

"When did you talk with him?"

"That same Sat . . . no, Sunday."

"And he hasn't called back or come by?"

"No, señor, not Ricardo. But another friend calls all the time, but I don't know his name. He told me to inform the police."

"So, then," Nogueira said, pretending to scribble in his little notebook, "your nephew doesn't come home Friday night; Saturday you begin to worry, and you go to the police on Sunday."

"That's how it was, señor. I was sure something had happened to him."

Manuel gave Nogueira a worried look.

"You see, I know my nephew. Maybe he does have a lot of faults. So does everybody else." She turned to Manuel. "And I do, too, I have to admit that, but he's a good boy. He knows I get worried if he doesn't call, and that's why ever since he got to be a teenager and started going out on his own, whenever he's staying overnight with some friend he lets me know, and says, 'Auntie, don't worry; I'm staying at so-and-so's house, you go to bed and get some sleep,' because he knows that otherwise I won't sleep a wink. My Toñino's a good boy, and he'd never do that to me."

She put the handkerchief to her face and wiped both eyes. She was weeping. Manuel was startled; he hadn't realized it.

"Something terrible has happened, I know it has," the old woman moaned through her tears.

Nogueira stepped forward and put a sheltering arm around her shoulders. "No, ma'am, you'll see, he'll turn up. He'll be out there someplace with some friends, and he must have forgotten to call."

"You don't know him," the woman protested. "Something must have happened, because he knew he was supposed to put the drops in my eyes." She gestured toward the row of medicines on the sideboard. "He always puts them in for me, twice a day, morning and evening. Days and days have gone by, and I haven't used them because I can't do it by myself." She unfolded the handkerchief, covered her face with it, and sobbed.

Nogueira's lips were a sharp straight line under his mustache. Taking her by the arm like a prisoner, although with great gentleness, he guided her to a chair. "Calm down, señora. Stop crying and have a seat. Which drops are you supposed to use?"

She lowered the handkerchief. "The ones in the pink carton, two in each eye."

Nogueira checked the instructions for the medicine, bent over her, and carefully applied the drops. "It says here everything'll look blurry for a while, and you shouldn't move until your vision clears. Don't worry, I'll close the door when we leave." He waved at Manuel and went toward the door.

"God bless you for that!" the woman said, still looking up toward the ceiling. "And please find my Toñino! What would I do without him?"

Nogueira paused in the doorway, surveyed the outside, and stared again at the oil stain on the tiles. He turned back. "Señora, does your nephew have a car?"

"Yes, he has one. I bought him one because he needed it for work, but then the job didn't work out . . ."

"Did you tell the officer you talked to that the car was gone as well?"

The woman put a hand to her mouth. "No. You think that's important? I didn't think of it."

"Don't worry, I'll tell my colleague. Just one more thing: What color is the car?"

"It's white, señor."

Nogueira closed the door carefully and blew out a long breath. The rain had stopped, but the humidity swirling about them had left everything glistening wet.

They walked away from the door. "White," Manuel said.

"Right," the lieutenant mused, "but that's not much help. It's the least expensive color and the one most frequently used for pickups. Lots of 'em out there in the countryside. I'd guess that just about every barn has one."

"Do you think she's right? Could something have happened to him?"

"Well, she's right about one thing. When it comes to cases like Toñino's the police don't waste too much time looking for them. He's a drug addict and a hustler. He might have gone off with just about anybody, without a second thought. Male prostitutes are like that. But . . ."

"But?"

"But I believe Rosa María. Sure, she's his aunt and thinks her nephew's a little angel, but the woman's practically blind, and the house is spick-and-span. I don't think she does the cleaning. Those twisted fingers tell me she probably has arthritis. And I don't know if you took a look at the list of phone numbers on the wall; he took the trouble to write them out with numbers large enough for her to read. I believe her when she says he always called when he wasn't coming home. My mother was like that. I found out pretty quick that it was better for me to give her a call than to find she'd stayed up all night waiting for me to come in. She'd be exhausted, and I'd have to put up with her scolding all the next day."

As before, when Nogueira realized he'd involuntarily revealed some aspect of his private life, he acted as if he suddenly felt vulnerable. He looked away, ignoring Manuel's surprised expression. The confession seemed that much more intimate after the man had shown an almost affectionate regard for the old woman.

Nogueira continued his list of observations. "It's not just the clean house and the phone numbers. The medicines are marked with the times she's supposed to take them, and they're marked in large letters to show what each is for. He takes care of his aunt, and, like she says, something must have happened to keep him from phoning. He knows all too well that the old woman can't take care of herself."

Manuel was skeptical. "A crocodile with a heart of gold."

"Sometimes even the worst degenerates have one. That's what's confusing. If the good folks were good and the bad ones were simply bad, the world would be a lot easier for everybody. On the other hand, his buddy's attitude bothers me. Ricardo; they call him Richie. The two are inseparable. The aunt calls to say the boy hasn't come home, and it doesn't worry him. So, two possibilities: Either he knows where Toñino is, or he knows what the boy's hiding from, and he figured out that the disappearance coincided with Álvaro's visit."

Manuel looked away in disgust.

"Could be that there's no connection," Nogueira admitted. It was the first time he showed any consideration for Manuel's feelings.

Manuel didn't thank him for it. He dodged the topic with a question. "And the other one? The one who's been calling?"

"Probably a client. His recommendation to call the police is a clear indication he doesn't know squat."

Manuel looked out unhappily at the houses spread across the Os Martiños slope below them. "Now what?"

"I take you back to the inn. Get some sleep. Both you and the dog look hung over." Café hadn't budged from his blanket on the backseat. "I'll talk with my contacts and get them to put the vehicle into the missing persons bulletin. Cars are easier to track than people. And tonight we'll drive out to Lugo to pay Richie a visit, and he can explain why he's not worried about his friend's disappearance. But first," he said, using his chin to indicate the house next door, "we pay our respects to the neighbor lady."

Manuel stepped forward and saw that the same old woman who'd seen them earlier from her ground-floor window was beckoning to them.

Stationed at her window, she was the living image of a malicious gossip. Her shameless peering at them when they arrived had suggested as much, and so did her expression when she came to the door. Her behavior was quite different from that of Toñino's aunt. This one held the front door open a crack and stuck her sharp nose through it to sniff at them like a bird dog. She opened it a bit wider, just enough for them to see she was wearing a housecoat. The lace edging of a nightdress was visible below it.

"You're from the police, right?" She didn't give them time to answer. "When I saw you I thought you were here for Toñino. Did they arrest him again? I haven't seen him for days."

Nogueira didn't answer her questions. He gave her a broad professional smile. "Good morning, señora. Would you be so kind as to give us a couple of minutes?"

The woman simpered, flattered, as she pulled tight the belt of her housecoat and reached up to finger her lapels in pretended modesty. "Well, of course. But you'll have to excuse me. With all the uproar I still haven't had time to get dressed."

"Oh, please don't worry, we understand perfectly. And we thank you for your kindness."

She stepped aside and opened the door a little more, enough for them to slip through into the house. The place smelled of chickens and cat piss.

"What a lovely house!" the lieutenant said, and walked over to windows hung with sheer curtains that gave an unimpeded view of every detail of the yard of the house next door. "And you're fortunate you can see so much," he added with a crafty smile.

The woman had gotten someone to build a bench that ran the entire length of the window. It was covered with cushions of various sizes and different fabrics she must have sewn for herself. Manuel noticed a sewing basket and a crochet project on the floor under the bench. An obese cat lay on the window seat, no doubt responsible for at least half of the stink.

"Well, I don't want you thinking I'm a gossip or anything like that. I'm not interested in other people's lives, but I really enjoy sewing, needlepoint, and crochet work, and since I have the best light next to the window, well, even if I weren't interested . . ." She shrugged.

"Of course, señora." Nogueira was firmly on her side.

"The truth is that I really do feel sorry for Rosa María. We've been neighbors for more than forty years, and we've never had any problems, but that nephew of hers! Her nephew is something else again. His mother abandoned him, and his father passed away, and I think Rosa María loved him so very much she just raised him wrong." That censure was severe. "Look, I never wanted to do him any harm, but I could have called the police a thousand times for the way he was always carrying on. Day after day we had people here yelling at his door, friends of his calling him early in the morning . . ."

"And lately?" Nogueira asked.

"Things have been quiet over the last few days. Well, I should tell you what happened last week." She was leading them on, well aware that Nogueira was getting more and more interested. "Well, it had nothing to do with the scandalous things that used to go on here. I mean, they weren't addicts or anything like that."

"Tell me about it," Nogueira requested with flattering attention as he walked her to the bench and took a seat beside her.

"Well, you see, Rosa María told me that her nephew was doing fine and had even started to work for his uncle at the seminary."

Manuel interrupted. "In the seminary? In the San Xoan seminary?"

"There's no other one," the woman replied tartly. "The prior of the seminary is Rosa María's brother and brother to Toñino's father. It wasn't the first time he hired the boy to help the gardener; small tasks and fixing things at the brothers' residence, but the boy never lasted long in any job, and this time was no different."

"Go on," Nogueira encouraged her.

"Well, the other day I was sitting here working when I saw—just the way I saw you today—a car stop in front of the gate. The prior of the seminary got out. He doesn't often come around, but I've seen him and I know him. Well, the thing is, he started beating on the door and shouting for the nephew. He and Rosa María were arguing at the front door, and she didn't let him in. Toñino didn't stick his nose out. He hid behind his aunt's skirts and argued from the inside of the house, but it was obvious he was too scared to come outside."

"When was that?"

"Early Saturday afternoon. After lunch."

Manuel looked at Nogueira in astonishment, but it was obvious that the lieutenant also had realized Toñino's aunt had been lying. She might have done so merely to justify her declaration he was missing; the rule is that no adult person in possession of his faculties may be declared missing until twenty-four hours have passed.

"Are you absolutely certain this was Saturday and not some other day? Friday, for example?"

"Of course I'm certain," she answered, annoyed. "It was Saturday."

"Could you hear what they were saying?"

"Officer, I could hear it because they were shouting. Not because I was trying to eavesdrop on my neighbors or anything like that."

"Obviously, señora!" Nogueira said again, although this time with a touch of sarcasm.

She didn't notice the edge in his voice. "The prior said, 'You don't know who you're getting involved with. This could be the end of me.' And then he said, 'Things are not going to stay like this.'"

"You're sure that's what he said?"

The woman appeared offended for a moment and then affirmed with great seriousness, "It was just like I'm telling you."

"Then what happened?"

"Nothing. The prior left, and right away Tonino got into his car and drove off. He's been gone since then. He's still missing."

CABALLEROS

The only sign for the Vulcan was a discreet illuminated plaque on a door so plain that had it been in an alley, you would have mistaken it for a service entrance.

He'd followed Nogueira through the rain after they parked a couple of blocks away. On any night other than this rainy Monday, the bar district would have been busier. Two boys smoking in the meager shelter of the overhang moved aside to let them pass.

The Vulcan's interior decorator hadn't applied much ingenuity to the design of the place. Dark walls with abstract designs in phosphorescent paint glowed under the neon lights. Even so, the crowd was lively, and several couples were dancing in a narrow space in front of the bar. Nogueira glanced around and strode up to a group of boys drinking bottled beer. "Well, what a coincidence. Here's Richie!"

The boy he addressed turned around sputtering and clearly annoyed, and his buddies quickly withdrew. "Fuck, Lieutenant, you gave me a hell of a scare!"

Nogueira grinned like the big bad wolf. He was enjoying himself. "Guess you were up to no good, then."

"No, no way!" The boy tried to smile. "It's just I wasn't expecting you."

Manuel thought Richie was probably in his early twenties. Maybe a little older, but he was certainly baby-faced. Manuel realized that he had no idea what Toñino looked like. Was he as young as this? Did he have that gaunt look that seemed to be so popular with hustlers?

Manuel felt ill.

Richie noticed. "What's wrong with your buddy?"

"Don't you worry about him, Richie. But come to think of it, that'd be entirely out of character for you. You don't worry even about your own crowd."

"I don't know what you're talking about."

"I'm talking about your soul mate, your bosom buddy Toñino, who's been gone for a week. You haven't even dropped by his house to ask about him, so I figure maybe you know where he is and why he's keeping his head down."

The boy started to say something, but Nogueira cut him off. "And don't think you can lie to me. I told his aunt not to worry, so now you're going to explain to me what your bud's mixed up in and why we don't have to worry."

Richie slowly deflated. "Well, listen, Lieutenant, I don't know nothing, right? Except for what he told me."

Nogueira motioned to the waiter, and three bottles of Estrella Galicia appeared on the bar. The policeman gave one to Manuel, then took the empty bottle out of the boy's hands and replaced it with a full one. "So tell me."

The kid took a swig before he spoke. "He said his luck had changed. Said he had something really big, and he was going to get a pile of dough."

"What was it?"

"I dunno. Didn't want to tell me."

"I don't believe you." Nogueira wore a bored expression.

"I swear, Lieutenant, he refused to say, but he was talking about changing his life, leaving all this behind." Richie waved broadly toward the bar. "It had to be something huge. The day before he got the hell out, he told me everything was ready. That's why I wasn't surprised he disappeared."

"You expect me to believe that your sidekick and lifelong friend vanished without leaving you a crumb or toasting his success with you?"

The boy shrugged. His expression was sullen. "What do you think we are—marines? We don't have no honor code or any of that kind of stuff. Yeah, we're friends, but that's how friends are around here, every man for himself. And if a guy runs across a good chance to get out and leave it all behind, you think he's not going to take it? I sure would."

"Did he say if this big deal of his had something to do with the marquis's family?"

"You talking about the folks up As Grileiras?" The kid smiled. "No, I dunno. I guess not. He had other business with that bunch."

263

"But you said it was something big. Blackmail? Maybe he was going to out someone as a user or talk about some client's kinky tastes?"

"What? That's crazy. Toñino's no fool. He knows his clients, especially the women, and he milks even the classiest of them. You don't kill the cow if it hasn't gone dry."

Manuel remembered Elisa running after Samuel through the garden and Herminia saying, *Her son saved her.* He turned away in disgust, left the bottle of beer on the bar, and walked away.

Nogueira caught up with him at the door. "He doesn't know shit."

They went out into the rain and walked down the deserted street toward the car.

They heard them before they saw them.

"Well, well, lookee what we got here!"

They turned around to find two grinning men standing in the middle of the sidewalk. Manuel noticed a third who'd stepped out onto the road from between the cars to block them off in that direction while keeping a nervous eye on the deserted street. Manuel thought he saw the blue lights of a police patrol car in the distance.

The first man spoke again. "This couple of queers've hooked up and are prancing off home to screw each other's butts!"

Nogueira raised a hand. "You're making a mistake."

The one who'd addressed them laughed as if that were a hilarious joke. The others didn't join in. The one who'd been in the road had now circled around behind them.

"He says I'm making a mistake; probably means they're not gonna stick it up their asses. They like sucking dick better."

"The one behind us is for you," Nogueira said to Manuel.

"Go!" Manuel responded and sprang toward the one at their backs.

The guy couldn't have been expecting it, because Manuel caught him full force in the left eye. He stumbled backward into the gutter and lost his footing, reeled against a parked car, and had to choose between putting a hand to his face and grabbing something to keep from falling. But he flailed out with a right hook that raked ineffectually across Manuel's left ear.

The other two froze at the sight of the gun in Nogueira's fist, aimed at them with the cold competent grip of a professional.

"And now what?" Nogueira challenged them, keeping them in his sights. "Who's the queer now? What have you sons of bitches got to say about that? Huh? Still planning on having some fun?"

"Nogueira," Manuel warned. The blue lights were coming slowly down the street toward them.

"Get out of here, you bastards!" the lieutenant said. He stepped to Manuel's side and stamped a foot on the pavement just as Herminia had done outside the kitchen to scare away the immense cat.

The two helped up the one lying in the road between the two cars. They left, half dragging him as they went.

"And next time I see any of you around here, I'll stick my pistol up your asses!" he shouted at their backs. That made them scramble faster.

Manuel and Nogueira went their way and turned the corner into the first cross street before the patrol car came abreast of them.

Nogueira didn't speak until they were in the car with the engine running. "How are you?"

Manuel was astonished by Nogueira's solicitous concern. He put his hand up toward the searing sensation across his ear but decided not to touch it. "All right."

"How about your hand?" the policeman asked, gesturing toward Manuel's still clenched fist.

"Okay. Swelling a bit, nothing special."

Nogueira slammed his fists against the steering wheel. "Goddamn good! You gave that asshole a fine lesson!"

Manuel nodded, releasing his breath in a long heave but feeling tension still scrabbling about his body like a living thing.

"Really good, Manuel!" the officer repeated boisterously. "And now we're going to get ourselves a stiff drink. We're a couple of Vikings, *qué carallo!*" He swore exuberantly. "I don't know about you but I need one!"

"Good idea," Manuel managed to answer. He was trembling all over.

∽❧∾

They slipped under the half-lowered metal shutter. Most of the lights were out, and chairs had been placed upside down on almost all the tables. A middle-aged man behind the bar was watching a boxing match on television. From time to time he refreshed the glasses of a couple of hardened drinkers and a gambling addict who fed coins into a slot machine the whole time Nogueira and Manuel were there.

They stood at the bar for the first two shots, but as they received the third Nogueira pointed toward the table farthest in the back by the door to the toilets. The stink of disinfectant was strong. Manuel was beginning to feel tipsy. The numbing effect of the booze dulled the throbbing pain of his hand. As he'd predicted, it had swollen considerably.

Nogueira appeared progressively more serene with each drink. "I greatly regret what happened earlier," he said with ceremonial politeness.

Manuel was baffled. "You mean what happened in the street?"

"I do."

Manuel rejected that. "Well, after all, it wasn't your fault—"

"It was indeed," Nogueira interrupted him. "It's the fault of all of us who think that way. Like those assholes do."

It dawned on Manuel what the man was trying to say. "Okay, then," he replied with equal seriousness. "In fact, I guess it was."

"I'm sorry," the lieutenant apologized again. "Don't know why things are that way," he added with the solemn emphasis of a drunken philosopher, "but the fact is—they just are."

"You are drunk," Manuel replied with a grin.

Nogueira frowned, raised one finger and pointed it at him. "I *am* a bit drunk, but I know what I'm saying. I was wrong about you. And when a man makes a mistake, the very least he can do is admit it."

Manuel regarded him with an equally solemn gaze and pondered how much truth lay in those words.

"I don't know why, really; I don't have any reason to hate queers."

"Homosexuals," Manuel corrected him.

"Right, what you said. Homosexuals," Nogueira conceded. "You're right about that; see what I'm talking about? It's a screwed-up way of talking. And truth is, when I see you having a coffee, say, in a bar, you know, that's 'normal'"—he gestured to indicate the quotation marks—"it doesn't cross my mind that you're gay."

"And what exactly do you think?"

"I mean that, just looking at you, nobody could tell you were . . ."

"But I am, Nogueira. I'm a homosexual. I have been since I was born, and whether anyone can 'tell' or guess just isn't the issue."

Nogueira waved grandly to dismiss that thought. "Fuck, it's so hard to talk to queers! What I mean is, you're a good guy and I'm sorry." He again became very solemn. "I apologize to you on my own behalf and on behalf of all the assholes in the world who have no fucking idea who you really are."

Manuel nodded, smiling at the man's awkwardness. He raised his glass to mark this conversion from homophobia. "I'll drink to that!"

Nogueira downed his drink without taking his eyes off Manuel. "Now that we know you're not a prissy little shit-faced queer, it's my turn."

Manuel nodded slowly and waited for it.

"I just want to say that sometimes we judge other people without bothering to get to know them. I'm not one to talk; I'm the first to admit it. But what I want to tell you, Manuel, is that I am not a son of a bitch."

"Listen, Nogueira—"

"No, no, let me finish. The other day you said I was a heartless bastard, a sadist who liked to see others suffer."

"That's just a manner of speaking—"

"And you were right," Nogueira interrupted him. "I hate the Muñiz de Dávila family. From the time I get up until the time I go to bed, I curse the air they breathe, and I'll be cursing them with the last breath I take."

Manuel looked at him in silence. He gestured to the bartender, who brought the bottle and filled their glasses again.

"Just leave it on the table," Manuel said.

The man started to protest, but Manuel slipped him a couple of bills from his wallet. The barkeep disappeared.

"My father was in the police too. One night it was raining, and there was an accident at a railroad crossing not far from here. He was one of the first to get to the scene. He was helping remove the victims from the vehicle, and a train traveling in the other direction cut him down. Killed instantly. My mother was a widow. With three sons. I was the oldest of the three kids."

"I'm sorry," Manuel muttered.

Nogueira's nodding head signaled acceptance of his condolences, as if he'd just lost his father. "Things were different back then. What he left and what they paid us wasn't enough to live on. She was a fine seamstress, so not long afterward she went to work at the manor."

"Up at As Grileiras?"

"Times were different. Ladies like the marquess were always having new dresses made, for everyday and for celebrations. Soon my mother was receiving commissions from other rich women; and after a while my mother was earning more than my father ever had. One afternoon she went to the manor with some dresses for the marquess to try on. Sometimes we'd go with her and play outside—see, that's how I know about the garden. I spent lots of afternoons waiting out there with my brothers. But that day we weren't with her."

Manuel remembered how startled he'd been by Nogueira's comment about the garden: *Really precious.*

"The lady of the house wasn't at the manor. They were all off somewhere, except for Álvaro's father, middle-aged, arrogant, and as macho as they come." Nogueira's lips set in a sneer. "I came home without warning because I'd skinned my knee playing soccer. I went into the bathroom and there she was. In the tub, but with her clothes on. They were twisted and torn, fastened up with a belt, and she was bleeding . . . down there. Her thighs were all bloody and the bathwater was red. I thought she was dying."

Manuel shut his eyes and pressed the heels of his hands to them, trying to chase away that picture.

"I was ten. She made me swear not to tell. I helped her get to bed, and she stayed there more than a week. All that time I took care of her and my brothers too. They were a lot younger. They had no idea."

"Good God, Nogueira!" Manuel muttered. "You were so young!"

Nogueira assented with a slow nod. But he gazed into the distance, years away in the past, seeing a very different night.

"One afternoon the marquess's car stopped at our gate. The driver brought a big basket to the door, with food, cookies, chocolate, ham, all kinds of things we never had. I remember my little brothers laughing like it was Christmas. The marquess went into my mother's bedroom, closed the door, and talked with her for a long time. She gave each of us a coin when she left. My mother told me she'd still be working for the lady, but she wouldn't be going back to the manor. From then on the driver picked up and delivered the dresses for fittings. Every once in a while he brought us one of those baskets with towels and sheets and fine bedclothes from the manor. My mother was a very courageous woman, Manuel."

"She had to be. Very courageous."

"She brought us up, me and my brothers, and she never complained. She did the only thing she knew how to do, and she never gave in. She never did, Manuel."

He saw Manuel wasn't following him.

"She died two years ago, really, really old." He smiled slightly. "When she was very ill and on her deathbed, she told me to open the huge clothes chest in her room. In there, carefully folded, were the sheets and towels embroidered with the crest of the Muñiz de Dávilas. Her closet was stacked high with them, too, from the floor almost to the ceiling. Can you imagine that? Not a single time in all those years had she used even one of those fine sheets. The day we buried her and came back from the cemetery, I made a fire on the patio and burned them all." He snorted with laughter. "I can still hear my sisters-in-law making a racket and calling me all sorts of names!"

Manuel joined in his laughter. For a while they both chuckled.

"They still tell that story every Christmas, those crazy bitches!" His laughter died away suddenly. He rose and jerked a thumb toward the door. "I never told anyone what happened to my mother. My brothers don't know and neither does my wife." He headed for the exit.

Nogueira didn't say a single word on the drive between the bar and the inn. It wasn't necessary. Manuel knew exactly how he was feeling. He remembered unexpectedly why church confessionals always have a screen between the priest and the parishioner. Lacking that protective separation, Manuel concentrated upon his own image reflected in the car window against the black background of the night.

When the car pulled up before the inn, Manuel asked, "Are you going to the seminary tomorrow?"

"Yes. I don't know if you're aware of it, but the prior says the buildings stand on land that belongs to the marquis. So now it's your land."

"If you want me to go along . . ."

"I'm still thinking about how to approach it. The prior and I have known one another for a long time, and if I get him riled he'll probably call headquarters and get me in hot water: 'Now the police are interfering with the Church.' I'll go solo, and we'll hold off on your visit until it becomes necessary later on. You have a certain standing as the owner of the property, but that old bird will clam up when you're there. So we'll see later on how we can approach it. If we have to."

Manuel got out of the car and took Café in his arms. The dog was sound asleep.

"Manuel," Nogueira called from the car. There was something strange in his voice. It took him a moment. "My wife wants you to come have dinner with us."

Manuel smiled, surprised. "Me?"

"Yes, you." Nogueira was obviously uneasy. "I don't know what we were talking about, but your name came up. I mentioned that I knew you, and it turns out my older daughter and my wife have read your books, and they're just wild to meet you . . . I already told them you probably won't be able to . . ."

"I accept," Manuel said.

"What?"

"That's a *yes*. I'll have dinner with the family. I'd be happy to meet your wife. When?"

"When? Uh, well, tomorrow, I guess."

Manuel stood in the parking lot and watched Nogueira's car disappear into the distance. He kissed Cafe's rough little head and walked smiling into the inn.

He needed to write.

∿❧∿

OF EVERYTHING HE REFUSED

One by one he opened the drawers of the dressing table, only to find them all empty. In the immense closet the few shirts Álvaro had brought hung perfectly ironed on heavy hangers next to the two jackets he'd left behind. They hung abandoned within the closet. Their movement in response to the opening of the door created a disturbing impression. He wanted to touch them, to feel the soft fabric, to let his fingertips search for the elusive presence of their owner.

DAMAGE CONTROL

The San Xoan monastery was commonly called "the seminary" by the people of the region, but there had been no teaching there for the past dozen years. The area previously dedicated to the parochial school had been converted into a hostel for pilgrims and spiritual retreats. Nogueira found such exercises absolutely ridiculous. As far as he was concerned, a vacation wasn't a vacation unless he could sprawl out in the sunshine with a cold beer on his belly.

The policeman had phoned the prior that he'd be dropping by to pay a call. The man had definitely sounded nervous and hesitant. He insisted on knowing the reason for the visit.

Nogueira had sidestepped the question. "The subject is somewhat delicate. I prefer to discuss it face-to-face." He was pleased with his counterthrust.

A chilly "As you wish" from the prior had ended the conversation. Nogueira saw the prior waiting outside for him at the gate to the gardens, the church, and the residence. The man seemed extremely jittery; he greeted his visitor with the usual courtesy and escorted him to the office without the usual spiel about the beauty of the grounds. He offered coffee and Nogueira accepted.

The prior took his place behind the imposing monastic desk. "Now, Lieutenant, perhaps you can explain how I may be of assistance."

Nogueira sipped his coffee and took his time. He admired the portrait hung above the fireplace on one side of the room. He appeared to be about to praise it when he looked at the prior and said instead, "Last Sunday your sister came to the station. She reported your nephew missing."

Nogueira watched for a reaction, but the prior's expression didn't change an iota. After a few seconds of Nogueira's unyielding silence, the prior gave him a slight nod.

The lieutenant pressed him. "How long have you known about this?"

"My sister telephoned me and told me. Tuesday, I think it was."

"And?"

The prior got up, heaved a sigh, and went to the window. "If you're asking whether I did something about it, the answer is no. I'm afraid our nephew has given us entirely too much trouble for me to be surprised by whatever he may be up to."

"I understand," Nogueira said, "but your sister says that with all his faults the boy is always considerate of her. He never fails to telephone when he's going to be out late."

"My sister has spoiled that boy. You shouldn't be surprised to hear her make excuses and defend him."

"As she did, for example, last Saturday when you went to her house?"

The prior gave him a surprised glance, perhaps tinged with alarm. "She told you that?"

"No, I heard it from the neighbor who saw you two shouting and arguing."

The prior busied himself with adjusting the position of potted plants so they faced the sun.

"What were you arguing about?"

"It's a private matter. Family business. Nothing important."

"Well, the neighbor said in her *statement*," Nogueira advised him, "that you seemed very angry. You were demanding she turn something over to you. She clearly heard you say it could be the end of you, and you weren't going to leave things the way they were."

The prior's face flushed with anger as he turned back toward the officer. "That old busybody should mind her own business!"

"I'll grant you the woman's unpleasant, but she's a credible witness. That's why I'm asking, you see. Your nephew evidently had been doing some odd jobs here, then you turn up at his home in a rage the very day he disappears."

"I don't know what you're insinuating, Lieutenant, but I don't like this at all."

"I'm insinuating nothing, Reverend Prior; in fact, I'm trying to do your family a favor, because your sister has been calling the station constantly" (a lie) "to ask what they're doing to locate Toñino. If she keeps it up, someone's eventually going to do something about it."

The prior blanched. When he found his voice again, it was barely audible. "Antonio took something from my office. It's not the first time he's stolen. But you know that as well as I do."

"What did he take?"

The prior held back for a couple of seconds. "Money." The lie was laughably transparent.

"No doubt you notified the police."

The prior again had to consider his response. "Lieutenant, he's my nephew. I don't want to disgrace my sister."

"I understand that. But if you know your nephew has committed a crime by stealing money from the seminary . . ."

"It was my money. He took it from my wallet."

Nogueira took his time. He let six seconds go by before he spoke again. "And *that* could put an end to you if it were known? *That* couldn't be left as it was? I don't know how much money you generally have in your wallet, but . . ."

"That old gossip got it wrong. What I said was, 'You'll do away with me,' referring to all the trouble he's causing."

"Uh-huh," Nogueira responded. He took another long look at the painting he'd seen when they entered the office. "I see you still have the portrait of the old marquis."

The prior seemed taken aback by that comment but recovered quickly. "He was a great benefactor of this institution, and his family continues the tradition."

"Oh, really?" Nogueira pretended this was news to him.

"All the buildings stand on his land."

Nogueira changed the subject and watched for a reaction. "His son recently died, as you know."

The prior looked down for a moment. "Oh yes! A terrible thing."

"I believe he attended school here as a boy."

"Yes, and so did all his brothers. Though he wasn't with us for long."

Nogueira got up as if to leave and stepped away to give the prior some breathing room. Then he turned and eyed the man. "Was Álvaro Muñiz de Dávila here last Saturday?"

The prior looked as if he were about to have a heart attack. "Saturday . . . No, no, he wasn't . . ."

"But he telephoned."

"No."

"His phone records confirm it."

The prior pressed two fingers to the bridge of his nose. "Yes. Yes, I'm sorry, indeed you're right, I'd forgotten. He did call, but it was a very brief conversation."

Nogueira stood like a statue, watching the man; he knew the prior felt sufficiently compromised already to provide an explanation without being asked.

"He wanted to be heard in confession," was the explanation. "I suggested a couple of possible times, but they didn't suit him. So we put it off."

Nogueira didn't say anything. He opened the door with arrogant slowness and exited at glacial speed. He even turned to look back, to provoke the prior even more. His farewell was casual. "No need to see me out."

He went out the main door of the building, inhaled the heavy humid air, and lit a cigarette.

A lay brother was strolling along the flagstone walk with his hands behind his back. He came up to the visitor with a smile. "I had that same vice for many years, but I quit many years ago. Food has tasted much better to me ever since."

"I should do the same," the officer said, falling into step as they went toward the gate. "But it's so difficult."

"Do as I do: pray for strength. God will assist you."

They walked past the open door of the garage where several cars were parked. Nogueira looked inside. "And you believe God pays attention to such things?"

"God pays attention to everything, great and small." The brother's cell phone buzzed. "Excuse me." He put it to his ear.

Nogueira gave him a little wave of acknowledgment and leaned into the garage. Inside were a tractor, a little motorbike, a 1999 SEAT Córdoba sedan, and a small white pickup with a dented front fender. He turned to speak to the brother and saw that the man's expression had changed. Still on the phone, the brother was looking up toward a second-story window where the prior was visible watching them. The brother pressed his phone to his ear. The men gazed at one another. The brother ended the call, went to the garage, and pulled down the overhead door.

When he approached the officer his face was anything but friendly and his words were curt. "I'll see you out."

✦

Manuel noted Nogueira's reticence as soon as they began the phone conversation. He'd expected it. Lucas had warned him, and he'd had the same experience. Very often a confession engenders feelings of shame and regret. Not because of the confession itself but because of apprehension that one might have been too hasty or confided to the wrong person. If kept secret, a matter that weighs heavily on the conscience may give one a feeling of invulnerability. Manuel assumed that after the lieutenant got over his brief boozy moment of exultant friendliness, he regretted telling the truth. And probably especially regretted inviting Manuel to his home.

The writer sidestepped the issue and kept his tone casual. "How did it go at the seminary?"

He had an idea the policeman was glad to have a different subject. Nogueira answered in his usual noncommittal style. "Depends on how you look at it."

Manuel smiled and let him talk.

"The prior didn't want to tell me anything, but by denying so much he actually wound up revealing a great deal. He says he was angry with his nephew because the boy took money from his wallet, but I don't believe him. He doesn't seem too worried about the kid's whereabouts, almost as if this has happened before. But the crunch came when I said Álvaro came to see him. He denied both the visit and the phone call. When I told him we had proof, his memory improved remarkably. 'Oh, yes, in fact he did telephone.' He claims it was to make an appointment for confession but they couldn't find a convenient time."

"I don't believe it. Lucas said Álvaro didn't go to confession, or at least not as a formal rite. I'll ask him again."

"There's something else. On the way out I saw a white vehicle that had a dent in the front right quarter panel, which might correspond with the damage to Álvaro's car. They practically threw me out when I tried to take a look at it."

"And now what do you suggest?"

"It might be a good idea for you to have a go, but you'll need to be subtle. I have an idea. I'll explain it to you after dinner and see what you think."

At least the dinner was still on, though so far Nogueira seemed reluctant to discuss it.

"Manuel, that's not the only reason I called. I want to warn you about something before you come to our house."

Manuel tried to make light of it. "I hope you're not going to tell me your wife's a bad cook. I was counting on a fine home-cooked meal."

Nogueira chuckled on the other end of the line. "No, nothing like that. My wife's a good cook, an excellent one, in fact. But we're going through a rocky spell right now, and you might notice some tension between the two of us."

"I understand, don't worry," Manuel reassured him quickly, hoping to avoid some lengthy explanation.

"And there's my older daughter. You know, she's a teenager, almost seventeen, and lately we haven't been seeing eye to eye. She failed her classes and has to repeat the school year. I haven't seen her crack a book all summer. I scold her and my wife defends her. We're always arguing."

"I'll see if I can help with that."

"And then there's the boy."

"I thought you had only the two girls."

"The boy's Xulia's boyfriend." He sniffed in exasperation. "I suppose he'll be there for dinner too. He's always at the house. He's arrogant. I can't stand him, and I'm sure my wife doesn't care too much for him either. But he's always hanging around, scratching his balls and looking like an idiot."

Manuel smiled as he pictured Nogueira's exasperation. "I can imagine it."

"Believe me, you have no idea."

❧

Manuel looked down at Café one last time before pressing the button. "Behave yourself now, little buddy."

Café's sidelong look suggested the dog was offended by the admonition.

The chimes died away within, and he heard a tumult and a shrill childish voice. A girl about eight years old opened the door. "Hi, I'm Antía. We were expecting you." She grabbed his hand and pulled him inside. Then the sight of little Café made her completely forget Manuel. "Oh, you've got a doggie! Can I pet him? Does he like kids?"

"Yes, you may," he answered. "I suppose he does, I don't know." He was overwhelmed by her childish eagerness.

"It's Manuel! He brought flowers and wine and a doggie!" she shouted down the entry hall.

Nogueira appeared in the door to the kitchen, relieved him of the wine, and brought him inside. A large table occupied the center of the room. By the stove stood a woman of about forty-five who was taking off her apron. She was extremely good-looking, with a dark complexion and long hair gathered in a ponytail. She held the apron behind her as she walked up smiling and offered him her hand.

"Manuel, let me introduce my wife, Laura. You've already met Antía, the little one who attacked you at the door." He turned toward a young woman who'd just entered the room. "And here's my older daughter, Xulia."

The handsome young woman was a teenage version of her mother, although she wore her long hair loose. She gave him a firm handshake and gazed at him with dark eyes that resembled her father's.

Manuel offered the flowers to Laura. "These are for you," he said.

"They're lovely, but you shouldn't have," she answered with a charmed smile, almost cradling the flowers in her arms. "I'm flattered," she said with a glance at her husband. "And I love your novels!" Her face colored with a bashful blush that captivated Manuel and astonished Nogueira.

Antía came into the kitchen carrying Café.

"Oh! I'm very sorry, but I don't have anywhere to leave him. If he's a bother I can take him out to my car."

"No, please!" the little one pleaded.

Laura was happy to reassure him. "Don't be concerned. I love dogs."

Manuel glanced at a boy who was already seated at the table. The kid hadn't looked up from his cell phone and seemed oblivious to them.

Nogueira jutted his chin toward the boy. "That's Alex, Xulia's boyfriend."

"Friend," the boy instantly corrected him. Nogueira was offended, but the boy's face remained blank.

Manuel could see very well why the kid's presence made Nogueira uneasy. Putting up with this zombie must be unbearable for anyone as temperamental as the lieutenant.

Nogueira busied himself opening the wine while Laura ushered Manuel to his place at the table.

"Alex, dear," she said to the boy sitting at the head of the table, "move next to Xulia and give that chair to Andrés."

Manuel was somewhat surprised by this. He detected a tension in the air.

"But I always sit here," the boy protested.

"But not today," the hostess replied, unyielding.

The teenager got up, making no secret of his reluctance, and plopped himself down two chairs farther along.

Nogueira took his place at the head of the table. Manuel realized he'd never before heard the officer's first name.

The policeman had told the truth: Laura was a superb cook. Manuel ate as he hadn't done in a long time, enjoying the conversation and the presence of the family, the joyful profusion of brilliant, fragrant dishes, an offering of Galician cuisine that manifested the typically excessive generosity of Galicia. Laura was pleased to introduce him to it. They talked a great deal about his novels, his beginnings, how he'd started writing, and literature in general. Laura had read extensively, had a similar taste in books, and appreciated his favorites. During the conversation Manuel saw her glance repeatedly back and forth between him and her husband.

"And tell me, Manuel, how did you get to know Andrés? He was terribly mysterious about it."

Manuel looked over at him. The lieutenant took the opportunity to get up to open another bottle of wine.

"In fact, he hasn't said anything because I asked him to be discreet," he said, well aware of the effect his words would have.

"It's for the next novel!" Xulia exclaimed. She exchanged a complicit look with her mother and turned enthusiastically to Manuel. "Tell me, am I right?"

"Well, you all understand that for now it's a secret, right?"

"Of course!" the women answered in chorus, clearly delighted with this confidence.

Manuel saw their admiring expressions when they looked toward Nogueira. That made him feel good.

"So your next novel will be set here in the Ribeira Sacra?" the girl probed.

Manuel smiled but didn't confirm it. "It hasn't been decided yet. It's at a very early stage and I'm getting to know places and events; your father is helping me a great deal with all that."

"Excuse my daughter," Laura said with a smile. "I've followed you from the first, but Xulia discovered your novels only a little over a year ago. She read every one of them in no time at all, and I'm afraid she's become a real fan."

"You don't say! Thanks, Xulia. What else do you read?"

"About thirty-five books a year, mostly detective stories and history, but I like yours the best."

"What?" put in Nogueira. "They must be novels then, since you never open your schoolbooks." His comment provoked a grimace from his daughter and a stupid little snicker from Alex, who didn't look up from his phone.

Laura gave her husband a reproachful glance. She got up to clear the table and serve dessert. Nogueira was quick to volunteer his assistance.

"Xulia wants to become a writer," Laura said as she placed before Manuel a tray with slices of cheese, slices of pie, and quinces.

He let the girl see he was intrigued to hear it. She blushed but nodded to confirm her mother's comment. The teenager with his cell phone snorted in derision and slumped so low in his chair that his chin was at the level of the tabletop.

Nogueira was clearly offended by the youth, but he spoke to his daughter instead. "That's a good one! And with the kind of grades you get in school, how could you even hope to be a writer?"

Laura, again seated beside Manuel, sat looking on without comment, apparently amused by her husband's growing exasperation. She seemed to be counting the seconds till he blew his top.

"Oh, Dad, there you go again!" Xulia complained. Ignoring her father, she turned to Manuel. "This year I got distracted from my schoolwork," she said, lowering her chin in a penitent expression that looked rehearsed, "so I have to repeat the year. But from now on I'm going to take it seriously."

"From now on," Nogueira mimicked her. "That's exactly what you've been saying all year. And what happened? You all but dropped out."

"Except for literature."

The teenager next to her guffawed, and Nogueira turned to glare at him. "Like to share what you think's so funny?"

The boy grinned and wagged a finger at Xulia. "A writer?" he asked, and snorted some more. "Wait and see how they laugh their asses off when she tries to tell 'em that!"

Xulia flushed deep red, and it wasn't from embarrassment. Her chin lifted; her demeanor was calm and dignified. She addressed the boy imperiously. "Alex, why don't you go home, and we'll talk about that later."

"What?" he replied, stunned. "I thought we were going out." He raised his phone to show her the screen. "The Panorama Band's playing in Rodeiro!"

Antía saw Manuel was baffled, so she explained. "He's looking at Galician Bands."

Manuel shrugged to show he was clueless.

"Galician Bands," the little girl said. "It's an app that tracks which bands are playing, every day."

Nogueira elaborated. "That's all they think about. They spend their summer running after the bands from town to town, from one village to another. But when it comes to studying?"

"Dad!" shrieked Xulia. But she immediately turned back to the boy. "You heard me. It's time for you to go home. We'll talk about it tomorrow." She spoke with a chill finality, an attitude that Manuel assumed she'd inherited from her father. It reminded him of the lieutenant's tone when warning him he'd take a blabbermouth writer off behind a mountain and shoot him.

The teenager looked unhappily at the platter. "But I haven't had dessert yet!"

Xulia refused to be moved. "Get out of here, Alex!"

Laura got up, fetched a piece of aluminum foil from the pantry, wrapped up a slice of pie, and handed it to the boy. He accepted it gracelessly, scowled, and left without saying goodbye. When the door closed behind him, the girl, who'd watched his every step, turned back to Manuel.

But it was the little girl who spoke first. "Sorry about him. The poor kid's kind of a dummy. One time he stapled his pants to his ankle."

Xulia was not amused, and she elbowed her little sister. Manuel saw the closed expressions on the sisters' faces and smiled slightly. "He stapled his pants to his ankle?"

Xulia looked back at him. Despite herself, her mouth curled into a grin. She broke into giggles that set the rest of them laughing too.

Encouraged by their reaction, Antía continued. "No, honest, the cuffs on his pants were so long they were dragging on the ground; so he took my stapler." She raised an admonishing finger, a gesture that was for all the world like her father's. "Without permission! And he tried to fix them and wound up stapling his pants to his ankle."

They enjoyed their dessert, along with other tales of Alex's misadventures. Laura served coffee and an aromatic local brandy. Manuel caught sight of a restrained smile playing across Nogueira's lips beneath the mustache as he sat at ease at the head of the table. He admired Laura's orchestration of the dinner, the way she urged each of them to participate, the way she handled the tensions with the husband she'd been tormenting but whom Manuel was sure she still loved.

"We can get together sometime if you like," Manuel said to Xulia. "I can suggest some titles that'll be a good deal more interesting to a future writer than my novels. But more than anything, you have to set your own goals." Xulia was enchanted by his offer, especially when she noticed her father's skeptical expression. "We all go through a bad spell from time to time. We get distracted or sometimes we just can't concentrate, and we get the feeling there's no reason to go on." Manuel kept an eye on both Xulia and her father, hearing his own voice as if that reminder were coming from somewhere far away—with valid advice he'd forgotten in the rush and confusion of recent days.

"You see?" Xulia said to her father.

Manuel completed the thought. "Above all, we must keep those bad times from becoming a way of life."

Nogueira replied to his daughter. "You see?"

Xulia looked at her father. She nodded.

It was two in the morning when Manuel said farewell to Laura and Xulia at the front door.

Antía lay curled up on the sofa with Café. Manuel called the dog and saw him hesitate, reluctant to leave. The reason wasn't hard to guess.

Thick mists had settled in the cold night air, considerably lowering the temperature and transforming the streetlights along the road into swirling presences, like a holy company of whirling dervishes stationed mournful along the road. The prospect of lonely solitude that night made him yearn to turn back to that welcoming home. He wanted another coffee at the big table, another warm farewell embrace from Laura. She had easily extracted from him a promise to return.

Nogueira had gone ahead of him. He was waiting where Manuel had parked his car in one of the orange pools of light. Manuel placed Café on the backseat and fished Álvaro's thick jacket out of the back. He put it on, for he had a feeling he was in for a discussion that might take a while. Nogueira hadn't escorted him to the car just as a courtesy.

Manuel was the first one to speak. "Thanks for the invitation."

Nogueira looked back at his house, barely visible through the mist. Manuel knew he was checking to make sure his wife wasn't watching. The lieutenant lit the cigarette he'd been wanting for hours. He took a hefty drag. The smoke he exhaled rose in blue swirls into the cold Ribeira Sacra night, so laden with humidity and the odor of the distant river.

Nogueira nodded without taking the cigarette from his lips. He waved away Manuel's words.

Manuel looked him straight in the eye. "Laura is charming."

The lieutenant took another deep pull and blew the smoke out in a sharp gust above their heads, watching Manuel all the while. "Drop it," he said.

"I didn't say anything, Nogueira—"

"Just drop it."

Manuel inhaled the night air and then let it out in a long slow sigh. "As you like. But thanks anyway. It was a very pleasant dinner."

Nogueira nodded, content with his success.

But Manuel hadn't given up yet. "I wouldn't get too worried about a girl who reads thirty-five books a year. I think she knows what she's doing. She inherited her mother's intelligence and her father's balls."

Nogueira turned to look out at the street. His expression was as grave as ever when he turned back, but Manuel was sure he'd smiled.

The officer took an envelope from the inside pocket of his overcoat. "These are the documents you gave me. We're lucky Álvaro kept all of his receipts. We were able to chart a relatively good map of his movements on the last day."

Manuel nodded. The receipts were for the cash purchases Álvaro had preferred to make instead of charging expenses to a card where they could be tracked. Like the second telephone and the portable GPS navigation device, they provided clues that were proof, or maybe just evidence, of his intention to cover his tracks.

"We knew from his call records that he telephoned the seminary at 11:32 a.m., and we estimate it took him half an hour to get there. There's a receipt from the service station in San Xoan, printed at 12:35; he probably stopped there after leaving the monastery. It's a shame this isn't an official investigation. This was only a week ago, and we could still get the video surveillance from the gas station. The cashier would probably remember the car, since it would stand out around here. Almost everyone buying gasoline there is a local, and he'd remember an outsider. That wouldn't prove that he'd been to the seminary, though. As long as the prior denies it, it's still his word against our hypothesis."

Nogueira handed him the envelope. "These were with the papers you gave us. Something to do with the winery. Nothing to do with the investigation, and maybe the executor needs them for the business."

Manuel slipped them out of the envelope, glanced through them, and put them away. "Why is the prior lying?"

Nogueira gave him an appreciative look and seemed to reflect for a couple of seconds. "The reason the prior is lying, the reason his sister is lying, too, the reason people lie at all—your guess is as good as mine. Sometimes a lie conceals a crime; sometimes it's a cry for help; sometimes it's an attempt to cover up something so stupid it's too embarrassing to admit." He looked out into the darkness. "But we've got plenty of reason to be suspicious: the white paint left on the dent in Álvaro's vehicle, plus the damage to the front of the white pickup. And the fact that it's ten days later and no one's taken it to a garage for repair. His desire to keep it out of sight bothers me; so does all that shit about the nephew." He shook his head. "I don't believe the kid took any money. He's a junkie, and of course junkies steal. Leaving a wallet where he can get at it is an open invitation. But the facts are that Álvaro phoned both the nephew and the prior, and it's almost a sure thing that Álvaro was at the seminary to discuss something we don't know about." He looked Manuel straight in the eye. "That something was important enough to be the first thing he went to deal with as soon as he arrived from Madrid on an unscheduled visit."

The weight of that evidence forced Manuel to agree. Nogueira lit another cigarette, inhaled deeply, and continued the narrative, enumerating events on his fingers. "A few hours afterward the prior turns up shrieking like a banshee at the sister's house where the nephew lives; the kid told a friend he's got his hands on something that could set him up good, but now he's so scared he doesn't stick his nose outside even though his uncle is screaming, 'This could be the end of me.' The prior leaves, Toñino gets into his car and disappears. And all of this on the day Álvaro was murdered."

Nogueira fell silent. Manuel could almost hear the sparks as the neurons in the brain within that deceptively bullish head worked on the puzzle.

"What are you thinking?" Manuel asked.

"The only thing I can say is that this is getting more and more complicated. There has to be a loose thread somewhere. One we can use to start to pick it all apart."

"On the phone you said you'd had an idea."

"Yeah, I'd been working on a plan, and now that I've seen the reactions of my wife and daughter, I'm sure it'll work."

"What do you have in mind?"

"Look, neither the prior nor any of the brothers is going to say anything if we ask them directly."

"And?"

"You're this famous writer."

"Okay. And?"

"You're famous, right? I didn't know it because I don't read that kind of stuff, but other people know who you are. Take a look at the way my wife and daughter reacted. A colleague told me even the captain asked you to autograph a book."

Manuel nodded.

"You got to admit, then, that people respond to celebrities. And that's what you are."

"Okay, great, but I don't know where you're going with all this."

"How'd you like to go undercover into the seminary?"

AN IDIOT STARES OUT
AT THE SEA

He got up early even though the night had run very late and he'd written for several hours after that. He was stimulated by the idea that at last he had a plan, something to do on his own initiative. It was nothing like the previous day's feeling of helpless inertia, following Nogueira's instructions but convinced nothing would come of it.

He phoned Griñán to set up a meeting. They agreed on noon.

He called Mei. She could hardly believe it. She wept and laughed at the sound of his voice, telling him over and over how sorry she was about the way things had turned out. It took quite a while to calm her down and assure her that he was feeling better, he'd forgiven her, and he wasn't holding any grudges.

"Listen, Mei, in fact I'm calling to ask a couple of favors."

"Of course, Manuel. Anything."

"Álvaro was enrolled in the school of the Salesian Brothers in Madrid from the age of twelve. Call them and ask them for the exact dates. Tell them he died, you're his secretary, and you need the information for the obituary."

"All right," she replied, sounding as if she were taking notes. "That's one thing. What's the other?"

"I need to talk to my agent. And, well, you know, Álvaro always took care of that."

"Manuel," she sighed, "I didn't want to bother you, but in fact both your agent and your editor have been calling, trying to contact you."

"Did you tell them anything?"

"No, Manuel, and that was really hard. You've been away for more than ten days now. Manuel, everybody here at the firm has been taking care of business, and of course the employees all know. I was practically prostrate, in tears all day long. I couldn't hide it. But everything's starting to get weird. What are we going to tell our clients? He's been gone so long now that some of the employees are asking who's in charge. They're wondering what's going on."

Manuel didn't know what to say. He hadn't been expecting this. He had no answers.

"Manuel, I understand you don't have time to deal with all that. But I really need some guidance, something I can tell them."

He felt an icy chill go down his spine, as if someone had dumped a bucket of ice water over him. He froze in place, unable to respond. He tried to think. Álvaro's agency wasn't very large. Four employees, maybe five. He couldn't remember.

"How many people work there?"

"Twelve, including me."

"Twelve?" he repeated stupidly.

"Yes." She didn't say it, but Manuel could imagine what she was thinking: *Didn't you know, Manuel? Weren't you paying attention? How is that possible? This was your husband's business; you attended company parties and had meals with us, Manuel. You should have known!*

"Tell them not to worry. I'll call you later and we'll talk," he promised. "But right now I need my agent's private number. I don't want to call her office."

He jotted down the digits and ended the call, all too keenly aware of reproaches Mei hadn't voiced but which were echoing through his mind. Because the answers were all negative. *No, I didn't know how many employees Álvaro had; I wasn't aware how much the firm had grown. I didn't know that in no time at all the five or six employees had become a dozen. I didn't know how much they were billing.* As for the list of clients, the only time he recalled having seen their names was on the meeting schedule Álvaro kept posted on the refrigerator.

He saw the worn copy of *The Man Who Refused* on the nightstand, the same one he'd autographed for Álvaro more than twenty times during the course of that scorching hot bookfair in Madrid. He'd taken the title from an ancient Basque tale about the food of evil. According to legend, whenever we deny a true thing, that thing becomes the fodder for dark forces. The thing denied dissolves, fades, and disappears. In the folktale a peasant lies and denies having an abundant harvest, so the denied portion becomes the lot of evil. If cattle give birth to ten heifers but the farmer tells his neighbors there were only four, the other six belong to evil and die soon afterward. The same curse affects a foresworn bastard child or a denied lover, and woe upon whoever claims that a hidden treasure doesn't really exist.

Everything denied becomes fodder for evil; when renounced by the legitimate owner it fades away as the dark underside of the universe collects its due.

The publication of *The Man Who Refused* came less than seven years after the dark night his sister closed her eyes forever. Soon after her death he felt the urge to write. That was a first for him; he'd never before considered writing fiction about his childhood, his parents, his sister, and their miseries. He'd kept the promise she'd pressed from him: he refused to be vulnerable to her demise. He'd suppressed tears at her passing, for each time they welled up he heard her insisting, "Don't ever cry. When you were little you wouldn't let me sleep, and if you weep, I won't rest in peace."

There came a morning when he discovered to his horror he could no longer see her face or recall her scent. Those memories had been erased, because in his determination to deny, pain had dedicated him to *no*. That *no* was devouring him. It was making him disappear as if he'd never existed. On that day of revelation he began to write.

For five months he bled onto those blank pages, and those months of tears and anguish left him completely exhausted. He chose the title *The Man Who Refused* because the manuscript contained everything he'd tried to suppress and put into writing everything he'd denied for so long. It was a hit and was still his bestselling novel. He never spoke of the events that had driven him to write it, and he swore to himself he'd never write anything like it again.

He looked toward the shabby desk in the corner of his room at the inn. Brilliant white pages covered with dark close-written lines were piled on the dark wooden desktop. Even at that distance he saw clearly the title he'd inscribed at the top of each page: *Of Everything He Refused*. Those four words had presented themselves spontaneously, almost as if a spirit had dictated them. They constituted the continuation of his earlier novel and an admission he hadn't been telling the truth. The title echoed Álvaro's call for him to look at reality without flinching. They were an exhortation to sincerity, the most profound declaration of love ever made. He had rejected that call like some willful child, and his adamant reaction had barred Álvaro forever from being completely open.

He rummaged through the stacked manuscript pages until he located the photo Álvaro had kept in the safe, the photo Manuel had been avoiding because it made him acutely uncomfortable. Now he understood why.

In the picture Álvaro was looking at him, but he was staring out to sea. Manuel experienced again that familiar sensation that something was missing, something had been overlooked. His feeling of loss was compounded because he saw that on the day that image was taken, it captured the pretentious self-regard of a writer who claimed an intimate knowledge of the very truths to which he'd deliberately turned his back.

Manuel had regressed to a childlike dependency, trusting Álvaro to take care of every trifling detail. He left real life in Álvaro's hands and hid himself away in his dream palace of crystal, where he squatted beside its inexhaustible font of stories. That unreal world became his daily routine. Álvaro scrupulously safeguarded him and maintained the balance between that world and demanding reality. For years Álvaro took care of the practical details of managing the contracts. He negotiated deadlines, advance payments, international contracts, and percentages. He made sure taxes were paid. Álvaro worked through the tangle of vulgar, necessary, and distasteful details that Manuel wanted nothing to do with. He'd handled it all, sparing Manuel from the annoying commonplace demands of the outside world by arranging his trips, reservations, and interviews, dealing with phone calls, acting as his gatekeeper, and tending to everything from the most important issues to the least significant details.

No, he didn't remember the agency's employees. He doubted he'd be able to put names to more than three of them. That morning he hadn't been able locate his agent's phone number, and he'd realized to what an amazing extent he'd lived like an idiot staring out to sea. He'd absentmindedly let Álvaro assume his burden of reality, the portion of existence assigned to each human being. Álvaro had carried both their loads, protecting him and shielding him as if he were somehow privileged.

A genius or a mentally incompetent dependent.

Or both.

He couldn't face opening the book to reread the dedications he'd written fifteen years earlier. They were made out to the man who became his husband, the man he loved, the man who had become his greatest vulnerability. The heavy import of the new title obliged him to undertake a clear-eyed reexamination of their photo. He returned the book to the nightstand and carefully propped the photo against it. The spine of that oft-handled volume was worn and tattered, but the title, *The Man Who Refused*, was still legible.

He picked up his phone and punched in one of the numbers Mei Liu had located.

⁂

"Oh, hi, Manuel! How are you? I've been trying to get in touch with Álvaro for days."

Manuel smiled. His agent's eager energy made him think of her as a hot wind blowing over him and sweeping away his indecision, pressing him to share her unlimited enthusiasm and join her constant march forward.

He was tempted to keep Álvaro's death from her, because he knew she loved him too. The warmth with which she spoke of him made that very clear. Manuel knew she'd have preferred to deal with Álvaro. Her daring and unremitting determination were more in tune with Álvaro's amused audacity than with his own soft-spoken reticence.

"Anna, I have bad news. Álvaro died in a traffic accident last week. That's why he didn't return your calls. It's why neither of us did."

"Oh, my God!" She said nothing more, and after a minute Manuel realized she was weeping. He gave her plenty of time. His eyes focused blankly on middle distance as he listened.

Then came questions he left mostly unanswered, accepting her grief as sincere, and appreciating her natural instinct to protect him. As always, she was at his service.

"Manuel, don't worry about a thing, I'll take care of it all. I'll call your publisher right away." She caught her breath with difficulty. "Last time I spoke to Álvaro, he said you were finishing *The Sun of Tebas*. We agreed to publish in time for Christmas, I'm sure you remember, but if you're not up to it, we can push it back to January or until National Book Day in April. I'll get you all the time you need. Think it over; you don't have to decide right now. Take some time for yourself."

"I'm writing," he muttered.

"Oh, that's good, of course. I don't know how things were when . . . Are you really up to it right now? Maybe you should put it off. Like I said before, we can postpone publication."

"I'm writing another novel."

"What, a different one?" Her natural instinct as a literary agent was immediately aroused, and he felt that wind of enthusiasm beginning to blow.

"I'm not going to give them *The Sun of Tebas*, Anna. I don't want to publish it."

"But—"

"Oh, maybe someday, I don't know. But I certainly don't want to publish it right now. The novel I'm writing now will be the next on my list."

She protested, reminded him of his responsibility and the engagements already made, attributed his refusal to the confusion of the moment, to the rush and course of events. Thinking ahead as always, she urged him to take time to think before making such a drastic decision.

He dismissed all her objections with a single sentence. "Álvaro didn't like it."

She had no reply to that.

"Anna, I . . . I need a favor from you."

"Of course, whatever you want."

"I'd like to gather some background for a novel about a monastery in Galicia."

❧

By noon the sun had warmed the area and at last dissipated the cloud banks that had covered the Ribeira all night and most of the morning. He found Griñán courteous but distant because of their most recent encounter, though relieved and perhaps even flattered to be asked for his professional services. In ceremonial demonstration of his dedication, the administrator put on his reading glasses to scan the papers Manuel extracted from the envelope Nogueira had given him the night before. Griñán made the arrangements within half an hour with a couple of phone calls.

"You're staying, aren't you?" The administrator escorted him to the door. "I ask, because the other day . . . and considering what you're doing now . . ."

Manuel smiled. He opened his mouth, perhaps to reply or perhaps to confirm that conclusion, but he found himself at a loss for words. He'd spent too much time looking out to sea, and he didn't know what to say.

"I'm going to get to the bottom of it," he called back in a determined voice as he stepped into the elevator. Griñán was left standing in his office door, nonplussed.

With Café at his side Manuel negotiated the curves and turns of the road down the slope to the *Heroica* winery. The main gate was closed today and the place was quiet. The numerous cars parked in the winery lot testified to the many employees hard at work decanting the juice after the first filtration. He parked outside and called Daniel's number.

"Are you at the winery?" he asked, thinking he should have called ahead.

"Yes. Are you coming to visit?"

Manuel smiled. "Come out front."

He still had the phone in his hand when he saw Daniel slip out beneath the half-closed metal shutters that ran entirely across the front of the building. The cellar master wore denim overalls. He smiled in surprise to find Manuel leaning against the car.

"Say, what are you doing here? Why didn't you tell me you were coming? I'd have had them cook lunch on the grill!"

"It's just for a minute," Manuel apologized. "I don't have much time today, but I wanted to come show this to all of you." He held up the envelope that contained the documents.

Daniel gave him a puzzled look.

"These papers concern the terrain you mentioned the other day. You were right. Álvaro arranged for the purchase and the contract was ready to sign. And because of what happened he wasn't able to complete it. I thought the men would be pleased to know."

Daniel removed his gloves and took the documents in hand. "That's marvelous!" He waved toward the warehouse door. "Come on, you should come inside to tell them yourself."

Manuel declined with a smile. "You do it. I . . . well, we had our celebration the other day, didn't we? Today I have to . . ." He waved vaguely toward the road up out of the ravine.

Daniel gave him a big smile and extended his hand. "Really, you have no idea how much this means." He held up the documents, visibly moved. He shook Manuel's hand and just as he seemed about to release it, he impulsively gave Manuel a big hug. He stepped back, slightly flustered. "Thanks, boss!" He backed away toward the warehouse door, never taking his eyes from Manuel.

"Just one more thing," called Manuel.

The cellar master suddenly realized that he was holding the documents. "Oh, of course!" He came back and held them out.

"No, I wasn't referring to those," Manuel said. "They're copies for the men; they can have them. I was going to ask you about the motorboat we took from Belesar to go downriver."

Daniel grinned and took out a bunch of keys. He found two and offered them. "You know, after all, it's yours now. Don't worry, if you can drive a car, you'll do fine as a boat captain."

SQUAWKS

Manuel made a reservation at a steak house the innkeeper had recommended, and at nine o'clock that evening he was waiting patiently for his guests to appear.

He hadn't had much difficulty convincing Lucas of the need for a get-together, but Nogueira had been far less willing.

"Shit, Manuel, he's a priest! How do you think he's going to take it? He's not going to like it."

"Not at all, Nogueira. You don't know him at all. He was a close friend of Álvaro, ever since they were kids, and he's the only person around here Álvaro stayed in contact with all those years. Álvaro trusted him, and so do I."

"Wait and see," was Nogueira's response. "But I'm not convinced. How did things go at the seminary?"

"Just as we expected. My agent telephoned, and the heavens opened as soon as she mentioned my name. She told them I was in the region gathering background for a new novel, and I wanted to learn more about the monastery. They fell all over themselves offering to help. They're expecting me tomorrow morning, but I think it's important to talk to Lucas first. He attended school there, and he was Álvaro's best friend. If anything related to that place comes up, Lucas can help us out."

The trio's first few minutes at the steak house were marked by an awkward formality, but with the fireplace blazing, the proprietor serving up abundant measures of home cooking, and the bottle of *Heroica* Manuel had chosen from the wine list, they all relaxed.

They'd gotten to coffee when Manuel laid out the plan for Lucas. Nogueira was somewhat dismayed to hear Manuel outlining what they'd learned about the disappearance of Toñino and the prior's bizarre reaction.

Nogueira took the floor. "He denied the call, the visit, and even the fact Álvaro studied at the seminary for a while. Blanket denial. That seems significant."

"Maybe not. Álvaro wasn't there for so very long—from the age of four until he was twelve," Lucas responded. "We were in seventh grade when he left."

"Between seventh and eighth?" Nogueira asked.

"No." The priest paused as if to consider the importance of what he was going to say. "In fact he left in the middle of the school year."

Nogueira and Manuel exchanged a quick glance.

Manuel made a guess. "Did they expel him? Was that the straw that broke the camel's back? Is that why his father sent him to boarding school in Madrid?"

"Not exactly," Lucas responded, "although I remember there was a rumor to that effect at school."

"So what happened? Do you know?" asked Manuel.

"Álvaro told me many years later. All I remembered was that there was a huge tumult. One of the brothers committed suicide by hanging himself from the ceiling beam of his cell, and apparently Álvaro found him." Lucas looked at Manuel, clearly surprised. "Didn't the prior mention that?"

Manuel shook his head wearily. "No. No, he didn't."

Lucas did his best not to acknowledge Manuel's sour look. "Of course, the official version was quite different. They told us Brother Verdaguer had died during the night. That was all. And not a word about Álvaro, despite all the rumors. All we knew was that Álvaro was in the infirmary, very upset, and they called the marquis, his father, who came to get him. Álvaro didn't come back to class or to the school."

Nogueira was obviously intrigued. "Did you ever ask him about it?"

"Of course, the next time I saw him, quite a while later. He told me that finding Brother Verdaguer dead left him in a state of shock. At first they tried to hush it all up. They sent him to the infirmary, but when he'd been there for hours and showed no sign of improvement, the prior got worried and finally informed his father. The prior and the marquis decided that the best thing to do was to get him out of there. They thought he'd have difficulty getting over it if he stayed. The next thing we heard was from his brother, Santiago. Álvaro was at a school in Madrid. I saw him one or two more times back then. He was changed; he seemed unhappy. I was just a boy, but I could see he didn't want to discuss it. Then he didn't come back anymore, and it was years before I saw him again. When I was going to be ordained, my mother sent Álvaro an invitation through the school in Madrid. He came to the ceremony, and we stayed in contact after that."

Nogueira spoke up. "How about his brother?"

"Santiago stayed at the seminary school. Actually, Santiago seemed to come into his own once Álvaro was gone. I think he'd always suffered from a mixture of admiration and jealousy, and with Álvaro gone he perked up. His grades improved. I had to repeat a year, so he caught up with me. He was one of the best students in our class, right up until we graduated. Then he went to university."

"Were you friends?"

"Friends? I had to explain that to Manuel the other day. Except for Álvaro, the members of the Muñiz de Dávila family look down on the rest of us mere mortals. I'm the son of a schoolteacher, and I was there on a scholarship. The other boys were from good families—or, at least, from wealthy families—but not one of us had parentage like theirs. I very much doubt Santiago had any real friends among those boys."

Manuel watched Nogueira nodding slowly as Lucas spoke. The priest's description of the Muñiz de Dávila clan seemed to have gained him some points with the policeman.

Their after-dinner discussion had taken quite a while, and they were the only clients left in the place. Nogueira took out a cigarette and held it up for the proprietor to see. The man nodded, went to the front door, and locked it.

"With your permission," Nogueira said to his table companions.

They made vague gestures of dispensation. Nogueira took a deep drag on his cigarette. "I was a young cop back then, and I wasn't assigned here. But I seem to recall my brothers mentioning some story about a monk who got hanged. What can you tell me about that suicide?"

"Well, I don't remember much about him. He taught in the primary school. The official version is that he died in his sleep, but it was rumored that he killed himself. He was known to be suffering from cancer. It was in the final stages and he was in great pain. I'm inclined to share the view that the Church authorities were trying to cover it up. That's all too common, I'm sorry to say."

Nogueira was pleasantly surprised. "You don't approve?"

"Of course not. I'm not justifying suicide, but I can understand that the suffering might have been unbearable. Times were different then. There were fewer ways to alleviate pain than we have today, and you can't judge others unless you've endured similar pain. But facts are facts."

Nogueira approved.

Manuel was fascinated by the story. "Álvaro didn't tell you any more than that?"

"No. I asked him when we got together again, but I really do believe he'd managed to forget it. Or at least to blank out most of it."

Nogueira also seemed disposed to poke into the background of those events. Manuel saw his brow was furrowed and he was taking only small pulls on his cigarette. Manuel wondered what the policeman was thinking, and he didn't have to wait long to find out.

"My theory is that while Toñino was working at the seminary, he found something he thought he could exploit for a lot of cash. But the fact that a priest with terminal cancer maybe cut things short wouldn't cause a scandal," Nogueira reflected. "Probably just the opposite. Both the suicide and even the seminary's handling of it might be viewed with sympathy. Times have changed."

Manuel had come to the same conclusion. Was Álvaro just an unfortunate child traumatized by his discovery of a dead body? Or had he been suddenly expelled for cause? If so, for what cause? Why? What had he seen?

⁂

For the first time since Manuel's arrival in Galicia, the morning dawned clear, bright, and cloudless. He chose his clothing carefully, and before going to the seminary he stopped in a small stationery shop to buy a binder, adhesive tape, a couple of notebooks, and half a dozen ballpoint pens. He expected that these items might provide a certain amount of cover for his mission.

He parked by the gate and said goodbye to Café. The creature watched him with that hangdog attitude and curled up, resigned, on Álvaro's thick jacket.

Manuel saw a young brother coming toward him down a stone walk sunk into an impossibly green lawn.

The man sent to receive him couldn't be any older than thirty. "Good day, señor Ortigosa, I'm Brother Julián, the librarian." He had a strong Mexican accent. "The prior isn't here; he had some personal business to attend to. He won't be back until tomorrow, but he's instructed me to show you the monastery and help you with whatever you may need."

Manuel didn't hide his disappointment. "Oh, that's too bad! Don't take it wrong, but I was hoping to speak with one of the older brothers, so he could describe the days when the seminary had a parochial school here."

"Yes, señor, no need to worry about that. Your agent informed the prior of your interests. He can answer your questions tomorrow when he returns, but meanwhile Brother Matías can help you. He's the most senior of us. He retired years ago, but his mind is sharp and full of memories and stories about those times." He grinned. "And believe me, he never misses a chance to share them."

Brother Julián escorted him for a two-hour tour of the seminary buildings and grounds, stopping along the way to greet the monks, fewer than a dozen of them, who lived there. They were expecting him and more than a little excited to be receiving a writer. Brother Julián had assured them he was quite famous. The brothers were elated at the thought that Manuel might be planning to set his new novel in their monastery.

He remained carefully noncommittal. "I'm trying to get an idea of student life in the seminary back then. I haven't worked out the plot."

They visited San Xoan church, the annexes, patios, kitchens, the refectory, and the chapel. The former infirmary had been preserved as a showplace. Its iron bed frames and glass display cases with sinister-looking medical instruments regularly delighted the many physicians who booked rooms to enjoy the peace and quiet of monastery hospitality. A small museum featured an impressive collection of lacquer boxes that would have enchanted any antique dealer. Former classrooms had been transformed into austere but well-equipped guest rooms with private baths for guests participating in spiritual retreats.

The shelves of the spacious library were set within the stone arches of the monastery cellar. Both the books and the furnishings had been preserved and exquisitely cared for. He noticed a huge dehumidifier and a modern forced-air heating system that maintained comfortable conditions in a space that must have been humid and gloomy in the past. The inevitable electric cabling fixed high on the walls provided lights, power, heating, and high-speed connections for the state-of-the-art computer equipment used by Brother Julián.

"I've been here for two years, and I have to admit that I've spent most of that time in here," he commented with a smile. "I see myself as heir to the traditions of those pious monks who dedicated their entire lives to transcribing a single book. I do a similar task, but with technology that's a good deal more modern." He waved toward the long ranks of metal shelves that filled an unlit section of the library. "And less picturesque."

The bound documents looked old but they seemed to be very carefully arranged.

Manuel was impressed. "Don't tell me those are the seminary files."

The brother nodded, clearly pleased to see he appreciated the work that had gone into them. "They were all like that when I first got here. There'd never been a trained brother-librarian here before. Various brothers—I call them the library rats—had undertaken to maintain the books and files. They meant well, but they did it according to the holy inspiration of the moment." He chuckled. "When I got here, not a single document had been digitized. Files and ledgers were piled in cardboard boxes against the back wall, almost up to the ceiling."

"How far have you gotten?"

"To 1961."

Álvaro hadn't yet been born in 1961. If the school records hadn't been scanned, he wouldn't have a prayer of finding a clue to what happened the year Álvaro was expelled.

Manuel's expression must have betrayed his disappointment, for Brother Julián was quick to respond. "I know what you're thinking: that you won't be able to get an idea of school operations over the last fifty years. I heard that's what interests you. No need to worry!" He went to the computer that occupied his desk. "It's always the same story: those who have no understanding of IT think that digitizing a file is like putting slices of bread into a toaster. When I saw the amount of work required, I convinced the prior to hire consultants to scan all the documents." He tapped an icon on the screen that opened to display a slide show of scanned images.

Manuel felt a huge sense of relief. "That must have been a great help."

"You have no idea! Though I do feed them in by hand, file by file, the contractor's work facilitates the task enormously. They scanned each document, some of which were in very poor condition, and they digitally enhanced records that had become almost illegible. They arranged them by years in these cartons." He drummed his fingers on the lid of one of them.

Manuel looked about hesitantly at the massive monastery tables positioned about the room. "Where should I sit?"

"Oh! You can use my desk and computer. The prior told me to make sure you had access to whatever you wanted to see." He smiled. "It's too bad this monastery doesn't own any literary treasures that require special care. The only rule is that in order to respect the privacy of those concerned, one is not allowed to copy or download any file containing confidential information. Of course, I don't believe you're interested in anything of that kind. If your aim is to get a picture of the way the seminary operated, I suggest you concentrate on the photo archive. That's right here. I can print a copy of anything you find useful."

Manuel thanked Brother Julián for the attention, and for the first hour he paged through the scanned documents in chronological order. The collection ranged from individual school records to commercial invoices. Special items included scans of the formal renunciations of the world signed by those becoming monks and documentation for infants left on the monastery doorstep during the civil war. His occasional comments were well received by the brother-librarian.

Then he turned to the photo archive, as suggested.

Lucas had said that both he and Álvaro had been enrolled at the age of four, so depending on the cutoff dates for the classes, Álvaro would have first attended with the class of 1975–1976 or that of 1976–1977. Manuel reviewed the kindergarten class lists and found Álvaro's name under a school photo of a child with hair carefully parted on one side who had a big smile for the photographer. He further satisfied his curiosity by identifying Lucas Robledo. He had to smile at the little face with enormous eyes and a surprised expression. He also found Santiago. Unlike his elder brother, Santiago seemed thoroughly intimidated by the photographer.

Manuel worked his way forward through the photo archive to 1984, the year when Álvaro left the school. He searched for Álvaro's student file. The accompanying photo showed a young teenager with the same confident gaze as in the photo Herminia had given him. Only the first semester of grades was recorded, and they were remarkably high. There was one further note: *Transferred to another school.*

Manuel decided to use other search criteria. He typed *transfers* but got no hits; he checked *departures* and turned up a number of files. He swiped through them and saw that the contracting firm had made the mistake of filing transfers, expulsions, and deaths together.

He found Álvaro's report cards with grades and teacher comments for each subject. The last of them went only to early December, and the rest of the card was blank. Disconcerted, he worked his way back chronologically, studying the report cards, and thought he recognized a name. He realized why it seemed familiar when he checked it against the notes he'd jotted down the night before during the conversation with Lucas. Verdaguer—that was the monk officially reported to have died of cancer but who was suspected of committing suicide.

He noticed that the order in which the contractor had placed the files corresponded to the chronology of the departures. He paged back further and found that December 13 was a remarkably interesting date. On the same day Brother Verdaguer's death was recorded, Álvaro was transferred, and a Brother Mario Ortuño left the establishment.

He opened Ortuño's file and found no photo. Brother Mario, in charge of the infirmary, had witnessed the death certificate for Brother Verdaguer. His signature appeared just beneath the illegible scrawl of a local physician. Much to Manuel's surprise, the certificate stated the cause of death as *self-inflicted.*

So despite the rumors and what everyone suspected, it appeared there'd never been any official attempt to cover up a suicide.

Brother Mario Ortuño had made a "voluntary departure" that same day.

His file showed he'd been born in Corme, A Coruña, the youngest of three brothers. He'd entered the monastery as a novice at the age of nineteen; he'd remained in the institution until the day he witnessed Verdaguer's death certificate. Álvaro was expelled the same day, leaving school directly from the infirmary.

Manuel scribbled the information in one of his notebooks, closed the file, and then called out to the librarian. "Brother Julián, what's a 'voluntary departure' of a monk?"

The young man came over, intrigued by the question, and took a look at the screen. "It's rare, but sometimes it does happen. That's when a brother decides to renounce his vows and leave the order." He took a seat next to Manuel and did a quick search. Brother Ortuño's file appeared. "Well, for example, as you can see in the case of this brother, he had a crisis of faith. I assume it must have been very serious. In most cases an effort is made to counsel the individual and bring him back, or perhaps transfer him to another house of the same order, or prescribe spiritual exercises. But here the prior decided to send this brother home." He went back to the work he was doing with his laptop.

Manuel pretended to work for a while longer, flicking forward through the images and stopping briefly at random until he was sure the brother-librarian was absorbed anew in his tasks. Then he typed *infirmary* into the search field. Hundreds of hits popped up. He did a secondary search for Álvaro, but none of the infirmary files were associated with his name. He tried the date instead, and a document appeared. He examined it and couldn't suppress a gasp of surprise. The resolution of the image was good, and he could read the infirmary roll of admissions and discharges. The pages were ruled so that admissions and corresponding departures were recorded on the same line. Beneath the boxes for date and time was a line for the class year and the name. There, in elegant handwriting reminiscent of bygone times, the record read simply *Muñiz de Dávila*. Under that in a larger space entitled *Diagnosis* the same calligraphic script appeared:

> *The child shows evidence of significant* ▇▇▇▇▇▇▇▇
> ▇▇▇▇▇▇▇▇▇▇▇▇▇▇ *the initial*
> ▇▇▇▇▇ *examination disoriented and confused* ▇▇▇▇
> *a slight fever, though incompatible* ▇▇▇▇▇▇▇
> ▇▇▇▇ *eight o'clock,* ▇▇▇▇▇▇▇▇
> *Therefore I recommend that he be* ▇▇▇▇▇▇
> *Given the circumstances* ▇▇▇▇▇▇▇▇
> *I can state that the child* ▇▇▇▇▇▇▇▇
> *by his primary care physician or a specialist, I earnestly request and am*
> *confident that* ▇▇▇▇▇▇▇▇▇▇
> *for the health* ▇▇▇▇▇▇▇▇▇▇▇
> *This being my solemn obligation, I so declare and record it, and I pray that God may guide us.*
>
> *Signed:*
> *Brother Mario Ortuño*

❧

The record filled a whole page. Considering Ortuño's precise handwriting, it must have been extremely detailed, but the record had been censored with the sort of ominous heavy black markings that he recalled having seen used only on records of summary executions during the civil war and in intelligence reports from the First World War.

He checked behind him to make sure that the librarian was still busy and then captured the image with his cell phone camera. He spent the next half hour swiping through blurry photographs in search of Mario Ortuño. He felt an urgent desire for a good look at the man who'd written an infirmary report so horrific it had been censored almost in its entirety. He wanted a picture of the monk who'd voluntarily renounced his vows after writing a report of which only fragmentary passages remained: *The child shows evidence of significant . . .* That man had left the monastery the same day Álvaro was withdrawn from school, and those few words constituted the only remaining record.

He couldn't get the phrase out of his head: *The child shows evidence of significant . . .* Was the shock of seeing the dead body serious enough to prompt the heavy censoring of that report? Yet there'd apparently been no effort to cover up the suicide. Was this the document that Toñino had found and for which he expected to get a princely payment? Or to be more precise, had Toñino gotten his hands on a document that provided the missing information?

Manuel looked over at the long stretch of metal shelving crowded with cardboard boxes that extended out of sight into the darkness. Even if an uncensored copy of this report did exist, he didn't see how Toñino could have found it here. The likelihood was simply too remote. No, whatever he'd discovered, the document had to have come from elsewhere.

"Do you know the prior's nephew?"

"Toñino?" The surprise in the brother-librarian's voice made Manuel want to bite his tongue.

"I don't know his name; in fact, I don't know him at all." Manuel had to improvise. "But this morning I stopped in the village, and a woman there asked me if I was the prior's nephew who was working at the monastery."

"Yes, sounds like Toñino; there's not another nephew. But I don't know how anyone could have taken you for him. He doesn't look at all like you."

"He was working here?" Manuel asked in what he hoped was an indifferent tone.

"In the library?" The librarian chuckled. "No, I doubt he's ever set foot in a library. He was painting rooms in the hostel and the prior's offices, I think, but just between the two of us, he's a disaster. And that woman needs to have her eyes checked as soon as possible."

Manuel didn't find a photo of Mario Ortuño anywhere in the archive, but he had no problem finding plenty of pictures of events with Brother Verdaguer. It was easy to see why Lucas had called him one of the most beloved of the brothers. Chubby and with pink cheeks that stood out even in the black-and-white photos, he turned up leading sports teams, excursions, and games. Though he always wore the robe of the order, it was apparently no hindrance in competitions. He was shown posing with the sports teams and their trophies, as well as directing the Christmas choir. In one of the most bizarre images, he was playing Basque handball against the side of the church, his habit held up almost to his waist with one hand while he punched the ball with the other. Manuel asked Brother Julián to print that photo in a batch of about twenty. The carefully chosen miscellaneous collection included photos of Brother Verdaguer with schoolboys, aerial views of the buildings, and old snapshots of classrooms. He left the librarian busy at work but only half-convinced by Manuel's assurances he'd be able to find his own way to the orchard. That's where the elderly Brother Matías whiled away the hours.

"I'm sure it was for a woman," Brother Julián commented as Manuel was leaving.

Confused, Manuel turned and gave him an inquiring look.

"A woman; the reason for Brother Ortuño's crisis of faith. The record shows he was twenty-five years old when he renounced his robes. It had to have been for a woman. Otherwise he would have come back."

Manuel just sighed.

Once outside, instead of heading for the fields behind the monastery, he went in the opposite direction, hoping not to run into any of the monks. He found the garage as described by Nogueira, its doors standing wide open. He took from his pocket the roll of adhesive tape he'd purchased that same morning, tore off a length, applied it to the scraped edges of the dent on the pickup truck and jerked sharply. Small flakes of white paint remained stuck on the tape. He secured them by winding the tape back onto the roll.

⁕

The librarian hadn't been kidding when he said that Brother Matías loved to talk. The man told long, rambling stories about the students, the orchard, the greens he enjoyed cultivating in the garden that had kept them alive during the war, and how he eventually found himself hating Swiss chard. The brothers had gotten into the habit of calling it "monk-killer," because they'd been reduced to eating little else during times of great hunger.

A long narrow stretch of garden plot separated the orchard from the cemetery. As they strolled through the area, the monk pointed out the oldest graves, some from three hundred years before. They were marked by plain stones set in the ground. The austerity reminded Manuel of those at As Grileiras, though this cemetery mostly featured stark iron crosses with plaques recording names and dates, unlike the Galician stone crosses at the estate.

They walked in silence among the graves. Manuel stopped before each one to read the inscription. Eventually they came to that of Brother Verdaguer. "That's odd!" he exclaimed.

The elderly monk appeared surprised. "What do you find odd?" he asked in a slightly defensive tone, looking down first at the little cross and then again at Manuel.

"Nothing, but I was taken by surprise. The name reminded me of what I read about him this morning. I happened to come across a death certificate that recorded him as a suicide. I thought the canon prescribed a different burial regime for suicides."

The smile dropped off the monk's face. He walked away, obliging Manuel to hasten to get an explanation.

"Things have changed considerably in recent years. Our consensus was that Brother Verdaguer should be laid to rest with his brothers. This man was afflicted by a cancer that caused him terrible suffering." His extremely serious expression lent weight to his words. "The illness was lengthy and debilitating, and he steadfastly refused all treatment. He put up with extreme pain, far more than most humans could have endured, but it exhausted him. He was completely drained, and he choose to give up the fight. We did not approve, but only God has the authority to judge him."

Manuel lowered his voice. "I'm very sorry if I stirred up painful memories. I didn't mean to be insensitive. It's just that his name caught my attention."

"Never mind. I'm an old sentimentalist, and I'm a bit tired. Perhaps you'd best come back tomorrow. I'll stay here a bit longer to pray."

Manuel saw that his guide really did look fatigued. His extreme thinness accentuated his frailty. He looked as if he might snap in two at any time.

"Of course, just as you like, Brother Matías." He gently patted the elderly monk's shoulder and turned toward the exit.

Manuel looked back before he disappeared around the corner of the main building. The old man stared stonily at him from the center of the cemetery.

BELESAR

He drove aimlessly, taking a long trip to nowhere as he struggled with the contradictions. Random images from old photographs rose before him, and his heart begged him to reject them, to flee, to run and hide from impending horror. It was as sharp and unnerving as static electricity preceding a howling thunderstorm.

He pulled up in front of Nogueira's house, not knowing how he got there or why he'd come. Or what had driven him here in search of the refuge he so desperately needed.

He called Nogueira's number, but a recorded voice informed him it wasn't available. He started the engine and took a last glance at the house. Just as he was about to pull out onto the road, Laura appeared at the door and gestured at him to stop.

She reached the car before Manuel could turn off the engine. She rested her hand on the door next to him. "Andrés isn't home. He went to Lugo on an errand. Were you supposed to meet him? He didn't mention it."

Manuel shook his head slowly. "No, we hadn't arranged anything, it's just that . . ."

Laura's sunny expression gave way to one of concern. "Has something happened, Manuel?"

He raised his eyes to her. She'd crossed her arms, rested them on the bottom of the open window, and leaned down to pose her chin on them. Her eyes and expression were warm and sympathetic.

Manuel gave her a barely perceptible nod that admitted his distress. In that moment of intimacy he closed his eyes, knowing that the weight upon his soul had begun to overwhelm him.

He looked up and surprised himself by repeating Daniel's invitation to the most beautiful place on earth. "Are you doing anything right now?"

❧

Rocked by the waves from a passing yacht, the motorboat pitched against the mooring of the jetty. Xulia and Antía resisted the impulse to abandon ship, held one another tightly in the stern, and endured the rocking as they watched an otter deftly picking river mussels off the pilings of the pier.

They'd driven between the double rows of chestnut trees with golden fruit that shaded the road down to the Miño River. After departing Belesar port they gazed enchantedly at the expanse of *muras* that sustained the slope and the orderly terraces planted with grapevines. They floated down the winding watercourse, passing over seven sunken villages flooded long ago, ghost dwellings beneath the waters. He repeated almost word for word Daniel's comments on the first boat trip, surprised to find that he'd retained them despite his former lethargy. He felt content. He turned to smile at the girls listening wide-eyed to his spiel, and he stifled the voice within that had begun to ask what was going on.

Later, seated beside him on the terrace overlooking the river, Laura smiled as she listened to her daughters' laughter. She liked Belesar. She wondered momentarily why they'd never visited it, even though she knew the answer: it wouldn't have made much sense to torment the girls by driving them to the Miño and then refusing to board the tourist boats for the river excursion. She drank some wine and inspected the purple ring it left along the rim.

Laura didn't care for boats, she hated sailing, and she hadn't set foot on a jetty since she was a child and a violent storm had changed everything. Today she'd recognized in Manuel's gallant gesture the love imprisoned within him, gagged and bound hand and foot, sentenced forever to the darkest depths of his soul. She recognized a kindred soul, a man who had taken ownership of his fears. Her heart had yielded without protest to a suffering greater than her own. She calmly scrutinized her new friend through the lens of the crystal wineglass. Each swirl of the liquid it held left faint purple traces of the *mencía* grape.

Manuel ran his finger along the path taken by a drop of wine from the mouth of the bottle down the side and across the label. He contemplated the metallic gleam of the letters boldly inscribed across the label to proclaim the name of the wine: *Heroica*. He tilted his head to the side and regarded that brave declaration. His brooding expression betrayed his unhappy thoughts.

Laughter interrupted his reflections. He looked out at the river and saw a dream come true—the three girls from the other day again rode their curious craft downstream. Their legs were tanned and their arms were strong, and their hair was carelessly tied back into ponytails dangling under their straw hats. They shrieked and laughed. The music of those voices rang like the notes of wind chimes moved by the breeze. The spectacle of those lovely river nymphs filled him with inexplicable joy. He saw them look up distractedly toward the terrace, and he followed a sudden impulse to wave. All three saw him but they didn't react. His sense of magical connection vanished, breaking the spell and making him feel ridiculous and quite old. They didn't remember him, and why should they?

Then one of them gave him a huge smile and cried, "It's the marquis, girls! It's the marquis!"

The other two responded with such a joyful outcry that it attracted the attention of everyone on the terrace. The girls waved their hats, overcome with laughter.

One of them cupped her hands and shouted, "Hey, Marquis, Daddy says hello! Come visit us soon!"

"I will," Manuel murmured, as he watched them dwindle into the distance in their curious craft. His voice was so low that only his new friend Laura heard him.

"You'll never be able to leave this place," she said.

He gazed calmly at her. That affirmation would have seemed a curse to him just days before, but now he took it as a prediction of good fortune, one of those wishes that fly against all logic. As if to counter his doubts or perhaps to create even more, Laura added, "It gets into your blood. That's what's special about this place. Be careful; it will enchant you, and you won't be able to leave."

He didn't answer, although he could hardly credit her prediction. The magic of the river; the peace of mind he'd thought forever impossible until the grape harvest at *Heroica* restored it to him; the easy familiarity of the river nymphs— all were very powerful, but they couldn't make him forget the real reason he'd remained.

Sipping this wine was like taking communion. Suddenly he found it difficult to swallow. He looked at the bottle and that single word in Álvaro's writing. He again brushed a finger along the silver gleam of the letters.

Laura looked at him in sudden surprise, as if she'd just discovered his deepest secret. "Manuel, you're not just doing research here, are you?"

He looked up and found Laura watching him. He finished tracing the legend on the label and then rested his hand upon the table. He replied with infinite sadness.

"No. I'm not."

⋆⋆⋆

Night fell rapidly. After a cloudless sunset the heavens didn't darken but instead turned silver. Their brilliance threw into sharp relief the silhouettes of the trees that lined the road to Nogueira's house. The policeman leaned on the porch railing and puffed placidly at his cigarette as he enjoyed the quiet of the gloaming and the silence of his empty house. The evening cool contrasted with the heat of that summery day as breezes entered through the wide-open front door. He looked up, attracted by swooping swallows snatching the mosquitoes that had begun to gather as the streetlamps turned on. He saw Manuel's car approaching. He continued enjoying his smoke until he caught sight of his wife in the passenger seat. He swiftly stubbed out his cigarette and hid the butt among the blooms of a hanging plant.

The car stopped and his daughters popped out of the back, Café following close behind. Little Antía ran up and hugged him excitedly. The words tumbled out of her. "Papa, you know what? Manuel has a boat and he took us to Belesar and all down the river. They've got seven villages under the water with churches and schools and everything, and we saw the grapes they picked over the weekend, and he treated us to snacks. Mama, Xulia, and I are going back, and they'll let us pick grapes in the *ribeira*. Isn't that great? Will you come, too, Papa?"

Delighted by her enthusiasm, Nogueira kissed the crown of his little daughter's head. She wiggled out of his grasp and flung herself into the house with Café on her heels.

Manuel got out of the car as Laura came around to say goodbye. Xulia walked past her father and greeted him cordially. "Hey there, Papa!"

He turned in surprise. He couldn't remember the last time his daughter had spoken to him that way—unworried, relaxed, without a trace of the tension and veiled dislike that stabbed his soul every time she spoke to him. He suddenly recalled the little girl she'd been until not long ago, the child who ran to the door and threw herself into his arms when he got back from work.

Nogueira stepped down onto the walk and got to the car as his wife thanked Manuel with a hug. The policeman felt a pang of jealousy.

She gave him a look. "I saw you smoking!" Her voice was stern, but she broke immediately into a smile that belied the rebuke. "And don't leave cigarette butts in the flowerpots, or I'll kill you!" She headed toward the house without another word.

Nogueira came up to Manuel, who was trying to hide a smile.

"I got your message. The meeting with the priest is on for nine o'clock tonight in the same place as yesterday, but you know, you might think of taking your phone calls from time to time."

"I was driving."

Nogueira gave him a sidelong look. "Uh-huh. With my family. You might have told me that too."

Manuel got into the car and beckoned to Nogueira. He waited until the former policeman was also inside. "I hope you don't mind. I finished early at the seminary, and it would have been a shame to waste such wonderful weather. I enjoy boating, and I thought they might like it. I came by, but you weren't here."

Nogueira didn't comment, but when Manuel started the engine the policeman said, "Aren't you forgetting something?"

"If you mean Café, I'll pick him up when I get back. Your daughter adores him, and the feeling seems to be mutual."

"How'd it go with our friend the prior?"

"Well and not so well," he replied, with a smile and the ambiguous taciturnity more typical of Nogueira. "The prior wasn't there. Their story is that he had to travel for personal reasons. I'd rather give a full report when we see Lucas, because I think he can offer us some insights about what I found. But in the meantime, this is for you." He held out a plastic bag with the roll of adhesive tape he'd used to collect the paint samples. "I suspect this and the samples of the paint left on Álvaro's car will give the lab enough to determine if they're identical."

Nogueira nodded appreciatively as he peered at the sample in the clear plastic bag. "Keep this up and you'll wind up as a detective someday. Going back to the monastery tomorrow?"

"I don't think I should," Manuel said with a shrug. "I'm afraid I screwed up my chances by asking about Toñino. I realized it immediately and tried to cover it, but chances are the brother-librarian will mention it to the prior."

⚜

Lucas was waiting by the fireplace when they got there. The splendid cloudless day meant that unfortunately the countryside cooled off fast in early evening. The restaurant parking lot was about a hundred yards from the entrance, and Manuel had put on Álvaro's heavy jacket to walk that distance. He'd kept it in his car since Daniel had given it to him.

Manuel saw the priest start in surprise at the sight of him but let it pass without comment. He was intent on filling them in on the results of his seminary visit and couldn't hold it until after dinner. "The prior wasn't there. They said he'd been called away on personal business. I met Brother Julián instead, a young monk who's been working full-time for the last two years on organizing and digitizing the archives. Just as we hoped, they gave me the full tour and offered to assist me in any way they could. At first I expected it'd be difficult to get away and sniff around, but once he'd explained the library setup and the digital archives, he set me loose on his computer. I found school records for Álvaro and his brother. And yours, too, Lucas," he added with a grin. "You were a very handsome little boy."

Lucas smiled but disagreed. "Afraid not; neither handsome nor little."

"Álvaro's permanent record runs to December 13, 1984, and ends with the note that he transferred to another school. But get this: I did a word search for departures, and I found Brother Verdaguer's death certificate. The cause of death is very clearly specified as suicide, contrary to what we thought."

"So they didn't try to cover it up after all," Lucas said. "Maybe the story about him dying in his sleep was something they just made up to shield the boys."

"I remember you said yesterday that Álvaro spent several hours in the infirmary after he found Brother Verdaguer."

"That's right. It seems he discovered the body that night, they took him to the infirmary, and they didn't tell his father until the next day."

The host arrived with several platters of meat, potatoes, and salads and spread them about the table, but for the moment none of them touched the food.

Manuel used his cell phone to display the photo he'd taken in the monastery library. "If I'd asked him to print this for me, that would have been a dead giveaway." He pointed to the document with those ominous black lines smeared across it. "This is the report the infirmary director wrote that night. The only uncensored parts are the name, the time, and the first words of the report: *The child shows evidence of significant* . . . and a few irrelevant phrases that throw no light whatever on the state the child showed 'evidence' of."

The expressions on the other two men's faces had changed. The officer took the phone and enlarged the photo to study the details. He was astonished. "This has been completely blacked out!"

"What do you think was in this report?" Manuel asked. "What could have been so horrible? Do you really think that the child's condition, no matter how scared he was, required a whole page to describe it?"

"A fine bunch of schemers!" Nogueira muttered under his breath without looking up from the screen.

Lucas's face had gone pale. He seemed to want to say something, but he managed only to shake his head and utter a choked "My God!"

"And here's something a good deal more suggestive," Manuel continued. "That same day, December 13, Brother Mario Ortuño, who had been in charge of the infirmary up till then, renounced his vows and left the monastery. The prior's report recorded it as a crisis of faith."

"Lucas, do you remember him?" Nogueira asked. "Brother Ortuño?"

"Yes," the priest replied in a low voice, searching his memory. "He wasn't a teacher. It's true, he left the school, but back then I didn't connect it with Álvaro's departure. I assumed he'd been transferred. That's not unusual in the monastic orders."

"Did you see what time Álvaro was admitted to the infirmary? Four o'clock in the morning! Doesn't it seem strange for a child to be up at that time of night? I don't know about you, but when I was twelve I went to bed so tired I slept like a log." He turned to Lucas. "You told me Álvaro was dedicated to sports, so he was one of those kids who couldn't stand still. You'd think he'd be dead to the world at that hour."

Lucas agreed, obviously baffled.

"What was Álvaro doing in that monk's cell in the middle of the night?"

It was a question without an answer. The three men exchanged glances, keenly aware of the foreboding implications.

"And then there's the question of Brother Verdaguer," Manuel added. "At the monastery they make no effort to hide the fact that he took his own life. That's what the death certificate shows. When I mentioned it today to Brother Matías, one of the oldest monks there, he said all of the monks agreed Brother Verdaguer should be laid to rest in the monastery cemetery despite the circumstances of his death. He said Verdaguer had gone through a lengthy illness, he'd refused treatment, and the pain had become unbearable. He made his choice. They didn't agree, but they didn't judge him. They left that to God."

"Along the lines of what I told you yesterday," said Lucas.

"Yes, but something doesn't fit, it seems to me," Manuel replied. He took from his jacket pocket half a dozen of the photos Brother Julián had printed for him that morning.

Brother Verdaguer appeared in each of them, playing games or practicing sports or posing with teams and their trophies. The most striking was the one that showed him playing Basque handball with his habit hitched up.

Manuel pointed to it. "The camera imprint shows this one was taken December 11, just two days before he took his own life because of the terrible pain he was supposedly suffering. I don't know about you, but this doesn't look to me like a man suffering a long and devastating illness." He tapped the photo with his index finger. "He's the picture of health."

Nogueira was the one to put into words what all three were thinking. "I don't want to jump to the conclusion that someone was abusing the boy, even though these signs are consistent with all the cases of abuse I saw in my career. We need to consider the alternative: maybe the boy saw something he shouldn't have. Hanging is the method most often used to conceal a murder by faking a suicide. The claim the brother monk refused all treatment might be their way of explaining the absence of any medical records of an illness."

A cover-up; the concealing of a murder. But if so, a murder committed by whom? Manuel had been asking himself that question all day long, and the obvious answer, the one he still refused to accept, resounded in his mind along with the words Mei had reported. He was haunted by that insistent voice from a phone booth in Lugo. Someone had tried to warn Álvaro not to take a threat lightly because someone else was aware of it. Someone knew he'd killed and had proof of it.

He was tormented by the knowledge that he was withholding Mei's report. He looked at the two men at the table with him and felt he was both their ally and a traitor to them. But despite the terrible impact of Mei's report, he was unwilling to share it. Especially now that it would seem even more damning, given the horror of what he suspected had happened that night. It was possible, just barely possible, that a distant night of horror might explain Álvaro's silence and his estrangement from that eerie world. Manuel's reason and his whole life hung in the balance. If only he could stop asking himself whom Álvaro could have killed! Fran, his own brother? Verdaguer? Both of them?

Lucas silently studied the photo displayed on Manuel's cell phone, the heavy black censor lines, and the signature. "Do you think Toñino found this?"

"No. When I asked Brother Julián if Toñino had access to the library, he practically split his sides laughing. He said the boy was there to paint a couple of guest rooms and the prior's office, that's all."

"So he must have found the document there," Nogueira concluded.

"If so, it wasn't this version." Manuel pointed at the screen. "It might have been the uncensored original. This one would have been useless unless he already knew the details. Given the dire nature of the events, the prior would've had every reason to keep it under lock and key in his office. It's highly unlikely Toñino would have come across the censored version in the mass of scanned documents."

Nogueira agreed. "Whatever Toñino came across had to have been clear as day. He has no way to contact Álvaro, so he approaches Santiago and demands three hundred thousand euros for it, an amount his buddy Richie said would allow him to start a new life somewhere else. Santiago has no way of directly contacting his brother, either, so he calls the administrator and makes up this tall tale about a horse, knowing perfectly well his brother will call. As soon as they talk, Álvaro comes here and goes directly to the source—that is, he goes to see the prior. They talk, the prior makes the connection. As soon as Álvaro leaves, the prior goes to the nephew's house, throws a fit that the neighbor overhears, and after he leaves, Toñino drives off in his car, a white car—but not the same model as the monastery pickup with the dent corresponding to the one on Álvaro's car."

Lucas turned off the phone and carefully placed it on the table. He pushed it away from him. He looked directly at Nogueira. "Do you think Toñino could have killed Álvaro?"

The lieutenant thought about it. "I've known the boy for years. He's never been involved in violence, and he doesn't seem the sort to get aggressive. He'd be more likely to run for his life. But everything suggests that Álvaro was very angry, so if Álvaro caught up with him, there could have been a confrontation. And anything could have happened."

Don't you threaten me. Manuel recalled those words. Was Toñino the one who was threatening? Did Toñino call from the phone booth?

"And how does the monastery pickup truck fit into all this?" Lucas asked.

"I don't know yet," Nogueira said, "but the witness heard the prior shout that this could be the end of him. If Álvaro threatened him—well, it all depends on how desperate the man felt."

The restaurant owner came to the table looking extremely concerned. "Gentlemen, what's the problem? Is something wrong with the meat? Would you prefer something else?"

The trio looked down at the platters of untouched food.

"Man, we're sorry," Nogueira apologized. "We were so caught up in our conversation we didn't even notice." He took a slice of meat.

The owner examined the spread, frowned, and gathered the platters. "But, gentlemen, it's stone cold! Give me a moment, and I'll bring you more, straight from the grill. But please eat. Such waste is a shame, and you'll find nothing better than what we serve."

He returned shortly with other trays and stood over them long enough to make sure that they actually did dig in.

Manuel was the one to break the silence. "I've been puzzling all day about what could have happened. I haven't been able to keep that censored report out of my mind. I've been speculating all sorts of horrible things." He put down his fork.

Nogueira responded. "You said you wrote down the information about that Ortuño guy."

Manuel nodded.

"Give it to me. I'll call someone." Nogueira took the notebook page with the information, got up, and left the dining room.

He was back in less than five minutes with a grin on his face. "Good news! Turns out that the guy still lives at the same address. He was there the last time he renewed his ID card a couple of years ago. Of course when we visit we might find he moved or even died since then."

Lucas's eyes lit up. "Are you planning to go?"

"You can come, too, unless priests aren't allowed to take time off."

Lucas smiled. "I can arrange it."

When they left the restaurant Lucas gave Manuel the same wondering look as at the start of the evening. "Manuel, that jacket you're wearing . . ."

"It was Álvaro's. Daniel gave it to me the other day for a trip down the river."

"I know. I remember seeing you wearing it once, and when you came in, that jogged my memory. That's the coat he had on the night I thought I saw him by the church. He had the hood up, and I recognized it from the fur lining."

"But anyone could have been wearing it," Manuel reflected. "Daniel took it from the stables. When I took it back, he said no one would miss it. Álvaro left it there so he could pick it up to go out to the countryside."

⁂

Manuel parked in front of Nogueira's house and waited in the car while the officer went to fetch Café. He smiled when he saw the man carrying the little dog.

"Goddamn! Can you believe the child had it in her bed? And my wife didn't say a word." He put the dog into the car.

"And I'm sure you didn't complain, did you, Café?" Manuel reached back to pet the animal.

"They didn't complain either. They've already planned what they'll do tomorrow when you drop him off again. I'm telling you, they don't make plans like that with me."

Manuel gave the lieutenant an earnest look. "Nogueira, I hope it didn't bother you that I took Laura and the girls on the boat trip. When I left the monastery I was so upset I felt almost destroyed, and I needed to spend time with real people. Normal people. To preserve my sanity."

Nogueira nodded, moved Café to the backseat, and took the passenger seat. He left the door open. "Sure, I understand. Lots of times after work I felt like that."

"I'd promised Xulia a reading list and some advice, and it seemed like a good idea."

"Don't worry. Sounds like they had a real good time."

Manuel turned to face him. "You and Laura should talk."

He shook his head. "Drop it, Manuel."

"Laura is very special," Manuel persisted. "I think many men would be proud to have her at their side."

That irritated Nogueira. "You think I don't know it?"

"It gives me the creeps to see you fooling around with Ophelia and going to that crappy roadhouse."

"Drop it, Manuel," he said again.

"Talk to her."

Nogueira shook his head, stubborn as a bull.

"Why not?"

Nogueira blew his top. "Because I don't want to, Manuel!"

"That's not true."

"You don't know a goddamn thing! You met us two days ago, and now you think you can swoop in here and fix everything." Nogueira leaned back and when he spoke again, his voice was calm. "I know what you're trying to do, and I thank you for it. But it won't work."

"No, it won't," Manuel replied. "Not unless you're willing to try."

"She hates me, Manuel," he complained. "My wife despises me."

"I don't believe it," Manuel replied obstinately.

Nogueira looked at him in silence for several seconds and then turned his gaze away. "I've been sleeping in the baby's room for the last six years."

Manuel's jaw dropped.

"I've been sleeping in Antía's room since she turned two. Every night I have to rearrange the stuffed animals and the heart-shaped pillows and go to bed in her Minnie Mouse sheets." His voice was resigned. "Or the Disney princess ones."

Manuel was amazed and then amused. "But that's . . ."

"Yes, it's ridiculous. She doesn't let me change anything there, because it's our girl's bedroom, but I'm not allowed back in ours. For years Antía has been sleeping on a cot in our room, and I've been in hers. It's just another of the many ways she takes it out on me. You've seen the crap I eat there, right?"

Manuel had.

"She's starving me to death," he said with utmost seriousness.

Manuel would have laughed out loud if it hadn't been for the man's pathetic tone.

"You've seen how she can cook," Nogueira continued. "Well, for the last six years I've had nothing but boiled greens. She fixes all sorts of things for her and the kids, dishes I love. Stews, cakes, and pies." He sighed. "And I'm not allowed even a sniff."

"But what you're saying is . . . It's your house, isn't it? So you can eat whatever you want."

Nogueira denied it. "Everything she buys, everything she cooks, she wraps up in yards and yards of that goddamn plastic food wrap. It's easier to unwrap a mummy than to get a bite of food in my house. One thing in her favor: my dinner's always ready when I get home. If you call that crap dinner."

"Okay, Nogueira, I understand this is a sore spot, but I agree with your wife that you should pay attention to your health. I've seen you stuff yourself with enough cholesterol to choke a horse."

Nogueira grinned. "That's my revenge."

"If so, your revenge will be the end of you. I really do think your wife is concerned for your health."

"Don't you worry about a thing, Manuel. She couldn't care less. It's just that she knows I love to eat and I adore her cooking. It's one more way for her to torture me."

"Surely you're exaggerating."

"And then there are the girls . . ."

Manuel gave him a grave look.

"I almost can't believe the way they've been treating me since you turned up; but it's because of you, Manuel. The respect and admiration they have for you makes them see me differently. But over the last six years the tension between Laura and me has affected my relationships with my daughters. Laura has turned them against me."

Manuel started to protest.

"I'm not saying she fills their heads with nonsense. She never says a thing. But the girls see she doesn't care for me, so they follow her example. They treat me with the same scorn as their mother. Xulia and I can scarcely stand one another; I can't remember the last time she gave me a kiss, and we're always arguing. Sometimes I think her mother spoils her just to get at me. Like that jerk at the table. I can't stand the sight of him, Manuel, he drives me crazy. Sometimes I look at my wife and see she's just as exasperated as I am, and if she puts up with him, it's only because it infuriates me to see him in my place at the table with his nasty stuck-up little face."

The policeman sighed and lit a cigarette. He smoked it there where he was, perched on the edge of the passenger seat with the car door open despite the night chill, turning to blow each exhalation of smoke into the open air. "What screws me over most of all is the fact that now I'm losing Antía," he said mournfully. "She's still a child, but women are like that. One of them senses the hostility felt by another and the rest join in. Even if they don't know the cause of it."

"Shit, Nogueira, I don't know what terrible thing can be wrong, but I'm sure that you can resolve it if you really want to."

The man had a completely defeated look. "There is no solution."

"Were you unfaithful?" Manuel asked. "I'm referring to . . ."

"She doesn't care about that. I already told you she doesn't love me anymore. Maybe she doesn't know for sure, but she's no fool. She's bound to suspect."

Manuel considered Nogueira's comments in silence for a few seconds. "So why do you think she stays? Look, Nogueira, Laura is an amazing woman. She's clever, and she earns enough money not to have to put up with you if she doesn't want to. Besides, she's really good-looking, and she'd have no trouble getting another man." Manuel didn't miss the hard look the lieutenant gave him but he continued anyway. "And you're claiming that she's not sticking around to preserve your relationship with your daughters. So it seems to me that if she didn't want to be with you, she'd have been out of there long ago."

Nogueira glared at him.

"You know everything I'm saying is the simple truth," Manuel insisted. "And it comes down to the fact that since she hasn't left you, there must be something left to save."

"You don't know her. She hasn't left me because she intends to make the rest of my life a living hell."

"Then leave her; put an end to this torture once and for all. Give both of you a chance to be happy, even if it means you have to part."

Nogueira rejected that with a smile, as if the very idea of separation were unthinkable. "No," he answered. "Never."

"But why? Why would anyone deliberately choose to be unhappy for the rest of his life?"

Nogueira threw his cigarette to the pavement, where it rebounded and traced a path of burning ash through the air. He turned to Manuel in a fury. "Because I deserve it," he shouted. "I deserve it, you hear? Can you understand that? If she tells me to leave, I will, but until then I stay here and take it like a man."

Manuel didn't back down. "What did you do?"

Nogueira seized his lapels, and Manuel was sure the man was going to punch him. Their faces were inches apart.

"What did you do?"

Nogueira didn't hit him. Instead he let go of Manuel's jacket, put his face in his hands, and broke down. Hoarse, desperate sobs racked his body so violently they must have caused him physical pain. He pawed furiously at his eyes and the tears coursing down his cheeks, as if his grief made him loathe himself. He said something, but between the sobs and the hands muffling his words, Manuel couldn't make it out.

"What?"

Nogueira said it again, through his tears. "I raped her."

Manuel couldn't believe it. "Nogueira, what did you say?" Startled and frightened, he desperately hoped he'd just misheard. Surely his ears were playing tricks on him.

The officer stifled his sobs. He rubbed his eyes angrily and turned so Manuel could see his face and his expression of tormented shame.

"I raped her," he said distinctly. He leaned slowly forward from the waist as if in an act of contrition. "I forced myself on my wife, Manuel. I deserve to be in daily hell; whatever she wants to do to me, whatever punishment she dreams up for me, it won't be enough to atone for what I did."

Manuel couldn't move. The horror of that confession held him paralyzed and blocked his thoughts, kept him from saying something, anything, and prevented him from reacting. "For the love of God!" he managed to murmur.

In his mind there arose the vivid image of Nogueira's mother, barely thirty years old, injured and humiliated, begging her son not to tell.

"How could you? With what you'd seen as a child?"

Nogueira again covered his face with his hands, anguished and ashamed. Again he broke into sobs.

Manuel's feelings surged in confusion as Nogueira dissolved in tears. Manuel tried to think of something to say, but whenever he opened his mouth the man's horrible confession took his breath away and overpowered rational thought. If only he'd been able to utter the words the elderly monk had whispered over Verdaguer's grave, recusing himself from judging another human being and leaving that heavy responsibility to God instead. But he couldn't. He was appalled by the bestiality of it, the brutality of the act. And at the same time he was moved by the abject misery of the broken man beside him. A suffering sinner had opened himself, and the profound sense of a shared humanity both provoked rejection and made him feel complicit in evil, as if Manuel too shared the responsibility for all the horrors, humiliations, and affronts committed against all women everywhere from the beginning of time. And he saw the truth of it. Every man on earth, by the simple fact of his masculinity, is guilty of causing all that suffering.

He reached out, placed his hand on Nogueira's shoulder, and felt the man's body shudder violently. In answer, the policeman instinctively resorted to the gesture that Manuel had seen days before when Sarita attempted to console Herminia: he placed his hand over Manuel's, held it, and pressed it against his shoulder.

After crying for a long time, at last Nogueira was exhausted and as limp as a marionette whose strings had been cut. He lit another cigarette and smoked in silence, blowing the smoke sharply upward and out from the car. His gestures were slow and weary as if conserving his last reserves of energy. He gazed through the windshield toward the house, but his eyes were looking beyond their home, his wife, and his sleeping daughters. The misery in his face was proof he was envisioning his dismal future.

"I was drunk," he said suddenly. "Not terribly drunk, and I'm not claiming that excuses anything. The little one was about two years old. Laura devoted all her time to the baby, the way we'd done with the first one. I was earning enough money so we could afford for Laura not to work. When Antía was a year and a half old, Laura went back to her job. And then everything began to fall apart. It was my fault," he quickly added. "I'd always left the housework and childcare to her. That's how I was brought up. My mother always chased us out of the kitchen. Me and my brothers too. I know it's a shitty excuse, and I should have taught myself what my mother never did. It was okay when there was just Xulia, but with the two of them things got more complicated. Antía was teething and cried all night long. Laura got home exhausted from work, and then she had to take care of all the housework and both of the little ones. She was starting to neglect me. On the weekends all she wanted was to stay home. She cooked and did the laundry, and when she came to bed she wanted to be left alone. She didn't want to go out, she was always tired, and the few times we did do something we had to take the girls along."

Manuel listened in silence. He tried to hide his emotions, but Nogueira saw them in his face.

"I know you're thinking I was a shit-faced macho and I didn't deserve her. And you're right.

"One night I went out with some buddies to celebrate . . . something, I forget what, it doesn't matter. I got back to the house really late, and I'd had a lot to drink. Laura was back from the late shift at the hospital, and she'd been up with the little one. Antía had finally gone to sleep. She walked past me and tucked Antía into the baby bed. She didn't say anything, but it was obvious she was angry; she was like that almost all the time. I don't remember how I got to bed, but when she came back I jumped her." He fell silent.

Manuel knew the policeman was going to weep. This time his crying was slow and mournful. The tears streaked his face. The angry pawing and vehement rejection had vanished.

"I missed my wife. I just wanted to touch her. I swear to you, Manuel, I just wanted to hold her close. I don't know what happened, but a minute later she was screaming and crying, terrified because I was hurting her and pinning her wrists against the pillow. She bit me." He fingered his upper lip. "I'll have to wear this mustache for the rest of my life to hide the scar. That sudden pain woke me, like I'd been having a nightmare. I didn't completely . . . but I'd hurt her. I pulled back from her in surprise, not knowing exactly what'd happened, and I looked at her, and then I saw her panic and fright. She was terrified. Afraid of me, the man who'd sworn to love her and care for her! And I saw something else, Manuel." He turned to face Manuel fully. "I saw contempt and emptiness, and I knew at that moment I'd lost her forever."

"What did she say?"

Nogueira met his eyes. "Nothing. I crawled out of her bedroom that night, Manuel. I took some medicine and vomited my guts out, and I didn't even try to go back to our bed. I slept on the sofa. I was sure she'd never say a word to me again. She never stopped speaking to me. But whenever she does, her voice is so cold and hateful it's a constant reminder. That's why we're like this now."

"But did you discuss this with her?"

Nogueira shook his head.

"Are you telling me that in all the years since then, you never once spoke about what happened that night? That you've been sleeping in your daughter's room ever since?"

Nogueira didn't reply. He pressed his lips together and exhaled sharply through his nose in an effort to contain his despair.

"You've never asked her to forgive you?"

"No!" he shouted. "I can't, Manuel, I can't; when I look at my wife, I see my mother. I see her again with her dress torn to shreds, hitched up to her waist, her thighs covered with blood. I see her face and the way that bastard devastated her, robbed her forever. I can't ask for forgiveness, because what I did was unforgivable. I haven't forgiven that bastard, and she has every right not to forgive me."

NAUSEA

Tangled in shame and suspicion, Manuel couldn't sleep. His turbulent emotions nauseated him and refused to be quieted. Those thick black lines censoring the infirmary report, Brother Verdaguer's rosy cheeks, Nogueira's mother crouching in the bathtub with her torn dress up around her waist as she tried to wash away the horror, Minnie Mouse sheets in a child's bedroom. His body punished him with agonizing stomach cramps for his reluctant identification with Nogueira. Perhaps because he suspected that the lieutenant's suffering was equally psychosomatic. The lieutenant was hounded by the thought he was the same as the monster who'd raped his mother. Nogueira's hatred of the Muñiz de Dávila family mirrored the contempt he felt for himself.

Manuel's mind was in a whirl. He and Nogueira shared the pain of all men, the knowledge that the dragon we seek to overcome dwells deep within our own hearts. The fact that our quest for justice and restitution is lost in advance. That monster, our worst nightmare, is immortal. It will perish only on the day we sacrifice ourselves to all-consuming flames.

He was sick and tired of being buffeted by the world. He sought the refuge of sleep. He fled back to his palace.

OF EVERYTHING HE REFUSED

I came home without warning because I'd skinned my knee playing soccer. I went into the bathroom and there she was. In the tub, but with her clothes on. They were twisted and torn, fastened up with a belt, and she was bleeding . . . down there. Her thighs were all bloody and the bathwater was red. I thought she was dying.

I was ten. She made me swear not to tell. I helped her get to bed, and she stayed there more than a week. All that time I took care of her and my brothers too. They were a lot younger. They had no idea.

THE SIN OF PRIDE

Mario Ortuño was in his late fifties. His fierce eyes were distinctly unfriendly as he studied them from behind the bar he owned on Calle Real de Corme. Despite their protests, his wife, Susa, had insisted on accompanying the visitors there from their house at the end of the same street.

As soon as they stepped inside, she went to her husband. "Mario, look, these gentlemen have come all the way from Chantada to talk to you. Come out here and I'll take your place behind the bar." She stooped and slipped through the low access to the other side the bar.

He didn't react. He stared at them, long enough to make Manuel think he was going to stay where he was.

Ortuño turned to his wife. "Do us a favor, Susa, and fix some coffee." He bent low and came out through the same passage.

He pointed to the table farthest in the back and followed them there. "I should have guessed that yesterday's visit wouldn't be the end of it." He nodded toward Lucas. "You're a priest; no need to tell me." He stared suspiciously at the others. "But as for you two . . ."

Nogueira waited until they were all seated before making introductions. "Father Lucas was a student at the seminary, and you may remember him as a child from back then." His tone was brisk and entirely professional. "Manuel and I are investigating the events at San Xoan seminary on the night of December 13, 1984."

Ortuño's puzzled expression while peering at Lucas turned into one of surprise. His eyebrows rose; he appeared impressed. He turned to Manuel, who said, "We know you were on duty at the infirmary and you left the order the following day, stating you'd had a crisis of faith."

Manuel looked toward the bar, wondering if Brother Julián had guessed right and the lovely Susa had been the reason for that departure thirty-two years before.

Ortuño read his thoughts. His eyes flashed. "I married Susa almost ten years later. She had nothing to do with my decision to leave the monastery, the order, or any of all that."

Nogueira spoke up. "So the prior came to see you yesterday?"

"You might as well say he came for two entirely contradictory reasons: first, to refresh my memory; and second, to persuade me to forget everything." It was clear from his tone that he'd found both requests offensive.

Manuel, seated beside him, watched him closely. It wasn't yet clear whether the man was going to cooperate. But it was clear he was profoundly angry.

Nogueira was equally belligerent. "And which did you choose?"

"I made my decision back then, and it meant I had to leave the monastery. You think anything has changed my mind? Only Alzheimer's could ever wipe away the memory of what I saw that night."

Manuel swiped through the photos in his cell phone, located the photo, and put the phone on the table.

Ortuño picked it up, checked the heading showing the family name, and saw his own signature at the bottom. "Those bastards!" he exclaimed. "It shouldn't surprise me though. I assumed they were going to burn it. But I suppose they couldn't destroy a whole year's worth of admission notes. That would have been too obvious. We were halfway through December and the pages were numbered, so they couldn't just rip one out. And that's just like them; the Church has been as arrogant as the Nazis and the Fascists. It's never bothered to cover its tracks. When you're convinced you're eternal, there's no need to destroy documents. That bunch of senile hoarders never bothered to remove the evidence of their crimes."

Manuel recalled his first impression of the document. It had indeed manifested the arrogance and conceit typical of those who consider themselves above it all: the assumptions they were invulnerable, all-powerful, and therefore invincible. Like one of Franco's Fascist bureaucrats, some anonymous clergyman had applied thick glistening smears of black ink to blot out the evidence of atrocity.

"We need to know what was on those blacked-out lines. I have to know what really happened that night." Manuel heard the naked desperation of his own declaration.

Ortuño sat silently studying the screen and appeared not to have noticed his anguish. Susa brought them coffee. Ortuño poured sugar into his, stirred it slightly, and drank it straight off, even though Manuel found the coffee in his own cup still boiling hot.

"Brother Matías pulled me out of bed at half past three in the morning and said there was no time for me to get dressed. So I was still in my pajamas when he hustled me down the hall to Brother Verdaguer's cell. It was obvious something terrible had happened. Verdaguer was unconscious on the floor, red in the face and dripping with sweat, wearing only a shift. The prior was kneeling there trying to revive him, but nothing worked. A leather belt was wrapped around Verdaguer's neck and trailed across the floor. The belt from a school uniform. I saw the older boy first. Standing there stiff and straight like a soldier at attention, watching us with huge frightened eyes. The other child was on the floor curled up against the wall, hands covering his face, and crying his eyes out."

"There was a second boy in the room?" Manuel asked in astonishment.

Ortuño nodded.

"Muñiz de Dávila," interjected Nogueira. "That's why you didn't give a first name. There were two of them, the brothers. Álvaro and Santiago?"

Ortuño nodded. He looked miserable. "The other brother, the little one . . . because of the way he was huddling against the wall, I could see blood on his pajama bottoms. He'd pulled them up in such a hurry that the top wasn't tucked in, but even that additional covering wasn't enough to hide the blood. For a moment I couldn't move. My memory of that moment is particularly vivid because it seemed to last forever. Me staring at the older boy's horrified expression, the little one twisting and turning on the floor with his face turned to the wall, Verdaguer's dead body stretched out on the floor naked from the waist down.

"I didn't realize Brother Matías had disappeared until he came back into the room with a thick rope. The prior hadn't noticed me. He loosened the belt, undid it, picked it up, got up, and threw it on the bed. He saw me when he grabbed the rope from Matías. 'Take the boys to the infirmary, put them to bed, and make sure they don't talk to anyone. And don't you talk to them either. They're both in shock and they're delirious. The poor youngsters found Brother Verdaguer dead.' He pointed to the beam overhead. 'He hanged himself.'

"I tried to protest. *You are to say nothing. Obey me and do what I say.*' He stooped over the body and put the noose around Verdaguer's neck. Brother Matías had already knotted it. 'Brother Verdaguer has been in terrible pain for a long time. From cancer. The suffering drove him mad, and he couldn't stand it anymore. The boys heard his body hit the floor when the rope came loose. That's what happened. Right, boys?'

"The older boy said nothing."

"Álvaro." Manuel's voice was barely audible.

Ortuño looked at him, moved to hear that name. "Yes. Álvaro." That name lingered in his mouth. "He said nothing, shook his head, stood there staring at the body. I suddenly saw that he wasn't in pajamas, even though it was terribly late. He was in his school uniform, but without a belt. But the little boy did speak up. I heard him clearly. He lay there sobbing against the wall and wouldn't look at us, but he managed to say, 'Yes, that's what happened.'"

"His little bare feet were covered in blood."

"Bastard sons of bitches!" muttered Nogueira. Lucas heard the anguish in the policeman's voice and gave him a commiserating look.

Manuel read the lieutenant's mind and understood what was haunting him.

Ortuño continued. "I was horrified. I pointed to the bloodstains and protested to the prior, 'The boy's bleeding from . . .'"

"He didn't let me finish. 'This child suffers from colitis and an ulcerated bowel. The intense fright caused a vessel to burst and gave him copious diarrhea. It's a little blood, that's all. You heard what the child said.'"

"I said, 'Brother Verdaguer wasn't ill, and I haven't heard anything about ulcers or colitis. I'm the only qualified medical attendant here, and if he was ill, I'd have known it. He's injured, not ill,' I told him. 'I think we should call the police.'"

"The prior stopped what he was doing at Brother Verdaguer's neck, straightened up, and glared at me. 'You'll do nothing of the kind. I'm in charge here, and unless you want to spend the rest of your life at some outpost in the jungle, you'll do what I say.'"

"I went to the older boy, who was still speechless and couldn't take his eyes from the body. I tried to pull him away, but he refused to move. So I stood in front of him to block his view and said, 'We have to get your brother out of here.' That suddenly broke his trance. He nodded, grabbed his brother's hand, and shielded him from the sight of the body. But there was no need; the little one kept his eyes so tightly shut that he couldn't have seen a thing. The three of us went to the infirmary."

Ortuño paused, checked his watch, and glanced at his wife. She was tending bar and entertaining a couple of regulars.

"What's wrong?" Nogueira asked.

"Nothing," the man replied. "I'm wondering if my wife's going to tell me it's too early in the day to have a drink."

Nogueira agreement was emphatic. "That's an excellent idea." The others felt the same.

Susa was a bit taken aback, but she nevertheless brought them four glasses and a small bottle of local brandy. She expressed her disapproval by not serving the brandy and returning to the bar without a word. Lucas did the honors. Manuel saw the priest's hand trembling as he poured.

Ortuño took a couple of hefty swigs. "The little one cried all night long. He wailed even louder whenever I tried to approach him. He wouldn't let me tend to his injury. I couldn't even persuade him to take off the bloodstained pajama bottoms. It wasn't until the morning that his brother managed that. The child spent the night curled up in bed with his brother next to him. I asked the older boy to see if the bleeding had stopped and got him to convince the little one to take a couple of tranquilizers with some water. They didn't do much good. The prior appeared a couple of hours later with Verdaguer's death certificate, already signed by the physician. As the monastery medical attendant I was required to witness it. I signed. Before he left he warned me again, 'Don't speak to anyone.'

"He came back at eight o'clock in the morning. The little boy had finally fallen asleep. The prior asked me if the bleeding had stopped and told me to give him the boy's clothing. He wrapped it in a sheet and carried it off. Álvaro was still at his brother's side. He stared at the prior but didn't say a word. He had fire in his eyes.

"The prior came back around noon and told me what I was supposed to put into the infirmary notes: 'They had a very contagious influenza.' I told him that wasn't what the boy'd told me. He turned to Álvaro, who stood there like a soldier on guard. The prior made me wait outside while he talked to the older boy. When the prior left, the little one seemed calmer and even had a bit of an appetite. But the older one, Álvaro, hadn't changed. He still had that black look." He looked at each of the three men. "And let me tell you something. Álvaro was young, but after that night he wasn't a child anymore. I could tell he was feeling the same way I was. Call it the fire of righteous rage. I knew that neither of us was going to get out of this unharmed.

"That same day a chauffeured limousine came to pick up the older boy. I saw him standing in the hall with his suitcase while his father was inside talking with the prior. The marquis came out, gestured to the boy, and left the building. The last time I saw Álvaro he was in lockstep behind his father, carrying that suitcase. I was struck by the fact the father didn't bother to visit the little one. He marched Álvaro off. There was no argument, no shouting. I don't know what the prior told him; I just know that the father took the older boy away and I never saw him again. The little one, either, because after I drafted and signed my report, with no mention of influenza, I walked out of the monastery for the last time."

A tense silence descended upon the four men. Manuel picked up his cell phone and punched in a number. The others' expressions were bleak.

"Griñán, I need for you to tell me when Álvaro's family acquired title to the grounds of the San Xoan monastery." He waited in silence. It took the administrator less than a minute to bring up the information.

Manuel listened, ended the call, and put the phone back on the table. He pushed it away as if it were tainted by some terrible contagion.

"The old marquis and the prior signed the contract for the transfer of the seminary property in December of 1984. Up to then it had been owned by the monastery. The sale was made for the symbolic price of one peseta.

"They bought his silence. Paid him off with the land."

Lucas was thunderstruck. He served another round of brandy and tossed his down like medicine. Manuel looked at him in alarm. The priest's eyes glistened and blinked rapidly as he looked straight ahead at some invisible hell that seemed to have opened before him. Memories, comments, and stray words coalesced with brutal significance. Lucas raised his eyes to heaven.

Manuel wanted to reach out to him but couldn't. Ortuño's narrative had devastated him, too, like a plow ripping open the earth's surface and mercilessly bringing to light unimaginable horrors concealed beneath. And with that revelation returned the chill and lethargy that had immobilized his soul, the pain he'd managed to suppress in hopes it would never break free and force him to attend to it.

An irresistible tide of grief surged within him with such speed and force it swept him away. His vision clouded over and tears burst forth, so copious and violent they shocked his friends. The primeval force of that mute grief summoned them to embrace his pain.

Nogueira reached out and placed his hand on his friend's shoulder, reciprocating Manuel's gesture of the night before. Lucas's eyes were full of tears and anger; he rounded the table, dropped into the chair next to Manuel, and gathered him in his arms. Ortuño sat motionless, fists clenched in seething anger, lips bared in a fierce grimace; he looked toward his wife, who gave him a questioning glance from behind the bar. He nodded, then took Manuel's hand beneath the table. It lay motionless and unresponsive in his grasp.

Manuel wept. Tears flowed and spilled forth. Overriding emotion demolished his soul. Stunned and half-conscious, he was grateful for the battering that numbed his suffering soul with equal parts pain and revelation.

All four men were in tears. Ortuño, the former monk, had suffered sufficiently from life's misfortunes not to give a damn about the curiosity of the gaping clients Susa was herding out of the bar. When they were gone she lowered the blinds and locked the door. The dimness was relieved only by the low-wattage lamps at the bar and the dim daylight filtering through the transom windows in the back.

Sharing grief is the only way a good man can find release from his own pain. Each was afflicted. Nogueira carried within himself the devouring wolf of guilt for discovering himself to be that creature he most despised. Lucas, who'd been there on the day of horror and never known of it, now was horrified and frightened as he reviewed images that in this still hazy context took on new meaning. Ortuño, the direct witness of the horror, ferocious at being stripped of his faith, was still dragging the appalling events of that night behind him, serving a life sentence without possibility of appeal.

Manuel looked up at them. They were supporting him and keeping him from falling to pieces even as they themselves crumbled. These devastated and guilt-ridden men were nevertheless capable of empathy and pity. Manuel felt a profound gratitude toward them, toward all men who take responsibility for the horrors committed by others, who condemn themselves for injustices wrought elsewhere. He couldn't contain his tears. His very soul gave way, the final strong dike burst, the rush of emotion engulfed him so violently he struggled against the temptation to give up and drown. But he was not alone, for they were with him. He embraced Lucas, covered Nogueira's hand with his own, and met Ortuño's eyes as he returned the pressure of the man's hand.

❧

A very long time later newly brewed cups of coffee stood on the table. Ortuño stared downcast at them. His body language made it clear he was still deeply conflicted. With elbows planted on the table he leaned forward, his hands over his mouth, fingers intertwined, and he stayed in that position for a long time. He looked as if he were officiating at a ceremony or praying over the untouched coffee Susa had served them to help counteract the effects of the brandy. Ortuño sat as if hypnotized. His gaze pierced the veil of time and penetrated the shadows of the material world to return to that night.

"That was more than thirty years ago. I've never been able to forget those children. That night, the little one seemed to be recovering as the hours passed. The older boy, on the other hand, understood the enormous gravity of what he'd done, but a calm settled over him, as if the event were both devouring him and strengthening him. After the little one fell asleep I convinced Álvaro to sit down with me for the breakfast they'd delivered. His appetite amazed me. Years later when I served as a medic in Bosnia, I saw soldiers react the same way: they consumed their food with ferocious appetite but never looked at it. Their eyes were fixed on the void. When at last I managed to attract his attention back from that place where soldiers go, I asked him what had happened in Brother Verdaguer's room. He answered with the absolute calm of someone who's come to terms with disaster. 'What happened is that I killed a man.' And then he told me.

"Verdaguer gave special tutoring to boys who were falling behind, and apparently the little boy wasn't doing too well in class. Santiago stayed every afternoon for an hour of extra tutoring. That wasn't unusual; many boys received such help. But Verdaguer insisted on tutoring Santiago in his office. I don't know if the older boy saw something or the little one told him, but for a whole week

Álvaro went to bed fully dressed. Every night he got up and checked the dorm room his brother shared with another boy of his age. On that particular night sleep had overcome him and he was dead to the world. He woke with a start, and when he discovered his brother was missing, he ran to Verdaguer's cell."

Ortuño sighed and energetically rubbed his face, as if his hands could erase the revolting narrative. Susa, at his side, took one of his hands and trapped it between her own, immediately calming him. Ortuño gave her a grateful smile that expressed more than words could say.

"He entered the room and saw Verdaguer naked from the waist down. The man was hefty and fat. Álvaro didn't see his brother but there was no need. He heard the child whimpering and knew that the boy half crushed by the weight of that monster had to be Santiago. Álvaro didn't shout. He didn't say anything at all. He ripped his belt out of his trousers, leaped on Verdaguer's back, and wound it around the man's neck. Thrown off-balance by that unexpected attack, the man pulled away from the little one and fought back, tried to grab the belt and loosen it. He fell to his knees. The boy didn't let go. He told me the man stopped resisting immediately, but Álvaro held on tight. He was afraid Verdaguer would get up again. I remember Álvaro as tall and thin; he couldn't have weighed much, particularly compared to Verdaguer. But the man was already doomed. It's all in the physician's report. The violence of the first yank on the belt crushed his trachea. Even if the youngster hadn't kept pulling on the belt the way he did, the man would have drowned in his own blood in a matter of minutes."

Manuel closed his eyes and heard the Raven's message loud and clear: *The marquis smelled in him the cruelty and strength required to preserve his legacy, our family line, at any cost . . . He didn't disappoint . . . His father knew he wouldn't, because he'd proved himself capable of it before.*

Ortuño pointed to Manuel's cell phone on the table. "I wrote a detailed description of the two boys' physical condition. I left nothing out. I guarantee that you won't find the words *contagious influenza* anywhere. That's why they blacked out the report."

Nogueira spoke. "Did you take photographs? Did you keep any evidence? Is there any other document that records this event?"

Ortuño shook his head. "This was back in the 1980s. There wasn't a standard medical protocol for cases of child abuse. Or for any type of abuse. But I wrote a detailed letter of resignation explaining the reasons I felt impelled to leave the order, which I sent to the prior of the monastery, with a copy to the bishop."

"You're saying the bishop was informed?" Manuel was amazed. "Did he ever contact you?"

"Never. Anyhow, why would he? I wasn't going to make trouble. The accused brother was dead, the disobedient student had been expelled." Ortuño's disgust was apparent. "I suspect the prior was congratulated for his outstanding management of an extremely delicate matter."

Later they would remember how Mario Ortuño resolutely lowered the bar's metal shutters and walked home, supported by his wife. That afternoon little was left of the fierce gaze and dark expression that met them across the counter when they arrived. Exhausted and maimed by the past, he walked away up Calle Real. They took the road out of Corme.

Little was said during the drive. The story they'd heard lay heavy as a tombstone upon them, and that shared knowledge took its toll in the form of a silence heavy with Ortuño's final words: "Nobody knew. I said nothing about it until I told my wife many years later. I've thought many times about what happened that night and the following morning, and I swear to you that after I left the order, I thought seriously about going to the police. But what good would that have done? It would have been my word against those of the prior, Brother Matías, and the well-respected rural doctor who signed the death certificate. And even those of the children. I was sure Álvaro would tell the truth, but the little one had seemed so ready to embrace the prior's idiotic idea of staging a suicide. All that for what? The only result would have been an investigation that was likely to implicate a courageous boy who'd just done what had to be done. There was no one else to punish. Verdaguer was dead and was no longer a threat, and the little one had been rescued. I decided the best thing both for Álvaro and for me was to get out of there."

Nogueira's phone buzzed and broke the silence inside the car. Manuel had been wishing Nogueira would at least turn on the radio for some music. The lieutenant glanced at his phone and made a sour face. The sharp curves on the road between Corme and Malpica obliged him to keep his hands on the wheel and his eyes on the road. The phone went silent but began to buzz again a few seconds later.

"See who that's from, please," Nogueira said to Lucas, who was in the passenger seat.

In the backseat Manuel lay back with his eyes shut. Nogueira knew he wasn't sleeping—*Poor man, he'll be lucky ever to sleep again in his life!*—but he understood why Manuel preferred to close out the rest of the world.

Lucas took a look. "Ophelia."

Nogueira looked for a place to pull off and eventually found a tourist overlook at the edge of a deep ravine, lined by the tallest eucalyptus trees Manuel had ever seen. "Sorry. I have to return this call."

He got out and stepped away from the vehicle. From the car Lucas saw the lieutenant was surprised by what he was hearing. Nogueira was coming back to them when his phone buzzed again. He took the call. Lucas saw him stiffen visibly.

Nogueira opened the driver's door, leaned in, and called into the backseat. "That was Ophelia, the medical examiner. Early this afternoon they found Toñino's car along a rural road, half-hidden in the bushes. A hundred yards from there they found the boy dead and hanging from a tree. The duty officer called me as well; two days ago when I gave them a description of the car, they practically told me to get lost. Now the captain wants to talk to me."

Manuel leaned forward between the front seats. "Shit, Nogueira! I hope this doesn't make trouble for you. If it helps, I'll say I asked you to accompany me to Toñino's house. We never claimed to be policemen, and I'll swear to that if they want."

Nogueira attempted a smile without much success. He was clearly worried. "Doesn't mean a thing. Pure routine, you'll see. They have to ask."

Lucas spoke up. "Did he commit suicide?"

Nogueira just looked at him. He started the engine and pulled back onto the road.

Lucas wouldn't let it go. "You said he was hanging from a tree. Was it suicide?"

Nogueira stroked his mustache and mouth, as if holding back a reply. Instead of looking at Lucas, he kept an eye on Manuel through the rearview mirror. "Ophelia says the body's black as pitch, but she can see he was badly beaten.

His face is battered, and his clothing is the same as in the missing persons report. It looks like they beat him unconscious and then hanged him. The autopsy will provide more definitive results. She says that given the state of decomposition, he might have died the same day he disappeared."

Manuel steadily met Nogueira's gaze in the mirror and tried to work out the implications. "The same day Álvaro was murdered. So the two have to be related."

"Not so sure about that," replied Nogueira. "It seems likely Toñino was painting his uncle's office and came across Brother Ortuño's letter of resignation. A quick read tells him the information's worth a nice fat payment from somebody. He figures Álvaro and Santiago are probably good for three hundred thousand or more. So he calls Santiago and asks for it. He isn't counting on the older brother's reaction. Álvaro storms into the monastery demanding an explanation from the prior. When Álvaro leaves, the prior goes looking for his nephew, maybe to make him return the document but also to warn him things won't stop there. What caught my attention was the prior's reaction when I asked about the boy. He didn't seem to care where the nephew was, maybe because he already knew. Don't forget that at first he denied Álvaro came to see him. And then when he was forced to admit he got the phone call, he made up that crap about a request for confession."

"I guarantee you that was pure fiction," Lucas interjected. "That much I know."

"Other than that he didn't seem too worried. Maybe because he'd already taken care of the problem. Álvaro was dead. Now we know his nephew was dead as well. They probably died the same day."

"You really think he'd go that far to keep secret something that happened thirty-two years ago?"

"You'd be surprised what people are capable of. Even to hide things far less serious. Given what Ortuño told us, we know the prior's a man who won't hesitate to do anything it takes, no matter how drastic, to solve a problem. He had no scruples about disguising Verdaguer's death as a suicide and covering up sexual abuse at the school. And we have a witness who says he threatened his nephew. Ortuño just said the man was there yesterday trying to persuade him to keep quiet; how much farther do you think he'd go to protect the institution and his own reputation? Would he beat his nephew to death and string him up on a tree? Or ram Álvaro's car off the road? For all we know, he might be capable of anything. We already know that on at least one occasion he disguised a homicide by pretending it was suicide by hanging . . . but . . ."

"But he's seventy years old, maybe a bit more," offered Lucas. "He has some sort of bone disease, arthritis or arthrosis, he's relatively short, and he doesn't weigh much more than 150 pounds."

"You're right about that, I agree," Nogueira said. "It's hard for me to imagine him stabbing Álvaro in a struggle. And though his nephew wasn't much more robust and was fairly wasted by drugs, I can't imagine the prior beating the boy senseless and still having enough strength to haul him up a tree. That would require determination and the physical strength to lift a grown man completely off the ground."

Manuel watched Nogueira through the rearview mirror. He knew the lieutenant was avoiding his eyes.

"In any case we're just guessing. Without proof we're just making up stories," Nogueira concluded. "We'll have to wait for the results of Toñino's autopsy. And see if the lab can confirm that the paint scrapes on Álvaro's car came from the seminary vehicle."

"You left out one possibility," Manuel challenged him. "Maybe the prior had nothing to do with it. Maybe Álvaro managed to catch up with Toñino."

Mei Liu's report of those words was beginning to weigh heavily on his mind: *He knows you killed him.*

"Stop it, Manuel!" The desperation in Lucas's voice kept Manuel from spilling the rest, but didn't keep him from imagining the possible sequence of events. The unspoken possibility was becoming more and more real to him.

Manuel glanced up, and this time found Nogueira studying him. He knew the lieutenant was thinking the same thing. So he continued. "Suppose the two of them fought. Álvaro was a good deal stronger than the boy and could have beaten him and hanged him from the tree. Ophelia said that the wound in Álvaro's side resulted in slow internal hemorrhaging, and he would've had time to get back to his car and drive away." He heard again the Raven's ominous words.

"I'm astonished you can entertain such a thought," Lucas said hotly, turning to look at him.

"So am I, if we're talking about the man I knew. But it turns out that wasn't the real Álvaro, and I tell you frankly I don't know what his double would have been capable of."

"I refuse to believe it!" Lucas exclaimed fiercely.

"Remember what his mother told me," Manuel responded. "I for one haven't been able to forget it."

Lucas dismissed it. "I already told you she said it only to hurt you. She was deliberately planting doubts in your mind. Obviously you've allowed them to flourish."

Nogueira spoke up. "What did she say?"

"That his capacity for cruelty made him the perfect successor to his father. They were sure he'd do a good job; he'd delivered magnificently for them before. They'd always counted on him, because he'd done it before."

"And you think she was referring to what happened at the seminary?"

"There's something else I haven't mentioned. Nogueira, you already know most of this. A few days after Álvaro's funeral the police returned his effects. With them was a cell phone I'd never seen before, and when we checked the history there was one call from a public phone booth. Álvaro's secretary told me he used that phone exclusively for his business here." He looked at Nogueira, who nodded in confirmation. "What you don't know is that his secretary told me the day before Álvaro left to travel here, a call came in on that phone and she picked it up. The person on the other end said, 'You can't ignore it, you hear me? He has the proof, he knows you killed him, and he's going to tell unless you do something.'"

Lucas was so enraged he spun almost completely around. "For the love of God! Are you saying Álvaro was a murderer? Maybe you're right, Manuel, when you say you never knew him. But I did, and I'm telling you Álvaro was not a killer."

"What I'm saying is that I'm convinced it was his own brother who telephoned. Santiago must have been so desperate that somehow he managed to get Álvaro's number. It's not inconceivable that Griñán might have given it to him. When Griñán told me about Santiago's request for money, he said Santiago was in a hurry and very worried. Think about those words: *He knows you killed him.* The person who knew was Toñino, and Toñino turned up dead. According to the medical examiner he's probably been dead since the day he went missing, the same day Álvaro came back to deal with the problem. *Don't you try to threaten me.*"

Lucas furiously rejected the possibility, pressing his lips together in an expression of unyielding opposition and enormous anger.

Manuel's phone buzzed, suddenly loud in the confines of the vehicle. He looked down at the screen, about to turn off the phone. It was Mei Liu. He took the call, listened to her without saying a word, and ended it. The tense silence hung heavy inside the car like a looming tempest. He found himself missing his furry little friend, Café.

The final miles were driven in total silence. Nogueira pulled up in the parking lot, let Lucas and Manuel out, and took to the highway, this time heading for the crime scene.

A troubling tension hung in the air between Manuel and Lucas. Manuel went toward his car.

Lucas followed him. "Where are you going, Manuel?"

"I'm going to As Grileiras. You can come or stay here, but I'm fed up. I want an answer, and I want it right now."

Lucas accepted that. He went around the car and took the passenger seat.

REASON AND BALANCE

The light of late afternoon was fading fast. By the time they got to the estate, the last rays of the setting sun cast a golden glow across the front of the manor house that made it look deceptively welcoming.

They went straight to the kitchen entrance. As they'd expected, they found Herminia and her husband seated at the kitchen table. The two were holding hands and their faces were full of pain. Startled at the sight of Lucas and Manuel, the housekeeper leaped to her feet and threw herself in the priest's arms. "Oh, please, no! Please, not this." She broke down in sobs. They were shaken by her terrible distress.

Lucas was particularly alarmed. "What's the matter, Herminia?"

"You don't know? You're not here because of Santiago?"

Lucas, still holding Herminia close, glanced at Manuel in amazement. "What's happened to Santiago?" Manuel, baffled, threw up his hands.

Herminia dissolved in tears. "*Fillo*, this house is cursed. They're all dying on me! I'm going to lose all my darlings!"

Manuel turned to her husband. He sat watching, stolid and unspeaking, as if all this had nothing to do with him. Or perhaps as if nothing could surprise him anymore. Manuel racked his brain and managed to recall the man's name.

"Damián—what happened to Santiago?"

"They took him away in an ambulance. Catarina's with him. They say he took a whole pile of pills. If it weren't for the child, he'd be dead by now. The boy went into his room and was shaking him, trying to get him to wake up."

"Samuel?"

The man nodded. "He'd be dead if the boy hadn't found him."

"Where's the boy? Is he all right?"

Herminia pulled free of Lucas's arms. "Manuel, the child is fine, don't worry about him, he has no idea of what happened. The poor little thing thinks it was all a game. He's upstairs, and his mother is reading him a story."

Manuel crossed the kitchen and dropped heavily into a chair. Everything around him was collapsing. He tried to put his thoughts in order. He'd come intending to pin Santiago down, to confront him and wring a confession out of him. His mind called up the vision of the afternoon he'd glimpsed Santiago weeping alone in the dark church. Maybe Santiago had been weighed down by more anguish than anyone knew, more pain than he could bear.

Lucas got ahead of him. "What happened, Herminia? There has to be a reason for it. You know Santiago as well as anyone, and nobody suddenly decides to kill himself, not from one day to the next. What was he thinking?"

Herminia's lips twisted in a terrible grimace. Her distress disappeared in a flash, giving way to a ferocious look of absolute contempt. "Of course I know what happened. The same as always: that horrid old woman won't stop until she's buried all her children! Any sane person'd say she loves to see them suffer! That"—her face hardened, and she spat out the word—"bitch!" She paused. "Yesterday Catarina told us their big news. She's pregnant again. And, well, you know how Santiago is about such things; he's always worrying about her. They had an early supper and went to bed." She broke down again, weeping bitterly. "But that witch wouldn't let us celebrate!"

Damián raised his chin and looked at her, upset but resigned.

Manuel got up and reversed their roles. Just as Herminia had comforted him days earlier, he took her hands and led her to a chair; then, with her hands still in his, he sat close and let her speak.

"It was this morning. I was with Sarita, cleaning one of the rooms upstairs, and I heard them arguing. You already know I never go into her part of the house," she declared emphatically. "I saw him come out of there in tears. His mother stood in the door behind him laughing and carrying on, and she didn't care that Sarita and I were there. The old woman kept mocking him and laughed until she heard him slam the front door downstairs. I went to the window and saw him ride off on one of the horses; he always goes riding when he's upset. Except that he shouldn't, with his hand in a cast the way it is."

"Do you know what they were arguing about?"

Herminia shook her head.

"And when did all this with the pills happen?"

"Less than an hour ago. The boy was looking for someone to play with, went into Santiago's room, and thank God he went to tell Elisa his uncle wouldn't wake up."

"I had no idea about Santiago, Herminia," Manuel told her gravely. "I know you love him, and I'm very sorry about this."

She gave him a miserable little smile of appreciation for his sympathy.

"I'm here because I wanted to ask you a question."

Herminia's expression changed to one of puzzlement.

"About something you said the other day when we were talking about Álvaro and how they sent him away when he was only twelve. When I brought it up, you mentioned a certain day when something happened between Álvaro and his father."

Herminia looked away for a moment. "I wasn't talking about any particular day. They just didn't get along at all, and the school expelled Álvaro. His father was very angry with him."

"Yes, I heard what you said," Manuel replied patiently. "But they expelled Álvaro from San Xoan on December 13, and I just received a call from Madrid telling me he entered boarding school on the 23rd of that same month. I know something bad must have happened during those ten days to make them send away a child from a Catholic home the day before Christmas Eve."

"Nothing in particular happened." Herminia got up and busied herself with the pots on the stove.

"I know something happened between Álvaro and his father, something so serious that the marquis decided to get him out of the house as quickly as possible; his mother mentioned it too." He raised his voice and insisted. "Herminia, if you really and truly loved Álvaro, tell me what it was!" She turned. "Because if you don't, I'm going straight upstairs to demand an explanation from the Raven, and she'll take great pleasure in telling me as crudely and nastily as she can."

Herminia dropped her potholder and came back to the table. She took the same chair as before. Her voice was very low as she struggled to get the words out. Even though they were right next to her, Manuel and Lucas had to lean close to make out what she was saying.

"It was after they expelled Álvaro, just before the school's Christmas vacation. I remember because Santiago wasn't back home yet.

"The old marquis was out hunting. He always used to take Santiago along because Álvaro didn't like hunting, and, well, Santiago would do anything to please him. But that day he took Álvaro. They came back in the middle of the day, and the car stopped right here, outside the kitchen. A big SUV with a trailer cage for the dogs. The marquis was very angry. All that week, one of the dogs had been refusing to obey, and because of that he lost one of the birds. He let all the dogs out of the trailer, grabbed the one that had rebelled, and started kicking it. The animal was yelping so loudly that everybody on the estate heard it. I rushed out of the kitchen, all upset, because of the way it was howling. I thought a car had run over it. Álvaro ran over and got between his father and the dog. His father raised his hand, and it looked like he was going to hit Álvaro, but then he went to the car, took out his shotgun, and pushed it into Álvaro's hands.

"'That dog won't hunt. It's good for nothing. You don't want me to beat it? Then kill it!'

"Álvaro looked at the shotgun and at the dog, then with the gun in his hands he turned to his father and told him no.

"'What do you mean, *no*? Do it!'

"'*No*,' Álvaro told him loud and clear.

"'Up to you, then; either you do it or I will,' the old man said and stepped toward him.

"Álvaro raised the gun, put it to his shoulder, pointed it at his father, and squinted down the barrel.

"'I said *no*.' He was calm. He meant it.

"I looked up and I saw his mother watching through the upstairs window. Everyone on the estate had responded to the dog's howls just as I had, and they saw what was happening. I thought the old marquis was going to have a fit. That man expected everyone to obey him, and his son's disobedience would normally have driven him into a rage. But I knew that the real humiliation for the old marquis was the fact this was taking place in front of all those witnesses.

"Father and son, face-to-face, and neither was backing down. The rest of us held our breath. Then the marquis started laughing, so loudly everyone on the estate heard him, the way they'd heard the dog howling. 'No,' says he, 'you won't shoot a dog, but you're not so finicky when it comes to a man! Isn't that right, you little murderer?'

"Everyone heard every word. He called his own son a murderer. Álvaro kept looking him straight in the eyes and didn't lower the gun. His father turned on his heel and went into the house. He spoke to me when he went by the kitchen. 'Just like I said, Herminia. More balls than most men!'

"Two days later they sent Álvaro to Madrid. And the day the boy left, the marquis took the dog out to the highway and blew its head off; but at least he waited until Álvaro was gone. Damián buried it, but he had to clean its brains off the pavement. You may think I'm crazy, but I truly believe that deep down, Álvaro's father was afraid of him."

Lucas covered most of his face with one hand.

Manuel let out a gust of air before speaking. "Why weren't you willing to tell me this?"

Herminia waved toward Lucas's appalled expression. "Why? Simple—I didn't want you to think what you're thinking right now. Because Álvaro was good and virtuous, the best person I ever knew."

Damián had nodded at everything his wife said. She got up and threw open the door that separated the kitchen from the interior stairway. Elisa stood there horrified, her eyes full of tears. She stared wide-eyed at them.

Manuel was bewildered. "How long have you been eavesdropping?"

"Long enough, Manuel. Long enough to know that I'm not the only one who suspects Álvaro."

Manuel felt a terrific jolt. He'd been here for more than ten days, in this region that had given him a hostile reception beneath the milky skies of its rapidly disappearing summer, shoving into his face the harsh fact that his whole adult life had been based upon a lie. It had been a journey through a spiritual desert where each new revelation brought new humiliations and pain, almost convincing him to accept the evidence of deceit and betrayal.

He'd shut himself off, he'd given in. For days he'd been expecting that those specters Nogueira warned could be hidden in the depths would quit their watery graves and their bloated corpses would float to the surface. Each time he came across a trace of the man he'd loved, each time he glimpsed a possible justification for Álvaro's actions, another legion of drowned corpses emerged and left him bereft once more.

And then he reconsidered: like Hansel, Álvaro had left a trail of crumbs for him to follow. Rats had carried some off, birds had devoured others, and maybe some had decayed in the rain to become forever part of the earth. But devoted, energetic, and as determined as ever, Álvaro had laid down hundreds of them, thousands, along with the most important one, the one that was the key to all the rest.

For years Manuel had been an idiot looking out to sea. He'd allowed Álvaro to take care of him, and now he saw that was exactly what Álvaro had always done. Álvaro had been taking care of them all since he was twelve years old. One little boy caring for another, shouldering the responsibility of saving his brother from unthinkable horror; and in return his parents had despised him and repudiated him. An idiot looking out to sea; never again would Manuel be that, nor would he permit the rest of them to do that, even if it meant breaking their necks.

"Don't say that, Elisa."

"I resisted it, Manuel, I swear. I never wanted to think so."

"But . . . ?"

"But I heard what his mother said to him the day the marquis died, when Fran was crying and falling to pieces, clinging to his dead father's hand. She couldn't stand to be in the same room with Fran."

Herminia nodded solemnly.

"Fran wouldn't listen to reason. I couldn't get him to leave the body for even an instant. I was exhausted. I was leaving the room, ready to collapse, and I heard them. Álvaro was looking out the window, and she said, 'Now that you're the head of the family, it's your responsibility. You're going to have to do something about your dim-witted brother and that pregnant little slut of his.'"

"And what did Álvaro say to that?"

"He said, 'I know what I have to do.'"

Lucas objected. "That doesn't mean anything."

Elisa continued. "The next day, after the burial, Fran refused to come back to the manor. He made us all leave the cemetery. It was terribly cold, and it was threatening to rain. I came here, and I was watching from the window of our room the whole time. He was sitting on the ground next to the mound of earth the gravedigger was shoveling into the hole. I was worried sick. I didn't know what to do or who to turn to. He wasn't just grieving, he was raving, about to lose his mind. Then Álvaro appeared. He got down next to his brother, and they talked for a long time. It started raining, and they went into the church. Nobody had managed to convince him to come home, and I remember thinking it was a wonderful initiative on Álvaro's part."

"And you've changed your mind?"

"I don't know, Manuel. There's some dark mystery hovering around Álvaro in this house, and with what you just said . . ."

"What?!" Manuel exploded. "A child who refuses to shoot a dog, for God's sake! No matter how you look at it, that counts in his favor. He was just a little boy."

She rejected that, desperation in her voice. "A little boy who aimed a gun at his father; a little boy his father called a murderer; a child they feared so much they sent him away forever. His mother told him to take charge of his brother because Fran had become an inconvenience. An obstacle." She looked from Manuel to Lucas. "And neither of you believes Fran committed suicide."

Manuel was stung. "That has nothing to do with it."

"Then why did you ask me if I'd seen Álvaro that night?"

Manuel saw Herminia start in surprise. He'd asked her the same question.

Lucas raised a hand, almost as if asking permission to speak.

"Because I thought so too. In fact I saw his jacket or at least someone wearing his jacket, but that proves nothing. The jacket was kept in the stables, and just as you said, it was cold that night. Anyone at all could have put it on and gone to the church. In fact . . ." His words slowed and took on a sarcastic tone. "It seems that at any given time that night every one of you intended to go, or actually was there, or was lurking somewhere in the vicinity."

None of them replied, but they all lowered their heads as if to acknowledge the truth of his charge.

Manuel's fury grew. The silent cloud of suspicion hovering over them sparked with tension, like an impending thunderstorm.

He looked from one to another. Damián with the cap of quality cloth his employer had given him; his enigmatic lowered gaze was evidence of prudent discretion born of those many years of service to authority. Herminia, grieving and in tears, had always striven to be a mother, through good times and bad. Elisa, the intimidated and frightened little girl who let others make decisions for her.

He got up, crossed the kitchen in three long strides, and swiftly disappeared up the stairs.

"Where are you going? What are you going to do? Manuel!"

He took the steps two at a time, ignoring the protests behind him. He turned into the dark hallway lined with heavy closed doors and marched to the one at the far end. He knocked sharply, hammering the way the police did to make it clear he expected to be received immediately.

The marquess herself opened the door. "Señor Ortigosa, I was expecting not to have to see you here again. Apparently I didn't make myself sufficiently clear."

A television in the sitting area was on, and the nurse was seated in the same armchair as before. Manuel assumed it was her usual place. The attendant didn't bother to get up. Her only greeting was a vague glance, the sort one gives to an intruder who won't be staying long. Manuel was satisfied to see that the marquess wasn't going to invite him in.

"No, you didn't. You weren't at all clear," he said as he surveyed the woman standing before him.

She listened with her head slightly tilted and a bored expression on her face.

"What is it you want, señor Ortigosa?" she said at last. Her tone was impatient.

"You stated that your husband's choice of Álvaro as his heir was a good one, and that Álvaro had fulfilled your expectations of him."

She wrinkled her brow and shrugged at the obvious.

"Why did you send a child of twelve away from his home?"

"Because he was a murderer," she answered coldly.

"That's not true," Manuel protested.

Her attitude was that of someone weary of being retained at a function with a predictable outcome. She leaned against the door, looked past his shoulder, and saw the group that had stopped at the landing. She smirked. "Don't try to play games with me. The prior called me yesterday. You forgot to delete the computer history of the searches you made. You already know the truth. Álvaro killed a man in cold blood."

Manuel felt his own blood boil, but he lowered his voice to a whisper to keep those huddled at the far end of the corridor from hearing him. "You knew that? You knew what had happened, and despite that you punished your son and left the younger one there, pretending nothing had happened?"

"The only thing that happened is that Álvaro killed a monk, a good man dedicated to teaching and to God."

"That good man, as you call him, was a monster, a child abuser. Álvaro was only defending his brother, and you two sold him out in exchange for some miserable goddamn land."

"The contracts negotiated by my husband were entirely unrelated."

"So it's true? You left Santiago there, in a place that was a hell for him, and you sent Álvaro away from his family never to return, exiling him from the only world he knew. That was his reward for saving his little brother from a rapist."

She shook her head with a mixture of boredom and impatience. She even turned to glance at the television screen before speaking to him.

"Yes, a very fine story, but what can't be denied is that he didn't act like a twelve-year-old. He misinterpreted the situation. Children get carried away and imagine things. But he didn't run to fetch an adult, he didn't shout or strike the man; he seized him from behind and strangled him to death. Did you ever stop to think how long it takes to die that way? And if that's not enough for you, after he'd been in the house for a week after that incident, he was two seconds away from killing his father."

"He refused to shoot a dog," Manuel said in disgust.

"We got rid of him because he was a murderer," the marquess declared with the finality of someone who has just concluded a conversation. She straightened up and made a move to close the door.

"And why did you bring him back?"

She lifted one eyebrow as if the question were absurd. "For the same reason. We knew what would happen. From the moment his father died, everything began to fall apart. And he took on the job of setting the family's affairs in order. And I'm not referring only to the businesses, although, as I said, he accomplished that to my entire satisfaction."

"What do you think he did? What do you think you saw?"

She bowed her head before answering. "I saw Álvaro approach his father's grave. I saw him convince Fran to stop acting like a fool and go into the church. I saw him take care of the matter."

Manuel listened but shook his head in amazement. He'd reached his limit with this woman's wickedness. She discussed horrors with the same cold tone she probably used to give orders about housework.

"And you believe Álvaro killed him? You've thought that all this time? You actually believed Álvaro had murdered his brother to rid you of an annoying problem? You didn't know him. You had no idea of who Álvaro was!" His voice dripped with contempt.

"And you did?" She sneered. "That's why you're wandering around here like a soul in purgatory? Gathering up crumbs from Álvaro's life and trying to make sense of them?"

Her metaphor disconcerted him, for her reference to the insignificant bits that he'd been collecting matched almost exactly his thought about Hansel's trail of bread crumbs. He'd been reluctant to dismiss the marquess as a self-centered monster, but Lucas was right. She had a sort of sixth sense for any human weaknesses she could exploit.

As if to confirm that thought, she added, "Look, señor Ortigosa, I understand human weakness because I grew up surrounded by it. I've observed it all my life. I don't know if you think you're fooling anyone with your posturing and pretending to be outraged, but you don't fool me. I know that deep down you're perfectly aware of what Álvaro was."

Manuel couldn't find words to respond. He stood there gaping at her, frightened of her almost telepathic ability to read his mind, and furious at allowing himself to be manipulated like this. Each time he met her, the woman intimidated him and made him feel like a child in the presence of the queen. He'd stormed upstairs determined to obtain the truth, and just as before she'd thrown it into his face, crude and hurtful. But it was the truth, even so.

She shut the door in his face. For a few moments he stood there in the gloom of the hallway, so close to the heavy wooden door that he caught a whiff of its polish. He became conscious of the group at his back that hadn't dared enter the hall.

He turned and saw Elisa sobbing in Herminia's embrace. Lucas stood a few steps behind them, his face indiscernible because he was lit from behind, but his body language showed that he'd heard what the Raven said. Manuel walked toward them, and one of the doors along the corridor opened. A milky light from within spread across the carpeted passageway. Samuel's bare little feet appeared, and then they saw his smile.

Manuel looked at him and experienced such a surge of tenderness and love that he stopped short, unable to continue.

"Uncle!" The jubilation in his high little voice celebrated that word.

Manuel sank to his knees and accepted the child's enthusiastic hug. Samuel babbled on and on, a torrent of words, only half of which Manuel understood. But he nodded and smiled and made no effort to wipe away the tears bathing his cheeks.

"Don't cry, Uncle," begged the boy, pouting and trying to stop the tears with his tiny hand.

Manuel rose, took the boy's hand, and walked toward the women. Elisa threw herself into his arms, murmuring, "I'm sorry, Manuel, I'm so sorry."

He gave her a lifeless hug, looking over her head at Lucas, who was watching them closely from a few steps away. There was a determination in the priest's eyes that Manuel would later be grateful for, but at just that moment it was more than he could stand. Manuel looked away.

"Uncle, are you going away?"

Downcast, he looked into the child's eyes and answered. "I have to leave."

"Then I want to go with you!" the little fellow cried resolutely. "Mama, Mama, I want to go with Uncle!"

At that instant Manuel understood why Álvaro hadn't been able to renounce his inheritance, why he'd felt obliged to take care of them. Manuel gave Elisa a look and turned slowly to peer back at the dark door at the end of the corridor.

"Pack your things," he said. "I'm not going to leave you two here."

❧

Manuel crossed the inn parking lot to where his BMW stood at the far end of a long row of vehicles. The first soccer match of the season had attracted a large number of locals. Perhaps that was why Lucas had chosen to wait in the car.

He saw the priest leaning back in the passenger seat with his eyes half-closed. It was the first time Manuel had detected in him any sign of fatigue or defeat. Manuel appreciated and admired Lucas's ardent defense of Álvaro, especially in the face of possibly damning evidence. Lucas was a man of faith, and not just religious faith.

When he got to the car he realized Lucas was praying. The priest's usually mild and tranquil features were twisted in anguish.

Manuel knew the tide of his own grief had swept him into a wild, surging sea of emotion. People had reached out to him but he still felt marooned and cast away. Little Samuel's pleading voice had reminded him he wasn't alone in this directionless confusion. Now, standing in the darkness, he became witness to the spiritual torments of the man whose eyes he'd avoided, the man he'd considered entirely too assured.

The agonizing weight of their discoveries creased the priest's brow with pain. His lips were pressed together in desperation. None of them had spoken of the dark shadow of child abuse too often associated with the Church, but the stigma was too horrible for any righteous man to ignore. Lucas must be accusing himself of taking Santiago's moods and introspection too lightly.

Worse still was the revelation that Álvaro, always forthright, had kept abominable horrors sealed deep inside, for it raised the specter of deeper duplicity. What more might Álvaro have been capable of hiding? What else might he have been capable of doing?

Lucas crossed himself and opened his eyes. He saw Manuel, smiled wanly, and beckoned. Manuel took his place behind the wheel. "How are they?" Lucas asked.

"Samuel's very pleased and probably overexcited. Elisa says this is the first time he's ever spent the night away from the estate. I suspect he'll have a hard time getting to sleep."

"He's never been anywhere else? They never went on a vacation or spent a weekend at the house in Arousa? I know Álvaro's mother spends every June and July there."

"No, Elisa hasn't wanted to leave the estate since Fran died." He paused, recalling the young woman's grieving expression when she touched the cross on Fran's grave. "She felt it was important to stay to find out the truth." Manuel's eyes were heavy with regret. "I originally thought she was obsessed and trapped in denial. But now I see her instincts were good. She probably did in fact know Fran better than anyone else." *The way I knew Álvaro,* he heard his own voice from his subconscious. "She's resting easy now. They gave her a room next to mine. This place doesn't have the comforts of the manor, but it'll do for now. Tomorrow I'll see if I can find something better for them."

Lucas gave him a knowing look. "You've had a special rapport with Elisa and the boy from the moment you met."

"She's a bit like me, I guess—an outsider who came here under difficult circumstances. One more person who'll never be part of the family, someone they barely tolerate." He knew he was echoing the Raven. "But it's more because of Samuel. He's—I can't really explain it. It's like he's my own child. The way he recognized me and accepted my presence as completely normal. As if he'd been expecting me. And the way he talks to me! He astonishes me sometimes with the way he reacts and the things he says."

Intrigued, Lucas took Manuel's chin and turned the writer's face to the light as if to inspect it. Manuel batted the priest's hand away with a grin. "You see what I mean? It's true; the kid's got me wrapped around his little finger!"

"Yes, he's a firecracker, all right. Very mature for his age. Hardly surprising, since he's been surrounded by adults since he was born, with no companions of his own age in that palace. And he's troubled by his father's absence."

"Herminia said the same thing. She says it isn't healthy for a child to be brought up that way."

Lucas was concerned. "What exactly did she tell you?"

"Nothing, really," said Manuel, slightly annoyed. "She said that children in such circumstances can turn out to be strange."

"Herminia worries too much," Lucas said sharply. "She means well, but she's not always right."

That spurred Manuel's interest. "Are you referring to something in particular?"

Lucas sighed deeply. "One of the last times I was at the estate she asked me to 'take a look' at Samuel."

Manuel's expression was baffled.

"To 'take a look at him' as a priest," he explained. "I'm afraid that for once I have to agree with you. Sometimes regional folklore and superstitions are as prevalent as the teachings of true faith."

"Herminia thought Samuel was acting strange?"

"She's well on in years and grew up in a different time. She noticed something perfectly normal but didn't know what to make of it."

Manuel shook his head. "Just a second, your attitude confuses me. It seems contradictory. The innkeeper's wife told me about a child in her family who was 'haunted,' but her visitations stopped after a visit to the sanctuary. That's what I was referring to when I asked if exorcisms are done there."

Lucas didn't reply right away. When he did, the answer was circumspect. "I don't know if I can talk about this with you."

"Because I'm not a believer?"

Lucas didn't reply.

"I used to be."

"Before your sister died."

Manuel looked at him in astonishment. His sister's death was a forbidden topic, a catastrophe he never mentioned. Not in interviews and not in his author biography.

"How do you know that?"

"Álvaro told me. I already told you he spoke about you a lot."

"Álvaro."

"I have no trouble dialoguing with an atheist, but that's not you, Manuel. You're angry at God. I'm not judging you, but the reality is that you'll have to resolve that issue with Him."

Manuel smiled and shook his head. "What are you up to, señor priest? And we were getting along so well!"

Unmoved, Lucas studied him for several seconds. "The innkeeper's story is true. I see many such cases, especially toward the end of the year. Sometimes things are exactly what they seem."

"The child received 'unwelcome visitations'?"

"The child was inhabited. Possessed."

Manuel felt a chill go down his spine. He suppressed the shudder. "And that's what Herminia thought was affecting Samuel?"

"Samuel's just like millions of other children all over the world. He has a terrific imagination, and it's stimulated by constant exposure to adults. He's already reading simple texts. It's no surprise a child without friends should invent an imaginary playmate."

"Is that what it was about? An imaginary friend? I had one from the age of six until I turned eight, more or less."

"Just like Samuel. An imaginary playmate to fill a void. In your case, a void created by the death of your parents; and in Samuel's case there is so much more vacancy to fill. At times I've seen him all alone, talking, laughing, nodding as if listening to someone. And as I said, Herminia is a fine woman who worries too much. She's mistaken."

"Good God! The more I learn about As Grileiras, the more sinister the place seems. Now I'm even more convinced I shouldn't leave Elisa and the child there. Especially not after what I heard today. Never mind what Álvaro decided—his mother *asked him to kill his brother.* And Elisa has lived all this time believing Álvaro did exactly that."

Lucas nodded vehemently. "I've been thinking this over. It's important for us to discuss everything that happened today."

"What part of it bothers you?" Manuel replied defensively.

Lucas exhaled a long doleful breath. He was determined. "All of it, Manuel. Everything Ortuño said, what that horrible woman insinuated, everything. We absolutely must separate what we know to be true from the lies and insinuations. I listen to you, and it's as if you're willing to accept whatever anyone says about Álvaro. It's almost—excuse me, Manuel, it's almost as if you embrace absolutely anything you hear."

"You don't believe what Ortuño said?"

Lucas sighed, a sign of deep frustration. He closed his eyes for a moment. "I hate to say it, it's terrible, but I believe Ortuño word for word." He paused. "And what Herminia said. But we must separate that information from malicious stories circulated with evil intent."

Manuel stared at Lucas in silence. He chewed his lower lip and shrugged.

"Don't let that woman manipulate you, Manuel. She's still doing it, from afar. She's exploiting your vulnerability and feeding you her absolutely lethal poison."

Though aggrieved, Manuel had to acknowledge the poison. "She didn't need to feed me anything, Lucas. The poison was already inside. I didn't see it before, but everything we've learned has made the horrifying picture clear. I'm starting to see why Álvaro decided to keep me out of it. I'm to blame for that as well. I gave in and went along. I let him watch over me and take care of everything. I was perfectly happy to become an idiot. It wasn't all his fault, just as his mother isn't entirely to blame for what I'm suspecting now. How can I help it? Uncertainty begets suspicion. He hid things from me, or maybe I just didn't want to see them. We're a band of cowards, and he knew it. Álvaro was protecting me the way he protected all of them."

Lucas straightened up, turned to face Manuel, and waved away that thought. "No, no, no, Manuel! I won't have you wallowing in self-pity. Let go of all that. Give me the raw courage that sent you upstairs to pound on her door. I want the rejection I saw burning in your eyes when Elisa confessed her suspicions of Álvaro. Give me the rage in your voice when you reminded us of the boy who refused to shoot a dog, when you said he saved his brother from a monster."

Manuel understood and accepted that.

"That's the rage of the just, Manuel. It doesn't matter what anyone says. You and I know what kind of man Álvaro was. We *know*, Manuel. Isn't that true?"

Manuel inhaled deeply and kept his eyes on the priest.

Lucas continued. "And he was no murderer. What we learned today strengthens my conviction. He was just a child when he summoned the courage to defend his brother from a rapist; he paid dearly for it. I can't imagine how he must have suffered all his life under the weight of that knowledge, made all the worse by his family's repudiation. A man of that character doesn't murder his brother or kill a blackmailer. He stands firm and confronts his adversary."

A tear slid down Manuel's cheek. He resisted it and swiftly raised a hand in a violent, almost frantic motion to wipe it away. He lowered his chin. "No!" he gasped, his voice raw and hoarse.

"Look me in the eyes and tell me you don't believe what they're claiming," Lucas challenged him.

Manuel looked up, met his gaze, and said it again. "No! I don't."

❦

Nogueira's BMW pulled up alongside them. The policeman got out, closed the car door, and took his time. He leaned against the vehicle, lit a cigarette, and waited for them to come to him.

Lucas was annoyed by his nonchalance. "How did it go?"

"Well, better than I was expecting." He turned to Manuel. "You can rest easy. It had nothing to do with our investigation, or at least not directly. It was about a previous case of mine." He took a deep drag. "The death of Francisco Muñiz de Dávila."

"Fran?" Surprised, Lucas turned to look at Manuel.

The lieutenant nodded grimly. "Manuel, I assume you remember I told you it seemed strange to us at the time that, given his emotional state, Fran apparently took the time to lock the church door. We found no key, so we suspected someone else had locked it, pocketed the key, and walked off with it."

Manuel nodded.

"Well, today it turned up."

UNDER OPEN SKIES

Nogueira studied his cigarette. He took a couple of drags, exhaled a cloud of smoke, and clicked his tongue in annoyance. "They called me in to identify it, though there was really no need. It's one of a kind, and I'd filed a detailed description: 4.7 inches long, artisan silver with eleven small emeralds set in the handle around Fran's initials. Toñino had it. They found it when they examined the body. A colleague remembered I'd mentioned it."

"Are they sure it's the same one?"

"No room for doubt. The file contained the photos from the insurance company."

"And how do they think he got it?"

"Excellent question! And that's why they're reopening the case. They know Toñino was his supplier. In her statement, Herminia said she saw him on the grounds that night. They think he was probably there when Fran died." There was no trace of enthusiasm in Nogueira's voice. "They're looking at the theory Toñino gave him the dose, which seems likely, then dragged the body to the gravesite, left it there, locked the church door, and went off with the key."

"Along the lines of what you suspected," Manuel said. "Your idea that somebody moved the body. So you were right about that."

"Yeah, I was right," Nogueira echoed. He didn't seem convinced. He continued smoking.

"You don't look particularly pleased," Lucas commented.

"Because I'm not." He grimaced and tossed the cigarette butt into a puddle where it died with a hiss. "Why would that useless scumbag take the trouble to haul a dead body to the grave? There was a risk somebody might see him.

Assuming they screwed up the dose, why didn't he just leave the body in the church and be done with it?"

"I agree. It doesn't make sense," Manuel said. "Though I could see him taking the key. I heard that valuable objects disappeared from the church at least once before."

"A burglary?" Nogueira found that hard to believe. "I hadn't heard about that."

"More like shoplifting. Griñán told me that a couple of silver candelabra disappeared. Antique ones, very valuable, but there was no sign of a break-in."

Nogueira frowned. "I never heard about any such incident." He was searching his memory. "Might be a good idea if you dropped by the church on the estate to check whether anything else is missing."

"Sure, but why did Toñino have the key on him three years later anyhow?" asked Lucas. "That makes no sense. You think someone planted it on the body to throw suspicion on him?"

"Suspicion of what?" Nogueira shrugged. "For a closed case that was never investigated? Why? No one was suspected of anything, no charges were made, and now Toñino is dead. Álvaro is dead, too, so who would stand to benefit? There has to be a reason Toñino had the key on him when he died." He extracted another cigarette from the pack, studied it for a couple of seconds as if maybe the answer would be written there, gestured as if dismissing an idea, and then lit it. He looked very tired.

Lucas glanced at Manuel before he spoke. "We had a lot of revelations today at As Grileiras."

Manuel nodded.

Lucas summarized events for the policeman: Santiago's admission to the hospital, their conversation with Herminia, and what Elisa and the Raven had seen from the house on the night of Fran's death. The lieutenant's face was expressionless throughout the telling, but when Lucas had finished, he looked at Manuel.

"And now Elisa and the boy are with you?"

Manuel nodded again.

"I've been with the police for a long time, Manuel, long enough to know somebody might see something that isn't really there. If you doubt it, look at how Elisa's interpretation changed. First she assumed Álvaro persuaded Fran to go into the church to console him; now she's thinking it was a murder plot."

Lucas backed him up. "That's just what I told you, Manuel. We have to distinguish between facts and assumptions."

"It is however true," Nogueira admitted, "that right now Álvaro looks like a suspect. But the prior's actions are also suspicious. We know he's enough of a dolt to have gotten mixed up in something like this or even worse. I found it strange that he didn't seem particularly concerned about his nephew's disappearance, as if he either expected the boy not to come back or just didn't care. Maybe it had nothing to do with the boy's murder. But it's obvious to me Toñino wasn't going to be the reason for him to come clean about something he'd taken such pains to conceal. Let's not forget that Ortuño's account implicates the man in at least two felonies: covering up a homicide and failing to investigate sexual abuse of a minor. If the press gets hold of that, there'll be a huge scandal."

Lucas stated the obvious conclusion. "So he's probably holding something back."

"More than likely," Nogueira said. "At least for now. But depending on what the investigation turns up, we ourselves might have to provide that information."

"We?" Manuel asked, raising his chin, suddenly indignant. "Or you?"

"Manuel, I'm still a policeman, even if I'm officially retired. I warned you how investigations are. They can turn up things that are anything but pleasant."

"But that was when you said someone had killed my husband, not in reference to . . . all this!"

"Yes, but maybe it wasn't so complicated after all. I know how policemen think. It could have been a random sequence of events. Toñino finds the document, starts blackmailing Álvaro; Álvaro goes to the seminary because he knows the information had to have come from there; he locates Toñino—maybe he follows the prior—they fight, Toñino is killed, maybe by accident, and maybe he strings him up to make it look like a suicide."

"Then who killed Álvaro?"

"Maybe Toñino stabbed him during the fight and Álvaro drove away, then eventually lost consciousness and died."

"There's a better case against the prior than against Álvaro," Lucas put in. "He goes looking for his nephew at the boy's home; maybe he waits for him at the intersection, follows him, kills him, and hangs him. It wouldn't be the first time he tried to pass off a crime as a suicide. Then he finds Álvaro, they argue, he stabs him with something long and thin, and finishes him off by running his car off the road."

"I can't see it." Manuel shook his head. "Neither Álvaro nor the prior wanted the secret to come out, so why would he complicate things by murdering Álvaro? With Toñino dead, everything went back to square one."

"And the key?" asked Lucas. "Is there any explanation for that?"

"No, I already told you," Nogueira said. "It makes no sense to draw attention to a case that was filed away as an accidental overdose or a suicide and forgotten a long time ago."

"I'm not so sure," Lucas countered. "Elisa never forgot it."

"Close family members never do. It's easier to believe a loved one was murdered than to accept a suicide. But no one thinks so."

"I don't understand any of this." Manuel turned to look out into the dark night. His face showed his exhaustion and desperation.

"Listen to me, you two," Nogueira said. "Manuel!" His insistent tone brought Manuel's eyes back to him. "Forget all this speculation until we have the autopsy report. Ophelia will call me as soon as it's done. Then we base a hypothesis on facts. Empty speculation does us no good."

Manuel gave him a sullen look. "You'll call me as soon as you know something?"

"I give you my word. Now go up to your room." He glanced back toward the inn. "And try to get some rest. Tomorrow, no matter what the autopsy reveals, we have a long day ahead of us, together. Take my advice, Manuel, and try to get some rest."

Manuel nodded and gave in. He took a couple of steps toward the inn, hesitated, and turned back. "I have to go get Café."

"Leave him at my place tonight."

Manuel and Lucas exchanged a conspiratorial glance.

"Careful, Nogueira!" Lucas teased the policeman. "You'll wind up liking the mutt."

"Like hell I will!" the lieutenant exclaimed. He looked around at the parked cars and lowered his voice. "But it's really late, and I'll bet you the damn thing's asleep with my daughter."

With a smile Manuel walked away without listening to Nogueira's excuses. He lifted a hand in farewell on his way to the inn.

The others watched every step. As if by unspoken mutual accord they said nothing until the door had closed behind him.

Nogueira turned to Lucas. "What can you tell me about Santiago and this suicide attempt?"

Lucas emptied his lungs completely, then sucked air in. "He was a ticking time bomb. I suppose this blackmail attempt put him through hell all over again. It meant the secret he'd been carrying with him all his life might be exposed. He must have been terrified. He asked Álvaro for help, the brother who'd always defended him, and now, maybe as a direct result, Álvaro's dead. He's been under tremendous stress over the last few days. He's had sharp words with Manuel and even with his wife, the way Manuel tells it. He was very depressed. He had a similar serious depression when Fran died, and now what happened to Álvaro has thrown him for a loop. A few days ago Manuel saw him weeping in the church, and Herminia heard him crying this afternoon a few hours before the child found him. And to top it off, he's had at least a couple of confrontations with his mother. Herminia couldn't hear what they were discussing, but she did hear the dowager laughing at him. All that, added to her humiliation of him in front of Manuel the other day . . . I assume that it was just too much."

Nogueira had been nodding as he took all this in. His eyes were pensive. "You were his confessor, weren't you?"

"What are you thinking of?"

"Of the fact that the people in this family are devoted Catholics. Right? Even got their own church and their own priest."

"Don't go there," Lucas warned him, deadly serious.

"Take it easy, man!" Nogueira exclaimed, amused by the priest's reaction. "What I'm saying is that after a suicide attempt, surely the guy's going to want to make his peace with God. It wouldn't be out of place for you to drop by the hospital for a chat. I want to know if this was because of all that accumulated grief or if maybe something specific set him off. It'd be interesting to know what his mother said to him this morning."

"I'd been thinking of waiting till tomorrow morning. And you know, if he tells me something in confession . . ."

"Yeah, I know," Nogueira said.

"I may seem like an imbecile to you," Lucas went on, "but I think I was too hard on him. Now we understand he's been dogged by horror since childhood and by the lies he's been hiding all this time." Lucas looked out over the parking lot but he wasn't seeing the cars—memories overcame him. "He followed Álvaro around like a little puppy, and now maybe I understand why. That may have been the origin of his violent temper, his tendency to destroy his toys, his things, even himself." He turned toward Nogueira. "I accompanied him to the hospital when they told us of Álvaro's accident. They gave us the bad news there, and when he came out after identifying the body of his dead brother, he was in shock. He couldn't believe it."

The two stood there in silence.

"How does Manuel seem to you?" said Nogueira. "I'm worried about him."

Lucas nodded. "So am I. He's in agony. Given the circumstances, he's holding up pretty well; he's stronger than he looks. But even so he needs our support. Every new development turns up new complications. I think he's starting to see that Álvaro might have had very good reasons for keeping the truth from him. And now he's trying to come to grips with the fact that when Álvaro was only twelve, he killed a man. And wondering whether he was capable of doing so again."

"My thoughts exactly."

"Put yourself in his shoes and just imagine. If it's confusing for us . . ."

Nogueira nodded. He stared at Lucas so fixedly that after a time the priest began to feel uneasy. "What?" Lucas asked.

"I'm going to tell you something, priest . . ."

"Priest?" echoed Lucas. He had to smile. "So now I'm 'priest'?"

"You understand exactly what I'm saying," Nogueira replied, deadly serious. "As a secret of confession. One that's going to stay between the two of us."

Lucas nodded with equal gravity.

"They didn't call me to headquarters. They called me to where they found the body. Toñino's vehicle, a white car, was half hidden in the bushes. The crime scene team was working on it, so I couldn't get too close. But even from a distance you could see a number of dents. They'd already taken the poor bastard down from the tree, and the examiner was about to take the body away. I wasn't the only one they'd called. The prior was there. I assume they wanted him to identify the boy. We found ourselves face-to-face. He grabbed my arm, pulled me aside, and said, 'I told my nephew that with the marquis he couldn't expect things to go on like this. Álvaro was furious when he came to my office. I tried to warn him, but he didn't want to listen.'"

Lucas's eyes opened wide in amazement. "Do you think he'll say that in his statement to your colleagues?"

"No idea. There was something in the way he separated me from the others. Like I said before, it gives me the idea he's perfectly capable of clamming up to stay out of trouble. But I don't know." He clicked his tongue in annoyance. "Like I said, until we have the autopsy report and the investigation gets under way, it's all speculation. I don't want to upset Manuel with any more sloppy work."

"But if Toñino ran Álvaro's car off the road, who killed Toñino? What was the sequence of events? I don't understand any of this."

"That's exactly why I didn't want to tell Manuel about the dents. And why you're not going to tell him either."

"Or you'll take me behind a mountain and put a bullet in my head?" Lucas said and smiled.

"Like I said." Nogueira returned the smile as he looked toward the windows of the inn. "This has been a terrible day for him. I don't think he'll get much sleep tonight. The writer's no fool. He has to be thinking the same thing we are, that Álvaro could have been a murderer, and God knows I'm not referring to what happened that night at the monastery." He tossed his cigarette butt into a puddle and set off toward the inn. "Come keep me company. Aren't you hungry?"

Lucas trailed after him with a disgusted expression. "Doesn't anything ever rob you of your appetite?"

Nogueira paused to let the priest catch up. He put an arm around the man's shoulders. "Didn't I mention that my wife is starving me to death?"

Lucas laughed, thinking this was a joke. Then he saw Nogueira's expression. "How about if you tell me about it over dinner?"

◈

Manuel entered his room. He first turned on the light in the bathroom, which was opposite the door to Elisa and Samuel's room. He brushed his fingers across the wooden surface of the communicating door with its dozens of layers of paint. He stood there listening for movement on the other side. His eyes fastened on the well-lubricated heavy dead bolt, starkly new upon the old door. He lifted a hand and touched it, but as he shifted his weight, a floorboard creaked underfoot. Embarrassed, as if someone had caught him doing something inappropriate, he stepped back, which made the floor creak again. He turned off the bathroom light, went out to the hall, and knocked gently on Elisa's door.

She opened immediately. She was wearing thin socks and no shoes. She smiled and stepped to one side so he could see inside. The room was identical to his except for the double bed. Elisa had draped a blue scarf over the lampshade, so a melancholy light lay across the simple furnishings of the room. The television was on but the sound was scarcely audible. A cartoon sent bright bursts of color dancing across the pillows around Samuel's sleeping face.

"He just dozed off," she whispered with a smile. She stepped back in an invitation to enter.

He went to the bed with his eyes fixed on the boy's completely relaxed face. The child's eyes weren't totally closed. He must have fought off sleep as long as he could.

"Was it hard getting him to sleep?"

"The hardest thing was calming him down." She giggled. "I had him using the bed as a trampoline for the longest time, bouncing and pretending to be a circus performer. When I finally persuaded him to watch cartoons, he dropped off in less than five minutes."

Manuel looked around. "Is this comfortable for both of you?"

She held out a hand. When Manuel did the same, she took his hand in both of hers and beamed. "Thank you, Manuel. We're very comfortable here, really. Don't worry. I think tonight any place in the world would be better for us than the manor house."

He had an impulse to embrace her, but she anticipated him and threw herself into his arms before he could initiate a move. She was unusually tall, the same height as he was. He felt her face close against his and the fragility of the thin body in his arms. He remembered Griñán mentioning she'd been a model—*and a drug addict*, the voice inside his head admonished him. When she disengaged from the hug, he saw her eyes were wet. She turned away, demurely drying her tears.

She gestured toward the door between the two rooms. "Manuel, I unlocked it. If you want anything, just call from your room. There's no need to go out to the hall."

He realized that the wooden floorboards had advised her of his presence on the other side.

"Listen to me, Elisa," he said with a serious expression. "There's something I want to tell you."

She seated herself on the bed, put her legs in a lotus position, and sat there attentive.

"It's about what the marquess said when we were at the manor."

She sat motionless and silent, but Manuel saw that her face had become more somber.

"I can't tell you or ask you, or even feel I have the right to say what you should believe or not. But I hope with all my heart you don't believe what she said."

"Manuel . . ."

"No, don't say anything. But do you remember you told me you knew Fran better than anyone else?"

She nodded.

"Well, I knew Álvaro better than anyone else. I was confused and uncertain when I got here, but now I understand that though maybe I didn't know absolutely everything about him, I still knew him better than anyone else. Just keep that in mind. You might be hearing a lot of things over the next few days."

"I know what she said and why. I know her all too well. I'm aware that everything she does is deliberate, but just like you, I will not accept it. Do you understand, Manuel?"

"I do."

They looked back at the sleeping child. "There's a favor I need to ask of you, Elisa."

"Of course. Anything."

"Griñán told me there's a tradition in the family that each male family member is presented at birth with a key to the church on the estate."

She nodded.

"And I understand the keys are supposed to be buried with them after they die."

"True, but . . ." she said, "Fran lost his."

"Do you know if he had it the day of his father's funeral?"

"Yes. When I took him something to eat, it was next to him on the pew."

"Are you sure it was his, and not one of the other keys?"

"Yes, absolutely. They're all different from one another. You can tell them apart by the initials and the gems set in the head of the key. Fran's key had emeralds. I remember it well." She looked down for a moment. "When we both were still on drugs, I tried more than once to persuade him to sell it so we could use the money. But Fran respected his father too much for that. He always said his father would never forgive him if he did."

"But Fran didn't have it on him when they found him."

"We looked everywhere for it, but it was gone. It's weird," she said, twisting about to look into one dark corner of the room as if the memory was lurking there. "I remember my mother-in-law was extremely put out that the key couldn't be located for the funeral. That fucking bitch!" she exclaimed, narrowing her eyes in a scowl so furious and vindictive that it shocked Manuel. "Álvaro gave her his own key. Did you know that?"

Manuel shook his head.

"Did they make a key when Samuel was born?"

"Of course. You can imagine, what with their obsession with tradition. It never meant much to me. Just the sight of it evokes bad memories."

"I assume it's in your care."

"It's in a container for safekeeping, a kind of frame. Like for a picture, but deeper. Something you can hang on a wall and open up. A kind of receptacle."

"Can you lend it to me?"

She opened her eyes in surprise and even seemed about to ask him to explain. But he found her answer even more astonishing.

"Álvaro asked me the same thing the last time he was here."

He was paralyzed. He sat staring at her. "Elisa, do you remember what day that was?"

"The day he arrived. He returned Samuel's key that afternoon."

He reassured her. "So will I."

"Don't be silly!" she chided him with a smile. "My room and Samuel's are side-by-side with a door between them, just like here. The key's on the dresser in Samuel's room at the estate. You can take it anytime you like."

Manuel leaned down and gently kissed the child's cheek. He went to the door, his hands still alive with the memory of Elisa's vibrant slim body. He recalled her confession that she'd tried to get Fran to sell the key.

He turned to look at her. "Elisa, there's one more thing." He hesitated. "And perhaps it's a bit delicate. Remember I didn't know you before, and the only information I have about the family comes from what they themselves have been telling me."

She nodded and pressed her lips together, acknowledging she understood he was about to ask something of importance. "I've had a long time to face reality and my own past. You can ask me anything."

"I know you and Fran were in a Portuguese clinic for almost a year."

She sat still as a sphinx.

"I know you were already pregnant when you two came back and the old marquis was dying. Elisa, I know you're a good mother; it's enough just to see the wonderful job you've done with Samuel. But I know it's very hard to break a drug habit, and relapses can happen."

She began shaking her head from side to side, rejecting what she saw coming.

Manuel's tone was apologetic. "I have to ask, Elisa, I have to. Because someone made the insinuation. I don't believe it, but I have to ask."

She kept shaking her head in determined denial.

"Have you ever given in and taken drugs, Elisa? Even just once?"

She rose and stalked forward to face him. Her naturally blue eyes had darkened like those of a cat. "No!"

"Elisa, please forgive me," he said, turning to the door.

But she reached him before he could shut it. "Look in the second drawer of the same dresser where Samuel's key is on display. You'll find my medical reports. Our beloved mother-in-law forced me to submit to weekly drug testing. I was allowed to remain at the estate as long as I stayed off drugs. She threatened to take Samuel away from me, and she'd have done it if she'd had the slightest excuse. You can collect those reports when you go to pick up the key." She closed the door after him.

Manuel went into his room and turned on the light. For a few moments, leaning against the warm wooden surface of the door, he surveyed the room from that angle, just as he'd surveyed his own apartment days before.

The energy-saving bulb in the ceiling fixture cast a weak glow. It would gradually brighten as minutes passed, but until then its reduced illumination would bathe the furnishings with a miserably dim light that only emphasized the room's cold and desolate appearance. He glanced at the ancient radiator with its many coats of paint, reminding him of all the layers of fiction and reality he'd encountered. By way of greeting it emitted a clanking sound that signaled the heating was about to come on. He turned to gaze at the door between the two rooms. Carefully avoiding the floorboard that would betray his presence, he raised a hand to touch the dead bolt with the same care he'd have taken if manipulating an explosive device. He silently unlocked it and stood there examining it in silence for a couple of seconds. Then he quietly bolted it again with the same care.

He crossed to the bed as if responding to a call. The chocolate-colored bedspread, impeccably clean and carefully set, was the vacant stage for a white flower carefully positioned on the pillow. Without touching the blossom he looked again toward the door to the adjacent room. He was keenly aware he'd just unlocked that door and then bolted it once again.

"Why?" he whispered to himself. "What does this mean?"

He picked up the flower. It was fresh and fragrant, as if recently cut; its pale presence disconcerted him and roused a mixture of apprehension and a different, unfamiliar sensation. His eyes filled with tears; in wild exasperation he jerked open the drawer of the night table and threw the flower inside. He hated this narrow bed, so like a military bunk, and he knew his night without Café would be unending and as dark as pitch. The dog's furry presence, watery eyes, and even the gentle snoring had granted him comfort; perhaps he should have gone to fetch the creature, although he admitted to himself with a touch of jealousy that the little animal was becoming more and more attached to Antía. He knew he wasn't going to fall asleep, so why try? He turned on the television and lowered the volume. He took his seat at the desk and searched for the only place that offered him rest. He went back to the palace.

OF ALL HE REFUSED

Laughter interrupted his reflections. He looked out at the river and saw a dream come true—the three girls from the other day again rode their curious craft downstream. Their legs were tanned and their arms were strong, and their hair was carelessly tied back into ponytails dangling under their straw hats. They shrieked and laughed. The music of those voices rang like the notes of wind chimes moved by the breeze. The spectacle of those lovely river nymphs filled him with inexplicable rejoicing.

SUMMONING THE DEAD

At about 4:30 a.m. Manuel grabbed the bedspread, pulled it back, and collapsed onto the bed. He closed his eyes.

He opened them in sudden alarm. He'd fallen asleep. He looked down at the foot of the bed. It was dimly lit from the hall through the transom window. The brothers always left the corridor lights on so the littlest boys wouldn't be afraid of the dark. Álvaro looked down at his feet, still secure in the heavy standard-issue school shoes he put on again each night once he was sure his roommate was asleep. For the last week he'd remained fully dressed all night long. On watch. But tonight he'd drifted off; worse, he'd lost all track of time. Watches weren't allowed at the seminary, because the brothers said that boys who were always checking the time didn't concentrate on their studies. A large grandfather clock stood on the ground floor. Its chimes were audible throughout the school and seemed even louder in the middle of the night. He remembered hearing it strike three. Now this damned sleep had overcome him, and he had no idea what time it was or how long he'd slept. He got out of bed, alert to any change in the serene face of the motionless boy sleeping with his mouth open in the bed next to his.

He opened the door, slipped out into the hall, and made his way through the dark. He mentally counted the doors between his room and his brother's room. He put his hand on the doorknob. Carefully, as if it might explode, he turned it until he heard a click. He pushed the door, put his head through the gap, and surveyed the interior. He heard the snuffling breath of his brother's roommate, who'd thrown off the covers and was sleeping soundly in the bed nearer to the door. The other bed was empty. The gleaming white expanse of abandoned sheets showed its inhabitant had vanished.

He ran through the darkness toward the monks' cells. He didn't stop to listen or call out; he threw himself against the door, twisted the handle and shoved, knowing it would open because none of the doors in the seminary had locks. He didn't see his brother. But he heard him crying out in pain, crushed and buried by the shapeless mass. The boy was moaning from very far away, as if from the depths of a well or from a grave.

The beast kept at it, completely unaware of a new presence in the room. Álvaro didn't hesitate. He instantly released his hold on the knob and whipped the leather belt of his school uniform free from its loops. He grabbed it in both hands, jumped onto the man's sweaty back, and slapped the length of leather around the man's neck. The surprise attack staggered the monk, who let go of his victim and grappled at his neck in an effort to free himself. With all his strength Álvaro yanked the belt tight, and in just a few seconds he sensed the monster's flailing efforts losing their force. The man's legs gave out, and he fell to his knees. The neck gave way as the belt bit deeply into his throat. Álvaro wasn't aware of the moment when the man's trachea cracked. The man stopped moving, but the boy kept the band tight, pulling with a fierce tension that cramped his hands and turned his knuckles white.

When he let go at last, panting and trembling from immense effort, he looked down at the beast sprawled at his feet like some enormous safari kill. He knew the man was dead; he knew he'd killed him. That didn't matter to him, he realized, and he felt no guilt. But he knew he would have to pay, for something inside him had broken, something he'd never be able to recover. He accepted that responsibility.

The child was sobbing, face to the wall, wailing louder and louder, hiccuping. He was going to wake up everyone in the school.

～⚜～

Manuel sat up suddenly in bed. His heart beat wildly. For a few moments he thought he still heard the boy's heartbroken wails; confused, he looked around for the child until reality settled in and brought him back to his room at the inn. The boy's sobbing became the buzzing of his cell phone. Nogueira was calling him.

"Manuel, Ophelia just called. She gets off at six, and we agreed to meet at seven o'clock at her house. Do you remember how to get there, or do you want me to swing by to pick you up?"

Grateful for the intrusion, he brushed away the vestiges of sleep still blurring his vision. He rubbed his eyes hard and tried to collect his thoughts. "Did she tell you anything?"

"Nothing specific. She has news but didn't want to say anything on the phone."

"I'll be there at seven."

As he was about to step out of the room, his eyes went to the bolt on the door that led to the adjacent room. He looked around in an absentminded reflex to check whether his room was presentable. His bed was unmade, books and the photo of him with Álvaro were on the night table, and the handwritten pages documenting his visit to the palace were spread across the desk. Relieved to have remembered the squeaky floorboard, he carefully approached the door and listened. He heard nothing, but he did see flickers of light through the cracks and under the door indicating that the television was on. With the same care he'd used the night before, he unbolted his side and turned the knob until he heard a click.

They were both asleep. Their heads were together and their faces were relaxed, their appearance altering only with the bright flickering cartoon images that bathed their faces in a succession of different colors. He felt a pang of commiseration—not just for them or for himself, but an empathy with all the lonely, the abandoned, and the unhappy ones afraid to turn off the light when night settles over their souls. He remained standing there for some time, quietly watching the face of the sleeping boy: mouth half-open, eyelids flickering, his dark-complected little hand spread out like a starfish across the white sheet. He closed the door with the same care as before. This time he didn't bolt it.

❧

The medical examiner's car was in front of her house, and Nogueira's BMW was parked on the street. Manuel pulled up behind it, walked to the front gate, and leaned over to release the latch as he'd seen the policeman do. The open door to the garage revealed part of a woodpile and the rear of Álvaro's car, partly covered by a tarp.

The house was full of the aroma of warm bread and freshly brewed coffee. His stomach growled to remind him he'd eaten nothing since the day before. The examiner had set the kitchen table with breakfast mugs, and when he went inside he found her with the coffeepot in hand.

"Hello, Manuel, please have a seat." She waved toward the table.

She didn't ask but simply served coffee with milk in all three mugs. As they stirred sugar into them she placed before them a basket with aromatic slices of toasted Galician bread, dark and fragrant beneath a white cloth.

The three devoured this breakfast. Manuel assumed that the physician was politely abstaining from conversation until they'd finished. She spoke when they'd done so. "Everything indicates he may have been dead for thirteen days. Fourteen, if we accept the missing persons report from his aunt, though yesterday his uncle the prior said she'd probably gotten the day wrong, since he saw the boy in her house on Saturday. He claims he went there to have coffee with them."

"What a bastard!" Nogueira exclaimed. "So he didn't mention the argument, and I suppose he won't have said anything about Álvaro's visit to the seminary or their discussion there. Now he admits he saw Toñino on Saturday. He's covering himself, because things are getting serious now."

"We can assume they're both lying. The aunt, to call attention to her report of him as missing, and the prior, who seems to be the more accomplished liar. All he said was that they had coffee on Saturday at his sister's, and he hadn't seen the boy at all since then." Ophelia seemed about to add something but stopped herself. She shook her head. "In fact he was wearing the same clothes his aunt described when she went to the police." She turned to Manuel. "You need to understand that it's too early just yet to determine the exact date of death. I'm waiting for the results of various tests, concerning the maturity of the insects and larvae, the aqueous humor drawn from the eye, and other samples. But if you were to push me, I'd say yes, fourteen days dead, the same as Álvaro. The body is badly decomposed. We returned it to the morgue an hour ago in a sealed coffin. I don't need to say more. It was exposed to the elements the whole time. There was a fair amount of rain, but many afternoons were very hot; and it's an area with plenty of crows and magpies. Both are readily attracted to carrion, so you can take it as a given that the remains were in a deplorable state."

Both men nodded.

"Once I had it on the examination table and could take a closer look, I was able to confirm what I'd guessed at the scene: the victim's face had been badly battered. A cheekbone was fractured, a tooth knocked out, and the jaw was cracked in several places. And there was evidence of swelling of the anterior forearms." She raised her arms as if she were shielding her own face. "Clear indications of an attempt at self-defense. He got a thorough beating, and all those blows came before he died. We know that because the blood around the injuries had clotted; in addition, in his car we found a packet of towelettes, more than a dozen of which he'd used to wipe away blood. All of which leads us to believe that he was beaten, he had time to try to clean himself up a bit, and then he was hanged."

Manuel spoke up. "Could you tell what they used to hit him?"

"Yes, it was obvious: hands. Punches, blows delivered with fists."

"Correct me if I'm wrong, but I assume that the person who assaulted him would have marks on his knuckles. Isn't that right?" Manuel remembered the throbbing pain of his own hand after the altercation the other night outside the Vulcan.

"Definitely. He was punched so hard that a tooth was knocked out. That would inevitably have produced a corresponding hand injury. The knuckles would be skinned and the finger joints would be swollen. And it might be possible to check the corpse for the attacker's DNA."

"I saw Álvaro's hands," Manuel declared firmly, his voice betraying a certain sense of relief. "Well, one of them, that is, the right hand. Considering that Álvaro was right-handed, he could be assumed to have fought with that hand. Isn't that right?"

"Yes. I remember that as well. Both hands were clean and unmarked."

"Toñino was a hustler, a male prostitute," Nogueira interjected. "It wouldn't be the first time a john beat him up. Plenty of those clients are seized by shame and regret after the act. The events could be completely unrelated. A client could have beaten him before he met up with Álvaro."

"Or the prior could have. You saw him some days after Toñino disappeared. Did he have any marks?"

"None that I could see. But if the boy died Saturday morning, a lot of time had passed; a good ointment could have helped heal such injuries."

Ophelia nodded solemnly. "There's plenty more. Though Toñino's death was due to asphyxiation by hanging, the body also had eight puncture wounds in the lower abdomen. Eight deep wounds with narrow-entry openings. In Álvaro's case I used calipers to measure his wound, but I had no time to do more; for this case I was able to probe the wound. Though I certainly can't be a hundred percent sure, I'd guess Toñino was stabbed with an object very similar to the one used to attack Álvaro."

"The same person could have attacked each of them?" Manuel said.

"I hate to be the devil's advocate," Nogueira said, "but the fight could have involved just the two of them. Álvaro agrees to a meeting with the promise of payment, then when Toñino turns up, Álvaro kills him. Or the other way around. Álvaro refuses to pay him, Toñino attacks him, and stabs him a single time. Álvaro, who's much taller and stronger, disarms him and then stabs him several times."

Manuel had closed his eyes as if unwilling to be a witness to that theory. "Has the weapon been found?"

Ophelia first served another round of coffee. "Not yet. It's not in the car or anywhere in the vicinity."

"Though if Álvaro then took it, he could have gotten rid of it on the way, throwing it away along the road somewhere before his car left the pavement."

Manuel gave the policeman a baleful glare.

"There's one odd thing," she said, paying no attention to the tension between the two men. "I noticed it with Álvaro, and with Toñino too. There are more lacerations, so with Toñino it's more obvious. The stabs were delivered along a trajectory from left to right."

Nogueira's eyebrows went up and he grinned.

"Which signifies what?" Manuel asked.

"The murderer could be left-handed," Nogueira said.

"You can't count on that," Ophelia quickly cautioned them. "It's just a hypothesis for now. Without proper measurements of Álvaro's injury we can't even be sure they were wounded by the same object. And then other considerations enter into play, such as the position of the attacker at the moment of the assault. For example, if it occurred inside a vehicle, the attacker might have been forced to alter his posture. But the first suggestion, nevertheless, is that everything points to the assailant having been left-handed."

"Álvaro was right-handed," Manuel declared firmly, staring defiantly at Nogueira. "And Toñino?"

The policeman checked his watch. "It's early. I'll call his aunt later to ask. I have doubts about the prior. He was brought up in times when left-handedness had to be corrected at any cost, so . . . he could be left-handed but not appear to be so."

"And the blows to the face?" Manuel insisted. "Can you determine from trajectories if the attacker was right- or left-handed?"

Ophelia gave a start. "Hmm—now that you mention it, it's true that his face had been struck everywhere. That's to be expected if you're moving your head from side to side during the beating." She mimed defensive movements. "But the most devastating blows—the tooth that was knocked out, the fractured cheekbone, and the cracked portion of the jaw—were on the left side. That probably says his attacker was right-handed; though both fists are used in fights, it might suggest that the person who struck his face and the one who stabbed him weren't one and the same. And there's more: the attacker must have been strong. It's true that Toñino weighed only a bit more than 150 pounds, and he was thin and not very tall. At the scene of the crime I saw one sneaker was missing and the sock on that foot had slid down so far that it was dangling from his toes. At first I assumed that in the spasms that are typical when someone is hanged, he'd kicked off his shoe, but in fact we found it about thirty feet away, near the car. And during the autopsy I detected several antemortem scrapes and scratches on his heels. I think he was dragged that distance, and that would have required someone strong. You have to be muscular to hoist a person from the ground and hang him from a tree branch. Granted, he wasn't very high off the ground, but even so a lot of brute strength was required. That would leave marks on the assailant's hands as well, though less pronounced if the attacker was wearing gloves. We're examining the rope for any residue of skin or epithelial cells. But on first inspection we saw none."

The three sat in silence for a few moments. Manuel was the first to speak. "I think it's essential to establish the time Toñino died, since we already know where and when Álvaro ran off the road."

"Look, Manuel," said Ophelia with a sigh, "despite what you might have seen on television, it's very difficult after the first few hours to establish the definitive time of a death. Unless of course the victim's watch stops at that exact moment or you have a credible witness. In most cases, we put together a picture from various pieces of information and posit an approximate time of death. But after so many days the state of decomposition of the body makes it far more complicated. As I said, not until I receive the results of the tests I've requested, as well as the report from the technical examination of the vehicle, can we even begin to speak of making an approximation."

Manuel accepted his defeat.

"And another thing." Her face assumed a formal expression as she handed to him an envelope that she'd had beside her on the table all this time. "Here are the lab results of the comparative analysis of paints. There's no better way to get a quick turnaround than by paying up front. There's an exact match between the paint residue on Álvaro's vehicle and the sample you took at the seminary."

The two men exchanged astonished glances. Nogueira was the first to respond. "And you've waited until now to tell us?"

"Curb your enthusiasm, Nogueira. You of all people should understand that this has zero value either for the police or for the courts. The sample was taken by a private individual without permission or a warrant. We can't use it. It proves nothing."

"Dearest sweet little Ophelia," Nogueira replied as he snatched the paper from Manuel's hands. "I've been retired for ten days, but I still have a pretty good idea how to do the job. This test may not serve as evidence, but it's more than enough to justify a call on the prior."

"I'll go with you," Manuel said.

"No, Manuel, you'd better not. He knows who you are and that you've been investigating, but it won't do us any good if he makes the connection between us."

"Are you sure he won't cause you problems if you keep turning the screws on him?" Manuel asked.

"No, I'm not. I wasn't so sure last night, but my hunch has now been confirmed by the fact that he didn't mention anything about Álvaro, your visit, or mine. We already know the prior has his reasons to keep quiet; now we need to determine whether he's covering up only that night in 1984. Or also what happened the day both Álvaro and his nephew died."

"We're still not sure," Ophelia replied.

"Everything's pointing in that direction, though, isn't it? It's time to have a chat with him. I'll drop by to express my condolences and see how he's going to explain the business about the pickup truck."

Ophelia nodded but clearly was not happy about it. "What will you do, Manuel?"

"I'll go back to As Grileiras. After all, everything seems to begin and end there."

⁂

Nogueira looked up at the office windows on the second floor of the monastery. They reflected the gray morning sky, but beyond them was visible the vague shape of the prior watching him. The blurred shape retreated as soon as Nogueira looked up. The policeman's slight smile was hidden by his mustache. He lit a cigarette and took his time smoking it, giving the prior's mood time to transition from apprehension to anxiety as the man racked his brains trying to guess the reason for the lieutenant's visit.

He snuffed out the cigarette and amused himself a bit more by greeting the aged monks along his path, prolonging the conversations by asking about their health. By the time it started to drizzle he calculated that the prior must be properly wound up. He walked through the front door and went up to the second floor.

The office door stood open. As he walked toward it the lieutenant imagined an indecisive prior opening it and closing it repeatedly, trying to figure out how to receive him. The man was sitting behind his desk. In stark opposition to Nogueira's imagined picture, he made no pretense of being engaged with work. He wasn't wearing his reading glasses, and there was nothing for him to read. The desk gleamed bright and empty.

Nogueira shut the door without a word and crossed toward the desk. The prior stared warily at his visitor and waited to hear from him. Nogueira didn't waste his breath with small talk.

"I know what happened that night in 1984. I know what was blacked out of the document signed by Brother Ortuño. I know Toñino found the original in this office and decided to blackmail Álvaro Muñiz de Dávila, who came here to demand an explanation from you on the day he died."

As if activated by a spring mechanism, the prior flew to his feet, overturning the desk chair in which he'd been seated. He clamped a hand over his mouth in an unmistakable effort to keep from throwing up. He ran past Nogueira toward the bathroom door tucked between the bookshelves. Nogueira didn't budge. He heard the man vomiting, coughing, and panting for a long moment. The toilet flushed and water ran in the sink. When the prior emerged from the bathroom he was pressing a damp towel to his brow.

Nogueira ignored the overturned chair behind the desk. He set the visitors' chairs face-to-face, seated himself, and with a gesture obliged the man to take the other one.

The prior didn't need any more persuasion. All semblance of assurance had disappeared. He vomited out his confession with the same lack of restraint with which he'd purged his stomach.

"Toñino was like that all his life. He refused to study and he didn't want to work. It wasn't the first time I'd hired him to do odd jobs and repairs in the monastery. In a building as rambling as this one, there are always things that need attention, and instead of calling someone else I'd hire my nephew. No one can blame me for that. Last winter we had a problem with one of the roof gutters, and water leaked into a couple of the rooms; nothing serious, but it left stains on the ceiling. We waited all summer long to make sure they'd dried out completely, and it was just a matter of repainting the ceilings. He worked for three days. For once I thought things had changed for the better. He was engaged and responsive and seemed to enjoy the work.

"We were clearing out my office so he could paint it the next day." He lifted a hand and pointed to a yellow stain on the ceiling, above the window. "But he didn't come back. I have to admit I wasn't surprised. He'd dropped out like that before. Before he left he'd told me he needed some money, and I advanced him part of his pay; when he didn't turn up again I just thought he'd gone off on a binge. When he didn't turn up, I called my sister. But she told me he wasn't home. She was always making excuses for him, always covering up for him. I don't even know if it was true that he wasn't home." He shrugged. "So I gave up. The brothers helped me put things back in place, and I told myself yet again I should never trust my nephew.

"When Álvaro Muñiz de Dávila suddenly turned up here, I began to have an idea of what had happened. I suppose that when the boy was moving my desk, the drawer must have come out. It was always a bit loose. And it seems that the folder where that document was kept probably fell out, and he got his hands on it. As soon as Álvaro left, I went to my sister's house to try to talk to my nephew, but it was no use. He wouldn't even come to the door. I was returning to my car when I received an urgent call and drove back to the monastery."

"You're claiming that you returned to the monastery just like that, knowing full well what your nephew was up to, after you'd heard Álvaro's threats?"

"I swear to you—that's exactly what I did."

"You'd been taking all that trouble to conceal what happened here the night Verdaguer died, and for years you thought you had it all under control. But after I came here asking about Álvaro, you forgot your duties in the monastery and ran off to talk to Ortuño, the former monk, to warn him to keep his mouth shut. You're claiming you didn't try to shut the others up as well?"

The prior started to deny it, but Nogueira held up a hand to cut him off. "There's too much at stake. The rapist is long dead, but the scandal can provoke real problems for the monastery. And you can wind up in prison for covering up Brother Verdaguer's death with a fake suicide. Which makes you an accomplice to sexual abuse of a minor."

The prior moaned, covered his face with the towel, and leaned forward. Nogueira regarded him without the least sympathy, reached out to grab one end of the towel, and yanked it out of his hands. The prior, startled, jerked back and put his hands before his face as if expecting a blow.

Nogueira gave him a look of infinite disgust. His mouth tightened into a line as sharp as the slash of a knife. "You're right, you slimy piece of shit. I should break every bone in your body." He spoke in a derisive whisper, addressing the man with utter contempt.

The prior began sobbing in fear and babbled something incoherent.

Nogueira took out a cigarette and lit it without asking permission. He took one of those deep drags of his. "I'm going to tell you what I think happened," he said with glacial calm. "I think you waited for your nephew at the intersection in the Os Martiños neighborhood, you followed him, and when you were in an unpopulated area, you waved him down, and he stopped beside you. You're an old geezer, but you're a hefty son of a bitch, and your nephew weighed only about 150 pounds. I think you beat the hell out of him, stabbed him, and then strung him up on the tree where they found him last night. That's why you weren't a goddamn bit surprised he'd disappeared. That's why it didn't worry you."

As Nogueira told the story he was well aware of the viciousness required for such an explosion of violence. Ophelia was convinced that the individual who'd beaten Toñino wasn't the same as the one who'd stabbed him. Nogueira knew from experience that she was very rarely mistaken. But putting pressure on this asshole was giving him real satisfaction. Of all the depraved monsters he'd seen, he hated none more than the child abusers and those who covered up for them. He was certain that if he frightened the man enough, he'd scare out of him whatever truth he'd been hiding.

The prior sobbed and denied it. He threw up his hands and protested his innocence. There were no marks on his knuckles, but so what? Several days had passed. It wouldn't be difficult to find out whether he'd had any recently.

Nogueira resumed his story, watching the man like a hawk. "Then you met Álvaro Muñiz de Dávila somewhere along the highway to Chantada to tell him the danger was past, but he didn't make it easy for you. I assume he wanted the document; that's what I would have demanded to make sure this wouldn't happen again. Or maybe he was just fed up with all this filth and had decided he was going to publish it anyway. That would be the best thing, and it's probably going to happen." The prior opened his eyes wide in fright. "Yes, indeed, I do believe that's how it went down. You two argued, and you stabbed him. He must have been surprised to find a monk capable of such a thing. You gave him no warning. He was strong; he got into his car and drove away along the highway, but you had to make sure he wouldn't talk, so you followed him in that white pickup you're hiding in the monastery garage. You rammed his vehicle and drove it off the road. That's why you haven't taken it to be repaired. A scientific analysis confirmed that the pickup's paint is identical to what was left on the rear bumper of Álvaro's car."

That took the prior completely by surprise. He stopped his moaning. Gaping like a fish out of water, he rose to his feet and started pawing through a pile of documents in the in-box on his desk. "No, no, no, you're wrong. I have evidence, I have proof." He frantically searched through the papers. He picked each one up, checked the subject line and cast it aside. Most wound up on the floor. At last his face lit up. "You see? See this?" he insisted, shaking a paper so violently in front Nogueira that not a word was legible.

Nogueira snatched the document and recognized it immediately. It was the standard insurance form used by both parties to record the details of a traffic accident.

"Álvaro came to see me. It's true, he was very angry. He told me he wasn't going to be blackmailed, that he didn't care at all; as far as he was concerned everything might as well be published. He said I was the only one who had anything to fear, and if I agreed, he'd find some way to stop Toñino. He was leaving, but when he backed up he ran into the pickup we use for our shopping. It was in front of the garage. He was ready to settle the matter then and there. He filled out the forms with Brother Anselmo, who brought our copy to me for safekeeping. We've been expecting the insurance company to call, so that's why we didn't take the pickup to the garage." His voice was shrill. "And now I suppose nobody's going to cover the expenses!"

"Why were you hiding the vehicle?"

"I don't know. We saw you snooping around; we didn't know what you were looking for."

Nogueira sighed as he sorted through all this. "You threatened your nephew. You told him things couldn't remain this way, that he had no idea who he was playing with."

Now almost frantic, the man denied it. "It was just a way of warning him. I mean, warning him about Álvaro. I knew the boy intended to contact him; Álvaro wanted to go confront him. I didn't want to give him the address because I could see how furious he was. But he insisted and told me he wasn't going to leave until I gave him the boy's phone number. Toñino wasn't evil; he was impulsive and not too bright, but he wasn't a bad boy. I tried to make Toñino understand the seriousness of the situation, but he wouldn't even come to the door. He hid behind my sister's skirts."

This contributed nothing new to their understanding of the case. They already knew that Álvaro had telephoned Toñino that afternoon. The question was why, exactly, had he done so? To say he wasn't going to pay, or to set up a meeting with the promise of payment and resolve the situation by killing the boy? That thought brought something else to Nogueira's mind.

"You said that when you were at the door to your sister's house, they called you about an emergency at the monastery."

"Yes, I was going to explain that. Brother Nazario is one of the oldest of us; he's ninety-three years old. He got giddy, nothing serious; it had to do with his blood pressure. But he fell and broke his nose. It wasn't a bad injury, but he takes Sintrom, a blood thinner to prevent strokes, so his blood is slow to clot. He was bleeding heavily, and they had to call an ambulance. I spent the night with him at the emergency room, and they were finally able to stop the bleeding. Even then they had to give him a couple of transfusions. You can talk with him if you want. They released him three days ago."

Nogueira looked over the accident report. It was properly filled out with the time of the accident and a detailed description. The handwriting and the signature looked like those of Álvaro, and there was no reason to doubt their authenticity. "I'll need a photocopy of this document."

The prior nodded feverishly.

"And I'm going to verify what you said about the hospital. If you lied to me, I'll see to it they lock you up for child abuse. You'll see what kind of reception you get in prison." He took grim pleasure seeing the prior shudder and quake.

His cell phone rang, and he took the call. Later, once he had the photocopy in hand, he left the place, but not before giving the man one last threatening look.

Though he didn't relish the prospect, he drove toward the Os Martiños neighborhood.

INSOMNIA

The next-door neighbor opened her door and greeted Nogueira before he got close enough to knock. "Good morning, Captain!"

He could easily imagine her lurking at the window waiting for something to happen. Like a big lazy cat.

"Lieutenant," he corrected her.

"Lieutenant, captain, who knows the difference? Please excuse this poor widow's unfamiliarity with military ranks," she said and stood aside to invite him in.

He turned his face away so she wouldn't catch his look of suspicion and disgust. Had he detected a flirtatious tone in the old hag's voice? He assessed the situation. She'd called him more than an hour earlier, but she appeared to be wearing little more than a nightdress under her carelessly closed bathrobe. It left exposed a goodly expanse of a pale bosom mottled with age spots.

Nogueira took a deep breath to calm himself but immediately regretted doing so. The place had the same foul smell of untended cat litter he remembered from before.

He was determined to keep the visit as brief as possible. "So what was it?"

"You told me to telephone if I remembered something."

"Right, you already said that. On the phone. And what was it you remembered?"

Instead of answering immediately, the woman stepped past him and took her seat on the sofa by the window. "First I have to give you some background, so you'll understand why I didn't remember it before. That way you'll see I'm not making it up." She patted the place next to her on the sofa.

Steeling himself, the lieutenant sat as instructed.

"I suffer from insomnia, Captain. I'm still young and active, and I have to take a pill to help me sleep, but sometimes I forget it. It's always annoying when that happens, because I go to sleep right away, but without my pill I wake up less than an hour later. And if I don't take it then, I'm up all night."

Nogueira sat enduring this torture in the hope that something useful would come of it.

"Last night it happened again. I forgot my pill, I went to sleep, and at one in the morning, as usual, regular as clockwork, I was as wide awake as I am right now. I got up to look for my medicine. I keep it all up there in the dresser." She pointed to a piece of furniture upon which the cat was dozing. "When I passed by the window I looked outside, and I remembered that on the Saturday Toñino disappeared, I'd also forgotten my pill. When I got up that night to fetch it, I saw Toñino's car outside."

Nogueira gave her a look. His interest was piqued. "Are you sure of that?"

She gave him that pout of pretended offense and nodded. "Absolutely sure. But I needed to put you in the picture, so you'd understand why I'd forgotten about it and then remembered it only yesterday. Because it was the same situation. I didn't pay much attention to it then, because it wasn't unusual to see his car there. I was half-asleep, but I know what I saw; and not just that. I took my pill and went back to bed, but it always takes me a while to get to sleep again. That's when I heard the car engine start up. It went out of the drive toward the main road."

"This is very important," Nogueira said, fixing his eyes on hers. "Are you certain of the time?"

She flashed a proud smile. "Captain, it was one o'clock in the morning. I may not be as young as I once was, but when it comes to telling the time and other things, I'm as reliable as any watch."

A FALSE BACK

Manuel leaned forward to peer up through the windshield. The sky was still as leaden as it had been at dawn, as if day were never going to break, but the stillness of the early hours was gone, broken now by gusts of swirling wind that sent flying the first leaves to detach themselves from the trees. The rain began as he was driving to the estate. The melancholy of the weather, the rhythmic thump of the windshield wipers, and the absence of Café from his side amounted to an unbearable combination. The image of Antía hugging the little dog rose uncalled to his mind.

He parked by the gate, in the same place as the first day. Santiago was still in the hospital, so Catarina was probably with him. Manuel had no desire to run into the Raven or even betray his presence to the dowager. He raised the hood of the heavy jacket. Threading his way through the gardenia bushes, he made his way to the kitchen.

The black cat was on lazy guard before the door. The upper panel was ajar. There was no trace of Herminia or Sarita, but he assumed they weren't far away. Probably busy with housework, since the stove was hot and emitted the agreeable odor of burning wood. He stood there for a few seconds, considering whether to let them know of his arrival or simply to go look for the object he hoped to find. The door to the house stairs was open, so he went there.

He swiftly mounted the stairs, feeling like an intruder. Today, beneath the ashen sky, the central space wasn't lit by the wide beams of light that had so fascinated him during the first visit. The sullen light filtering through the high windows gave the marble the dull look of pewter and intensified his feeling of being unwelcome.

He counted the number of doors along the hallway twice to make sure of his destination, firmly gripped the icy doorknob and turned it. Before him appeared a sumptuously finished room that as Elisa had told him adjoined another. The door between them stood open. Expensive furniture chosen to last forever gave the child's bedroom a regal air. Like the chamber of some medieval prince, far too imposing for the antic existence of tiny Samuel the circus performer. The bedroom was scattered with toys, stuffed animals, fire trucks, and even a collection of toy motorcycles parked in a row along the dresser. It was obvious Samuel had slept with his mother ever since he was taken from the cradle. The traditionally furnished adjoining room was largely superfluous.

He located the display case on the dresser. On a blue silk cushion hung the ornate silver key set with sapphires around Samuel's engraved initials. He touched it and felt a shiver go up his back. The key was as icy cold as the doorknob. He held it in the palm of his hand for a moment or two, admiring the beauty of the artistry. He contemplated the macabre reality that the object had been crafted with the idea it would eventually be buried it with its owner. He put it in his pocket.

Just as he'd done with the doors along the hall, he counted the drawers to make sure he didn't open the wrong one. A black case was the only thing inside. He carefully unzipped it and found a sheaf of papers clipped together. Each bore the logo of a private clinic and provided a report of drug tests administered to Elisa Barreiro. They were in chronological order and went back to the final months of her pregnancy. The most recent was only a month old. The dowager marquess had been extremely demanding in her requirements, for Elisa had been tested for heroin, cannabis, cocaine, and even tranquilizers. All results were negative. He shut his eyes and heaved a sigh, feeling relief and a touch of shame at the memory of Elisa's offended look the previous evening.

Once outside, he raised the hood of Álvaro's jacket to shield himself from the rain as he hurried along the tree-sheltered walk to the church. There he was shielded from any surveillance from the manor, at least until he got to the churchyard. He tried Samuel's key in the lock of the massive wooden door of the church. At first it didn't seem to catch, and he wondered briefly if perhaps the jeweled silver key was merely symbolic, not crafted for the ancient lock. He pushed it in as far as it would go; twisting it, he felt the antique spring mechanism move and heard the echo of the click of yielding springs. The door opened.

Before entering he looked behind him and caught sight of a large black umbrella moving in his direction. Beneath it was Alfredo, the old gardener who'd served as gravedigger. The man raised a hand in a gesture that was both a greeting and a definite command to wait for him. Manuel tested the knob to make sure that it would remain unlocked. He slipped Samuel's key into his pocket.

"Good morning, señor," the man called out as he approached.

"Please call me Manuel," he responded and extended his hand.

The gardener took it in a firm grip. "All right then, Manuel. I was wondering if you could give me a moment." He looked back toward the path through the trees and peered toward the high windows of the manor visible above the treetops. "I tried to say something on the day of the funeral when you were standing by the grave."

Manuel nodded, recollecting. He'd had the impression the man was about to speak that day. It had slipped his mind afterward.

The gardener looked again toward the manor windows. "Perhaps we could have a word inside?" He jutted his chin toward the church door.

Manuel pushed the door open and gestured. It felt odd to be inviting someone into a place where he felt he himself had no right to be.

The gardener shut the door and made sure it clicked into place. Manuel played the host by inviting him to take a seat in the rearmost pew.

Perhaps the gloom inside the church called for quiet; the man spoke in a whisper. But his voice was firm. "I knew Álvaro from when he was a little boy. Well, I knew all the brothers, but I had a particularly good relationship with him. Santiago is like his father. He treats others, everyone, as if they're inferiors; and Fran, though he was a good boy, had his own ways. But Álvaro always took time to chat with me; he'd even offer to help out when he saw I had a lot to do."

Manuel nodded, beginning to feel that perhaps all the man wanted was the opportunity to present his condolences.

"I do all sorts of work here on the estate. Most of the jobs are fairly agreeable, but certainly the hardest of them is to serve as gravedigger. I don't do it alone those times when unfortunately it becomes necessary. I call in several of the tenant farmers to help. But I'm in charge, and I make sure it's done right. The day the old marquis was buried, Fran didn't go back to the manor; he stayed there, sitting on the ground next to the grave as I filled it in, one shovelful at a time. I sent away the other workers and I stayed behind as long as I could, because I didn't want to leave him there alone. He didn't complain at that, maybe because he knew that I didn't have any choice. I felt I had to be there. He didn't cry. He'd stopped that the moment we lowered the coffin into the ground, but there was something in his expression that was a thousand times worse. I can't really put it into words; it broke my heart.

"And then I saw Álvaro come down the road. He sat down on the ground beside his brother, and for a few minutes they were quiet together. Then Álvaro spoke. And the words he said to his brother were more beautiful than any I've ever heard. I'm no good at expressing myself; I don't have his gift, and I couldn't tell you exactly how he said it. But he spoke about what it meant to be a son, what it meant to hold a father's hand, that love was greater than any other power, and about knowing it would never be lost, and he also talked about what it means to be a father. He said that life was offering Fran a new opportunity, that the child his woman was carrying was his chance to become a father, to create for that child the love and caring he'd received his whole life long. And he added that Fran's child was a sign, a promise of good things, and an opportunity to do things right."

Manuel nodded slowly, recognizing the words that Fran had repeated to Lucas just a few hours later.

"Little by little his expression changed as he listened to his brother. Then Fran said, 'I think you're right'; and he said, 'I'm glad you're here, Álvaro, because I'm worried. Something terrible is happening in our family, and I can't help feeling responsible, because I know that when all is said and done, I'm the one that brought the demon into our house.' That's when the rain started, and Álvaro convinced him to go on talking here, in the church." The man looked toward the altar, where despite the gloom and the scant leaden light that filtered through the tiny windows high up just beneath the ceiling, the chapel's decorations of gold leaf gleamed. He turned to meet Manuel's gaze. "I'm telling you this because I know you're the head of the family now, and I believe you need to know that despite everything I've heard and whatever they may say, Fran didn't kill himself. And Álvaro had nothing to do with his death."

Manuel blinked in surprise, taken aback. Not for a moment had it occurred to him that the suspicions about Álvaro's role might be so widely held.

"The day Álvaro pointed the shotgun at his father, everyone on the estate was there and saw it. The worst part of it was that his own parents were the ones to spread the rumor the boy was dangerous," the man went on. "What do you think happened after his own father called him a murderer in front of everybody?

"The old marquis adored Fran, but everyone knew his mother couldn't stand the boy. And then when he came back with his pregnant girlfriend, you could see the smoke rising from her ears. You know what she calls her grandson?" Manuel closed his eyes and nodded in pain. "When after the old man's death Fran started acting in such a strange way, we all thought his mother was bound to throw him out soon. Or even worse. An estate is like a whorehouse; there are no secrets. As for me, you'll understand from what I've said that I'm long-suffering; I have sharp ears and an excellent memory."

Manuel said goodbye to Alfredo at the church door. He watched the gardener set off toward the path under the shelter of his black umbrella. Manuel turned back toward the church interior, after first closing the door and making sure it was locked.

The tiled floor amplified the sound of his footsteps, reflecting them to the vaulted ceiling as he walked to the altar. He noticed the tiny red lamp flickering in the chapel. He used the flashlight app of his cell phone and took a close look at the altar monstrance. The carved central panel was dedicated to Saint Clara, perhaps an evocation of the original name of the estate. On either side stood candelabra of antique silver, elaborately crafted and more than three feet tall, each supported by four massive metal feet. Manuel put a finger to the core shaft of one candelabrum and gave it a push. It didn't budge, for it was indeed extremely heavy.

A low door to one side of the main altar led to the sacristy. He had to stoop to enter. The interior was entirely of wood. Even the ceiling was covered with elegant wood paneling, almost certainly chestnut. There were no windows. He found the light switches behind the gray metal panel of a switch box incongruous in that setting. Each was labeled. He flipped the one for the sacristy; he bent to look out through the low door to make sure that none of the other lights had come on.

A heavy wooden table stood in the center of the sacristy space, surrounded by chairs upholstered in red. A row of heavy wooden lockers, chest high, ran all the way along one wall. On the table was a relatively stark reproduction of the main altar along with several sets of liturgical chalices and patens.

He checked the interior of each locker. One contained heavy boxes, some of which were difficult to open. He found paraffin candles and votive lights, reserved no doubt for special occasions; matches, lighters, and a collection of antique candle snuffers. Another of the lockers contained religious images, missals, and various Bibles—both for personal use and for the mass—and fine altar linens wrapped individually in clear plastic bags. The next locker was used to store large glass vases.

The last locker in the row appeared empty, but he was intrigued to note that it wasn't as deep as the others. He had to kneel in order to determine that the rear panel was, in fact, hinged, with a keyhole. Bright scratches on the metal showed it had been recently opened. He worked a finger into the keyhole and pulled, but nothing happened.

He turned his attention to a clothes locker with a collection of white vestments; an upper compartment held a colorful collection of chasubles, the outermost clerical garments, all carefully folded. And nothing else.

He knelt once more before the locker with the false back. He rapped softly and heard it was indeed hollow. He rose again and left the sacristy. He spent some minutes inspecting every inch of the floor beneath the pews, working his way eventually back to the main altar. He set his phone against the altarpiece.

With great care he placed one of the candelabra on its side and looked for the silversmith's mark, almost always placed in some concealed part of the artwork. This smith's chosen mark was a star somewhat resembling an asterisk, the points of which expanded into shapes that looked like ax blades. He set his cell phone camera to macro mode and took several photos. He did the same with the other candelabrum.

He checked his contact list and telephoned Griñán. The administrator's amiable voice greeted him immediately. "Good morning, señor Ortigosa. To what do I owe the pleasure?"

Manuel smiled, reproaching himself for his own susceptibility to the administrator's affable manner. "Griñán, do you remember you told me there'd been a theft from the church not long ago?"

"Yes, I don't know what the world is coming to. Somehow nobody was looking when someone got in and carried off two very valuable ancient silver candelabra. We don't know exactly when, but it came to light as they were preparing for the mass for the holy day of Saint Clara, patron of the church. As I explained, the church is opened only for special occasions."

"Yes, I do remember that. And you said Santiago moved heaven and earth to locate similar ones."

"Correct. He took personal initiative in replacing them as soon as possible. He found others that were very similar. Of course, they weren't as valuable as the originals."

"How do you know they were less valuable?"

"Because I authorized the payment, and they cost only a couple of hundred euros. And that's not taking into account the historical and artistic value of the originals; the silver alone was worth more than a hundred and fifty euros per pound. And they were very heavy."

"I assume they were insured."

"Yes, of course. We maintain a detailed record of all the estate's artworks. They're inventoried every other year. And the record is updated for each new acquisition."

"That leads me to suppose you'd have photographs of the stolen candelabra so you could make an insurance claim."

"Yes, of course. Although in that case don Santiago preferred not to file a claim; he was concerned they might increase the premiums, since only a few months earlier don Santiago lost a watch for which we did file a claim."

"Do you know if the theft was reported to the police?"

"Well . . . I suppose so."

Manuel said nothing for a few seconds. As he took time to reflect, he was aware of the unease of the administrator on the other end of the line.

"Listen, Griñán, I need you to do me a favor and to be very discreet about it." He added the caution more as a warning than anything else, and he knew Griñán understood as much from the tone of the man's reply.

"Of course. You can be sure of that."

"Get me copies of the photos of the stolen candelabra and the invoice for the new ones that were purchased."

The long silence that followed confirmed to him that the administrator was dying to ask him why; but the man replied only, "I'll take care of it personally. Right away—but it might take me a while."

"Griñán . . . I'll do my best to express my appreciation." Manuel ended the call. He didn't need to see the administrator to know that the man's face had just lit up.

He returned the candelabrum to its original position, and then on a sudden hunch he returned to the sacristy, knelt before the locker with the false back, and put Samuel's key into the lock. It fit perfectly, with none of the looseness he'd noted in the lock of the church door. He turned it entirely around and heard springs cede as the door opened. He was annoyed with himself for not having thought of it earlier. It was logical that such a ceremonially significant key would serve as the master for all the church locks. He pocketed the key again and put his fingertips into the gap to pull the door open, for there was no handle.

A round bundle of smooth fabric fell out of the locker. Its brilliant red reminded him of a theater curtain, but when he extracted it he saw a zipper and realized it was a sleeping bag. Just behind it were two glasses and a couple of bottles of unopened wine someone had carefully placed on their sides to keep the corks moist, a packet of wet wipes, a package of condoms, and a piece of carefully folded cloth. At first he didn't know what it was, but when he took it in hand he recognized it instantly. It was the cloth Santiago had been pressing to his face when Manuel saw him weeping alone in the church. The shiny fabric slipped between his fingers with the silken feel of lingerie. He raised it to his face and caught the smell of masculine perspiration and perfume. The fabric was still wet with Santiago's tears.

He laid out all these things on the floor and photographed them from various angles. He returned them to their cache within the locker and folded the chemise. After a moment's thought he opened the adjoining locker, took one of the linen altar cloths out of its protective bag, and used the bag for the garment instead. He folded the packet into a small tight anonymous shape and tucked it beneath his shirt.

He buttoned his jacket and closed the locker door. He turned off all the lights and left.

A SCHEME

The rain had lowered the temperature to the point it seemed almost chilly outside. Even so, Manuel chose to wait at one of the tables on the inn's exterior terrace, half-sheltered by the porch awning and the shabby parasol they always left open no matter what the weather. He'd come back hoping to see Elisa and Samuel, but the innkeeper told him a young man had called for them and they'd gone away with him. He found the door to the adjoining room open when he entered his room. The sweet smells of soap and baby oil hovered in the air, and for the first time since his arrival in Galicia, he felt welcomed into this space. That sensation was reinforced by the sight of a shopping bag with child's clothing left on the chair and tiny sneakers neatly set before the window; even more welcoming was the note Elisa had left on his bed saying they'd see him later. She'd signed it simply *Kisses from Elisa and Samuel*.

Manuel's phone sat before him on the terrace table—he'd checked the volume for the third time to make sure it was at maximum—along with the inevitable bar snack. Today they'd served a beef-stuffed fritter along with a steaming cup of coffee that was cooling rapidly. Through the thin vapor rising from his coffee he saw Lucas and Nogueira walk up. The priest took a seat next to him and Nogueira went into the bar to order. The lieutenant said nothing until everything had been served. Then he took out a document and handed it to Manuel.

"What's this?" Manuel asked. He was disconcerted by the sight of Álvaro's handwriting.

"It's the accident report form for Álvaro's car insurance. The prior tells me, and he's backed up by half a dozen monks ready to swear to it, that when Álvaro backed his car out after the discussion at the seminary, he accidentally hit the pickup parked there. They say he filled out the report and left. It seems to be in order; if you recognize his writing and signature, it explains the paint from the pickup we found on Álvaro's car."

Manuel nodded, his eyes fixed on the piece of paper. "That's his writing. But it doesn't prove the prior didn't kill his nephew or Álvaro. Just as you said, things could have taken some other course, some other sequence of events."

Nogueira chomped down on his fritter. "The prior took a call when he was standing at the door to his sister's house. I checked his phone's call history. One of the monks at the monastery had a minor accident. He's an old man, and he spent the whole night at the emergency room, and the prior was there with him. It's a public space with lots of video cameras, so it'll be easy to confirm his presence. You already know that Laura works at the hospital; I asked her to check, and the nurses remember him. He was there from five in the afternoon until the next morning."

"And so . . . ?"

"So unless we can find other evidence, that excludes the prior as a suspect in Álvaro's murder." He sighed and added, "And he couldn't have killed his own nephew either."

"I thought they hadn't been able to establish the exact time of Toñino's death," Lucas said.

"Ophelia just called. When they searched the boy's car the crime techs found one of those paper bags for Burger King carryout. There's one nearby that's open twenty-four hours, and the receipt inside the bag shows he bought it at 2:30 a.m."

"By which time Álvaro was already dead!"

"The techs are reviewing the video recordings from the drive-in to make sure that it was Toñino who picked up the food and not someone else. Cameras at places like that are generally of pretty good quality, as a safeguard against robberies. If the boy was captured on video, Álvaro can't be a suspect in his killing."

Lucas was confused. "Did you say 'someone else'?"

"I'm no expert on fast food, but my colleagues say it was a meal for two: two drinks, two hamburgers, a double serving of fries."

"Was he with someone?"

"That seems the most likely possibility. But instead of making up stories, let's wait for confirmation from the video."

Lucas nodded and looked at Manuel. "You see? I said we should trust our instinct. Álvaro was not a murderer."

Nogueira didn't share his elation. "I went back to talk to Rosa María's neighbor. She now recalls that at one o'clock that night she got up to take a pill and noticed Toñino's car parked in front of his house, and it drove off not too much later. That further excludes Álvaro, but as long as she's not confused about the time, it would also exonerate Toñino from any involvement in Álvaro's death. He couldn't have been in two places at the same time, and there's more than thirty miles between the site of Álvaro's accident and the aunt's house in Os Martiños. I think we'll have to call on señora Rosa María again; right now she's not at home. Her attentive neighbor tells me that she's at the funeral home sitting with the body of her nephew. The funeral is this afternoon. I think we can pay her a visit afterward to see if she can explain why she hid from us the fact that Toñino came back late at night and went out again, probably for a meeting with whoever killed him."

"She might not know," Lucas suggested. "She could have been asleep."

"After the confrontation with the boy's uncle and the boy's sudden departure, I doubt it. She herself said that she couldn't sleep whenever she was worried about him, and I certainly believe her."

Manuel appeared to accept that. He turned to the priest. "You went to the hospital this morning, didn't you? How was Santiago?"

"He was asleep, so I couldn't speak to him. I felt truly sorry for Catarina. She hasn't budged from his side since he was admitted yesterday. She's devastated. She told me Santiago was unconscious when the boy found him. They pumped his stomach as soon as they got him to the emergency room, and some of the pills were only partly dissolved; but the doctor estimates that he must have taken many more earlier. Those had broken down and were being absorbed. The man had to face too much in too little time: his father's death, Fran's death, and then, just as things were starting to stabilize, Álvaro's death, Catarina's pregnancy, and he . . . Well, we'd always had an idea that he was weak and unstable. All this just proves how vulnerable he is."

"Is there any possibility it wasn't attempted suicide?" asked Manuel. "Could he somehow have taken the pills by accident?"

"I'm afraid not. There's something you don't know. Yesterday afternoon before he took the pills, Santiago called me. I suppose it must have been while we were on the road between Malpica and Corme, where there's no cell phone coverage, since he got my voice mail and left a message. He wanted me to hear his confession."

"You think he was trying to reconcile himself before he tried to kill himself?" Manuel asked. "I thought that's something no devout Catholic would do."

"I know what I said about Fran's behavior, and I haven't changed my mind. That young man didn't commit suicide. But Santiago is different. What we learned yesterday fills out the picture of someone who was extremely vulnerable."

Manuel's phone buzzed and vibrated against the tabletop. It was Griñán. Manuel quickly picked up, answered, listened, and then ended the call. There was a ding, indicating he'd received a message. He opened it and placed the phone in front of Nogueira and Lucas so they could see the image.

"Do you both remember what I said about there having been a theft from the As Grileiras church about a month ago?"

"Yes," said Nogueira. "The fact that Toñino had the key strongly suggests that he had something to do both with Fran's death and with the disappearance of those silver antiques."

Manuel enlarged the screen image of the silversmith's mark. "Griñán told me that Santiago used his own funds to replace the stolen candelabra. Silversmiths have very distinctive hallmarks, like this one." He tapped the image, somewhat like an asterisk, with which the smith had signed his work. "So I asked Griñán to provide the photos they took of the originals for the inventory and insurance. I was sure whoever did the inventory would have recorded the mark. Antiquities are valued far more highly for the artist and the age of the piece than for the mere value of the metal." He then tapped his photo app. "I was in the church this morning, and I took several pictures of the ones that are there now." He again held out the phone. "Compare these with these photos taken for the insurance policy." He alternately displayed the photo app and the text attachments.

The two men studied the photos and looked up in amazement.

Nogueira took the phone in hand and looked closer at the silversmith marks. "They're identical!" Nogueira looked first at Lucas and then at Manuel.

Manuel leaned back in his chair with a smile as he took a sip of his coffee. It was cold. "Because they're the same candelabra."

Lucas shrugged and threw up his hands. "Are you sure?"

"At first I wasn't. I thought maybe the original set had included four candelabra and Santiago had somehow managed to locate the other two. But the certificate of authenticity submitted to the insurance company with the photos is very clear. The master craftsman created a single pair." He pointed to the screen. "This pair."

"You think Santiago faked a robbery so he could defraud the insurance company? And then after collecting he put the original pair back in place? That's a typical insurance scam," Nogueira responded.

"No, I think they really were stolen, and Santiago knew who did it. That's why he didn't go to the police or to the insurance company." Manuel was relishing the look of confusion on his friends' faces. "He managed to get to the thief, and he bought them back. Álvaro hadn't been at As Grileiras since early July, and the candelabra turned up missing in mid-August, so Álvaro hadn't seen the new ones. But as soon as he did, he knew something was wrong with that tale about a theft. He went into the kitchen and accused Santiago in front of Herminia: 'Who do you think you're fooling with this story about the candelabra?'"

"Why would Santiago do such a thing?" Lucas asked.

"Obvious. He was protecting someone." Nogueira stared at Manuel. "Someone very important to him."

Manuel nodded. "He was protecting his lover, the person he'd been meeting in the church sacristy for some time, the person he suspected of the theft." He took his phone back from Nogueira and swiped again until he came to the photo showing the contents of the sacristy locker.

"A hooker?" Nogueira asked, raising a hand to his mouth in astonishment. "Sorry, Lucas, but it's obvious. This is a fuck pad."

"In the church . . ." murmured Lucas, scandalized.

"It was the perfect place. No one would disturb them there. As you know, family tradition dictates that only the males of the family have the key to the church, and it's buried with them when they die. The old marquis had his, Fran lost his, and Álvaro provided his own so that it could be buried with Fran. That accounts for three. Only little Samuel's was left, and that's the one I used. But until now it has been kept in a display case, and Santiago knew that Elisa would never use it. That reduced the count of the remaining keys to only one, his own."

"So let's suppose he wasn't meeting a prostitute, since after all he was going to the roadhouse once a week or so; he'd just gotten his wife pregnant; and in addition it looks like he was having an ongoing relationship with some other woman—good God, what a sex drive!" the cop exclaimed. Manuel laughed out loud at that while Lucas tried to hold an expression of disapproval. "My hero!"

"No, not a prostitute. Not at all," Manuel continued, despite the interruption. "Someone who'd been seen by many, a regular at the estate. By Damián, by Herminia. The person Fran saw by the church, the reason he got so upset. That's what Fran hinted at in his confession, Lucas. He wasn't entirely certain by then, but he did suspect something terrible was going on, so much so that he told Álvaro that day by their father's grave. The gravedigger overheard them." He paused. "When you told Álvaro that Fran was terribly upset, Álvaro thought you knew. Fran had drawn the obvious conclusion: the dealer was lurking around the estate because he was going to meet a client. Maybe Fran saw them meet or go into the church together." Manuel's face was grim. "Fran blamed himself for allowing a demon access to their home. Richie told us Toñino still had business at As Grileiras, so we thought he meant drugs. I even began to think Álvaro might be involved. But Toñino wasn't selling drugs; or at least that wasn't all he was doing. 'You don't kill the cow if it's still giving milk.' Remember?"

Nogueira stared at him but said nothing. He was thinking. Manuel saw disbelief and acceptance contesting one another in his eyes. The policeman's expression darkened with gathering suspicion. "The lock hadn't been forced," he said.

Manuel nodded. "And Santiago wouldn't have left the church door open."

"No, I don't think so."

Nogueira said it. "Santiago knew immediately who'd done it: the only person who didn't need to break in because he had a key. And he had it because Santiago had given it to him."

Manuel nodded again. "Toñino. That's why he still had it on him."

Too agitated to sit still, Nogueira got to his feet to light a cigarette. He looked around as if seeking somewhere to go, but the rain steadily falling beyond the awning offered no escape. He was limited to the sheltered space beneath the umbrella. Seeking some release for his nervous tension, he resorted to shifting his weight from one foot to another as he stood there smoking.

"Even so," Lucas responded, "they've been trying for some time to conceive, and his wife was pregnant. You two told me that he goes every week to that roadhouse."

"Right, and he has to stoke himself up with drugs to get through it," Nogueira said, remembering what he'd learned from one of the women at the pickup joint.

Lucas couldn't believe it. "Manuel, are you sure of all this?"

Manuel reached into his jacket and took out the parcel wrapped in plastic. He unwrapped it before their eyes.

"Along with the sleeping bag, the wineglasses, and the condoms, I found this," he said. He shook out the garment and placed it in a heap on the table.

Nogueira took it in his hands and lifted it to see it better. As he stretched the woven garment it unfolded completely, and Nogueira found that what had at first looked like a woman's camisole was actually a man's sleeveless undershirt, the garment commonly worn by waiters in low-life bars.

"Shit!" the lieutenant exclaimed in disgust and dropped it on the table. "It's from some man and it's all wet!"

"With tears," Manuel replied. "Santiago was terribly upset and sobbing into it the day I saw him in the church. I thought it was because of his brother's death." He remembered his feeling of sympathy for such suffering. "He'd probably been secluding himself in the church to give free rein to his grieving, greater with each passing day after Toñino disappeared. I asked Griñán for a copy of the bill from the place where Santiago bought back the candelabra. An antique dealer in Santiago de Compostela. If the store owner identifies him, we'll have something to go on."

"Santiago and Toñino," whispered Lucas, bewildered. "I'd never have imagined such a thing."

"It seems to me, my friend the priest, that you're forgetting the most important point. I don't give a shit if Santiago was getting it on with Toñino; what I want to know is how the boy got the key. Maybe he stole it from Fran or maybe Santiago gave it to him, but one thing's for sure: the two were mixed up in this together. Elisa saw Santiago by the church the night Fran died, and she persuaded him not to go in. The fact that Toñino lifted things from the church wasn't a reason for him to walk around with the key. Even less so if it implicated him in Fran's murder. But now I understand why he had it—it was the key to his love nest."

"But Elisa saw Fran lock the church from the inside," Lucas objected.

"She saw someone, but the light was dim, so it could have been Toñino. Maybe they heard her coming, and Santiago went out to talk to her while his lover administered the dose that finished Fran off."

Lucas refused that interpretation. "I find that hard to believe. You have no idea how much Santiago was affected by the death of his brother. He fell into a terrible depression."

"Yeah, it must be fucking awful to do away with your own brother; regretting it afterward is the least you can do," the cop commented. "And besides, Álvaro asked me that day if Fran's death seemed normal to me; it occurred to me he might be asking because maybe he had something to do with it. Now I believe Álvaro suspected Fran's death might have been very convenient for someone. Let's not forget there were family members who found him hard to bear."

Both Manuel and Lucas nodded, considering that thought.

Nogueira waved a hand at the table. "I already paid inside. Send me a copy of that photo of the silversmith mark and let's go call on that antique dealer." He looked down at the fritters that had been served to Lucas and Manuel. They were untouched. "You're not going to eat those?"

Lucas, who'd already stepped away toward the parking lot, turned, took Nogueira by the arm, and escorted him away from the table. "Let's go! It'd be better for you to have a heart-to-heart talk with your wife, unless you're looking for a heart attack to make her a widow."

Manuel looked back in alarm at Nogueira. Did Lucas know something about his marital difficulties?

The lieutenant shrugged. "There you go. Six years of keeping it a secret, and in a single week I spill it twice."

Manuel nodded. "I agree with Lucas. Laura's the one you should be talking to."

"Oh, yeah, right! Right! *Carallo*, I will, but you have to admit it's a shame to leave those behind on the table." He took one last regretful look at the snacks but then stepped out into the rain.

⚜

Rúa do Pan was close to the cathedral. The shop interior was well lit and the business appeared prosperous. Two very young women were attending to the tourists in the front of the shop with displays of postcards, rosaries, and vials of holy water. The pilgrims' cheap rain ponchos resembled colorful garbage bags and made them look ridiculous.

Any visitor who happened to get past the storefront piles of cheap tourist knickknacks would encounter a more serious collection of antiquities. While the clerks fetched the proprietor from the back, Manuel looked over the articles on display. Nothing really appealed to him.

The owner, a thin man in his seventies, went directly to Lucas. "Good day, Father, how can I help you? Are you looking for any particular liturgical object? We're specialists here, and if you don't see it on display, we may have it in the storeroom. If I don't have it, I can get it the same day."

Lucas, who wasn't wearing his clerical collar, shook his head, surprised and discomfited.

Nogueira held up his cell phone with the photo. "How about you get us a pair of stolen silver candelabras?"

Manuel was amused to find Lucas immediately recognizable as a priest even without his collar, while the way Nogueira had thrust the phone into the face of the owner made it perfectly clear that he was a policeman.

The man heaved a sigh and put a finger to his lips in a plea for discretion. "Come with me." He indicated a door in the rear. He waited until he'd closed it behind them before he spoke. "I curse the day I trusted that fellow and bought the candelabra. They've been nothing but trouble."

Nogueira wasn't having it. "That's to be expected when you fence stolen goods."

"I hope that's not how you see me. Look, the boy swore they belonged to his family, and I had no reason to doubt him. He'd sold me something before, and there'd been no problem."

"A gold watch," Manuel interjected, much to the surprise of his companions. "Several months ago Santiago thought he'd lost his watch. He made an insurance claim, but he might have suspected something. And later when the candelabra disappeared, he was sure. Toñino finally told him where they'd gone. Santiago came here and recovered them. That's why they didn't file an insurance claim. He didn't want to get Toñino into trouble. Or maybe he was worried that the boy might tell them more than he should."

The owner accepted that version. "I don't usually deal in such articles, but I accepted it because it came from a client. I had no reason to doubt him, and that time there were no problems."

"I assume that he gave you proof of ownership?" Nogueira inquired.

"He gave me his word. Or perhaps you have the receipt for his watch?"

Nogueira gave the man an icy look that made him regret his impertinence.

"And who was the client who recommended him?"

"At the moment I don't recall. That was a long time ago. However, my custom is to hold a particularly valuable object back for a reasonable time before I put it out for sale. Just in case."

"Just in case it's hot," Nogueira said.

Lucas and Manuel gave him an uncomprehending look.

"He waits for a while just in case the police come asking about it or something in the papers suggests it might have been stolen. Standard practice among these appraiser guys."

The man clearly didn't appreciate Nogueira's explanation. "Well, there was no time for that with the candelabra. A man turned up two days later and claimed to be the owner. At first I pretended ignorance, to see if he was lying, but there was no doubt about it. He gave me a detailed description both of the articles and also of the boy who'd brought them in. He said he knew I had them. He wasn't looking to make trouble; he said he'd pay me whatever I'd given the boy, plus a premium for my trouble. All legal and aboveboard. He even insisted I make out an invoice."

Nogueira held up his cell phone with a picture of Santiago. "This him?"

The proprietor nodded. "He was a real gentleman, one of those with whom it's a pleasure to do business. And later, when I thought that at last I'd escaped the pernicious influence of those damned candelabra, along came another man asking about them."

"Another man?" Nogueira echoed him.

"Yes. When I saw him enter the shop, at first I thought it was the same gentleman. I don't see very well without my spectacles, you understand? I should wear them all the time, but I actually use them only for reading. When he got closer, I realized that though there was a certain resemblance, it wasn't the same man at all."

This time Manuel was the one to hold up a cell phone. With a picture of Álvaro.

"Yes, that's him. He was asking the same questions as you gentlemen: Who sold them to me? Who bought them back? And he showed me a photo too; and he was just as generous as the first gentleman. All he wanted was information. I gave it to him."

"What day was that?"

"A Saturday. Two weeks ago, I believe."

They forgot the antique dealer and exchanged glances. He peered from one to another of them.

"You knew that?" Nogueira asked Manuel.

"I suspected it last night. When I asked Elisa for the key, she told me Álvaro requested it the morning he arrived at the manor."

"Do you think he discovered the same things in the sacristy that you did?" Nogueira asked.

"I'm sure of it. And he needed to come here to confirm it, just as we have. He'd heard of Fran's fears before his brother died, and maybe for a while he dismissed them. But he was no fool. If he suspected there was something unusual about Fran's death, he was going to connect the dots. The blackmailer was the one his brother saw prowling around the church."

They went out and found the sky heavy with rain clouds. They made their way with some difficulty through the tourists who crowded the noisy streets around the cathedral. Nogueira checked his phone as they avoided tour groups trailing after their guides. Four thick heavy drops of rain were all the warning they got of the sudden downpour. It burst upon them, prompting cries and curses from tourists, who scrambled to shelter in doorways along the streets of Santiago de Compostela. The three men opened their umbrellas and quickened their steps up the center of the suddenly empty street. The rain was pounding down by the time they reached the parking lot. They tossed soaking umbrellas into the trunk and jumped into the car. The roar of rain against the roof was deafening. Manuel started the engine and turned on both the wipers and the windshield defogger, for the windows had misted over. Nogueira's phone rang. They sat in the motionless vehicle as he listened intently, thanked the caller, and then broke the connection.

"This is good news, Manuel," Nogueira said, waving his cell phone. "That was Ophelia. Her colleagues confirmed that the Burger King video clearly shows

Toñino at 2:28 a.m. He was alone and showed no signs of contusions or bleeding. Whoever beat him and killed him did it later, so Álvaro's excluded as a suspect both for the beating and for the murder. Because Álvaro was already dead by then. It doesn't clear Toñino of Álvaro's murder, though it's fairly unlikely that he would commit such a crime and then drive around for two hours and buy hamburgers as if nothing had happened. That'd require someone very cold and controlled; and believe me, that doesn't fit Toñino's character at all—he tended more toward the hysterical type—nor does it correspond to his behavior in the video. So we're back to someone unknown who first killed Álvaro and then murdered Toñino, most likely with the same weapon, just two hours apart. They estimate it's twenty minutes from Burger King to the place where they found the boy's body."

Manuel nodded, his face serious, but then smiled in relief when he sensed the weight of Lucas's hand on his shoulder. He said nothing, as if the rhythm of the windshield wipers had hypnotized him.

"Are you all right, Manuel?" asked Lucas.

"There's one other thing I can't figure out. It has to do with the other night. You told me Santiago called you to go with him to the hospital, because they'd just advised him his brother had been in a traffic accident."

"That's right."

"Did he say they told him there'd been an accident, or did they tell him Álvaro was dead?"

"That there'd been an accident. It wasn't until we got to the hospital they told us he'd died. I'll never forget the expression on Santiago's face."

"What time did he phone?"

"Five thirty in the morning. I picked him up at the manor house at six. We used my car. He told me he was too upset to drive. That didn't surprise me."

"You said that when you accompanied him to the hospital, you noticed that his hands were swollen. You even insisted he should let you to take him to a doctor."

"Yes; well, you know, that's how he reacts. He draped his overcoat over his right arm and hand. I saw that he was injured, but he covered it up and didn't want to talk about it. It was only later I learned what had happened."

"But Herminia told me he came into the kitchen when he got back from the hospital. She said that's when he punched the wall—when he told her Álvaro was dead."

"That means his hand must have been injured before he went to the hospital," Lucas said, suddenly aware of the inconsistencies in the story.

"But he wasn't yet aware his brother was dead."

Lucas hesitated, frowned, and obviously examined the possibilities, shaking his head each time he discarded one. Finally he said, "I'm sure that his hand had already been hurt when we got to the hospital. I don't know if it was serious, because he didn't let me examine it."

"Remarkable, wasn't it, that he asked you to drive?" Nogueira added.

"For the love of God!" Lucas was in great distress.

Manuel sympathized. "When Santiago got back home he realized he had to manufacture an excuse for the unfortunate state of his hands, and he played out that farce for Herminia." Manuel remembered the bloodstains bleached out of the wall and imagined the intense pain those blows must have inflicted. Perhaps very little faking was required.

"Well," said Nogueira, "so we know who bashed Toñino's face in. Which hand had the plaster cast?"

"The right one," replied Manuel, remembering the moment they'd shaken hands at Álvaro's funeral.

"All right, then. That corresponds with the trajectory of the blows to Toñino's face. It was Santiago; and Santiago might have killed him as well."

"Ophelia was suggesting the stab wounds could have been made by a left-handed assailant."

"Or by someone who had to use his left hand, because he'd already injured his right," the lieutenant countered. "If you think about it, that's very like Santiago: he's always been known for his fits of temper. Just the other day he slammed his fist into a wall while he was arguing with Manuel. And the Burger King visit fits as well. Who else could Toñino have been buying food for? He had a date with his lover."

Manuel remembered the Raven's tale of Santiago destroying his toys and then weeping over them for hours. Was that what he'd seen in the church? A spoiled child crying over a broken toy? He was weeping for a dead lover. And maybe for his dead brother or for his victims.

Lucas seemed very downcast. Nogueira raised a quizzical eyebrow.

Lucas's expression was compassionate. "It's horrible to think that someone may have lived like that his whole life. Pretending."

"I believe that the blackmail attempt made him lose control of the situation. We know the origins of his pain. For most of his life he hid the truth about what happened that night in the seminary. I think Álvaro told Toñino he wasn't going to pay and he didn't care If It came out that he'd killed a rapist while defending his brother. He had nothing to be ashamed of. But things were different for Santiago. He'd spent his whole life trying to please his mother and father, doing his best to play the perfect son, trying to distinguish himself from Álvaro. He couldn't bear the idea of what he saw coming. After he kills Álvaro he arranges a meeting with Toñino to try to convince him not to use the information, but Toñino refuses and that sends him off the deep end."

"Maybe," Lucas responded. "But I don't believe Toñino really intended to make it public. There's a big difference between making threats to get money and actually carrying them out. I think Toñino knew that sort of information is valuable only if it's kept secret. If the truth came out, his uncle would go to jail. His aunt would see that as a terrible disgrace, and he himself could wind up in prison for blackmail. If Santiago had intended to kill him, he could have done it any time after Toñino asked for money. Álvaro wouldn't necessarily have ever found out. And look at what Santiago just tried to do. For the love of God! He's tried to kill himself. The man is suffering."

"Look here, priest, I know a lot about suicides and confessions," Nogueira replied. "Plenty of times a suicide is as good as a confession, at least in my experience."

"And it takes two weeks for that sense of guilt to overwhelm him? Fifteen days after killing Álvaro and Toñino, and three years after killing Fran?"

Nogueira was indignant. "And what's so impossible about that? Fran told both Álvaro and you of his suspicions. Do you find it so improbable that Fran might have directly asked Santiago? Couldn't he have said he knew Santiago was sneaking off to get it on with his dealer-hustler in the sacristy? How long do you think it would have taken Fran to work out the truth? Fran was liberal and open by nature. His drug habit was already the cross he had to bear, and most likely he was pressing Santiago to confess. Santiago has been two-faced all his life, with lots of practice in lying. He lied to his own family, married a woman he couldn't love, had to take drugs to get it up to screw prostitutes to pretend to be a macho. He dragged his brother off to a whorehouse and forced him to go upstairs with a girl so nobody would suspect that he himself was gay. He must have been terrified someone might discover that. After the lengths he'd gone trying to conceal it, don't you think he'd do anything at all to keep up appearances? I told you from the beginning, these people are made of different stuff. For centuries this family has done whatever they damn well fucking please. And they still do, because for them only one thing counts: keeping their name unblemished, above anything else and at any price."

Manuel recalled Lucas's account of the pact with the devil the old marquis had proposed to Álvaro. Might he have offered the same deal to his second son? *Indulge in your vice with discretion so that nobody learns of it, and marry a girl from a good family.*

No, there was something in Santiago that seemed more like natural subjugation. Manuel saw it in that servile attitude the others described. He'd behaved like his father's lapdog, cowering, forever humiliated by the marquis, always trying to please but never succeeding. Could the trauma of that night in the seminary have been the reason he'd never come to terms with himself? Sexual abuses suffered in childhood disrupt the development of sexual identity and can leave an individual confused. It was clear Santiago had done all he could to make sure no one found out about his relationship with Toñino. But was that due to his own refusal to accept who he was, or had it been because of his ambition to have a role in his family? He'd seen from what happened to Álvaro that he'd face rejection if his own true nature came to light.

Nogueira regarded Lucas, who sat with his head hanging in misery. He became suddenly aware that he'd raised his voice. In fact, he'd been shouting. Sometimes he forgot whom he was talking to. He emptied his lungs and sought to calm himself. "Well, in any case, without evidence we still have nothing. Pure hypotheses. And I doubt Santiago will confess."

"I'm going to see him this afternoon," Manuel declared firmly. "I'll ask him."

Lucas looked up in sudden alarm. "Do you think that's a good idea?"

"I don't see any better way to get answers than by asking the person principally concerned."

Lucas appealed to the lieutenant. "Nogueira, aren't you going to say anything?"

"First we need to go call on Toñino's aunt. I hate to say so, but right now she's vulnerable, and if she knows something she might talk. And as for visiting

Santiago, it doesn't sound like such a bad idea, but don't for one minute even think about letting him know in advance."

Nogueira's telephone erupted in the closed confines of the vehicle.

"Hello, Ophelia," he said, looking over at his companions with a meaningful expression. "Yes. He's here with me . . ." He listened intently for several seconds. Then: "Terrific. I'm telling you, girl, you're a genius!" He ended the call. "Ophelia's hunch was right. You know we're checking Álvaro's phone calls, and I already told you about the numbers we found there. But while we were busy analyzing the records of his second phone, we neglected the calls from his regular personal phone. The last GPS position triangulated for Álvaro's telephone was when he called you fifty-seven minutes after midnight. He did it using his car's hands-free application, and right then he was at kilometer 37 on the highway to Lugo."

"What's there?"

"La Rosa. Our favorite roadhouse."

"He called me from there?" exclaimed Manuel. He didn't expect an answer.

"What did he tell you?" asked Nogueira.

"He said he was very tired. I remember he did sound tired. And very sad also, I don't know. It was strange, almost as if he had a premonition he wouldn't be returning."

Nogueira nodded, thoughtful. "My wife tells me that everyone facing imminent death is aware of it. It doesn't matter if it's cancer, a heart attack, or an earthquake. Or if he's going to get run over by a train. Laura says that they sense it a little ahead of time, their behavior changes, and they fall into a weird melancholy. A sort of acceptance of what's coming, as if they were about to begin a trip they can't postpone. And I guarantee you that nurses see lots of people die."

"Your wife is right," Lucas said. "I believe that too."

Nogueira looked at Manuel again. "Manuel, I'm very sorry, but the really important point is that if Álvaro called you from his car in that roadhouse parking lot, it was probably because he was there with Santiago. That would mean Santiago was the last person to see Álvaro alive. It directly implicates Santiago as a suspect."

"But we already asked your friend Nieves, and she said the last time Santiago was there was a week before Álvaro came back to Galicia. She wouldn't have forgotten something like that."

"Not if they went inside. But suppose they didn't?"

"Then what were they doing there?"

"Can you think of a better place for meeting a blackmailer than a crowded parking lot at a pickup joint out on the highway?"

"You think that's the place they picked to hand over the money?"

"It's a good place for it. Under surveillance but discreet at the same time, with an exit directly onto the highway and anywhere they wanted to go. I'm sure that's the place Santiago would choose."

Manuel heard in his mind Baby's comment about how vigilant the Mammoth was, making sure the girls didn't go out there for after-hours extra work, and he remembered the scrutiny the man had given him while he was waiting for Nogueira to come out. "If they were there, I have an idea who'd be sure to know."

"The Mammoth," Nogueira responded. He turned to Lucas. "Sorry about this, but tonight you'll have to stay home, priest. We're gonna go see a hooker."

"Several hookers," Manuel corrected him. "Plural. And I think we might go rattle Richie's cage again. There's something I want to ask him."

"I can wait in the car," Lucas replied in a dead-serious tone.

Manuel and Nogueira glanced at one another and burst out laughing. The tension that had been accumulating in the car suddenly dispersed. After a moment or two Lucas joined in. It occurred to him that the picture of the three of them laughing their heads off would probably be astonishingly similar to that of the three in tears together.

THE CROCODILE'S COLD HEART

Cars were parked along the road, pulled up onto the neighbor's graveled yard, or partly blocking the flagstone drive, but out of respect no one had parked directly in front of the narrow garage. The oil stain left by Toñino's car was still there; it cried out for attention like the blood left by Cain's murder of Abel. It gleamed with stark, grim rainbows in the wash of falling rain.

The gentle *orballo* during their previous visit was now a heavy rainfall, but the front door stood wide open. There was no awning to shelter it. They entered without knocking. About twenty people, mostly women, were in the kitchen and dining room. The prized dining-room table was covered with a cloth today, and for the first time the massive formal piece of furniture seemed appropriate in the crowded room. On it was an abundant spread of baked goods, meat fritters, and a couple of homemade cakes. Coffee cups from the elegant set of porcelain had been taken out of the sideboard for the occasion; several of the visitors had them in hand. Now several oil lamps stood before the image of the saint on the highly polished heavy wooden chest. Impassive within her shelter, the saint contemplated the mourning mortals.

Rosa María wore deep mourning. She sat surrounded by other women, some as old as she, all gaunt and severe. Declining the assistance offered as soon as she made a move to rise, Toñino's aunt got up, gave them a slight nod, left the group, and motioned to them. She went toward the rear of the house.

The bedroom was minuscule. The double bed, covered by a deep-purple comforter, was positioned against one wall, leaving just enough space for a dark little night table.

The old woman gestured to invite them to sit on the bed. She closed the door. Hanging behind it were various garments on clothes hangers; with the door shut their appearance was distressingly similar to that of a hanging human figure.

She stared at the hanging garments. "I'm getting help now from social services. A young woman comes to apply my eye drops, but she doesn't know where the clothes go. She just hangs things up here. They say soon they'll have someone who can stay longer." She turned to Nogueira. "Thank you for contacting them."

Nogueira made a little deprecating motion.

She pointed to the bed again, but they all remained standing, ill at ease and highly conscious of the awkward situation.

"I saw you go next door and figured she'd be telling you some story. That woman is always spying on the neighbors. Of course the poor thing has been all alone since her husband died, and that's going on eight years now. She seems to have been going downhill ever since." This thought appeared to worry her. She raised a trembling hand and covered her mouth.

She'd been weeping. Her features had the washed-out appearance deep grief leaves upon the skin. Her eyes, though red, looked healthier than they had during the previous visit. She dabbed at them constantly, wiping away secretions. Her cataract seemed not quite as milky.

"Yes, Toñino did come back that weekend. It was horrible, when my brother turned up that afternoon and said all those things. We do love one another, but we're always quarreling because of the child. He could never understand why I was so determined to protect him. But Toñino was tiny when his father died and his mother ran off. I tried to give him everything and took care of him the best I could. God knows I love him, and he loved me. My Toñino was a good boy." The woman fell silent and gave them a look of great dignity, as if daring them to contradict her.

Nogueira assented. "Of course he was, señora!"

She nodded in weary gratitude. "I was upset and worried, waiting for him to come back and explain. My brother was always going on about the boy, but I'd never seen him as upset as he was that day. I was afraid for Toñino. It was almost one in the morning when I heard his car. I stood there waiting for him. I'd been in such a fret I was too distracted to fix dinner. I was going to tell him he was putting me in a terrible fix, and I wanted to know if what his uncle said

413

was true. I never got a word out. He was beside himself. Maybe he wasn't my son, but I knew him better than anyone. I could always tell how he was feeling, just from the way he came into the house, and that night he was going to pieces. I had no chance to ask him, because he threw himself right into my arms, the way he used to do when he was little, and he said, 'Auntie, I made a mistake, I really screwed up.' I was dying inside."

The woman stopped speaking, and for a while she seemed to be studying something at Nogueira's feet. The men waited silently, hearing the growing murmurs of Rosa María's neighbors around the dining table through the thin panel of the door. She stood motionless. If she'd wept or at least covered her face, they'd have been less disturbed by her grief, but her listlessness and mute surrender were excruciating. Manuel gave Nogueira a questioning glance. The policeman's gesture in reply counseled patience.

The woman sighed. She looked around as if suddenly awakening. She was exhausted. Nogueira took her arm just as he had before and guided her the two steps to the bed. When she sat, Manuel heard the rustle of the corn husks in the old-fashioned mattress.

"'Auntie,' he told me, 'There's a man, a friend of mine . . . I found something at the seminary and I thought he'd be willing to buy it. He has lots of money, Auntie, so really he could have. I thought it would be okay. He was going to give me the money tonight, lots of it, but things got complicated. There's another man, a tough one, who said no. He's smart and he knew all about it. The same guy who went to the seminary and warned Uncle, and Uncle gave him my phone number. I thought everything was okay when Uncle left, but then that man called me. He was really angry, not afraid of anything or anybody. He threatened me, and I was surprised and scared. He hung up. But I was a fool, I see now, because I called him back. I thought we could still make a deal. I tried to convince him all he had to do was pay, and that would be the end of it. Auntie, I couldn't believe it. He said if that's what I wanted, he'd tell everything, and Uncle and I would go to jail, and you'd die of shame. It was like he knew us, like he knew everything about me. I didn't know what to say, Auntie. I just shut off my phone.'

"I threw up my hands and held my head, and he kept crying.

"'I swear I didn't think things would get this complicated,' Toñino told me. 'I thought it'd be like before. I wanted enough money to get you out of this shitty house, so the two of us could have a better life, the life you deserve and couldn't have because of me. And now everything's gone wrong. I swear, Auntie, I was never going to tell anyone, all I wanted was some money. My friend's a good man, I never wanted to hurt him.'"

Rosa María seemed to deflate in one long miserable exhalation. She looked up at them. "And what could I say? I stayed with him and tried to calm him down. I didn't know what to do. He said after talking to that man he couldn't decide what to do or where to go. He was too scared to go to that meeting. He'd been driving around like a lost soul, scared as a little child, trying to find the courage to come tell me about it." She subsided into silence, overwhelmed by fatigue.

"Why did he go out again? He'd already decided not to go to the meeting."

"A man called his cell phone. I know it was a man because I could hear a deep voice while they were talking. I don't know what the man said, but my Toñino cheered up a lot when he got that call.

"I heard him say, 'At home . . . I want to see you too . . . Okay.' And that was all. I saw the blood come back into his face. He said he was going out, and I tried to convince him to stay home because I had a bad feeling about it. He didn't listen. He changed his clothes, put on nice ones, and before he left he said, 'Auntie, maybe things will be okay.' The last time I saw him, he was smiling."

PROSCENIUM

Santa Quiteria Clinic exuded ostentatious luxury. The five-story building loomed in the middle of an expanse of extensive gardens, groves, and even an artificial lake. Manuel parked in the public lot that wrapped around the employee parking spaces near the elegant sloping drive. A circular flowerbed stood before the entrance. The place looked more like a palace or an embassy than a medical establishment. A black Mercedes at the entrance reinforced that initial impression.

Manuel was about to get out of his car when he saw two women come out of the main door into the portico of the main entrance, arm in arm with their heads close together. Catarina and the dowager marquess. Manuel sat and watched. The older woman raised a hand to signal the driver to wait. It was her car; that might be Damián's cap he saw through the car window. From where Manuel sat it would have been impossible to overhear them even if the rain hadn't been pouring down. Their expressions, body language, and gestures were clear evidence of the complicity between them. They now stood face-to-face, their hands intertwined. Their smiles and expressions showed their feelings of mutual esteem.

Manuel saw something move inside an ordinary white pickup truck parked off to his right and partly concealed by a large mimosa bush. A man sitting inside was watching the women with an interest as keen as his own. Manuel couldn't see who he was.

He looked back and forth between the watcher and the women. The two spoke for a while longer and then hugged warmly in farewell. The rear door of the Mercedes opened, and the marquess's nurse got out. She went up the stairs and gave her arm to the elderly woman just as Catarina had done. The two went to the automobile and left. Catarina went back inside the clinic.

Manuel got out. He opened his umbrella and held it to hide his face, just in case the sound of the closing car door caught the watching man's attention. He went around his vehicle, walked up to the passenger side of the pickup, and yanked the door open.

Vicente, Catarina's assistant at the greenhouse, was startled to see him. His bloodshot eyes and the tears on his face showed he'd been weeping for a long time. Manuel closed his umbrella and pushed a box of tissues, a pile of crumpled used tissues, and an overcoat to one side in order to clear the passenger seat. He glimpsed the butt of a revolver in the pocket of the overcoat. The gardener didn't move at first, but then he picked up the coat, threw it carelessly into the backseat to make room for Manuel, and again slumped over the steering wheel. He didn't bother to try to hide his tears.

"Vicente. What are you doing here?"

The man lifted his head and jutted his chin toward the clinic entrance. He shrugged. "I have to talk to her."

"With Catarina?"

Vicente turned to look at him, and his face betrayed his surprise. "You didn't know? She fired me."

That explained why the pickup no longer bore the nursery logo. Manuel looked behind and saw the truck bed was still loaded with tools, flowerpots, cable ties, and metal stakes for laying out hedges.

Into his mind came the echoing conversation between Vicente and Catarina he'd overheard in the greenhouse.

"Vicente, maybe this isn't the right time or place."

"She doesn't want to talk to me. I've been working with her for five years, and yesterday that horrible nurse came to the greenhouse and gave me this." He held out a creased envelope.

Manuel carefully extracted a sheet of paper as crumpled as the envelope. The notice advised Vicente Piñeiro he was immediately discharged from any and all activities having to do with the estate, instructed him to leave the premises at once, and enclosed a check for his salary, vacation pay, and all additional compensations, including a generous separation payment as thanks for his services. Manuel looked inside the envelope and recognized the gray-toned paper of a bank check. The bold sweeping script matched the appended signature of the dowager marquess. On the line for the amount she'd written *Fifty thousand euros,* a huge amount.

"She discharged me like . . . just like any employee."

Manuel remembered Griñán's comment: this family considered outsiders as no more than servants to be compensated for services rendered.

"I thought we had something special," Vicente said miserably.

Manuel remembered Catarina's comment in the greenhouse: *What you want is never going to happen, because I'm Santiago's wife, and he's the man I want to be with.*

"Maybe you were imagining—"

"No, Manuel!" He erupted in anger. "I'm certain, I'm not making it up, it's real!"

"Maybe so, and perhaps there was something once. But even so it looks as if Catarina has made up her mind. Don't you think so?"

Vicente sat looking at him gravely. The man's lips slowly puckered into an almost infantile pout, and tears again began to flow. Vicente covered his face with his hands and again put his head down on the steering wheel.

Manuel sighed. "Vicente, I think it's time for you to go home."

The man choked back his tears, took another tissue, dried his face, blew his nose, and tossed the wadded tissue on the floor. He admitted his defeat. "You're right. I should leave."

Manuel opened the door, but before he got out into the rain he looked back at the gardener.

"And . . . Vicente, I don't know why you're carrying a weapon, but nothing good can come of it."

The man dolefully contemplated the wrinkled mass that his overcoat had become and then looked back at Manuel. He nodded and turned the key in the ignition.

❧

Manuel stepped out of the elevator onto the fourth floor. He found no one at the reception desk or in the silent empty halls at this early hour of the afternoon. He followed the posted signs in search of the room number Lucas had given him. He located it at last at the end of a corridor, one side of which was entirely glass. A door in that hard transparent surface provided access to a fire escape. The rain and the low light outside rendered the smooth, unyielding surface as a long stretch of hopelessness reflecting his walking figure. Voices from the end room interrupted his moody thoughts. The door was ajar. They weren't shouting, but the tones were sufficiently heated for him to hear every word. He planted himself against the wall by the door and turned to watch the corridor behind him to keep from being surprised as he eavesdropped.

"You have to respond," Catarina pleaded. "You must make the effort!"

"Leave me alone! Go away!"

"I'm not going to leave. You're my husband."

Santiago mumbled something indistinguishable.

"Because I'm your wife, and we're family. Don't push me away, Santiago. Lean on me, let me take care of you."

"I don't want to live, Catarina. I can't go on like this."

"Hush! I don't want to hear that kind of talk from you."

"It's true. I don't want to go on. I don't have the strength."

"I'll give you strength. Our child and I both will—did you forget the child? Santiago, the baby we've wanted so much. We're going to be very happy, Santiago, I promise."

"Out!" he shouted. "Get out of here! Leave me alone!"

"Santiago!"

"Just leave me alone!"

Manuel heard her approaching the door. He felt the urge to retreat up the hall, but it would be absurd to try to pretend that he hadn't heard. He stayed where he was.

Catarina was wearing a light-blue dress of sheer fabric that made her look much younger. She carelessly clutched a coat and a purse. She gaped in surprise when she saw him and seemed to want to say something, but not a word came out. She didn't even close the door all the way behind her. She dropped her purse and coat, threw herself into his arms, and burst into sobs. He felt the warm press of that female body, short and strong but overcome with grief. She pressed her face to his chest as if trying to burrow into it, her hands like two small frightened animals seeking holds on his shoulders. He held her tight, taking in the scent of the shampoo from that mane of hair trimmed to the level of her chin, and he let her cry. He was deeply moved by the woman's strength. He had an intimation of what they must have meant when they said she knew how to maintain her place within the family.

Catarina gradually calmed down. She accepted a tissue from Manuel and didn't make the awkward mistake of apologizing for her behavior. She dried her face and then hugged him again, rose on tiptoes, and kissed his cheek. She leaned down to recover her purse and coat, pointed toward the coffee vending machine at the far end of the corridor, and walked in that direction.

She sank onto one of the plastic seats next to the machine, but waved away his offer of coffee, gesturing toward her abdomen.

"Oh, that's right! Congratulations!"

She smiled as best she could in the circumstances.

Manuel was so moved that he found himself apologizing. "I'm sorry you're being subjected to all this just when you should be celebrating."

"Oh, Manuel! Thank you so very much. You don't know how much I needed to talk to someone. This has been a terribly hard day."

He recalled the scene he'd witnessed when Catarina and the Raven had come out of the front entrance. The relations between the two seemed quite cordial. He wondered if perhaps Catarina didn't share that opinion or if she was deliberately not acknowledging that she'd already received support from someone.

"I can imagine. Do you feel all right?"

She smiled. "Yes, thanks, I'm fine, just worried, but I'm very happy you've come. I wanted so much to talk to you. Herminia told me Elisa and Samuel went away with you last night."

"They did."

"I'm not blaming you at all, and I do hope things work out. I adore Samuel, and now he's going to have a little cousin. I'd love to see them grow up together."

Manuel didn't reply, for he didn't know what to say. But he was aware that her affection for Samuel didn't extend to Elisa.

"How is Santiago?"

Her face darkened. "Terribly depressed. I've never seen him so bad." She put a hand over her mouth.

"Herminia told me that he went through a spell of depression after his younger brother died."

"Yes, he did, but it was nowhere as serious as this. He turned to me then, and I helped him get over it. But this time, I suppose it's not his fault alone. I should have realized that he was at a breaking point. He's so weak, so . . ." She shook her head, and for an instant her expression was vexed, almost angry. Or perhaps even something harsher. Manuel looked at her, disconcerted, and pretended not to notice, but he remembered the Raven's condemnation of Santiago in almost the same words.

"Catarina, I'd like to talk to Santiago; there's something I'd like to ask him."

Her first reaction was one of alarm, but she restrained herself and appeared cautious. She tried to smile but failed.

"I'm sorry, but it's just not possible, Manuel. Santiago's in a very delicate condition, and I still remember how he reacted the last time you two met. I'm not going to allow it, whatever you say. I must protect him, Manuel. I have to take care of him."

He had to accept that. He gave Catarina a dutiful hug before he left, but this time the embrace left him with a feeling of dismay. He didn't know whether to attribute it to his own sentiments or to the stiff reluctance he sensed in her embrace. She prolonged the contact, perhaps by way of compensation, and held his hand as they walked to the elevator. Manuel took no solace from her grasp, for it seemed to incarnate the ghostly presence of the Raven.

Rebuking himself silently for that reaction, he sought to compensate for it with an act of loyalty. "Catarina, when I arrived, I saw Vicente sitting inside a pickup truck in the parking lot."

"Oh!"

"I wouldn't bother you with it right now, but when I spoke to him I saw he was very emotional. He was weeping. I convinced him to drive home, but he seems determined to speak to you. I wouldn't be surprised if he came back."

Her mouth tightened into a hard line, an expression of annoyance or displeasure, as if instead of communicating the man's desperation he'd mentioned a plague of aphids threatening her plants.

"Well, you heard our exchange the other day. I finally had to fire him. It was very unpleasant. Vicente was an excellent assistant, but he's one of those people who doesn't respect boundaries or understand his proper place."

Without thinking Manuel dropped her hand. He was disappointed. Perhaps because he'd been expecting an expression of regret, some spark of humanity that might differentiate her from the rest of the Muñiz de Dávila family. Maybe Nogueira was right; maybe they were all the same.

The elevator door opened. Manuel stepped in and turned to catch her eye. "He had a pistol."

That did provoke from her eyes the glint they'd been lacking, but she recovered quickly. "Oh, don't worry about that, Manuel. Men are dramatic and exaggerated, but I know Vicente well. He'd never raise a weapon to me."

"But against himself, perhaps?"

She just shrugged. The elevator door closed.

❧

The rain didn't let up all day. The two weeks he'd spent so far in Galicia had taught him not to trust a brilliant cloudless sky, for he'd seen it close over in hours as the weather changed rapidly. On the other hand he'd also assimilated the locals' ability to intuit when rain would continue all day long. Madrid's rains were hectic, sudden, and impetuous; they dirtied the sidewalks and sent torrents surging headlong down the gutters, but all trace of them disappeared from the air as soon as the drops stopped falling. In Galicia, however, the earth soaked up water and welcomed it like a long-awaited lover. After a rain a humid presence lingered in the air, a barely concealed ghost ready to materialize at any moment.

He parked next to Nogueira's car and Laura's small van. He smiled when the girls' faces appeared at the window in response to the sound of his arrival. He stopped the engine but didn't get out.

He felt still confused and dismayed by the state in which he'd found Catarina. The *orballo* with its quietly relentless rhythm intensified those feelings. Sheltered within the car, he watched Nogueira's house through the windows and saw the image waver and blur as if the residence was melting. Misgivings again seized him. He was tempted to start the engine and drive off.

He faced his anxiety. "Screw it," he muttered.

Café had made all the difference. If anyone had suggested to him a couple of weeks earlier that the furry little fellow would become so important to him, he'd have laughed himself silly. But that's what had happened. His mood wasn't because of Santiago, the feeling of general melancholy, or the *orballo*; he was simply afraid that the dog wouldn't want to come back with him. He'd read somewhere that animals choose their masters. How could a boring writer hope to be more attractive than an eight-year-old playmate?

Nogueira came out on the porch and waved at him to hurry up. Manuel finally got out of the car and hustled to the door, hunching over both to protect his face from the rain and to avoid the policeman's gaze.

Café slipped between the man's legs and the doorframe. The dog ran toward Manuel, barking, yipping, and wagging his tail. Manuel stopped short, relieved and surprised, and bent down to receive his dog. The dog jumped up in an unsuccessful effort to lick his face. He grinned, trying both to calm the dog and yet to reward that celebration. Laura and Xulia appeared in the doorway next to Nogueira, and little Antía joined them. Manuel saw the child smile but recognized the same melancholy that had just abandoned him. He knew why.

He said nothing to Nogueira until they were alone together. Then he related the conversation with Vicente and after that the one with Catarina that had given him the eerie sensation of missing something, like listening to a grand symphony played by only half the orchestra. He was torn between his admiration for Catarina and his repugnance for her relationship with the Raven. He didn't know how to deal with this mix of prejudices and vague premonitions. He'd liked Catarina from the first moment he saw her. She had an innate elegance and that sense of class that made her very attractive, and obviously not only to him; but perhaps it had misled him into attributing exaggerated virtues to her, almost idealizing her. After all, she was a woman of flesh and blood, a person with human emotions, subject to human temptations. So what if she'd felt a passing attraction to a man who was a faithful assistant and admired those things she loved most of all? And did it matter if she secretly envied Elisa for her son because she herself hadn't succeeded in conceiving? And who cared if sometimes she felt tired, fed up with fulfilling the role of mothering a weak and willful husband? Would any of that diminish her grace and virtue?

Nogueira looked as if he were reading Manuel's thoughts, but he wasn't. "What's running through your head, writer?"

Manuel smiled. "Something occurred to me while I was driving. Something to do with what Ophelia said the first time we spoke. When she got to the scene of Álvaro's accident, there was already a rumor going around that a Muñiz de Dávila was involved. She said everyone was acting a bit strange."

Nogueira nodded. "I noticed that myself."

"And all this stuff about their influence and importance in the region . . ."

"Where are you going with all this?"

"Doesn't it seem strange that if people knew a Muñiz de Dávila died in an accident at 1:30 a.m., no one had the consideration to inform the family? That they didn't hear about it until the hospital called them at dawn?"

Nogueira nodded emphatically. He took out his phone. "I think you have something there."

✦

The hallway to his room at the inn always stood silent and dark upon his arrival. A monitoring system detected his presence and progressively lit the hall lights ahead of him as he walked toward his door. This time he was surprised to find the hall completely illuminated. Already on the stair landing he heard the unmistakable sound of cartoons coming from the open door to Elisa's room.

Café scurried ahead in that direction, but before the dog reached the door Samuel appeared and peered expectantly down the hall. He saw Manuel and shouted, "It's Uncle!" He turned and called into the room. "It's Uncle Manuel!" He hurled himself down the hall toward the man's arms.

Manuel hoisted him high, and as always had the impression he was embracing a big slippery fish with ideas of its own. He felt those small sturdy arms around his neck, the softness of the boy's skin against his face, and the moist lips of the child's kiss.

"Hello, dear heart! How was your day?"

"Really good!" the little fellow replied. "I met Isabel and Carmen. They're my cousins. I didn't know I had cousins!"

"Was it fun meeting them?"

The boy affirmed it with great emphatic nods.

Elisa smiled from the door to their room. "Hello, Manuel!"

Manuel put the child down and gave her his hand. He felt a little hand thrusting into the pocket of his heavy jacket. He reached after it and felt the silky surface of petals. He knelt and gazed into the eyes of the boy, who responded with a smile. Manuel took the gardenia from his pocket and held it before him.

He saw surprise in Elisa's face. She came forward for a closer look. "Did you put that flower in there, sweetie?"

Samuel smiled happily. He had. "It's a present!"

"It's very beautiful," Manuel said in thanks. "And tell me, have you been putting flowers in my pocket every day?"

Samuel put a finger in his mouth and nodded shyly.

Manuel smiled. He'd been so startled by the appearance of those flowers in his pockets, but they'd simply been the gifts of a child.

"Have you been giving Uncle flowers without telling me, you little rascal?" asked Elisa, amused.

"It's just . . . It's 'cause it has to be a secret."

His mother was intrigued. "A secret?"

"He told me to put the flowers in there and not tell anybody."

Elisa looked at Manuel in confusion, then turned back to her son. "Who told you to do that? Samuel, it's okay to tell me."

This sudden intense attention bothered Samuel. He pulled loose from Manuel. He ran toward the open door of his room and called back, "Uncle, it was Uncle who asked me to!"

"Uncle Santiago asked you to put flowers in my pockets?"

"No!" shrieked the boy as he reached the room. "Uncle Álvaro!"

Manuel instantly felt nailed to the spot. He heard again Lucas speaking about the boy's active imagination and imaginary friends. Oh, little Samuel! He tried to hide his agitation, but when he raised his eyes he met Elisa's gaze.

She seemed almost ashamed. "Oh, Manuel, I'm so sorry, I don't know how . . ."

"Don't worry about it. It's nothing." He took her arm. "It's just that he took me by surprise. I was finding these flowers every day, and . . ."

"I'm really sorry, Manuel, I don't know what to say. Maybe he saw Álvaro do that sometime. It was a habit of his."

"Yes," Manuel answered in a neutral tone.

❧

He had dinner with Elisa and Samuel in the inn restaurant, laughing at the boy's antics. Samuel kept slipping bits of his own meal beneath the table for Café.

Manuel enjoyed Elisa's company. She'd changed; it was as if by getting away from As Grileiras she'd shed a veil and had left behind her sepia tint of sadness. She was no longer the image of an old photograph, for she smiled, chatted, laughed, and scolded Samuel half in jest. Manuel had the idea he was seeing her alive and in charge of her own life for the first time.

They were laughing at something the boy had said, and at that moment Manuel became newly aware of his feelings. He was flooded with waves of love, bewilderment, and the fear of not seeing them ever again. He sensed Elisa's importance to him and his love for Samuel. He smiled broadly.

Elisa spoke and pulled him out of his reverie. "I called my brother. You remember, I told you about him? He's married and has two young daughters."

"Samuel mentioned it. He seems delighted with his two cousins."

"Yes, he is." Elisa smiled. "It seems terrible to me now that we deprived him of the pleasure of meeting them. One more mistake on a very long list," she accused herself in a matter-of-fact tone. "But we talked a lot today. I think things will work out between us." She reached out to cover Manuel's hand with her own. "And you had a lot to do with it. If you hadn't helped me, I don't know if I'd have had the strength to leave that place."

He shook his head, minimizing his role. "We're all stronger than we imagine ourselves to be. You've taken the first step. Anyhow, you have your own allowance and can live on your own."

"It's not that, Manuel. It was partly because of Fran; I felt that he was holding me there. But it's the family too. I don't know if you can understand, Manuel, but life on a big estate is easy. It's nice to feel you're one of them, even though I knew they were putting up with me only for Samuel's sake." She watched the boy playing with Café. Manuel remembered Catarina's distinction between her feelings for her sister-in-law and those for her nephew. "But there's something different in that family, and it's both terrible and fascinating. Everything flows along on the estate, life goes on, it's serene and without surprises, and it was what I needed. Or at least that's what I thought for a while."

"And now?"

"I'm starting to think seriously about what you said about living away from the estate. My brother thinks it's a good idea. Samuel could see the rest of his family, too, that way, and next year he'll start school, and . . ."

"That's wonderful," he said, putting his other hand over hers. "But, Elisa, what I was trying to say the other day in the cemetery is that it's your life. Yours and Samuel's. Take all the time you need to think about what you want to do, and once you've decided, I'll help. But it has to be your decision, not one made by the Muñiz de Dávila family or by your brother or by me. It's *yours*, Elisa."

She nodded and smiled.

A DEATHLY FEAR OF LIGHTNING

Laura closed the book she'd been reading when she heard Nogueira start his car engine.

She'd listened for more than fifteen minutes through the half-open window behind her as her husband and older daughter talked on the porch. She hadn't been able to hear everything, but there hadn't been any silences. She'd even heard laughter. There was no reason to have expected him to come in to say goodbye before he left. For years the two had scorned that very French custom of elaborate leave-takings, so she'd have thought nothing of a wordless departure just a couple of weeks earlier. But tonight his uncommunicative manner aroused an ancient ache she thought she'd overcome. She got to her feet and left the book on the armchair. On her way out she smiled at the sight of her daughter Antía, who had yet again fallen asleep on the sofa despite her mother's repeated urgings to go to bed.

Xulia was reading, leaning back on the swing that took up much of the porch. This had been her favorite place ever since her father had installed it when she was only four years old.

"Your father left already?" she asked, even though the answer was obvious. Only her van remained parked in front of the house.

Xulia looked up from her book and took her time answering. "Yes," she replied, wondering what was going on with her mother. "Did you want to tell him something?"

Laura looked into the distance as she leaned against the porch railing. She didn't reply, perhaps because she needed to ponder the answer. Did she in fact want to tell him something? She thought she detected a faint flash of light on the horizon, and she stood up straighter to study everything going on out there so far away. Or was it perhaps that she wanted him to say something to her?

"It's not important," she responded, her eyes still fixed on the distant line between earth and sky.

"I think it is," replied her daughter, with the seriousness of which only a teenager is capable.

She was startled by the girl's tone and turned to glance at her. She was almost certain she'd seen something in the distant sky.

"I heard you two talking," she said, still closely watching the sky. "But now I think there's a storm coming."

Xulia gave her a condescending smile. She knew her mother well: an intelligent, capable woman, rational and self-possessed, who was nevertheless terrified of thunderstorms. She checked the weather forecast on her phone. "There's no storm in the forecast, Mama."

"I don't care what the internet says," Laura answered stubbornly. "We'd better go inside."

Xulia contemplated the night sky, calm and sprinkled with stars. But she didn't protest. She knew that it was a waste of time to try to argue with her mother when it came to storms.

Laura hated thunderstorms, and she also hated their effect on her. They drove waves of terror deep into her soul. That absurd panic merely intensified her irrational hatred of the storm and conferred upon it the identity of a living thing, a conscious, enraged creature and a deadly enemy. She didn't believe in hunches, premonitions, or mystic signs. In the time since she'd married her policeman, she'd had to deal with all-too-justified anxiety when he was on night shifts. Early in their married life she'd stayed awake night after night imagining the worst: her husband dragged beneath a truck, run over by a car smashing through a checkpoint, shot by some criminal late at night or by one of those drug smugglers said to move tons of cocaine across Galicia in the course of a single night.

Her husband knew how to take care of himself, and he was no longer on active duty. He'd probably gone out for a drink with Manuel, and yet the fact he'd left without a word, as well as the storm she glimpsed in the distance, had reawakened an ancient fear lurking deep within. She lit the oven and kept a close eye on the inexorably advancing storm. Its lightning flashes threw the profiles of the hills into sharp relief against the sky.

Laura crossed the kitchen, silent and intent as she set out in a row the ingredients for the cake he liked so much.

"Are you making a cake now?" asked Xulia, looking up toward the kitchen clock where the hands pointed to 11:00 p.m.

The window that she'd left wide open so as to monitor the progress of the storm across the horizon was suddenly lit by a blinding lightning flash.

Xulia wasn't surprised. She knew her mother'd had a sixth sense for storms since that time long ago when Laura's father died at sea in a raging storm.

Laura didn't answer her daughter. She began mixing the ingredients, but her mind was far away, focused on that terrible night.

Laura's mother had waited at the port for hours, hoping to see the boat return. When night descended and the storm tore inland across the seacoast, a group of kind souls, all women, appealed to her and almost physically dragged her back home. Laura's mother collapsed in tears the instant she stepped across the threshold. Terribly miserable, she huddled on the floor and moaned. "Now I know he'll never come back."

Her mother was now more than eighty years old. She lived alone and proud in that cottage by the port. She did her shopping, went to mass, and lit a votive candle every day before the photo of the husband who'd never returned, the image of that beloved face she couldn't forget but Laura could hardly remember.

Once Laura asked her, "How did you know? How did you know Papa wouldn't come back?"

"I knew it when I gave in and left the port without him. For years I cursed those women for persuading me. They forced me to betray my vow and return home, but I was to blame. I gave up and abandoned all hope. That's why he never came back."

Xulia silently watched her mother prepare the batter and put the cake into the oven. Xulia particularly noted Laura's worried expression and the distraction with which she dried her hands with a dishcloth. Her movements were careful and deliberate but her anxiety was obvious. Laura peered vigilantly back and forth from an invisible chasm just in front of her to the roiling advance of a storm that now covered the horizon.

Xulia looked out when she heard another thunderclap in the distance.

"Give me a hand," her mother said. "Your sister fell asleep on the sofa."

"As usual," Xulia commented.

"Turn down the covers, so I can put her to bed."

Laura lifted Antía. She smiled at the thought her little one would soon be too big and heavy to carry.

Careful to keep Antía's feet from hitting the doorframe, she made her way around the furniture toward the bedroom the two of them had shared for six years. She paused in the hall and reflected. The sleeping child started to slip from her grasp; with a little upward thrust she secured the girl in her arms. Antía was already almost too heavy for her. She turned toward the hall and spoke to her older daughter. "I think it'll be better for her to be in her own bed."

Xulia made no comment. She entered quickly and turned down the Minnie Mouse blanket. She kissed her mother and went to her own bed, knowing she wouldn't sleep. She'd remain awake until her father returned, and she thought that would be a good thing. She knew the background story of ports and storms, and at the age of seventeen she was of the opinion that going home makes sense only if someone is waiting for you.

⚜

The hot-pink neon of the roadhouse flickered across the faces of the two men in the car. Manuel turned to check on Café. The dog gave him a sidelong look from the customary place on the backseat.

"Looks like Lucas took our advice to stay home and not visit the hookers."

Nogueira was surprised. "He didn't phone?"

Manuel checked his call log. "No, he didn't."

It was still relatively early, and only a couple of cars were parked there. The bouncer's barstool was visible on the porch, but the Mammoth was nowhere in sight.

"Ophelia and I worked up a list of all the people we remember seeing at the scene of the accident. I've started calling them, but most of them are on the night shift, like Ophelia. If she's not too busy, she'll do the rest to see if anyone contacted As Grileiras about the accident before the hospital did."

The towering figure of the Mammoth came around the side of the building. He was zipping his fly, a gesture that explained his temporary absence. The bouncer surveyed the parking lot and spotted their vehicle; he paused for a moment in the falling rain to study the two men inside. Before the cowboy decided whether to investigate, Nogueira and Manuel got out. The Mammoth went back to his post.

Perhaps because he was royally bored with the almost-deserted parking lot, the Mammoth was more than willing to fill them in.

"Sure I remember him. My job is to keep an eye on the cars out there, so I'm always here. Our little Nieves won't let me go inside even to take a pee. Don Santiago's a regular and he's very generous. When the lot is full he generally asks me to keep an eye on his car to make sure that no drunk sideswipes it."

"So you remember them."

"Sure. It was a Saturday. That's when I really have to be on the lookout. You know what they say, 'Saturday's the day for a roll in the hay.' The lot was full. It's not like that on Sundays; Sundays are for the family." He grinned, and his obviously false teeth flashed under the neon lights. "Two cars showed up and stopped at the far end of the lot, close to the road, but they didn't pull into the parking spots. That almost never happens; usually the new arrivals park, if only to avoid blocking the exit. I was going to go check on them, because sometimes we get drug pushers trying to sell their stuff here, and I have to chase them off. Our little Nieves doesn't want the place to get a bad reputation."

Manuel smiled.

The irony was lost on the Mammoth. "I knew it was okay when I saw don Santiago. Some guy got out of the other car; I've seen them together sometimes. They didn't talk for long, but they were shouting. I couldn't hear what they were saying, because the music from inside is pretty loud. But I could see don Santiago was really pissed off. He got into his car, slammed the door, and drove away, leaving the other guy just standing there."

"That was all?"

"Well, the guy was looking out at the road. Then another vehicle pulled up. I noticed it because it didn't turn in from the road. It came from the pine grove over there." He waved toward a clump of trees beyond the parking lot. "Sometimes sweethearts park in there, you see." He gave them a conspiratorial wink. "It was a pickup truck. Came from the left along the dirt track and stopped next to the guy. A woman got out, and they talked for a while."

Nogueira turned to scout the far end of the parking lot. "It's pretty far away. Are you sure it was a woman?"

"Not tall, hair down to here," he said, placing the fingers of his right hand across his throat. "And she was alone. She left the door open, so the interior light was on, and I could see there was nobody else with her. They talked for a bit, said goodbye with a hug, then he got into his vehicle and drove away; she did the same."

"They hugged one another?"

"Yeah, sort of to say goodbye, a couple of seconds. Well, that time of night I wasn't paying very close attention. A client came out to say something, and when I looked back, I saw the two had gotten back in their vehicles and were leaving."

"Can you remember what time of night this was?"

"About one in the morning."

"And the vehicle. Can you describe it?"

"Hey, man, I couldn't see the license number or anything, but it was a white pickup truck. There was some kind of design on the side, kind of like a flower basket. Yeah, that's it, a basket of flowers." He smiled, pleased at his recall. "Like I told you, I keep an eye on everything here." He grinned. "That's my job."

"A pickup with the design of a flower basket on the side," Manuel said when they returned to the car. "That's the pickup Catarina's assistant drove. And the bouncer practically gave us a description of her."

"We already know why they were arguing: Álvaro told Santiago he wasn't going to pay any blackmail money. That must have really riled him."

"Yes, but he left. And Álvaro was still alive then."

"Then Catarina turns up. What was she doing here?"

"No idea. But Catarina always seems determined to protect Santiago," Manuel said, remembering the conversation in the clinic as well as her exasperation at taking care of her good-for-nothing husband. "Maybe she thought he was in some sort of trouble and followed him here."

Nogueira pressed his lips together and grunted. "Hmm."

"What is it?" asked Manuel.

Nogueira had just started the engine when his phone buzzed. It was Ophelia. He put it on the speaker so Manuel could hear her.

"Well, just as we suspected. Someone did report the accident to the Muñiz de Dávila family."

"Who called?"

"One of the traffic cops. Pereira, that's his name. Says he saw no reason not to. He spoke to Santiago at about two in the morning, give or take."

"At two? So right after it happened."

"Correct. He said Álvaro had died in a traffic accident and everything suggested he'd run off the road. He did mention the dent and paint scrapes, and he said the police hadn't yet discounted the possibility that a white vehicle might have been involved. Sounds like he got a bit ahead of himself, trying to be helpful. But that's not all." She made a dramatic pause.

"*Ofeliña! Que non temos toda a noite!*" Nogueira exclaimed. He tried to hurry her along.

"*Voy, home!* Two days later Santiago called to thank him. Pereira didn't mention it, but I assume he got a cash tip. And Santiago asked for a favor. He said the nephew of an old lady who'd been employed at the estate had disappeared; the old woman was very worried and had reported the boy missing. Santiago said he'd appreciate it if they could find the boy or his car. He even gave Pereira the license number."

"It had to be Toñino's license number," Nogueira said.

"And did he? Did he contact Santiago later?"

"Yes, he did. Yesterday afternoon at about five he called to say they'd found the boy's body. Said it looked like a suicide."

Manuel clutched his head with both hands. "So he didn't kill him. He didn't have a clue, didn't know Toñino was dead. When he found out, he was so devastated he tried to kill himself."

"That's what we think," Ophelia responded.

"Then why was he sobbing into the boy's undershirt in the church days before that? Don't you think that suggests he's guilty? And that he already knew?"

"He was crying because he'd lost his lover," Manuel said. "Toñino's aunt said a friend was calling every day to ask for him. We know that wasn't Richie; I suspect that'll be easy to verify, because I'm sure it was Santiago. He was weeping because he thought Toñino was stonewalling him in revenge. Santiago beat the crap out of him but didn't kill him. Santiago didn't know Toñino was dead until yesterday. That's why he kept calling the aunt to ask about him. Santiago urged the aunt to make the missing persons report. He even took the risk of asking the trooper to call him if anything turned up. He wouldn't have done that if he'd known the boy was dead. And yesterday the trooper called and said Toñino had committed suicide. That was the same night he'd been beaten up. Santiago blamed himself. It was more than he could stand."

Nogueira remained silent as he put the pieces together. "Let's recap. Santiago leaves Álvaro after arguing with him when they were supposed to turn over the money. The trooper calls him that night to say that Álvaro is dead and a white vehicle might have been involved, so he assumes that means Toñino. But Toñino has no idea. He even goes to Burger King to get food for both of them, thinking they'll meet to discuss it. Santiago turns up in a rage and gets carried away, bashes the boy's face in, because he thinks the kid just killed his brother. He beats him till he gets tired or Toñino manages to convince him he had nothing to do with it. And he's alive when Santiago leaves him. Fuck! I think it all fits. That explains the bloodstained wipes in the car. Toñino was alive, and he was tending to his injuries before he was killed."

"There's more," Ophelia added. "They just called to tell me. Toñino had his cell phone with him. The battery was flat; it was wet and contaminated by fluids from decomposition, but we got it to work. There are lots of unanswered calls. Three from his buddy Richie, fifteen from his aunt, and more than two hundred from Santiago. Including voice mails that were as desperate and pitiful as any you could imagine. Santiago's calls completely exhausted the battery. They're going to interrogate him first thing tomorrow."

A MISSION

Elisa stood in the bathroom door, watching her son. Seated cross-legged on the bed, he was absorbed in television cartoons. They'd gone back to their room after saying goodnight to Manuel, but from then on Samuel had been acting strangely. The previous day the boy had kicked off his sneakers and bounced on the bed like crazy; this evening he was silent and unresponsive. As soon as they'd entered the room he'd asked her where the phone was. When she told him it was in her pocket as usual, he said, "Not that one. The phone that's here." She hadn't even noticed there was a fixed phone in the room. It stood on a bedside table. The oddest thing was that Samuel made her check to see that it was working. Wondering at this, she lifted the receiver and confirmed there was a dial tone; she even put it to the boy's little ear so he could hear it too. She thought perhaps he was missing the familiar surroundings of the manor house. She knelt before him. "Do you want to call someone? Do you miss Herminia? Should we call the house on the estate?"

Samuel looked at her with a grave expression. He lifted his right hand and ran it through his mother's hair, gently separating the strands. There was a twist to his mouth Elisa had never seen before. His expression was patient and reassuring, as if their roles had become reversed and she was the little girl. He was keeping something from her he wasn't going to explain. "I have to wait for Uncle to phone me."

"He told you he was going to call?" She tried to reason with him. "It's very late. Maybe he meant tomorrow."

Again the boy ran his hand through her hair with infinite care. "It's a mission, Mama."

"A mission?" She entered into the game. "What kind of mission?"

"Something I have to do for Uncle. And I can't go to sleep until he calls."

Confused by this, she'd smiled indulgently, trying to assume her role as mother again and understand her son's actions. First there'd been the gardenias he'd put into Manuel's pockets, and now came this weirdness . . .

"But just a little while longer. It's very late, and you need your sleep."

Samuel shook his head with a determination new to him, patient and grown-up, as if to say, *You don't understand anything*. He took off his sneakers and settled on the bed to watch television. Elisa retreated to the bathroom door. She busied herself pretending to take off her makeup and brush her teeth, but in fact she'd posted herself there to observe him and monitor this new and entirely unfamiliar behavior.

She saw him laugh at SpongeBob as he always did. He gradually settled back against the pillows, and she thought maybe he would forget his notion that his uncle would call. Maybe he would at last give in to the sleep heavy in his eyes. He yawned several times. She saw him close his little eyes. The day had been intense and full of emotion; away from the estate and meeting his cousins, he hadn't stopped for an instant; he had to be exhausted. She watched him with a loving smile and carefully moved toward him as she mentally counted backward from ten. That was her little ritual: if she got to zero without the boy opening his eyes, that meant he was deep in sleep. Nine, eight, seven, six, five, four, three . . . Samuel opened his eyes and sat up as if he'd just heard a call inaudible to her. She stepped back in confusion, and her gaze followed his to the telephone. Samuel nodded as if remembering something, or as if someone had reminded him of his mission. He sat up straight and pushed away the pillows, resisting their temptation, once again focusing his attention on the cartoons bathing the room in their colorful light.

OUTCRY

The Vulcan was just as deserted as La Rosa roadhouse. They spotted Richie as soon as they stepped inside. He was drinking alone, facing the bar and ignoring the few clients swaying on the dance floor.

Nogueira clapped his heavy hand on the kid's shoulder. It looked as if all the boy's bones would give way beneath that weight like a collapsing house of cards.

He grunted, turned, and dully acknowledged them. His face was gaunt and emotionless. Manuel felt sorry for him. The boy was mourning. Nogueira must have seen it, for instead of hassling him as he had before, he patted the kid's shoulder, more gently this time, and motioned to the waiter for a round of drinks.

They took a couple of long swallows of beer before anyone spoke.

"Listen, Richie," Manuel said, "there's something I need you to explain about what you told us the other night."

The boy drained his beer and stared into space. Manuel knew where the kid was; not too long before, Manuel himself had been staring into the same abyss.

"You two were looking for Toñino," the kid said. "You were worried about him, and if it weren't for you, he'd still be out there. On the mountainside."

Manuel agreed and put a hand on the boy's shoulder.

"Will it help you get the bastard that did that to him?" Richie hadn't moved. His eyes were still unfocused and far away.

"I don't know. I'd like to say it would, but I just don't know."

Richie turned and met his eyes. He seemed to have made his decision. "What do you want to know?"

"You said that Toñino had 'business' at the estate. That's the word you used. You said, 'You don't kill the cow while it's still giving milk.' Tell me what kinds of business he had there."

Richie's expression was very serious, and for a moment Manuel didn't think he was going to answer. But the boy shrugged, sighed deeply, and said, "I guess that now Toñino is dead, it doesn't matter anymore, right? It's not going to hurt him any, and I don't give a damn if it gets those bastards into trouble. Toñino had a gold mine up there on the estate, first with Fran, and then he'd been seeing Santiago for a good while. That was a different kind of business. He always said Santiago was in love with him, and, well, I'm not going to say that Toñino was indifferent. He didn't mind being loved. Santiago's a good-looking guy and has lots of dough. Sometimes Toñino would deal him some drugs. Cocaine, mostly. Why are you asking about him?" Richie's eyes were suddenly feverish. "You think he had something to do with what happened to Toñino?"

"We know he didn't. We're sure of it."

The boy's features relaxed. He slowly shook his head. His eyes again lost their focus and he stared into space. Nogueira gestured impatiently. He suspected that the boy's confused state was due to something in addition to just unhappiness.

"Richie, listen closely," Manuel said firmly, regaining the boy's attention. "There was one more thing. You said Toñino knew his clients, especially the women, and you mentioned a 'classy' one. I thought you were referring to Elisa, Fran's fiancée, but I now know with absolute certainty she's been clean for years. I want you to tell me who else on the estate was buying drugs."

"Elisa? Yeah, I know who she is. Nah, not her. She'd have a fit if she saw us anywhere near her boyfriend. You know what they usually say: it's like tobacco; those who condemn it most are the ones who used to be slaves to the habit. But considering how things turned out, it's pretty obvious Fran went back to it."

"So who else, then?"

"The other one, the gorgeous one, stuck-up, I don't know her name. Her parents were aristocrats, too, marquises or something. They have an estate on the road to Lugo."

"Catarina?" asked Nogueira from close behind him.

"Yeah, that's her."

Manuel looked past Richie's shoulder at Nogueira. "That doesn't seem possible. She's been trying to get pregnant for years. She doesn't even drink coffee."

"Oh right!" exclaimed Richie. "You think she's not a druggie? She likes the real strong stuff. Look, I don't know if she stopped using lately, but I tell you I saw her with my own eyes. One time I went to the estate with Toñino. He knew a back road, and she was waiting for us close to the church. We gave her the junk, she paid us, and we beat it out of there."

"What did she buy?"

"Heroin."

Nogueira pushed himself out of his chair and looked at Manuel, alarmed by the seriousness of what it looked like they were about to confirm. He stepped close to Richie. "Listen to me real close. Think carefully about what you're about to say."

The boy's expression and nod showed he understood the gravity of the situation.

"Do you remember when that was?"

"Sure. It was maybe two . . . no, three years ago, and I even remember the date: September 15. My mother and grandmother are both named Dolores, and their saint's day is on the 15th. Toñino came to my house so I could drive him to the estate. He didn't have a car yet, and my mother made him come in and have a piece of cake. It was the 15th of September. If I ever forget that date, my mom'll kill me."

ECHO

Lucas rode up in the elevator with a nurse who looked down with a disgusted expression at the puddle spreading across the linoleum flooring from the tip of his umbrella. "Sorry," he apologized. "With this storm I couldn't help getting drenched."

He breathed in the humidity exuded by his dripping raincoat into the confined space of the elevator. He had the odd sensation that at any moment it might rain even in there. The nurse said nothing.

The doors opened before a nursing station where another woman was seated. She greeted them curtly and pointed to the office door.

The nurse rapped on the door and opened it without waiting for a reply.

The center of the room was occupied by a conference table with twelve chairs. Three physicians—one male and two female—were sitting at one end. Catarina was at the side, her back to the vast window. On that rainy night the thousands of drops trickling down the outside surface had transformed it into a mirror, glistening like silver and reflecting everything within.

One of the women rose to greet him. "Good evening. You must be Father Lucas. I'm Dr. Méndez; we spoke on the phone. These are my colleagues Dr. López and Dr. Nievas, and you already know Catarina."

Catarina came to greet him with a quick kiss on either cheek. She was pale, seemed worried, and was clutching a small bottle of mineral water. It was unmarked, for she had picked the label into tiny pieces that lay scattered on the table.

The physician continued as soon as Lucas was seated. "Catarina tells us you know what's happened in the last few hours. Santiago took an overdose of the sleeping pills he regularly uses. Luckily we got to him in time, and the dose he absorbed wasn't fatal. He's been asking to speak to you since the moment he regained consciousness."

"Lucas, I don't agree with this," Catarina said. "You were the last person he phoned before he overdosed. I'm sure you know as well as I do what that means. I'm afraid of what might happen. I'm scared this might be his way of saying goodbye."

Lucas nodded to acknowledge the gravity of the situation, but one of the woman physicians responded. "We understand your worry, Catarina, but my colleagues and I agree that this meeting could have a positive effect. Knowing he's a devout Catholic, we believe he might find it easier to speak to his spiritual adviser than with us. We've kept him under close observation all day. And we all agree: Santiago is unhappy and determined—that's not untypical of would-be suicides—but his mind is clear."

"How can you say he's not deranged?" Catarina protested. "For the love of God, he tried to commit suicide, and this wasn't the first time!"

"It's very common to think that those who decide to commit suicide are out of their minds, but that's not necessarily the case. Or at least not most of the time. No one is entirely certain what causes depression." The physician paused. "Right now he's despondent, but that doesn't mean he's incapable of getting past it. He did so once before, remember. It's been documented that in many cases of depression, each successive episode is worse than the previous one. What interests us most right now is drawing him out of his isolation so he can speak of what's causing him such pain. We haven't been able to help him at all, and we believe that the fact he's willing to speak with his confessor is a hopeful sign."

Catarina rejected the doctor's proposal. "He speaks to me. I'm his wife, and I know him better than anybody. Santiago is . . . he's like a little child. When he's frustrated or angry he does and says things he regrets afterward. He's always been like that, since he was a little boy. I know him very well, and I've learned not to take it to heart. I can tell when he's letting his emotions run away with him and when he's telling the truth. He's shouted at me every time I've seen him today; he's said horrible things; he's pushed me away; but I know him. He's doing it because he's in pain, and that's why I believe it's too early to talk with him. Why don't you give him a few days to calm down? I'm sure that whatever Santiago might say today will only give you the wrong impression of him, and my duty is to protect him. That's what I did when his little brother died, and I was able to bring him back to himself."

The physician nodded. "Certainly, we understand your misgivings, and your determination to protect him is laudable. But we believe that right now it's fundamental to draw Santiago out of this self-imposed isolation. We hope Father Lucas can convince him to accept help in getting through the bad patch he's going through right now. In any case, opening up to someone will be his first and most important step toward getting better."

"I absolutely refuse," Catarina persisted. "You don't know him. If I allow this, he'll only get worse."

The three doctors looked at one another. This time the male physician was the one to speak. "I understand your view, Catarina, but I'm on the board of directors of this clinic. I sought the advice of our legal counsel before we decided to call Father Lucas in. We cannot deny spiritual counseling to any patient who asks for it. This institution is religiously affiliated, but even if it were not, we are psychiatrists, and our view is that spiritual assistance to the patient is always beneficial."

"Then I'll go with him. I promised I wouldn't leave him alone, and I intend to keep my word. We have no secrets from one another. He's suffering terribly, and just as when you were examining him, I won't let him be interviewed by anyone unless I'm there at his side. I already told you this morning that if you don't respect my wishes, I'll take him back home."

Lucas cleared his throat to get the attention of all those present. "I am a Catholic priest, and it is my duty to attend to any of the faithful who ask to be heard in confession. I don't know if you are Catholics, but you should be aware that whatever don Santiago may tell me will remain under seal of confession and cannot be revealed." He turned to Catarina. "I've known Santiago since we were boys together, Catarina, and I've been his confessor since I took my vows. I've been a friend of the family for years, and I officiated at your wedding at As Grileiras. But today I'm not here as a friend but as a priest. Santiago tried to call me yesterday before he took those pills, and I believe that if I'd only been able to speak with him, I could have dissuaded him."

"He's out of his mind, Lucas! You can't imagine the kinds of things he's saying. He's drugged up and excited, spewing wild nonsense." She was terribly upset. "I don't want to leave him alone."

The physician opposed her. "He's in full possession of his mental faculties. There are no drugs in his system other than traces of the sleeping pills he takes regularly. In our opinion he is no more affected by drugs than he would be any other day."

Catarina was sputtering in frustration. Lucas got up and went to sit beside her. "He's asked to be heard in confession. That's one of the most important sacraments of our faith, and no one other than the penitent and the priest is allowed to be present. It cannot be recorded, and nothing of what he tells me may be revealed."

"Nothing? Whatever he may say? Not even to the doctors?" Her tone was one of distrust.

"Nothing," Lucas reassured her. "The secret of confession obliges me to remain silent about everything he tells me. Catarina, confession is a solace to the soul." He took her strong but small and visibly shaking hand in his as he addressed the physicians as well. "The joyful sacrament that frees us of our afflictions is neither medical treatment nor a legal declaration."

The physicians' faces showed their disappointment. The female doctor who'd spoken looked at her colleagues and sighed, then turned to Lucas. "Very well. We understand the requirements of the rite, and right now the greatest problem facing us is the patient's isolation. If you are able to break through to him, we'll consider that a success. We'll be understanding of the fact that you can't share the details of confession, but we hope that you'll be able to persuade him to embrace life. And that you'll inform us if he remains determined to commit suicide."

Catarina was sharp with her. "He just told you. The secret of confession means he's obliged not to divulge anything he's told."

"Even so," the physician said, fixing her gaze on Lucas, "if after your session with the patient I should personally ask you for guidance on the best way to proceed with his case, you'd be able to tell me not to worry or, alternatively, to be extremely vigilant, wouldn't you? That means you wouldn't be reveal-ing any secret; you'd only be giving me your best guidance on what attitude I should take."

Lucas nodded. "I will give you my sincere guidance." He rose.

The physicians escorted him to the door of the hospital room. He checked his phone one last time and turned it off. He turned to them just before he went in. "I request your absolute respect for the sanctity of confession. No one is to come in or to interrupt us in any way until we've finished."

He closed the door behind him. A terrified Catarina looked on.

GARDENIAS

Manuel raced up the stairs, certain there was no cell phone coverage in the Vulcan's underground locale; besides, the loud music would have kept him from hearing anything. And his own sense of decency wouldn't allow him to make the call from such a sordid hangout.

The rain had dwindled to a gentle *orballo* that still obliged the smokers to crowd together beneath the overhang that provided scant shelter at the bar entrance.

He stepped out into the night, brushing past the men without heeding their annoyed looks and muttered comments. He walked far enough away to be clear of them and then tapped in Elisa's number. His fingers trembled as he fished in his jacket pocket for the flower Samuel had given him.

He heard Elisa answer immediately. "Manuel, is something wrong?"

"Elisa, I'm sorry to call so late," he apologized. "I hope I didn't wake you."

"No, we weren't asleep." She sounded agitated. "Oh, Manuel, what's going on?"

"Why do you ask?"

"Samuel refuses to go to bed. He's been sitting on the bed waiting for something for the last two hours. He told me he couldn't go to sleep because you were going to telephone him. Did you promise that? Did you say you'd call him before he went to bed?"

"No."

"So what's going on, Manuel? Why did you call?"

"Elisa, will you let me talk to Samuel?"

She was silent for a moment. "Yes. Of course." He heard a rustling on the line and imagined the child sitting on the bed.

"Hello, Uncle Manuel." That adorable voice came through loud and clear.

"Hello, darling boy," he answered with a smile. "Last time we talked, I forgot to ask you something." He found himself caressing the petals of the flower.

"Yes."

"Uncle Álvaro asked you to put gardenias in my pockets."

"Uh-huh."

"And did he say why you needed to do that?" he asked cautiously.

"Yes."

"I forgot to ask you that. Will you tell me now?"

"Yes."

"Why was that?"

"So you'd know the truth."

Manuel looked at the gardenia's waxy whiteness, and its masculine scent carried him back to the interior of the greenhouse. Notes of music blended with the perfume of thousands of gardenias. The impression was so strong that for a moment he seemed to have been transported back in time.

"Thank you, dearest."

He heard more rustling on the other end and Samuel's voice, directed to his mother. "Give me my pillow, Mama. Now I can go to sleep."

Manuel broke the connection and noticed the blinking icon advising him that he'd received a voice mail. Who the hell kept leaving those voice mails? He saw Nogueira climb up the Vulcan's steep staircase and push aside the youngsters clustered there. Nogueira got to him just as he opened the voice mail. He turned the speaker on so the policeman could hear it too.

"Listen, Manuel, I've tried to call but I guess your phone's turned off. I'm not going to be able to join you tonight. They just called me from the clinic where Santiago is; he's asked me to hear his confession, and apparently the doctors consider that a good sign. I'm headed that way now. I'll call you when we've finished, unless it's too late." A beep signaled the end of the recording.

"When did he call?" Nogueira asked.

"At ten thirty. I left the phone charging in my room during dinner," Manuel said, regretting that decision. "He must have called then. I didn't notice until just now."

He called Lucas's number but a recorded voice advised him that the number was turned off or out of coverage.

"She refused to let me in to see him," Manuel said. "She used the excuse that she was protecting him, but obviously she was protecting herself. She must have done it. Somehow she must have given him the overdose that killed him. And three years later she murdered Álvaro because he was about to blow her world apart." His eyes filled with tears, and he had to swallow a thick knot in his throat before he could continue. "She followed her husband that night, and when she saw Álvaro refusing to pay, she took care of it. If you think about it," he said with a bitter smile, "a hug looks the same as the position she had to take to stab him. I'm sure he didn't know what was happening until it was too late. She took care of both brothers, and finally they had what they wanted. Santiago is a weakling who falls apart under pressure, but she knows how to manipulate him. She isolates him from everyone else until she gets him under control again. But this time it was different, and the difference was that Santiago was in love with Toñino."

Nogueira nodded emphatically as he followed the train of logic. "Do you know what this means? Santiago's going to commit suicide; he has nothing left. But he wants to confess first, and he knows she won't let him. A confession is the only way he has of communicating the truth. He has to isolate himself from her in the company of another person."

Manuel was already on the way to the car, and the policeman raced after him.

The lowering storm pushed across a sky of otherworldly light.

NEVERMORE

Vicente's face felt taut, wizened, and salty. He brushed it with his frigid but sweaty fingertips, feeling the silky smoothness of skin washed with tears, stiff and tired. The gardener looked into the rearview mirror, trying to make contact with the eyes in that empty reflection. He didn't know how long he'd been there, but there'd still been light in the sky when he arrived. Now the night was so black that the far-off flashes of the approaching storm had jolted him out of his lethargy. His chest ached from all his weeping; he felt as hollow as a broken and discarded drum, empty and immense. In contrast, his stomach seemed to have contracted into one great cramp with no room for anything. As if to test that thought he gulped down the thick, hot saliva that had accumulated in his mouth. He felt its acid sink deep into his gut, provoking a heave he barely managed to suppress. He looked up at that threatening sky and then over to the exterior lamps bathing the front of the manor house in that atmospheric but totally inadequate light.

He got out of the pickup and felt the stirring breeze, forerunner of the storm. Lightning again lit the heavens sufficiently for him to look down and realize the shabbiness of his attire. He grabbed his raincoat and covered himself. It wasn't much more presentable. The wind flattened it against his figure, and the lower edges flapped as he walked toward the manor.

Herminia started in surprise when his blurred and altered face appeared at the window in the kitchen door. She opened the door, pressing her hands to her chest and laughing as she scolded him. "What, Vicente, *home*! What a scare you gave me!" She ushered him in. "Come in, hurry up! What a little rogue! You look like a ghost!"

Damián, seated silently at dinner, gave him a mystified look as he observed Vicente's dark stubbled face, shaking hands, and swollen eyes. Alarmed now, Herminia scrutinized him, trying to identify some hint of catastrophe; she'd become an expert at that, and these days the prospect of disaster seemed to loom over them. "Something bad's happened . . ."

It was more of a statement than a question.

"No," he denied it hoarsely. The sound of his own voice frightened him. He cleared his throat. "Herminia, tell the señora marquess I want to speak to her."

Damián's spoon stopped halfway to his mouth. He rose and signaled Herminia he would go.

Herminia gaped at him in surprise. "So something's happened?" she insisted in alarm, glimpsing dimly the arrival of the disaster that she'd tried to keep from imagining throughout the day.

Vicente shook his head and tried to steel his nerves. It was obvious Herminia and Damián didn't know he'd been fired. And why would they? Why would masters bother to inform servants of their decisions? A bitter smile spread across his face, but even so he appeared sufficiently self-possessed to reassure Herminia.

Damián came back to the kitchen a minute later. "The marquess says you may come upstairs."

Vicente took the staircase and went down the dim hallway, attracted by the warm light thrown across the corridor by the open door of her room, a rosy rectangle painted across the dark wood floor. Vicente stopped in the doorway and looked inside. The dowager marquess reclined upon a sofa. Although the temperature in the room was comfortable and she was wearing a sweater with a rolled collar, she had a blanket over her legs. Across from her the nurse crouched before the hearth, feeding a fire that had filled the upstairs suite with scents of the forest.

Hesitant, he rapped softly on the heavy wooden door that must have been left open for him.

The nurse didn't move, but the dowager raised a hand as pale and withered as that of a corpse to beckon him in. He crossed the threshold and was immobilized by indecision. Should he close the door or leave it as he'd found it? He felt nausea wash over him again. He was nervous and ashamed. He knew the nurse wouldn't leave them in private, for she never left her mistress. Anguish surged in his chest, stifling him, and he feared he wouldn't be able to speak without sobbing. He decided that although everything was sure to come out—everything always did, here on the estate—he wanted the fewest possible witnesses to his impending collapse. He shut the door behind him and walked straight forward, his gaze lowered, aware of the thick carpet beneath his feet and sensing from afar the eyes of the great lady, calm, motionless, and indifferent.

For seconds that seemed interminable to Vicente, the three of them remained fixed just like that: the nurse taking care of the fire, he standing like a cowed prisoner facing the scaffold, and the marquess with her eternal pallid grave decorum.

"Good evening, señora. I apologize for intruding at this time of night, but I need to speak with you."

She sat motionless, as if she hadn't heard a word. Vicente was about to repeat himself, but the marquess raised her hand and gestured impatiently to signal him to continue.

"It was . . . well . . . It's because of the fact, I'm sure you're already aware, that I've been dismissed. Again."

"What was your name?" she demanded.

"What?" That's all the reply he could manage.

"Your name," she said again impatiently. She snapped her fingers to call for the nurse.

"Vicente," he whispered.

And almost at the same time the nurse responded, "Piñeiro, Vicente Piñeiro."

"It's these horrible pills I take," the dowager commented to the nurse. "They leave my head entirely vacant." She sounded annoyed. She looked back to the man, and with her characteristic dignified severity instructed him. "Come to the point, señor . . ." She snapped her fingers again.

"Piñeiro," the nurse prompted her.

The dowager nodded, apparently satisfied with her prompter's performance.

Vicente gulped down another of those balls of acid saliva. The burning rejection of his stomach forced a shudder he couldn't hide.

"I've been employed for five years on the estate, assisting Catarina." The very act of pronouncing her name came out like an anguished moan and robbed him of all courage. "I've been very happy all that time, I've enjoyed my work very much, and I've done my best, not only fulfilling my regular duties, but also working with a devotion I believe far exceeded what one might normally expect of an employee." He raised his head and saw the dowager still motionless, regarding him without any indication his words were having an effect. Or that she was even attempting to understanding him. He paused.

She merely waved at him to continue. "Señor . . ."

"Piñeiro," the nurse's emotionless voice repeated.

"I believe I already asked you to be brief. What is it you want?"

He swallowed another caustic globe of saliva. This time it made him slightly dizzy.

"What I want is"—his breathing accelerated; he was panting as he continued— "to have my job back. I need to come back to my work on the estate." He stepped toward the old woman, but she stopped him instantly by raising one perfectly drawn eyebrow to signal beyond any doubt that his approach was not allowed.

"What you're requesting is impossible. I do regret it," she replied, without a trace of regret in her voice.

Vicente began stubbornly moving his head from one side to the other. "I beg you, señora, I don't know what mistake I might have made or how I might have displeased the family, but I beg you to pardon me and allow me to return to my work." He heard his voice break as he pleaded.

The old marquess again lifted a hand, this time to stop him. Only when she saw he wasn't going to continue did she lower that hand. She pushed aside the blanket with an elegantly graceful motion and slid her legs off the sofa so she was in a normal sitting position. "Señor . . . Piñeiro, wasn't that it? The truth is that I don't know the point of all this. As you just stated, you have provided your services to this estate for the last five years. I'm not familiar with the details of the contracting process, but I understand that you were not a permanent employee. Unless I am mistaken, you had a time-limited contract. Isn't that correct?" She looked at the nurse, who confirmed it. "We no longer require your services. I see no reason to make a drama of this."

Vicente was shaking, but even so he found the courage to reply. "But . . ."

The old woman lifted a hand. She had reached the limit of her patience. "There is no 'but.' You are wasting my time. I am appalled to find you so discourteous. Can it be that you're not aware of the current circumstances of this household? Events that I have no reason to explain to you have brought us to the decision to dispense with your services."

"But Catarina will need help. Next month we have several floral events planned, and we've already confirmed our attendance—"

"In all sincerity I tell you I believe Catarina will not be attending those events. She will dedicate herself in the coming months to her husband and to the care of her own health, now that she once again is with child."

The despairing grimace that had planted itself upon Vicente's face froze when he heard her last words.

"Catarina is pregnant?"

"The matter does not concern you, but yes, she is."

"Since when?"

The elderly marquess gave him a calculating smile before she answered. "She is almost four months pregnant. This time we waited a prudent length of time before ringing the church bells."

"Four months," he whispered.

Suddenly he felt that all the air seemed to have gone out of the room. The gardener gasped and felt cold sticky sweat break out upon his brow. He staggered to one side and looked around for something to grasp to keep himself erect.

He found the back of an upholstered chair, and without asking permission he stepped around it and sat down. Exhausted and confused, he struggled to speak. "I have to speak with Catarina."

The old dowager glared at him with contempt. "And why do you suppose she would wish to speak with you?"

The gardener's expression was almost joyful. "You don't understand. This changes everything."

"You're mistaken, señor Piñeiro. I most certainly do understand. Everything. And it changes nothing at all."

His sketchy smile went rigid. "But . . ."

"As I said, you are no more than an employee who provided services, and that is all you were for Catarina. Your work is done. We no longer require your services."

"No," he replied, raising his head to look directly at the woman for the first time. "You know nothing about it. Catarina . . . appreciates me . . ."

The dowager maintained her scrutiny of him, glancing away from time to time to exchange an expression of bored impatience with the nurse. But she did not interrupt the tirade that followed.

"Catarina is better than the rest of you. I know she's at the clinic taking care of Santiago, but when she comes back and learns you've fired me the way you did before, things won't stay the same. She'll hire me back. She'll come find me the way she did before when you fired me."

Definitely losing her patience, the marquess waved to the nurse. "You tell him, please."

The nurse smiled and sat up straight like a dog encouraged to demonstrate a trick. "Señor Piñeiro, Catarina was the person who ordered your dismissal."

"I don't believe it. It's like last time; you people fired me, but she came to find me and bring me back."

"Are you really so obtuse? Ah, God grant me patience!" exclaimed the old lady in disgust. She held out a hand to the nurse for help in getting up. She looked at him as if expecting a reply. "I'm sorry, but no, señor Piñeiro, Catarina will not be contacting you again. You are no longer needed. We have made certain everything is in order."

Terror filled him. "What do you mean?"

"It's not unusual for a first pregnancy to result in a miscarriage. Catarina lost the baby in February. The creature wasn't properly implanted, and I suppose she was too hasty when she announced it at Christmas." She smiled with vicious delight. "A regular Virgin Mary."

"That's when you fired me," he babbled.

He was so dazed that he had to use his fingers to count the months. He tapped each against his knee like some drunken pianist. It couldn't be. It was impossible, because it was mad. It couldn't be, because it changed everything. "But she came and hired me again. That must have meant something. It had to mean something!"

The marquess conceded that point. "Of course it did. After she was released from the hospital we needed your services again."

Vicente's fingers kept hammering out melodies on his knees. He opened his dry, sticky mouth. It filled with the burning, cauterizing saliva that had seared his insides. "She said they'd taken out her appendix," he cried out in disbelief.

"Señor Piñeiro, you shouldn't believe everything you hear. Do as I do; put your faith in numbers." She touched her thumb to one finger after another in serene imitation of his frantic counting. "Numbers don't lie."

He pushed himself up, staggered as if drunk, and tried to go to the door. He had to get away. He stumbled against the chair he'd been sitting in, turned it over, and almost fell. He felt a powerful cramp in his gut. All that burning bile he'd swallowed gushed up into his throat in an unstoppable torrent. He fell to his knees as he shook and twisted like a poisoned animal. His vomit was a living creature, a thick serpent of lava that had devoured his bowels, drowning him, choking him as it erupted roaring from his stomach, through his mouth, through his nostrils. Crouching on all fours on the marquess's beautiful red-and-gold carpet, he vomited out the hell he'd been swallowing gulp by gulp for hours and hours that day.

A crystal clear vision presented itself to his soul and replaced the chaos that had reigned there. Confused calculations that had seemed so misleading just a moment before aligned themselves in his mind with cruel clarity: the dates, the frigid dismissal, the flattering reconciliation, the tempered charm, the occasional crumbs of love. They explained everything he'd found incomprehensible, moments of passion broken off an instant later and replaced with indifference. Catarina had used him. Like a credulous idiot he'd played the part of a hired stud.

He got to his feet, stepped across the puddle of vomit, and walked away without looking back. He got to the door. That's when he looked around. His esophagus burned as if he'd swallowed shards of glass, his lips were swollen, his face was still stained with the vomit that had erupted from his nostrils and mixed with his tears. His humiliation was complete. He fumbled in the pocket of his raincoat in search of a handkerchief and encountered the solid, comforting presence of the revolver. Like a miraculous remedy passed down from his ancestors, he felt its comfort running through his veins, his skin, and his blood, healing him, cauterizing him, reviving his dead flesh and zombielike body. Another wave of clear-eyed comprehension swept away his sluggish thoughts, and he knew what to do at last. His hand refused to budge from its reassuring contact with the weapon, so he wiped his face with the other sleeve of his raincoat. "That child is mine. The world will know about it."

She sniffed and exhaled, shaking her head in negation, almost amused by these events.

He didn't like that at all. Because he'd hoped, no, he'd been *sure* he would defeat her. Or at least surprise her.

"Don't talk nonsense. The child is ours. Your contribution is complete. Your work is done, and we will not require your services in future. We've been very generous with your compensation, and we trusted you would be reasonable. However, if you persist in your unreasonable behavior, I will crush you."

Vicente looked back, comforted and calmed by the cold authority of the weapon under his hand. Its influence seemed to have overcome the fever previously burning in his head and consuming his thoughts.

"You keep thinking you're special, don't you?" He left his post by the door and stepped forward toward them again. "You think we're still back in the days when your people were all-powerful, that *poden mexar por nós*, piss all over us, and people would bow and scrape when you passed as if it were an honor to have you walk all over us. How do you propose to threaten me? Can you keep me from finding work in Galicia? Will you bankrupt my business?" He laughed loudly. "And what do I care? What's the limit of your influence? Asturias or León; I'll move to the other side of the country if necessary. I'll emigrate if I have to, but that child will bear my name because it's mine. And even if I have to sue in the court in The Hague, I will claim the paternity of my child."

The marquess appeared to be impressed. She closed her eyes for a couple of moments. Vicente saw via the thin line below her lids that her eyes were jumping wildly, like those of a sleeping demon. She opened them then and looked at him, and at that moment he knew that he was looking directly into her soul.

"Catarina will say that you raped her."

He didn't react. He couldn't.

"We had to fire you at Christmas because you behaved like a cad. But despite that, heeding Catarina's generous spirit and her pleading, we took you back. But your fixation on my daughter-in-law only got worse. We have confirmed that several people on the estate were witness to confrontations when Catarina had to treat you firmly. She is too good-hearted, and she refused to see that you were dangerous. But then it was too late."

He started to object.

"We've kept the brassiere you tore off when you raped her. The straps have traces of your DNA."

"That's not how it happened and you know it!" he said. He remembered the silky garment dangling from his fingers.

"My nurse swabbed poor Catarina, and we carefully preserved the evidence in a rape kit. We will both testify that we were strolling in the garden when we heard my daughter-in-law screaming for help. When we entered the greenhouse we saw you attacking her."

"That's not true!" He raised his voice and gripped the butt of the revolver in his pocket.

"You threatened her and said you'd come back and kill her if she said anything. She'll still live in quiet terror as long as you remain silent, but if you talk, she will collapse and have to tell this horrible story. Tell me: Who's the judge going to believe?"

The violent quaking of his rejection shook his head and extended to the rest of his body. "No, no . . ."

She smiled, exposing her scarlet gums, then clamped her mouth into a cruel smirk. "Forget the child. We've finished here. Get out! Señor . . ." She glanced at her nurse for a prompt.

This time Vicente was the one who smiled.

He took out the revolver and aimed it at her face. "Piñeiro. Señor Piñeiro. I'll see that you never forget my name."

He fired.

The marquess stood there motionless, shocked, then the terrified expression on her face was replaced by a smile both of appeal and panic revealing her deepest feelings as she released her breath with a whoosh and inhaled the acrid smell of gunpowder. But she hadn't been hit. The nurse had leaped in front of her mistress, raising her right hand as if in an absurd attempt to catch the bullet. It caught her in the chest, just between the collarbone and the swell of her breast. A black hole appeared in her uniform, and the impact of the shot at close range threw her backward over the marquess. The nurse was robust, one of those German tanks, tough and loyal to the end, and she'd seized the barrel of the revolver with her left hand. If Vicente hadn't been holding it tight, she would have torn it from his grip.

As it was, grabbing the barrel as she did changed the line of fire but yanked Vicente's finger, firm on the trigger, all the way back. The gun discharged again. The second shot blew the nurse's thumb off and struck her mistress in the gut. The women's screams united in one overwhelming shriek. The marquess's howl of pain overrode the nurse's intense, contained groan as the woman fell lifeless between the tea table and the hearth, where the fire was roaring at last. The dowager pressed her hands to her stomach, overwhelmed by pain and then collapsed gasping back onto the sofa she'd occupied when Vicente arrived.

She screamed no longer but stared down at the open wound in her abdomen. Blood welled up in ominous slow pulses like the sluggish seep of an overflowing fountain. Vicente heard her heaving gasps, almost a parody of a pregnant woman struggling against labor pains. Her grimaces of mad desperation rendered her features pale and demonic. She was suffering; the intense pain was obvious, and the torment was eating her alive. It barred her departure and refused to let her release the groan she was suppressing so as not to go mad with pain. Her lips were moving, she was saying something. Her eyes were set, and she was whispering.

Vicente couldn't hear what she was saying. He went to the sofa where the center cushion was already stained dark red, and he put his face close to hers.

He shouldn't have, for as soon as he did, she opened her eyes. He realized that the demon wasn't unconscious. She was wide awake and smiling.

"You are dismissed, señor . . . What was the name again?"

He straddled her. Her hot blood drenched the thighs of his trousers. He raised the revolver and smashed it into that demonic face. Once; again; again and again, until that smile was gone.

Then he blew his brains out. He had to use both hands because the revolver was slippery.

A TEMPEST

Nogueira's phone rang as soon as he pulled out of the lot. The lieutenant passed it to Manuel. Manuel turned on the speaker so both could hear.

It was Ophelia. "Nogueira, I just heard it on the police radio—shots have been heard at As Grileiras. Several units have been dispatched. An armed assailant went into the manor. There are reports of several victims."

Nogueira glanced at Manuel. "Where do we go? To As Grileiras or to the clinic?"

"To the clinic." Manuel remembered the polished revolver butt in Vicente's raincoat so clearly that he felt like he could reach out and touch it.

He pulled out his phone and found Herminia's number. It rang and finally lapsed when no one answered. He tried again. Just as he thought it was about to go to voice mail, he heard her distraught voice.

"It was Vicente. He turned up here pale as a ghost, and he wanted to see the old marquess; we asked her, and she agreed. I don't know what he said, Manuel, but we heard shots."

"Is he still in the house?"

"He's upstairs with them. There's not a sound, Manuel. We heard a lot of shots and I think they're all dead."

"Herminia, lock yourselves in the kitchen until the police get there."

"Yes, sir," she responded submissively.

The suspicions growing over the last few hours had become a certainty: Santiago's collapse, Vicente's desperation, the Raven's wings sheltering Catarina.

"Herminia, what were Santiago and his mother arguing about yesterday? It was after Catarina told everyone she was pregnant, wasn't it?"

Her weeping became a wail. "Oh, my God!"

"Tell me, Herminia. You know, don't you?"

"It hadn't crossed my mind until Santiago reminded me of it a few months ago."

Manuel listened. It was all beginning to make sense.

THE JOYFUL SACRAMENT

The light from the fluorescent tube lamp over the headboard fell across Santiago's head, leaving deep dark shadows where his eyes and mouth should have been visible. He was strapped in a sitting position, quiet and alert, and Lucas had the impression he was smiling. The priest paused, listening to the patient's heavy breathing as he opened the case containing the liturgical articles used for confession. He unfolded the stole, kissed it and put it around his neck, then uttered a quiet prayer requesting God's help and the strength to carry out the sacrament.

Lucas went to the bedside. Standing next to Santiago he crossed himself and began the ritual. A lightning flash reflected from the ceiling and cast the stark pattern of the barred window across the floor of the room. Despite the elegance of the appointments at the Santa Quiteria Clinic, they were nevertheless in its locked psychiatric ward.

Santiago responded as required. "Hail Mary, full of grace . . ."

"Born without sin."

"Forgive me, Father, for I have sinned." His voice was calm but determined. "Lucas, I'm going to kill myself."

Lucas demurred. "Santiago, don't say that. Tell me what's causing your anguish. I'm sure I can help you."

"No one can help me now." He spoke with absolute serenity.

"God can help you," Lucas replied, seeking to call Santiago back to this life.

"Then God will help me die."

Lucas stood silent.

"Do you remember when we were boys, Lucas?"

The priest nodded.

"Something terrible happened to Álvaro and me at the seminary." He stopped. A few seconds passed. Lucas realized Santiago was weeping.

The tears trickled slowly from his eyes and fell onto the sheet folded across his lap. Santiago seemed not to notice.

⁂

It seemed to him an eternity had passed since he entered the room. Lucas felt exhausted and overcome by a sorrow so profound he knew it would own him forever. He closed the door behind him and went forward blindly, letting his feet carry him to the group of chairs by the coffee machine. The hall, deserted earlier, seemed now vibrant with the energy of those who'd been there during the day. The trash basket was overflowing with little paper cups, and nearby he saw the distinctive splatters of coffee stains on the floor and wall. Yearning for the comfort of the womb, Lucas settled into the chair closest to the machine, leaned against it, felt its warmth and quiet hum. He rested his elbows on his knees, put his head in his hands, and tried to pray, aware that if any support at all was forthcoming, it had to come from God, for no one in this world could help. Santiago's words continued to echo in his mind like a handball bounced off the front of a building; they bounded back and forth, drove him frantic with their mad trajectories, with the perfect angles of their rebounds and the maniacal rhythm of the game. Ticktock, ticktock . . . Not a single impact was random. Each and every trajectory was predetermined, a suffering accepted in quest of greater conquest.

He could almost hear the smack of leather against stone. Ticktock, ticktock . . .

He opened his eyes and looked up to find Catarina before him. She loomed over him with a smirk on her face.

He tried to say something but couldn't. The only sound he produced was an exhausted exhalation of defeat.

"I tried to warn you."

He nodded.

"I told you he was out of his mind. But you refused to listen."

He nodded again.

"I just checked on him. He's sleeping like a baby." She smiled and took the chair next to him. "I assume you've lifted a great weight from his soul."

The soft chime of an elevator door opening was followed by hurried footsteps and the sound of a heavy wind. They heard the crash of a glass door flung back against a wall, and the current of air from the elevator shaft rose to a howl. Lucas and Catarina leaped to their feet in alarm. From one end of the corridor, Nogueira and Manuel ran toward them; at the other end the immense glass door before the fire escape hung wide open. By some miracle the double-paned glass was still in place, but it was cracked and splintered from top to bottom as if struck by a lightning bolt. The strong pull of air from the elevator shaft sucked rain into the hall so fiercely that by the time they reached Santiago's room, they were soaking wet. The same deathly white light fell from the fluorescent lamp across the bed; along its sides the padded belts that had been restraining Santiago hung loose and empty.

Manuel and Nogueira raced to the fire escape and tried to guess where in that black night he could have gone. Lucas hesitated in Santiago's room, almost lost his footing on the wet sill, and had to grab the doorframe to keep his balance. The belts dangling from the bed looked like limp, lifeless arms and hands. Lucas sensed Catarina at his side and turned to glare at her. He was scandalized. "You undid them!"

His voice was nearly inaudible in the howling wind.

Catarina raised two fingers and placed them across his lips, in a gesture of defiance that between any other man and a woman would have been extremely sensual. They seared his flesh, but not with lust. She stepped so close that Lucas caught her perfume of freshly watered gardenias.

"He was very tired, he needed to sleep, and he couldn't turn over because he was belted down. I didn't think it would do any harm to loosen them a bit," she whispered into his ear. "I thought he'd be at peace after confessing. You said he'd be joyful. And you said you'd keep his secrets."

Lucas was so furious he could hardly see straight. He shoved her away and hurried toward the fire escape. Several female nurses and two security guards came running down the corridor. Lucas realized then that beneath the howl of the storm an alarm was clanging, surely set off when the emergency exit was thrown open.

Water and wind beat against his face and body, instantly soaking his clothing. It was as if a bucket had been dumped over his head. He squinted into the darkness. The roar of the storm was deafening. He shouted to Manuel and Nogueira, but his voice was swept away by the wind. He slipped, fell forward, and felt metal bite into his knee. He struggled back to his feet, clinging to the railing, and became aware of a vibration along the hollow metal rail. It seemed to come from above. He climbed the steps, guided by the handrail, only half-aware of the turns in the staircase as he struggled up one step at a time and finally reached the landing.

The profound darkness along the side of the building contrasted with the brilliant spotlights that illuminated the front of the flat roof and the tall blue letters that formed the name of the clinic. Lucas shaded his eyes with one hand and caught sight of the three men just a few yards beyond the sign. He hobbled in that direction as quickly as he could.

The spotlights lit the flat roof as brightly as an airport landing strip. Their hot white brilliance in the beating rain rendered Santiago's hospital pajamas blindingly white. Soaking wet and plastered against his body, they looked like a shroud. He was standing on the parapet and had turned to face his pursuers.

"Don't come any closer!" he shouted to make himself heard over the roar of the storm.

Manuel stopped, fully aware he was the closest to Santiago. He looked back for Nogueira, but the glare behind him revealed only three dark silhouettes, two men and a woman. He recognized them from their shapes but couldn't see their faces.

"Listen to me, Santiago! Please, talk to me," he said, trying to gain time even though he was sure there'd be no reply. That's why he was startled to hear Santiago's voice loud and clear in response.

"There's nothing to talk about!"

"You don't have to do this, Santiago. There are better ways to resolve everything."

Raucous laughter met his plea, followed by a pause and mournful reply. "You have no idea."

Manuel looked around again, seeking help from his friends, and saw they'd moved forward to his side. Nogueira's lips were drawn back in a snarl Manuel had never seen before. Lucas was weeping; despite the torrential rain whipping against them it was clear that he'd dissolved in tears. And Catarina . . . Catarina was smiling. Manuel stared, transfixed, incredulous at her expression. It was subtle but undeniable, the tranquil expression of someone awaiting the denouement of a perfectly executed performance and the final curtain.

Manuel took one step forward. "Santiago, we know it was Catarina. We have a dealer who's willing to testify he sold her the drugs that killed Fran."

"I administered them," Santiago responded, unmoved.

"That's not true, Santiago. You fell apart, crazy with pain when you heard your brother had died. It was Catarina, and she murdered Álvaro too. Vicente let her use his pickup that night. She followed you."

"I did it," he said again. "Álvaro refused to pay the blackmailer to keep our secret."

Manuel took another step. Santiago did the same and now stood inches from death.

"I know why you think you should do this . . ."

"You don't know a goddamn thing!" he cried.

"You're doing it for Toñino."

Santiago's face contracted in intense pain, and he doubled over as if he'd just been punched in the stomach.

"Santiago, he didn't commit suicide!"

Santiago's face was a mask of immense suffering.

"Did you hear what I said, Santiago?" he called, louder this time. "Toñino didn't kill himself!"

Santiago straightened up again, confusion clouding his face. "You're lying! The police officer told me. He was despondent, and he hanged himself from a tree branch. He killed himself!"

"The policeman was wrong. The body had been there for more than a week, and that was just their first guess. I have Lieutenant Nogueira right here." He waved toward the officer. "He can confirm to you that during the autopsy, they discovered the stab wounds just like those Álvaro received."

Manuel saw Santiago's gaze shift to Catarina and knew he'd planted a doubt.

"Don't listen to them, darling," she called sweetly. "They're trying to confuse you."

465

"Catarina followed you that night when you left Álvaro behind. And after the police called late that night, she followed you to your meeting with Toñino. She saw you beat him, and after you left, she finished him off."

"That's not true!" she shrieked.

Manuel was on fire. Rage and pain blazed within him. The icy rain pelted his face and soaked his body, and he knew all the water in the world wouldn't be enough to extinguish the fire inside him. He looked down at his hands, brilliantly lit by the intense white beam of the spotlights, and he saw bright vapor steaming off his skin. He was flooded with the blazing enlightenment of a savage mystic vision and saw with absolute clarity what had happened. He again looked at Santiago and perceived a fire within him as well, but a different sort of blaze, one Manuel had experienced all too fully, a fierce combustion of doubts, questions, and awareness of betrayal.

"Álvaro didn't die in an accident. His car ran off the road because he passed out from internal bleeding. She stabbed him in the parking lot at La Rosa after you left. She's always seen you as completely inept, an idiot she has to clean up after, and that's what she was doing. She followed you to your meeting with Toñino and finished him off for you."

Manuel's instant declaration made Santiago wail like a baby. The marquis rubbed his eyes with the helpless gesture of a woebegone child.

Manuel remembered Vicente's desperation, his tears, the raincoat and the weapon, the tools thrown helter-skelter about the bed of the pickup, the buckets, the metal stakes . . . He put his hand into his pocket and took out the gardenia Samuel had given him because someone had told the child to do that, so he would understand the truth. The flower seemed a sudden vision, illuminated from within by an intense glow. Its perfume spread through the air as if the torrential rain had intensified it a thousandfold, precipitating the same dizzying sensation that had struck him down in the greenhouse. He turned toward Catarina. Her eyes were fixed upon the flower as if in a trance, and he had a vision of her on that distant afternoon, smiling and *extending her left hand to him*, obliging him to shift the boy to his right in order to shake it.

He held up the flower and shouted so Santiago would be sure to hear. "She stabbed Toñino eight times with one of the stakes from the gardenia beds."

Certainty gives only momentary relief, for truth is always overwhelming. You can assimilate it if it comes to you gradually, just as the earth of Galicia absorbs the water falling from the sky; but when truth washes over you like a tsunami, it causes as much anguish as the blackest of all lies.

Santiago was no longer looking at him. His eyes were turned toward Catarina, but he wasn't looking at her either; he was seeing straight through her with the gaze reserved for those about to die, the look that marks the instant when they see the border between this world and the next, and that boundary starts to dissolve.

That may have been why she didn't react. She knew him too well; she saw he'd rather die than face humiliation. He'd been pretending all his life, trying to be and to appear something other than what he was. He was weak. She knew him well. Perhaps that's why she gave him that last brilliant smile.

He turned toward the vast empty space and seemed to look out expectantly toward the dark horizon, perhaps seeing something out there visible only to him. He turned his head and shouted over his shoulder. "Father Lucas! Father Lucas! Can you hear me?"

Struggling against his grief, Lucas responded. "I'm here, my son." His voice rang out loud and clear through the rain.

"Father Lucas, I release you from the seal of confession!"

"No!" screamed Catarina.

"Did you hear me, Father? Did everyone hear? I renounce the secret of confession! Tell them everything!"

He jumped.

SALUTE AND BOW: THE CURTAIN FALLS

Oh, yes, he thought as he looked into the sky, *what a fine expert I've become: I thought it was going to rain all night.* Clouds masked the heavens, but now as only a thin veil across the sky. For a moment he caught the glimmer of a pale and faded moon that immediately hid itself as if in vexation. The immense storm clouds were gone. The flash and rumble of their spectacular progress were still perceptible in the distance, but their fury had ceased.

Patrol cars, flashing blue lights. Manuel saw Ophelia arrive almost at the same time as the local authorities. He accepted the coffee a young policeman held out to him. From the shelter of the front portico of the clinic, he saw Nogueira in lively conversation with his superiors. Or former superiors. Or whatever. For a moment he had misgivings and worried about the consequences for Nogueira when they learned he'd been mixed up in this business, but their close attention as he spoke, firm pats on his shoulder, and the grin on Nogueira's face reassured him.

He was more concerned for Lucas. When Santiago threw himself from the roof Lucas had dropped as if shot. He'd knelt, his hands over his face, racked by sobs that shook him as if some trapped creature were fighting to emerge from inside him. The water on the flat roof was ankle deep, for the drains had been overwhelmed by the torrent. Manuel and Nogueira had lifted the distraught priest and half-dragged him back to the stairs, down and through the smashed glass door, and out of the storm. Lucas seemed to regain his calm once they were back in the orderly and regulated interior of the clinic. His crisis of grief ended. Despite Nogueira's initial opposition he insisted on going with them to Santiago's body to confirm his death and administer extreme unction. He refused an offer of dry clothing and declined to accept anything to drink. He went to pray in the clinic chapel until the police arrived.

Manuel was stationed so he could see Lucas. The priest was now seated in one of the upholstered chairs in the well-appointed office put at the disposition of the police for their preliminary investigation. Manuel couldn't hear them, but he saw Lucas taking small sips from a water glass. Lucas appeared collected. He was speaking calmly and deliberately to an officer, laying out the story as if it were simple and straightforward.

He also saw Catarina. She was handcuffed in the back of a police cruiser with a policeman at her side. Her hair had begun to dry and curl, framing her face with a natural simplicity that made her look younger. Unlike Lucas, she had accepted the offer of other clothing. Someone had provided a white blouse, and they'd put a thermal blanket around her shoulders. Manuel found her very beautiful. Nogueira materialized beside him as he was contemplating her.

"They'll permit it, but for no more than five minutes. And you're not to touch her for any reason. I'll escort you." Nogueira clasped his shoulder and looked him straight in the eye. "Those are the instructions. And this from me: it's a bad idea. But if you're determined to do this, keep in mind I said I'd vouch for you. Don't you fuck me over!" They crossed the drive together.

Nogueira opened the door of the patrol car, exchanged a couple of words with the policeman beside Catarina, and walked away. The other policeman got out and followed Nogueira.

Manuel had nothing planned. He didn't know what he was going to say. His request to speak with her had been spontaneous, the expression of a wish he assumed could not be fulfilled. But what he hadn't expected and couldn't have imagined in his wildest dreams was her response. Those serene eyes met him calmly and without a shadow of pain. He found himself wanting to see her frightened. He'd have given anything to find some emotion, any emotion at all, disturbing the eternal elegance of her face.

He looked at her and she looked back, completely in control and without a trace of agitation. Catarina, the woman they'd all said knew her place better than anyone.

Her calm annoyed him, and he tried to disturb it. "I don't know if you've heard. The old marquess is dead. Vicente turned up at As Grileiras a few hours ago. They talked and he shot her dead. Then he blew his own brains out."

He detected an almost imperceptible start. She hadn't known. She took a breath and then released it slowly before replying. "My mother-in-law was elderly, she'd had a good life, and in recent years she's suffered terribly from arthritis. As for Vicente, well, he never knew his proper place. That became obvious some time ago. I should have dispensed with his services earlier."

Manuel shook his head in astonishment. Catarina spoke with the same calm as if her aged mother-in-law had passed away peacefully in her bed and the problems with her employee were merely minor indiscretions.

"And Álvaro?"

She returned his gaze, then closed her eyes for a couple of moments as if signaling this was difficult; but no such sentiment was to be heard in her voice. "I won't be so gauche as to apologize, Manuel. That would hardly be appropriate. But the fact is that I had no intention of killing Álvaro. It was sudden and unpleasant, a problem I had to solve in the spur of the moment. If Santiago had told me everything from the start, Álvaro would never have known. But my idiotic husband fell in love with that despicable boy, and he had such a romantic notion about this attempt at blackmail." She smiled, recalling it in amazement. "Can you imagine that? He argued in favor of it: 'He doesn't have a cent, his father died, his mother walked out, and he's living with his sick old aunt.'" She shook her head as if describing a naughty child. "I tried to explain that a blackmailer always comes back for more. How long would three hundred thousand euros have lasted for a wretch like that? But it was too late. Santiago was sure Álvaro would pay up, and he'd already told him. Álvaro was here the next day, and he suspected there was more between Santiago and the boy than just a ransom demand. I followed Santiago to the lot outside the roadhouse where the payoff was scheduled. I heard Álvaro insisting he wasn't going to pay. He said he was fed up with all the lies. As far as he was concerned, everything could be made public.

"Santiago ran off and went home to cry, like always. I looked in the back of the pickup and saw the gardening stakes. I got out, grabbed one, and walked up to him. Álvaro was a bit surprised to find me there, but he still reached out to hug me."

Catarina shrugged at the inevitability of what followed.

Manuel recoiled. A horrified expression appeared on his face and tears filled his eyes.

"Álvaro left. I went back to the pine grove alongside the parking lot to wait for Toñino, but he didn't turn up. I decided he wasn't coming, so I went back to the estate."

"And when they called Santiago about Álvaro's death, he thought Toñino had something to do with it. He arranged a meeting. And you followed him."

"The business with the boy had nothing to do with Álvaro. It was different, and not nearly as difficult. Santiago left the boy too battered and dazed to put up a fight. I went to his car, knocked on the window, he opened the door and got out. You already know what happened then. I stabbed him."

"Eight times."

She appeared unmoved. "And hanged him. That seemed entirely fitting for such vermin. Santiago refused to listen to me, and I knew there'd be no end to it. He was a threat to our family."

"He wasn't. Santiago was right. He was a little lost boy who couldn't foresee the consequences of his own actions. Álvaro had convinced him to forget the whole thing. That's why he didn't show for the meeting at La Rosa."

Catarina raised an eyebrow for just a moment as she took in that unexpected news. "Hmm. Irrelevant. How long do you think he would have held back? It wasn't the first time he'd stolen from us. He'd have been causing problems in no time at all. It had to be done, but I wasn't expecting Santiago to take it so hard. He was so weak, so weak and vulnerable he made me want to throw up. Someone called him to say the boy was dead, so he staged his little spectacle and tried to commit suicide. And then came another complication: before I knew it, Herminia had called an ambulance and the emergency team was all over him. I couldn't keep them from carrying him off to the clinic."

"Like when Santiago fell into that terrible depression after you killed Fran. You kept him locked up in his room, caring for him and spoon-feeding him until you convinced him that it was all for the best. That you'd done it for the two of you, and everyone was better off."

She gave Manuel a look of surprise. "For God's sake, Manuel, don't be such a child! Santiago wanted exactly what I did. What do you think our relationship was based on? Love, maybe? Oh please! Santiago had been the old marquis's devoted little dog, always trying to please him but always finding himself humiliated and despised. Always the same story. The old man never let Santiago do anything, never even allowed him to manage his own money, and when Fran came back it was pathetic to see the old man slobbering with delight over his favorite son. When the old marquis got sick and Fran was in rehab, we were sure the old bastard would name Santiago as his heir. But he died and left it all to Álvaro, his wayward son, the black sheep of the family. Despite everything he favored Álvaro over the good and loyal son who lived with him.

"It didn't turn out too badly though. Álvaro didn't want anything to do with all this. He was never here. But the title went to him, so Santiago had to put up with being just the brother of the marquis . . . And Fran! You have no idea, Manuel! He fell apart when his father died. He was a drug addict and a coward, a shell of a man, and he was bound to die of an overdose eventually; and besides, Santiago couldn't keep his mouth shut, so Fran started to suspect something strange was going on. He said as much to Santiago, and the big idiot repeated that in confession. And afterward he came crying to me, the way he always did." Her voice went into a scornful mocking treble. "'What am I going to do? How shameful! He's going to tell everyone, and I won't be able to show my face!'"

"I hope you're not claiming Santiago killed his brother Fran. We have evidence that you bought the heroin."

"Oh, of course I bought it! I knocked him over while he was praying, and his head banged against the pew. He was unconscious when I gave him the dose. Santiago whimpered and whined the whole time, and he almost screwed everything up by moving the body from the church to their father's grave. He thought it would be 'undignified' just to leave it in the church. But of course he found nothing undignified about meeting his lover there. Everything would have been fine if my stupid husband hadn't lost his head over that good-for-nothing and had just let me take care of everything. But that was Santiago—hysterical and crazy, a real drama queen. Ever since he was little, according to his mother. But make no mistake, Manuel, he wanted exactly what I did. The difference was that he didn't have the guts for it, and afterward he was eaten up by guilt. But never for too terribly long; after the first phase of regret and repentance, sobbing and beating his chest, he revived and was a new man, ready to enjoy everything I'd gotten for the two of us. You're not going to make me feel guilty, Manuel. I don't believe in it. These Catholic penitents have never impressed me. Am I any worse than he is, simply because I have no regrets? Was he better than I was because he was sorry about what we'd done?"

Manuel regarded her, still amazed. There was no doubt about it: Catarina knew her place better than anyone, and she'd applied all her strength and ingenuity to maintain it. She was that rare embodiment of the self-regard of the aristocrat, the people Nogueira had said were more able than any to emerge from scandals and the afflictions of poverty with their heads still held high. And an unmatched actress. He remembered her pretense of wiping away tears after the encounter with her husband the day he first met her. As well as the fragment of her conversation with Vicente he'd overheard in the greenhouse. Theater, all of it, magnificently executed acting aimed at creating a desired effect; she'd even had the calm audacity to tell him she realized he'd overheard. No, there wasn't a shred of repentance or regret; she held her head high as any queen, her gaze serene and her eyes calm, showing not a trace of grief. He again thought he'd have given anything to see her frightened, to find some trace of fear in those eyes.

He was about to get out and close the door when a question occurred to him. "Tell me, was it worth it?"

Her head moved as if to say nothing could be more obvious. "Of course. I won't be in prison forever, and in my womb I bear the next Marquis of Santo Tomé." She glanced down at the slight bulge visible through the blouse and looked up again in arrogant pride.

Manuel's frozen, grieving lips quivered. That tic caught her attention. Her expression changed when she realized he was grinning.

"I suppose it must have been quite difficult for Santiago to go to bed with you."

"But he did."

"It's not Santiago's child," he said, regarding the bulge.

"Officially, it is."

"He knew. That's why he went to talk to his mother after you announced it." She sat there impassive. "And managed only to get her to mock him yet again." She waved away his comment. "My mother-in-law knew how to set priorities. She was a great lady."

Manuel looked at her in regret. If only she were to show emotion. Any emotion at all. "Santiago wanted a son. He truly did. And the fact you hadn't gotten pregnant worried him a great deal. When you had a miscarriage a few months ago, something made him suspicious. He brooded on it for quite a while and began to wonder why you were 'working' so much." He paused. "I had a very interesting phone call with Herminia today. Turns out that his suspicions prompted him to remember something he'd almost forgotten, something his nanny remembered when he asked about it. When he was sixteen years old Santiago had the mumps. It's a childhood disease, but it can be very serious in older patients. In teenagers it can cause fever and inflammation of the testicles, sometimes resulting in masculine sterility. That incident had been forgotten until it began to look like you two were having trouble conceiving. When you became pregnant and had the miscarriage, Santiago arranged for fertility tests."

There it was: the fear in her eyes.

"You're lying," she accused him. "I'd have known about it."

"The test results were sent to the only person he could trust—Herminia, his nanny."

He shut the cruiser door but turned to look at her one last time. He saw it clearly, even through the thick glass window. Now she was terrified for real.

GOING BACK HOME

The river gleamed below them. He hugged Samuel, put him down, and felt a knot in his heart as he watched the boy clamber up the slope to his mother. She was laughing in response to something Daniel, the cellar master, had said. Smiles all around. It occurred to him that those two were getting along very well. He settled next to Lucas on the stone *mura*, warm in the midday sun, and looked around. He recalled again the enologist's comment the first day they'd met: *You won't believe me, but when I first came here I hated the place.* He took a deep breath and marveled at his own former ignorance.

"Have you thought about what you'll do with the estate?" Lucas asked.

"I haven't decided yet, but I'm interested in the notion of converting it into a tourist attraction. A dignified one. That way we could keep all the employees. Herminia and Damián could stay where they are, and apparently they're not averse to the idea. In any case I won't do anything too radical. When you think of it, Samuel's the marquis now, and perhaps someday he'd like to live there. It's the family seat, after all."

"And how about you? Did you ever think about moving in?"

"No." He smiled. "It wasn't Álvaro's home; I don't think he ever felt comfortable at As Grileiras except in the garden, and neither do I. I need something much quieter and smaller, a place where I can shut myself away to finish my novel. Nogueira told me there's a cottage for sale in his neighborhood. Maybe I'll drop by to take a look."

"Hold on, just a minute. Let's not change the subject. You said you're finishing your novel?"

Manuel smiled, a bit astonished by his own words. "Yes, in fact, I'm finishing it. Whenever I heard stories about writers producing novels in just a few weeks, I always assumed those were fairy tales. You know, PR nonsense writers made up to embellish their reputations. But it does happen. It's been"—he searched for the exact expression and found it—"like bleeding myself dry." He considered the heavy implications of that expression.

He sat there brooding in silence. Lucas detected his melancholy and returned to the earlier topic of conversation. "Going to see a house! So, then, you're thinking seriously about staying in the area."

"I don't know if it'll be permanent, but with every passing day I understand better why Álvaro was attached to this place, and right now this is where I want to be." He raised his wineglass and caught a reddish reflection of his own face.

The vineyards now held no sign of the dark grapes with frosted skins that had hung there only a month earlier. The proud expanse of leaves that had sheltered them had now turned a deep red, a color close to that of the wine, and in the soft breezes they produced the visual impression that the entire Ribeira Sacra was blazing with an internal fire risen from the earth through dark twisting grapevines now in their last gasp of glory. Until the next harvest.

Daniel came up to them carrying a bottle with the distinctive white label and the sweep of metallic script lettering of the single word upon it: *Heroica*, inscribed in Álvaro's proud and valiant script. They held up their glasses to be refilled with the festive red wine. Without moving from the warm *mura*, they turned and saw Nogueira arriving with his wife and daughters. They'd stopped at the entrance to the winery to chat with the men who were beginning to place the meat on the grill. Café caught sight of little Antía, scurried out from his resting place between his owner's legs, and raced to meet her. The girl received him with a joyful shriek. Xulia waved in greeting from the parking area. From where they sat they saw that Nogueira and Laura were holding hands.

"It looks as if they finally had that conversation," Lucas said with satisfaction. He raised his glass.

"It does," Manuel replied. He glanced in their direction and clinked his glass against Lucas's. "I'll bet they have."

When Nogueira arrived he carried a wineglass Daniel had made sure to fill on the lieutenant's way to them. He settled beside them and from the inside pocket of his hunting jacket, he took out a small package neatly wrapped in colored paper and topped with a bow. In that by now familiar style of misdirection he ignored the men's intrigued glances and motioned toward the boat moored below and rocking on the surface of the river. "You're going to have to lend it to me more often. I've discovered that river cruises put my wife into a very romantic mood."

"Whenever you like," Manuel replied with a grin. He pointed to the package. "And now are you going to tell us what you have there, or do we just have to die of curiosity?"

Nogueira held out the package. Manuel peeled off the tape and began to remove the wrapping paper.

"It's something that really fucking bothered me," Nogueira commented, enjoying the puzzled expression of the two other men. "I'm goddamned annoyed to have to acknowledge that you were right, even if only partly right."

Manuel had finished unwrapping the present and now held in his palm a square carton about the size of a fist. He opened it and found the portable GPS that had been missing from Álvaro's car.

"I turned headquarters upside down and got everyone to search for it. And like I said, you were partly right: someone had carried it off."

Manuel raised his eyebrows.

"But not a policeman," Nogueira added quickly. "One of the tow-truck drivers, an apprentice who'd been on the job barely two weeks. They fired him for stealing."

Manuel smiled. "Thanks."

"But I was right when I said no policeman took it," he added quickly. "I already told you that we police officers aren't thieves!"

The three broke into laughter. Daniel called out from the grassy terrace and summoned them to eat.

Manuel started to get up, but Nogueira detained him. "Just a minute. I've had it charging all night so you could turn it on. Like I said, this gadget can tell us where Álvaro was going when his car ran off the road."

Manuel looked down at the screen. The dark brooding feelings from which he'd managed to struggle free over the past month stirred again. He felt them squeeze his heart. "I don't know if . . ."

"Do it," the lieutenant insisted.

Manuel pressed the button to turn the apparatus on. It lit up immediately and displayed icons for its various functions. With a fingertip he tapped the square containing the history of recent routes. The screen lit up with a map. It was labeled *Home.*

Manuel's eyes filled with tears. He felt both his shoulders gripped and knew those were Lucas's hands.

He heard Nogueira's voice. "He was going home, Manuel. He was going back to you. When Álvaro knew he was dying, he didn't think of any other place in the world. He was going back to you."

ACKNOWLEDGMENTS

I'm grateful for the collaboration of all those who made their talents and knowledge available to me to help this story that has lived in my mind for years to materialize into the tangible reality we now have in our hands. Any errors or omissions, and there may be many, are entirely my responsibility.

To Elena Jiménez Forcada, veterinarian in Cintruénigo, Navarra, for her guidance on veterinary matters concerning the dogs and horses that appear in this novel.

To Jean Larser, because the phone calls that fill one with energy and the courage to go on almost always have a good friend on the other end of the line. Thank you.

To J. Miguel Jiménez Arcos of Tudela for his professional guidance concerning the effects of a certain drug. We'll leave it at that and let the others speculate! ;-)

To the *Guardia Civil* and especially to the officers and troopers of the headquarters in O Carballiño in Ourense, and especially to Corporal Javier Rodríguez for his indispensable assistance.

To the municipality of Rodeiro in Pontevedra that has been welcoming me and my family for lengthy stays over the years.

To the Vía Romana wineries of Ribeira Sacra for serving as my inspiration for the *Heroica* winery.

To the Center for Wines of the Ribeira Sacra in Monforte de Lemos, Lugo, for teaching me about the proud tradition of producing wine as it has been done for two thousand years, and to the guides of the tour boats of Belesar for making me fall in love with the winding course of the Miño and its seven submerged villages.

To Michael Meigs, Kelli Martin, and Gabriella Page-Fort for their passion, attention to detail, and professionalism in making the novel available to English readers everywhere.

To my sister Esther, the most passionate enthusiast for Galicia; I will never be able to thank you enough for revealing to me this incredible, powerful, and ferocious place.

A Nosa señora do Corpiño. As is her due.

ABOUT THE AUTHOR

Photo © 2013 Alfredo Tudela

Dolores Redondo studied law and the culinary arts before writing The Baztán Trilogy, a successful crime series set in the Basque Pyrenees that has sold over 1.5 million copies in Spanish, has been translated into more than thirty-five languages, and was adapted into a popular film series.

Twice nominated for the CWA International Dagger Award and a finalist for the *Grand Prix des Lectrices de Elle*, Redondo was the recipient of the 2016 *Premio Planeta*—one of Spain's most distinguished literary awards—for her stand-alone thriller *All This I Will Give to You*, which has also been optioned for feature film and television development and will be translated into eighteen languages.

Readers who want to learn more about Dolores Redondo and her work can do so by visiting www.doloresredondo.com/en.

ABOUT THE TRANSLATOR

Photo © 2017 Steve Rogers

Michael Meigs reviews theater and translates literature from Spanish, Swedish, French, and German. Since 2008 he has published the online journal *www. CTXLiveTheatre.com*, which is dedicated to live narrative theater in Austin, San Antonio, and the rest of central Texas. He served as a diplomat with the United States Department of State for more than thirty years and was assigned abroad with his wife, Karen, and their children, Nina and Lamar, to Africa, Europe, South America, and the Caribbean. He has graduate degrees in comparative literature, business, economics, and national security studies. Michael serves as a pro bono interpreter and translator for refugees and asylum seekers. He is secretary and bursar of Gilbert & Sullivan Austin and a member of the American Theatre Critics Association, the American Literary Translators Association, Swedish Translators in North America, and the Austin Area Translators and Interpreters Association.